MW01126474

ARAUCO

A NOVEL

John Caviglia

April, 2013

For Nita —
a great friend & neighbor.

For Barbara

Copyright © 2012 John Lawrence Caviglia

All rights reserved. No part of this book may be reproduced or transmitted in any form or by any means, mechanically or electronically, including photocopying, recording and retrieval system, without prior written permission from the author, except in the case of brief quotations embodied in critical articles and reviews. Contact: http://arauconovel.com

Cover illustration: Tyler Jacobson
Book design: Rosamond Grupp

ISBN: 978-1479383016

Printed in the United States of America

Table of Contents

Foreword

Having invaded the Americas, Spaniards conquered the Aztec and the Inca empires. In 1540, Pedro de Valdivia led an expedition south from Peru across the Atacama, the bleakest desert in the world, into the land now called Chile. There, he founded the present city of Santiago. Taking his conquest south, he encountered those who called the land he had invaded *mapu*—the Mapuche, people of the land—who resisted the *conquistadores* as no others ever had before. This novel narrates the beginning of a three hundred year war.

John Caviglia

Preliminary note: The characters depicted in this novel are largely Spanish and Mapuche—the indigenous people of the land now called Chile. As Mapudungun, the language of the Mapuche, will be unfamiliar to almost all readers of English, I have provided a Mapudungun/English glossary at the end of the novel. The same glossary is available, with illustrations, in the author's blog: http://arauconovel.com.

BOOK ONE

Prologue: The Beginning *(Mapu)*

The sun was dying in *fucha lafken,* the great sea, but Ñamku, shaman of the Mapuche, did not see it. Behind him, the sacred volcanoes of the ancestors soared into the sunrises of the past, and he did not see them. Breathing deep, he removed his mask. Opening his eyes, he spread his arms to embrace darkness. This night the *pillañ*—the ancestors—would speak to him.

Mapu shivered as the ancestors danced over the great sea, their garments glimmering from earth to sky. These fires of air that did not warm, and dwarfed volcanoes, flames that hung and trembled like transparent cloth, were signs. For as it had been before, so would it be again. The sacred volcano, Lonkimai, would speak to the Mapuche with his burning tongue.

Ñamku loosed his long white hair, remembering how as a child he groped with toes for clams…. Waves beat his legs like a slow, cold heart, fear telling him he did not know what lived there. In time, as shaman—*machi* of the Mapuche— Ñamku learned to become what he then feared. He had been blind *kufull*—the clam—wearing a stone, burrowing with his tongue. He had walked sideways as a crab. He had been other creatures of the earth and air. But what he had most feared becoming was what now he was—an old, white man with red eyes, unmasked only in the dark, living with the dead.

He unclasped his left hand, revealing what he held—two small crossed sticks, made of gold. And from them hung a man—a *che* carved from bone—wearing only a dark loincloth. This *che* was white as he, with a wound bleeding on his ribs, wounds also on his hands and feet. People from beyond the desert to the north had brought this thing resembling nothing he had ever known.

Like the bone seed of fruit—hard but not dead—the bone *che* slept, and Ñamku intended to take him into his own dark to sprout. The ancestors were wise and powerful, and Ñamku knew his whiteness had chosen him for this moment. Lonkimai would speak to him this night.

Those who brought the bone *che* said it was the *pillañ* of white men with hair on their faces that had appeared from *fucha lafken.* They were both warriors and sorcerers, and their clothing blinded like the sun.

All *che* were not albino as Ñamku was, alone in his whiteness and pain, power and apartness, strange to his kind, seeing the world through red eyes … and an entire people, all of them white, was unthinkable. Ñamku was made *machi* by his difference. For many to be like him was impossible.

Dusk was done—Ñamku saw—taking up his *kultrung*. And the sacred stones, the seeds, inside the drum began to speak. The ancient skin pounded like an ageless sea as Ñamku sang the beginning for this new beginning....

Kaikaifilu, death as water,
Kaikaifilu, the black serpent,
loosed his tail as the waters of the air,
on the rivers of the mountains,
on the shores of the great sea.
And mapu *drowned in Kaikaifilu, death as water.*

Kaikaifilu drowned the mountains,
drowned all creatures large and small,
drowned the creatures of the land,
drowned the piru, luan, pudu, pangi.
Kaikaifilu drowned the creatures of the sky.
Mañke, peuko, tiuke, ñamku.
And in his coils Kaikaifilu drowned the che.

The thrum of *mapu* was now moving the *kultrung*, its skin the hollow ribs of the *pillañ*. Behind him—Ñamku knew—the distant tongue of Lonkimai was burning.

Heat crawled his glowing backbone to the old white stone that was his head, and that pulsing flame grew into a burning tree as his heart stuttered with the *kultrung*.

Trentren. Trentren, life of mapu.
Trentren. Trentren, life of the che.
Trentren. Trentren, enemy of Kaikaifilu.

Trentren lifted mountains, speaking with a flaming tongue, telling the *che* to climb his mighty shoulders as he rose.

And Ñamku was on fire....

Climbing the shoulders of Trentren, *che* fled the black water. Those that did not reach summits turned to fish, seals and whales. Those who collapsed upon the shore turned to frogs and salamanders....

Then Ñamku sang the quieting of waters, the marriage of the *pillañ* with *domo*, the women who reached the peaks. He sang the birth of the Mapuche—children of the earth—rescued from the waters of Kaikaifilu.

Ñamku sang that he might see, sang that he might hear ... shimmering light dancing into his mind. He saw the glow explode into many flaming, spotted puma ... the violence of falling stars followed by a milky dark, like fog lit by a new moon....

The whiteness brightened....

And Ñamku saw nothing but himself outside himself, white against the white, searching ... seeing nothing.

Yearning to hear, he heard nothing. Emptying himself, he waited for the simplest sign, the slightest whisper....

And when Lonkimai at last stopped speaking, Ñamku knew he had been given waiting as his vision. Then with wonder much like terror, he knew that the *pillañ* were waiting with him. The bone *che* brought a beginning that to their wisdom was as mist and silence. He had been made white to wait, white to prepare for the moment being born....

And one more time, the bone *che* shook *mapu* with the imminence of what was to be.

Chapter 1: Sevilla (Andalucía, 1539)

Having traveled far from the Extremadura of his birth, Juan de Cardeña was dazzled by the whitewashed dwellings of Andalucía under their sun, astonished by the opulence of this Spanish south. Millet, wheat and barley nodded in the waver of afternoon heat. Vineyards, gray-green olive groves, nameless plants and fertile gardens embraced the dwellings that strung the road like beads of an enormous rosary. His burro kicked up puffs of dust.

Dust to dust, thought Juan, for summer brought Black Death ... as in 1530 when all his family died, and Providence left memory as the price of survival. Too terrible to summon, the images would visit of their own savage will. Like the Black Death itself, remembrance was a foulness born of heat....

He woke in darkness, heart pounding, saw light sifting through closed shutters. Mother sprawled in a corner, eyes red, not breathing. Father moaned for mercy where he lay, persistent as an insect. By him something moved.... Sister...?

Juan crawled over ... touched a rat ... and screamed the high scream of the very young.

Here always—like a door—memory mercifully slammed shut.

Having spared Juan, God turned him into one who enjoyed only the company of books. Even Father Davila Sosa—who found this infant cursed by Fortuna whimpering in a cart filled with corpses and took him in, loving him as the offspring denied him by the cloth— was as a stranger to him. Twice a father, he was somehow less than one.

Juan was given to waking trances that were terrible but endurable, as one might have a nightmare knowing one was dreaming. And so now, with a start, he awoke to his companion....

Pedro Gómez de San Benito towered beside him on a fine blue mule, magnificent, though he was dusty and rumpled, sleeves smeared from being used to wipe his nose, for— as he said—the use of fingers was a sign of sissies. And he would darkly add, a handkerchief was signs of worse.

In truth, Pedro had much in common with Negrito—the capuchin monkey he brought back from the Indies—habitually perched on his left shoulder. *Ceteris paribus*, both were wide of shoulder, long of arm, short of leg, and had mobile mouths. Yet the feature they most shared was hair, for tufts erupted from Pedro's ears and nose, while unruly mats crept down his hands in dark promise of what his clothes concealed—and one might add, concealed always, because as a devout *cristiano* he would not unclothe his shame to sleep or wash, even to cover a whore. Therefore—like every other soldier—he stank. Nonetheless, he was stunning in apparel never before admired in Spain, taking both civilization and barbarism to their extremes. Defying every precedent and sumptuary law, Pedro had breached the battlements of decorum in Extremadura like a cannonball fired over continents. To Juan—who admired the Apocalypse—the first vision of Pedro was a second Revelation.

Like their fathers before them, the wealthy of Extremadura wore black … the material rich, tailoring refined, with starched, white ruffs an immaculate exception at the neck. And their jewels—preferably pearls—were modest. In short, in dress, the nobility imitated the *cuervos*—or crows—as the clergy were popularly called. In total contrast, Pedro was a peacock to himself.

He conceived his 'indument'—for so he always called his finery—while roaming Spain, Italy, the Indies. The foundation was Venetian, as in his opinion the gallants of that ancient city-state were first in fashion. To that impeccable base he had added tributes to his native Spain, as well as accents observed here and there—galloons, aglets, etc.—the whole finished off with an Inca flourish in Peru, for when the overarching concept at last saw light, the Indian seamstresses improvised upon their ignorance, confecting a triumph more extravagant than the conceiver had conceived. To this day Pedro was stunned by his own presence.

"*Pardiez*, am I not a thing of wonder!" he would exclaim to Juan. "I know nothing about stitching, and those Inca savages had no knowledge of Christian dress, much less Venetian fashion. Which all goes to show that a single ignorance is nothing, but that two ignorances combined can beget miracles." And he would pivot to display the undeniable….

A crimson velvet doublet, padded at the shoulders, was embroidered in gold thread with battle scenes. Slashed sleeves—galloned—allowed peeks of violet silk. Plumes of birds that never flew Christian land raked a wide-brimmed hat. Riding boots—tooled with Inca scenes—snugly fitted over purple and orange hose. Over the whole billowed a black cloak lined with red silk, covering both the immensity of Pedro and the hindquarters of his mule.

Metal glittered in the frippery…. The scabbard of Pedro's sword, in filigree, depicted jaguars crouched in jungles, while the enormous hilt was bound by twisted silver thread. A barbaric golden sun with an impassive human face—its rays depicted as outstretched arms—hung from his neck. Rings on both hands depicted human skulls grinning in intaglio. And, in tribute to civilization, Holland cambric exploded at his neck, his wrists. As for ruffs—which were at the sartorial moment huge—Pedro did without, for in his words, putting your head upon a platter tempted Fate … therefore, a simple collar.

Of this magnificence the codpiece was the keystone—purple, embroidered, padded … with bombast, Pedro specified, not the perfumed handkerchiefs of dandies, or a bumpkin's bran, just good old, soldierly cotton. But, as a last touch, he had bent to winds of change by including a purse in the conception. And, Juan thought, secretly, that Pedro had managed to make himself uneasy at this last flight of fancy, for he commented—far more than once—that metal *there* was good as armor, in a crux.

In Juan's opinion Pedro was confusing his *cojones* and *doblones*—his balls and his doubloons—yet did not dream to say so. One did not joke with Pedro about God, manhood or honor—that trinity created by the Almighty for cold steel to defend.

No one had ever fought Pedro and lived … save Juan, who was his student in the knife, that subtle, arduous art.

The first blade Pedro gave him had the simplest of bone handles, yet on its edge an angel could not dance. Juan learned the stone, the strop—the perfecting of the perfection—and the holding of it, against the arm to block, spin, slash. Usually the tip was forward, edge down—the exceptions would come later.

Juan practiced until the day Pedro let him unsheathe a damascened blade he had once taken from the body of a Moor. Crows observed with interest as in sopped shirts and hose they rehearsed the dance of death…. Shuffle … balance at all costs. Move. Beginners' eyes betray their blades. Focus on the expert's gut … no one goes anywhere without it.

"See," Pedro would say, flowing with the economy of water, feinting, lunging with extraordinary grace where least expected. So it went, day after day, when books had once been Juan's single discipline. And he applied himself as a convert to a faith.

Father Sosa observed all this with wrenching guilt, in full knowledge that Juan was emulating Amadís de Gaula, Child of the Sea, orphaned hero of the *libros de caballería* to which the good priest himself had introduced him. For—despite a life entirely lived in wrenching poverty—Sosa had managed to acquire priceless manuscripts damaged in a monastery fire, trading for them a sack of chickpeas and a pig. Burned as these volumes were, much remained legible, so that Juan knew Amadís trained with weapons as a youth. And in his innocence he had imagined fighting as analogous to telling rosaries—skill descending like the Holy Spirit, from above. Instead, as he found out, learning the blade was arduous labor.

He could not have had a better guide for this violent path. Pedro Gómez de San Benito left Extremadura as a young man to fight in the Italian campaigns, where the Spanish *tercios* were the wonder of the world. Then he sailed for the Indies, serving in Mexico under Cortéz, growing obscenely wealthy, acquiring gold, land, Indians…. But the natives who did not die of overwork, pox and suicide, escaped. The gold slipped through his hands. And—as land was useless without Indians to work it—Pedro returned to conquest, acquiring a second fortune in Peru under Pizarro, this one large enough to survive a year of true excess. In time, bored by peace and debauch, he returned to the Extremadura he had left over twenty years ago, to rediscover this was the place he never wanted to see again.

He headed for Sevilla, as by imperial decree all fleets sailed for the Indies from that port. And he took with him Juan de Cardeña, rescuing the child from a senile village priest. He would show Juan the world! Cloak billowing, he announced in the tavern where he spent his days that—*Pardiez!*—he would take Juan to the Indies, make of him a man.

Despite his gratitude to Father Sosa, who had taught him to read and write both Latin and Spanish, and also tried his best to be a parent—countless onion omelets!—Juan was in raptures. The Indies, with all that glittered in their promise! He would walk the pages of *romances* with Amadís de Gaula, Orlando Furioso. He was a page to a knight errant, a *caballero andante*!

At their parting, Father Sosa wept as he handed Juan a package, prostrating himself beside the road as if he could not tell his sorrow from some kind of penitence. And only that night did Juan discover that—in addition to a loaf of bread, and yet another onion omelet— he had been given the two volumes of **Amadís de Gaula** least damaged by fire.

Looking like a water strider, a far horseman raced toward them over the mirage of highway heat and thundered by in dust reeking of horse and sweaty leather. Juan twisted to look back. The royal mail!

Nothing was faster. From wherever the peripatetic court of Carlos V happened to be— relays spaced two to four leagues apart, horses at a gallop—His couriers covered thirty leagues a day when the poor trudged four, the well-off rode a comfortable six, and the wealthy went no further in the dubious pleasure of a litter borne by mules. To ride like the wind to far corners of the empire—Flanders, Italy...! Juan thanked God he lived in an age that had so shrunk the world. The Indies! He would experience what the immortal Pliny never penned in his **Historia Naturalis.** And with him he had Pedro, that living book of marvels....

"Gold, *hijo*. In unimaginable quantity, none of it coin. The Incas have no money, strange as that might seem. They think gold to be the tears of the sun—the most important of their many gods—which is why you find it in the temples. If you could have seen the one in Cuzco, so rich they called it Coricancha—place of gold—bounded by an immense wall, around which was a frieze of gold plates tall as I am! But that was as nothing to the interior. The very Pope for all his riches would have shat his vestments in the anterooms ... of which there were scores, crowded with the ransom of emperors. And *they* were nothing, compared to the sanctuary, bigger than a cathedral's. There, on the west wall, was the golden disk of the sun—maybe thirty *palmos* wide, the rays another four. The pupils of the eyes were made of emeralds, mother of pearl for the white. And the eastern door was placed so that in the morning the sun shone on his own face, lighting the huge interior with his reflections. There were silver vases there also, taller than a man, filled with *choclo*."

"*Choclo?*"

"A savage grain also known as maize, for the Inca do not grow civilized crops. They consume *quinoa* and *choclo* instead. And—*Voto a Dios!*—they do not eat meat!"

Juan was no longer listening, for they had crested a hill, and in the distance were crenellated ramparts.... Sevilla! Richest city in all Spain. House of gold. Ivory tower. Window to the Indies. There was a saying: *Quien no ha visto Sevilla, no ha visto maravilla*—He who has not seen Sevilla, has not seen a miracle. And—although some called it Babylon— Juan believed this with all his heart. Nothing would surprise him here—not heroes on battlements, magicians, flying dragons, evil dwarfs....

Flower opened to the sun, Juan turned his head as they approached. Towers flanked the entrance. By them, blood-crusted stakes displaying the impaled heads of criminals whose rank had earned them decapitation. Not far away were the remains of common criminals—garroted, then drawn and quartered. Children were throwing stones, making the hunger of the assembled crows a matter of life and death. They had killed one, which they dismembered and impaled—childish copy of the adult display. The stench, thought Juan, would not be half so bad if the crows could have their fill....

He stopped his burro to look into eyes that had survived the birds but lost their shine, like fish not fresh. The head stared from under heavy, half-shut lids, with a grimace expecting the ax in perpetuity. A fly landed on the tongue, walked in.

Hammering his donkey with his heels, Juan fled into Sevilla.

Pedro told him they had time to kill. The fleets sailed twice for the Indies. In May or June, for Mexico, in September for Panama and Peru. As it was August, they would find an inn. Tomorrow they would go to the whore's quarter, the *mancebía*.

Juan shuddered, for he was not just virgin, he was a fearful and ignorant virgin, having been raised by that rare phenomenon, a celibate village priest—for as the saying went, a priest without children was a priest without *cojones*.

And the good Father was rarer yet, for he could read and write. Tales of chivalry comforted his chastity, yet he was not profligate. Although in Spain *libros de caballería* and *romances* were breeding—in his words—like locusts happy with their desert, Sosa remained faithful to his supreme love, **Amadís de Gaula**. A few other *romances*—**Orlando Furioso** at their head—he admired esthetically, as a knight the beauty of a damsel to whom he could not plight his troth. The rest he disdained as the promiscuous trash that printing had made available to all—these texts like whores, revealing far too much in promise of the rest.

And so it was that **Amadís de Gaula** summed Juan's sexual education, these volumes in which the love of knights and damsels was life itself. Deprived of love, a knight languished … could even die. And only true love made disporting with a maiden possible. A marriage ceremony was not necessary, as Juan well knew, since the vows of true love were holy before God—so had King Perion of Gaul and Queen Elisena plighted their troth in secret, begetting the hero Amadís himself.

How then, at the *mancebía*, do what there was done! How 'disport' with an unknown to whom Juan had plighted nothing, someone probably ugly as cross-eyed Rosa, the gypsy who initiated all the men in the village of his birth! Worse, Juan did not know what 'disport' *meant*. The Church taught that man should be on top … but where, there? Where the entrance clothed forever by The Fall? If in bushes much like his—as he had heard—how find it amid complications, concealed like partridges…?

To Juan, woman was *terra incognita*, and *that* was how he wanted her, as in the wondrous maps that inked discovery about a blank. In unknown lands the love of knights and damsels was consummated. There they 'disported' on the white of pages—so to speak. In consequence, from books Juan had learned not one thing useful about the actual acts of love. And to think that to Pedro and every other male in Christendom this great mystery was familiar as blood sausage!

They clattered, hooves echoing, into narrow streets flanked by high, whitewashed walls. The twined ironwork of doors revealed glimpses of courtyards in chiaroscuro, pillars, plants and fountains afire in violent light … the rest impenetrable dark. Above their heads bright canvas, faded pale—pleated so that it could be folded to the side—hung from roof to roof, providing shade. Geraniums in hanging planters glowed like silent coals, for the streets were deserted. Sevilla slept her *siesta*, balconies empty, vivid shutters closed.

The inns were overfilled by the imminent departure of the fleet, but Pedro knew one where the *ventero* owed him a favor. They tied their mounts in the courtyard, where the poorest travelers slept. The list of prices, set by the Crown, was posted by the door—a *real* for a bed, another for the meal, a third for the candle and the service. The innkeeper—who reminded Juan of olives, for he was plump, dark and oily—bowed them into the murky space that served as dining room, kitchen, and dormitory. At the center was a fire, and above it a hood that captured what it could of smoke. An iron cauldron simmered over flames that over years had layered the rafters with unctuous soot.

By it was the long table where at every Spanish inn the guests were served from that perpetual pot—the *olla podrida*—of which you never knew what was put in, or when, for as the level dropped more was added, an uninterrupted simmer turning its contents into a bubbling gelatin punctuated by shards of bone. Scooping it with bread, travelers rehearsed canonic jokes—what better way to dispose of rats and rotten meat, nagging wives, unwanted children…?

Pedro held court, Negrito on his shoulder, regaling the travelers with tales of the Indies.

In time the *ventero* lit tallow candles and stuck them into loaves of bread, their wavering light reflected on a tabletop polished to a greasy mirror by homespun sleeves. His daughter decanted into the jugs and wineskins of the guests, replenishing her supply from pigskin bladders hanging from the rafters. A merchant—from so far away that, *there*, they drank beer—muttered that the stuff might have been drinkable if it did not taste of 'hog leathers.' Everyone drank to that, including the foreigner, who had downed quantities of the abomination. But by now the gathering was toasting everything, sodden imaginations reeling.

A butcher, spattered by the blood of his calling—arrived from afar for the seasonal slaughter in Sevilla—asked Pedro about Indian women. Did they have one breast, two twats, what…?

Belching, Pedro resumed his tale. "Indian women are like everybody, not like in the books of this Pliny my young friend so admires, who claims that in Africa there are men with feet on their heads, a finger growing up their arse, and eyeballs between their legs." The assembly echoed Pedro's guffaw. There were catcalls, comments….

"What a view!"

"Are the women of Africa blind?"

"So where are their *cojones*?"

Juan studied the runs in his hose as Pedro attempted to salve the situation. "Just a joke, *hijo*. Why not tell these good people what Africa is *really* like."

Juan stuttered, "The Monocli have just one huge foot. And they jump like fleas."

Someone tittered.

Frowning at the culprit, Pedro urged Juan on.

"They're called the Umbrella Foot Tribe because in hot weather they lie on their backs and rest in the shadow of their foot."

"More, more!" someone gurgled hysterically.

Juan rushed on. "There are the Astomi, who have no mouths. And although they have a hairy body, Pliny says that they are very delicate."

"Just like Don Pedro," some drunk shouted.

Pedro heaved to his feet, hand dropping to his hilt. Negrito bared yellow fangs and slapped his bicep. The drunk hurried out the door.

Juan continued into utter silence, "The Astomi dress in cotton and eat nothing, sustained only by breathing air and delicate aromas. While traveling they carry roots, flowers and wild apples, because they can be killed by stronger smells."

In the resulting uproar a voice stood out. "Now we know why there are no Astomi here in Spain. They've been wiped out by the inns." Improbably, it was the innkeeper who had shouted this, swept away by general hilarity.

Juan was mercifully forgotten as Pedro—who led in drink as in all else—resumed: "Indians are like us, but the same, though like us the women differ from the men. But they are unlike us in being all alike—no blue eyes, no red hair, no freckles, no blondes—all dark as the devil. Still they're much the same as us, and with all due respect—here doffing his hat at the innkeeper's daughter and winking at the assembly—Indian women fuck normal." He lowered his voice. "But they do things The Church never thought to forbid...."

Every mind in the room ran amok as Pedro triumphantly belched, savoring the hush he had created.... Then he snored and slumped, forehead thumping the table.

The guests who had not passed out wrapped themselves in cloaks on the floor, or left for the few straw-stuffed pallets they had paid for, to battle the vermin guarding the portals of oblivion.

As one lifting a dead horse Juan tried to get Pedro to his feet, seeing that now the butcher was staring in their direction. Then—Mother of God!—he remembered that he had left his weapon in his saddlebag.

He shook Pedro. Nothing....

Juan looked up to see a long, thin knife materializing in the butcher's hand. Unsteady as he was with wine, the butcher's eye was cold as he approached....

"Pedro!"

Negrito hoo-hooed, scurrying under the table. Pedro's eyes opened, barely. Juan could only see the whites.

The butcher was almost on them.

Juan bellowed, "*Dios ayude, y Santiago!*"

Pedro surged to his feet, responding to the battle cry. Juan gripped the butcher's knife arm and bit deep, was rewarded by a screech. Closing his eyes, he ground his teeth, tasting metallic blood, and was felled by something heavy as a grain sack....

When Pedro at last lifted the butcher off Juan, he saw that his forehead was caved in, the head of grinning death stamped there in low relief.

"An Indian sort of joke," Pedro told Juan, when next morning they sat to break their fast, after eloquence—and gold—had convinced the representative of the Crown, the *alguacil*, that they had killed in self-defense. "Their slingsmen carve messages on clay balls, to print them on the bodies of their enemies.... This, I had done to my rings."

Pedro had been silent until now, for his headache was the size of empires. And he was devastated by guilt—that his drunkenness had almost killed them both. "I owe you my life, *hijo*. And such a debt Pedro Gómez de San Benito does not take lightly."

Then, embarrassed, he turned to the *ventero*, asking a question that caused the ripe fruit of dread to drop squarely in Juan's lap....

Yes, Liliana of the amazing melons was still a working woman....

"*Pardiez!*" Pedro exclaimed, turning to pummel Juan, " My *hijo* deserves the best. Now, how about some food as what will give us vigor." They ate as Pedro talked of whoring.

In Juan's Extremadura women spread their legs for money or as a favor, or simply casually—never for him, of course. And here Pedro was describing an actual *profession*! Juan could not believe that *putas* spent their working lives on their backs, paid to be filled by males. Did they drip? Did *it* accumulate?

Pedro was explaining that they provided a service regulated and taxed by the Emperor. In return both the *putas* and society were protected. For example, whores could be not be married or virgin, or veil themselves. They wore low-cut dresses, so as not to be confused with decent women. Physicians inspected them. And in larger cities they inhabited a walled quarter, the *mancebía*—Valencia's was the best, but Sevilla's was not bad.

Done with his morning pork, Pedro insisted that it was time. So—too soon for Juan—they surrendered their weapons at the *mancebía* gate as law demanded, entering a street flanked by houses with gaily-painted doors and shutters. Avoiding the early sun, *putas* sat their porches under the iron lamps that would illuminate them at night, bantering with early customers. It was much like any street of shops, but here the vendors were the wares.

They wore velvet and silk, breasts shoved up and out, necklines lower than the possible. They stood hipshot. They winked and wiggled, lifting petticoats, baring legs above the knee. One bent to fool with a shoe, and down her bodice Juan saw far more than he ever had before.

His stretched, old codpiece now betrayed an erection. And he was reminded of when, as an acolyte, he faced the congregation, priest elevating the monstrance containing the body of Christ as, in sacrilegious imitation, Juan's cassock was also elevated below.

A *puta* leered. "Eh, *guapo*. Let Sofía handle your problem."

Another, eyes rimmed with kohl, shouted at her retreating business, "Your problem is so little I'll do you for half price."

And when Pedro unwisely swore to God that they would shut their traps or he would shut them for them, the chant began—"Little problem! Little problem!"

As *putas* they did not like lost business. As Spanish they had pride. And the Crown, which tolerated no disruption in its revenue, protected the *mancebía*.

Liliana had been alerted by the uproar, and like an Amazon with two breasts she towered over her threshold in low-cut, crimson velvet.

Suffering Jesus! Juan could not look into her eyes, so dark were they with deep amusement.

Women made Pedro nervous, and he generally avoided them save to copulate—for like cannons welded, not cast, they could explode in your face. He fumbled for his sword, and in its absence stuck his thumb under his baldric. "This is my *hijo*, Juan," he bellowed. "I'm paying."

Juan did not dare ask God for help, much less the Virgin Mary. But as Saint Francis of Assisi had been licentious in his youth, to him he implored—let her not say I have a little problem! Would the gentle saint, who loved all the little creatures that so promiscuously begat, comprehend his yearning?

Ignoring Pedro, Liliana examined her customer, who seemed to be studying the cobbles beneath his feet. Lifting his chin with a forefinger, seeing that the dark-flecked hazel eyes were close to tears, she breathed into Juan's ear, "*Caballero*, pray come in."

The interior was shuttered, allowing shafts of light into the monastic room, which held an oak chest, a table, two chairs, and a cot. A cot!

Juan's stare did not turn it less normal. He saw that a crude ceramic cross hung over it, given strange life by casual tools. Christ looked both tired and bewildered.

Liliana made conversation in a husky contralto, pouring into wooden cups, inquiring about his journey. They drank the sweet, astringent, amber wine of the South. They ate toasted wheat. It did not take long for Juan to tell her about everything—the death of his family, Father Sosa, his study of Spanish and Latin, the *romances*, Pliny, *terra incognita*, his dreams ... all with an erection.

Then he was fumbling with her points—as she called them—undressing her with wooden fingers. And when her tongue flickered in his ear Juan was paralyzed for good. He watched as she sat down, naked, on the bed. A shaft of light illuminated the gentle hollow in her throat.

She leaned over to unlace his codpiece, Juan wishing that the black plague had killed him young. Then his *thing* was out and bobbing. She took it in her hand, and endlessly Juan came, seed plopping on her cot.

She comforted. Such things happened, *querido*. He had spirit to waste.... And she took him to the table.

Juan sat on the cold cane of a chair, feeling that strange relief which could follow disaster. Thank Almighty God—it was over! But he was wrong. Liliana sat on his lap, kissed him softly.

Juan blurted that the Church forbade this position.

No matter, she said—between kisses—she had done it this way many times with priests. Besides, there were no witnesses.

What about Christ Almighty Crucified, staring at us from the wall? thought Juan as she straddled him, taking his hands to her breasts, telling him what to do and how much she liked it. She began to moan—which made him moan. She asked him to suck her nipples. He rooted like a shameless hog.

Juan was in heaven at the consummation, not minding at all that he sinned by doing 'it' sitting. He wanted to plight his troth ... take her to the Indies.

Brisk, she said, "*Querido*, it is time to go."

He protested, but she was insistent, "Go tell your friend he needs to pay me."

Pedro—who dispatched whores efficiently as enemies—was long done with two and working on his thirst in one of the many taverns of the *mancebía*. He asked no questions, cracked no jokes. And he paid Liliana a large sum, for Juan had taken the time of four.

At the street corner that would erase Liliana from his vision forever, Juan turned to look. She waved....

He ignored Pedro's banter as they walked on, scarcely seeing Sevilla. What they said was true—when you came, you died a little death. Some said you came brains, some said sweetbreads. You never were the same again....

They emerged into a thoroughfare. The clamor of the street—the vendors, rumble of carts, and clop of hooves—was tossed back by the walls. A pair of gypsy beggars sang, clapping a rhythm ragged as their dress—stuttering hands playing with the echoes. Their Spanish words were set to Moorish melody—a high undulating wailing which returned Juan to curiosity.

Singing was just one legacy of the Moors, who dominated Andalusía for seven centuries before being conquered militarily, then converted, or evicted, by Ferdinand and Isabella. And Sevilla was one of the last bastions of their stay. Here, the yearnings of their desert souls remained visible in the architecture, the gardens, the food, and in the passion for concealment that turned the backs of Moorish houses to the street—these coffers for their women.

The *cristianos* scarcely modified old Moorish custom. Decent women only risked the street veiled and accompanied by a male relative or female servant. The truly reputable hid their faces and were led like the blind. However, there were women who briefly revealed an eye with forbidden coquetry. Laws against this shameless practice were passed to no avail ... the left eye of certain *sevillanas* was flirtatiously displayed.

Juan asked Pedro, "Why not the right?"

"Custom, *hijo*. They say some who reveal their eyes are whores, and some are noblewomen who debase themselves to flirt, even with slaves."

Why whores? Juan wondered. Required by law to bare their heads, they bared far more. If law allowed they would bare *everything*. But they were wrong to display themselves at all, he decided. The more you saw, the more they reminded you of livestock. But every veiled woman was a princess, for there was *something* about an eye. Unlike the thighs and udders of the *mancebía*, human eyes were not simple meat—though those of sheep were eaten. Eyes were windows to the soul. And this *sevillana* that just passed—he was sure—had looked at him.

She was small, wearing pattens—wooden overshoes with thick soles that elevated her above the filth of streets. And to judge by the livery of her servants, she was born to wealth. Juan imagined following her home, whispering at a grated garden door ... arranging a tryst. Her unveiled face was pale in starlight. The scent of oranges suffused the air....

"*Clavos de Cristo*," Pedro grumbled, "swoon some other time. We're heading to *El Corral de los Delicios*—The Square of Delights—and you need advice."

As the Eldorado of Europe, Sevilla attracted criminals as a corpse did maggots. Since the courts were corrupt, only those who could not afford a bribe went to the garrote or ax. And in a quarter surrounding the cathedral—ringed by the chain separating civil from religious authority—cutthroats, ruffians and thieves were subject only to the laws of the Church ... which is to say immune to justice. For crimes against God, the Church had the Inquisition. Secular sinners merely needed to confess and do their penance to be forgiven. In consequence, shriven criminals created a Gehenna about the cathedral that was renowned in all of Spain. And one of the two squares in it, *El Corral de los Delicios*, was said not to contain a single honest man.

Where they were going, Pedro said, you could have what you wanted for a price, and if that price was on your person you were in danger. He counseled Juan—slash, when the time comes. Just leave your mark. Killing got you into trouble. He chuckled. They would give these amateurs a tiny taste of war.

Since Columbus, ships sailing for the Indies had been crewed by sailors unwillingly recruited, usually from prison. And those who boarded voluntarily—more often than not—had good reason to depart. The voyage required desperation, for the hardships were many, the pay low, and Death was the only shipmate always to survive. Scores fled the law. And many of them were from the impoverished province of Extremadura. Pizarro—said to have been a swineherd—was born there. Consequently, *El Corral de los Delicios* was thronged not only with cutpurses and cutthroats, but also by their departing cousins in crime—soldiers and sailors drinking time away until the fleet departed.

Pedro took Juan to a tavern on the square that was named—with some irony, Juan thought—The Garden of Earthly Delights. The door, a pointed arch, opened to a courtyard surrounded by a colonnade. Overhead a balcony soared, elaborately carved with Moorish arabesques. At the center a fountain played—liquid tongues pouring from the mouths of lions. Candles lit the tables. Encapsulated by exquisite architecture, hunched over wine, every patron appeared to conspire.

Pedro recognized two veterans of the Italian wars, and greeted them. Bearing the scars that marked them as the fools of courage, drinking to no tomorrow, they were proud men, because the troops trained by *El Grán Capitán* were the best in Europe. Ruffians they might be, yet their discipline in combat did not have its equal. They drank, talked tactics, and traded yarns with Pedro. And—as this was their first trip to the Indies—they convinced him to describe Peru.

"The gold there would make reliquaries for every scrap of every saint that died on earth and went to Heaven, down to the last hair, splinters of the True Cross, and drops of Blessed Mary's milk ... hallowed be Her name."

The imp of storytelling had betrayed Pedro again. Jokes about the corruption of the Church were expected. Most men and women of the cloth were no less carnal—and venal—than every other mortal in this fallen world ... perhaps more so, appetites whetted by abstinence. Even reliquaries were ridiculed, for counterfeits abounded. But as for Mary, Mother of God without sin conceived—this known fact not yet official—even soldiers did not take Her Name in vain.

Spanish armies had God The Father at their head. He was The Judge, condemning or forgiving—which was to say that He worked for His Eternal Living—largely concerned with sending you to Hell. But Mary was simply there to intercede, having no other chore in Heaven. No matter how sinful you might be, she folded you in the blue mantle of forgiveness, and to soldiers—who needed forgiving more than almost anyone—her worship was ideal. Yet when the fighting moment came Spanish soldiers called upon the saint they called Santiago. The Father might judge, The Virgin intercede, Their Son redeem—and only wild-eyed theologians knew what the Holy Ghost was up to—but Santiago fought. In blinding armor, riding from High on a white horse, he miraculously intervened in the reconquest of Spain. Witnessed by thousands, he galloped from clouds that revealed the Heaven he had just come from, smiting Moors with the sword of God.

The day wore on to evening in *El Jardín de los Delicios*, comrades wetting tales of campaigns with wine. And candles had long been lit at all the tables when a voice hissed, "Pedro Gómez de San Benito, we meet again."

Pedro stood, hand on hilt. "*Pardiez*, De Hoz!"

Tension sputtered as if a fuse were lit, for De Hoz was flanked by four armed men....

Not liking this stranger—with his perfume and foppish clothes, his sneer made permanent by a harelip—Pedro's comrades rose as one.

Chairs scraped on flagstone in *El Jardín de los Delicios*, men backing to the walls to watch, yearning for the insult that would make honorable retreat impossible.

But Juan's spirit abandoned him to hover above his body—as it did sometimes before sleep—and it said, "I'm tired, Pedro. See you at the inn."

Catching up with his *hijo*, Pedro studied him, perplexed. Was he a coward, or cunning beyond his years? They had been outnumbered five to three, Juan a mere liability. De Hoz was a superb bladesman, his companions seasoned soldiers. And behind the table, they had been at a tactical disadvantage.

A half moon shone, the only other illumination passing torches. Juan plodded like a donkey bearing a fat prelate—good as blind—probably thinking about some book. Hah, hah, and hah! Writing was supposed to make you smart ... instead it made you talk like a moron and walk like a weary *burro*. But maybe he was judging Juan too harshly, Pedro thought. Faced with two desperate situations in as many days he had acquitted himself admirably in both—his strategies unorthodox, yet effective. And—despite his reading—his *hijo* had courage. He had stood beside him in the tavern, unwavering, when all he had was a knife in his sleeve to pit against the sword of De Hoz, who had killed more men than there were books in any library Pedro knew of.

Death had been Pedro's closest companion for more years than he cared to remember. Now, he had a closer one. Something that was not fear made him hesitate to fight in *El Jardín de los Delicios*—and this something had nothing to do with honor, comrades or the Crown, or God Himself Almighty. What happened there had everything to do with a puzzling child. Pedro was no longer free to be himself.

They arrived at the inn as dawn was breaking, slept until hunger woke them. And then Pedro sent for pork, his meat of preference. He made a point of eating great quantities, cutting off gobs, twirling them in juices, sticking them in his mouth with his knife, chewing and belching, grease glistening on his beard—where he could lick it later. Pork was meat delicious in and of itself, of course, but more importantly it was a demonstration of his Spanish purity of blood—*limpieza de sangre*. No Jew he, by God! So, this morning, Pedro gobbled the incarnation of his denial of fallen races, saying that today could not be spent on pleasure. They needed passage to the Indies and—*Voto a Dios!*—*that* would not be easy at this late date.

They walked to the Arenal—what the *sevillanos* called the expanse that lay between the walls of the city and the river Guadalquivir serving as its port. When fleets were preparing to depart there was not space in all Sevilla to house the goods. The excess was therefore stored on the shore—olive oil, wine and ceramic tile from Andalucía, cloth from Castile, mercury from Almadén, used to extract silver in the mines of México. Since Spain produced only a fraction of the necessary, merchandise came from much of Europe—Normandy wool, Angers linen, Italy brocades. To fit out the fleet, hemp rope from Hamburg. There was ordnance—powder and shot, wads for the cannons, long ropes of match and pyramids of cannon balls. For the passage, there was dried herring and eel, salted cod, smoked beef and pork, barrels of flour and ship's biscuit, olives, garlic, raisins, tuns of wine—not water, for it spoiled at sea. Livestock was brought to slaughter—immense flocks of chickens and ducks, droves of calves, pigs, and goats, herds of sheep and cattle. Provisioning the two fleets left Sevilla with no month of ease. The Arenal was a perpetual fair that turned to bedlam at the end. And there was nothing like it in God's world.

Juan had not dreamed so many languages existed. Not just the dialects of a Spain still imperfectly united—Catalan, Aragonese, Galician. There was Portuguese too, and French, and northern languages Pedro could not name—beer drinkers! There were versions of Italian—Venetian, Sicilian, and, especially Genoese, for they were formidable merchants and skilled sailors. As for the goods…! You could get lost in casks and tuns, bales and boxes, sacks stacked high as houses, the little space between plied by ox-drawn carts, drovers shouting for pedestrians to make way.

They did not find passage that day, and that evening Pedro brooded in his cups, rambling on about De Hoz…. No one was quicker to take offense. No one could so bear a grudge. In the use of a sword he had few equals, but he still preferred a knife in the back or a hired ruffian. Sucking wine from his beard, Pedro sighed, saying they had served together in Peru, where De Hoz had been Pizarro's friend. And one day De Hoz made some stupid proposal. Unfortunately, everyone had been drinking *chicha*—a kind of Inca wine—so he, Pedro, blurted out something about hare-brained ideas, not even mentioning harelips. And De Hoz had drawn his sword. So, there they were, lost in Inca mountains, freezing and starving, enemy campfires all around, and the lame brain wanted a duel to the death about his lip. Pizarro did not allow it of course, but De Hoz had never forgiven or forgotten. And now he was returning to the Indies and Pedro wondered why. As Pizarro's confidante he had become fabulously wealthy and returned to Spain to marry, maybe settle down. God only knew what he was doing in *El Jardín de los Delicios*. He should be on his estates with his wife, who was rich and by repute not bad … hem … in both upper and lower story.

Pedro lapsed into moody silence, and Juan was about to go to sleep when he heard, "*Bolsillos.*"

"What!" With a start.

"De Hoz had pockets, *hijo*—holes sewn into your clothes to hold things, so you do not have to put them in your purse or sleeve. They were the rage in Italy when last I was there."

Pedro was jealous, Juan realized. And he headed for bed, mystified until he perceived that, having no rival in war, Pedro had met one in 'indument.' De Hoz had brilliantly included a detail omitted from his own creations. And now—*pardiez!*—pockets were denied Pedro, for how could he appear to imitate…?

Next morning Pedro broke his fast with *pajaritos*—songbirds plucked, gutted and fried whole. You grabbed the legs and ate, starting with the head. Pedro consumed dozens, happily crunching.

Juan did not himself enjoy this dish, which inescapably reminded him of cats eating mice. Francis *was* his confirmation name, after all—after he of Assisi. He ate bread pudding instead, and drank baptized wine.

Pedro said he knew a Genoese trader—Giambattista di Lorenzo—who owed him a favor or two. And—although he had no ships of his own—he had influence. Pedro grinned, rubbing thumb and forefinger together. All Genoese had *that* weakness. And since the Crown allowed only Spaniards to trade in the Indies he might find Pedro useful. They would dress in their best to see him.

The street where Di Lorenzo lived was narrow, houses turning blank backs to traffic, and little wonder. Juan was used to wayfares fouled by 'servants,' as chamber pots were called. But the stench of Sevilla! Not just human waste, but garbage, festered in the heat, overlain by the excrement of the emaciated packs of dogs multiplying on that fare, so numerous that from time to time they were killed in special hunts.

In Juan's village, pattens were the ostentation of wealthy women. Here, the elevated clogs were a necessity and Juan was grateful for the boots Pedro bought to replace the sandals of his youth.

The door they arrived at was sky blue. They knocked and a small window opened, framing a face that was absolutely black. *Negro* slaves were almost unheard of in Extremadura. In Sevilla they were prized as docile, unlike Berbers and Turks. Rarity made them more valuable, and it was considered the height of fashion to be escorted by the blackest of the black, dressed 'Moorish style'—that is, in caftan and turban.

This one was not the brown of leather or *serrano* ham, like some that Juan had seen, for his black rivaled the habit of Dominicans. And when the door opened Juan could not help but gape. The *negro* wore the blue of the door, gold rope as girdle—the very livery of those escorting the girl who had revealed her left eye! And now, this creature plucked from dreams was bowing, saying master would be with them shortly.

Like *El Jardín de los Delicios* this mansion was built about a courtyard, a balcony giving access to the rooms of the second floor. Supporting it all, arches writhed with intricate carving, but—unlike the *yesería* of the tavern—these arabesques were brightly painted, and the whitewashed walls were tiled shoulder high with interlocked designs in saturated hues. This—thought Juan—was less a house than a jeweled casket.

The courtyard was a geometric garden immaculately trimmed. A desert people, Moors were captivated by vegetation. Who else would name a capital after the pomegranate? But they loved water more. And denied representation in art and architecture—their women veiled—their sensuality found an outlet in their play with water.... At the four corners of the courtyard gryphons gushed from bronze tubes set in their mouths onto marble troughs. In them, water rippled in a pattern gently dying into an octagonal, central pool. That placid mirror reflected the garden, the surrounding arches, the swallows swooping above, scissored wings cutting the blue clarity of Andalusian skies. And always, the liquid sound....

The graying man—politely bowing as he waddled in their direction—was in no way a Moor. However, his somber attire was the very essence of Castilla. Di Lorenzo had become fabulously rich in Spanish camouflage—though he had not dared to fabricate progenitors back to El Cid, as many did when *limpieza de sangre* decided everything that mattered. It was good to blend with the background when you were breaking the letter of the law.

Foreigners trading in the Indies employed Spaniards as their agents, and the Crown winked a Royal Eye at this, content to get its third. However, Di Lorenzo's wealth was built on caution, and although fabulous riches were pouring in from Mexico and Peru—with which the Emperor financed his addiction to religious war—He was always profoundly in debt. The day would come when too many soldiers, their pay too long in arrears, would be needed for another campaign against Lutherans, and the Crown would confiscate the wealth of foreigners, and for this Di Lorenzo was prepared. He had an estate in northern Italy where he could retire—for there he had gold and silver illegally smuggled out. But now that the riches of Peru had begun to pour in Di Lorenzo had decided to retire a little wealthier, a little later. He needed a reasonably honest Spanish rogue, willing to just reasonably break the law and not take advantage of his patron by walking away with profits that legally were his. Pedro Gómez de San Benito was quite possibly that man, and it was said he had the ear of Pizarro himself.

Di Lorenzo welcomed his guests, leading them into a room furnished with Moorish comfort, Italian elegance and Castilian severity. Oriental carpets glowed on the tile floor, where ottomans, sofas and cushions in rich fabric vied for splendor. Flemish tapestries hung the walls— among them a Susanna naked at the spring, lush woods revealing portions of her nakedness, while here and there through leaves, the eyes of elders stared. A table inlaid with ebony and mother of pearl was flanked by straight-backed chairs carved so as to intricately burrow into flesh— magnificent examples of Castilian furniture as penitence.

Oil paintings portrayed martyred saints, and Juan approached a triptych of Santa Olalla flayed by Romans. To the left Olalla chained at her trial. At the center her dismembered body on a table in the countryside, her flayed skin elevated by a centurion, looking like a painting in the painting. And at the right Olalla was whole again, ascending into clouds of Heaven, welcomed by gestures of the blessed.

Varnish, thought Juan, washed pale gold over martyrdom, so that seeing it was like looking through summer air into another world where all was small and perfect, luminous. This was how God saw man, he decided—living, suffering and dying, going to Heaven or to Hell, at once. To His Eye in some way a whole human life was a triptych—simultaneous and distant, a beautiful design.

Pedro and Di Lorenzo sat at their table, politely chatting. Casually, Pedro mentioned that his young friend—now frozen before a painting—was a lover of fine art. Then like chess masters, soldier and merchant engaged in the treacherous simplicities of the opening game.

Negotiations concluded to the satisfaction of both, Di Lorenzo invited his honored guests to—as he said—partake of his poor repast…. A flight of stairs led to a room opening on the courtyard through windows with pointed arches that filled it with light and air—not like the stifling houses of the Spanish north Juan knew, where windows covered by oiled parchment shut out heat and cold, most light as well, sealing in the odor of chamber pots.

According to custom, the room was divided by a carved railing. On one side were chairs and a table for the men. On the other was a platform covered with oriental carpets, strewn with cushions on which women could recline. Centuries of warfare summed this space, Juan thought, so that it figured forth a Spain which fought the Moors so long it wed the enemy.

Pedro glanced at Juan uneasily, comforted to see that he had managed to sit down. Then, at his ease, he swilled aged wine, downed olives and *empanadas*—these pastries baked and fried, stuffed with delicacies—sighing with pleasure in anticipation of the meal to come. The obese Genoese was no Carlos V, to dine on millet, lentils and little else, and little of *that*, at that.

Servants entered bearing pickled tongue, pigeon pâté, chicken stewed in wine and—that edible Christian shibboleth—pork ... in this case rolled and stuffed with sausage, pepper and garlic. With it arrived an exquisite blancmange ... clove an Italian touch. After, came platters of figs, oranges and melon slices, grapes and pomegranates, almond pastries and—a crowning touch—sweetened egg yolk spiced with cinnamon and shaped into tiny fruits and animals. Forks were provided, but Pedro in this rare case did not approve of an Italian innovation. Knives did everything just as well in his opinion, and other things much better, like trim your beard and toenails. And, when it came to fighting, a fork was a joke.

Di Lorenzo had included a signal honor with the meal, for his wife and daughter reclined beyond the rail—odalisques nibbling from silver platters set on low ivory tables. A *sevillano* would be absolutely scandalized, but none was present, and the Genoese had set a scene that worked wonders for his business in the past.

Licking his knife, crunching almond pastry, gulping white wine fromVenetian crystal, Pedro eyed the blonde and blue-eyed, opulent wife—a magnificent, example of what money could buy in northern Italy.

As for Juan, he was in love with the daughter, and it had happened as love must—the first sight a blow from an exquisite mace. He was in Heaven, and the food was ash. His mouth was dry. The wine was vinegar. On a Sevilla street the veil of Isis had been rent, revealing a left eye, and here it had been lifted from a beauty too great to be endured. He could not look and could not look away. Constanza di Lorenzo! Her very name was music!

Hebrew by his Ark, Juan worshipped as he ate. Her eyes were a cerulean blue shaded by lashes long and dark—enchanted pools in shadowed grottoes, they reflected summer skies. Her ebony hair, caressed by silver nets, swung over fingers that were tapered alabaster, and from time to time she would rub them in perfumed water poured by servants. Then sometimes she would glance—at him!—aloof, while toying with meat and pasty.

Juan was going downstream fast, Pedro decided, for—while not entering into trances—

he was eating like a famished beggar and swilling priceless wine like water. He fidgeted. He blushed. He blanched. And he was still eating from the huge platter of blancmange placed before him when first he saw the daughter of Di Lorenzo.

Holy Mary, help my *hijo*, Pedro prayed, for this was puppy love. Next, Juan would kneel and sigh, reciting verses from **Amadís de Gaula**....

Juan sighed.... Horrified, he tried to turn this revelation into a cough—a deep mistake, as his mouth was full—and he shut his lips on the contrived explosion. Blancmange taking a bad turn—he gagged.

Pedro hammered Juan with a hand like a *serrano* ham until—from inner depths and with an awful retching sound—blancmange was ejected, to glisten on a priceless carpet.

Mea culpa, mea maxima culpa, Juan prayed, eyes closed as he knelt by the rail that forever would separate him from perfection. Images of flagellants following the crucifix in Holy Week flashed by his eyes, and with the distant intensity of the dying, knowing that nothing worse could happen now, he opened his eyes to see Constanza one last time, her mouth opened wide with astonishment.

She had noticed him on her way to Mass, briefly baring her left eye in that small rebellion of her sex against perpetual incarceration. What was this modestly dressed youth—handsome, and about her age—doing with a peacock of a soldier...? She had risked a second glance.

Exquisite as Constanza knew herself to be, never had she been worshipped *instantly*, and this was causing her to dream of some impossible revelation of her own—a wink?—when Juan knelt before her, pounded on the back by his gigantic companion, to eject blancmange.

If this was love's strange tribute, Constanza wanted nothing of it. Intending to leave, she was unable, chained to the entreaty in his eyes.

In his misery and ecstasy Juan had repeatedly drained a cup kept full by hovering servants, and so he was unsteady as he rose. Blancmange accused him from the carpet, staring back with a blind man's eye. Juan scooped it up.

Cuerpo de Dios! what to do...? He needed a pocket ... had none. His purse was out of the question. Bowing with a flourish he considered his velvet cap, dropped in the gobbet and hurried from the room, concentrating.... *He must not put it on*!

Pedro was forced into ignoble exit yet again, but this time the departure was less a solution than a problem. Food was uneaten, wine not drunk. But above all, he had no letters of passage or credit from the merchant they just insulted. Muttering obscenities into his beard, licking it for wine and cinnamon syrup, Pedro lumbered after Juan, cursing the printing presses that now swarmed Spain like lice. Sit *him* on the throne and he would burn them all!

Luckily, he caught up with Juan before he came to harm, staggering with wine and despair, cap extended like a beggar's.

That evening, both silent at their meal, Pedro emptied his *bota*, devising repairs to their enterprise. As for Juan, he was remembering the Amadís de Gaula who—unjustly spurned by Oriana—vowed to spend his remaining years praying in a hermit's hut. The greatest knight of history had been loved by the most beautiful queen ever to exist, the wheel of fortune taking the hero higher than any before or after, creating the tremendous measure of his tragedy. But never having risen, Juan could not fall. Black Death should have killed him as a child.

Next morning Pedro was firm. "*Hijo*, I am off to see Di Lorenzo by myself. Explore if you must—but, *pardiez!*—you will do this with an armed companion. I have made arrangements with the *ventero*."

Juan sat listless for a time, then dressed in a white linen shirt with lace at neck and wrist, gray hose—the codpiece modestly padded—a doublet of black embroidered velvet puffed at the shoulders, matching velvet cap.

When this, his best outfit, was first discussed, Pedro grumbled at Juan's monkish taste. What next, lentils for pearls? Juan needed something with—for the love of the living God!—color and fashion. But as Juan remained obstinate the result was compromise. He chose the absence of color, the severe cut, Pedro the magnificent cloth. Therefore Juan left in subdued finery, defiantly alone. As a *cristiano* he could not commit suicide, but if Pedro courted death for lucre and enjoyment, Juan could tempt it with indifference. Sevilla was dangerous, but no courage equaled despair. And the *negro* in blue had intrigued him.

Juan went to the cathedral, where slaves were sold on the steps of the west facade. There the Portuguese—who more or less monopolized the trade—hawked *moros* and *negros*, barking in their peculiar accent. Business was brisk before the sculptured portico portraying The Last Judgment. Almighty God, Jesus Christ, the Blessed Virgin, and an assembly of saints and angels looked down at the commerce going on, unmoved … for the Christian tradition of selling heathens into bondage was centuries old.

Today more *moros* than *negros* were being auctioned, more men than women, some children. A shackled Saracen with the eyes of a bird of prey was on the block, staring at the crowd. Born to sand and solitude, he would die in his captivity, Juan thought, as all Indians did in Spain, needing freedom as they needed air.

He headed for the Arenal, thinking of *negros*, deciding that Di Lorenzo had the blackest in Sevilla, which was to say in Spain, since only Lisbon had more slaves. In Extremadura it was said the South was like a chessboard—black and white in equal number.

He entered the Alcaicería, a walled quarter which was guarded, such were the riches it contained. Here, the costliest merchandise was displayed—pearls and other gems, crystal, enamels, coral, feather fans, brocades, silks, gold and silver worked into exotic forms.

Juan passed the royal prison on Sierpes Street, an enormous building recently constructed. Ferdinando and Isabella had spent some of the tidal wave of wealth from the Indies on public architecture—this phenomenon without precedent in Spain. Not long ago the only large buildings were castles and churches. Now there were royal hospitals, and prisons towered above the cities. And in Extremadura returning *conquistadores* were erecting grim palaces of stone, displaying the wealth to be found elsewhere as islands in the grinding poverty that made exodus the necessary dream.

Juan came to Sevilla's abattoirs, largest in the world, built to provision the fleet—that city floating on the sea. Striding through driven beasts Juan paused at a bridge over a tributary of the Guadalquivir, where gutters spewed the offal of slaughter, a sight suiting his mood.

He strode to the Arenal, where a bridge built over boats crossed the river. And there the awaited moment came....

Two men barred his way. "What have we here," said the larger through teeth black with rot. "A peacock with no tail feathers. Must be a hen."

The other—who had lost an eye and not bothered to blind the socket—replied, "We'll have to see how many fingers fit the ass ... see if it's laying eggs."

They laughed.

Having his pride, Juan drew his knife.

"*La guaguita tiene navajita*," the larger mocked, arching back to roar.

"Baby's got a little knife. Baby's got a little knife," one-eye echoed....

Sick with shame before the assembled crowd, Juan cried out, "*Caballeros*, on your guard."

They laughed, and did not draw their enormous knives.

Juan was despairing, thinking he would not be allowed his honor, when the voice he would never forget spoke—a cadenced treble—menacing for all its melody. "*Pardiez*, one of you ruffians will fight this *caballero*, and I wager ten *reales* he will win."

Turning to face his savior, Juan understood the silence of the crowd.... A figure dressed in blue had spoken, and by his side crouched four immense, armored mastiffs, leather collars set with bright, honed blades. Unleashed, the war dogs were quivering with blood lust....

With an elaborate bow the vision addressed Juan. "Nuño Beltrán de Mendoza at your service, *caballero*. I see that you have encountered riff raff."

Juan returned the bow.

"I admire courage," his savior said, as the gathered crowd began to form a ring.

Mendoza began taking bets, the odds being long.

After a whispered argument, the cutthroat with the rot-dark smile swaggered up.

Juan unlaced his doublet and tossed it aside, knowing there would be no rules, honor demanding only that blood be drawn.

"Begin," cried out the man in blue, and—floating far above his body—Juan saw what then transpired with God's own candor....

He was tiny in a circle of shouting men.

Pedro taught him what to do. *Never* grapple with a larger man. Keep your distance. Forget the battles of books, do not go for the heart ... dart in and slash, dart out. Tire him. Bleed him. Move! Your best weapon is your speed. Your second is your youth. Your blade is but your third.

They feinted for eternities until the other leapt, knife extended for the kill.

But the eyes of Rotten Mouth betrayed him....

Juan spun to the side, slashing the knife arm to the bone.

Again— as if swimming through molten glass—the two circled in the trembling heat of Andalusía. The other gasped for breath, now, threadbare shirt so sweaty it showed every matted hair.

Juan whirled in, thinking to cut with his arc, but the other dropped to seize his ankle, and when his back hit sand it was like being kicked by mules.

He somersaulted backward as a knife descended. Seeing legs ... he kicked between. The other doubled over.

Juan slashed and rolled away.

Rotten Mouth screamed, bright blood running down homespun to the straw-stuffed rags he used for shoes, and he was lame as they returned to circling, the Arenal drinking his blood as in a bullring. The moment of truth approached....

Suddenly, Juan went blind, launching himself sideways so wildly he rolled into the legs of the crowd.... He leapt to his feet—still in the circle of Hell that despair had chosen for him—sand falling from his eyes....

Rotten Mouth stumbled.

Juan leapt in and out, leaving the knife in him. But Rotten Mouth did not fall with the uncanny silence of a fighting bull. With a wordless keening renewed by every shuddering breath, he gripped the hilt of Juan's knife with both hands, as if he had just stabbed himself. Then his legs began to run to take him from his death. Instead they spun him like a slowing wheel....

Mendoza said, "That *hideputa* will soon look the Devil in the eye. Better leave with our winnings before the *alguaciles* get here."

Rotten Mouth was simply shivering, now, no longer spinning.

The dogger reached down to yank out Juan's knife, and wiped it on the shirt of the dying man. "A mercy, really," he offered, handing Juan his weapon. "He'll die the sooner."

And leading Juan away Mendoza said, "If that scum had been a bull, I would give you both his ears."

Chapter 2: The Ocean Sea (1539)

The pinnace of the *Santiago de Compostela* labored through a moonless night, surrounded by the riding lights of anchored vessels—unsteady stars beneath a steady heaven. At the bow a sailor held high the vacillating flame of their own lantern, leading them through the maze of galleys, *naos* and caravels. Odors commingled over the tranquil Guadalquivir—of hemp and tar, the reeking woolens sailors wore every hour of every day. Cargoes lent hints of olive oil, wine, salt herring, cod, and unknown things.... This was the perfume of leaving Juan thought, for on this September morning he would be sailing for the Indies.

A looming darkness blotted out the dawn ... a hail and response....

Juan scrambled up a rope ladder, in awe of the dim forest of masts and spars above, the tracery of cordage. He thought of God sketching on the black canvas that was Chaos. And soon the breezes of the risen sun drove a slow roil of cumulus southwest.

All Sevilla was congregated on the Arenal. Today the die was absolutely cast, and no sweet terror was its equal. At a time when Fortuna sat at God's left hand, Sevilla wagered for the highest stakes. The arrival of a successful fleet would daze Croesus. Hundreds of ox-drawn carts transported treasure to the *Casa de Contratación*. And when the riches overflowed the dungeons guards stood by the excess piled in the streets. Or, a shudder of Fortuna's wheel might sink the fleet, bankrupting the largest peaceful enterprise in the world. But on this bright day the *sevillanos* celebrated, disaster a distant thing. Astrologers considered the aspects favorable, and if the stars misled Sevilla Almighty God would not, blessing the expedition as bringing Heaven's light to benighted Indian eyes. Mass was celebrated on the shore upon an altar containing a fragment of the foot of Christopher, patron saint of travelers.

From the gently rocking deck Juan heard Gregorian chant solemnly floating over water. And after the *Ite missa est* a salvo tore the silence. The demi-culverins—largest ordnance of the fleet—the mortars and falconets, thundered and barked, the oak ship shuddering with recoil. Tatters of acrid smoke dispersed as chanting sailors turned the capstan, weighing anchor. Others sped up ratlines to where the pennant of empire floated from the mainmast, the twin gold eagles glorious in the wind.

Juan turned to the plump youth beside him, leaning on the rail. "Isn't this...?" he said. "What a thing...!"

The young sailor replied, solemn as a Thomist agreeing to transubstantiation, "The fleet is a thing indeed." And there was a twinkle in his eye.

His name was Gil, and he was a *gromete*—an apprentice seaman. He added with a wink that he was the 'duck fucker,' caring for the animals on board. But he was also the trumpeter, he proudly added. His father taught him to play—God rest his soul!

Gil's candor made it all pour out of Juan—his orphanhood, a life made bearable by *romances*....

The *gromete* cut Juan's babbling short by saying he could not read. Patiently, then, he answered questions.... Twenty leagues to the Mediterranean, an easy day's sail, but they would anchor before they got there, as there was no moon and the shoals at the mouth of the Guadalquivir were treacherous. God willing, tomorrow they would be sailing salt.

And this was a *nao*, not a caravel—bigger by many tuns. Also, *naos* were not clinker built, which meant the planks did not overlap. They were butted and caulked with oakum.

Oakum was hemp and tar. And a tun was the wine cask ... with which someone once decided to measure the size of ships. Juan could see them in the orlop if he wanted.

The orlop was the lowest deck. They were standing on the spar ... and no idea of why three masts. *Naos* had three, or they would be something else. The front one was the fore. The middle was the main. On the poop was the mizzen.

Yes, the mizzen probably should have been called the hind mast. And yes, the name was strange. And no, he didn't know where the word came from. "Maybe they put a mast where it was mizzen."

Inspired by his wit, Gil stalked like an actor in a comedy, looking everywhere but in the right direction, saying, "The mast is mizzen." Doing a double take he cried, "Aha, it's on the poop deck!"

Hooting, they collapsed. And there they were, pounding oak with their fists, kicking heels in the air, when a body towered over them....

Juan's heart plummeted. From the pinnace, the **Santiago de Compostela** had seemed a floating world. Yet aboard it was a small space to share with Pedro, after Nuño Beltrán de Mendoza....

After killing Rotten Mouth, Juan went to a tavern with the dogger, stunned by what he had done, needing to get drunk. Over a glass of wine he studied Mendoza, who had the lean elegance of bullfighters, and pallor perfected by a broad-brimmed hat. Blue as imagined tropic seas, his eyes were flecked with gold. White-blond hair fell to the blue silk of his shoulders. He was an angel on earth—calm as a Heaven glimpsed through the clouds of altarpieces, revealing a frozen turbulence of seraphim—for never did he display emotion. His rare smiles were scarcely seen, and then sardonic. Drinking, he stayed sober. Speaking, he was most abstracted when most intense. His dogs perfected his absence from the world, Juan decided, by creating the limbo surrounding him. In brief, Mendoza was everything hulking Pedro was not. And the contrast was unavoidable when Juan returned to find him snoring by his wine.

Pedro woke to tell him they had passage to the Indies, pulling vellum from his sleeve. They danced madly about the room, sat for a celebratory cup ... Juan mentioning the knife fight.

Pummeling his *hijo* Pedro bellowed, "We'll make a bladesman of you yet." And all was well until Mendoza's name was mentioned.

"*Hijo*," Pedro said abruptly sobered, "as God lives, Mendoza is a faggot and devil, his name infamy in the Indies. In my opinion he has less conscience than his dogs. As president of the first *audiencia* in Mexico he captured Tangaxoan, the *cacique*, or head, of the Michoacans, and to extort gold from him he had his family devoured by dogs before his eyes. Then he put him in stocks and roasted his feet over coals, basting them with a marinade of olive oil and garlic, saying that was what you did with pig's trotters, after all. Tangaxoan died without a sound they say, as dogs fought over his flesh."

Juan was speechless, Pedro remorseless. Mendoza's specialty was the *montería infernal*, the infernal hunt. He ran down Indians as one ran down game.

Pedro pleaded. "*Hijo,* it is one thing to kill warriors in combat, but to hunt down women and children ... feed them to dogs...."

Juan stuttered that this could not be true.

"No one—ever—gives me the lie!"

For an intolerable moment they were eye to eye ... and then Juan turned his back.

Pedro handed him his passage to the Indies before leaving, saying he did not want him here when he returned.

Juan walked Sevilla like the Wandering Jew, footsore, famished. At nightfall he spent his one *ochavo* on an *empanada*. He roamed, eating his spicy, meat filled bread, fearful that his throat would be slit if he dared sleep. The second day near sunset, hunger overcame pride.

"Join me," Mendoza offered, with a tightening about the mouth that might have been a smile. He added, "There are not that many men worth feeding."

So now, 'sailing salt,' Juan had nothing to do. He avoided the stern castle, where Pedro spent his time. And as Mendoza was self-absorbed, he turned his attention to the cats conscripted from the alleys of Sevilla. Vicious and unnamed, they were welcomed no more than the vermin they suppressed, and it was impossible to approach the mangy things. A grizzled deckhand told him he should befriend a rat instead, since he seemed to have ... that kind of liking.

Juan pretended to absorb himself in the slow passing of the dun and lavender coast.

That night he made his bed on deck like the sailors, his bundle his pillow, cloak his blanket. A sliver of moon shone through rigging to where he lay by livestock— pigs and chickens not grudging him their company, as Pedro and the crew did. In his place what would Amadís, the hero, do? The cold moon hovered over swaying spars, distant as Mendoza.... And Juan fell asleep under stars that brought ill fortune only, thinking of how beautiful malevolence could seem.

Next morning he watched sailors wolf a breakfast of rough wine, ship's biscuit, garlic and salt sardine. They primed the pump and turned the capstan, chanting as fetid water coughed into the scuppers. They were swabbing the deck when Gil sauntered in his direction. Dark eyes laughing, he asked Juan what it was like to live in a *romance*.

"No fair maid in sight. Otherwise not bad," Juan lied.

Gil had been on duty since four, he said, and intended to sleep until noon watch. Why not meet when he was off at two?

Reading Juan's face he chuckled, saying, "You'll know, the change of watch is called."

Juan had heard the *gromete* by the steersman chant, now and again, unaware that this comprised a singing clock. How could a simple seaman know the time?

Gil laughed. "There's an hourglass—the *ampolleta*. I turn it when the sand runs out, every half hour."

Time was important to monks, Juan knew. They prayed at *matins, compline, vespers*. Heaven had told them when to toll their bells. But no one else kept time and life went on just fine ... except for sailors. Why? The wind blew. The weather varied. This all happened at God's unmeasured pleasure.

Gil said the crew needed to know their watches, which changed every four hours except for the one after noon—the dog watch—which was split in two. This meant that every day the sailors were on duty at different times. And as he had just finished the graveyard watch—from midnight to four—he was dead on his feet. Time to sleep.

The **Santiago de Compostela** was running with the wind—a bone in her teeth, as the sailors said. And when Gil left, Juan mused about their language—unbend the mizzen, belay the backstays, tighten the spritsail sheet, grease them parrell trucks.... The *nao* was a new world to itself, speaking a language that sounded familiar only if you did not listen. And when you did it was the gibber of Cipangu.

When he woke, Gil took Juan on a tour of the orlop. Deep in the ship a sailor and *gromete* were preparing the evening mess. Pork and sausage—made from entrails stuffed with chopped livers and lights, blood and garlic—sizzled on spits. Gil coaxed one from the cooks, to share with Juan. "These are the good times," he said. "Soon it will be wormy biscuit and salt fish. And when the wine runs out—if it doesn't rain—we'll be drinking water you wouldn't wash your ass with." Back on the spar deck, sucking his fingers, Gil concluded, "But that's only for us hands. You and Mendoza will fare better."

"What do you mean by *that*?"

"When we're picking grub from hardtack you'll be feasting on chicken and quince jelly."

He explained that passengers and officers were allowed personal provisions, and Mendoza had brought with him eight plump hens, a suckling pig and two large chests of food, no doubt filled with fine wines, orange marmalade, honey, figs and raisins ... maybe even spices. The *gromete* stared at the horizon. "You don't want to hear this, but I'll tell you anyway. The sailors hate Mendoza, not you. He brought his reputation with him from the Indies and he's taking it right back. If I were you I'd have nothing to do with him."

Juan asked no more questions. But Gil had provided sobering confirmation of Pedro's opinion of the dogger.

They sighted Grand Canary on September 15th after a week of extraordinary weather, the wind so constant the *nao* well as sailed itself. This steady, untroubled pace was the sort of magic that books had led Juan to expect, but to the sailors it meant chores. Therefore—ritually as they complained about bad weather— they now complained of good. They swabbed the deck, mended tackle, did the thousand other duties set aside.

And with Gil's instruction, Juan could now understand their peculiar speech. The **Santiago de Compostela** was "*el rocín*"—the broken down horse. A ship in general was "*el pájaro puerco*"—the pig bird. If sailors wanted food it was "*pon la mesana*"—set the mizzen. If they spilled something it was, "*como achica*"—see that pump suck. As for farts, "*Ay, de popa*"—watch out aft!

Yet the *nao* did not lose its aura of miracle. Devouring *romances*, perusing maps, Juan had somehow imagined ships as willingly transporting you to your desire, the wind existing to display the pennants that in illustrations rivaled sails for size—both indicating to him the femininity of vessels. He learned instead that wind propelled the obstinate *nao*, its ponderous sails set by dint of hard and risky labor. Still and all, he remained astonished that the wind could blow one way as the *nao* went another—a phenomenon even Gil could not explain, attributing the ship's behavior to the captain.

Gil had been wrong in insinuating intimacy between Mendoza and Juan, but he was otherwise right, for they ate far better than others on the *nao*. Mornings,

Mendoza fussed in the orlop, stripped to an immaculate shirt, supervising the basting of his meats with olive oil and pepper … or perhaps cinnamon, preserved lemon rind and quince. Gil also had been right about the chests, having omitted only the preserved lemons and olives, pickled hare and candied orange rind.

When the one cooked meal of the day was eaten—after Mass, at noon—Mendoza and Juan sat apart from the rest. Usually the dogger ignored Juan as he did all others, yet he made a point of conversing at their meals, usually about the banquets he impossibly assembled in the stinking bowels of the vessel. They were invariably strange, and often delicious.

One morning Mendoza said they would celebrate his saint's day with a special meal, explaining that though he used ingredients Aztecs lacked—chicken, bread, black pepper—he made it in *their* style. He handed Juan a bowl of the dark and foaming liquid he had been beating. Intensely bitter, the beverage vaguely tasted of clove, strongly of something else.

"*Chocolatl*," Mendoza said.

"Not bad," Juan responded, more honestly than he expected, licking the aromatic bitterness of the New World from his lips. Then came the main course—suckling pig cooked in an unimaginable sauce … based on *chocolatl* and chilies, as Juan found out. Sucking useless air, weeping helplessly and nodding that it was good, Juan chewed, Mendoza uncorking *jeréz* when at last he finished. Snuffling, wiping his eyes, Juan wondered why his teacher seemed pleased with his performance.

"A hybrid dish," Mendoza said, pouring. "Spanish meat with Aztec spices. And since you have passed this trial by fire … one last thing." He extended a bowl filled with speckled paste. "Something I dreamed up. Try it on bread."

Sipping *jeréz*, Mendoza talked about Spaniards and Aztec food. We clamor for wheat, he said—and, would you believe it, barley! We dream of oranges, reluctantly eating maize. We yearn for pork and beef, rejecting what meat there is in Mexico, especially *iguana* and those little Indian dogs, both of them delicious. Of course we turn up our noses at Indian spices … and was not this ironic when spices brought Spain to the Indies in the first place. But it is ridiculous to try to make the Indies into a New Spain. Just look at the names—New Granada, New Córdoba, new this, new that—meaning that we want old Spanish this, old Spanish that…. We leave Spain because we cannot stand it, and having crossed the Ocean Sea we dream of nothing else. The *conquistador* has no real appreciation of the new, wanting only to make his fortune and return to build an ugly palace towering over the pigsty of his birth, but not before he does his best to transform the Indies into the nightmare he left behind."

Mendoza shook his head with pity. "You should have seen the City of Mexico when we arrived. There was an immense palace in which the simplest things were astonishing, for to their rulers life itself was an art. And I am not just referring to the miracles they fashioned from the gold we Spanish are obsessed with. Far more interesting were the every-day objects fashioned from wood, bone and shell ... from gourds! Their ceramics were extraordinary. They made capes entirely covered with brilliant feathers! And in the palace was an enormous complex built only for unimaginable beasts and birds—not animals to be ridden, shorn or eaten—just there to have their rarity admired.

As for the act of love, Atahualpa's harem was expert in refinements that must have taken centuries to perfect. They made the most beautiful Spanish woman, trained to flop on her back and grit her teeth, resemble a plank offering her knothole. And of course there was Aztec cooking, of which you here have a distant imitation."

Mendoza watched with interest as Juan dipped into the speckled paste.

"When you think about it," the dogger continued, "the wealthiest Spaniards live austerely in dank and drafty, stinking homes. Or they kneel on stone in an equally drafty church, praying for good reason to be dead and gone to Heaven. And imagine that—weapons and armor aside—the only Spanish art is religious...! Now, picture your companions and the swineherds who lead them, ignorant of everything fine and beautiful, turned loose on the palace of Atahualpa.... I am accustomed to death of course, but there is a moment I will never forget from the sack of Mexico. Some soldier raped one of the emperor's concubines as I watched. Exquisite, in the flower of her youth, she was perfumed and pampered, trained from childhood in every refinement. Too frightened and ignorant to know better, she began to do to the *infante* what she had been taught, and as a good *cristiano* the *infante* slit her throat for these sins, raping her as she died. What I saw that day became to me an emblem of Spain's passion for the Indies."

Aghast, Juan looked down to parse the porridge he was eating ... bland, only slightly fiery, and —Thank God!—only slightly spicy. The texture was smooth, though something stuck between your teeth....

Mendoza resumed. "The true alchemy in the crucible of the Indies is the transforming of a man into one who does not turn down 'different' pleasures. Take what you are eating as an instance, keeping in mind that Mexicans prize their insects and their grubs, which they cook a thousand ways. Grubs are in fact the pork of a people that had only small dogs and lizards as meat until we came along. In particular there is a grub that burrows into the *saguaro* cactus, of which there are heaped baskets in the markets ... a stunning sight—nothing but squirming, infinitely tender flesh. The grub is the perfect meat animal if you think about it—size being the only problem—for nothing is discarded. They can be steamed in leaves and baked, roasted on hot coals, simmered with spice. Raw, mashed with avocados and chilies, they are excellent. Each town has its recipes, for the possibilities are infinite with a base so bland. Today, I thought to invent my own."

Juan stopped chewing....

"So," Mendoza asked, "what do you think of my creation? These are grubs knocked from hardtack, roasted and ground with flour, spice, *jeréz*, then heated over coal." He searched Juan's face for clues. Had he misjudged him?

He had not, and as the shuddering jaws began again to move Mendoza said, "Sailors despise what crawls in biscuit, while the Aztecs would see these grubs as far more succulent. Consider the Indies as a fresh way of seeing what was always before your eyes. Come on, confess that properly prepared grubs are far better than ship's biscuit."

"I do," Juan admitted as Mendoza poured resinous, wonderfully cleansing *jeréz*....

The trades continued steady. The sun was warm, air crystalline.

And in the *nao* rats and vermin swarmed—the philosophic sailors saying that they always appeared around the Tropic of Capricorn. Impossibly, the ship stank worse than the city of Sevilla. Every morning the pumps spewed sludge that was unimaginably foul, for in the time-honored tradition of the sea anything could be tossed into the bilge. On the orlop the cooks relieved themselves into water slopping over ballast. If they were lazy, chicken feathers, entrails, remnants of slaughter also were tossed in. The cauldron slowly cooked in tropic heat like a huge *olla podrida*, depleted only to be refilled.

Gil was stoic. "Ships smell, that's all. She'll be rummaged when we reach shore."

Twelve days out from the Canaries the trades died. The hands gambled about the calm, and then—needing more exciting gambling—they held a cockroach race.

The carpenter erected temporary canvas by the track, which ran from the mainmast to the forecastle door, the crew reasoning that the contestants would sprint toward the stink. Most of the money rode on the back of El Toro, an enormous insect. Thick as a thumb almost, he was the property of Gil.

When the roaches were released they ignored both the track and the distant fetor of the forecastle, El Toro scuttling beneath the canvas barrier and disappearing under the crowd. The other racers—with the uncanny talent of their kind—squeezed into tiny cracks. Only one managed to stagger erratically toward the goal, before collapsing....

Maestre Yáñez, owner of the triumphant insect—named Sinvergüenza—crowed that the secret of this victory was his diet. No hardtack. Just wine and salt. A roach ran better when lean and drunk.

The crew—their excitement rivaling the Diet of Worms, for intense argument falling short of bloodshed—ignored the death of Sinvergüenza. The loudest, who had bet on El Toro, claimed that a deliberate foot had created his disappearance. Yet he could not prove the smear to be a roach. And indeed, dark splats accumulated between the daily swabbings of the deck, due to the sailors' spitting habit.

Backers of El Toro declared the race forfeit, since the only contestant on the track would never make it to the finish, being dead. Incensed, the owner pointed out his roach was the only one to race, and to his credit he died trying. So it went, tempers sputtering on short fuses until the captain, fearing violence, decreed that Father Marmolejo would pronounce the verdict.

Rodrigo González de Marmolejo was a product of the reconquest of Spain, a *clérigo batallador*—a fighting cleric—far more comfortable with his sword than with Aquinas. He could craft uplifting sermons about sin—Beware damnation!— but the actual complicated workings of theology rendered him impatient. Therefore he asked Juan Lobo—fellow Dominican, a man of immense and fervent erudition—to take his place.

Next morning the *nao* fidgeted through Mass, and after the *ite missa est* Lobo leapt to the point as to the jugular....

"Our Savior instructed us by parable. It is therefore appropriate for us to examine the roach race as exactly *that,* a parable. Hermeneutically, the theological problem hinges on the virtues of courage and self-control as defined by Aristotle in book three of *The Nichomachean Ethics* and elaborated upon by Aquinas in passages that I will later cite. If memory serves, Aristotle stipulates that self-control is most concerned with the appetites we share with animals. The *self* of self-control, that is, refers to yearnings we share with lesser beings, of which the roach is but one example. In this light, Sinvergüenza is a figuring forth of our animal self. He is—or was—an incarnation of man's desire as base."

Lobo paused, delving passion and memory. The rigging groaned. The sailors sighed.

"Aristotle refers to self-control in matters having to do with food and sexual intercourse. Yet—as Aquinas clarifies—it is meaningless to apply the notion of self-control to passions such as music, which we do not share with roaches. Allow me then to elaborate his point—that courage is the highest manifestation of self-control, violating that deep urge we share with every other animate being, which is survival. Courage is self-control in the face of death, and there is no denying that as every other cockroach succumbed to its lower self, scuttling for cover, Sinvergüenza ran his race, and in so doing perished. The conclusion follows by analogy—Sinvergüenza, parabolically speaking, was the only moral roach."

Lobo went on to cite Maimonides, Avicenna, Ibn Gabirol ... but the disgruntled crew no longer listened, whispering....

"Cockroach self-control can kiss my ass. The bug was drunk."

"Should have crawled up Aristotle's crack. Give him something *deep* to think about."

The crew dispersed. And—grumbling soon replaced by tedium and bad temper—they argued about what had caused the failure of the trades.

The coin of nautical ill fortune had two sides, of which the face was religion and the obverse superstition. Disaster was brought about by sin, and for this the antidote was penance and Masses. Or misfortune could be caused by the breach of unwritten nautical law—a hatch cover upside down, a printed page destroyed.... And of course, nothing was worse than having a woman aboard. A vessel could also be dogged by mishap if a silver coin was not heeled under the mainmast. More important, a tree that grew with an unbaptized infant buried beneath it had to be used in the construction. Barred from Heaven, the innocent soul haunted the vessel, bringing good fortune ... so Gil told Juan. He did not know where they got dead, unbaptized infants however, but in Sevilla everything had its price....

Juan imagined the soul of the tiny, naked child, glowing, floating through rigging, keeping forlorn watch by the mast of the only parent it ever knew. What if the *nao* sank? Would the shining infant be released from bondage, going to Limbo ... or be condemned to hover forever by moldering timbers in the deep...?

There was no respite to the awful calm. Tempers smoldered, and—on the seventh day—exploded, when Mendoza walked by sailors breaking into laughter, slapping knees, looking at him sideways.... The dogger spun about. "I know something about training animals," he said. "I need to know which one of you told the joke about me."

Four dogs sprang forward at his invisible command. The terrified sailors backed away, leaving Gil to stand alone.

"So what's the joke...?"

The *gromete* squeaked but failed to speak. Two mastiffs went to flank him.

Mendoza's foot began, improbably, to tap.

A sailor stepped up, head jerking as he knelt, afraid to speak but more afraid that if he did not he would shit his morning raisins in his hose. And when he repeated Gil's joke, Mendoza laughed. In the silence, the silvery sound was uncanny as a Gloria sung *a cappella,* in that cathedral without echoes which is the Ocean Sea.

"What is your name, child?" the dogger asked the *gromete*, who was shivering as with ague.

Receiving no answer he continued. "You need to realize that what will befall you now you have brought upon yourself. The dogs, the crew, the friend who betrayed you, and I, are here but instruments of a higher principle, not unlike the Holy Inquisition.

Approach," he ordered. "You question my manhood. Let us see you come into your own."

Leading Gil to the mainmast, he prompted, "Lick it." And the *gromete* did as told.

"Do it sideways."

Gil did.

Finally, "One more time and leave it out."

Head craned, tongue moving like a snail's long, slow foot, Gil embraced the instrument of his torture.

Then, with the flicker of a blade, Mendoza pinned his tongue to the mast.

The *gromete* attempted a scream … managed only a gargle. Spasmodically, his hand groped for the ivory handle he could not see.

Mendoza warned, "If you or anyone else so much as touches this instrument of instruction, I will have the dogs kill and eat you." Then with a sweeping gesture, "The day will come when you will thank me for this lesson."

He faced the stunned assembly to say, "You must agree that the punishment befits the crime, for it was his tongue got him in trouble."

Mendoza then sauntered to the stern castle, and ascended its ladder. Leaning on the rail, he contemplated the empty mirror that was a windless sea under a cloudless sky.

A rivulet of blood ran to the deck, heading for the scuppers. Gil was gurgling what might have been *piedad*…! Pity! But the cry was largely incomprehensible, a note deep in the throat that brought to mind a *vihuela* with bass strings wound too tight, the gut about to break.

First to react, Marmolejo ascended the stern castle. "In the name of Merciful God, release this child."

Mendoza replied too quietly to be heard below.

And Marmolejo prostrated himself, as before God at his ordination, while on the deck the captain conferred with his mate, weighing fear and justice, meaning and consequence, for the matter was complex. There had been an insult before witnesses, but for a *caballero* to duel with a *gromete* was unthinkable. And unusual as the punishment was, it fit the crime, as Mendoza quite rightly pointed out. Also, the *gromete* should survive—a flogging did far worse…. The scales of justice tilted toward Mendoza.

Ignoring for a moment the impromptu trial, Juan saw—vivid as the blood welling from Gil's tongue—that Mendoza was marooned on a desert island of the spirit, without even other devils for his company, there perfecting the impregnable fortress in which he had his being. Juan wondered what occupied his hours, what furnished the chambers of his mind? Were there dungeons in which even *he* could not tolerate the darkness…?

Gil's blood slowly crawled the deck as he embraced the mainmast, unable to quiet a convulsive shuddering. And then he fainted … tongue ripping free.

Whispering a *Pater Noster*, Lobo took a half step forward. A mastiff sofly growled, the low sound menacing as the hiss of a drawn sword. Dogs could be like magic blades wielding themselves for men, thought Juan, having no mind or mercy of their own.

And it was then Mendoza whistled quietly to his dogs, calling them off.

As Lobo hurried to Gil's aid, Juan ascended the forecastle. And to the velvet back he said, "Pedro was right, you are a monsterMendoza fixed him with his unearthly eyes. "Gil failed his test, and you are failing too."

"*Hijo de puta*," Juan hissed, prepared to die.

The dogger shrugged. "Just between us, you are right—my mother was a whore. But be thankful no one heard." And—losing blue eyes in the sea—he said, "You must admit that you have learned from me."

Juan silently agreed. He had been taught Honor once again—this summit of Hispanic law—which made of every man a God punishing crimes against Himself.

The next day Juan ate sailors' food, alone. The wine was gone, the water rancid. The hardtack teemed with maggots. Olives and raisins were a distant memory. And once reborn, the wind was scarce relief, for you cannot drink the trades.

Juan nursed Gil. As he could not speak or eat—and scarcely swallow—Juan softened hardtack with the putridity that passed as water on the ship, spooning it behind the awful wound. Gil would gag ... spit pus. One day he hurled his trumpet overboard.

The cattle in the hold became Juan's company, attracting him with their profoundly gentle, liquid eyes, fringed by lashes that would make an Andalusian beauty weep with envy. Something like love lived in a cow, thought Juan, as calm acceptance. Eden must have looked upon the world with eyes like this, before all sin and subterfuge. No distance there, as in Mendoza. Mutely the eyes said, *All that I am is here*, these eyes that Jesus chose to see him at His birth.

Juan whispered, "I'm here too," embracing the enormous accepting neck, weeping without sound.

A heavy hand fell on his shoulder....

And when Juan walked out to see a world alive with blue and white immensities, Pedro was his friend again.

The hardships redoubled. The wormy biscuit stank of rat piss. The onboard stench increased. The *nao* was a floating hell, but little did Juan care, for he had Pedro back. The crew as well was friendly, after his public rupture with Mendoza. And for the same reason the Dominicans sought him out.

They found the young adventurer to be astonishingly educated ... reciting Pliny by heart! In turn Juan encountered such learning as Father Sosa never dreamed existed, for Juan Lobo was a Humanist, an inexhaustible fountain of this new learning. Disciple of Erasmus, admirer of Juan Luis Vives and Thomas More, he was fluent in Latin, Greek and Italian, conversant with English, Dutch and French, able to read a smattering of other languages, including Hebrew....

Apprenticed to a typesetter in Barcelona as a youth, Lobo discovered a vocation that he fanatically pursued. To him printing was not just the pressing of black marks on paper. He loved books almost as living things—the gloss of vellum, jet of ink. Above all he loved the texts he printed and could not read—Latin, Greek ... Arabic! He touched them and they spoke to him in tongues. He yearned for entire libraries he could not comprehend, books ranging from floor to ceiling like the blank forehead of God. And he toiled at his press, perfecting his craft, until at last his savior came. An errant savant, a wandering Humanist who desired to print a Greek text he had translated, annotated and glossed, found Lobo, admiring both his work and his keen love of learning. They wandered Europe from patron to patron, press to press—as well as to the homes of Humanists—arguing old and new ideas into the night.

Lobo met Erasmus and More, and carried with him everywhere his cherished, autographed copies of **In Praise of Folly** and **Utopia**. But the more Lobo learned of Humanism the better he understood that life should be right principle put to practice. What had Erasmus gleaned from his scrutiny of the ancients—Cicero, Quintus Curtius, Pliny, Seneca, Suetonius, Publius Syrius, Terence, Aesop, Aristotle, Demosthenes, Euripedes, Galen, Socrates, Josephus, Libanus, Lucian, Plutarch, Ptolemy, Xenophon, and the rest...?—that their wisdom was as nothing if it did not interpret Christianity for the betterment of man.

Lobo fasted for five days, praying ... and became a Dominican. Then he lost himself in the religious ferment of the time until—sick at heart of defending ceremonies and observances in which he did not believe, weary of sophistry— he took **Utopia** to heart and sailed for the Peru that was the inspiration for that ideal society. Perhaps perfection did not there exist, but he believed that man was educable. He would write on the blank page that was Indian innocence, creating a second Paradise on earth....

Flesh long ago consumed by fires of intellect, he was all bone and nervous sinew. A freckled forehead towered like Gibraltar over deep-set eyes. The unkempt reddish hair about his tonsure seemed to glow—a pyre lit by language. Spidery fingers sketched out truths ... or stabbed, quashing errors wandering the air like insects sent by Hell. Lobo quoted, elaborated and extemporized, the alembic of his mind distilling arguments to essences. Juan imagined that, left to himself—like Pliny's *astomi,* Lobo would purge himself of all of material substance, becoming an iridescent spirit.

He had his themes, the foremost being *Dulce bellum inexpertis*—War is sweet only to those who have not known it. And footnotes to *that* could last late into the night, Humanism on display atop the spar deck hatch as Juan's mind ultimately wandered…. This was no Thomist but a tome, an excess of More, a book on shanks, a library on fire, a man improbably begotten of Guttenberg and God.

"*Conquistadores!*" Lobo would huff, derisive. "We fought for centuries to wrest our land from Moors, only to free ourselves by turning into the slaves of war. Deprived by victory of combat, we sailed far horizons in search of carnage and found the Indies. Now we must save *them* from our past."

Unfortunately for Juan, the very past Lobo derided was enshrined in his own beloved *libros de caballería*. According to the Dominican, chivalry was the bloodbath of a dying society misrepresented as a Golden Age. Destroying that old order, point by point, Lobo built a new City of God upon the ruins—a utopia with no princes or poverty, no ignorance, no property, where all shared work and gold was fashioned into chains to fetter slaves.

In awe, Juan was yet left cold. He appreciated the exotic touches—that, for instance, in **Utopia** the priests' garments were feathered. The rest bored him. The cities were invariably eight leagues apart. The clothes were everywhere the same. All ate the same three meals a day. To Juan, More's dream resembled more a gaol than an ideal. He imagined its citizens as having the faces of clocks….

The ship sailed. Lobo lectured. Juan listened.

Taciturn by his *hijo*, Pedro picked hairs from his nose, to fling into the wind.

One tropic evening—Lobo lecturing on **De Copia** of Erasmus—the thought came to Juan that books and loneliness were linked inextricably. Were the priest's pale eyes as mirrors, reflecting the library within…? Did he actually see *out*…? Juan was disturbingly reminded of Mendoza. And it seemed proper, of a sudden, that king Utopos formed his society by severing an isthmus, creating an island of perfection by separating his people from mankind.

Winking at Juan, Pedro farted—long, loud and foul.. No island he. And Juan took guilty pleasure in winking back.

The morning of October's final day dawned calm, the sea a glass. Gil was emaciated, unresponsive. His tongue had swelled into an obscene leech feeding on his blood, so that he could no longer close his mouth.

"Gonna be a bad one," an old salt said to Juan, spitting over the rail toward a disturbance on the horizon.

The cloud grew in speed and size until a charge of Titans obscured the sky, lashing it with lightning, racing across flat, gunmetal seas. Sailors swarmed like squirrels, battening hatches, setting storm lines, reefing sail as the storm churned implacably toward them—a wall confusing sea and sky. Pedro yanked Juan below decks.

The impact heeled the ship hard over, and the two tumbled into the hay stowed there for cattle. The *nao* slowly righted, groaning, plunging on a sea gone mad. Juan and Pedro braced themselves against each other as the vessel bucked and soared. An oil lamp madly swung, illuminating terror-stricken sailors, singling out hands clasped in prayer, emptying eye sockets with blackness. Every shadow writhed. And all that was not tied or nailed down acquired life, bewitched. A marlinspike flew like a bird, and landed to tumble on the deck. Sailors stalked it on hands and knees, as if it had acquired personal malignancy.

Seasick, Juan rushed to the door, pushing against the weight of water that held it closed. Might as well die out, as in.

He erupted into darkness, deafness, blindness, and slammed into something. Drawing breath to pray, Juan found he was in agony, gripping ratlines stretching into Hell.

Lightning revealed the ship suspended over green, translucent water.

A flash lit the bowsprit, lost in churning foam, and ... was someone there?

Juan waited for the coming bolt, and in its stutter saw a man, arms spread against storm sail like a bird nailed to a wall. Submerged to the waist in an ebony surge of water, he was screaming ... or laughing. The next flash he was gone.

Unable to move, to breathe, cry out, Juan prayed to *Stella Maris* until his eyes opened once again—not to eternity but to a lesser dark, a greater quiet, a huge familiar hand....

He told Pedro about the bowsprit.

"I'm sorry, *hijo*. Gil is missing. Sleep if you can."

When Juan woke Pedro snored beside him. His ribs hurt too much for him to stand, so he crawled to the door, found the line leading to where he had been flung ... and there was nothing at the bow, where Gil defied the Ocean Sea. Juan clung above the churn of waves, imagining the body sinking in the blue, slow hair drifting with deep currents, releasing silver bubbles of what had once been life.

With a blinding crash, lightning struck the mainmast, shattering rigging, and the *nao* was aglow with the cold fire of the unearthly corposant. These flames consuming nothing were a sign from Heaven, a compact with an unseen Presence, and—like the descent of Moses with his tablets—a token of protection. This first morning of November—All Saints' Day—the holy dead were with the ship....

In Juan's mind Gil was transmuted into the unbaptized child, guardian of the *nao*—a presence manifest as light. Now his own hands shone—no less than the three masts—Juan knowing he had managed not to die again.... And his spirit soared, light as any albatross....

Below him, the three masts of the **Santiago de Compostela** were a burning Golgotha. He turned his head, and—far away—phosphorescent waves were breaking on black shores....

Pedro woke him. "*Hijo!* Land!"

"I know," Juan said. "I saw."

Chapter 3: The Bone *Che (Mapu)*

The condor floated toward the far immensity of *fucha lafken*. Below him, streams in the mountain gorges twined to become the tumult of the Rankil, the Filacura—these rivers fed by mountain snow, falling, foaming, ultimately uniting as the Fiu Fiu. In the distance Lonkimai spewed grumbling smoke, a tortured umbilicus uniting earth and sky, alive with lightning.

Admiring *mañke*, Ñamku strode on with grace that time had not encumbered. A hooded tunic of bleached leather hung to his knees. His feet and legs were stitched into the same. From his neck hung a pouch of white hide worked with a pattern of black beads. And his *kultrung* was suspended from his shoulder on a braided thong, so that with a chinking whisper the sacred stones within the drum—*llanka* and *likan*—echoed his stride. He wore a black wooden mask with slits at eyes and mouth, and above it his headdress—a white hawk, wings buckled, talons outstretched, fierce eyes turned to yellow stone. Ignoring time, the spirit forever plummeted....

Like bone, feathers outlived memory and flesh, yet they were fragile. For this reason, Ñamku released the spirit hawk only at sacred times, at night. For many moons of planting Ñamku the machi and the hawk that gave him his name had scarcely known the light of day. But now that the *machi* had many fewer moons of life remaining than there were moons of memory, the *pillañ* had spoken and all had changed.

After his vision Ñamku spun in milky whirlpools from which menace threatened to be born, until at last he heard a voice. Waking, he saw the young woman he knew as Lleflai, back turned, shoulders square, facing *fucha lafken*. Voice quivering, she spoke his name again.

A brave young *domo*, Ñamku sadly thought, knowing why her courage was required. Lleflai was apprenticed to a midwife, and his niece, Rayentru, was with child.

"*Mari, mari*, Lleflai."

Starting like a deer about to flee, she yelped, "*Mari, mari*, Ñamku."

"I know why you are here, Lleflai. Let your young legs lead the way. And tell the midwife these old bones will follow."

She was over the cliff in an instant, down the abrupt path.

To the basket Ñamku took to *machitun*—his healing ceremonies as a *machi*—he added a pouch of the seeds that fathers chew after a birthing, to bring the vision that named the *pichiche*. And to the pouch that held the dried eyes and tongue of the *machi* who taught him—and those of Katrinir, who had been his love—he added the bone *che*. Then, past and future pendant from his neck, he descended the mountain.

Rayentru was his niece, when to a *che* no relationship was closer. And Ñamku feared for her. Birth for a woman of her *kuyen* was difficult. To one so delicate it was dangerous. Yet it was her fragility that made her beauty so extraordinary, reminding him of *pingda*—the bright hummingbird—suspended in a cloud of wings, nourished by the souls of flowers.

Ñamku walked hills cascading to the great sea, emerging at last from dimness into the shock of light as—a flash of black and white—startled *keltewe* took to the air with raucous cries. He passed fields of *uwa*, the tall stalks climbed by squash. He passed a garden lush with *poñu*. Dogs barked in a clearing where a *ruka* exhaled smoke. By it a spring bubbled through bamboo into a mossy, hollowed log. Ignoring the barking, Ñamku walked by, keeping a polite distance.

Mapuche lived isolated in a *ruka*—sometimes more— near kin, yet always at a distance from others less related ... and the solitary heart of the *machi* approved. Che were not as sea birds, crowded cackling on guano-covered cliffs. Like Ñamku they lived only with their families. Unlike hawks, however, the *che* united to make war. Ancients spoke of *winka*, a strange, fierce people that appeared from the north. To fight them the Mapuche allied in the *wichanmapu*. Like ants the *winka* crossed the Fiu Fiu, and like ants they had been crushed, although countless *weichafe* died in the joy of battle. And the *winka*, having stained the water and the land with blood, were halted at the Fiu Fiu. So had it always been. So it would always be. The courage of the Mapuche would keep them free.

Wraith on a forest path, Ñamku ignored the whirr of insects, the chink of his *kultrung*, the song of a distant *diuka*, for he knew the belly of Rayentru held green fruit. Her time was to have been in *weda antu*—the bad days—when *che*, their stomachs shriveled, planted seed.

Ñamku valued his solitude, but there were times when he regretted it. If only he had been with Rayentru! Perhaps there had been sorcery. Or perhaps she saw the *waillapeñ*, that foul creature of the night that lusted after *domo*, knowing he could never have one. No man had ever seen this monster and lived, but Ñamku knew him to be naked, small and black, misshapen, sometimes shrunken with a hairless tail, sometimes with fingers like the legs of a spider.... The *waillapeñ* was always different, always terrible. For a domo to see him was disaster. And if she were with child she would birth monstrous children—*ankeñ peñeñ*.

Ñamku came upon Lleflai squatting by the trail, waiting to escort him into the forest, for the birth could not take place in a *ruka*. If a child—a *pichiche*—first saw light in one, evil would befall the newborn and all who lived there. So a simple shelter was built at a distance, always near running water. Ñamku followed his guide along the burble of a stream, listening to her nervous chatter.

Since it was not yet her time, no shelter had been prepared, and although the waters of Rayentru had broken yesterday, her *pichiche* had not yet been born. She was growing weak, no longer able to squat and grasp the two poles driven into the ground beside her. And she was bleeding badly. The midwife wanted to crush the head of the child and pull it out before it was too late both for the *pichiche* and the mother, but Rayentru had refused, weeping and asking for Ñamku.

The midwife had been insulted. This was only a difficult birth after all, about which not even *machi* knew more. But the birth was going badly, and if sorcery was involved she did not want to be accused. Also, inside Rayentru there were too many heads and legs. Rayentru would give birth to *ankeñ peñeñ*. Fearing that the niece of a powerful *machi* would die and she would take the blame, the midwife sent Lleflai.

Rayentru was lying in a clearing by a stream, on a blanket stretched over mounded fern, bare legs dark with blood. Near her, a fire smoldered beneath the pot where the midwife brewed her medicines. Ñamku thought she might be dead already—so pale was she, so still—but in her neck he found the flutter of the bird of life.... He touched the swell of her *kepam* as the midwife and Lleflai retreated, averting their eyes from his bared hand, for rumor whispered that it was death to see the machi in the flesh.

Something monstrous moved beneath his touch—not one head but two, maybe another—*pichiche* who would be smothered in mud, if born. But born they would have to be for Rayentru to survive. Ñamku knew that a Mapuche, child of the earth, turned his head to *mapu* at birth. Those who turned their heads to *wenu*, the sky, desired to be born as birds. You could trick them into life on earth by upending the mother, so that they mistook earth for sky. Such a *pichiche*, once born, would continue to yearn for the freedom of the air. So had it been with him.

Gently probing, the machi discovered that there were three *pichiche*. And as Rayentru was far too weak to stand on her head Ñamku sent Lleflai hurrying off. She returned with two of the other wives of Kuriñam, husband of Rayentru, carrying the loom on which she wove her blankets. Ñamku lashed his niece to the frame and propped it upside-down against a tree.

Rayentru woke to pain—the moon above her feet in a dimly smoky world—to the awarness that her child was not yet born, to a soft chant and a familiar mask.

"*Mari, mari*," she whispered." "Ñamku, am I dead? Is my *pichiche* dead? Are you visiting the dead?"

"*Mari, mari*, Rayentru. You and your *pichiche* live."

Then, "Push," he said.

He is a tree, Rayentru thought—pushing although pushing was impossible—drawing on his deep-rooted strength. She was a sapling bending to winds of pain, seeing between gusts that Lleflai was prostrate, distant. Rayentru wondered at her tears, for this was so beautiful, this dance with the wind that Ñamku was teaching her, the dance he sang—this dance of breath.

A *pichiche* emerged, then another. And at the end of a path lit by fire, by stars exploding in her eyes, a third.

Rayentru then lay upon her loom, three *pichiche* naked on the numbness of her breasts. There was one more thing to do, but her arms, her mouth, her eyes would not do her will. Summoning all her strength, Rayentru opened her eyes to the mask and whispered, "Put my arms around my pichiche, please." Then as her eyelids slid like silent stones, returning her to a dark without a moon, she breathed, "Ñamku, you cannot let Kuriñam kill them."

And with that, her labor was ended. She could no longer hear, but did not need the answer, her blood flowing through the door of life after her *pichiche*, soaking the unfinished blanket on her loom.

The domo keened—*atrutrui!*—stealing glances through the whipping of their hair, not at the untidy mound which was Rayentru and her *pichiche*, but at the hawk suspended, silently shrieking over new life, new death.

What was Ñamku to do with *añkeñ peñeñ*—these pale children of sorcery—squirming like maggots on the corpse of their mother? There would be a *machitun*, and the one responsible for this sorcery would be discovered. There would be blood and vengeance…. The keening of the *domo* cut through his grief and anger, asking him to join them, yet he could not, for Ñamku was a man and was not. But he was *machi*, and he would not allow the death of these *pichiche*.

He stood, for the newborn needed to be bathed—so had it always been, the mother bathed her child and herself. Not tonight, and the midwife hissed that she would not wash these monsters. Three! These were not che but dogs or *degu*, offspring of *wekufu*, or fathered by the *waillapeñ*! They would die anyway, being so small and weak, and if they did not they should be smothered!

Lleflai took pity, cradling the *pichiche* in her arms. One by one she immersed them in the stream, removing the blood of birth. Then she dried the tiny, shuddering bodies, wrapped them in a blanket and returned them to Ñamku.

The *machi* stroked the forehead of Rayentru with the clumsiness of grief, studying her hollowed eyes. She was gaunt from her ordeal, skin tight against fierce bone, and he thought with pride that his niece—no less than he—was a hawk. He took up the *pichiche* and followed the keening *domo*, at last allowing himself to weep, trying to plan but with little hope….

Kuriñam, husband of Rayentru, had to be persuaded not to smother the *pichiche* in mud or drown them, or expose them in those places where scavengers had created a scatter of small bones.

The procession wound through darkness, the *machi* lost in revery. Much as he mourned Rayentru, he knew that death was what she most desired after her husband, Likanpan, had been killed in a blood feud. And not just his death was impossible for her to endure, for as a widow she was required to wed his brother, and Kuriñam was a *wentru* she would never have freely chosen.

In battle Kuriñam was courageous, in friendship steadfast. Trusted in counsel, eloquent, he possessed every virtue of a *weichafe*—a warrior—almost to dangerous excess, as jealousy provoked sorcery. But he had five wives when Rayentru came to his *ruka*, and all but Ayelewei—her sister—were jealous of her beauty and her weaving, eager to poison what happiness remained in her life.

Rayentru remained faithful to Likanpan, her growing belly protecting her from the right of Kuriñam to couple. Now—the *pichiche* born—her soul had left its body of its own accord. She had died at peace, her children in his hands. And Ñamku would not violate her trust.

The *domo* bearing the corpse wound their way through darkness. Had he been alone Ñamku would have removed his mask. Daylight blinded him and made his eyes water, but they were keen at night, when through the mask he could only see blurred forms. Still, accustomed to near blindness, he made his way, hearing the rustle of bare feet, the far whisper of water, the faint hoot of a *quilquil*, until a bonfire stained the night with brightness.

Field and meadow sloped to the *ruka* on the hilltop where Kuriñam waited. The bearers set the loom before the headman—or *longko*—joining the *domo* huddled to the side. The only woman to approach was Ayelewei—sister of Rayentru and first wife of Kuriñam. She knelt by the corpse, keening.

All Mapuche dressed in dark wool—black and gray, less often the green of granite, brown of shale, somber reds of clay—these colors of the earth. But now like the sky descended with unknown purpose—flickering through shadow toward Kuriñam—Ñamku was the white of clouds of *wenu mapu*, home to the *pillañ*. He strode into the firelight, intending to hand the *pichiche* to the *longko*, but the arms of Kuriñam remained implacably crossed.

Ñamku set down his bundle to greet him.

Kuriñam had a long mustache, was lean and lined, forehead plucked so that his brow was high under his headband. His hair was braided to below his shoulders—a sign that too much time had passed since war. Disdaining the chill in the air he wore only a *chiripa*, the loincloth revealing the taut body of a seasoned warrior.

Crafty and swift, tireless as he was strong, he had earned the single earring that proclaimed him *longko*.

And before him stood Ñamku, greatest *machi* of the Mapuche. It was said that he became invisible at night and could turn into a hawk, a *kilkil*, or any other creature. It was said that he spoke with animals and the *pillañ*, and commanded the spirits of the dead. It was said as well that he *was* dead and that only his voice was left behind, inflating his clothes as breath does a bladder. Ancients who remembered him as a child said his hair and skin were white as clouds from birth, and that his eyes were red as coals, but cold. No one remembered why he had not been smothered at his birth.

The *machi* addressed Kuriñam, "Rayentru is dead, but she has given you two sons and a daughter." He revealed the *pichiche* as *domo* wailed. Rayentru had died begetting *añkeñ peñeñ*. What could be more terrible?

With a gesture Kuriñam severed the braid of sound, proclaiming, "These are not my children." And into the silence he had created he said, "There were portents. A *kilkil* hooted three times the night that Lonkimai spoke. This evil before me was foretold—these are not *pichiche* but grubs that soon will die."

True enough, thought Ñamku. The infants did look like grubs—or new-hatched birds—through whose skin one dimly glimpsed blue things. And now they were mewling at the chill.

Kuriñam said, "Smother them."

Ñamku hesitated before saying the unforgivable.... "You say that these are not your *pichiche*, but you neglect to mention that Rayentru was not your wife. You took the wife of your brother into your *ruka*, yet no bride gifts were given, and she never let you lie with her."

Kuriñam was numb with fury at hearing what he knew was whispered behind his back. The bride gifts were not important—the exchange usually a token in these cases. Yet the last claim cut deep, as true.

If Rayentru was not his wife, Kuriñam replied at last, who then would decide the fate of these grubs?

Quietly, Ñamku said that he would ask Likanpan.

The kin of Kuriñam exhaled as one, fear supplanted by speculation. Likanpan had not been dead two *kuyen*, so that his soul might be lingering about. Talking to him should present no problem to a *machi* who spent more time with the dead than with the living.

"Very well, then," Kuriñam hoarsely said, "I give these grubs into your keeping, *machi*."

"The *pichiche* need to eat."

"The hunger of *añkeñ peñeñ* does not concern me!"

Ignoring his anger, Ayelewei stood, saying, "I will nurse the children of my sister."

Kuriñam could kill his wife, but not tell her what to do when her mind was made. And as he loved her deeply, he shrugged, wishing he could salvage this situation with his club. Then—wisdom drowned in rage—he cried out, "If Rayentru was not my wife, as it has been claimed, then her corpse will not lie in any ruka of mine." And he stalked in, slamming shut the bamboo door behind him.

Rayentru could not be buried until the matter of the *añkeñ peñeñ* was settled, so *domo* laid her out in an abandoned *ruka*, placing her belongings beside her corpse. Fearful that her soul—the *am*—would resent such treatment, they swept the floor and scurried out.

Ayelewei wrapped the *pichiche* in soft wool, nursed them, sang, and rocked them. Ñamku built a fire.

And then in silence the *machi* and the sister mourned the Rayentru who was departing, loved the Rayentru who remained. Her *am* had left her but would linger by the places and people that she loved, passing through the smoke of the *ruka* fire, leaving eddies twined with darkness. Even so, her soul soon would leave for Ngulchenmaiwen, island of the dead.

Ñamku had taught Rayentru a song as a child, of which her beauty was the seed, and he the soil of *mapu*.

Hummingbird
You do not see her when she is before you
Hummingbird
The rainbow is a cloud of wings
Hummingbird

Ñamku sang with the voice of a girl, at one with Rayentru the child. And until dawn his voice pursued the smoke billowing with her soul, as slowly the fire died.

Ayelewei—whose name meant laughing—heard him and remembered, smiled, fed the *pichiche*, then wept, thinking that even spirit fathers were Mapuche. Would Likanpan do his harsh duty from beyond death…? She dozed, the *pichiche* on her bare breasts beneath a blanket. And as dawn invaded the *ruka* door she laughed, soft and low.

Ñamku understood—this was a *domo* not even lonely in her sleep. But it was time. He bathed in the stream, shuddering at this immersion in first-forgotten things, surviving the shock of life again. Returning, he found Aylewei smiling as she snored, the *pichiche* cradled in her arms.

He left to find Kuriñam.

Likanpan lay in a *wampu*—the dugout canoe he had used in life—boarded over and set upon a platform in a clearing. By it the plants once trod by mourning now grew with reckless gladness. And there a basket bleached by the sun was empty, the food Rayentru brought her dead husband consumed by the forest. A bowl and cup, a bone *pifilka*, and a *chiripa* frayed by mice survived. Admiring the beauty of the weave, Ñamku knew that Rayentru died on a blanket she had been weaving for the dead.

Roaming, Ñamku found flowers for the basket. And ignoring those that stood around him, he sat, chewed a seed. He chanted, chewed, his *kultrung* commenting with a rustling chunk. He felt a numbness of the lips that spread, turning his head—tooth bones moving over seeds—into a mask beneath a mask. He grew hot ... and hotter, as his skull became a husk echoing with the thud of hearts, loud and louder, faster, more confused. His blood turned to waterfalls roaring through his ribs....

Now Ñamku was empty, of tooth and tongue, seeds and flesh. He was a hollowed stone, and his red eyes were jellyfish in darkness, pulsing, spreading tentacles, yearning for light until glowworms spun pale green globes that grew and turned orange, spinning, making the cavern that was his stomach churn. Then a wind blew out his eyes through a tunnel of whirling light.

The spinning stopped. And—as if the sky had fallen—stars pulsed about him like living hearts that were not hearts but the eyes of the *pillañ*, alike in death, eyes red as his. Ñamku wanted to say, "I need to see, not to be seen," but his lips had vanished.

Ñamku burned and waited—teeth cold in a mouth emptied by the wind.... He waited until his mouth filled with glowing eyes and the deep shudder came, ejecting vision into the air, a sputtering arc over the mountains. There his eyes became serene, his fingers light and hollow, tingling, growing feathers.

And Ñamku shrieked with joy, having left heavy bone behind. Empty as a flute, he soared, free of *mapu* as the dead.

Dead, now, he saw his body far below, surrounded by the specks that were the kin of Kuriñam. And folding his wings he plumeted ... to find the *am* of Likanpan beside his body. The soul had the firm transparency of an eye.

"*Mari, mari*," Ñamku shrieked, "I have questions for you."

Likanpan said, simply, "The *pichiche* will live." Then the *am* floated up, disappearing, naming the children as it left ... Ñamku repeating for all to hear.

"The firstborn will be a warrior called Lautaro."

"The second will be *machi*."

"And, " Ñamku whispered as he collapsed, "the *domo pichiche* will be named Raytrayen."

Kuriñam—who appreciated this spirit session little less than an arrow in the eye—said, "I have heard." And he headed for his bed, wishing he had more than just one door to slam behind him.

Chapter 4: *Kalku (Mapu)*

Lleflai was born like all the people of the earth. She was held over a fire and stretched, that she be strong. Her umbilical cord was coiled and buried. She was bathed in a stream, swaddled and strapped to a cradleboard—a *kupulwe*—leaving her arms free. A cap of dry moss was placed on her head. Like every other newborn, she was carried on her mother's back in the *kupulwe* when she left the *ruka*, suspended from a tumpline. Or her cradleboard was propped nearby as *ñuke* went about her tasks. This was *admapu*—Mapuche custom—the way things should be. And according to *admapu* Lleflai would one day have grown and married, becoming a mother like every other ... but she did not.

One morning her mother went to the spring, leaving her with Antiao, her brother. The boy lifted the *kupulwe* with mighty effort, bouncing it and crying 'cha' each time it struck the floor, as he had learned from watching mother. When his sister laughed the soundless laugh of infants Antiao wanted to do more. Propping the cradleboard by the firepit he picked up his *pifilka*— the bamboo flute made for him by *chau*. Lleflai waved her arms wih pleasure at his music.... And the cradleboard toppled.

Hearing screams, *ñuke* dropped her bark pail at the spring. Madly she raced through gardens, lashed by *uwa*, ensnared by vines. And she burst through the door of the *ruka* into the reek of burning hair and wool, the sweet odor of grilling meat. Then, taking her *pichiche* in her arms, she looked down upon her with a grief she would take to her grave. Lleflai had fallen face first on coals, and through black, blistered lips she wailed, a wordless keening....

As the *kupulwe* toppled, the arms of Lleflai extended with a reflex ancient as her innocence, fire levitating toward her eyes. But the Lleflai of then did not know fire as fire, just as the Lleflai of later would not know that, falling like a living crucifix as she did, had spared her hands and arms, while the *kupulwe* spared her body.

Lleflai remembered nothing. Not the agony of weeping in bandaged darkness. Not the salty fire of tears. Not the moons that turned her face into a living mask. And her parents—slain in a feud—did not live to tell her what she did not remember.

Fire shaped a face that Lleflai saw only through the averted eyes of others. And when she apprenticed herself to a midwife so ugly that she might have shown mercy, Lleflai asked the old one to be honest. The crone spat into the fire pit, saying Lleflai could kill fish just by looking into a stream. No need to poison the water, she cackled.

Lleflai then felt her face, as she often did, finding a familiar ruin. Scars had tugged her nose into a twisted beak and buried her eyes in crumpled pouches, clawed her lips from her teeth. She did not need touch to know she hissed when speaking, like a wind through reeds. But her hair was thick. Like all *domo*—and some men—she never cut it. Unlike others she did not bind or braid it, letting the black weight veil her face.

And the *pillañ* gave her another gift as well. Wandering in her solitude, she fed the forest birds. Singing with them, she learned their speech. Birds were her only friends, until her difference was made right....

It seemed fitting, then—when the moment came—that she go to live with Ñamku and care for the *pichiche*. She was in her own way masked, and birdlike. Even so, *kuyen* ago, Lleflai surprised herself by saying, "*Mai. Yamai*"—Yes. Yes, of course. She would.

Face veiled by hair she said she understood that she would not be his wife. *Yamai,* she whispered when agreeing was no longer necessary, through ruined lips, through the long veil of hair that hid her tears, knowing that she would be a mother, with *pichiche* to love and care for. No longer would she be alone. And so Lleflai—whom the *che* came to call *Umeñdomo*, or Birdwoman—climbed the mountain to the cave in which Ñamku lived, to stay.

Che said that *lolo*, the cave, had been inhabited by *machi* since the waters of Kaikaifilu retreated to the great sea. Far larger than any *ruka*, its chambers were hollowed from living rock in the struggle of the beginning, when the earth opened its mouth to scream defiance at Kaikaifilu and forgot in the joy of victory to close it, leaving a stony throat open to the sky....

Emerging from *lolo*, turning his back to the dazzle of sunset, Ñamcu admired *dewiñ*— the distant mountains. And when his eyes could tolerate the sea he turned....

He stood by his *rewe*—the sacred pole sunk into the earth, with steps cut in it, so every morning he could climb to pray. He was on a shelf of rock looking out over treetops from which the mountain tumbled, purple in twilight. Smoke skeined from *ruka* in the hills below, the sight sweeping to the great sea, where the sun walked a distant, crimson path to be reborn. Ñamku wondered how *che* who were not as he could endure all this with open eyes. It was good, he thought, that hearts were not stopped by beauty ... or their own land would long ago have killed the Mapuche.

Shrill whoops ... and a naked *pichiche* appeared on the path up to the cave, running with the rolling effort of the very young, ecstatic as the world lurched by. A girl followed ... then a boy, crying high with joy—much like a bird. Ignoring Ñamku, they swept by like the winds of *kuru waleng*.

Lleflai—having taken the *pichiche* to the stream—followed them at a gentler pace, hair wet and bound to her head, eyes smiling at the *machi* through their scars.

Already they had habits—she took the *pichiche* to bathe at dusk, when Ñamku would be waking to the night. Then he would leave to do what *machi* did—turn into a bird, speak to the dead—she did not want to know....

The first morning at the cave, food was set beside the fire pit—roots, berries ... honey. So it went. Never meat or fish. Never *uwa, poñu, dawe*. No wonder *che* believed Ñamku was made of air. Eating as he did he *should* be dead. *Pichiche* could not grow strong on this....

She descended the mountain and returned with seed ... planted a garden in a clearing below the cave. Awaiting harvest, she made *chine*—bamboo sieves. With them she caught *puye*—the tiny fish glittering in streams. She did not trap small birds as others did, catching *degu* instead, flooding their burrows with water, and netting them when they ran out. Lleflai did not believe—as others did—that they were not fit to eat, like their cousins the mice. She and the *pichiche* were well nourished, but Ñamku, who ate her bread, left her stews and soups untouched.

Mornings he would be in a recess of the cave behind a hanging made of pelts, where he kept his *machi* things. Usually she only met him once a day, but she had never seen his face, his hands. What some *che* proposed could possibly be true— that his clothes were like bladders inflated by his voice, for he was an *am* that left its body and forgot to leave the living. These rumors she could not deny. Yet Lleflai did not care, glad to be *papai* to the *pichiche*....

It was Ayelewei who begged Lleflai that she be their mother.

She had wept, having grown to love them. These were obviously not *añkeñ peñeñ*. Even Kuriñam had grown fond of them—she suspected—although he never said so. She saw no good reason to exile them to a far off cave. But Ñamku said all this was necessary. The *pillañ* had told him so....

She recounted to Lleflai the moment in which Raytrayen finally earned her name—Flower in the waterfall. Carrying a fistful of flowers, the child fell into a stream and sat, as infants will, and then began to eat the bouquet. Laughing helplessly, Ayelewei added that the *am* of Rayentru would be pleased at the name of her daughter, for it recalled her own. Lleflai hardly heard her, never having seen *pichiche* so beautiful.

Now—weaned and plump—they were hers. They had grown, fussed over, largely unpunished, especially the *wentru pichiche*. This fostered freedom of spirit, for nothing was more important than to nurture the Mapuche will not to submit. Lleflai had now been with them since the last planting moon, and she could expect to have them to herself until the boys began to learn fighting from *weichafe*. Raytrayen would be hers until she married. Lleflai could wish for nothing more … yet she could fantasize. The *wentru pichiche* would stay with her, since there were no warriors in the cave to teach them war. And Raytrayen would not marry. Lleflai could always hope. In the meantime she labored to earn their love with indescribable happiness, chirping and whistling from twilight to twilight, and after sunset by firelight, for the *pichiche* were her life and breath.

She cut up her best *kepam* to make them clothes. She taught them not only the language of *che*, but the speech of birds as well. She pulled on their noses to make them long, arched and beautiful, like the beak of a *raki*, as Mapuche noses should be. She kneaded their heads to make them round. When food was abundant she was not satisfied. She learned to spear large fish, cooking them in clay, on coals. She made a loom, and when it was completed walked down the mountain carrying the *pichiche*. She returned late the next night from the *ruka* of Kuriñam, staggering with weariness, laden with the children and the wool she had acquired. And with it she made a blanket, for the cold moons were coming.

At dawn Ñamku entered *lolo*, pausing by the gentle breathing of the *pichiche*. Under their guanaco pelt they seemed a creature with one body, three heads, and too many limbs—one hand holding a *pifilka*. Near them Lleflai had collapsed against her loom, fingers of the left hand threaded through the warp, as if in dreams she planned to weave herself into her work.

As did all makers, Ñamku thought, living in what they made as *pellu*—the soul—did in the body, though this was something he had never done. Making was a becoming of yourself, and 'not himself' was what Ñamku had learned to be. Still, his being had been captured once….

He sat cross-legged in his alcove, holding a carving in each hand. Katrinir was no larger than a thumb, fashioned from a root. Steamed and polished, coaxed and carved, the spirit of the wood had united with the maker, creating this otter—his totem. In his other hand Ñamku held himself fashioned from shell as a hawk, his eyes *likan*, wings curved in a down stroke. Dark otter, white hawk … these creatures of the water and the air were made to fit as one. Ñamku cupped them in his hand, and the bird of memory flew. So many places to alight!

Long ago, when the sky called his *pellu*, captive in his body, and Ñamku roamed *mapu* empty as a net catching nothing, one *antu* he walked by *fucha lafken*. The coast was rocky there, stripped by the storms of the cold moons. He found a sheltered cove, and in it, a grotto. This was before Ñamku chose to live at night or knew his mask, and so it was that—dazzled by sun and sand—he met his love as a speaking shadow….

The voice in darkness said, not "*Mari, mari*," but, strangely, "*Amukilmi*." Do not go. And only then he said his name, Katrinir.

In the dimness Ñamku at last saw him sitting on sea-polished stones—serious, as he would always be—selecting one to hand him. Ñamku closed his eyes, to feel with the hungry fingers of the blind. Long and smooth, it had a fracture as a mouth. No teeth…. This was the head of a bird that did not exist.

Then—as if already inhabiting his thoughts—Katrinir asked the first of the questions that would one day make Ñamku what he was. "What *pellu* is in this stone?"

"That of *umeñ*—a bird, but without the body of a bird. This is a bird that cannot fly. One that does not exist."

Katrinir quietly replied, "Think again…."

And in all his life to come Ñamku never ceased to wonder at the ease with which love had placed his problem in his hands.

The second day at the grotto Katrinir handed him another stone. Of this one the great sea had decided to make a seal arched by the moment when—emerging into light to breathe—it returns to the blue welcome of its home. Adding nothing, Katrinir had incised the head, giving it the whiskers and round eyes of the seal, so releasing a trapped life.

And so it was from that time on—stones and seals, the sea, the moon. After Katrinir, *nothing* was the same again.

The day came when he produced a mask—bamboo stained black, cowries for the eyes, a slit the mouth. Ñamku was perturbed, not wanting to seem what he was not. But Katrinir only said, "You peer through your fingers when the light is bright. As for the black…?" He shrugged.

Katrinir was not attractive in the usual ways—tall and very thin, hair brutally cropped short. But—here Ñamku became defensive with himself—Katrinir did not care about unimportant things. And his eyes were truly extraordinary. "Kind, deep and wise, gentle as his fingers," the Ñamku of the present said, just as the Ñamku of the past always had. And just as then, he wondered how fingers so like bones could be so soft.

Katrinir was older, which made it the more remarkable that he was not *weichafe*. White, red eyed, Ñamku could never have been a warrior. But Katrinir…?

He asked him why.

"Every maker must destroy, but destroying without making is a different thing. By this I mean that *che* make nothing, for *mapu* exists already. *Che* of course make bowls, *ruka*, and many other things. But the trees and rushes, do we make them…? A *che* cannot even make soup. *Pillañ* cannot make soup. Can a *che* or a *pillañ* make the *piuro*, the *poñu*, the *uwa* that go into the pot…? No … for they made themselves already. Thinking that we are making soup, we are merely killing living things in hot water. This is why Kaikaifilu lives in every *che*, not as an evil in us but simply as what we are.

A maker cannot be a warrior, although the two are similar. Both use tools—the spoon maker to kill and shape a tree, the *weichafe* to kill others. But the maker kills to make, the warrior just to kill—and *that* is why I will never be one. Respecting the many *pellu* of *mapu*, I work to release these souls like a midwife. Wood can be a cup ... a stone a seal. A bone can sing. The tree, the stone, the bone, die to allow a second birth. The maker is a midwife that kills the mother to save the child, and that is the great sadness in his heart. But when warriors make things from those *they* kill—cups from skulls, drumsticks from long bones—they do this not to liberate a soul but to possess it."

Waking, Ñamku argued with Katrinir in the present, as he had so often in the past. "What if *che* you love are killed? What if the *winka* that invaded had enslaved us? What would have happened if Mapuche were makers only, not *weichafe* protecting us with their lives?"

Fully awake, now, Ñamku knew that there would never be an answer to his question, and he wondered what *wenu mapu* had intended by Rayentru's death. Was it right to kill a *domo* so perfect, to create the future of the *che*? Was her death necessary? If so, of what beginning was her death a part? Sick at heart he wondered what the *pillañ* intended for the three *pichiche*, for him, and for Lleflai?

Greeting her on the path that morning, he thought that she made the beauty of every other *domo* far too easy. How much more interesting was hers, soul shining through her scars, reminding him of quartz lifted to the sun....

He said to her, "I will be gone two *antu*." And he added, "You are *kume ad*."

As the *machi* strode from her astonishment, having told her she was beautiful, Lleflai did not know she had just heard the dry humor of Katrinir—the only humor Ñamku had—this visitor that moved in for good....

Before dawn next day, Ñamku was cross-legged at the grotto by the sea, thinking it strange that after the many moons and deaths this place remained the same. The sun rose here as it always had before. The same waves of the same sea washed the same pebbles of the shore. But was there a distant head, bobbing in the dazzle of light...?

How often had he not seen Katrinir return from beyond vision, a speck pulsing on water! "If then ... why not now!" his soul cried out, for the swimming of Katrinir had always been a wondrous thing. Like *antu* he would disappear in *fucha lafken*. Like *antu* he was reborn. And the habit of this impossibility lived in Ñamku, who still somehow expected to see him return from death.

Like his totem, Katrinir could swim with breathtaking ease, and it was uncanny to see him approach the beach with playful mastery, only to stand and totter on the stony shore like ordinary *che*. Ñamku knew something of that feeling, when as a weightless bird he returned to laboring on *mapu*, comic as a duck.

When Ñamku asked Katrinir how he swam so well, he was answered with that faint smile of his, which reminded the *machi* of banked coals sensed only by a hand hovering over ash.

Katrinir said, "A *pichiche* learns walking from the *pellu* inhabiting his bones ... and, as a child walks, a young seal swims. The difference between *che* and the other creatures of *mapu* is that only *we* desire to be other. A seal wants only to be itself, do simply what it does." So, he had swum with seals, Katrinir said, the yearning to be other pressing him against the edge of death until swimming changed his soul. He ended, "I fear for you always, Ñamku, as sometimes I fear for myself, but more. You must not confuse the need to soar with the desire to die."

And so in the present, scratching at the wound that was a life never to be healed, Ñamku remembered days spent with Katrinir by the sea—the swimming, the long talks, the far longer speaking silences. Together they swam so far out that the mountains strangely did not shrink, but grew. Numbed in body, souls glowing, they returned to peace together at the shore.

Startled into the present by what seemed a head in the sea, Ñamku wondered, if not Katrinir, who...? The head was his and could not be, but in matters of the spirit the *machi* did not trust accident. Sometimes the *pillañ* gave you questions tiny as eggs beneath a water lily leaf. The answer lay in a patient waiting for emergence.

But patience caused nothing to appear today, and Ñamku began the long, long walk back to *lolo*, certain that what was coming would happen in its season, like dragonflies in a stream, still trapped in their husks, swimming up in their desire for wings....

A faint, wrong sound. A sneeze...?

Ñamku was tired, yet his senses were not dulled by fatigue, or lack of food and sleep. Vision had accustomed him to the extremes that attacked his body to free his soul. He thought of death as a sea that had shallows from which he could emerge after discomfort. And in these shallows, the dead nibbled you like minnows in a stream.

The same faint sound...!

Taking off his white tunic he slipped on the black one in his *wilal*—the basket he always carried on a journey—and ran to shadows under a huge *peweñ*. There he hung his tunic, where trembling moonlight seemed to give it life, and backtracked silently to a boulder he had just passed.

His pursuer soon appeared, too noisy to be a *weichafe*, and little more than a *pichiche* ... awkward. The burden on his back was not on straight, forcing him to do a twisted shuffle.

From the boulder Ñamku dropped, soundless as *kilkil*.

But his wisdom had failed him, for this was no *pichiche*, swinging a stick at him....

Lights skittered in Ñamku's head, as in his visions. He thought he had been blinded, then realized his eyes were closed. And when he opened them he saw that his attacker was already far away.

Ñamku ran, head spinning, summoning the speed to see a black figure against moonlit water, the burdened creature twisting to look back before plunging into *fucha lafken*. And scanning that immensity, the *machi* knew he would not see the head appear again.

He slumped and sighed, felt under his hood—not surprised to find a lump, sticky with blood. And he smiled, for never had he been struck so hard by insight.

The day that Ñamku left, Lleflai slept little. The second day she did not sleep at all. The third, resigned to dread, she emerged from *lolo* to sit beneath the peaceful harvest moon, recalling that the *pichiche* had been born in the moon of earthquakes. Waiting for the *machi*, she envied *mapu* its quiet sleep until, near dawn, a shadow loomed....

Ñamku...?

Unmasked!

In black!

Back in the cave she tossed tinder on coal, afraid to see his face, for this would be the first time. But ... white, pallid, emaciated, he smiled.

His white hair black with blood! Gentled by fear, her fingers found nothing but a nasty wound. She washed it, bandaged it with moss ... covered him with a blanket. Soon he was snoring.

She had to conceal his face! Not with the mask—that sacred thing! Chirping with distress Lleflai found a basket, thinking that it would let in air, and covered his head without touching his wound. Then she collapsed beside the *pichiche* and fell instantly asleep.

Ñamku woke to a throbbing headache and sat up with care, as if his skull were a raw egg about to topple from some high shelf. He was masked, but firelight gleamed through many tiny eyeholes. This was no mask he ever wore.... He reached up to touch, and heard Lleflai whistling with a laughter echoed by the *pichiche*.

The great *machi* of the Mapuche, basket on his head, looked like a mushroom examining its cap.

The laughter stopped when the basket came off, revealing a pained smile.

"*Mari, mari*," Ñamku groaned.

"*Mari, mari, chau*," the *pichiche* politely fluted.

He surprised them all by sitting at the fire pit unmasked. Touching his wound, he winced and asked—perhaps a little spitefully—"Anything to eat but *degu*?"

Ñamku was handed cold, boiled *poñu*—the long, thin potato with blue skin and pale flesh that made him think of cold fingers ... and Katrinir. He ate with appetite, wishing he could chew with teeth not fastened to his head.

Lleflai blushed, knowing her eyes were doing a peculiar dance. She would steal a glance at Ñamku and look away, afraid to have him see her seeing. In fact, she was doing exactly what she detested in others, for this was how *che* had looked at her since she was a *pichiche*. So, as one might bring a finger to a flame and there hold it steady, Lleflai looked into the red eyes of the *machi*. Reflecting firelight, they resembled those of *pangi* surprised by torches in the night ... but they were gentle.

Pleased, Ñamku said, "It is time for the *pichiche* to have a father with a face, and it will not hurt you to see me, either. More *poñu*?"

There was, but the children were eager to leave for the stream. And it was then that Ñamku astonished Lleflai by joining her, saying he could eat as he walked. The *pichiche* raced ahead down a path beaten hard by generations, under the canopy of ancient, moss-draped *peweñ*, singing like birds. They disappeared around a bend through arches of bamboo, their chirps and whistles, childish shouts, part of the forest song.

Lleflai had said nothing, asked nothing, yet Ñamku explained, "If I am to teach the *pichiche* I must join you in the day."

She would—she thought—sooner have been struck by lightning! The children had been given to *her* care. Did he not trust her...? Had she not taught them well? Was it not *domo* who raised *pichiche*? Did all her labor—her love—count as nothing? She was desolate.

She was furious! Ñamku would not pull on the noses of the *pichiche* or knead their heads! She did not even know if he could cook. How *would* he feed them?

Lleflai knew that her fury stemmed from her fear that her children would leave her for the dead. But who was she? Just the ugliest Mapuche *domo* ever, knowing no more than any other, save that she sang like *diuka*, *meñkutoki*, *loika*, *trengko*. What she had to offer was as nothing to what Ñamku could—things so wonderful, so mysterious, she did not begin to know what they might be. She was a fool to have been happy.

Snared by pain, like a wounded bird, her mind fluttered to escape. Lleflai forgot the path, forgot that she was walking. She did not know that her erect back was bowed, that she was stumbling on stones familiar as her feet....

"*Ñawe*," Ñamku said, "forgive an old fool."

Lleflai snapped. "Forgive *what*?"

Then—seeing the great sadness in his eyes—she whispered, "*Yamai*, Ñamku, I forgive you." Yet she did not know exactly what it was that she forgave.

The *machi* finished his *poñu*, and she watched him replace his mask, as if this gave their short exchange a ritual closure. He turns *everything* to magic, thought Lleflai.

They reached the pool where the *pichiche* waited, leaping in with glad cries when they arrived. Ñamku stripped at the shore, and—with a sidewise slip—he swam. Lleflai saw it all—all white—and, in utter contrast, the black wound....

She undressed, wondering why his blood was an exception to the whiteness, like his eyes. And she swam, cold water tugging at the hairs of her arms, her legs. Her nipples grew erect. They were like beans, she thought—the nipples seeds on mounds of earth—that, wakened by water, wanted their round backs to break free. Then she *was* a seed unfolding from the streambed, plump leaves open to the welcome of the sun, knowing that her body had grown beautiful.

How wise Ñamku was to know her need, to give the *pichiche* the fierce love of a *domo* who thought never to conceive, and at the same time heal her shame. She walked from the pool wringing water from her hair, and—making a silent promise to herself—fastened her *kepam* only at one shoulder, leaving the other bare as married women did.

Like a fish, Ñamku had been swimming underwater. His head appeared, long hair streaming like pale seaweed. And he seemed to smile. Had he noticed her shoulder? Or was his smile simple pleasure? Was it the pain in his head? Was he blinded by the day?

Lleflai bobbed her head and sang. She was *trengko*—the mockingbird, singing—happy again.

On the way back Ñamku asked her, "Does *trengko* have a song that is his alone?"

Annoyed at being tested, Lleflai simply said, "Birds listen to their own kind, and *trengko* is the only one that pays attention to the others. Imagine if there were as many kinds of *che* as there are birds, and we could all talk like each other! When I began to sing I learned from all until I realized the *trengko* knew their songs already. And then I sang, and sang his songs until I was as much the *trengko* as I could be—the one who listened to them all...."

Ñamku gave her thoughts a twist. "The *trengko* is the only bird resembling *che*, the only one wanting to sing like another." Then the mask hovered above her, like a full, black, speaking moon, "It is important to *want* to be yourself."

"I do," Lleflai countered firmly, although her mind was spinning. If being *trengko* was like being *che*, wanting to be *trengko* was wanting what she already was....

The *machi* said, "It is good that you are *trengko*, yet do not leave yourself out of dislike." Shaping his message to her love, he added, "Return to yourself as to your *pichiche*."

And once they arrived at *lolo*, Ñamku astonished her by asking, "So did your mother forget to pull on *your* nose, leaving it short and tilted, like the beak of a songbird?"

That said—taking up firewood—he entered the cave. Lleflai followed with more wood, laughing, thinking that if her mother *had* pulled on her nose, it would have come off like skin from boiled chicken.

She found Ñamku prodding the fire, asking for *kallfu poñu*—blue potatoes. From her garden, Lleflai thought with pride.

A new routine began—the stream at twilight, both morning and evening. Sometimes Ñamku was with the *pichiche*, always teaching in some way. Lleflai helped when she could. The *machi* knew *mapu*, but she knew children. She tempered his instruction with laughter and song … about a wet little hummingbird … a hawk that waded in too deep … a bird too solemn to sing.

Unmasked, the *machi* would join her in *lolo* sometimes as she went about her tasks, and she never spoke first, as was proper for a *domo*. But one night she was bold enough to say, "There is a hive in that dead *koyam* beyond the spring…." She had been yearning for honey, more for the *pichiche* than for herself. And she added, not wanting to seem to be suggesting *anything*, "The children found a mouse skull … and we heard bees." Getting honey was work for *wentru*.

Ñamku knew that hive—but did not say so—giving Lleflai the satisfaction of a rich discovery. He told her he would see to this tomorrow, thinking he had been too long neglecting both the love of others and the pleasures of *mapu*. Lleflai was offering him a great sweet to salve his bitterness.

Ñamku went to the hive next morning —that body with unnumbered hearts— and built a fire of choking smoke upwind. After most of the bees had left or died, he chopped with his ax, lungs burning with smoke and effort. And when the tree fell at last, late in the day, he pulled out masses of dripping comb, the ruptured cells oozing honey, as if the light of *antu* had congealed into gold bee-blood. Other cells spilled larvae with blind, black eyes, dark organs visible through milky flesh, like the *pichiche* at their birth. Ignoring stings, Ñamku licked his fingers as he worked. Then—bent under a great weight of sweetness—he set off for *lolo*. Everyone would gorge. Then Lleflai would labor with fire and basket until the honey and the wax were pure.

Ñamku often took the *pichiche* on forest walks, having made them pouches— dark versions of his own. They returned carrying sticks with curious shapes, polished stones, berries, insects, leaves fresh and wilted, flowers. Often they were chewing on something.

Seldom did the *machi* speak to Lleflai. And often he required no answer. On the other hand, he sometimes answered questions she had not asked, as when one night he said, "The children are learning how to smell, touch, and taste *mapu*, to know each thing and creature in its place."

This was not the answer Lleflai expected to a question never asked. She had simply been wondering why Ñamku took it on himself to teach the children *everything*.

"As a plant is rooted, so are Mapuche—we *are* the land, our being tangled with that of every other living thing—so that when *mapu* lives, we live, and when it dies, we die. And since we *are* our land, I am teaching the *pichiche* how beautiful they are."

Lleflai was not persuaded, thinking her little part of *mapu* plenty. She could admit to being—as the *machi* said—the children and the cave, its contents maybe, and her garden, the stream in which she fished and bathed. More, she did not want.

One evening Ñamku took out the bone *che* and talked about it. Refusing to look at the awful *kalku wethakelu*, Lleflai stubbornly pounded salt into strips of *degu* meat, unable to believe that the fate of the *pichiche* had something to do with *that*.

She pounded. He talked. And when the meat was ready to be dried, she slumped over her metate.

Ñamku was not fooled—Lleflai had just pretended to fall sleep on salted *degu*. Still, he was relieved that he had not revealed to her the secret to which he had been building—he knew how Katrinir had returned, twisted and burdened, from the dead.

Long ago, Rayentru had come to him alone and weeping. She had been raped, she said, while her husband had been gone. Now she was with child, but if her husband found out she would have to hang herself from shame. He, her uncle, had to revenge her!

Ñamku had refused, curtly. He added, more gently, that he had foresworn revenge. Kind at last, he said it would be better if he did not know who did this awful thing.

Rayentru was too astonished—and too furious—to respond. This rejection was impossible. *Admapu* allowed him, her uncle, *nothing* but revenge!

Thinking for a moment, Ñamku suggested, "Why not tell your husband that you would like to spend some time with me, learning herbal medicine? Your interest in this is well known."

This was not the answer Rayentru had been seeking, but she did as he suggested.

The *pichiche* that she birthed had short legs and a humped back. His head was twisted to the side. And he returned their wonder with the dispassionate slate-blue eyes of the newborn, not knowing that he had to die.

Rayentru was defiant, and it took an *antu* of argument for her to leave her *pichiche* in the hands of Ñamku, alive.

But, what of her revenge? Remembering her humiliation, her pain, her undying hate, she paused before she left, to scream, "Kurufil *raped* me! And you will do nothing about it...! What kind of Mapuche are you...! What kind of uncle...!"

Ñamku had promised that her child would live. He swore also that Kurufil would one day suffer for what he had done, and know why.

When she left, the *machi* fed the unnamed *pichiche* the milk of *luan*, meditating his rash promise, until only one solution seemed fitting—that the black snake bite its tail....

The *machi* entered the hollows of memory with the shudder he once knew as a child, when—gathering *kollof* at the seashore—he reached into an underwater recess and pulled out a hand embraced by an octopus. The past could be no less cold, no less clinging, and it could look back unblinking....

When Katrinir came to live in *lolo* he was content as a maker of small things, uninterested in being *machi*. This greatly troubled Ñamku, since by not taking an apprentice he betrayed the trust of generations of his teachers. For this reason his greatest love was also his greatest sorrow, until the day the stranger came....

All *ruka* had dogs to announce visitors, but not *lolo*. Therefore the few who came to the cave were at a loss. Usually they cleared their throats. Sometimes they sneezed. This visitor began a pleasing song instead—about fishing with torches in the dark. Ñamku went out to meet him.

By the young stranger sat a *wilal* that seemed to contain his possessions—an unspoken declaration of what he proposed. Dressed only in *chiripa* and necklace—white beads intense against a dark throat—he had nascent breasts, and his long hair was braided to his waist....

Ñamku rudely barked, "Who *are* you?"

The stranger stuttered, "Kalfil. Son of Katripan."

Ñamku thought he knew his *ruka*. If so, the youth had walked three *antu*. He relented and they talked. Kalfil said he would do anything to be apprenticed....

His was a very strange enthusiasm, for *machi* were born different or created by unwelcome accident. Ñamku was white. His teacher had been struck by lightning. Another that he knew found his calling when he fell from a *peweñ* while picking nuts. Some were summoned by nightmares. No one *wanted* to be *machi*.

When Ñamku asked him *why*, Kalfil was evasive.

Ñamku thought him far too beautiful. What about Katrinir...?

But—on finding out—Katrinir only said, "He cannot live with *us*."

Kalfil built a small *ruka* not far down the mountain, covered his breasts with a *kepam*, removed his necklace, and seemed to ignore the fact that Katrinir never spoke to him.

And in the many *kuyen* that followed Ñamku taught Kalfil much of what he knew, until the day prepared by his blindness came…. Having been to a *machitun*, he was returning to the cave exhausted by the lack of sleep, the endless dancing, the potions that brought vision. Each time it was more difficult to return from the attack on the body that released the bird of sight, he was thinking … when at a turn of the path he found six eviscerated toads set in a circle. And at the center was Katrinir's totem—the tiny otter he wore around his neck

In that instant, Ñamku knew he had outlived happiness, for Katrinir was dead, or dying.

Forgetting exhaustion, Ñamku sped up the mountain, as if he could outrace certainty.

Kalfil of the treacherous humility had done this. Hate? The silence of Katrinir? Jealousy? Maybe a simple demonstration of—*this* I now can do to you! Needing you no longer, I leave my warning.

Machi did not kill, but healed. Therefore Kalfil was *kalku*. Perhaps he had planned this from the start.

Katrinir had made it to the ledge, lips cold as the stone on which he lay. Ñamku put a feather to his mouth … found breath. He cradled his head, put it on his lap, kissed him and wept, heard a whisper….

With the simplicity of the dying, Katrinir said, "I love you."

Then, "I feared you would not return in time."

Fainter, "If you kill him you will no longer be yourself. My *am* will not find you."

Finally, "He watched…."

It was the spirit hawk that heard these last words—faint as the rustle of a mouse in leaves. Then the head slumped back, long neck vulnerable forever.

Toad poison kills with cold, like *pillel kuyen*—moon of wishing for the sun— and Katrinir's frozen tongue no longer moved. Yet his soul managed to say, "Kalfil is evil, and revenge will make you into what he is. Promise me you will not kill him."

Weeping, Ñamku said, "*Yamai.*"

Then he thought he heard, "So, great *machi* can make great mistakes."

Katrinir was not smiling. But then again, he never really had.

Ñamku put him on a rack above a smoking fire, not wanting him to decompose. He had to fell and hollow out a tree large enough to hold the body, owing Katrinir nothing less. But before he did this—with a rage great as the waves born of *nuyun* that emerge from *fucha lafken* to snap trees like reeds—Ñamku attacked the *ruka* of Kalfil with bare hands and feet, until he was bleeding from the violence. After, he burnt the ruin and cursed the ashes.

And when Ñamku at last covered the smoke-black body of his love with a lid of wood he began to live only in the night—with the dead—until the day Katrinir returned from the great sea. Not that the *machi* was a fool, to think he had been hit on the head by his love. Having no bodies of their own the *am* of the dead sometimes used the living—as they spoke through Ñamku, for example ... as they hooted through *kilkil*. He knew exactly who had hit him, and he knew even where the twisted creature lived, for there he took him....

After a *kuyen* of indecision Ñamku had carried the twisted child of Rayentru—and the *luan* whose milk he had been feeding him—to where it was rumored Kalfil lived in *renu*, the cave of a *kalku*, practicing sorcery. It was also said that he changed his name to Kurufil.

There the *machi* saw smoke emerging from a promontory—a black jumble of rock kept naked by the pounding sea, and he watched from afar as a *che* wearing a *kepam* emerged. Convinced that this was Kurufil, Ñamku left the *pichiche* and the *luan* beside the entrance. And by the child he set a blanket and a basket of food.

This was done, not often. Women who for some reason did not want their *añkeñ peñeñ* killed would sometimes give them to *kalku*. And the sorcerers turned these monstrous children into *ifunche*—dwarves with swollen bellies, eyes and rectum sewn shut, legs broken and attached to the nape of their necks, heads turned backwards.

As *machi*, Ñamku knew some things that *kalku* did—about poisons, mostly. Yet there was much he did not know about their evil. It was a mystery to him how you could turn *pichiche*—even misshapen ones—into *ifunche*. No matter. What he was doing served his vengeance, and he watched from hiding as Kurufil took the *añkeñ peñeñ* into the cave. Unsuspecting, he would turn his own child into an abomination.

Ñamku never told Rayentru. And she never knew of their revenge. Nor could she know the cost....

Many moons ago, guilty of blind arrogance, Ñamku had outlived happiness. The day he gave the *pichiche* to Kurufil he outlived good as well, tasting the terrible joy of being *kalku*. And little matter that it was only that *one* time. From some evils no *che* can return, himself again.

Chapter 5: *Ifunche (Mapu)*

Before *renu* there was nothing.
Outside *renu* there were words.
You lived alone with Chau, in *renu*.

You had no age, no mother, and no word for either.

The only other *che* was Chau. But there was also Ñamku—tiny, made of sticks and dressed in white, his head a small black gourd with shells for eyes. Real white hair was on his head, and he was kept in a hole in the wall. You knew he was the enemy, not knowing what that meant except that enemies were hated … and You knew hate.

There were other *che*, Chau said—more words about outside. The floor of sand and stone, the rock walls and fire he tended, his *chiripa* and blanket, the darkness beyond the firelight, these and food were the only important things. Everything else was words.

Never having known a garden, You could cook. You had never seen willow thickets, bamboo, or rushes in the wind, yet You made boxes and baskets from what Chau brought. Not knowing living trees, he carved bowls and spoons out of what came from the land of words. You knew work—and the word for it—laboring with pleasure in his making, not knowing what to call his loneliness.

You knew poisons, for Chau brought him toads to gut and cook, turning their anger into ill smelling, deadly juice. You knew other poisons too. And You knew *renu* well as his toes. But more than anything, You knew that Chau was always to be obeyed.

A bird, some insects, found their way into *renu*. The bird first smelled, then dried. You kept the feathers. He put the insects in a small bark box. One of them was green and blue with legs ending in sticky claws—this was the greatest wonder in his box.

You did not know the moon, only the word. Above—where smoke went out— he could see light. When it was pale Chau called it *kuyen*, which did not make sense, for this word also meant many days. At other times the smoke hole glowed intolerably bright, creating light in which dust burned like very tiny coals. *Antu* was the word for that bright hole.

And there were many other dark, nameless holes in *renu*, which was too big for words.

When Chau woke he gave You lessons, then left through the only door You knew. And when he closed it You was left with work and nothing else to do. When it was done, You learned the dark.

Renu had many, many passages he explored with his fingers. There were also smaller openings where You could lie feeling safe, doing nothing. You did not know why he liked darkness. But he sometimes thought of the toads Chau brought for You to gut and cook, hopping to escape their basket, always failing to make it to the dark.

When he was older, You began to climb, and *Renu* was much bigger than he imagined. There were high walls and crevices You followed, learning strength and memory. One *antu* he found a high passage unlike all the others, blocked by a rock, where through a hole You could throw pebbles into echoes of a far larger place.

The rock became his enemy, and for *kuyen* You attacked it when Chau was gone. It would slightly move, and settle back—a back and forth unmeasured—until one day You fell onto the sand floor of the cave, embracing the enemy he had pulled free, feeling something he had never felt before....

You was hurt but hid his wounds. And when Chau left, he slid through the opening he had made into a place maybe even larger than outside—tunnels branching through darkness without end. There were chambers, tight passages, sudden drops. Yet You—ignorant of many things—was a stranger to fear also.

One passage had a gap into which You almost fell. And through it he dropped a stone that clattered a long breath later. He backed away, returning only when his secret led him to nothing but dead ends. Finding a narrow ledge above him he swung out over nothing, fingers creeping, finding cracks, growing numb ... until his feet touched stone.

You again was in a tunnel, feeling his way until he found a chamber like none before, dimly lighted by a crack in the ceiling. He was standing on black pebbles. There was water! You knelt to drink. It was bitter and he spat it out, noticing that it was slowly moving up and down. The water breathed!

From that day the chamber of breathing water drew You as his deepest secret. He felt under the water with his hands, his feet, in it to his neck. One *antu* he paddled, gagging and spluttering, to where the water ended at a wall and had no bottom.

The *kuyen* came that—shivering with cold, and something he could not name—You began to learn underwater as he had learned darkness. He found that the blank wall sloped and turned into a tunnel. The secret of You, beginning with a door, maybe ended with another....

Lungs bursting—*antu* after *antu*—You swam the tunnel. He broke fingernails, banged his head, scraped on rock. Eventually, something in You screamed he had to breathe. By doing this You learned when to return. You tried again and again. He went further and further, until the *antu* came he knew he could go no further and return—his door was good as closed by water. Having become accustomed to what he could not name hope, You felt something else he could not name—despair.

He abandoned his secret, tried not to think about it, until one *antu* he realized that he could not leave through the secret door *because* he intended to return. What if he kept going…? The tunnel was probably too long for breath. But what if it was not…?

You returned to the door.

Almost from the first he had counted strokes as on his fingers, and when he reached *kiñe epu kuq*—one two-hands—You started over, never swimming farther than *kechu epu kuq*—five two-hands—when he would turn back. This time You would not….

At six two-hands You still powerfully swam. He came to a bend, hit his head on a rock, lost count … calling it *pura epu kuq*. Then it was *mari epu kuq*—ten two-hands! Having reached the end of counting, he touched the ceiling. Was it sloping up…?

You exhaled the last of his air in this door without end— eyes closed tight, for there was nothing to be seen. And he decided to die seeing….

Lungs burning, You broke through a bright ceiling that shattered to reveal immensities. He gasped for air, seeing what he had never known or imagined he would know—a place filled with light and without walls.

"This is *outside*," You said to himself, shivering with cold, admiring what he would later know to be *antu*, setting through cloud over the great sea.

You returned to *renu*, calling his new secret *dumiñantu*—by which he meant light after darkness. And it did not take long for You to discover that his door—like the one Chau shut—led to the same outside. He was not disappointed, however, in discovering wonderful things he had only known as words.

One day—swimming underwater as You always did—he came up to take breath and saw two *che* sitting in a strange, long thing. You swam closer and surfaced to look….

The *che* were like each other, and like Chau, although their hair was shorter and they did not wear *kepam*. They were somewhat unlike, but were similar as toads to toads, or fish to fish. You had assumed *che* were as different from each other as he was from Chau. Yet neither resembled You. Forgetting fear You swam too close and looked into astonished eyes….

You dove, swimming far as he could, escaping. And from that day he was tormented by the need to know what he was. You began to walk the land, hiding by paths he took, finding no *che* like him. There were small ones, big ones, *wentru* and *domo*—as Chau had said—their bodies all much the same. Not one had a hump. Not one resembled him. You shared only his face with *che*.

The rumor spread like a forest fire—an *ifunche* had been seen swimming near the cave of the *kalku*. And Chau found out.

You had been beaten often with bamboo … never with a club, and never with such rage. You would tell how he got out or it would get much worse!

Biting his tongue, You refused to answer. Chau kept on beating him, screaming that he was just a toad with the head of a man.

You knew he was not a toad, but what Chau screamed gave him an idea that burned through the pain. Toads had toads, fish had fish, *che* had *che*. Why could not You have another You?

Done with threats, Chau tied You down and struck his leg hard with his club— twice, to make certain. And he looked down at the *ifunche* writhing soundless as a severed worm, disturbed by the intelligence in his eyes, wondering how the face of an *añkeñ peñeñ* could be so beautiful. Untying him, he asked himself if jealousy had some small part in what he had just done.

Having bitten his tongue through, You spit blood as he crawled into the cave, and Chau found him later where he had fainted. To punish him he pulled on his broken leg, making the bones sound like insects creaking. You fainted before Chau put on splints, setting the leg wrong, so that it would heal shorter, foot turned to the side.

The sense of humor of the *kalku* was aroused by his creation, for the foot of the *ifunche* was turned the same way as the head. He chuckled, thinking that now You could half walk in the direction he was looking. And he thought that the punishment fit his purpose. You would find it far more difficult to escape. Also, as more monstrous he would be more useful, inspiring greater fear in *che*.

You left for *dumiñantu* before his leg had healed, taking as much food and water as he could. And—for *antu* he could not count in darkness—he climbed and crawled. You withstood the pain, but almost fell to his death, before he finally rested by the breathing water of the door. There, You slept and hated until the food and water were gone. Then You swam the door, unhealed bone grinding.

You made a home of twigs and leaves, far from *che*. He created a walking stick that would also serve as club, and never strayed far from the water into which he could escape. You was always hungry. But You, unable to name happiness, was happy.

One *antu*, swimming, You saw a *che* by the shore that resembled the little

Ñamku in *renu*. He swam closer, becoming certain that this was the enemy of Chau and You. Feathers were on his head, and Chau said he turned into birds. His white body and black face seemed right.

You swam toward him, underwater—long as he could—knowing he was in danger. But You had learned that the greatest danger could bring the greatest good. Close as he dared—watching from low in waves—You approached, and when Ñamku disappeared into the forest he followed, struggling to keep up with the swift, white figure. Farther from water than he had ever been, yearning for he knew not what, You hurried until a dark form dropped soundlessly beside him....

Striking with his stick, You ran for water, and got away.

By putting leaves on his clothes You had learned to disappear into the forest. Dogs could smell You, however, and he avoided *ruka*. You found *che* in other places—a good one was where *domo* washed clothes at a stream. He waited until they came, hiding with a patience learned in darkness, as *antu* created tiny changes about him. You learned much from listening to *domo* talking ... and once they spoke about You. They called him *ifunche*, describing You, saying to a *pichiche* that if he was not good You would come and get him.

At last You knew the truth, so slow in coming. He was an *ifunche*.

You *was* small, his head turned to the side. And You *had* once served Chau. If nothing else, that made him what he was, even though the holes of You were not sewn shut, neither foot went near his neck, and You had his back—not his belly—swollen.... Also, his tongue was not split like that of a serpent. But none of this mattered, for You would rather die than serve Chau again....

And so it was that—having been twisted by *wenu mapu* for unknown purpose—You became a shadow in the forest, creating what he would become in solitary innocence, hate, and yearning.

Chapter 6: Cuzco (1539)

Pedro and Juan rode with a band of heavily armed and armored *caballeros,* every one of them a ruffian to the core.

"Gallows bait, I will admit," Pedro had explained to the *hijo* of his heart, preparing him for the crew assembled in Panama. "But they are harder than horseshoes. More important, they are comrades, and whatever a comrade might be in the eyes of Heaven, he is the one who will cover your ass on this earth, because if he does not, his own sorry ass will be blowing in the wind."

Still and all, thought Juan, these criminals they trusted their asses to were worse than the butcher who almost slit their throats in Sevilla. Besides, he and Pedro had but one ass each, which they could cover mutually. But he kept his peace.

Sunset overtaking them, they forged on under a gibbous moon. Better Cuzco than a bivouac, and there was no getting lost on Inca roads, for all led to the capital. When at last they clattered through deserted streets Juan was too exhausted to notice much, retaining only the din of hooves, and the jangle of cascabels echoing between stone walls.

Next morning he and Pedro were on foot, their horses hired only for the journey. Juan had broken his fast with *papas*—fleshy Inca things, mild and mealy, with only nourishment to recommend them. In Peru you ate *papas,* just as you breathed thin, cold air.

Juan followed Pedro down an alley, squinting in the glare of mountain mornings, drinking in exotic sights, and thinking that—despite the interest of the scene—it disappointed. Never had he thought to imagine an imperial city populated by dark and stolid, heavy-lidded, flat-faced peasants. Pedro was right—Incas *were* all the same, interesting only because Juan never saw their like before. And Cuzco was not the expected hub of empire, either. Monotonous, it called to mind Latin verbs learned by rote—*Sum, es, est. Sumus, estis, sunt.* These astounding walls were a materialization of *to be* when that verb was all one knew. They *were,* and they said nothing more. Pressed into a single facade, the whole was starker than convent walls. Could Peru be more monotonous, even, than Extremadura…?

Alike, unadorned, a single story—though tall—the walls were pierced by trapezoidal doors, the windows were simple holes. However, the stones between were of astounding size, all different and miraculously fitted. Cuzco had been erected by simpletons with the brawn of giants and the skills of masons from the Age of Gold.

Juan was halted by a cornerstone, which was—Suffering Jesus!—the size of Spanish rooms. He glanced, to see Pedro's broad expanse dwindle down an alley, yet still took the time to examine the immaculately quarried edge, unable to fit a fingernail. Juan was reminded of a pomegranate—plump grains pressed against each other, shape adjusted to the plenitude in the crimson and crunchy, juice-spurting confines of the skin. Salivating, remembering that his breakfast had been potatoes, Juan scanned the alley to find Pedro gone.... *Virgen Santíssima!* He must have taken some turn in the labyrinth, leaving him with murderous heathens! Merely colorful before, the Incas now seemed to threaten as they passed with averted, menacing eyes. Juan rounded the next corner at a dead run, his boot hitting something that jounced over cobbles.

He had kicked a brown, disintegrating ball. But what he interrupted was no game....

Three *infantes* in rusty, blood-smeared armor were hacking drunkenly at an Inca prone on the street, his tunic so soaked with blood that rivulets ran from the fringes. Weeping women knelt by him bowing, wailing in Quechua, touching their foreheads to the cobbles and extending their arms, bringing their fingers to their lips to make a kind of smacking sound. It looked to Juan like they were praying for food. A large basket lay on its side between them.

Weary of martial arts, the soldiers stopped worrying the corpse. A fat one lurched toward the women mimicking their bows, bringing grimy fingers to his lips and making smacking sounds. "*Cuchicuchi,*" he said, "*cuchicaca.*" He turned to wink at his companions. A tall *infante*—vivid Inca cap atop his helmet—elevated this Quechua joke to the sublime by crowing, "*Incacaca.*" All roared at that stroke of genius.

The fat one belched and hiked up his harness ... approached the bowing women. "You Incacaca fuckers can take that Incacaca fucker," he said—gesturing toward the corpse—"and get it off this Incacaca fucking street, dry it into a mummy for all I care. Just more dried shit in this shitty place full of shitty dried Indians." Rotating unsteadily, he gestured. "Fucking place. Only fucking *chicha* to get drunk on, and not a white cunt to be had."

Bleary, he considered the prostrate women, realizing that his mouth had brought an idea to his head, for one of them was a girl and he liked them young. He could stick it to virgin Inca beard right here and now. Was he too drunk for a hard on...?

"My cup," the tall *infante* roared, studying the ball Juan had just booted, lifting it by the hair. "*Cagüenlostia!* My cup's nose is broken!" The *infante* elevated a crumbling head.

An image flashed into Juan's mind, of Salome and the dripping trophy of her twisted love. The eyes of John the Baptist were closed, peaceful in his wrinkled parchment face....

The *infante* roared, "Kick my head, you little fucker! Break the nose! I'll teach you to kick my head!"

Juan was about to draw his knife when Pedro materialized by his side.

The tall soldier dropped both sword and head, for—peering over Pedro's shoulder—Negrito created a two-headed, hairy apparition. The *infante* belched with horror.

"It's good you did not fight my friend, *pardiez*," Pedro commented, departing. "He would have made *charqui* of you."

Propelled forward, Juan looked back. The Inca women had resumed their bowing and finger smacking. The fat *infante* was lurching toward the youngest. The tall *infante* was holding up the broken head and—eye to eye—exclaiming, "Incacaca, I'm going to cook your *charqui* off." Tucking his prize under his arm he proclaimed, "The hell! A cup don't need a nose."

Pedro explained to Juan, "The *infantes* hoped something valuable was in the basket, and got annoyed when they only found a mummy...." He strode on in troubled thought. They still owed a fabulous sum for the horses. He had letters of credit given him by Di Lorenzo, yet had given his word to use them to his patron's profit. Needing employment, he had arranged an audience with his former commander, Pizarro, now Governor of Peru....

Juan was not to be put off. "What's a mummy? Why was the soldier going to make a cup from the head? What's *charqui*?"

"A mummy is a dead, dried Indian. Probably just throw them on some mountain, for in Peru everything left out dries up. *Charqui* is strips of meat hung out until it's dry as mummies. You could make boots from it. Even *papas* are better."

For Pedro to admit that a potato was preferable to meat was a secular sort of blasphemy. And Juan was stupefied, as if he had caught Saint Francis of Assissi dining on a songbird, claiming that it was good to eat a tiny child of God....

Now his *hijo* was walking backward, gaping at something. Pedro placed a hand on his head, powerfully rotating until the child walked facing forward, and went on. "Mummies are outlawed now as heathen. Used to be that Incas worshipped them. *Voto a Dios*, the mummy of the Sapa Inca lived in his palace for a year after he died, just like he was alive. They changed his clothes, prepared banquets for him with everybody eating and drinking and talking to His Royal Highness, pretending he could hear—wouldn't be surprised if they put him to bed with the wives and concubines they killed when he died. After a year, the mummy was put in Coricancha with all the Sapa Incas that came before him, and his palace and possessions were kept as a shrine. Every new Sapa Inca had to accumulate palaces, women and treasure from scratch." Pedro shook his head with sadness, at such stupendous waste.

"They paraded the mummies like the statues of Holy Week. And when the

Church put a stop to this pagan nonsense, every mummy that could be found was burned—Christ, did that stink! Mummies seem dry, but they're hard to catch on fire. And as here there aren't any scrolls with pictures on them like in Mexico, we used llama dung to light them. I suppose a lot are still hidden … mummies, I mean."

Juan was plaintive. "What about the cup?"

"Oh, *that*—Incas make flutes out of the long bones of their enemies, as well as knuckle rattles, drums of stomach skin, etcetera…. After a victory they have a regular band. And sometimes they turn the skulls to cups—cut off the top, line the inside with gold or silver, make a gold base and stick it in the backbone hole. You can spit in your enemy's face while drinking from his head." Pedro chuckled at his joke.

Juan was reminded of reliquaries— brown saint's knuckles set in gold, splinters of thighbone embedded like strange toothpicks in silver settings, twists of hair on the faded satin of a monstrance, scraps of cloth preserved in jeweled caskets…. And inescapably, he imagined the mummy skull transformed into a gold-lined cup—reliquary of Saint Incacaca. Dear God in Heaven! Juan remembered being an altar boy as Father Sosa elevated the host. And now he saw not the monstrance, but the reliquary of Saint Incacaca elevated at the holiest moment of the Mass, the cup opening puzzled eyes as Father Sosa intoned, "For this is my body…."

"Wait outside," Pedro said to Juan curtly, passing through a massive trapezoidal door flanked by Spanish guards, intending to negotiate employment with Pizarro.

Eventually he emerged, waggling a fat purse. "Coin of the realm. Wahaaa!" He cavorted, Negrito clinging to his beard to keep from falling.

"Hayaaa!" Taking Juan by the hands he did a dance. "I am a captain!"

And they headed for the nearest wine.

Cuzco was paved for the ages, the flagstones polished—but not worn—by traffic, for here existed no iron-banded wheels or hooves. This was a mystery to Juan. Why did a people without carts or beasts of burden—except *llamas*, which hardly counted—need thoroughfares built to withstand centuries and the march of armies?

Seeing that Juan was staring at the street—a sobering sight—Pedro prayed, "Dear Santiago, saint of warriors, help my *hijo*, crazed by reading. Turn the child around. You know how good he is with knives … just wait until he learns the sword."

Having just successfully emerged from touchy negotiations, Pedro decided he might be able to tempt the saint. "If only he abandons letters, Juan will send many Indians to the Hell where they belong, and help bring those that deserve it into the fold. Please do Heaven this favor. Amen."

They arrived at the quarters Pizarro had assigned them.

"Only five servants," Pedro groused. But—cheered by money in his purse and richer prospects in the offing—he barked orders, putting the Indians to work with a shove, a Quechua word or two, and Spanish imprecations modified for Juan's ears.

Providence had given Pedro a son purer even than monks, when to him being excessively holy—eating locusts like Saint Anthony and fighting nothing but temptation—seemed a nasty exaggeration of virtue. Yet he did not want Juan to become the sinner he knew himself to be, therefore Pedro kept strict rein upon his tongue, determined to wean Juan of books without having him fall prey to the many temptations of a soldier's life.

Cheerful, he waved his *hijo* off, saying they would eat later.

Juan explored the former palace—a maze monotonous as Inca streets. Passages led to courtyards surrounded by empty rooms, leading to yet more stone passages … more rooms. The place, stripped of everything of value, echoed with the absence of the past.

He walked the ruin, feet crunching broken pottery, pits and seeds, dried husks of maize, bones sucked for marrow. Guinea pigs scrabbled in the detritus.

Led by smell, Juan discovered the latrine—chosen, he supposed, for its distance from the entrance and its absence of a roof. He pissed and left. Where Spaniards lived the Inca women did not clean, just as they ceased to sweep the streets.

"Come and get it," echoed down passages.

Pedro had spent a fortune on a proper banquet. No *papas* cooked over burning turds tonight! He had the servants take down some rafters and build a genuine Spanish blaze, over which was spitted—*mirabile dictu*—an entire suckling pig. No more porkers in Peru than fingers on your feet, Pedro bragged, and the governor had thrown in Madeira, *gratis*! He toasted Pizarro. They drank. Again they toasted, waiting for the meat to be done. Impatient, they cut bloody slices. Exquisite! Pedro toured his beard with his tongue for marinated morsels.

At the evening's highly drunken end Pedro assumed his role as father, booming, "Time for bed." He beckoned and three Inca women walked in, kneeling to bow … not bringing their fingers to their lips, Juan noticed, like the ones by the mummy.

Sick at heart, he indicated the youngest.

"Knew you would choose her," Pedro commented, leaving with the other two. And taking them to his room he plied them with his beef, after which he enjoyed the untroubled sleep of money and Madeira.

Not Juan. The fragile girl was strangely dressed and stony as an Inca wall. She arranged herself on the one straw pallet in the room, arms crossed like the statues of church coffins. Tears trickled down her cheeks. Awkward, Juan gestured for her to stand.…

Then, somehow, she was weeping on his shoulder and he was swaying back and forth—fighting tears of his own—patting her back, amazed that simple Spanish gestures could work their comfort on a heathen.

She leaned back to massage her nose with the back of her hand, studying him from Inca distances. Beneath strange lids, her eyes were the darkest he ever saw, filmed by her victory over tears. She was breathtakingly beautiful.

Tapping himself in the chest, Juan said his name.

"Uan," she managed. Then she was struggling with, "Ca ... ca..."

Juan put his hand over her mouth, shaking his head.

She pointed at herself, saying something impossible to pronounce.

"Huai ... na," Juan repeated.

She giggled.

Exhausted and more than just a little drunk, Juan tried to lead her to the pallet in the room—only to sleep, of course. Huaina stopped giggling, panic in her eyes.... So, they slept arms around each other, slumped against a wall that had withstood earthquakes, conquest and the slow tooth of time.

In the morning Juan found himself in bed with Huaina, who was crooning what sounded like a Quechua lullaby. How they had gotten there he did not know, but both were clothed. She was crying as she softly sang, and—morning light flooding into his consciousness—he realized that her world had ended with his advent.... "Forgive me," he pleaded.

She nodded.

Only later—reliving their little time together—did Juan realize that Huaina could not have known what he had said ... and God only knew what Inca nods meant, but at the time he had been comforted.

Consuming breakfast pork, Pedro was surprised to find his *hijo* silent about his performance, although he rattled on about the girl herself. Ah, well.... Pedro was mellow, for the Madeira cask was still wonderfully full.

He topped off—and admired—the silver Inca vessel he held. The stem was composed of four naked, squatting men, supporting the cup on their heads much as Atlas supported the world. Their arms were tied behind their backs, which made them prisoners. They were *orejones*—Inca nobles—earlobes stretched by gold weights. In Spain they would be gargoyles, here they were a vessel reminding Pedro of a compass with four dongs indicating the cardinal directions. He did not like many Inca things, but this cup pleased him.

Juan nattered on.

Pedro could not fathom him. Sometimes his *hijo* just sat quiet as a poleaxed pig ... sometimes not. Maybe he was in love, unable to tup a woman without adoring her. But, had he even been between her legs?

"She *is* special," he boisterously agreed. "An *accla*. Not many left."

"*Accla?*"

Pedro said they were selected from all the Inca empire as children for their beauty and talent, then sent to places much like convents where they were taught dyeing, spinning and weaving, making *chicha*, so on and so forth. When they were about thirteen they were taken to Cuzco during the festival of the sun to be presented to the Sapa Inca, who decided their fate. Those that struck his fancy he selected as concubines. Others he bestowed to nobles who had earned his favor. A few were sacrificed ... and Pedro did not know why. The rest returned to their convents to spend their lives making fine cloth for the Inca, *chicha* for the religious ceremonies, etc, etc.

Voto a Dios, you deflowered a virgin, " Pedro bragged. "In Spain no virginity is certain, but here it sometimes is. If there is even the slightest suspicion, an *accla* is hung by the hair until dead, though sometimes they bury them alive. So if you find a live one you know she has not ever had a ... hem ... flute in her ... hem ... pitcher."

Muddled by Madeira as he was, Pedro yet managed to realize his euphemisms made unhappy bedfellows, as the flute was an instrument that men were said to play by themselves. He raced on, hoping to leave language in his dust.

"I got yours from an Aragonese who had a small supply. They're only good for once of course. A live *accla* is a virgin *accla*. That's why so few are left."

Juan was appalled. "You mean that when she leaves Huaina will be killed!"

Shrugging to indicate that Indians settled their own affairs, Pedro said that his own *acclas* had already left looking like ordinary Indians. Who was to know?

Huaina entered, wearing her tunic of white alpaca.

If Pedro did not believe she was still virgin, why should an Inca...? Juan could hardly believe it himself.

Huaina dropped to her knees, bowed to Juan.

He asked himself—what did you die of, hanging by the hair...? And springing to his feet, he knocked cup and bowl aside, sending the bones of breakfast flying.

"*Sálvate!*" Save yourself!

Ignoring Juan she turned her back and left.

Pedro finished his cup, wiped his beard with a caked sleeve, and strode out shaking his head.

That evening Pedro reminisced about the early years of conquest—the glory of Cajamarca, the capture of Atahualpa, the room filled with the gold of ransom, his execution. He progressed to Diego de Almagro—Pizarro's partner in the conquest of Peru and his own captain. How, with a large expedition he went south to conquer. How in the land called Chile they found little gold, much suffering, and hostile Indians. The expedition was a disaster—as Juan knew—but there was worse. While they were in Spain—he and Juan, that is—Almagro treacherously took Cuzco, rebelling against Pizarro and the Emperor. A battle had been fought and the wretch he once trusted and admired was defeated. Then he was garroted and beheaded ... as was right and just. Gloomy, Pedro yanked a hair from his nose and studied it, torn between his devotion to Almagro and his duty to the crown.

This was not a man made for civil war, Juan thought.

Sighing, Pedro said all this happened just last year. From there the cart went downhill fast, for those siding with Almagro still were causing trouble—the men of Chile they called them. And the Incas had seized the opportunity to rebel under Manco Capac. The puppet emperor of the Spaniards had cut his strings, was doing a war dance on his own.

No longer listening, Juan wondered how long it took to die, hung by the hair? Or would Huaina be buried alive? She would close her eyes and mouth, death falling on her as dank weight....

In the following weeks Pedro attempted to fulfill his agreement with Di Lorenzo, waving letters of credit before Spanish faces—good as gold! To doubt Di Lorenzo's word was to doubt his own! Soon all fled at his approach.

Evenings, Pedro returned to his cups, saying that paper promises were worth a fly's fart, and he was no Jew to grovel for money. Thinking of insects, he would rummage through his beard for one that he could pop—ridding the world of another bloodsucker.

Such credit as existed in Peru was secured by handshakes, not signatures. And at the end of the day, *conquistadores* prized the tools of conquest above all. Wine and women, food and clothing could be had as rapine if you had the sword and horse, while the gold was only good for gambling. If you won you gambled more. If you lost you looted more. In Peru the wheel of fortune was a treadmill. Like Di Lorenzo's parchment, gold was only valuable in Spain.

Juan asked Pedro, one evening, "Did that *infante* really eat a gold nugget every day, and raffle off his shit?"

"*Voto a Cristo!* He sold tickets and then duck-walked as he crapped, leaving them in a row, calling out their numbers as he went."

The next day Pedro came home cackling like a maniac. He had found a Catalan returning to Spain who knew Di Lorenzo's credit to be good—a greedy *hideputa* who would be rich as the Pope if he made it back alive, and wouldn't mind being a little richer. Pedro waggled his hips lewdly as he could, displaying the heavy purse between his legs.

The haggling took two days, preparing the shipment another three. To Juan the ingots were unimpressive—dull, immensely heavy, crated in tiny boxes borne on poles. There were curios also—monkeys and extraordinary birds, a chest full of capes made of feathers and bat fur, sumptuous alpaca blankets. And the Catalan threw seven Inca concubines into the deal for free, as he had a wife back home.

Juan ignored the sudden harem, causing Pedro to be concerned. It was common knowledge that a man came brains, and therefore abstinence could build dangerous pressures in the head. One morning he went so far as to allude to the butcher's dog—asleep by beef!

The harem vanished in any case, three evaporating into the night, two contracting pox. The rest just died as Indians did, and Pedro had to make do....

In Inca days whores plied their trade in huts outside Cuzco, shunned inside the city walls. This tradition flourished in the chaos after conquest—the supply of women widowed and dispossessed swelling to meet the needs of the invading army. Pedro took to spending his nights with these *pampairunas*—women of the fields—paying them with potatoes.

One morning, Pedro returned to break his fast with guinea pig. Now that his purse had hollow cheeks, he no longer disdained what he called 'Inca rat meat,' grateful to consume what grew on feet, at least. Speaking through saliva, 'Inca rat' and *chicha*, Pedro said that Inca Manco had taken to the mountains. And—thank Providence!—Pizarro had ordered troops to the high peaks where the rebels lurked. They would chop them fine as onions! Why, only one hundred and eighty some Spaniards slaughtered the mighty Inca army at Cajamarca, think of what they would do with this rabble! Maybe he would be rewarded with a decent *encomienda*.

Inca Manco wandered the peaks between Cuzco and the coast, descending to raid plantations and caravans, massacring travelers. When he managed to cut off and slaughter a band of thirty Spanish, that was the last straw. Francisco Pizarro sent an expedition commanded by his brother Gonzalo.

They heard Mass by torchlight and marched at dawn. Juan and Pedro walked with those who could not afford a mount, though many of these men were richer than Iberian dukes. With them marched Indian allies and porters carrying food and equipment, for horses were far too valuable to be used as pack animals, and *llamas* too likely to lie down and spit in your eye when you complained. Incas, however, would shoulder enormous loads if only you provided *coca*. Perhaps they were even grateful, for previously only *orejones* were allowed to chew it. Spaniards encouraged this habit in any case, as it made the Indians tractable and decreased their need for food. And—no less durable than their men—the women served a double purpose. The *infantes* had their joke—In Peru you could fuck pack animals from the front.

In two days the expedition was deep in mountains. Juan had thought himself accustomed to the *puna*—that elevated plateau which was heart of the Inca Empire—but nonetheless his heart pounded and head ached. The cobbled road was narrow, often a contorted staircase winding over certain death—and no wonder the Incas had no wheeled vehicles, for they would have had to carry them.

They crossed bridges that seemed made by human spiders, webs of fiber over water far below. Juan's stomach churned with vertigo on the swaying things. The horses had to be blindfolded to be led across.

The first camp was in a valley between peaks, where only moss and lichen grew. Wrapped in cloaks and *ponchos* they attempted sleep in the bone-numbing cold. Then they walked days through barren wilderness.

One night their guides vanished. Next morning the Incas attacked. First the thunder of boulders, then a shower of missiles as archers, slingsmen, and spearmen sprang from hiding above them like tiny puppets in a deadly show. A barbaric blare of conchs began the Indian charge, and Pedro rushed to where the van engaged the enemy.

Juan was left behind in uproar. A horse with an arrow flopping in its eye bucked and fell. Juan went to help the *caballero* pinned beneath the kicking beast ... was struck a glancing blow by a hoof. Shoulder numb, Juan realized that the clamor of battle was fading into distance.

He walked through scattered bodies, the wounded making low noises that sounded apologetic. And at last he found Pedro dispatching an Inca who—improbably—held a sword. Half the arm went spinning, along with the weapon. Then Pedro beheaded him, blood spurting as it was said to do in the *romances*. The eyelids on the severed head trembled, Juan noticed, although the eyes were dead. The Indian wore the simple tunic of the Inca male, fashioned richly—a stylized bird repeated in red and yellow between black squares. A small shield with the same bird motif lay beside him. His only armor was a leather helmet painted black, with a tuft of crimson feathers. His legs were bare, with tassels at knees and ankles. Fascinated, Juan watched death work on the warrior. His eyes had died before his heart, he thought, for blood pulsed feebly at the neck....

Needing to loot—and reluctant to have Juan see it—Pedro fretted as his *hijo* gawked at a simple corpse. It could be awkward to be a father in the field. Juan at his side, they might well leave Peru, for all its riches, poorer than they came.

That evening, after they built a fire from grass and Inca clothing—which produced more choking smoke than heat—Pedro explained that this had been a mere skirmish. And Inca weapons were a joke—bronze spears, slings and wooden clubs, for the love of God!—their armor leather, sometimes quilted wool. Inca were quick, all right, but what good was being quick if you were dead?

In the *romances*, Juan was thinking, bravery was everything. Was it simple foolishness in Inca? How could they run to certain death, screaming with enthusiasm? When overwhelming numbers attacked Amadís, the hero *knew* he would emerge victorious. Was that valor or simple butchery? Maybe brave and stupid were two sides of the same coin. This 'skirmish' had been a slaughter of heroic idiots.

Pedro busied himself by cleaning the sword taken from the Inca—a scrub with sand and coarse cloth, followed by a polish with wool cut from some corpse, and finally … a greasy rag. You had to protect metal from water, Pedro explained, even in dry climates. In Spain there were fine oils for this purpose. Olive oil worked well too. Why, running the sword through your beard was better than nothing.

"I learned this trick when fighting for Cortez," Pedro said, displaying his rag. "See?"

"See what?" replied Juan, who had been attempting to reconcile the beauty of the *romances* with the horrors of the day, seeing only that this rag seemed to have hairs.

"Human skin polishes better than horse hide." And with pride Pedro handed Juan the gleaming weapon. Wanting his *hijo* to admire the whet and workmanship, the chasing of the hilt and—above all—the quality of the restoration, he spread his arms in a triumphant extension of his grin. "You can fight in the next battle."

Then he clapped the black helmet with crimson plumes he took from the corpse, on Juan's head. Handing him an Inca shield, saying, "Just look at you!"

Juan felt he had become a composite monster—merman or chimera—or more to the point, something like Pedro in his finery. The shield was leather over wood, and on it rows of llamas alternated, black and white. The Castilian sword was ornately chased with gold. If fools are clothed in motley, then a fool am I, Juan thought. The feathers of the helmet were his cockscomb.

Pedro was hurt that Juan did not seem pleased. "Don't worry, Indians will skewer themselves for you." He drew, saying they were like a thorn bush. Lunge, and your point gets in, but you get pricked right back. Then he's dead and that's good, but you're dead and that's bad. You had to clear his weapon first. Pedro demonstrated, sweeping air with hissing steel.

There was no avalanche next morning, just a trumpet sounding as Indians sprang from shadow. Juan had slept in battle gear. Up and running, groggy, he realized that he left his shield behind as he reached the Spanish line, which presented a wall of metal to the Incas charging in suicidal masses. Nothing here for him to do. The flanks, he thought, seeing a cliff to the right, boulders at the left. He trotted over and was hammered to the ground by a form dark against the sky. He rolled, saw the Inca lift a mace….

Juan leapt to his feet, ready to defend himself with—*clavos de Cristo!*—nothing! His sword had flown! The Inca charged. Juan dodged, seeing a hand holding a knife…. His hand and knife! He never wanted that damn sword anyway.

Shield high, obsidian glittering on his mace, the Inca charged again. Juan pivoted, shifting the knife to his left hand—point back, blade out—tight against the forearm raised above his head. He could now block if the Inca reacted quickly. Or he could slash…. He slashed, as he had a thousand times before with Pedro—who was always miraculously not there. This time, the shock almost took his knife.

The Inca staggered, arm half-severed. Mace gone, bleeding in gouts, he circled Juan, shield his only weapon.

Soon he would bleed to death, and Juan spun—needle of a slow, deadly compass—at last registering Spanish shouts. Battle over, *infantes* had congregated to cheer the duel.

The Inca leapt in, screaming….

When Juan came to, icy water was running down his neck, Pedro having packed snow on his head and clapped on his helmet to keep it there.

"*Hijo*," Pedro said, beaming. "He hit you with his shield, but I clove him from helmet to tackle."

Another tale is born, thought Juan, walking with legs like jellied lamb to where the Inca had been flung by death … seeing that Pedro had, of course, exaggerated, for the legendary cut did not extend below the ribs. Snow was wedding the body to the ground, the flakes pristine on bright Inca wool, but melting in the blood. Juan felt numbness climb his body to his mind—an absence of emotion that turned into the clarity of hindsight—seeing the Inca lift his leather shield to Pedro's blow. And little as Juan knew Aristotle, he yet felt an explanation of that moment resided in The Philosopher's analysis of causality. Several 'causes' conspired to kill that Inca— including Pedro's sword as proximate—but the efficient one was habit, for he had lifted a useless shield….

He found his sword and handed it to Pedro, saying, "Thanks, but this is yours."

Rejected both as father and instructor, Pedro was profoundly saddened. First women, now swords … next, indument…?

They built a fire of broken spears, and inside a dead man's helmet Pedro made *charqui* and *chuño* stew. They ate.

Warm and full, at last, Juan cleared his throat. "You know how in the Bible it's: 'Not I, but Christ in me.' Well Pedro, when it comes to fighting, *you* are in me."

Juan was right—but mostly wrong—thought Pedro sadly.

"*Hijo*, I deserve no credit for the gifts God gave you. You were a fighter before I ever handed you a knife."

And Pedro spoke the truth, as his heart knew it. Generations came and went, father handing a weapon to his son. So had it always been. "Consider a longer blade," he added.

And that night Pedro held an internal conversation, for as Juan was honest, so had he to be, admitting that he had been made uncomfortable by one so gifted. Graduating him to the sword would have kept him a student for some while longer…. But in the end, it all boiled down to pride, refusing to accept his *hijo* as a man.

Your son was grown when he could kill you.

Chapter 7: Valdivia (Peru, 1539)

The Incas led them through a wilderness that seemed to hold no breathing being but for the condors wheeling overhead. Arid, wind scoured, void as the stomachs of the expedition, these altitudes were beautiful nonetheless, washed by twilight with corals, ocher, violet, and hues for which Juan knew no name.

There were skirmishes, yet never a pitched battle. The *charqui* was rationed, *chuño* and *choclo* short. When the horses could no longer bear them the *caballeros* walked, abandoning their armor, leaving a metal trail of gorgets, cuirasses and greaves as record of their futile wandering.

One day a hungry arquebusier killed a low-flying condor and spread out his prize. An unhealthy black, the huge beast of the air had a fleshy featherless head that looked as if red cheese had melted on it. Over the eyes a mass of crumpled meat was cocked, a nightcap from a nightmare, and from a feathery slit in the neck hung something like a flaccid tongue. The ruff of white feathers at the neck, the baldness, the eyes sunk in creases, made Juan think of aged ministers from Hell.

The day came that Gonzalo Pizarro decided they had been made fools of long enough, ordering the expedition back to Cuzco. That very evening Pedro sold Juan's sword and gambled away the *pesos*. The only worthwhile things that Indies coin could buy came from Spain, anyway, and for these items the prices were exorbitant. A horse cost twenty five hundred gold *pesos* or more, and wine a king's ransom. Genuine Iberian whores—far scarcer than pork—could name their price. Such was the demand for these 'squirrels'—for they were said to shelter themselves with their tails—that some were richer than Spanish noblewomen, importing tapestries, gem encrusted crucifixes and luxurious beds for the cheerless Inca interiors in which they spread the priceless pallor of their thighs. So it was that for an ordinary sword Pedro got enough to make a man rich in Spain, though in the Indies it would not purchase a dead burro. In the field, gold was but a load.

Pedro was melancholy—back from the campaign—as for the first time in his career he had not risen like rich fat to top the military stew. And not having nothing much to do, the next day he took Juan to see Sacsahuaman—the Inca fortress brooding over Cuzco. To get there was something of a walk.

Sucking on a *bota* as punctuation, Pedro lectured as they went.... Cuzco was designed by Inca Pachacuti to resemble the puma, sacred to these Indians. The head was a great natural outcropping. Two rivers—the Huatanay and the Tuyumayo—

flowed by this promontory, shaping the back and belly. Cuzco was built between them. And on the head, created by the gods, was a fortress built by man.

Once on the parapets, immense beyond belief, Juan decided that Sacsahuaman confused architecture with God's earth. The stones! Pulled leagues, some had been abandoned on the way. They made him think of houses with no interior space.

Pedro talked curtains, salients, bastions, the glacis, cross fire and artillery, an impromptu essay which compared Sacsahuaman to the fortifications of the Italian campaigns, the first in Europe designed to withstand a siege with artillery more modern than bombards—that is, cannon firing stone. About to analyze the *trace italienne*, he decided his *hijo* was not listening....

Silent, they had returned to Cuzco's streets when an Indian sprinted by pursued by *infantes*. Following, they found him cornered at an alley's end. Unarmed, he snarled. His teeth were filed to points, his naked torso corded tight as the strings of a *vihuela*, face tattooed into a savage mask. This was no Inca.

Pedro opined, "The savage will sell his life dearly. And those assholes think so too, or they would have attacked already. Ten *pesos* to your one he buys something with his death ... an eye or ear maybe."

Then a door behind the Indian opened, exhaling an apparition which made every Spaniard present catch his breath. The Blessed Virgin was known to visit man, and *She* the disembodied vision seemed to be, her countenance floating in an aureole of ruddy gold, the sun of afternoon catching her hair obliquely with a shaft. Below, a black dress blotted out her body ... an accident of light, yet—to minds attuned to miracle—a miracle it was. Her nimbus was her copper hair, and in her hand she held a comb, transformed by the spirituality of the moment into an emblem.

The vision spoke. "Attack an unarmed man! For shame!"

She stepped into full illumination, her outstretched hands pale in a foam of lace.

The *infantes* edged ahead, for a mere woman stood between them and their sport.

Pedro kicked the legs out from under one of them. And drawing his sword, he stepped over his groaning form to stand beside the vision. "Five armed men against a naked Indian!" He spat. "*Pardiez*, you make me ashamed to be Spanish."

Drawing his knife, Juan went to protect Pedro's left, seeing that the apparition beside them was holding a long hairpin, low and steady.

Her eyes were green as the seas of Panama. And Juan was in love forever.

Pedro said, "The party's over."

Muttering like monks at *matins*, the *infantes* turned to go.

She lifted burnished hair, twisting casually, and curtsying with unimaginable grace she thanked the *caballeros* come to her rescue. Inés de Suárez was at their service, begging pardon for the informality of the meeting. Would they accept her hospitality...? And turning to the Indian—erect as a post by her door—she signed that he too could enter.

Having totally forgotten him, Juan was shocked to see that the savage was tattooed with cryptic symbols.

Inés again gestured ... to no response. Sighing she led Juan and Pedro in while completing the casual architecture of her hair—transfixing Juan as well, as if hairpins were Cupid's darts, her hair somehow his heart.

"Indians!" she exclaimed, tilting a firm chin up. Then, "Welcome, *caballeros*."

Juan almost gasped, for the room was a riot of color. Blankets and feathered cloaks blazed on walls. The floor was layered with Inca tapestries. Spanish chests bound by iron were overlain by barbaric cloth. Colorful curios of the Indies were everywhere.

As for Pedro, he perceived—Could it be?—wine! Then he focused on a proper hearth, holding a fire of wood— not turds—where a fragrant haunch was sizzling. He sniffed. Olive oil? Oregano? Body of God!

And Juan found himself comparing Inés de Suárez to the equally pale Constanza di Lorenzo, thinking that the Sevillana would now forever seem too languid, too recumbent. He wished that he were older, more experienced. He did not mind at all that she had freckles.

"Pray sit, *caballeros*," Inés said.

Juan sat and prayed. "Dear Saint Francis, a rake in youth, were I not a fool, what would I do?"

Father Sosa had taught him that as saints were occupied with many thousands of requests, most of them foolish, prayer should be clear, specific. But in this instance Juan was terrified of being clear, and his desires were impossible to specify.

A spark leapt to a tapestry by the hearth.

Juan sprang to protect this prized possession of his love, smothering the small coal with his hand.

She came to touch him with a tapered finger reminding him of candles. The nail was pink—a perfect almond. Taking olive oil, she rubbed it on his blister.

None of Juan's prayers had ever been answered so quickly, wonderfully and subtly. He thanked Saint Francis from the bottom of his heart.

They discussed tapestries. At some point she laughed, head tossed back, eyes in shadow, throat warm with light. She poured Spanish wine. And when the meat was done to what Pedro pronounced "rare perfection," they feasted, Inés producing a second miracle—fresh wheaten bread!

She demurred at their delight, saying that in the lowlands of Peru Spanish wheat grew well. The crust, perhaps, was not as crunchy as it might be....

Inés had a knack for putting men at ease, and when Pedro began to pick his teeth with his knife—this sign that he was done with serious eating—she asked his opinion of the situation in Peru.

Sucking on marrow, Pedro contained a fart. And despite his deep conviction that women were limited—as the old toast proposes—to the two ends of the corset, from this moment on he treated Inés de Suárez with his own version of respect.

Gonzalo Pizarro was organizing an expedition to the east, he said, where cinnamon was said to grow. He had been thinking of taking part, even if it meant riding into the valley of death looking for tree bark. Strange miracles could happen in the Indies.

Why jungles? Inés retorted. Even Incas loathed them. Your armor rusted. Your feet rotted, and your toes fell off. Black flowers rooted in your ears. And in jungles there were no riches, just Indians with bones in their noses inventing stories about gold ten days away. Mexico and Peru—their wealth beggaring the imagination— were both in highland valleys. If she were a man she would not go east with Gonzalo Pizarro to rot in jungles. She would go south with Pedro de Valdivia.

Pedro had, respectfully, to disagree. Only a handful of supporters of Almagro— fearing for their lives in Peru—had signed on for this march to hell. Valdivia was an extraordinary captain, but—begging her pardon—he was insane to think of going to Chile. Almagro had returned with a tiny fraction of his expedition after an odyssey of suffering imposssible to describe. Down *there,* you could walk on salt forever.

"Almagro just went so far."

Pedro was incredulous. How far did one need go, to die? He had *been* to Chile, for the love of God!

Inés changed tack…. To the south—it was said—an Amazon ruled an empire where the streets were paved with gold. A similar rumor led Pizarro to Peru, and even though the streets were stone the wealth had been incalculable. No one claimed anything like that existed east, which is why men were being lured there with cinnamon, of all things. Had they come so far—suffered so much—to end up peeling jungles! Valdivia knew better. He had vision. And he needed soldiers like Pedro and Juan. The tougher the expedition, the tougher the men needed for it…. Inés made it sound more like a compliment than an invitation to a likely death, when she asked them to see Valdivia with her.

Pedro was not swayed, though charmed and in his cups. He had been south already.

Wooing Pedro, Inés had forgotten Juan, and he was able to study her pale intensity, her animated gestures. The coal of her hair burned through her shawl. Her nose was piquant, upturned, sprinkled with constellations of faint freckles.

"There is no better captain in the Indies. Give him a chance." Inés was becoming desperate.

And it was then that—thinking her bread and wine, cunning and charm, would come to nothing—she succumbed to her desire and improvised the legend she would one day become. "I, at least, will go to Chile with him."

Valdivia had never proposed anything of the sort. What he did was bow and scrape, and talk about the Indian problem—which, for a woman, was the servant problem. He also often commented on the extraordinary weather of Peru, in which sunburn and chilblains could coexist. He rendered her furious, in short, avoiding every subject of importance in deference to her delicate incapacities—though she could ride as well as any of the men he gambled with. Above all, he ignored the fact that she had a mind of her own … and a good one at that. To him she was an ornament, when all she wanted was to be a part of his endeavor.

In Peru a Spanish woman needed male protection to survive with her honor intact, and high protection to prosper. Inés had therefore—and in this she was honest with herself—pursued Pedro de Valdivia from the start as the most attractive of the men of power. But that had changed. Inés did not yet actually *admit* to herself she was in love, but Valdivia was the reason she was doing everything in her power to recruit hulking Pedro and Juan of the hazel eyes and serious eyebrows. Her captain was in desperate need of men. She needed for him to need *her*. And tonight she had failed.…

She leapt to her feet, digging in her hair for a pin, screaming, "No, Don Pedro! No!" But she was far too late.…

Without warning, Pedro had drawn a knife and—demented—slashed at Juan's throat. But, miraculously, the child survived, casting himself aside. Now they stalked each other like cannibal spiders, manic grins on their faces. Men!

Indignant, but no fool, Inés noted that their violence had been a dance. Nothing had been broken or knocked over. And Negrito—on the table eating bread—casually ignored them both.

Pedro grinned at Inés. "You would need more than a hairpin," he said.

She rearranged her hair. "It's late, so why not spend the night? I have Spanish beds."

In Peru by and large, Spaniards slept on the floor as Incas did. Yet what rendered the proposal extraordinary was that it came from an unmarried Spanish woman, making it the next thing to an offer of her body.

Stifling a rich burp with his hand, Pedro thanked her. And—soldier that he was—he made it to his feet, astonished that a woman this beautiful, with a reputation for virtue without equal in Peru, should want to sleep with *him*. He would have simpered if he could.

She left Pedro on the promised mattress, however, departing with her candle.

"*Buenas noches, caballero*. Perhaps tomorrow you might give Valdivia a chance to make his case."

He had been outmaneuvered Pedro thought. Inés was after Juan, *pardiez*. And good for him! Pedro truly liked her. And in all truth he was relieved at this development, never having slept with a woman beside whom he could not—for example—fart. Why forsake one pleasure for another?

But Pedro was twice mistaken. Inés tucked Juan in as mothers might, offering a cheek for a kiss. Breath fragrant with clove she said, "*Guapo*,"—just like Liliana!— "I am not ... insensitive, to your interest, but I am old enough to be your mother. Can we not just be friends?"

She appealed. "The Indies need men like you. Too much talent here has been devoted to melting empires into ingots. Chile will be a new start for the New World—a place where gold does not corrupt the heart. Valdivia does not so much want to conquer as to colonize, therefore men of little vision and great greed think he is mad." And—with a misty look that set the seal on Juan's eternal yearning— she said, "Valdivia is a dreamer."

She loves him, thought Juan, appalled.

"Excuse me for rattling on," Inés concluded, shifting her weight so that her thigh was in incredible proximity to his arm—without making actual contact. "Would it be so hard for us to be friends?"

Juan plighted his troth. "No ... yes. We are, *señora*."

And touching his cheek lightly, saying, "Call me Inés," she left, trailing a faint cloud of clove.

Once in her room Inés knelt on flagstone and prayed—her Paters and Aves rote—for she despised her deceptions of this night. An Amazon kingdom? Ha, ha, and ha! What she wanted was a Valdivia so far south that his wife would never dream of going there. In Patagonia he would be hers alone. And Heaven would forgive her for egging poor Juan on. Of *that* Inés was ashamed, but—God knew!— she was profoundly lonely in this land of enigmatic Indians and Spanish men who saw you as two holes—the empty head above, and the one they yearned to fill below, you were so white and rare.

Clearly Juan was different. Never had she seen such love look back at her, bereft of artifice and hope. Valdivia loved her too, she imagined, but if so in a distant and far more dominating way, without a trace of desperation. This somehow made her sad....

She woke with the crucifix of her rosary pressed against her forehead. And contemplating the brutal, crimson imprint in her steel mirror, she remembered girlish dreams of riding horses farther than any woman had before....

That very morning—after a sumptuous breakfast—she convinced Pedro Gómez de San Benito to meet with Pedro de Valdivia. But he had left to recruit.

The month and more that Valdivia was gone made Inés, Pedro and Juan into a trio of unlikely friends. Days they spent together. Evenings, Pedro gambled at the *bodegón* of Francisco Martinez Peñalosa, gladly emptying both his purse and his *bota*.

Pedro and Juan all but moved in with Inés—her place so much more comfortable—and the improbable arrangement worked well. Pedro was drinking wine, eating the best food south of the equator, and actually enjoying talking Peruvian politics with a woman. Elbows on the table she would cradle the pale oval of her face in the perfection of her hands, rapt in listening. Or, fiery, she would pace to argue. With Juan she mostly talked books—though she could neither read nor write. She knew of Amadís de Gaula, and was somewhat intrigued by this hero, distant in time and place. But she was terminally impatient with Pliny and More's **Utopia** ... and the very *thought* of writing made her restive.

"Where are the books about the here and now?" she asked one day. Staggered, Juan asked back, "Why read about what you can see and touch?" Ideally, words transported you to better times and places.

Every past was once a present, she replied, and every other place was *this place* for someone, then. Why wait for a later and an elsewhere?

She had a way of striking Juan dumb.

They scoured Cuzco, collecting more Indian things to crowd her place, bringing back pottery, feather work, weavings, wood carvings and *quipú*—those intricately knotted strings, so utterly unlike books. As for Pedro, he collected but one thing, showing up one evening with a cup made from a human skull, and saying, "Won this work of art at dice...."

Gold lined the cranial cavity. The cup's foot—jammed into the neck bone hole—was gold. The eye sockets had emeralds for their pupils. To Juan, it seemed an obscene parody of green-eyed Inés.

As if she had read Juan's mind, fairly glowing with outrage, Inés hissed, "Pedro Gómez de San Benito, upon my father's grave, if you drink from that obscenity in my house, you will never set foot here again."

The condemned vessel disappeared with Pedro into the night.

And when he returned Juan almost 'killed' him for the first time. Pedro had attacked according to their evening ritual, with a sweep of the knife that should have cut Juan's head off. But he ducked, drawing, knife tight against Pedro's 'purse.'

Pedro said, "I would rather die."

Juan declared his own death as well.

Like a bishop hushing a cathedral, Pedro lifted his hand high and whispered,

"Wait!" And disappearing, he returned with a package of oiled parchment that he handed Juan, making a ceremonial leg.

From the wrapping a Toledo blade emerged. The bolster and finger guard were chased in gold with Moorish filigree, and Pedro had Inca artisans reset an exquisitely carved bone handle on the tang. "Check it out," he coaxed.

On the one side of the handle was a tiny battle scene, resembling a storm with a man at its eye, holding a knife. On the other was a library wall. God only knew how Pedro communicated what was foreign to himself as to the carver—and indeed, to Juan—but there books were, looking like grains of *choclo*. And on the spine of one, not so tiny as to be illegible, was the title—Juan de Cardeña, *Maestro*.

Celebrating, Negrito did limber handsprings on the table.

Inés thought to herself that some male rituals were like strange marriages ... and indeed, she was dewy eyed. Then as the three embraced—sober as Cardinals electing Popes—her hand was nudged....

She had inherited Juan's first weapon, and that night she took it to her bed, crying outright, knowing how precious it had been to him. How easily a soul could pass into a thing!

In some way subtly strange, the knife created greater intimacy between Inés and Juan, so that when Pedro left to gamble next evening he confessed to her his unrequited passion for pale Constanza di Lorenzo, making of it a joke of course, and obviously omitting the blancmange incident.

Emboldened by his trust Inés sketched her own history—somewhat amended, for why undergo the travail of the Indies, if not to remake yourself...?

She was—she said—a single child, mother dying at her birth. Her father was that empoverished *hidalgo* of the jokes—too noble to work, too proud to beg. And he had no idea of how to raise a daughter. Had she been male, he would have taught her to ride and fight, hunt and drink. Instead he taught her only to ride astride, omitting the rest. And when he died young of apoplexy she was of an age to marry, with no family that she knew of, so she lived by herself in a ruinous pile of stone.

Still, those were good times. She liked to ride, be alone. Men did court her, and she turned them down, loving nothing more than taking to the hills on Duque, last of her father's horses. He was old and slow, almost blind. One day he broke his leg in a rabbit hole....

"I walked home and came back with an ax and father's sword, not knowing which to use."

"Merciful God in Heaven!"

"Poor Duque. He was not just my only companion, he was my ride into the village. And as I could not afford a *burro*, I was stranded. I had food—chickens and eggs, my garden. I also had my sewing, which gave me a modest income. But there was talk. Why was I living by myself, unmarried? Why had I rejected all my suitors? Women would turn their backs when I walked into the village. This could not go on, and I asked the best suitor of the lot if he was still interested. So, I got married because my horse was blind.

My husband's relatives never accepted me, thinking I put on airs. And as the months passed, I did not conceive. Then when my husband left for the Indies, his family was free to hate me. My only comfort was that I had not borne a child. I sewed, and sewed, and saved enough to buy a *burro*, then sewed some more, and saved enough to follow my husband to the Indies. In Panama I was told he was in Venezuela, but when I got there an *infante* that sailed with him said he died on board, never even making shore. So there I was, in godforsaken Venezuela, with no place to go. And it got worse. The *infante* who told me of my husband's death offered me a *peso* to share his bed. And when I refused he tried to force me."

"No!" Juan exploded.

"That's when I taught myself to fight with hairpins. And not long after that I met Valdivia in the midst of hellish jungles. I was footsore—for my *burro* had gone lame—filthy and mud spattered, soaked by one of those showers that there explode from the blue…. How I hate Venezuela! Air so wet you cannot breathe! And it's full of creeping things. Sometimes, when you slash with a machete at a vine, it bleeds. Snakes! Leeches!"

"They think Eden might be somewhere in Venezuela," Juan offered. But she ignored him.

"So I stumble out of a jungle swamp and *there* Valdivia is up on his horse—Apollo in his armor. I almost cried when I saw myself reflected on his steel, rat's nest holding up my hat. Worse—to make walking easier—I tied up my skirts."

"And…?"

"He did not tell me he was wed. As they say, every married man is a bachelor, once past Gibraltar."

And with that revelation Inés cut short her narrative, saying she sailed to Cuzco on a ship captained by Rodrigo de Grijalva, in 1538.

With a rudeness he hoped their new intimacy might ignore, Juan asked her why she still wore black. She was so alive—and so in love with color—that it nagged.

"Black," she said, putting on the flat, broad-brimmed black hat she invariably wore outdoors, "is dramatic. Black makes men respectful. And black becomes me. Black *has* become me."

She posed in radiant demonstration, tugging out tortoiseshell combs, her copper hair sputtering like sparks against the black velvet of her shoulders….

Pedro chose that moment to sweep aside the blanket standing for a door, announcing that Valdivia had returned, recruiting no one.

Blanching, Inés braced a hand on the table by her.

"But I signed us up. We're all going to Chile—a small purse now, and horses for us all. Not bad, *amigos!* "

Inés sat as if her hamstrings had been scythed.

Pedro had resigned himself to the inevitable, Juan insisting like a pregnant mule that if Inés went to Chile *he* would too. This insanity was clearly important to the child, and there was precedent in any case, for this was not the first madness of which Pedro had been part. If Valdivia went to Chile, sure as the damned went to Hell, Inés would follow, Juan hot on her scent. But his *hijo* could not brave the many dangers by himself. And also, Inés was now very like a comrade. Therefore Pedro sought Valdivia out the instant he was back in Cuzco, volunteering in the face of his surprise, using shock as a lever in the bargaining....

And there Inés was, slumping like a puppet with severed strings.

Pedro pleaded, "You *said* you wanted to."

She came to life. "Old bear," she crooned. "Dear old bear." She danced up to hug him, crooning, "Wonderful old bear."

Then the trio joined in a tight wild knot, Juan and Inés orbiting Pedro's mass, spinning in an orrery of gladness. As for the death that waited south, let it yawn.

Next morning they went to see Valdivia.

The Lieutenant Governor—now just shy of forty years—was a living legend. He had fought for Carlos V in Flanders and the Italian campaigns, returned to Spain, married, and after ten years in Extremadura embarked for the New World, leaving behind his wife, Doña Marina Ortíz de Gaete. He spent a season in Venezuela, emerging with his life, no gold, and a reputation as one of the best captains in the Indies. Then he surfaced in Peru in 1537, five years after the conquest of the Incas, a time of tension in the Spanish ranks. From the first, Valdivia was devoted to Francisco Pizarro, who recognized his talent and appointed him *maestre de campo*—second in command, and leader of his armies. And when—after Almagro's return from Chile—civil war broke out, it was in this capacity that Pedro de Valdivia routed the rebels at the battle of Salinas. Thanks to Valdivia, Peru was under Pizarro's thumb.

The Governor was generous, granting Valdivia the valley of La Canela as his *encomienda*, which produced two hundred thousand gold *pesos* a year. He also gave him a silver mine in Porco, worth that and more. Valdivia was the richest man in Peru after Pizarro himself. And it was at the zenith of this triumph that he asked permission to explore the south, requesting to be named Governor of the lands he would discover. Pizarro initially turned down the lunatic petition. But giving the matter thought, he agreed to name him Lieutenant Governor of southern lands if he renounced his *encomiendas*.

Valdivia accepted in April of 1539.

Peru was stunned. Almagro had returned from Chile with no gold and one eye missing. The one hundred and fifty Spaniards who went with him, at least as many horses, and *yanaconas* numbering in the thousands had perished there. No one was surprised when Valdivia's recruitment met with failure.

Therefore, neither was it a surprise that the Lieutenant Governor accepted Pedro's offer with open arms, more than hinting that if his present *maestre de campo* were to die—this being likely, as he was old—Pedro would be next in line. They drank deeply, talked particulars, agreeing that Juan would have an *encomienda*.

Man of great momentum, Pedro pleaded for Inés, promising to be responsible.

Valdivia replied that perhaps it would be better if Señora Doña Inés de Suárez were under his *aegis*.

Pedro could not tell an *aegis* from an egg, but caught Valdivia's drift. In a coop with far too many roosters and one hen, better that she be under the top cock's wing, so to speak. Yet Pedro wondered how Valdivia would explain to Pizarro that his esteemed lieutenant—a married man—was taking his mistress on the expedition.

Valdivia revisited that same predicament once Pedro left. In Peru, ambition created an undeclared civil war among the captains, and in this struggle Inés would be a serious liability. No one cared about fornication with Indian women, invisible in every way that mattered. But in this empire where power was granted by an emperor who was a veritable monk, to take a Spanish mistress in the public eye would be the worst of politics. Some rival would use Inés to undo him.

So, power or passion…?

Valdivia did not waver in his decision. Others were perhaps more beautiful, but no other had her copper-haired fire. And she fit a man's world surprisingly well. He had not taken his own wife to the Indies, for example—that languid, puffy dumpling. Yet never imagining that Inés would consort with a married man, he had desired her with polite respect, a distance she herself maintained.

Here, Valdivia's thoughts turned darker. What had *happened* in his absence? Inés was presently cheek by jowl with the most tireless drinker, gambler and wencher of the Indies—a legend of heroic excess. The whole thing puzzled. What changed the mind of Gómez, who turned him down before? Not Inés! Not when she could have any Spaniard in Peru, including himself, and probably Francisco Pizarro. Logic led him to Juan de Cardeña, whoever he might be, this 'friend' that *had* to come along. Valdivia awaited meeting him with far more pique than pleasure….

And when the three recruits walked in, he lifted an eyebrow at the thought that he had promised three horses, two of these priceless animals carrying a woman and a boy. What had his cod up been up to? Even if the child—as alleged—could write, how could he be worth a horse? Was this stripling bedding her...?

Valdivia glared. "*Un rapaz!*"

Instantly, Pedro was an irate fort. "*Señor*, he is my closest friend, and I would trust him with my life." He spun on his heel to leave.

The Lieutenant Governor sprang to his feet, beaming. "*Señor* Don Juan, any friend of Pedro Gómez is a friend of mine. I welcome you to the expedition." He embraced the boy.

Then as the ticklish matter of Inés remained, Valdvia bowed. "Doña Inés, what a pleasure to have you join us also."

Valdivia turned to Juan. "Don Pedro says you read and write. Is that in Latin?"

"*Sí, su señoría*. Also in Spanish."

Impressed but doubtful, Valdivia said, "Please be so kind as to take this page and read it." He gestured to where he had been working.... Juan read with difficulty, faltered and confessed, "God's truth, this scrawl is hard to read."

Fond of quoting Caesar, Valdivia was far more educated than most soldiers, and had been able to nurture a reputation that he was something of a scholar. Yet he had penned the blotted page himself, and was not so vain as to suppose that the problem lay with Juan. When it came to concept and general composition, Valdivia had few equals. Yet he embraced no illusion about his calligraphy—his letter being erratic, his spelling worse. This made a secretary necessary and he had already hired one—a puffed, unctuous toad whom he despised—postponing paying him until departure. In the interim he had been putting quill to parchment himself.

"Hem ... I agree. Hard to read. Now, could you take dictation?"

After, Valdivia pronounced the hand superb. And like cannon fired by slow match, he concluded, "Would you do me the honor of assisting my personal secretary, Luis de Cartagena, in the expedition to Chile, a position which will of course be reflected in your *encomienda*."

Juan managed broken thanks.

Expansive, Valdivia toasting their future, pouring from a wineskin balanced on his armored forearm. "To Pedro Gómez, right hand of my *maestre de campo!*"

They drank.

"To Juan de Cardeña, right hand of my personal secretary."

They drank, Valdivia refilling with a practiced squirt.

"To Doña Inés de Suárez ... angel ministering to the expedition."

Valdivia knew she cared for the sick and wounded, including Incas. She also kept animals and tended a garden in which she grew plants both civilized and savage. Nonetheless, no military expedition had ever included what Valdivia now proposed....

Knowing the offer an honorary sop, Inés still glowed. He had called her an *angel*! Damning her blushing, cursing her freckles—but keeping her composure—she raised her cup. "To Valdivia!"

To that, also, they bent elbows. After, they drank to everything else—save mules and Indians—managing to empty the capacious wineskin.

That afternoon Juan, Pedro and Inés slept a badly needed *siesta*. Valdivia did not, for in the alembic of ambition alcohol had set his thoughts on fire. "*Alea iacta est*," he murmured in his cot, being in awe of Caesar without having read him … as he was of Alexander, never having conquered. He would leave for Chile, with or without an army.

Next morning he called on Inés de Suárez, with whom—as he found out—Juan de Cardeña and Pedro Gómez de San Benito spent their days. Presumably, he was visiting to talk to his Next to be Second in Command, but he had a deeply shrouded motive. With the decisiveness he displayed in battle, Valdivia had determined to abandon distant siege and press a true attack upon the charming widow. Therefore he brought with him Indians bearing rare wine and a far rarer suckling pig, squealing with terror as it hung from a pole, trotters up. Hospitality would demand he join the feast, which would take hours to prepare, during which time he would mine her bastions.

Success in war demands a concentrated division of attention of the captain—who must comprehend the parts of an evolving, unpredictable, complex whole—and of this Valdivia was a master. So it was that—while talking recruitment, armaments and routes with Gómez, and future duties with his new assistant secretary—he touched knees under the table with the delectable Inés....

The route to Chile was the most difficult decision. There were two ways to get there—the *altiplano*, high in the *cordillera*—and the Atacama Desert. Pedro Gómez had traveled both with Almagro, going to Chile on the high road, returning by the low. And he insisted that of those two hells the desert was far preferable.

Inés was thinking she never met a man so commanding as Valdivia, although physically he did not stand out, which made his attractive force the more remarkable. Of medium height and wiry, in dress he avoided refinement. Yet on his charger he was a very god. His Italian armor—no less polished than her own steel mirror—framed a face in which mustache and beard were twirled into a trio of stilettos. Yet all that paled beside his glance—proud and brooding, brooking nothing, his were the eyes of an emperor. Inés imagined armor that revealed only *them* … and his hands, strong, yet eloquent. Valdivia had the eyes of a Caesar and the hands of—God forgive her!—a lover. Her husband—God rest his soul!—had always mounted her both mathematically and theologically—three times a week, never on Sunday. The eyes and hands of Valdivia promised greater adventures....

The evening drawing to its close, Pedro and Juan took to their beds. And lingering by the door with Inés, Valdivia wondered what her knees had told him.

She extended a hand only.

Valdivia brushed it with his lips, thankful for some reason that this woman was more complicated than Italian fortifications. Hat in hand he bowed—the sweep of plumes turning his failed campaign into the wit of friends—and spun to leave, his cloak a huge black bloom.

Pedro and Juan busied themselves with preparation in the following days, Inés with her many interests, and their evening feast became a habit. Cuzco now considered her the mistress of Valdivia, and although in this she took great pride, she did not turn the rumors real.

She treasured their chaste proximity, for now he talked to her as to one of sense and insight, not some adornment in a skirt. He inquired about her duties as Ministering Angel—the gardens, the ill, the orphans—this ministry he had more ratified than created. In plants Valdivia had no interest whatsoever, but about men he listened with deep attention, priding himself on knowing his command, and fond of saying, "*No por acero, por amigos se gana la batalla.*" Friends, not steel, win battles.

Inés perfectly agreed. And since undue familiarity with the troops was to be avoided by their captains, she performed a vital function. If Valdivia could be said to be the trunk sustaining the enterprise, then she comprised the branches touching the many leaves—not just the relatively few Spaniards, but also the *yanaconas* in their multitudes. This mattered.

One evening, when Valdivia and Pedro left to gamble, Inés confided to Juan that Valdivia said she was his Mediatrix to the Troops. "Can you believe it," she cawed full-throated. "Might as well be called an Immaculate Gunner." Yet she joked not just out of pride, as she had attempted to mediate for Juan himself … and she was nervous.

Valdivia had taken her aside to say that he regretted having promised Luis de Cartagena the position of secretary to the expedition—this swine being the only one available at the time. Now Juan made him regret his promise. However, as his sword was his sword, so was his word his word. This created a problem. He did not want to hire Luis until the expedition left, but he needed someone in the interim. Could she persuade Juan to do be his secretary out of friendship, on the side, for free…?

Their growing intimacy had created a candor in Inés that Valdivia prized with reservations—as if her tongue were a strong and willing mule that did not always take him where he wanted. Therefore he awaited her response uneasily.

"You mean that Juan will work for nothing now, and this Cartagena pig will be hired when we leave at last, for pay!" She was more furious than she otherwise might have been, as the pig in question had once propositioned her.

Valdivia made calming motions with his hands. "My fiery angel, you know how short of money the expedition is. I just thought that, as Juan is so close to you...."

The Lieutenant Governor raised his eyes to that Heaven in which saints were well aware of the difficulties of his enterprise, allowing the silence to reverberate. "Friendship has no price," he argued. "Besides, I promised Juan a horse."

Inés had reluctantly agreed, deciding that this would further Juan's career. But when he swallowed her bait with an alacrity she considered excessive—peeved at shouldering the entire burden of indignation—she pointed out that he would be working for free in the stead of a swine that would get all the money and glory.

Juan replied that as he liked to read he liked to write. And never in his life had he been paid to do anything, anyway. He was thrilled.

That evening he took dictation from Valdivia, and writing replaced dueling with knives as Juan's after-supper ritual. Pedro would leave to gamble, revolted that the martial moments he had shared with his *hijo* had degenerated into language, until one evening Inés asked Pedro if he would teach her to use her knife.

They chose a distant courtyard for their lessons. There they sparred in a ring of torches held by astonished Incas, Inés impressing Pedro both with her courage and the patience with which she died. One evening, having become skilled enough that her skirts were an encumbrance, she dismissed the torchbearers. Lighting the many candles she had brought, swearing Pedro to eternal silence, she removed her skirt and petticoats.

"Let's mix it up."

"How can I fight if I can't look?" Pedro whined, having turned his back.

"You're breaking your own rules. If you don't look, I'll kill you. Just pretend that I'm a boy."

He stole a glance over his shoulder. She held her guard, wearing a black bodice, dark hose. Her hair was stuffed into a brilliant Inca cap. And for that matter, her legs tended to the boyish ... but if she's a boy, Pedro thought, then I'm Mother Superior. Never had he seen a woman in hose, for holy laws put skirts on legs, lest men's eyes be led to that convergence which was their pleasure and her shame. But on Inés now, fortunately, a skirt brutally chopped off hid that delta with a thousand names.

Pedro cleared his throat. Theirs was a friendship he treasured as a sexless thing, and *there* her legs were, next thing to bare, when even whores did not display above the knee. *Putas* showed their tits is what they did, revealing goods above the belt—that equator set by God for the beginning of important veils.

Inés leapt forward, prodding Pedro's kidney with her point. He dropped to a knee, creating distance and clear space with a sweep that would have halved the pupil of two weeks ago. About to yell never to surprise him like that again, he remembered that surprise was the name of the game. She was shuffling, feinting … lunging!

Pedro sidestepped, her knife just short of his throat. Two more inches to her arm and he would have been a dead man. So, drawing a deep breath ... he killed her.

She smiled as she dressed. "Thanks, Pedro. You are a wonderful friend."

He decided that the contest had been unfair. "I was staring at your legs."

"I counted on it," she replied, leaving the room in a wind of skirts.

"I never taught you *that!*" At this moment, for some reason, he was reminded of the pudgy altar boy he used to be.

"You are unbeatable," she shouted back. "I needed the advantage."

In retrospect, Pedro did not regret glimpsing those long, wonderfully rounded legs. And that night he dreamed The Fall of Man with a difference—The Tree of Knowledge had women's legs in hose instead of branches. And not an apple on it.

Juan's respect for Valdivia reached new highs in the taking of his dictation. With a staccato delivery—sometimes turned into a stutter by the speed of his thoughts—he composed marvels of Spanish prose.

Valdivia was corresponding with Lucas Martínez Vegaso, a merchant who had been with Pizarro at the capture of Atahualpa and become fabulously wealthy. And on October 10 of 1539, Valdivia and Vegaso signed a contract penned by Juan. The entrepreneur agreed to supply the equivalent of nine thousand *pesos* in horses and cash in return for one half of the expected profit. Since a horse cost at least two thousand pesos, Vegaso's offer was absurd on the face of it. Yet if a man of this stature followed Valdivia's banner, perhaps others would too. And from that day momentum gathered. Valdivia had sent letters to those returning from explorations of the territories surrounding Peru, and received promises that over a hundred would meet him on the journey.

The ship's captain, Juan Bautista de Pastene—his good friend—wrote from Panama where his vessel was being careened, promising to arrive when Fortuna permitted. Jerónimo de Alderete—who sailed to the Indies with Valdivia and shared the failure that was Venezuela—wrote that he had broken his sword arm in a fall that killed his horse. When his Indian wife died of pox—which should happen shortly—he would pursue a rumor of a fabulous empire to the northeast. If it did not materialize, he would join him.

The wheel of Fortuna had begun to elevate Valdivia from the nadir where he lingered since April. But, in December, he stormed in to say to Inés and Juan that Sancho de Hoz—that reptile with a rapier—was in Cuzco. He had gone to Pizarro with what he claimed were royal decrees proclaiming him Governor of southern lands. And he proposed—ha, ha!—to make him his lieutenant.

Too stunned to respond, Juan and Inés merely gaped.

Pedro, who had been grooming Negrito, roared, "*Qué cojones!*"

Valdivia buried his dagger in the table with a violence that toppled candles and made Inés leap to her feet. Then with quiet venom he proposed, "Let's see what Pizarro does." De Hoz had been Pizarro's secretary until 1535, when he renounced his position to return to Spain and marry. The Governor knew him too well to trust him.

Pizarro met with the interested parties in late December, and Valdivia returned home more drunk on triumph than on wine. "The hare-lipped *hijo de puta*," he crowed, "has a decree that makes him governor of all the lands to be discovered south of the Magellan straits. Very well then, let him govern penguins." Valdivia began to waddle in armor. A ruler of penguins, he lisped commands to his black and white nation. "Swim," he ordered. "Sit on eggs."

"So...?" Inés was annoyed to see Valdivia's intelligence drowned by wine. "The decree makes him a Governor. What does that make *you?*"

"I was about to get to that. De Hoz and I are partners now. He has agreed to provide the expedition with two shiploads of materials and men, meeting us in the South."

Pedro cried out, "Beware! De Hoz is a scorpion in a boot."

"I know," Valdivia said, winking. And—as the spring of the enterprise was now wound far too tight—he handed Inés a purse, asking her to arrange a party.

The fragrant room was crowded with men. A fire crackled under spitted meat. Along one wall were wineskins, slack as pigs at ease. On a long table at the center were pyramids of roasted chicken and mountains of fresh bread. As the centerpiece, *empanadas* were arranged like bricks into a fort with sausage cannons. Raisins—soaked in *aguardiente*—were stacked like cannonballs beside them. The drawbridge was made of breadsticks, the moat filled with white wine, and in its clarity swam fish shaped from the strange fruit of Peru.

Knowing that his purse could not have purchased *this*, Valdivia raised a brow when Inés greeted him. Blushing, she touched both cheeks to his with the welcome of a wife. And arm about his waist she called out, "*Caballeros*, fill your cups. I have a toast." Vessels dipped into the moat.

"I drink to riding with Valdivia into the future!"

And when the company deeply had, she breathed in his ear. "*Querido*, see to your guests."

Alea iacta est, Valdivia murmured to himself, too stunned to improvise. Inés had just turned Cuzco's rumors true. She was now his mistress, and every man in the room was dying with envy.

When all had staggered off, Valdivia gently embraced Inés, and she released herself as gently. Returning, she handed him a purse larger than the one he gave her, saying she had sold everything not needed in the wilderness, save for this and that, and a few pearls. In addition she had called in favors, which had left her with one feast, one purse.

She shushed his objections. "Less can be more," she said demurely....

Her room was small, warmed by fire, dim. She tugged out combs, loosing the torrent of her hair, removing clothing Valdivia could not name until only something filmy draped her, bare arms milk in candlelight.

She breathed, "Less can be more. But sometimes, nothing is better."

"We will ride light," he groaned.

Like Adam and Eve they had much to learn, the first time reminiscent of married beds, though more athletic. The second, Inés ended up on top. The third was like a dream on horses. And the fourth—near dawn—Valdivia was no longer an arquebus that had to fire or fail.

He awoke late.

Blanket about her, sitting on the bed, Inés watched as he dressed, then handed him her mirror to help in the repair of his mustache and beard.

"So you do lick and twirl," was her only comment.

Stiffly he replied, "I left the wax at home." Her nibblings had caused the problem in the first place.

Shafts of morning that had evaded shutters burned the floor, casting Inés into soft darkness, and in this penumbra her face was wondrously pale. The night—Valdivia noticed—had shadowed her eyes with violet. Perhaps, like gold, all perfections needed alloy, not to be too soft.

"I love your hands," she said.

In love with her entirety, the Lieutenant Governor of lands yet to be discovered left disoriented, apprehensive. Not just The Church but the memory of his wife—a saint!—made him feel a looming retribution....

Doña Marina Ortíz de Gaete—who was raised by nuns—considered her marital duty to be the only necessary sin. In her eyes The Fall was exactly as it sounded—Eve *fell* onto her back, and Adam jumped on top of her, to do Evil. Obliged to perform a reenactment of this, she wore layers upon layers, so that Valdivia had to delve through sweaty complications to find the unmoved seat of his desires. Also, she would bring a rosary and pray out loud—as one condemned, offering the wrong end to the ax—when all Valdivia wanted was simple silence as he took his pleasure. The Aves! There were acts to which you did not summon the Mother of God, by God!

One night, after an evening at the *bodega*, Valdivia forbade both the rosary and the wool. Doña Marina fought tears and put on her shawl, saying that she needed to confess before she did anything like *that*. She returned, saying that the priest had said she could wear wool. And while she agreed to set her rosary aside, she reserved the right to pray in silence. So, from that day Doña Marina went silent. Yet she did not, truly, Fall. This was God's Will. Amen.

Walking the streets of Cuzco, Valdivia shrugged off his misgivings. Stripped of riches, he had won a woman who was a far greater prize. Yes, less could be more! But—thinking realistically—less in some areas might prove to be far too little. He needed more Indians. He needed maize, *llamas*, guinea pigs and the cages for them, nails, powder, shot, casks for water, wine and mercury—not to mention horseshoes, bits and stirrups, leather for the traces, pig iron and the blacksmith to work it. Another arquebus or two would help. And it would be even better to get his hands on war dogs, trained and armored, which were far more valuable than horses.

Before he walked a block the Lieutanant Governor had forgot the night, lost in logistics. He recalled that Nuño Beltrán de Mendoza was in Peru. And though the dogger had once refused him, he decided to send a letter. Time was short, and the conquerable world immense.

Juan had never been so busy. He had dictation to take, records to keep. Valdivia trusted him to compose entire letters, giving him gist to be fleshed out. The one to Mendoza made him tight-lipped … but he did not comment.

In his rare leisure Juan was learning a little Quechua with Inés—which Valdivia considered an extravagant waste of time. Translators were always to be found, springing up after conquest like mushrooms after rain, making the acquisition of heathen speech unnecessary. And—theologically speaking—in *his* humble opinion it was the Indians that needed to learn Spanish so they might be saved, not the reverse.

Inés was making Juan rethink the *romances*. No palpitations or uncertainties, just a delight in her beauty and warm, intelligent companionship. She skimmed over decorum with the incomparable lightness of insects that dimple bright water with their walk.

One morning Juan arose hungry from his cot. A stolid *chola*—dressed in bright but faded, ragged wool—squatted by the fire. With Quechua and sign language she communicated that Pedro had left. Juan sat to what remained of breakfast—a *guanaco* leg so ripe he spat the first bite, unable to tolerate what Pedro called 'nice bloom.'

He made do with maize cakes and potatoes, trying out his Quechua by saying *choclo and papa*—the latter—by a freak of coincidence—pronounced much like the Spanish word for Pope. She nodded taciturn approval.

Encouraged, he progressed to simple sentences. She laughed and laughed. To her, Juan thought, he must seem a cow attempting Castilian. Why even attempt correctness?

"*Apuapu, apu baba, sí, bayamba,*" he improvised.

She giggled helplessly, her teeth that white which Indians kept into decrepitude. "The better to make mummies' grins," as Pedro said.

"*Ave ave, apure cavi, bombadebaba.*"

Juan was now combining false Quechua with Latin and Spanish, waggling his eyebrows at the *chola*, and she was choking with laughter. If the Pope was a mealy vegetable in her language, anything was possible.

"*Epopeya. Poca papa. Ay caramba!*"

She collapsed, hiding her hysterics under her shawl, sides heaving under washed out wool.

Now, Juan imagined a cow lithping Cathtilian. "Thith ith moooothic," he lithp-mooed.

At this, she did not laugh.

Perhapth she had never heard a lithp. And of course she never thaw the thecretary to Don Pedro de Valdivia sthrut. Wide-eyed Indians—like children—brought out the infant in a man. But hith sthmall thilly thecret wath thafe with her.

Then Juan was walking to his work, thinking Cathtilian was thimply thilly, when Pedro approached him, cloak billowing like a gathering storm.

Wondering what news could be this bad, Juan stopped in his tracks.

"I was at Valdivia's. Nuño Beltrán de Mendoza, that ... *pato* was there."

Pedro spat. "He has been hired—actually *hired*—with the promise of an enormous *encomienda*." Yanking hairs from a nostril, he added, "It could be worse. He'll join us later in the Atacama."

"We need this devil," Juan responded, feeling the measure of his distance, not just from Spain, but from his chilhood.

Departure being imminent, Valdivia took Juan, Pedro and Inés to claim the promised mounts. Pedro's was an immense black gelding with heavy fetlock feathers. "Just like me, big and long in the tooth," Pedro crowed, feeding him a *choclo* cake, naming him Huracán.

Inés gasped at hers, a white mare. "She's beautiful! She cost far too much!"

Valdivia basked in the setting sun of impulse. It had been either this Arabian or two arquebuses. "Good horse for a desert," he replied.

Juan inspected the bay being walked toward him, of no great size but excellent configuration. Looking him in the mouth, Pedro pronounced him maybe three years old, adding that the deep chest promised stamina.

"I name you Amadís," Juan said in awe, never having owned anything nameable. He was now a *caballero*.

Three days later—in the chill of Andean dawn—the confusion of departure coalesced into an expeditionary column, Valdivia resplendent at the van. Alvar Gómez de Almagro, *maestre de campo,* rode beside him. Inés rode with Juan, who twisted on his saddle to see the column strung behind—the pack animals, *llamas* and mules led by Indians, the flanking *caballeros*, Pedro among them. Bringing up the rear was the standard-bearer and Luis de Cartagena, with whom no one wished to ride.

An unnumbered *yanacona* horde carried the burden of civilization—plows, hoes and spades, scythes and mason's tools, a multitude of other iron objects they only knew as heavy. Heavier were the barrels of wine and oil, and—load for the strongest—diminutive casks of mercury for extracting silver. Pig iron marched one ingot to an Indian. An anvil was borne like a potentate upon a litter. A youth received the honor of bearing the executioner's ax, which from time to time he brandished. Others bore caged ducks and chickens, pigeons, geese and guinea pigs. The larger animals were driven—guanacos and llamas, sheep and goats, colts and fillies too young to be laden, a few pigs.

Under the attentive eyes of Inés traveled the seeds of Spain, sewn into bags and now on Indian heads, as well as the plants of civilization, potted by the Ministering Angel. Like Pedro, Juan could hardly tell one green thing from another, yet he knew from Inés that a variety of grapes and fruits, including the orange and the fig, were represented.

Her plants, Pedro's indument and steel, my books, Juan thought. We pack what we most cherish. And he touched the saddlebag that held **Amadís de Gaula**, remembering the night before departure....

He was reading, Inés potting orange trees. And Pedro, who was oiling his sword, grumbled, "No books or plants went into Noah's ark that I know of, just a lot of meat on the hoof." Pedro was smug, having scriptural precedent for what one takes into disaster.

Inés had countered, "No swords on the ark either, that I know of."

Recalling yesterday, Juan worried about today's Inés—withdrawn, crooning into her horse's ear to calm her.

"High spirited," he commented. "Have you named her yet?"

Unsmiling, she replied, "*Blanca Rosa del Desierto*."

"White Rose of the Desert." As if you named yourself, Juan thought.

She asked, "Did you know Valdivia told Pizarro I was going as his servant?"

Studying the passing scene, Juan shrugged. He had penned those very words.

"Why didn't you tell me? I thought you were my friend."

Juan miserably shrugged, again ... by which he meant he loved her far too much to wound her.

She insisted. "Don't you know how much this *hurts* me, Juan...?"

What could he do but nod his yes. He knew.

And he looked south to hide what was surely in his eyes.

Chapter 8: *Ngillatun (Mapu)*

In the last of *filla kuyen*—the hunger moon—Andalikan strode soundless through a forest soft with fog and pale with dawn. *Kula* arched over him, the thick bamboo a tunnel through milky light in which the crowded leaves were like suspended knives. Around him the immense trunks of *peweñ* rose into dimness, so tall he could not see their needles worn as topknots.

It was a good morning for a kill and Andalikan was weary of the food of the moons before harvest—parched *uwa* boiled with wood ash, fermented *poñu*, shriveled roots, dried fish. He had red blood hunger.

Coming to a fallen *koiwe*, he climbed the enormous mossy trunk. Arrow nocked, he listened as light grew.

Soundless, a form flitted by ... a *domo* in a dark *kepam*.

The time was wrong, for what women gathered could wait until *pangi* was in his lair. Her solitude and silence were also out of place. Intrigued, Andalikan ran after, sprinting through bamboo, pounding around a bend.... She was motionless, face shadowed by her *ekull*. A hand fumbled in her mouth.

What *was* she doing!

Andalikan needed to apologize, but had to know her name to greet her.

The *domo* looked up.... Kurufil!

The black lips of the *kalku* opened in a toothless yawn, laughing without sound. A black snake flicking a forked red tongue slipped from his mouth, sliding in and out, obscenely growing ... flying to strike him in the chest.

This was a mortal sting, Andalikan knew, for such a *wekufu* no *che* survived. With horror he saw the snake fall to the ground and crawl back to Kurufil, who snatched it up. Laughing silently, the *kalku* vanished into bamboo.

If a *kalku* killed with sorcery he was tortured and burned alive, the ashes scattered, condemning his evil soul to wander. The punctures on the chest of Andalikan were the proof that would unleash just such revenge, and he began to run ... but his legs—which were as the sinewed trunks of trees—soon tired. Cold caused his entrails to heave like icy snakes. And when Andalikan began to stumble he knew that he would die too far from ears that had to hear him. He was weak, so weak the heaving of the forest made him fall. But it was the *pillañ* who had brought him to his knees, he thought, for blurred before him he saw the path that led to the cave of Ñamku. Revenge gave him the strength to crawl.

Time slowed, but he was slower. Slow knees. Slow hands. Slow tongue repeating the horror it must remember. Numb, he reached for spinning branches, roots that vanished from his hands. Then he was a blind worm crawling....

Brushing her hair outside *lolo*, Lleflai admired the play of sunrise over fog below. Hearing a faint moan she dropped her brush and went to check.... She screamed.

They dragged Andalikan into the cave. He was delirious, cold as Katrinir just before his death. But the pulse was steady.

Indicating the punctures on the chest, Ñamku told Lleflai to suck there and spit, wash her mouth out with water, and keep on doing it. But she *must not* swallow! He needed to make medicine.

Lleflai had never even *touched* a man. Sucking on the breast of one she did not know was just not possible. And he had been pierced by a *wekufu*! What if she swallowed the snake or thorn, the lizard, worm ... thing of evil! Eyes enormous in her ravaged face she shook her head, refusing. Ñamku had to understand she could not die—not now—not when at last she had begun to live!

"You must, to save him."

Shuddering, Lleflai sucked. Her unbound hair cascaded over the *weichafe* as she sucked and spat and rinsed—over and over—into a bowl. He rolled his head from side to side and gasped for breath. She thought she heard, ""*Kewen* bit me."

He persisted. "The black tongue with the red tongue."

Her saliva was cloudy and astringent at first. When it turned pink and tasted of blood, Lleflai rested, weeping. The handsome young *weichafe* was dying. And she might die too.

Ñamku hurried in, pounding something in a bowl, telling Lleflai to bring hot water.

"Black snake ... black tongue," Andalikan said, briefly waking, belly hollow as a rotten log.

"I know," the *machi* said. "Drink this."

Andalikan did, and slumped.

The *machi* could not rest that night, remembering that Katrinir disapproved of his study of poisons, feeling about them as he did about war—that the Mapuche would be better off with neither.

Ñamku had argued, "A warrior knows war to defend himself and his family. A *machi* knows poisons to defend against *kalku*."

"But do we *have* to be this way?"

"*Mapu* was begotten by the war of the beginning. Kaikaifilu is still with us, and we must fight him."

"Kaikaifilu lives *in* Mapuche, not out there somewhere. Do we need to *welcome* him?"

"Without war the Mapuche would be something else."

"Perhaps 'something else' is what Mapuche need to be."

That first day of argument ended in separate convictions never aired again, a conflict buried, not forgotten. And from that moment, in fond complaint, Katrinir called Ñamku *Mapuche*, and he in turn called him *Kangen*—something else—each knowing that, where love abides, differences can bind.

Next morning, groggy, Andalikan ate *degu* for the first time, finding the rodent surprisingly good. Beside him Ñamku sat unmasked—white, ancient, gaunt, his eyes like *antu* seen through clouds of a cold moon. Lleflai was telling the *pichiche* they should throw their bones into the fire pit.

She was attractive despite her face, thought the warrior—strong arms softly rounded, hair long and fragrant. And she was gentle as her *degu*.

Andalikan stood to say what he must. "I was bitten by the tongue of evil and I live. For this I thank the *pillañ* who brought me to the cave. For this I thank Lleflai, who cared for me. Above all I thank you, Ñamku, for returning to me my *am*. Ask what I can give you in return."

When the *machi* merely nodded, Lleflai stood to say what she had been thinking about all night.

"Andalikan, son of Likankura, for myself I ask nothing, yet I fear for the *pichiche*. They are Mapuche but have no *weichafe* as father. They are Mapuche but for a mother they have a *domo* with no living kin. I fear what will become of them in our solitude."

She was weeping now, tears running crooked scars, unheeded.

"My love for them wanted them for myself only, and this is not right. For Ñamku and for me to live apart is *kume mognen*. For the *pichiche* it is not. They are as seeds fallen on stone.

There is much Ñamku and I can teach them, but there is much we cannot. The *wentru pichiche* will not learn the ways of *weichafe*. Raytrayen will not learn to weave with beauty as her mother did. The wisdom of Ñamku saved their lives and gave them a mother who loves them more than words can say. Yet his wisdom and his love, *my* love, are not enough. Andalikan, son of Likankura, I can tell you this as something that I know more than anyone would wish—deprived of their people, the souls of these *pichiche* will shrivel as they grow, and one day blow away, leaving their bodies empty."

Ñamku grunted with unspoken admiration of the sacrifice she was about to make.

"Look upon them, son of Likankura, and ask yourself ... are these *añken peñeñ*?"

She gestured, that the sight speak for itself.

"I request of you one thing—and one thing only—that you be as uncle to them."

Andalikan had expected to be asked for a *luan* … blankets. Nothing like *this*— little less than adoption. An uncle was in many ways a father to the children of his brother, the day-to-day duties were not his, yet he shared the great responsibilities. A brother also customarily took the wife of his brother in marriage when he died, and his children as his own. But … the children before him were *añkeñ peñeñ* renounced by Kuriñam, *pichiche* that should have been killed at birth! He hesitated.

Shaking with grief, certain that the silence of the warrior meant rejection, Lleflai said, "I have spoken."

Overwhelmed by pride for her, Ñamku stood to say, "What she requested, so do I."

Andalikan did not then vacillate. "So it is, and so it shall be—these *pichiche* are of my *kuga*, always welcome in my *ruka*." He boomed, "Come to me *malle fotem, malle ñawe*."

And as the frightened *pichiche* went to hide behind Lleflai, Ñamku smiled with deep approval, then went to seek the counsel of a wakeful night.

Like wind-borne threads, memories unraveled in his mind, so that he was unable to create whole cloth from stray events—the death of Katrinir and Rayentru, the birth of the *ifunche* and three *pichiche*, the bone *che* … and now, Andalikan.

Unmasked in darkness, Ñamku took the pouch that held the dried eyes and tongue of his teacher and Katrinir.

The dead you knew in life visited as ghostly bodies. If you had not known them, they came as voices or animals—sometimes as a bat or owl at night, or in the day, perhaps, as a fat, green fly. The dead forgot the living as the living did the dead, but their forgetting was far worse. And their bodies faded with their memories, leaving voices in the shadows dying into darkness. So it was with Kalfuñam—the *machi* who taught Ñamku. Absent-minded in life, he was so much more so in death as usually to be absent altogether. Part of this was anger that an uninterrupted line of healers had ended with his apprentice. He resented Katrinir also, for refusing to be *mach*Ñamku sipped the potion that took him to those shores of a death from which it was increasingly difficult to return. The *kuyen* would come, he knew, when he would sink into the sea of vision to remain, breathing with the dead.

He waited for dried eyes to swell with vision, dried tongues to swell with speech. He waited until he spun—dry leaf through sparks, igniting—waited until he landed on the cold water of a whirlpool, where he was quenched. There the eyes of fish spun with him, turning … turning into the turning eyes of the *pillañ*.…

The voice he heard was peppery. "You have my eyes, so use them. You have my tongue, so speak." Departing, Kalfuñam whined, "Why not summon he who shares the pouch that should be mine alone?"

Ñamku's mind was clear, although his eyes were blind. Like *kudellkiñ*, above him swirled the eyes of the *pillañ*. Never had he gone this deep to find his love.

He tried swimming … but had no arms, drifting deeper, deeper, until a nose nudged him, moving his helpless body upward. He broke surface, frantic, searching for Katrinir….

"Mapuche."

"Kangen!"

Katrinir did not waste time with greetings. "You must remain yourself, Ñamku. If you seek revenge I will not know where to find you, and you will live alone with evil."

Having no bodies, the dead touched the inner warmth of men directly, their breath passing through living ribs. Ñamku felt it as a small momentary chill, and he recalled that in life the nose of Katrinir had been icy as if he were dead already … especially in bed. He smiled.

But Katrinir had no interest in old times. And he had counsel….

Earthworms were the silent tongues of *mapu*, he said. Torn from the earth, they spoke for the earth by saying nothing. Eat dirt, he suggested with a fading voice. It will improve your silence and your humility….

Ñamku grew to like being an earthworm, eventually knowing his very little very well. But when finally he breathed air again he had lost his memory of vision. There was something important he had to see, to say … and he could not.

Lleflai took a stick from the fire pit, rushing in to where she had never been before. Legs crossed, eyes closed, Ñamku was strangling.

She took a quick step in darkness, whirling her brand, seeing that his tongue filled his mouth. The noise waking her must have been caused by his attempt to speak. He was breathing well however, probably just doing *machi* things…. Backing away from what she should not see, she thanked the *pillañ* for giving her a difference that did not make her *machi*.

Late next morning Andalikan was enjoying *uwa* and *puyen* stew, well spiced, praising Lleflai, when Ñamku emerged unmasked, haggard. Greeting then briefly, he said. "Son of Likankura, the *pillañ* have told me that this will be your revenge."

Magically he plucked the bone *che* from the air and held it high, floating in firelight—uncanny emanation of the dark. Slowly, the *wethakelu* spun.

Andalikan examined the tiny *che* that looked nothing like Kurufil, and asked, "Will the *kalku* be fastened to a tree, then cut to pieces, burnt, the ashes scattered?"

"His death will be very terrible."

The *machi* was not *exactly* being honest, having no clear idea of what the fate of Kurufil would be. But to spare the *ifunche* he had to postpone his master's death.

He changed the subject. "Tell no one what happened here. Tomorrow we will all go down the mountain"

"As you have no *ruka* there, I would be pleased if you stayed in one of mine."

Laden, they left under a brilliant sun. Slowed by the *pichiche*, they spent the night on a mountain flank. The sun was low next day, when Andalikan at last introduced his wives—Wispu and Liftuipani—saying that the *ruka* of his first wife would be available until another could be built.

The new dwelling was soon erected in a clearing half circled by a limpid stream. Snow-topped, Lonkimai loomed in hazy distance. There was an excellent garden spot—the soil deep and black, nourished by the floods of spring. Lleflai loved the spot. And she soon acquired a friend.

Wispu—first wife of Andalikan—was loved yet childless and lonely, having only given birth to a dead *pichiche*. When no other was conceived—after drinking numberless foul concoctions—she turned to cooking, as if filling her husband's belly could make him forget that hers remained empty. Andalikan was as well fed as a Mapuche could be, yet the day that he said he was taking a second wife, she perfectly understood, for *wentru* needed to father warriors.

Liftuipani had the teeth—and pointed nose—of mice. And she was fertile as a rodent, whelping yet another child every year without fail. Jealous of Wispu, her cooking and her beauty, she mocked her barrenness, so that Andalikan was forced to build another *ruka* to separate them. Better the dangers of excess, than a battle under his roof.

One *antu* Wispu came to see Lleflai, saying that, as she did not have a loom, maybe it was time to make one. After that she was a daily visitor, bringing the seed of *uwa, poñu, penka*. She brought wool, a spindle … helped spin yarn. She showed her where to find the root of *nalka* to make black dye.

Taking Lleflai as an adoptive sister was not easy, for Umeñdomo was shier than her birds. But as patience drew her out Wispu learned her heart was gentle as her face was scarred. By the time the first blanket was finished they were fast friends, and the *pichiche* were calling Wispu *chuchu*.

Lautaro prized the company of his adoptive uncle, Andalikan, delighting in their war games, especially dodge-the-rock. And—although the *weichafe* was expert at barely missing—there were days when the *pichiche* returned proud with the blood of battle. They fashioned a small bow, blunt arrows.

Laku—or grandfather, as they nicknamed the second born for his seriousness—participated in the war games, but he far preferred the company of Ñamku.

Raytrayen spent her time gardening, gathering, cooking and weaving with the *domo*. *Chuchu* and Lleflai showed her how to pass the shuttle through the warp, how to pack the wool. They made her a miniature loom on which she wove a tiny blanket.

Ñamku returned to healing and soon was busier than he desired—presiding at *machitun*, dispensing love potions, herbal medicines and endless advice. In exchange he obtained two *luan*, *rali*, raw wool and yarn, chickens, seed, a family of ducks.

In the moon of new fruit, no rain fell. Passing clouds released their water only on the mountains, so that the rivers ran but the gardens withered. *Longko* Kuriñam declared a *ngillatun* to pray for rain.

Lleflai and Wispu prepared *mudai*, chewing *uwa* and spitting into bowls until their jaws were aching. Wispu brought dried strawberries, roots and freshly gathered leaves, which they chewed and spat as well, to give it special flavor. Later they would filter the fermented mash through a basket. When the milkiness had settled they would pour it into pots.

They made flat bread from *uwa* and water only … no fat or salt, as was proper for a *ngillatun*. They fed *uwa* and *dawe* to the duck and chicken selected for sacrifice, as the *pillañ* would want them plump. And the evening before the ceremony Andalikan slaughtered a young *luan* and sprinked its blood on the parched ground to attract the rain.

As *luan* were too few to be eaten often, nothing was wasted. Some meat was cut in chunks and wrapped in leaves. Some was sliced fine, pounded with salt. Bones were broken for their marrow and tossed into a soup pot, slivers saved for needles. The hide was scraped, then rubbed with brains and set aside to cure. The little that was left went to the dogs.

The morning of the *ngillatun* dawned clear. Those living near rose early. Those who came distances began to walk the day before. *Wentru* played *pifilka* as they walked, the rivulets of sound running to pool in the clearing where the *ngillatun* was to take place.

Wentru played *trutruka* also, made from *rengi*, a bamboo. Although a few were coiled and carried by one man, most were great instruments three *nufku* long, thick as a wrist, tightly covered with dried tripe. These it took two men to play—the bearer in the front, blower in the rear. A good player could produce a wonderful low sound.

Ñamku, Lleflai and the *pichiche* walked with Andalikan and his *pu kiñeche*—the extended kin—leading two *luan* loaded with food and jars of *mudai* sealed with beeswax. Leaning into tumplines, all were joking, laughing, teasing. The *ngillatun* was a serious thing—for if the crops failed every *che* would suffer and the old and sick might die. But at the gathering there would be relatives, old friends and acquaintances, daughters married into distant *ruka*. For everyone—after the two *antu* of ceremony—there would be feasting. And for the young men and women, there was the prospect of many others of their age. The moon would be full. They would dance into the night. And they would couple, bringing fertility to a yearning earth.

Ñamku walked separately, rapt at the warble of the *pifilka*. *Che* would listen and respond. Others played melodies by themselves—self-absorbed as birds proclaiming territory. And there were those who remembered older music. From time to time a *trutruka* blared, heedless of the swarm of lesser sounds.

He stepped into the blinding light of the clearing.

Ayelewei ran up to embrace the *pichiche*. Kuriñam had told her not to fuss over the children, but she had decided to disobey, briefly. If she bent his patience to the snapping point everyone would be sorry.

Men prepared sun shelters from saplings, thatched with leaves and grass. Boys took charge of the sacrificial animals. *Domo* cooked. As the most important of the *longko*, Kuriñam directed the preparations, avoiding Ñamku, Lleflai, the three *pichiche*. He also ignored Andalikan and his kin ... his greeting curt, almost to the point of insolence.

A respected warrior, Andalikan had never been snubbed before. But stony-faced, he kept his peace. And there were those who whispered loudly that the ignoring of *admapu* brought disharmony—*añkeñ peñeñ* should be smothered at birth. Andalikan ignored them as well.

The clearing was a hundred *nufku* wide. At the center, the trunk of a *maki* stripped of bark was set into the ground. Four shorter, sharpened stakes were set symmetrically around it. This done, a circle five *nufku* wide was traced in the dust, post at the center, outlining the *parufe*—the sacred precinct of the ceremony. There the women arranged the food they brought, but only on one side—stacks of flat bread on wooden plates, jugs of *mudai* and wooden cups half filled the circle. Outside the empty half, a stack of firewood was piled.

Kuriñam gave the signal to begin, and all gathered in silence about the *parufe*. Inside the sacred circle were the *longko* and the men helping with the sacrifice. Two lit the fire as four brought up a white, female *luan*, and pressed her to the ground. Kuriñam—flint in hand—looked to the sun in silent prayer, then dropped to one knee by the animal, cutting, wrenching, taking out the beating heart so quickly that the shuddering animal only produced a smothered bleat. Kuriñam held up the heart, still spurting blood.

The crowd cried, "Ya-ah!"

Kuriñam impaled the heart on one of the four sharpened stakes.

"Ya-ah!"

The crowd dipped fingers in the blood, sprinkling the *maki* trunk.

Chickens and ducks—all white and female—were brought up to be beheaded in turn, blood splashing the trunk until it ran red.

Facing the sun, Kuriñam prayed to Chau, asking him to send rain and make their harvests bountiful. From memory, he invoked Tranmaleufu and Konweniri, great *longko* of ancient times, as well as many others. Although the prayers were long and repetitive, all listened in a silence interrupted only by the flies and sacrificial animals.

Done with praying, Kuriñam tossed the *luan* on the bonfire—now leaping with high smokeless flame. Other *longko* did the same with the pile of chickens and ducks. so that the blaze spewed greasy smoke, filling the clearing with the reek of burning hair and feathers. Kuriñam began a slow beat on a *kultrung*, which *machi* echoed. To the side, *trutruka*—propped on forked sticks—blared. *Domo* formed two circles about the *parufe* and danced in opposite directions, rising and falling with a hopping step. The *wentru* surrounding them played *pifilka*. When this had gone on for some time Kuriñam stopped drumming and cried out, "Ya-ah!"

"Ya-ah!

The *wentru* joined the women, making four circles in which the men and women alternated, clasping hands—never a married man with his wife. This dance continued until the sacrifices were consumed by fire, when Kuriñam gave the sign for rest. All went to the shelters to drink *mudai* and quietly chat until it was time to sacrifice the second *luan*.

Each *antu* of the *ngillatun* four *luan*—and many chickens and ducks—were sacrificed. The cycle—sacrifice, prayer, dance, and rest—repeated itself four times. By the fourth round the sun hung low and red, and the old, were in the shelters with the *pichiche*, cooking.

The long walk to the *ngillatun*, the dancing, heat, *mudai*, made the young light-headed. Some flirted with their dancing partners—and there was nothing wrong with this, if the solemnity of the ritual was maintained. Yet Tuiñam—son of Kuriñam—was fuming. Pichikan—nephew of Andalikan—had been making eyes at his younger sister, Kurui.

Tuiñam ignored the fact that he had himself been making eyes at the plump Pushmei—as was normal for a young man at a *ngillatun*. But it was not right for the kin of one who adopted *añkeñ peñeñ*—kin of a weakling who had been shunned by his own father and ignored the insult—to eye his sister... especially because she was eyeing him right back. Tuiñam suspected that she would join him in the woods that night, to do exactly what he hoped to do with plump Pushmei....

The only weapons allowed at the *ngillatun* were sacrificial knives, or he would have skewered the seducer with his spear. Instead he strode over and told his sister through clenched teeth that she had no shame. If *che* like Pichikan were not good enough for her father, they were not good enough for her. And if she did not immediately return to the sun shelter, he would drag her there by her hair.

Kurui, who loved her older brother deeply and had never known him to act like this, was frozen in mid giggle.

Pichikan remained calm, a smile slowly fading from his face as a crowd gathered. This insult might lead to a death, and that to a blood feud. Worse, violence at a *ngillatun* would enrage the *pillañ*, dishonor everyone present, and threaten the purpose of the ceremony, which was restoring *kume mognen*.

Weichafe entrusted with preserving the peace of the *ngillatun* came running. Usually they only had to contend with *ngollife*—drunks. From time to time there was a scuffle. Such events were rare however, and those responsible were made to leave, disgraced. But how deal with sober warriors at the edge of combat? Interference risked widening the war.

Kuriñam strode up, and lifting high bare arms smeared with the unwashed blood of sacrifice he said, "No son of mine will disgrace the *ngillatun*."

To Pichikan he said, "The apology must be mine. It was my lack of … judgment, that provoked my son to his exaggeration. To make amends I invite you and your *pu kiñeche* to share food and *mudai* with me tonight after the last sacrifice."

And to all he said, "Violence cannot be permitted at the *ngillatun*, yet there has been an insult which also cannot be ignored. I suggest that when the ceremony is over we hold a contest that does not draw blood."

"As you say, Kuriñam." Pichikan was relaxed, but grim.

"*Mai, chau!*" Tuiñam stalked away.

The crowd dispersed into shade to discuss the incident in low voices over *mudai*, drought forgotten.

The ceremony began again. At sunset, during the fourth dance, Kuriñam ceased tapping his *kultrung* and raised his drumstick high, crying, "Ya-ah!"

"Ya-ah!"

Stunned by the sun and the beat of drums, smeared with blood, stumbling from endless dancing, the *che* consumed flat bread and *mudai* in the *parufe*, then left to feast in their own shelters. Families wandered under the rise of the full moon, talking quietly. The *ngillatun* was not yet over and the young were waiting for the dancing to begin again.

Andalikan and his *pu kiñeche* visited Kuriñam, polite…. The day had been hot but the *ngillatun* excellent. The flat bread was abundant. The *mudai* could not be better….

Pleased, the *pillañ* stirred a breeze from *fucha lafken*. The full moon floated higher. *Kultrung* and *pifilka* played. The young sought out the young to dance—some in circles, some in lines, many in pairs. Husbands danced with wives. Men danced with men. Women danced with women. The old danced with memories. Ñamku—who only danced with the dead—watched as Tuiñam paired with Pushmei, Kuriñam with Ayelewei. Pichikan danced with the beautiful Waltuipan. Wispu danced with Lleflai, laughing. And the *pillañ* danced with the living, laughing also. Ñamku could not see them, but knew that they were there.

Then one by one, in twos, in groups, the dancers returned to their shelters—or paired to walk away—the balance of pleasures shifting. Ancient custom allowed young *domo* to lead *wentru* by a rope tied to their *penun* when the moon was full ... but not tonight, as the occasion was too solemn.

Ñamku went to lie by the *pichiche*. Wakeful to the danger that was Kurufil, he and the silent moon watched over the sleep of innocence.

In the morning an inconstant wind brought deepening cloud. The round of sacrifice and prayer, of dance and rest, resumed beneath a sky become slate black. And when Kuriñam cut out the heart of the fourth *luan*, the wind went wild.

Raindrops splashed on the beating heart as *che* danced with *meulen*—the whirlwind.

"Ya-ah!"

The sky drowned the blood of sacrifice, washing the impaled hearts, and the sound of prayers was lost in hammering rain. Dancing resumed in a downpour swept by wind. The drums—dropping in pitch, as they grew sodden—stopped. But the dance continued with the joy of rain in a dry moon.

The flat bread was disintegrating, *mudai* diluted in its cups. Fortunately, the meat had already been roasted, so that *che* feasted in shelters that did not protect against the torrent. Spread-eagled, children made mud birds. Seeing them, Pichikan lay down to make one himself. And he was laughing with the *pichiche* when Waltuipan came up to run her hands down his body, fingers tapping with the rain down to under his *chiripa*. Then she was crooning to her handful as it grew. After that— since they could not stand—they tried to crawl away entangled. Failing, they tried rolling, laughing in the rain ... never making it to the forest. But it was now very, very dark.

Ayelewei left her shelter when the *pichiche* were asleep, knowing that her husband would confuse his climax with a skillful kill, and whoop. In their *ruka* she did not mind, but here it might be noticed. So—at a safe distance—she gasped and he ululated on a wet blanket spread on moss. Then they talked, entwined in positions loving habit had perfected....

She was proud of him. It had taken courage and wisdom—she said—to take the blame for his son.

But it was *he* who had made the huge mistake, he countered. Andalikan was once a friend. And Pichikan was a perfect match for Kurui. Not for the first time in his life, Kuriñam cursed his temper and hard head. Ayelewei chuckled, saying that Kurui did not have marriage on her mind last night.

Next morning—heavy, steady—rain fell from clouds the *che* could almost touch. The contest between Tuiñam and Pichikan was postponed.

Returning to her *ruka*, Lleflai found that the stream cupping the clearing had spilled its banks, flooding the garden. She imagined green leaves dancing beneath the water with the glad end of thirst, then, wondered if the garden still *existed*.

She slept, waking to *antu* shining on drowned earth, and saw that the *ruka* sat on an island in a stream grown to a river. Where the garden had once been an eddy swirled. Near tears, she waded in, groping for *uwa* underwater. Finding them, she pucked like a rooster to his hen on finding a fat worm—a signal for the children to come for something good. The *pichiche* joined her, and they all danced the dance of gardens saved from drought and flood—arms the grateful leaves, heads the nodding tassels.

And when the stream once more ran its banks, Lleflai brought order to her garden, tucking roots into mud blankets, staking toppled stalks, sowing new seed in new soil, washing silt off leaves. Finding her at it, Wispu laughed helplessly—almost toppling into muck—saying that at last she knew what made Lleflai the best of mothers.

In the *ruka* they sipped hot tea, Wispu saying she had news…. Tuiñam had challenged Pichikan, and it was decided to have the contest a *kawiñ* at the *ruka* of Kuriñam—a sign of friendship between the *kuga*—and Wispu thought it a wonderful idea. Now that the drought was over they might as well eat. Besides, it was a terrible thing for *weichafe* who were friends to risk a *malon*. The feast would turn the contest into just another game men played in their unending dreams of war. They would get drunk, becoming closer friends. And for once the women could enjoy themselves as well.

And Wispu said as she left smiling, that tomorrow she would come help wash the garden….

Andalikan, his wives, children and kin—including his brother, Kanicura, and nephew Pichikan—left at dawn with Lleflai and the three *pichiche*. Ñamku came as well. They arrived in the second sun of walking, lighter than they left. Not a little *mudai* had been consumed by the *wentru*—emptied jugs dropped to be picked up on the return.

Awaiting them, Kuriñam had attempted to lift his spirits with *mudai* in anticipation of the competition. However, the more *mudai* he downed the more he was convinced that the son he deeply loved—strong and skillful as he was—would lose, this truth more evident with every cup. Kuriñam was belligerent and thirsty, old and thirsty, sad and thirsty, confused and thirsty. And more *mudai* made him feel older, more confused, more belligerent, more thirsty.

Ayelewei came to where he sat belching by the fire pit, asking permission to warm her old bones and speak her mind.

Kuriñam nodded assent.

She told him that his son was going to lose, and the *mudai* his father had been drinking would change nothing. She was no *weichafe*, but neither was she a *wed wed*.

Now Kuriñam was *annoyed* and thirsty. He *knew* Tuiñam was going to lose, he said. So why not drink, if drinking changed nothing, anyway? He muttered that it was easier to lose oneself than have a son defeated. And this was not a fair contest anyway. Pichikan was a mountain, not a man! Besides the choice of contest would be his as the one insulted, and he would pick something like who could hold an immense log overhead the longest—a test requiring strength, not skill.

Ayelewei replied that Tuiñam was a son *any* father could be proud of. He would do his best no matter what the contest. And losing, he would probably do better than anyone but Pichikan.

She concluded softly, "Tuiñam is not the only impulsive *wentru* that I love. Maybe he was wrong in what he did, but he did it for what he thought our honor. Now you know and I know—and he knows with everybody else—that he is going to lose. But you could not tell it to look at him. How could you be more proud?"

Lightly touching the arm of Kuriñam, Ayelewei added that he did well at the *ngillatun*—the *pillañ* demonstrating this with rain. All *che* looked up to him, she most of all. Why not stop muttering into *mudai* about what could not be helped? Why not take pleasure in the coming day?

Kuriñam knew that Ayelewei had wanted the *kawiñ* to go well, in part, out of her affection for the three *añkeñ peñeñ*. He did not hold this against her. She was young when he stole her from her *ruka*—he ululating, she laughing with joy as he bore her away, and as the *kuyen* passed he had come to trust her judgment as deeply as he counted on her love. There were those who thought her empty-headed, and yet it was from her that Kuriñam had learned that grimness should not be confused with wisdom. And now—with shame—he saw his always-smiling wife not smiling, more worried about him than about having her firstborn lose his contest.

He had to tease at least a grin from her, he thought, placing a hand on her knee....

Ayelewei had not expected *this*. Shaking her head to say—Not here, not now, not with all the kin out there to hear you whoop!—but everything she did and said was contradicted by her grin. His other wives were younger, yet she knew herself his favorite.

With a war cry Kuriñam leapt. But—for all her plumpness—Ayelewei was agile. She eluded him for a turn around the *ruka*, hissing for silence, smothering her squeals.... And so it was that war whoops told the weary kin of Andalikan they reached their destination.

All feasted that night around a bonfire going to ember. After, the *wentru* spoke in the formal language of oratory taught to *wentru pichiche* from childhood. All dwelled on the importance of friendship between those not of the same *kuga*. No one mentioned the insult. The will of the assembly was made clear by indirection, settling the matter without voicing it.

Pichikan listened, distant and polite, Tuiñam brooded, equally polite. No *weichafe* mentioned the challenge until eventually Kuriñam formally asked Pichikan, son of Kanikura, to select the contest....

Sleepy as the assembled were—and befuddled by *mudai*—they paid attention, for bets had been placed. The odds were heavily in favor of Pichikan, all assuming he would choose a challenge that demanded strength, endurance. There were a few *weichafe* taller than Pichikan, but none approached his size or power. The betting was complicated by the fact that from his youth he was fond of dangerous challenges. When little more than a boy he invented a game called 'pinecones.' He and his friends hung upside-down by their knees from the branches of a tree to see who would be the first to 'get ripe,' and fall. He had swum the Fio Fio with rocks tied to his feet. He had raced naked in Winter, jumped from cliffs into the great sea, survived bareheaded butting contests, and invented combat with a variety of weapons—including a long-handled wooden spoon he liked so much that he became adept, calling it a *kurawutrutref*, and claiming it was better than a sling. Then there were his improvements on the usual eating and drinking challenges— for example, *puyen* eaten live. The list of his mad challenges being endless, the gamblers had an endless topic for discussion. But all this talk in no way changed the odds....

Pichikan rose to speak. "Three spears will be tossed from thirty paces. The target will be the size of a hand."

The assembly dispersed gabbling like spring frogs, for the choice was insane. Every *weichafe* was comfortable with a variety of weapons, but while still young they chose one in which to specialize. Pichikan was adept with the war club, Tuiñam with the spear. And the size and distance of the target were also insane.

Next morning a target was chipped from the bark of the tallest *peweñ* at the clearing edge.

Millanam—son of Mariñamku and cousin of Tuiñam—was sent to stand behind the tree to create a record of the contest by removing the spears from the trunk and placing a small stone where they had struck.

Pichikan paced the distance, dug a line in the ground with his heel, stood to the side.

Hefting his spear, Tuiñam tested the breeze. Taking five long strides from the line, he turned to face the target. Drawing a deep breath, weapon extended behind him, he ran and cast with a war cry.

The throw seemed perfect, but there were gasps of horror. Millanam had chosen to prove his courage—and faith in the skill of his cousin—by emerging to stand beside the tree. The spear flew endless instants, thudding into the trunk less than the span of a hand from his ribs. He tugged out the weapon, broad smile on his face.

For a *weichafe* to endanger his life in peace was necessary sometimes, at others not—and to do so at any time was his right—but Millanam had complicated the challenge. The *longko* conferred, deciding that both contestants must throw as if he were not there. More important, if Pichikan should wound or kill Millanam, it would not be held against him or his kin, for this was a risk freely taken.

To this Mariñamku agreed. Severe, he told his son of the decision, adding that one who chose this path should walk it so that it was not to the advantage of either side.

Pichikan tested the freshening breeze. From the line he measured his paces back. Waiting for quieter air, he ran and cast.

Millanam appeared again, the spear buried perilously near. He placed the stone.

The next cast of Tuiñam was *in* the target! Whoops and war cries echoed back from a silent forest, for now not a leaf moved or creature cried, and Pichikan threw into stillness.

His spear was also in the target. Uproar!

Meulen—the whirlwind—spun in the clearing, and clouds piled over the great sea. Like a live coal tossed into a cooking pot, the dying sun seethed, turbulence boiling into air that glimmered with lightning over *fucha lafken*. The *pillañ* raced toward *mapu*, bringing war and turmoil.

Tuiñam cast…. And the flash, the slam of wind, the crash, were one. Intolerable light froze the sight of Millanam speared and flung back … dark mouth open in a cry. The tree by him smoked and sputtered as he pushed himself to his knees, long spear protruding from his chest….

Mirañamku ran up to set a foot on his son's shoulder, pulled, blood bubbling when the shaft was free. Millanam struggled to get up, and collapsed. He whispered, "*Kiñe*," shuddered and stopped breathing … breathed again.

The father said *yamai*—thinking that another whisper might kill his son. And gathering him into his arms he took him to stand behind the *pewen* for one last cast.

Rain was not yet falling—yet the winds warred—as the *che* returned to their places silently. Ignoring the whip of his hair, Pichikan waited for the calm that would not come, and threw....

The spear went wide with wind or purpose, missing Mirañamku, who had emerged holding his dead son.

The rain was sudden, savage. The spiraling wound on the *peweñ*—smoldering in the downpour—had cut through the target, so that the stones from every cast were gone. The tree was hissing.

The corpse was washed by *domo*, lashed to a ladder and propped up. Food and drink for the *am* were placed on the floor beside it, women wailing as they worked. *Atrutrui!* The mother smeared herself with water and ash. Kneeling at the feet of her son she ripped at her face with fingernails, turning it into a gray-white mask streaked with blood and tears in which the mouth gaped black. Rivulets of blood ran through the ash. She tossed her head, and bright drops flew.

Mariñamku embraced Tuiñam, saying that this death was the will of the *pillañ*. Then he rose, silencing the *domo*, saying the same to all his kin.

The women wailed. And the father joined the *wentru* circling the *ruka* with their war cries, banging spears, preventing *kalku* from stealing the soul of the newly dead.

And it was then that a *che* ran up, wearing only a *chiripa* and headband. The foot of a *pudu* hung from his neck. A *werken*!

It was an honor to be a messenger, these *weichafe* chosen for swiftness and stamina. Also trained in memory, they learned lengthy messages and repeated them word for word, even after a run of *antu*.

The *che* were devoured by curiosity. *Werken* always brought distant news, often of war. Yet this messenger did not carry the blood-smeared arrow.

Kuriñam emerged to welcome him.

"I have a message from Michimalongko. Greetings to Kuriñam, son of Pailakura." The *werken* inquired into the health of Kuriñam and his kin, one by one, this remarkable feat of memory creating time for the *che* to ponder the one thing they knew—Michimalongko lived in one of the last river valleys before the desert. For him to send a *werken* this distance—not for war—was unimaginable. If the moment were not so formal they would have been chattering like crickets in the heat....

The message was short when at last it came, and unexpected as the recent lightning bolt. "*Tefa petu nguiueiyu*—I send you this."

Unwrapping a bundle the messenger went on. "*Werken* brought these *wethakelu* across the great desert. They belong to *che* such as none have ever seen. Most are white. One is said to be black. Some have eyes blue as *likan*. Their hair is brown and black, yellow and red—never blue like their eyes." To the astounded listeners these beings sounded more like parrots than like men.

"Some are spotted. Many are *che* from the waist up, enormous *luan* from the waist down. These have four legs, two arms and two heads—one like a *luan*, one like a man."

All this went beyond belief. There were evil beings that were both *che* and animal—*ngurufilu* for example, had the body of a serpent and the head of a fox. However, these were creatures of the night. And no *che* who saw them lived.

"Many have tails on their faces."

Some stifled laughter at these *che*, who had their ends confused.

"They speak a language no one has heard."

A drunken *weichafe* called out, "Maybe we have, if it comes from the end with the tail."

There was stifled laughter that Kuriñam suppressed with a raised hand.

"Their *wentru* shine like silver and are hard, so that no weapon hurts them. And they carry sticks that strike with lightning."

The *che* exhaled as one, at this coincidence foretold by the extraordinary death of Millanam.

Gesturing at the objects spread on the ground, the *werken* continued, "These *wethakelu* were abandoned by them—except for the one in leather, which was taken from a sleeping *lik winka*.

Kuriñam—then all the *che*—crowded to see them. A curved, flat stick with holes all along it, which was no stick. Long bent thorns, which were not thorns. And the *wethakelu* covered in leather. A *pichiche* bent to sniff it.

Kuriñam lifted the stick with holes. Heavy! A weapon?

The *werken* was not done.

"I, Michimalongko, have sent these things brought to me across the great desert. I ask Ñamku, who is white like *lik winka* and speaks with the dead, to examine them and tell us what they mean." He concluded, "The *lik winka* have killed many *che*. We are preparing to fight them. I have spoken."

Kuriñam told the *werken* that Ñamku had been here but left. No one knew where he had gone.

Che crowded around the messenger offering food, *mudai*, asking questions.

How many *winka* were there? Did they have tails only on their faces? Were they only white and black, or were they other colors…?

Only *lik winka wentru* had tails on their faces.

Did they have white hair and red eyes, like Ñamku?

And it was then—as if summoned by his name—that the *machi* walked up to say, "I, Ñamku, greet Michimalongko." And his message was astonishing as it was brief. "I will come myself, to see these *lik winka* and speak with you."

"I will bear your words to Michimalongko." Accepting dried meat and water, the *werken* loped away.

That night, as Ñamku was examining the *wethakelu,* Katrinir appeared without summon … and he was irritable.

"Answers are all you ever want of me!"

Then gently he said that he was sorry, worried, wishing he *had* answers.

"Go see for yourself then," replied Ñamku, testy himself. "Ride a cloud. Come back and tell me."

Saddened, Katrinir said he should not expect too much of the dead.

Ñamku persisted. "What about Lleflai? Will she choose to go?"

"Of course."

"We will all go. I feel it in my bones."

"What you feel in your bones old man, is old age."

Then Katrinir talked about making. You made what you were. You were what you made.

And Ñamku wondered then—what were the *lik winka* who made these *wethakelu*…?

Next morning, he chose Pichikan and Tuiñam from the *weichafe* who offered to go with them.

Eight left on the long journey *piku.* One was a very old, white *machi,* who had returned to the living. Another was a disfigured *domo* who had learned joy and talked with birds. Three *pichiche* went with them as well.

Two *weichafe* led the way, one armed with spear and knife, another with club and spoon. And with them all, traveled a dead maker.

Chapter 9: Atacama (1540)

Valdivia planned to retrace Almagro's return to Cuzco from Chile by following the *altiplano* to Lake Titicaca, veering there toward the Southern Sea through Moquegua to Arequipa—that last outpost of civilization, one hundred and forty leagues distant. There they would prepare for the final effort—through Tacna to Atacama la Chica, on to Atacama la Grande, then to the nightmare of the desert proper, where geography was swallowed by the blank of maps, and men walked nameless ground....

Over the precipitous miracle of Inca roads they marched not to the pace of the *infantes* or the impossibly laden *yanaconas*, but to the amble of the pigs—four leagues to the good day. The cold of the *altiplano* was not to be imagined, the wind a thing of evil.

Not a week out of Cuzco the horse of Alvar Gómez de Almagro missed its footing and tumbled down a cliff. They buried the *maestre de campo* in a cairn and ate the horse raw, fires being impossible in the wind. Valdivia appointed Pedro Gómez de San Benito his successor.

Fortuna smiled next evening, for Francisco de Galdanes joined the company, having ridden at a pace he claimed was doubled by the wind. Not long after, two shivering *infantes* overtook them, as well as yet another *caballero*—Juan de Almonacid. The eleven Spaniards who left Cuzco were now fourteen, but—a few leagues out from Arequipa—Francisco Martinez, merchant, was wounded in a skirmish with Indians and sent back to Peru on a litter pulled by a mule, accompanied by two *infantes*. The expedition was eleven once again.

Valdivia stopped at Tacna for Holy Week, there creating a makeshift altar from boards and barrels, although they had no priest. He proved to be clairvoyant, however, when four *caballeros* rode up, Juan Lobo among them. A priest at last, in time for this holiest of weeks! And two old friends of Valdivia came with him—Alonso de Monroy and Diego de Cáceres. The expedition was now fifteen! The joy! They heard Mass and slaughtered a suckling pig.

Yet fifteen they remained far as Tarapacá, where Valdivia—wrestling with decision—conferred with Alonso de Monroy. Lean and dour, clean-shaven the long of a blue jaw—that rarity among *conquistadores*—Monroy was born into a noble family fallen on hard times. Having lost his wife and children to the plague, and his estate to creditors, he left Spain with little more than his weapons. In Peru his courage had been legendary. Scrupulous, caring of his men, he was Valdivia's trusted confidant.... And today he had no doubts—they could not conceivably survive the Atacama with this number.

"I'll go back to Peru and recruit," offered Pedro Gómez, "if I can take Juan with me...."

Doom and disaster, mummies, gloom and disaster. Pedro had nattered on about nothing else those endless days on horseback, rehearsing the failure of Almagro's journey south with the obsession of one with an unhealed wound too itchy to ignore and too painful to scratch.

Pedro's pessimism began in Peru, where they recruited not a single *infante*. Since then they had driven themselves and their mounts to rejoin the expedition, and all Pedro could talk about were the days of living, walking death.

Juan hardly listened as Pedro repeated himself, monk muttering his beads. *Soroche*—a nausea without end, and a beginning long forgotten, that sent your head into a spin so that the mountains lurched with every step. You stumbled, sucking useless air, seeing nothing but the *poncho* of the man ahead—that fool one step closer to nowhere. You heard nothing but the wool-muffled clank of his armor and your own, ignoring both, ignoring your stink—familiar as the garlic on your breath—ignoring the corpses above all, as being what you soon would be.

Following a trail marked by the bodies of the past, the column left its own dead—like a snake shedding flesh, not skin. Spaniards and Incas, men and women, livestock, horses, even the hardy llamas died of hunger, cold, exposure, wind. At these altitudes the heart could simply stop. And there were those who lost the will to move their boots, for there was peace in ceasing. Pedro once saw an *infante* on his hands and knees, head hanging like a horse abused, as a companion kicked the steel over his ribs, crying, "Rise, and walk!" The *infante* shook his head at every kick, much like a stubborn bell. Left behind, he would freeze in that position, sustained by rusted metal and the denial of everything but denial itself.

Conquest—Pedro mused about Almagro's fatidic expedition—was a gamble in which you staked your life for gold, playing with your sword. When you lost, you lost your life. When you won, you gambled gold. You gambled your life so you could gamble gold. But with Almagro, everyone lost. He led the largest gamble of the Indies, dwarfing the rabble of Cortez—not to mention Pizarro's few. Five hundred men! And the tenth to survive returned with nothing but memories of a freezing hell going down, a desert hell returning. Now Valdivia intended to do the same with fifteen! Pedro stood in his stirrups, so his ass could freely comment on this madness.

That evening as they were sitting by a dung fire, eating *charqui* and *choclo* cakes baked hard as Inca roads, Juan urged Pedro to speak again. Better tales of doom than listening to the winds of wastelands....

The dead, Pedro said, assumed every posture conceivable. Sitting of course, backs against rocks. Some died standing, kept upright by the wind. Pedro had seen an Inca frozen in mid-bite, the *charqui* in his teeth looking like a mummied tongue stuck out at the fools who persisted on what the *infantes* called 'the high way to nowhere.'

Jokes being the only remaining pleasure, the *infantes* used the dead as comic raw material. There was no changing the position of the frozen and dried bodies, so they would set them upside down, or put two together lewdly. One *infante*—sick-drunk with altitude—made a compass from an Inca who had died spread-eagled, balancing her on a rock so that each limb indicated a cardinal direction. But as the men were mostly too exhausted to move the mummies, they found it easier to imagine the postures. Having nothing else to bet on, they had Postures of Death contests, awarding prizes for the best at the end of the day....

There was the Posture of the Former Shepherd who—absent his beloved sheep—still died smiling, gap-stopper in a llama's frozen end. Many imaginary dead died shitting. One got turned into a kind of tripod by his frozen turd. Then there was the *infante* who found ice by a corpse, put it in his helmet to make himself some water, and discovered that he had thawed a brewer's fart ... so that he had a meal. That posture would have gotten the prize, but the losers claimed that a fart was not part of a Posture if not attached to the dead.

Pedro ruminated entries, expurgating.... There was the monk who met his maker while yanking on forbidden fruit, dying as he came and leaving frozen gobbets hanging in the air like little clouds....

That night, attempting sleep, Juan decided that Pedro's stories were very like the mummies in them. They needed soaking in imagination, the way you soaked *charqui* in water, to make them palatable. And—now that he was living a true adventure—he realized that **Amadís de Gaula** left more out than even Pedro. The dreams of his youth had no real meat on their bones....

A vision of the monk tugging at forbidden fruit floated from the darkness. No face in the hood. A pale, hairy hand. Black wool. Yellow banana? Yes, that would be the fruit. No other in Spain was suitable—save perhaps the fig ... but what about the gourds in these Indies?

Juan imagined the monk tugging members of every shape, size and hue, gaudy against his black habit. On second thought, gourds were inappropriate, as connoting dugs.

Days, Pedro labored to illuminate the text that was Almagro's expedition, turning the margins intricate with commentary. *Soroche* made you dizzy, nauseous, gave you indigestion even when you had not eaten. You burped. You threw up rancid air. Noses bled for no reason. Men blacked out and kept on walking. Men blacked out, got up, and headed in the wrong direction. Men blacked out for good. Envious marchers crossed themselves at the bodies they passed, thinking it better to die getting nowhere than getting killed when you arrived. The antidote for *soroche* was garlic. Everyone chewed it, even rubbed it on the gums of horses. The joke was that—marinated—the horses tasted better when they died.

Dried by day, frozen by night, the dead marking the trail turned to *charqui*. The flesh was edible, you just had to decide on your degree of repugnance. Most of the animals had been consumed already—though the meat was like leather sewn to bones by a demented cobbler. The fresher human dead were far more edible, and when their hunger became intolerable some *infantes* feasted. Of course, Pedro had never consumed *this* abomination, but those who did became picky ... tongue and liver were said to be best.

Nauseated, Juan changed the subject.

The Incas who guided the expedition sent messengers ahead, so that when the column came to Indian hamlets—usually by rivers—everything remotely edible was burnt or hidden. Like a dragon heralded by its own deadly breath, the column walked through devastation. Pedro sighed. "A march like that can leave you bleak as the fucking ground you walk on."

How could you get lost on the way to nowhere, Juan wondered, except by *getting* somewhere?

After two months of brutal travel Pedro and Juan rejoined the expedition at Tarapacá, arriving while Valdivia had left to scout the route.

Inés was sitting by a fire. Rising, and crying out with happiness, dispensing with formalities she embraced them as dear friends, touching cheeks as she kissed the air.

Did they bring good news? she asked, Negrito leaping onto her shoulder. Gently scolding the *homunculus*, Inés leaned forward to embrace Juan a second time, head tilted to await the answer.

"We recruited no one."

Incredibly, she chuckled, the throaty note becoming unforced laughter. And she was still smiling when she sat them by her fire, saying gladness could make you a little crazy sometimes. "I know you did your best," she added, as Juan and Pedro gluttonously ate. "Maybe I want too much, when I have all I really need—my two Pedros and my Juan, my plants and animals. What more could I ask of God?"

A llama with a broken leg had been slaughtered that afternoon, a haunch apportioned to Valdivia, and Ines was sharing the bounty. With a half-smile she watched her friends consume astonishing quantities, in carnivorous heaven. It was good to have them back alive, to feed them, to relish the surprise she was about to share....

The men of Los Chunchos, led by Francisco de Villagrán—as well as many others—had arrived while they were gone recruiting. "Counting you, we now number a hundred and six *cristianos*."

"*Cuerpo de Dios!*" Belching, Pedro stood to scrutinize the campfires—as if they could reveal this arithmetic miracle occulted by the night.

"Anyone I know?" he asked, fearing traitors in the number.

"Probably the half," Inés responded with a wicked grin. "Villagrán was your gambling companion in Cuzco, as I recall. Then there are the brothers Alderete—Jerónimo and Juan Fernández—also your gambling companions." Inexorable, she went down the list of friends and fellow gamblers—these near synonyms for the *conquistador*—ending with the priest, Rodrigo González Marmolejo....

Pondering the data, Pedro concluded that with this godsend they had now more or less the equal of Almagro's force on his return from Chile, after he had lost almost his entire army. He took the bone he had just gnawed clean, and—placing it upon a stone—smashed it with his sword hilt. Sucking marrow he ruminated the fact that they had gone from a dead certain to a merely uncertain disaster. But his pessimism was lessened by the fullness of his belly, and then by a thought that caused an erection to begin to throb against his steel. There had to be hundreds of *cholas* out there—though no one really knew their numbers—women of every age and size, every one of them constructed for what he needed. Wiping grease from his beard with chain mail—that habit combining hygiene with the never-ending battle against rust—he excused himself, saying he would go pay his respects to Don Francisco de Villagrán.

After he left, Inés commented that Pedro was a mountain crossing a desert. And having made Juan smile, she came to sit beside him, taking his hand. "We are few. But the fewer, the more magnificent, is it not like that in books?"

"*Sí.*"

Inés had a heart-stopping habit of looking Juan in the eye from close, her breath fragrant with clove—this scent that had pervaded his dreams since he met her.

She smiled, saying that she had to go check her pigs. A pregnant sow was about to litter.

Appointed Ministering Angel of the Expedition by Valdivia, Inés had made the honorific sop her responsibility. She ministered to the sick—mostly *yanaconas*. She attended to the miscellaneous wounds that were part of every expedition. She provided comfort and counsel to both Spanish and Indian. Inés was physician, mother, and—since until recently there had been no priest—spiritual advisor to the entire enterprise.

She was also in charge of the herds and flocks that the colonists had brought to recreate their civilization in the heart of an unwilling wilderness. There were uncounted chickens, geese and real ducks—not Inca ones, with combs like crimson caps. There were four pigs—three sows and a boar—sheep, goats, a lamb, a ram and ewes, and of course the horses, mules and sundry burros ... but no cattle, for they were far too expensive for Valdivia to afford.

Inés was also keeper of the plants. She tended to the pips, the pits, the seeds, the scions and roots of oranges, lemons and figs, apricots and peaches, plums and melons, grapes—as great a variety of the fruits and flowers of Spain as she could buy and beg before she left, including wheat, barley and millet. A forest traveled potted on the heads of porters, and watering these plants was her greatest challenge. Thirsty *infantes* grumbled, seeing precious liquid given to a fucking stick.

One morning Inés found all her trees kicked over. She pruned and repotted, furious....

Valdivia lectured the expedition—these plants were *absolutely not* to be touched by anyone except the *yanaconas* assigned to bear them. The penalty for an Indian would be death, for a *cristiano* a stiff fine. And from that day—despite Valdivia's murmured objections—as many pots as could fit spent the night in their tent, so that they made their bed in a garden.

Inés also had to protect her animals from the larceny of the expedition, for *infantes* were not innately colonists, and they were furious at having to eat desiccated Inca roots when all about there was meat cackling in baskets and bleating on the hoof. One night two chickens disappeared, and Inés took to making a public daily count of every cage with an Inca who kept tally on his *quipú*. The March day came that—responding to a smothered cry—Inés found *infantes* slitting the neck of her fattest ewe.

She insisted to Valdivia—who made it so—that the culprits be fined heavily and get none of the meat. And from that day she made it clear that every plant, every animal, was under the mantle of her protection—which was to say Valdivia's—and that for the life of even the oldest and toughest rooster the culprit would answer to the Lieutenant Governor himself.

In revenge, the *infantes* that slaughtered the ewe composed a litany titled **Mediatrix of the Barnyard**—

Fowl Guardian.
Duck Protector.
Mother of Sheep.
Tower of chicken shit.
Hole for a Goat.

This last was a not very obscure reference to Valdivia—whose stiletto beard was a signature feature. Yet the litany progressed no further, for the listening *infantes* were outraged at this insult to the Mother of God, to Valdivia, and above all to Doña Inés, who was almost sainted by the men. It nearly came to swords.

Choosing not to assist at the sow's labor, Juan was staring into a death of embers when Pedro returned, saying that he paid his compliments to Francisco de Villagrán, then went to rub his giblets on a skinny one, for there was not a plump one left.

Done with pigs, Inés reappeared by the fire saying that the litter would not arrive tonight. The sow was sound asleep and snoring fit to pop her snout. Inés hardly slept, herself, that night, worrying about Valdivia, and even more about his wife. Not hating that woman was a struggle. She prayed every day for the Virgin to protect her ... just as she prayed that she remain in the Spain where she belonged, for in the Indies pious frailty could not survive. Let her devote her life to prayers and embroidery. Half the world was not room enough between, and Inés knew she would not truly rest until the Atacama was behind her.

She sought solace thinking of the new recruits. Most came from the failed conquest of the Chunchos—these Indians of some vague and distant region, who were intelligent and made bread good as wheaten, it was said, from a root. But they had not even the *idea* of gold, as it turned out. The second band to return was gaunt and grim, on foot, having deserted their captain, Diego de Rojas, who had led them to a land populated by ants and demons. And the last to straggle in came from looking for the legendary Mojos—whom they never found—having suffered the indescribable. Of these three hundred, fewer than eighty survived. They had eaten insects and snakes, and walked some seven hundred leagues, surviving to be too emaciated to recognize each other....

When Inés slept at last, she dreamt that she was starving.

In the morning, Juan went with Pedro to greet the newcomers. For the *maestre de campo* this was a duty, for Juan pure curiosity. And even to him—who had heard everything there was to hear about disaster from Pedro—the arrivals were a mind-wrenching surprise. These were not men but armored bones, harboring an unquenchable lust for gold.

Juan decided that some things you had to see to know. Hearing about disaster turned it distant, or maybe not so much distant, as small, like scenes in manuscripts that fit into a capital O—these martyrdoms you could not hear or touch.

Sangre de Cristo! A blasphemous vision was materializing in his mind! Attempting not to imagine a beautiful, naked martyr, Juan went to a new arrival, stuck his nose in his armpit, and inhaled deeply. Too startled to take offense the *infante* gaped. Gagging at the stench Juan walked away, happy to have deleted virgin martyrs from his mind.

He noted that the arrivals had not shaved or cut their hair—or bathed—maybe since Spain ... or maybe never. Matted hair dangled from their helmets. Their beards were tangled, greasy, sometimes braided. Stained, and pitted with jungle rust, the armor that survived was so rotten Juan wondered if could stop a blow. Long decomposed, the leather buckles of the armor had been replaced by vine, frayed rope, scraps of poncho remade as twine. Nothing Spanish that could rot remained. They wore motley Indian cloth instead—stolen from the dead, taxed from the living. But they still had the weapons needed for the wager that was the Indies, and these were immaculate. Their swords shone. Their spears could split a hair. Even the arquebuses—with all their complicated parts—gleamed inside oiled, protective rags.

The armed ghouls grew homesick around their fires that night. They spoke of wine, olives and Spanish women. They remembered boots and Spanish women. They lusted for pork rinds, oranges and Spanish women. They grew nostalgic about thyme, church bells, and Spanish women dressed in black, women that prepared your daily meat—*Pardiez!*—and never heard of *papas*.

Spain had rotted from these men, thought Juan, as flesh from some soft fruit, and their dream of Spanish women was the stone remaining. And this was true for him as well, for Inés had roots deep in his Spanish soul.

Valdivia rode in the next day, jubilant. April had come and gone, De Hoz not arriving as promised. Their contract was void. And wasting no time he dictated a letter to Francisco de Pizarro, asking that he be named sole commander of the expeditionary force.

They lingered at Tarapacá until—one bright morning, blinding as every other— they marched for Atacama la Chica, where the desert was said truly to begin.

Moving on meant arguing over future *encomiendas*—a pre-apportioning which had no end. As men arrived, the shares were readjusted. Fractions were split and shaved, renegotiated, reapportioned. The complexities were Byzantine. And Juan recorded it all, Luis de Cartagena happy to have him do the work, giving him insolent instructions as he trimmed his fingernails with tiny silver scissors. Only when Valdivia walked in did Cartagena return to business, barking peremptory commands.

One evening Juan went to visit Lobo, finding only Marmolejo at the fire both priests shared. The prelate rose to embrace him, extending a depleted *bota*. Like every *caballero* the priest wore armor, but with one difference—on his breastplate blazed the crimson cross of Calatrava. *El clérigo batallador*—the fighting cleric— was what the troops called him.

They chatted, Juan asking where he had been before joining up with the expedition....

Marmolejo did not know where, exactly, for these were places without Christian name. And where was Lobo? Juan wondered out loud. He missed him as he missed books, for the monk was much like a library crossing a desert on a mule.

As if summoned, Lobo appeared, greeting Juan, saying he had shriven yet another *yanacona* dead of pox, and two of calenture. He proposed a walk.

Being all bone from the start, Lobo could not conceivably lose weight. So, since God and weather had spared his cassock—and the enormous wooden rosary that he wore as belt—he seemed much the same as when Juan first met him. But sadly, these days the fires of his enthusiasm were damped. He could not understand how the Indies that inspired More's magisterial volume fell so short of utopian possibility. Much of Inca society before the conquest was admirable—property held in common, the absence of hunger and abject poverty, for example. Everyone who could work, did. Those who could not were provided for by the state, which stored surplus grain for times of hardship. The sum of Inca civic virtue was impressive. Still and all, their success in the temporal plane was undone by their failures in the spiritual. Their ignorance of writing was inconceivable! And they had princes! War! Not to mention human sacrifice! Lobo groaned, crossing himself. *Utopia* was not *here* he exclaimed, not now, not in the places and peoples he had seen. But it was not too late.

His voice rose, pale eyes blazed, fingers stabbed at desert stars....

It was time—he said—to abandon the failure of futures dreamed by pasts, time to realize that *Utopia* existed not in a book, or land, but in the minds of men. And the time was now, the place was near, for to the south lived Indians with no princes or property, no gold or precious stones ... just as in *Utopia*. The Atacama had protected the innocence of these children of God—the Araucanos. They were said to be warlike, but surely they would beat their spears into plowshares when given the vision of God! Above all, there was no corruption there, for their hearts and souls were as clay unformed. On the wheel of faith, in the hands of God's potters, they would be turned into the chalice of the new communion of man. *Utopia* was not insular by accident. The new Eden could be nothing less than an island in this fallen world. And that land south of the Atacama, east of the *cordillera*, west of the Southern Sea, north of nothing known to man save for the straits of Magallanes, *was* an island, thorough as any sea could make it. Chile was the Fortunate Isle.

Here's one empty-handed potter, Juan thought, as Lobo's hands stopped gesturing at stars and disappeared monastically into their sleeves.

Lobo began to pace again, head bowed, shaking his head. "Who really knows," he said at last, "what the Indies might contain. Why, in my travels from Peru, while profoundly lost in jungles, I came across a tribe of naked, tattooed savages, whose language contained sounds greatly resembling those in Hebrew. Perhaps these were descendants of the lost tribes of Israel."

"What?" Juan exclaimed, his incredulity causing Lobo to launch himself into seas of erudition, oars of rhetoric whipping a froth of scholarly asides....

There were few explanations of how Indians came to the Indies—rigorous enough to mention, that is. In order of increasing credibility, Berosus—suspect chronicler—claimed that Hespero, legendary twelfth king of Spain, sent a fleet westward more than a millennium before the birth of Christ....

Lobo hooted, slapping a bony hip in derision. Ha, ha! A king of Spain before there was a Spain! Might as well believe in the *romances*!

More believable was Aristotle's ***Mirabilibus aut Seculationibus***, in which The Philosopher mentioned a Carthaginian voyage to a fertile island beyond The Pillars of Hercules. Still—in Lobo's opinion—the translation into Latin was too corrupt to be reliable.

Then, the inescapable Atlantis—referred to by the even more inescapable Plato—created the possibility that some of its inhabitants sailed away as the ground sank from under their feet. Nonetheless, impeccable as was the source, Lobo thought this single citation a tenuous hook on which to hang such tremendous freight.

Therefore the most probable hypothesis, in his opinion, was that the ten lost tribes of Israel had peopled the Indies, for had they turned up anywhere else? It was a shame that Indians did not write, for the diacritical marks of Hebrew were unmistakable.... And here Lobo began to produce noises in pairs, presumably comparing Hebrew with the tongue of a descendant of the ten lost tribes of Israel, now located deep in swamps.

Juan had to agree that the sounds were very similar. But he could not tell which was Hebrew, which Chuncho.

That was *exactly* the point, responded the Dominican, triumphantly cackling. However—taken from his steamy village—the presumed descendant of the lost tribes did not survive his first week in mountains, dying before a single of his sounds could be identified. He had spoken Hebrew to the Indian for hours on end, and the savage was attentive ... sometimes smiling uncertainly, as if on seas of ancient memory a sail appeared on the horizon. But there were contraindications. He was not circumcised! And sad to say, his canine teeth were filed to bat-like points.

When all was said and done, Lobo could not understand how a people of the desert ended up in a wilderness where soil and water combined into something too thick to drink and too wet to walk on. Thank God that his own poor mule lived long enough to preserve him from contact! The *infantes*—Lobo brooded—were in that morass to their knees. They lost their boots to rot. Soft as soaked bread, the flesh fell from their feet. More food for the leeches—he added with a snort—that *there* span your hand, crawling the ground like snakes with heads erect. And from the trees they dropped on you like a fat, black rain.

Producing Chuncho sounds again, Lobo wondered why a descendant of the lost tribes had not understood a single Hebrew word containing the very sounds he uttered daily?

Just as **Utopia** had left Juan cold, the ten lost tribes left him skeptical. How could they possibly have gotten here...?

Inés hooted with skepticism when Juan went over it, though she could not actually *deny* anything touching on The Bible. She and Lobo considered each other wrong in the head—he thinking of her 'lightness,' she of superfluous baggage.

She said to Juan, "If the ten tribes were *that* important, God would not have lost them."

One dazzling morning Juan was trotting by the straggling column when the newcomer whose armit he had sniffed stepped into his path. He dismounted as the *infante* shambled over, seeing that it was the usual soldier—leather and rusted mail overlaid by greasy Inca wool. A livid scar beside his mouth gave him a leer displaying decayed teeth layered with yellow incrustations. He had the forehead of a Negrito and the eyes of a cunning pig.... And he had come to avenge his insult, thought Juan as—too close for comfort— he looked him in the eye. Incredibly, the breath of the present stank worse than the armpit of the past.

Winking, the *infante* turned to the gathered troops with the elaborate bow of an actor at his prologue. Solemnly, he lifted the tail of Juan's horse. With a flourish, he sniffed its ass.

Even the Indians roared. The *infante* bowed, sauntering over to consider Juan from fetid closeness. And—a glitter of anger in his eyes—he displayed a palmed stiletto.... Then he turned away to play the crowd, miming the soldier tripping on his spear, followed by the soldier who—seeing a spear between his legs—yanks on it to create an astonishing erection. He concluded by turning his helmet sideways to bless the multitude as a mitered bishop.

Pedro found out, and keeping his eye on the stirrup he was mending, commented, "I hear you did not fight today."

"Right. No fight."

Morose, Juan picked at *choclo* grit between his teeth. The encounter had the whole camp chuckling.

Eyes still on his stirrup, Pedro said, "He loves both obscene jokes and fighting. But mind me though, his idiocy and fighting go hand in hand. No one is more unscrupulous or less predictable. He shocks men into laughing ... surprises them into dying. He was on Almagro's march, you know. The worse it got the more he laughed."

"The mummied compass?"

"There were details I left out."

"The frozen fart?"

"Of course."

"So what's his name?"

"Ask him and he'll tell you that the envious call him Esteban, his full name being Esteban Ana."

"Este Banana!"

"*Sí.* Saying that was what his mama named him for—in awe when he was born—so long was it already that the priest used it to sprinkle the entire church with holy water without having to remove him from the font. Once, when I told him I was glad I was not named for *my* banana, he said it was better than being named after a *pedo*—a fart—with an *r* in it. And he turned to fart my name quite well.

He claims his bum fiddle can play music, and that he's going to teach it to speak."

"If he's not really Esteban, what do they call him?

"Cacafuego, a name well earned, for no one lights farts better. He maintains that when his ass learns the alphabet he will set his words on fire—like the Holy Ghost, no less. Tongues of flame will descend from the Heavens to his head, go clean through and out the other end."

Stirrup mended, Pedro saw that Juan's brows were knit into a serious bar.

"Be careful with this man, *hijo*. Do not let his idiocies make you take him lightly. He will play the fool, yet that makes him no less Spanish, and he will let not even God joke about his honor." Delicacy prevented Pedro from going further, for he had a suspicion of what happened and did not want to cause his *hijo* shame. But the question wormed out of itself. "In which hand was Cacafuego holding his spear?"

"Don't tell me he's right-handed!"

Juan wondered if Amadís de Gaula—living by chivalric codes—could have been 'surprised' into dying by this foul jester. He imagined Amadís, slumped over his trencher, carving knife in his heart, as a dark figure vanished into curtains. And this returned a measure of Juan's pride, his weakness being that he too much resembled the Hero of Heroes.

The next day Nuño Beltrán de Mendoza rode into camp with his dogs, never volunteering where he had been, what he had done. And he was not one to take a casual question casually.

His dogs were sleek, well fed. And he was—as always—immaculate in blue. The broad-brimmed hat, the pallor, perfect cloth and manner were the same—

although whisking desert dust from velvet with his handkerchief had become
something of a tic.

And he looked at Juan as through one absence at another.

For this small mercy Juan thanked God, wondering at the sleek vigor of the
dogs, the health of the dogger himself—which extended to the plumpness of his
mules—when the expedition now approached starvation. Mendoza and his beasts
had food. And—sure as God was in His Heaven—the chests borne by the mules
were full.

Valdivia granted Mendoza an *encomienda* that outraged the *vecinos*, and the
expedition marched as usual from that day, but it seemed to Juan that—as with
cankered fruit—a worm gnawed at its heart.

The dogger kept to himself, cooking from his chests, hunting with his
greyhounds as the mastiffs guarded his belongings, letting neither man nor beast
within the void of their attention. And he would return with meat he never shared,
causing bitter whispers. The soldiers were on short rations of *choclo* gruel, *choclo*
cakes, *chuño*, *charqui*—moldy raisins if they were lucky—all washed down with
muddy Adam's ale. This, as the dogger feasted on jam and roast hare, even wine,
for one of his mules bore counterbalanced skins. The expedition was eating worse
than Mendoza's dogs.

The march grew more arduous—an unremitting sun by day, at night the bitter
desert cold ... and always, little food, less water. Near Atacama la Chica they
came to a dry riverbed where they found scant forage for the beasts, nothing for
cristianos. The messengers of Manco Capac had been there before them....

Valdivia ordered the column to continue to Atacama la Chica. He would take
ten men and the strongest horses and ride to Atacama la Grande, where Francisco
de Aguirre and his men had agreed to meet them. Riding fast enough, far enough,
they might surprise the savages before they vanished with their food.

Weeks ago Juan had thought himself in the desert proper, only to find the
dryness growing dryer, the bleakness bleaker. The distant *cordillera* invisible
behind hills to their left, they walked from river to distant river, all of them
running roughly parallel toward the Southern Sea. You marched as if crossing an
enormous tilted washboard, down to a river with its abandoned Indian villages,
up into an arid waste where there was nothing for the eye or appetite but scrub,
cactus, and the hares that—like magicians—the greyhounds of Mendoza captured.
Then again you descended to the brackish rivers that often vanished altogether. In
the Atacama there was no rain, only melt water from the mountains. And in this
season the thirsty desert absorbed it before it reached the sea. Yet the portable oasis
of Inés—swaying on the heads of *yanaconas*—lived. Indians dusted the plants,
evenings. And they held improvised parasols over them during the heat of the day.

Pedro was overseeing more than a hundred Spaniards, a thousand or so Indians, sundry *negros*, herds of disorderly animals, and he walked the camp after the evening meal—as Valdivia did—giving orders, checking men and gear, returning late.

Juan and Inés talked in his absence, feeding their fire with resinous desert wood that created explosive, smokeless light.

Inés was troubled. Mendoza had requested permission—of her!—to track the vanished Indians.

Why in Valdivia's absence? How stupid did he think she was? How weak? She *knew* Mendoza wanted to feed Indians to his dogs. She *knew* about the meat markets in Peru where the cuts were human, hung like the hams of hogs. She *knew* Mendoza had been returning unsuccessful from his hunts. His chests were full of figs, jams and spices, but what he needed was meat, and not just for him. The whole thing was an insult to her intelligence.

Juan pointed out that the Indians Mendoza would be hunting down were enemies. The rules of war obtained.

"To kill Indians might be right. Feeding them to dogs is wrong, for they have souls. The Emperor said so. And when they die they need to be buried undigested, to rise whole at the Last Judgment."

To that Juan had no response, thinking only that if you were buried in the Atacama you might participate in the Last Judgment whole, but very dry. Silent, he entered his tent, expecting abominable dreams.

A shriek pierced the woolen wall.

Inés!

Juan jerked upright, tangled in his blanket.

Pedro attempted to exit without bothering with the laces of the door, some of whose knots popped as others tightened. He took a vicious backhanded sweep with his sword, shearing an opening but also cutting a post, collapsing the tent.

The outraged cry, again, "Who *are* you?"

Crawling, shoving heavy wool aside, Juan felt his hand emerge into the coolness of the night. He followed it and was out, disoriented, as Pedro bellowed muffled war cries from his self-imprisonment.

Inés was calmer now. "What *do* you want?"

Figures slipped past Juan, melding with the dark. Oriented by her voice, he lit a stick with last night's fire. Knife drawn, he entered her tent....

In her tented orchard, indomitable, Inés searched the air with a knife that had the delicacy of a blind man's stick. Potted trees had been upended, spilled their dirt, been trodden on.

"Pero Sancho de Hoz!" she exclaimed as Juan's light entered.

Juan could not believe it either.

"In my tent! You boot my trees!" And she did not utter all....

De Hoz had stumbled on pots, and in his floundering groped Inés where no friend—and certainly no enemy—ever had. She sputtered, unable to utter public words.

Juan saw De Hoz remove a handkerchief from his sleeve, concealing a dagger in the process. He noticed also that his forehead bled. Inés had caught him with some blind sweep.

The traitor dabbed at his wound with one hand, flicking potting soil from his hose with the other, as men ran up with torches and drawn swords.

Inés turned to the reinforcements. "*Caballeros*, this is under control. You will do me the favor of searching the camp for intruders." Dressed only in a cotton shift, she radiated calm authority. How beautiful she was, Juan thought, in white.

"*A sus órdenes, señora*," the men chorused.

The camp was roused, fires flaring, the tent of Inés ringed by armed men in shirts and hasty armor. She tossed on a cloak, unaware that she had begun to use her knife to put up her hair. Defiant, she finished that familiar task, which gave her a warlike look—blade through her bun.

To De Hoz she said, "This is an outrage!"

He scattered potting soil with his scented handkerchief as he bowed. "There is no cause for outrage, *señora*. It is simply that, after a long and difficult journey, I came to pay my respects to Don Pedro de Valdivia."

Horse feathers and hen's teeth, Juan thought. Bah!

Only then did Pedro burst onto the scene. Wild-eyed from combat with a tent, wielding his enormous sword, he was prepared to halve whatever culprit like an orange.

Seeing De Hoz he said, "Doña Inés, *a sus órdenes*." One word from her and he would cleave the *hideputa* from harelip to tackle.

She offered no such encouragement, saying to the assembled men that she desired to speak with the *maestre de campo*.

When all had left, Juan blurted that De Hoz had a dagger up his sleeve, no doubt intending to kill Valdivia.

Her knees—firm through the ordeal—shook. And she sat. "Sweet Jesus!"

Pedro exploded, saying he would gut De Hoz, and striding out the tent to do exactly *that*, when Inés stopped him.

Having him gutted would give her wonderful pleasure, she said, but this would have to wait. As De Hoz had his authority from Pizarro, only the Lieutenant Governor could order violence to his person. Also, since De Hoz would not have dared the assassination himself, it was a plot.

Pedro left to dress—not wanting to confront the traitor dandy in his nightshirt.

And having dispatched a messenger to Valdivia, taking command of a militant band of men, he found De Hoz whispering to a huddle.

If he had not convicted himself inside Valdivia's tent, De Hoz was doing so now, for with him was every malcontent in the expedition—Juan de Guzmán, brother of the Diego that slaughtered the ewe and composed the litany, Antonio de Ulloa, Diego de Ávalos, as well as the rogues De Hoz presumably brought with him.

Arrogantly rising, the traitor fluted through his harelip, "What kind of camp is this, that anyone can wander in at night unchallenged?"

Pedro was too furious to speak … and too ashamed, for there was truth in the charge.

De Hoz hissed—viper that he was—"I believe it is *your* duty to assign the watch and see it properly maintained. You can be certain Don Pedro will hear about this."

The restraints in Pedro snapped like anchor hawsers in a gale. He took a step … took another, drew his sword in a huge sweep.

Recoiling, De Hoz drew as well.

Then every sword was out.

Here was the end of the expedition, thought Juan numbly. Valdivia's dream would be cut short by civil war.

But, miraculously, Pedro found some anchor deep in duty. Pale with fury, he half-sheathed his sword and spat—close enough to the boots of De Hoz for the miss to be an insult, far enough away that it could seem poor aim.

And he collected himself. "I answer only to Valdivia."

He spat again—a gunner working on his range—yearning for the conspirator to draw … but, nothing.

Pedro slammed his weapon into its sheath and left.

Inés said they must act as if nothing happened, their only hope being that Valdivia would arrive in time.

Returned to the ruin of their tent, Juan and Pedro decided to sleep under the cold brilliance of desert stars—so much nearer than those of wetter lands.

"I'm proud of you, *maestre de campo*," Juan said, whacking Pedro … which was like hitting the side of an ox.

"What for?" Pedro grumbled. "Shredding the tent? Playing the coward?"

"Don't be silly. You did the harder, wiser thing. Being *maestre de campo* makes you think with something beside your sword arm."

Pedro hawed and snorted, retorting, "De Hoz is vulture-fodder, anyway. When Valdivia returns, the traitor will ride the horse foaled by an acorn." Gruffly he added, "Thanks *hijo*. Now go to sleep."

Juan faced the strangeness of the southern firmament above him with much to think about and more to worry over. Even conjugating the Latin verb *dormio*—in every person, singular and plural, the present and imperfect, future and perfect, pluperfect and future perfect tenses, together with translations into Spanish—did not summon sleep. He gave up at 'he or she will have slept,' to contemplate the slow wheel of alien stars.

When they marched, De Hoz openly rode with the malcontents, speaking in conspiratorial whispers and displaying the document signed by the Emperor—his claim to lead the expedition.

There was nothing Pedro could do but swallow bile. The majority of the men remained true to Valdivia, yet if the revolt gained momentum De Hoz would attract opportunists desiring to be on the winning side. At some point the scales would tip to mutiny.

Pedro fumed, weighing his chances of killing De Hoz and getting away with it. Maybe he could provoke him to a duel. Maybe he should just take his sword and join the crack on his lip to the one on his ass. The problem was, if he did *that* Valdivia would have no choice but to hang him as the ordinary soldier that he was. And this Pedro definitely did not want, having seen too many hangings.

Juan rode with Pedro in the van, thinking that the expedition had taken an asp into its bed, like Cleopatra. Better an honorable expedition of ten than that number increased by villains. He searched for hope in the roll of barren hills before them and, incredibly, saw a tiny cloud in this cloudless hell. Dim and low— over the hill of their horizon—it grew to the size of an outstretched thumb. And in it steel glinted….

Pedro whooped, spurring his horse into insane gallop down the rocky slope, taking a perilous short cut toward the summit of the next rise, for life was again worth risking. And soon he was a silver beetle crawling up a rise.

The miracle had come about.

On his exhausted mount—having ridden all the night—Valdivia thundered up with his *caballeros*, reining in a lathered horse. Pedro cantered down the column to where De Hoz and his conspirators—army in the army—marched together, making show of their increasing strength.

The *maestre de campo* boomed, "Pero Sancho de Hoz, Diego de Guzmán, Antonio de Ulloa, Diego de Ávalos, you are all under arrest. The charge is attempted murder of the Lieutenant Governor and conspiracy to mutiny. You will surrender your arms and horses at once."

The four hesitated, but dismounted, making a pile of swords, spears, maces. Valdivia ordered them clapped in irons. And from that moment they walked under the merciless desert sun in the armor of horsemen, with the added weight of chains. Whatever their eventual fate, these would be remembered days.

Valdivia had good news for Pedro and Inés. He had come upon Francisco de

Aguirre and Rodrigo de Quiroga at Atacama la Grande, as well as fifteen *caballeros* and ten arquebusiers—the remainder of the expedition to Los Chunchos. And they surprised the Indians before they vanished, so that they were able to confiscate everything edible. Now the expedition could rest and recover, build reserves.

When they camped, Valdivia interrogated the conspirators singly, first saying to each that their guilt was a foregone conclusion. All that remained was the confession.

Hoping to trade betrayal for clemency, Ulloa was the one who broke. They planned to assassinate Valdivia with daggers bought in Arequipa. When he was dead—De Hoz told them—the expedition would acclaim him Lieutenant General of lands south of Peru.... De Hoz had entered the tent by himself, and they waited until it was clear that his attempt had failed. So they had done *nothing* really, except listen to bad counsel, bitterly regretted. Ulloa begged for mercy, pointing out that the Emperor himself signed De Hoz's claim.

Valdivia only said that—as here there was no wood for a gallows—the formal sentencing would take place at Atacama la Grande.

The conspirators walked, chained, under the merciless desert sun. As the armor of a *caballero* was not designed for this, they developed sores rubbed bloody by the coarse cloth they wore, stinging with the salt of sweat. Ulloa went down on his knees to beg.

They could remove their armor, as all their property was forfeit anyway, said Valdivia. But they must wear their chains.

De Hoz walked the thirty leagues to Atacama la Grande in six days, wearing only a filthy shirt and hose. Yet he still had on a pearl and diamond earring, a gold necklace thick as thumbs, a bracelet, half a dozen rings. Pedro commented that it was bad enough when you threw pearls to swine. It was worse when the porker wore them.

At Atacama la Grande they found the promised food and water. Celebrating *infantes* threw themselves armored into the water of the catch basins, the desert momentarily forgotten. And there, Rodrigo de Quiroga blushed and stuttered as he made his leg, greeting Inés.

This amused her, for the rumor—so persistent as to be likely—was that he had been smitten with her in Cuzco. But whatever his past feelings, Quiroga was lovesick *now*, or she was not Inés de Suárez. To be desperately admired could cause pride, of course, and with this sin she did not intend to struggle. Quiroga was tall, slender, broad of shoulder, and—though younger than Valdivia—looked up to by his men. And she admired the stuttering captain herself, enough *not* to use him to make Valdivia jealous. However, Inés knew that she was not made for uncertainties of the heart. Valdivia loved her, but he was not hers in the eyes of

Heaven. And on Earth, quite possibly, he was not hers to keep. In the game of life, Quiroga would remain a card up her sleeve.

Valdivia ordered a gallows built from the poles of Indian huts. When this was done he required his *maestre de campo* to bring him the four conspirators.

"Pero Sancho de Hoz, Diego de Guzmán, Antonio de Ulloa, Diego de Ávalos, you are guilty of mutiny and attempted murder. By the authority conferred upon me by the crown I sentence you to death by hanging. You may have this day and night to reconcile your souls to God. In the morning, you will confess yourselves after Mass. Then justice will be served."

Ulloa crawled sniveling to where Inés and the priests stood beside Valdivia. He kissed the hem of their cassocks and her skirt, babbling pleas for intercession. Pedro spat—not far from the recumbent sight—muttering that if they could not live like men of honor, they could at least die as such. They were a disgrace to Spain.

To Juan this execution seemed a parody, Ulloa too much the fool, De Hoz too bumbling, to be tragic. The manacled dandy was now on his knees, snot running from his nose, beating a breast covered in filthy wool, a pearl like a pigeon's egg hanging from his ear. This was too bizarre to be happening.

Grudging pity had cooled the long-simmering fury of Inés. De Hoz indeed once groped her breast, but—in the light of retrospect—by accident. Valdivia's sentence was beginning to seem excessive. She took Father Marmolejo aside and they agreed to plead for a judgment less harsh. Mutinous these men might be, yet they had murdered no one.

To them Valdivia replied, "My assassination did not fail for lack of trying. An example must be made." He waited then, for Inés to voice the answer he himself could not propose....

"Why not just have De Hoz return to Peru, along with his accursed document?" Nodding sagely, Valdivia refused, as he had to.

The same sun rose over the same hills in the same bleached sky the next bleached morning, yet all were in a gala mood. Any execution was a holiday, and of the various kinds a hanging was the best. The garrote just turned them purple, making their eyes bulge with blood. The ax was a better show ... quickly over, however. Stringing them up gave you the real dance of death.

Valdivia broke his fast with appetite, listening to Inés point out that the whole thing could backfire like a rusted arquebus. De Hoz—for the love of God!—had the backing of Pizarro, who created the partnership in the first place. Hang him, and Valdivia would at some point be brought to trial, perhaps even executed. De Hoz *was* guilty, yet could one string him up because he walked into a tent at night, knocking over orange trees? As for the so-called mutiny—De Hoz had an arguable right to represent the Emperor.

Finishing his meal, Valdivia commented that it was better to handle present problems in the present. The future always changed them, seldom for the better.

Crude but serviceable, the gallows was shaped into a T. Two of the condemned would be pulled up together, balancing the structure. They would not be dropped, for the flimsy structure would not stand the shock.

Lobo as his acolyte, Marmolejo sang High Mass before the tree of justice towering behind him like a cross.

"*Introibo ad altare dei.*"

With a shiver Juan thought that of these Latin words, each was one fewer. To the condemned this Mass was like a speaking hourglass.

"*Ite missa est.*"

Pedro organized the hanging. Ulloa—selected to go first with Diego de Ávalos—was unable to stand. Disgusted, Pedro said there was rope enough to drag him up from where he knelt. Checking the nooses, he awaited orders....

Valdivia proclaimed, "Pero Sancho de Hoz, Diego de Guzmán, Antonio de Ulloa, Diego de Ávalos, your crimes merit death. But as Almighty God is just so also is He merciful. And as does He, man must temper justice with mercy. His representatives on earth, Fathers González Marmolejo and Juan Lobo have counseled that I spare your lives. Yet your crimes are too great to go unpunished. You will therefore return to Peru, taking only what is necessary for the journey, and your remaining property will be confiscated. Until tomorrow's dawn you will remain in chains. That is all. This assembly is dismissed."

Few were happy with this startling reversal of the day, especially Pedro. And that night he returned from a meeting with Valdivia incoherent with anger.

Who *are* these 'two less than lice?' Juan asked of his outburst. What *is* the problem?

It turned out that Valdivia had decided that De Hoz and Ulloa would remain with the expedition— even though Inés and every *caballero* summoned to the meeting had bitterly opposed.

"He must have his reasons," Juan proposed, unable to conceive of one.

Pedro violently undressed and flung himself upon his cot.

Diego de Guzmán and Diego de Ávalos began the long walk back to Cuzco the following morning, accompanied by Indians. And for the two months spent in Atacama la Grande, de Hoz was chained and guarded, although Valdivia allowed him to resume his dandy's outfit. As for Ulloa, he seemed to have won Valdivia's confidence and was allowed to circulate without guards. The gallows, however, were not wasted…. A certain Escobar— *infante* and unvarnished partisan of De Hoz—had also been pardoned by Valdivia. But when Pedro went to release him he drew a concealed dagger and stabbed him in the back, drawing blood through chain mail.

Valdivia sentenced him to hang soon as confessed, saying to the priests that the time and place for mercy were not here, not now. To his captains Valdivia said he could stomach crimes against his person, not against *them*.

Inés pleaded. This was stupidity, not mutiny. If men were hanged for idiocy, why not hang half the expedition?

Valdivia had thought Inés deeper, subtler. And he thought that there were times, no doubt, when intercession drove even Almighty God to become irritated with Mary. Yet he was patient.

"No one cares about this fool."

Escobar was strung up.

The scapegoat struggled and shat his hose, as Juan expected. But no one had told him that the crowd would cheer the moment, holding their noses. Also, no one told him that the tongue of the dying man would protrude, an amazing blue.

Pedro remarked that the mutinous asshole was bouncing hard on purpose. Everybody knew that the more you jerked the quicker you died. Only the pious kept still as possible, so as not to make it suicide.

And it was then that Escobar dropped through the little air that separated him from life, for the rope had snapped with his exertions. *Yanaconas* cheered. *Cristianos* crossed themselves, some reverently kneeling before God's decision. To acclamation, Valdivia commuted his sentence. But Escobar had to return to Peru.

Pedro was thoughtful. "Think about it, *hijo*. Valdivia could not execute the men of a mutiny that had De Hoz as its head. Neither could he let them get away with it. So he scares them into kissing the skirts of women and priests. Now De Hoz is humiliated, still in chains. Ulloa is pissing his hose at the memories. The rest are starving as they fight Indians and their way to Cuzco—probably already dead. And now, the failed execution means that God has put His seal on it all."

Pedro danced his admiration of Valdivia—ponderous yet light—with a grace that he attributed to wine and the exercise of the sword. "*Voto a Cristo, hijo*, if it had been up to me I would have halved De Hoz in that tent like a grape, chewed him up and spit out the seeds. And *that* would have been a great mistake."

The *maestre de campo* had fogotten gloom, for his blind impulse of that moment had stood the test of time, this time.

Juan thought, however, that Pedro had not reasoned the situation through. Not only could Valdivia not execute De Hoz, he could not return him to Peru, to plot.

What—he asked Inés that evening—if De Hoz were not the fool he seemed?

What if Valdivia had been in bed, and De Hoz not tripped on trees? If he *had* succeeded, what version of the event would have survived to reach the Emperor?

Inés said that De Hoz was a simple hissing fool—deadly as a snake, no more intelligent. Valdivia was just giving him the slack with which to hang himself.

Dreading the day he would march in chains again, De Hoz requested an audience with Valdivia, and they spent two days in a sweltering Indian hut. No record was kept. The third day— the twelfth of August of 1540—Luis de Cartagena was summoned to draw up their agreement. De Hoz renounced the rights and privileges bestowed upon him by Pizarro, dissolving the partnership into which he had entered with Valdivia. In return he would be part of the expedition, with a status corresponding to *hidalgos* of his importance.

De Hoz walked from the hut a free man, but without a weapon. That part of the agreement was not put in writing.

Inés fumed like a banked fire as, next day, the immense snake of man, animal and goods began to labor south. Within a week every mind had turned to survival. There were no more rivers, only meanders of dusty green. There, they would dig and drink the buried, tea-like fluid, rich with bitterness.

At one such place Valdivia declared a day of rest, the third week out from Atacama la Grande. Here there was water, however sour, and tomorrow was Sunday.

Then they began to cross a dead land under a sky that stared back like a blind man's eye....

The Atacama emptied the mind like memories of childhood, compressing months into unchanging days. A breakfast swallowed with foul water. A Mass. A march. A rest under a pitiless sun. Another march. An evening camp. Thin blankets for an icy night.

Memories not the same were few, like the first sight of a *salar*—salt flats stretching far as the eye could see—a crumpled, silver mirror for the sun. After that, salt dust covered everything ... and no way to wash it off. Your eyes burned. Your thirst tasted like minerals.

Another memory ... of *camanchaca*—morning fog invading the desert from the sea. You rode, slow as snails, in the comfort of an absent sun. And being blind was good. No need to see a place you hated.

The *camanchaca*, thought Juan, was like the memory of the Atacama—that rosary of days in Hell—a present to endure ... a future to undergo ... both indistinguishable from the memories that brought you there.

You survived to forget.

Chapter 10: Santiago (Nueva Extremadura, 1540)

Swans. Liliana's breasts. The hamlets of Andalucía.

In Latin, *alba*—white, or fortunate—as in the auspicious albatross. *Alba*, the tunic over the black cassock of a priest. In Spanish, *alba* the dawn. *Alba alba*—white dawn. Fortunate white. Fortunate dawn. And in Quechua, *camanchaca*. *Camanchaca alba*—white fog, white dawn … this luminous opacity through which Juan rode.

He could feel himself hope, hear himself breathe. *Camanchaca* turned you on yourself, seeing nothing, bathed in light.

His extended hand was dimmed, not white, although Indians called him that. Ahead, the faint blot that was Inés floated, white horse consumed by fog.

White horse, white rider.

Black dress, black hat.

Juan imagined her from the front, eyes suspended in a blank, and a faintly rosy, silent mouth....

Sounds drowned in *camanchaca*, and when you spoke you talked to phantoms. In *camanchaca* you were alone with others. Vision's cables to the world were cut. Thoughts floated on inner tides....

Inés was white—under her clothes—on a white Arabian in a white dawn, wearing the black of mourning, cassocks, ink.

Liliana's breasts and thighs. The offered host. And in Latin, *album* was a book....

On the blank page called *camanchaca* Juan saw a naked woman, white in fog. A creator sketched in hair and eyes, delicate nostrils, a refined chin—freckles!—nipples and a navel, a small, dark cloud below.

Black Mass was being said, over a white woman.

They were riding on a morning like every other, Valdivia marching despite complaints—they could not find their cocks to piss, grumbled the *infantes* ... or see their boots, to miss—until the sun risen over the *cordillera* burnt through fog like a hot coin. The muffled clanks and cascabels, creaks and muted conversations grew distinct. Inés appeared. And then beyond her ... green.

Dismounting, Valdivia knelt to lift his inverted sword as an impromptu crucifix. The Copiapó! They prayed.

Arrived at the river they found the few Indians not yet vanished. Sullen, they claimed they had no food, no gold. The women too were missing, save for crones too old to flee. The messengers of Manco Capac had again preceded them.

Valdivia called a meeting, saying they had water, but not food. Jovial, Diego de Cáceres proposed they eat the more tender women. Mendoza—who never joked—suggested he use his dogs on the Indians. They tended to talk when they saw one of their own devoured.... But Inés was vehemently opposed.

Valdivia took Pedro aside, quietly ordering him to put some Indians to the question ... and by evening they knew where the food and women were hidden. The expedition ate well for the first time in months.

Juan confronted Pedro on his way to the stockade where the natives were confined.

"How many did you torture?"

"Two," Pedro sighed.

"How could you!"

"Indians are enemies. War is war. A soldier is a soldier. An order is an order." These simple verities should have been enough, yet Pedro was aggrieved enough to amplify. "Where would our Empire be, if protected by women and priests? Nowhere, is where. We would be living under the heels of Moors, the sons of slaves, and slaves ourselves." Pedro grew heated. "*Pardiez*, you have no right to blame me for doing my duty! I got results. We're eating." He did not add the good news—that the younger of the two sons of the *cacique* survived. Torturing children was an unfortunate thing, but with their lies savages brought serious consequences upon themselves. Also, the father had not been touched ... just made to watch.

Pedro walked off to ply his meat to Indian tenderloin, leaving Juan to explore his shame. As a consequence of torture he had eaten half a chicken and two small animals—perhaps *chinchillas*, although Indians grew them for their fur. There were *papas* too—not dried—tasting delicious for the first time ever. He summoned a glorious belch. Maybe Pedro was right. The Indians had conspired against them, after all. Who—If not the Devil?—made pagans refuse food to the starving men bringing them salvation?

The Copiapó was not just the last of the desert, it was the northern boundary of the territory Valdivia had been granted. He erected a cross, claiming lands south for the Emperor, naming them Nueva Extremadura after his native province. He never liked the word 'Chile' anyway, for Almagro had turned it into a synonym for failure.

Mass was sung by Marmolejo, who slipped a chasuble over armor and set his sword where he could reach it. After, he donned his tunic emblazoned with the cross of Calatrava and taught the assembled Indians to kneel before it.

Turning to civil education, Valdivia explained to the surly natives their rights and duties as subjects of the Crown. An interpreter translated into Quechua—this language many Indians of the South were said to understand....

They were now subjects of His Majesty, Carlos V, their lands his lands, His law their law. As loyal vassals they would be treated fairly. However, there would be no mercy for those who transgressed against His edicts. In addition—as His subjects—they were now children of His God, entitled to baptism and instruction in the one true Faith, this precious gift that would allow them to enter Heaven. In return they would be taxed like every other subject—in animals and crops, as they had no gold. Finally, they would be required to work for those who were assigned their religious instruction.

The Indians listened, hostile, and what little they understood, they hated. Their homes and food had been taken, their women raped, their children tortured.

And the Spanish were deaf as the Indians. Who would even consider an *encomienda* by this trickle of a river in the desert's hostile lap?

By evening every native not shackled or confined had vanished, leaving the expediton in possession of abandoned huts. They ate and rested, mended equipment.

Valdivia however, busied himself with creating a chronicle of the expedition. Intense, he twirled his mustaches as he dictated....

Juan came to understand that, for reasons of statecraft, what secretaries perceived as History was an interpreted—sometimes expurgated—thing. For example, the journey to Tarapacá was ignored until De Hoz appeared on the scene, when he was almost overlooked by Clio's pen. No attempted murder. No sedition or trial ... *and*, no agreement leaving Valdivia in sole command....

To see De Hoz smudged upon Valdivia's page—though not erased—still deeply troubled Juan. The man was base, mutinous, evil, a self-annointed nurse for treachery impossible for sane men to understand. Yet he was the villain called for by the narrative, and Valdivia almost cut out his part. As for Nuño Beltrán de Mendoza, he was not even mentioned—although, interestingly, the torture of Indians was.

Diplomacy could ruin drama, Juan concluded

And when the chronicle was transcribed, October was almost on them.

Three Spanish straggled into camp the day of the feast of San Olselmo, thin, thirsty, exhausted. Juan Jufré and Gáspar de Vergara, dispatched by Valdivia to Tarapacá to recruit, were returning empty-handed when they met up with Juan de Almonacid. And as if these few had breached some dike, next day a small army rode cheering into camp—Gonzalo de los Ríos with twenty *caballeros*, a dozen packhorses and mules, and well over a hundred *yanaconas* with their loads, bringing the number of the expedition to nearly one hundred and fifty.

Pedro strode off in a swirl of cloak. Puzzled, Juan followed.

"What's the matter?"

"Them as just rode in is the matter. I would as soon lose twenty as acquire these hell-sent swine."

"What! We're an army now."

"We *were* an army. Now we're mutiny about to happen. Gonzalo de los Ríos is like this with De Hoz." Pedro held up his index and middle fingers tight together.

Juan considered the new arrivals, remembering that Valdivia's greeting had been far more courteous than cordial. That of Inés had been perfunctory ... and now she was tucking wisps of hair under her Andalusian hat—hiding that light— as De Hoz embraced the ample De los Ríos. He embraced a second.

"Who's that, Pedro?"

"More trouble, named Chinchilla."

The burly soldier looked nothing like the tiny rodent save for his incisors, revealed by a smile of greeting.

Pedro blew his nose violently with his fingers, demonstrating in this manner how—given the chance—he would eject traitors from the body politic. "Here comes Inés," he said.

That night she was adamant with Valdivia, who grumbled that she was making much of little. De Hoz was under guard, allowed no arms. The viper's teeth were pulled.

Teeth of dragons, Juan thought, sowing a harvest of armed traitors.

Livid, Inés said that to govern a Lieutenant Governor needed to see what was before his eyes.

Valdivia nodded pleasantly, suggesting with a greasy grin she try the meat, which was done just right.

In her agitation Inés had allowed it to be grilled to cinder. He had been tunneling like miners through coal to reach the blood, he said.

Too angry to respond, Inés seared Valdivia with the green flame of her eyes and strode out the door to see to her animals.

A litter of pigs—born in wilderness—had prospered under her care, surviving the length of a mighty desert uneaten, sharing the sustenance of soldiers who considered their own hunger more important. It infuriated the *infantes* that their food ate their food. This miracle had not been easy for Inés. Nor was the salvation of her ducks. When they arrived at the Copiapó she released them from their cages, tying twine to their legs so they could swim without escaping. In their filthiness they half sank, so that only their heads and tails were visible, making them look like floating, feathered snakes with beaks—a sight both hilarious and sad. But today her ducks were floating fat and high.

Contrite, Valdivia came to join her, accompanied by Juan and Pedro, and they all laughed about the day ducks sank, avoiding the true topic on their minds.

That evening Valdivia asked Pedro his opinion of the new arrivals.

The *maestre de campo* said that De los Ríos and the others—especially Chinchilla—itched to conspire. Juan Salguero—who guarded De Hoz—reported that six or seven had whispered with him for hours. The fuse was lit, and soon the expedition would be blown all over the landscape. And he was not just talking grumbling, he was talking civil war. The omens truly boded ill. His friend Juan Romero told him that when these men came he had been slaughtering a rabbit that quivered three times before dying. Pedro crossed himself at this worst of signs.

Worrying his beard, Valdivia said he would think it over … and the following day Fortuna dealt the card bringing him back into the game. Juan Ruiz—a former member of Almagro's expedition, bold in his criticism—urged other *infantes* to follow the rebel banner of De Hoz.

Valdivia had been inclined to ignore the ravings of wild-eyed Ruiz. And the journey to Chile had further addled the wit of this poor soul who—from the moment of his recruitment—was like the idiot that seems to wander every Spanish village, regarded with a vaguely holy awe. But one day Ruiz went far too far. In the presence of witnesses he said to De Hoz that if he walked in his boots he would already have destroyed Valdivia.

This was the provocation that the patience of the Lieutenant Governor had waited for, and he sentenced Ruiz to immediate hanging, though it was night. As there was no time to erect a proper gallows, he would be pulled up into a tree.

Juan stood in the flicker and stink of torches. Shriven, Ruiz was dragged weeping to the noose, digging in his boot heels, flanked by priests.

And when the condemned levitated into torch-lit leaves, wildly kicking, Juan reached for awe—wanting to resonate with some tremendous chord—and failed. He felt simple shame instead, one with the crowd that cheered when Ruiz shat his hose.

Rebellion grumbled in dark corners, Valdivia keeping his counsel until the expedition departed Copiapó. And three days later he left the column to reconnoiter.

The next day Chinchilla addressed the crowd after Mass. He was prepared to kill Valdivia, and he asked for support. De Hoz leapt to his feet, crying, "Behold your new *maestre de campo*."

Pedro Gómez accelerated like an avalanche, drawing his sword. But Inés got to Chinchilla first, ordering him disarmed and clapped in irons. The mutiny was quelled, and when Valdivia returned Chinchilla revealed every detail of the plot. But Valdivia surprised everyone—including the culprits— by executing no one.

The company around Juan's fire was gloomy that night. Valdivia left with Pedro for the evening rounds. Inés mended a skirt, morose, introspective. Juan left to seek companionship.

Marmolejo dozed by a blaze as Lobo read Erasmus. He greeted Juan curtly, returning to his text. He had hoped to have in him a disciple, but the lad was clearly under the thumb of uncouth Pedro and Valdivia's unlettered concubine.

Depressed, Juan headed for his blankets. Feeling his way through darkness, he heard a heavy raindrop on a tent ... another. In the Atacama! He searched unwinking stars for cloud, heard another plop. He extended an open hand. A horse screamed.

Someone leapt up to piss on a nearby fire, yelling 'fuck the fuckers.' The steaming coals exploded. He screeched....

Cacafuego! And by his fire's light an arrow quivered.

"Shit!" yelled Cacafuego. "I burned my dick!"

Juan drew his knife.

Cacafuego thought this so funny he stopped rubbing spittle on his member and began to hoot.

"Hoo, hoo, the mighty warrior. Yank out your prick instead."

And in fact there was no enemy to be seen, nothing to be heard, save for the camp's commotion. The *infante* insisted. "*Cagüenlostia*, I mean it! Yank out your prick! I'm out of piss, so help put out the fucking fire! Or stomp it with them fancy boots."

Of course, Juan thought, fires were what the Indians were aiming at. Unlacing, he pissed on sizzling ember.

Thunder came in their direction—Horses!—a stampede under starlight, gathering tents, flapping and pounding like a single infernal animal. Juan heard a howl of agony ... two ... a shouted curse cut brutally short. In an instant he would be trodden like wine grapes. He turned to run and a hand sat him with a thump. Cacafuego yelled, "Don't fucking move!"

Sudden shock catapulted the *infante* onto Juan. A horse shrieked, and a floundering bulk—half tent, half horse—occulted stars and parted the stampede, which roared its way around.

Juan smelled burning wool. He was lying on the coals that piss had not put out. He yelped.

Rolling free from under Cacafuego—thank God for chain mail!—Juan bent over the motionless *infante,* detecting fetid breath. Shuddering, he removed his cloak to cover him.

Sunrise revealed less harm than chaos. Tents were scattered like laundry by a cyclone. Men sifted through the confusion. Pigs rooted. And by Juan's side an enormous horse lay dead, the shaft of a broken spear jutting from its chest. By it Cacafuego snored, breath steaming in the morning chill, purple lump on his forehead.

Pedro appeared, asking what had happened.

Cacafuego stopped snoring and distinctly said, "Ask my arse."

Grinning, Pedro did. The *infante* produced a wavering bleat, and sighed, shamed by his apprentice mouth. Then, blaming his concussion, he lapsed into unconsciousness.

Juan was awestruck. "Can he truly make it *speak*?"

Pedro wrapped his cloak around him, saying, " God help you, *hijo*, I think he likes you. In any case, he saved your life."

"What?"

"Infantry tactic. He rested the spear butt in the fire pit and the horse impaled itself. If the spear had held, Cacafuego would be fine."

They found Inés kneeling by a *yanacona*, blood bubbling from his mouth. She looked up and smiled weakly. Taking Juan's hand she pulled herself up, green eyes shadowed by violet. "Three dead," she said. "And this one is the next."

Juan went to help with her traveling oasis, which had suffered. Inés knelt by a tree that would not make it and wept, racking sobs bowing her to the ground....

As a young male in love what could Juan do but something wrong? He comforted, "It was only a fig ... I think."

She began to hoot with grief, and he rocked her in his arms as the Virgin her crucified Son—that ancient cadence of nurture and grief, human beginning, human end.

Inés said, "You get attached to what you cross a desert with."

What...?" Valdivia asked, arriving.

Armed patrols became routine. Wanderers were attacked, some wounded— not seriously, save for Francisco Rodríguez, who went to pick cactus fruit and got an arrow in his throat. Pedro found Juan armor that he wore with his Inca helmet.

The Indians attacked every night, and in short weeks the column lost over thirty *piezas*, four horses and a goat. The animals were butchered. The Indians were buried. If too wounded to march they were abandoned with food and water. The number of bearers was dangerously shrinking, and rebellious. Their spokesman—an *orejón* with earplugs long gone—said that the mighty armies of the Sapa Inca fought with the savages south of the Copiapó. Many Inca died attempting to conquer this land where there was nothing of worth but the land itself, for he regretted to say his people had exaggerated the riches to be found. The Sapa Inca—who had conquered the four corners of the world—halted his armies after great bloodshed at a river called the Fiu Fiu and there set the limit of his reign. It was said that the savages on the other side ate people and drank blood. It was also said they could fly and turn into fish. To cross the Fiu Fiu was certain death. Even to approach it was dangerous. Did he have to point out that thirty-two of his people had died or been abandoned, and almost that number still bore their loads wounded, afraid to be left to be skinned alive or eaten by these savages? They must turn back.

"Never," replied Valdivia. "Conquest is dangerous. Tomorrow we march." And so they did.

Cacafuego had taken to winking and pointing at his ass when Juan rode by, and Juan would nod and ride on. One morning he made the mistake of asking what he wanted.

"Ask my arse."

There were guffaws from witnesses as Juan entered into the drama, sweeping off his feathered helmet, bowing, saying, "Arse, pray speak."

Bending, the *infante* produced an 'rr,' an 'fff,' and a prolonged 's'—somewhat off.

Thinking he heard echoes of the consonants of the lost tribes of Israel, Juan asked, "Was that Spanish?"

Insulted, Cacafuego said hith arthe had thpoken Castilian. Had Juan not caught the lithp?

Pedro rode up in rescue, asking if Juan wanted to go scout, and they galloped off. Scouting, you rode with the wind in your face, leaving the expedition to its barnyard crawl.

They had trotted perhaps five leagues through bleakness scoured by deep ravines—a long day's march for the expedition—when they came to a defile not wide enough for three to ride abreast. The place stank of ambush, Pedro growled, drawing his sword. And as if that were the signal, a horde of shrieking Indians flooded the gap ahead.

War was noise—thought Juan—now that he had come to know it. Stones and arrows thunked as the horsemen in the van slammed into Indians so packed that they could scarcely fight. Pedro swung his sword like a scythe through upraised arms. Hands and weapons flew. The horses reared and pirouetted, lethally striking, trampling downed Indians until their hocks dripped blood. Ignoring the arrows and futile blows, the *caballeros*—with the economy of harvesters beginning a large field—methodically were swinging....

When one in the killing row ceded his place Juan's horse surged forward— wild with blood-scent—rearing to strike with hooves at a yellow face striped black, which bloomed crimson and disappeared. Another hairless head now stared at

Juan, mouth gaping in an unheard scream, and he stuck his sword in it. To the side a flicker of black ... and his arm grew numb. He backed his horse and another horseman took his place.

Soon, pandemonium retreated up the defile. Pedro cried, "Santiago!"

They spurred their mounts, slamming into the retreating warriors from the rear, crushing and scattering, treading bodies under iron like red grapes. Juan grew tired, for the sword was heavy and it sometimes stuck in bone.

Hundreds of Indians died in a vivid blur until Juan could hardly lift his arm, yet every Spaniard was unharmed, save for one who preposterously lost an ear protected by a helmet. The *maestre de campo* and Villagrán decided that it was time to call a halt, as the canyon was already in deep shadow, and night would favor the enemy. They ate standing by their mounts, conferring.

Villagrán was of old blood, and appeared—Juan thought—to have been given a perpetual headache by consorting with lesser mortals. Slow to speech, he was also slow to stop once started, apparently considering the last word his by ancient feudal right. "Their tactics have changed, *caballeros*," he declared, voice resonating in the caverns of his nose. "They offered us pitched battle, and we could ask for nothing better. The more of them we kill, the less they will nibble our flanks."

"*Por Belcebu!*" a weary *caballero* interjected, "These Indian *hideputas* don't *know* when to stop getting killed. They're like earthworms. Cut one in half and you make more."

"Like the miracle of the loaves and fishes," someone commented.

"The miracle is their stupidity," another added. "They were fighting their best war, keeping out of sight, circling like a pack of dogs, and now, simple suicide. If they want to die so badly why don't they just kill themselves?"

"All right," Pedro said, "they're suicidal, but their numbers have no end."

"Good thing they can't flank us," Villagrán offered into the silence created by that tiring truth.

"Why not outflank *them*?" Juan cried out, impulsive.

Villagrán stared over his nose in disbelief, like a supercilious llama. Protégé of Pedro Gómez Juan might be, but he had no hair on his face below his eyebrows.

"How to get there?" Pedro wondered, pulling on his beard ... then answered his own question. "Down canyon, the sides are less steep. We'll see in the morning if we can find a way up."

Juan was wakened by Pedro's light rap on his helmet. He was leading the flanking party, and would his *hijo* like to come?

They set off, silent as iron-shod horses could be, which is to say with a huge clatter. Finding a gully exiting the ravine, they trotted parallel to it at a distance. Juan was shivering, exhausted, proud. Yesterday's butchery did not seem chivalric, yet at this moment he felt himself a knight-errant. And under moonlight this wild land was an extraordinary sight. Dawn was breaking behind the *cordillera*, casting a milky pallor.

"Few Indians attack at night," Pedro commented, low. "But sure as Christ is God there will be whooping at first light."

Peaks were being illuminated by dawn—in purples, pinks—when Pedro found the gully that he wanted. Trotting down, they heard the roar of combat and spurred their horses toward echoes of the battle, amplified by the canyon as by some stone instrument. Riding around a bend they attacked the Indians from the rear. *"Dios ayude, y Santiago!"*

Attacked from both front and rear, the Indians became compressed into a mass so compact that some added a second level to the combat, climbing onto shoulders. When killed, they floated on a sea of men. But their savage suicidal urge must have reached some inner limit, for they began to scale the defile and the *caballeros* hacked at legs. Then it was over.

The dead and wounded almost reached a horse's chest, and they had to clear a path through the carnage to regroup with Villagrán. All were proud of Juan, yet he was despondent. The Valley of Death—as he called it from that moment—was in no way noble, but more like pounding people in a *metate*. Stomach churning, he flung his bloody sword away.

That evening Pedro cleaned and oiled his armor, glancing at his *hijo* while going over the battle with Valdivia. What did it mean, strategically, that the savages had progressed to confrontation?

Mending in twilight, Inés also glanced at Juan from time to time. Something was bothering her hero.

Juan knew Valdivia would not take his problem seriously, and Pedro would feed him banal soldiers' pap. Even Inés would not understand. She was too, what...? Spanish, was what she was. Her heart was warm and wonderful, but fierce. She hated Moors and Jews, despite her ambivalence about Indians. Lobo was the one to understand....

Juan found him praying on his knees on stone, and said, "That battle was horrible."

"Dulce bellum inexpertis."

"It's sweet indeed, in books."

"Have you come to confess?"

Juan knelt to be blessed, and as war was not in breviaries, he wondered what to call his sin.

"Bless me Father, for I have sinned," he said, "I killed many Indians. I do not know their number."

"Did they attack you?"

"Yes."

"Would they kill every member of the expedition if they could?"

"Yes, Father, except maybe for some *piezas*."

"Then, my son, you did not sin. You protected the expedition, and by extension Holy Mother the Church, for whose message we are the living vessels."

Juan wept into his hands.

Lobo urged, "*Hijo*, of all cruel necessities, there is none more than war. But think, where would Spain be if she had not fought the Moors? Even **Utopia** had its soldiers...."

At this not-so-distant echo of Pedro defending torture, Juan thought that—of all people—Lobo missed the point. "Almagro came before us, making them our enemies."

"What did he *do*?"

"He killed them, took their food. And their women had ... bad things happen."

"Should they seek more civilized redress I would gladly plead their cause, but can I do this if they kill me? These savages are worse than Chunchos, and I only hope that, south, they will more incline to love and learning. But I have serious doubts about that."

Lobo made the sign of the cross over Juan, adding, " You are the first to confess to me the killing of an Indian, and may God bless you for that. Though what you did was in no way good, it was right and just. Go in peace."

Pedro was sitting by a dying fire, whetting a sword. "*Hijo*, are you all right?"

Juan shrugged.

Giving the blade a last polish Pedro held it out. "I believe this weapon fits your scabbard."

Absorbing Juan's shrug, Pedro persisted. Too large and deadly to have to lie, he hated falsehood anyway, on principle. Therefore he had to stick a little finger in his ear and search for wax, before producing his diplomatic enormity—"*Hijo* ... hem ... you must have dropped your sword...."

"*Muchas gracias*," Juan said, moved by the transparent beauty of the fabrication, for he was being offered love in the only version Pedro knew. Lobo was right—if they could, Indians would kill faithful Pedro, brilliant Valdivia, Inés of the burning hair.

"Sheathe it," Pedro urged, uneasy.

Immaculate, the edge cut the night with a perfect line of reflected fire, making Juan realize that in wilderness nothing was straight as swords. Here there was no truer rectitude, and in that light Pedro was the counterpart. Heartsick, Juan slid his steel into its oiled fit.

Just as well, for they had ridden to a place where violence suffused the very air.

The land had changed, alive with shrubs and small trees reminding Juan of laurel and acacia. The river valleys seemed an untamed Andalucía. And the natives—who called themselves Picunche—fought with absurd tenacity, ignoring defeat after defeat, their ferocity increasing, as the land grew greener … as if here rain watered not just plants, but courage.

At Valdivia's insistence, Inés put on a vest of quilted wool, dying it black to match her skirt. A helmet she would *not* wear, stating that she would sooner have an arrow through her head than wear a smelly pot. She had a point, since helmets were often used for cooking, and the remaining food combined with sweat to form a nameless compound that *infantes* claimed would stop a blow as well as steel. Most helmets stank.

Inés also protected her larger animals. 'Pigs in quilt' became a joke … and one day *infantes* strapped a discarded helmet on a boar. *Don Jamón de la Cocina Negra*—Sir Ham of the Black Kitchen—they called him, intending to put a pointed beard and mustaches on him too. Shocked, Inés forbade this parody of Valdivia.

Horses were lost to Indians, but no Spaniards. There was a steady attrition of *piezas* however. Sending no further delegation, the Indians kept up the unhurried pace that would carry them to the world's end under amazing loads, if only they had their *coca*. However, at the valley of the Coquimbo, the expedition woke to find that most had vanished. They took with them items intended for trade—hawk's bells, small metal mirrors and glass beads…. The executioner's ax also turned up missing.

Burdens were redistributed, impossibly loading the remaining *yanaconas*. Some surplus was loaded on warhorses. Much had to be left behind, so that they feasted on what could not be carried. What remained they burned along with the fields and huts of the Indians.

They marched. Uncounted Picunche died, uncounted *piezas*. A horse was lamed and slaughtered. One *cristiano* lost an eye, another a finger. A certain Díaz was mortally wounded pursuing a Picunche. He threw his lance and missed, and somehow managed to impale himself on the butt of his own weapon. It took two men to pull it free, he screaming all the while.

During the Requiem Mass sung for his soul a miracle happened—rain, that forgotten blessing—and many knelt to pray. The more practical collected water in their helmets, where it made thin soup of last night's meal. The cynical survivors of Almagro's disaster said that soon a daily rain of water would accompany the daily rain of arrows. The wetter this land, the more vicious its Indians, giving you a choice of death by thirst or arrow.

At the valley Almagro called Chile—and the Picunche Aconcagua—the fighting intensified as predicted, not so much a change in kind as in relentlessness.

The passes were blocked with logs and stones, forcing the Spanish to dismount and climb to fight, or else waste time in flanking. Also, the Picunche were learning about horses.

Every league was contested. And the nights, if anything, were worse. Three *cristianos* perished in as many days—counting Díaz—when not one had died in the Atacama. Tortured Indians revealed that Michimalongo—a great *toki*—led the resistance. He had sent runners everywhere with arrows dipped in blood. It was said that if the *lik winka* continued their advance all the *che* to beyond the Bío Bío would be united, as against the *winka* that came before them.

Valdivia released captives bearing trinkets for Michimalongo, promising more gifts if he would only meet in peace. Daily attacks were the only response, and the expedition was growing sullen, mutinous....

One evening, Valdivia snapped at Inés as she was leaving to see to her animals. "Time to tuck Don Jamón into bed, eh?" The Lieutenant Governor spat into the fire, "*Cagüenlostia!* I hate that *hideputa* pig!"

Every soldier swore, of course—this being as much part of the calling as the sword—yet never had Juan heard Valdivia this foul before Inés, even when drunk. The pig had touched his quick. Had he *heard* about the helmet and stiletto beard?

At Valdivia's words the head of Inés jerked sharply to the side, as if physically struck. Love offering no defense, she stiffly strode away.

Juan ran after, and she took his hand in the tremble of her cool grip.

"I will not cry over a pig," she said—Juan thought—ambiguously.

"Valdivia didn't mean it."

Inés had mercy, saying only, "Mean *what*?"

"To hurt you."

"I'm not hurt. I'm furious!"

"He needs you," Juan pleaded. "And we need *him*."

"I know," Inés sighed. Proud head bent, she wrapped her arms around herself—a fighting ship upon a sea of grief. Valdivia had begun to fail her.

When they reached the sty, Juan blurted, "He's jealous,"

Inés could not believe him. "Of a *pig*!"

"He showed signs," said Juan, improvising. "You must admit this is a handsome porker."

On the spot they rechristened him *Don Jamón de la Barba Ausente*—Sir Ham of the Absent Beard. And Inés was smothering laughter—exploding with it—pounding Juan on the back, when Valdivia walked up.

"Am I interrupting something?"

The Lieutenant Governor was piqued. He had come to apologize to a devastated lady, and there she was, cackling and shrieking. It hurt him that she took his nastiness so lightly.

Inés pivoted, and—with the solemnity of queens bestowing knighthood—tapped Valdivia's shoulder, saying, "You are forgiven."

They exited, she whispering clove scented words into his helmet.

Juan was left with Don Jamón, who masticated with the shallow philosophy of his kind, slobber dangling silver from his snout, no less oblivious of the disasters threatening the expedition than of the fact he owed his life to Inés. By ignorance, this boar was blessed. If things got worse, Juan thought, he would be jealous of a pig.

On the morning of the feast of Santa Lucía— the thirteenth of December, 1540—Valdivia sat his horse in silence before a river valley stretching blue-green under serried hills that rose to mountains. Be this nowhere—or not—they had arrived at last.

East, loomed snow-capped mountains. Copper in color, they were shadowed with purple. To the west a lesser range hid the Southern Sea. South, hills displayed a muted palette—dove gray, uncertain greens, the dull orange of old brick. This valley, cupped by heights, was broad and fertile—a forested bowl. Here and there were wisps of smoke amid meadows and irrigated fields. Through it all wandered a quicksilver river, splitting to create an island with two hills.

Juan asked himself—What was an isolated valley in an isolated land, with an island in the river at its center … if not an island, in an island, in an island? This new Eden, were it such, was figuratively thrice walled. Could this be Lobo's Fortunate Isle?

A spring breeze promised heat. Insects chirped and whirred with placid voices. A cloud of yellow butterflies flickered by with silent purpose. Valdivia reached for the image of the Virgin painted on wood that always hung from his saddle, and kissed it. "God be praised!" he said.

Uncontested, they reached the island and set up camp beneath the eastern hill which split the river like a boat's prow, Valdivia christening it Santa Lucía after the day of their arrival. In the meadow where they camped, pink and purple flowers grew. Inés was ecstatic over the pasture, the fields, the abundant water, but did not like the woods. No one liked woods.

Valdivia and Pedro agreed that the island was defensible. The hills could be fortified. There was water in case of siege, timber for palisades….

Juan ignored their considerations, thinking the place beautiful—not just because memories of the Atacama made every other place seem better. Though verdant, this valley held nothing like the obscene growths of Panama, and here the temperature was perfect. In addition, there had been no Indian attacks. The huts they came to were empty as the fields, the only fires distant. Maybe their travail was over.…

He set up tent with Pedro, and after helping Inés with her animals, walked to the river and along the bank, removing his boots when out of sight of camp. The river here was wide and deep, clear over stone. He knelt and drank … came to where a sandbar embraced a pool under overarching trees. A gray bird with a black head sang with a tumbling trill. The pool was dappled by shadow. A school of fish hung suspended there like glittering fingers, heads pointing in the same direction.

Juan capered barefoot on the sandy shore. And since dancing in steel was absurd, he stripped to shirt and hose, trying to remember when last he was this foolish. Sillier yet, he removed what little clothing remained and waded into the river, thinking that—although here he did not recognize a single plant or bird—water was everywhere its blessed self. He sank until the chilly pleasure reached his chin, his tackle floating, then exploded to the shore in a shower of spray and hopped to warm himself.

He sat—feet piercing clarity—examining a body he had not seen for months, his hands like gloves tanned on his pallor by the Atacama. And on his hands the hairs were gold … much darker against the whey of untanned skin. Light on dark, dark on light. I'm white and Indian both, he thought. I'm motley, yet more white than not. Fish nibbled on the hairs of his legs, a wonderful sensation. Did they eat hair? He closed his eyes, tried not to giggle. Then he realized that he was famished, and in the pool were fish….

He knotted the ankles of his hose—which badly needed washing anyway—and with them herded a school to shallows, trapping so many darting fingerlings that he filled his helmet with them. They seemed untroubled as they flopped—eyes round and clear, fish-faces expressionless—making Juan wonder if they knew fear and pain.

Inés was delighted by the helmetful, tossing the contents whole into a soup. By way of celebration she added spices from Peru. And Valdivia passed around a skin of rancid wine that he had hoarded, which made of it the perfect evening.

Wakened by roosters, Juan crept out his tent. Stars were still visible, the sun a pale promise over the *cordillera*. Only the guards were awake, cloaked at their posts, making him think of chessmen bored with waiting for the next move. Juan was let pass, for the secretary to Valdivia was said to be too refined to crap outside his tent.

He had wading on his mind instead, and this morning the pool was as magical but different—a silver mirror over which mist writhed … *houris* in a twirl of veils. Crowding the banks were crimson flowers, shaped like trumpets, and about them tiny insects hung suspended in the air, a sentient dust. Juan heard a hum … saw a jewel feeding on a blossom, tiny in a fog of wings. The back was emerald, shining also with gold and ruby. The breast was white, speckled like ermine. Afraid to frighten this denizen of a fairy world Juan held his breath, and saw the second tiny miracle. Twin jewels floated in the air, sipping from crimson trumpets.

They flicked from sight, and Juan made out a shadow in the woods … dressed in black with a featureless black face, blank as the yawning mouth of Hell. Juan grabbed his armor and ran, sprinting by the startled watch at the gate, dodging early risers, bursting into his tent with a violence that had Pedro reaching for his sword.

"What, *hijo*? *What!*"

"I saw an Indian with no face!"

Pedro pulled on his boots, preparing for war but not expecting it. Juan was surely seeing things again, and … why was he wearing only boots and wool? "Put on your armor," he chided.

Juan exhaled and obeyed, grabbed *charqui* and ate. He was saddling his horse when trumpets sounded the alarm

Indians were emerging from the forest at the clearing's edge and massing there, so numerous they seemed a single thing, arranging themselves according to weapon. In their order they reminded Juan of grains of maize, though he had never seen a menace so immense.

He galloped off to search for Pedro, but the confusion was too great, the battle developing too rapidly. The Indians were already in motion, keeping formation as they broke into a run, hoarsely roaring now—a surf.

The Spanish line of battle formed as a crescent to protect the camp. Juan spurred Amadís to join them at the left, seeing that Pedro was by Valdivia at the center. Not more than fifty *caballeros* ranged themselves against the tide of warriors.

Horsemen hurried up, adjusting armor as they rode. Marmolejo joined Juan, silver hair escaping from his helmet as if a halo had slipped down to frame his face. No less calm than in confession, he told Juan to stay close. God would protect them.

Behind them the many *infantes* with their spears, and the few arquebusiers, assembled. *Yanaconas* deployed to the flanks, readying their primitive weapons. Juan made out the attackers as painted men, mouths open in wild stuttering screams, naked legs a blur in the meadow's green….

Valdivia raised his sword and spurred his horse. "*Santiago!*"

Amadís surged forward.

The armored charge slammed the warriors in front against the rows behind, creating a windrow of dead and floundering wounded. The disciplined Indian ranks became disorganized as they pressed forward over bodies, falling to the work of hooves, swords, maces, lances. Yet the savage discipline held.

Now every *caballero* was engaged. One went down floundering, buried by exultant Indians … dying—as it was discovered later—of a spear in the eye. Eager to kill before they died themselves, Picunche were sinking weapons into the belly of the great downed beast.

Marmolejo led the charge exacting justice—Juan at his side—and the battle soon merged with memories of battles past. Perhaps Valdivia could tell one carnage from another, not Juan. Indians *always* outnumbered you, yet only so many could fight with you at once, which made them resemble water. You could drown in a tiny stream or in the Ocean Sea, or you could swim in both if you knew how. Whatever their number, when you fought Indians you did exactly the same thing to survive. You confronted perhaps two to five, who fell, replaced by others. You grew used to your living and their dying. Victory was as inevitable as weariness and sunset.

Today gradually became different, the disciplined Indians driving the Spanish crescent of *caballeros* back into the line of *infantes* and arquebusiers—there held in reserve with Mendoza and his dogs.

An order echoed down the line. The *caballeros* pivoted and galloped through sudden gaps in the line of *infantes*, quickly closed. The spearmen dropped to a knee, creating an uninterrupted row of honed steel at the height of a man's belly. Behind them the arquebusiers—matches trailing smoke, weapons propped on forked sticks—waited for the command to fire over their heads.

Tasting victory, with a scream of joy the Picunche charged.

Valdivia barked orders. One third of the horsemen would flank the Indians to the right, another to the left. The last third would back up the *infantes*. Himself a part of that number, Juan saw that in an instant the arquebuses would fire. In another, the Indians would impale themselves on the spears of the *infantes* and overwhelm them with their numbers. An instant after that they would overrun the arquebusiers before they could reload, and he would again be fighting. Incredibly, the inevitable Spanish victory was beginning to resemble a defeat.

Hearing thunder greater than that of guns, Juan looked up to see that gloom had overspread the sky. The clouds he had admired by the pool had grown into an echo of the struggle on the ground. A tormented sky the gray of lead was now attacking the *cordillera*, and so it was that Juan actually *saw* the miracle. The arquebuses fired, and he was blinded. Shielding his eyes he thought the clouds had parted briefly, so that he glimpsed the sun. The coincidence was extraordinary—of flash and salvo—as if the roar of firearms required lightning.

Later he discovered that appearances had deceived him. Clouds had parted, not to the sun but to Heaven Itself. At the time—cursing himself as a distracted fool—Juan scanned the scene for the Indians that should have overrun the *infantes*, perceiving none in his dazzlement. Sight returning, he saw the Picunche now disorganized. A handful broke and ran, followed by hundreds. Then thousands turned their backs and raced in chaos for the forest, shouting.

Incredulous, Juan contemplated the rout, as if he had blinked and opened his eyes to a different world … and in the end, this battle proved no different after all. The *caballeros* sent to flank the Indians began to kill them, as Juan's companions spurred their horses through the *infantes*, eager to compound the victory. "*Dios ayude, y Santiago!*"

Juan sat his horse, having no stomach for this seal on victory—though Pedro argued that the first principle of war was to kill as many enemy as possible in the shortest possible time. If you shrank from *this* you were good as dead yourself.

The *caballeros* pursued the Picunche far as the forest, killing hundreds, taking captives. And when the prisoners were interrogated, the strange day grew stranger. Speaking broken Quechua to the *yanaconas*—who translated into broken Spanish—the Pikunche told a story which was in every way contradictory, save for the fact that a bright warrior appeared from clouds, killing with lightning.

An excited *infante* said the savages were right. With his God-given eyes— *pardiez!*—he saw Santiago descending from Heaven on his white horse, sword raised to smite the heathen. Others added detail…. Santiago's armor was a blinding mirror crusted with precious stones. White plumes nodded on his helm. His horse—shod in gold—galloped down shafts of light. He fought the entire Indian army, killing hundreds, before disappearing into clouds. The very Santiago who fought the Moors in Spain, today had turned back Indian hordes. A miracle!

Juan cursed himself for missing the only wonder in his life, though he had been staring at its glory. Had he been blinded by Santiago's armor? Scanning memory, he caught no hint of helm or sword, white plumes, jewels, golden horseshoes….

Marmolejo had seen only the backs of Indians attempting to evade his sword. However, hearing of the miracle he interviewed witnesses, who provided testimony convincing in its lack of contradiction—same bright armor, same sword, same white horse. Through interpreters Marmolejo asked Picunche captives why they fled, and they described a man in the clouds.

Pillan, they insisted—a word difficult to translate through Quechua to Spanish. Marmolejo gathered that a *pillan* was a dead man in the clouds … in other words a saint. This became unassailable proof, as issuing from the mouths of the unwilling infidels themselves. The Spanish might have seen what Spanish hearts desired to see. For Indians to *invent* Santiago was impossible.

Removing his helmet—as if suddenly in church—falling to his knees, weeping with joy, Marmolejo declared the miracle a solid fact. And he sang Mass on an impromptu altar made of boards lashed to the forked sticks of arquebuses. To commemorate the miracle Valdivia ordered a church built at the foot of the hill Santa Lucía.

That evening, at the insistence of his *hijo,* Pedro rode with him to a pool in the river, finding only the water and unhealthy proliferation of greenery that he expected. Pedro had a profound mistrust of forests. They reeked of ambush—especially in these parts, where trees grew Indians like nasty fruit. Were he God, he would eliminate all plants not useful, replacing them with grapes. As for the river he had been brought to see, he liked it little more, for in water one could drown.

Juan saw that the hummingbirds were gone. Two apparitions in one day, he thought, one that he alone had seen and Pedro now discounted, and the descent of Santiago in his radiance, which he managed to miss while looking straight at it.

"Pedro," said Juan, "I saw the sun when all others saw the Saint. I think I was just blinded." Feeling unworthy, he asked, "Did *you* see anything?"

"I was busy fighting."

Pedro was testy, not mentioning that in his experience, worst soldiers experienced apparitions best. In his many years, in battle, never had he even *glimpsed* Santiago out of the corner of his eye. And he was chagrined that the patron saint of fighting men—whom he revered little less than the Virgin—should be revealed to such *infantes* as upon whose boots he would not bother spitting. Also, he was doubly depressed that today things were looking grim before the miracle. The saint obviously felt that his chosen people had botched the battle and intervention was necessary to set the martial muddle right.

The camp was not depressed, however, abuzz at the phenomenon, and the last of the wine was broken out. It was rancid, musty—indescribably foul after crossing a desert in bladders. Yet it had kept some blessed kick. Juan abstained after the first taste.

As neither Inés nor Valdivia witnessed the apparition, they interviewed the priests. Particularly puzzling was the fact that no *yanacona*—and only a handful of *cristianos*— had seen Santiago in his glory, while many Picunche captives had....

Inés proposed that Picunche witnesses to the glory had their feet slowed by awe, and therefore were captured in larger numbers. Valdivia disagreed, thinking they would be the fastest runners in the bunch.

Perhaps Santiago appeared largely to those he meant to kill, Juan suggested, lamely.

Lobo pointed out the not insignificant number of Spaniards who saw him. And he offered the possibility that, like children, in their innocence Picunche were closer to God. Therefore He granted this vision to them.

Unconvinced, Valdivia was truculent. If these Picunche 'innocents' had been part of the Children's Crusade they would have overrun the Holy Land in weeks!

The battle was going from bad to worse before Santiago's intervention. What these savages were innocent of was of peace! And what about the *yanaconas*? he somewhat nastily inquired of Lobo. They were "childlike," too, and not one had seen Santiago.

Incas were not *exactly* Indians, Lobo responded, distracted, wondering if Santiago had different criteria for manifesting himself, and what they might be, or mean.

The argument grew protracted, and it was halted—not settled—late at night by Marmolejo, who had been silently eating with the appetite of warriors. Politely belching, benevolently he blessed his friends. "My children, as I see it a miracle *is* perplexing, else it would have another name." This mildly said, he retired to sleep.

"*Quod erat demonstrandum*," Lobo muttered, sarcastic, following after. No one had been swayed to his argument for Picunche innocence. And—in deep, sad truth—he was losing his own faith in Indians.

While getting into bed, Valdivia proposed to Inés that they call this place Santiago, and she replied that this made more sense than anything else she heard that evening. Inés agreed with Marmolejo that excessive discussion of matters of faith led to quibbling and heresy—as in distant northern lands where they drank beer and opposed the Pope. Lobo had always been suspect to her as a disciple of Erasmus. Everybody knew that this monk was little better than a Luther.

Taking to his cot, Juan thought that 'nowhere' was exactly where you were when you stopped marching south. Also, 'nowhere' was where you ended up when you stopped arguing about miracles. In some way 'nowhere' *was* the miracle, like the jeweled birds by the river. And what of the Indian with the black, blank face?

Two apparitions in one day—one black, one bright ... one visible, one not. Two mysteries and one miracle ... one interesting to one, the other intriguing all. The symmetries and differences seemed related. Was this constellation of meaning simply a fabrication of his mind?

Black and bright. White knight. Black pawn.

Out of armor and in wonderful thick wool, drowsy in his warm corner of 'nowhere,' Juan slept with mysteries erased by waking.

Chapter 11: *Welen* (Valley of the Mapocho, 1540-1541)

Silent as an otter, brilliant moon lighting his path, Ñamku swam the Mapocho, senses heightened by great danger. Soon he would be face to face with *lik winka*. This was the fate that made him white. And it awaited him, across the river at Welen … that hill Pikunche had named Sorrow.

They reached the Mapocho after a walk of a half *kuyen*. And he did not discuss the mysterious *wethakelu* with Michimalongko, the *toki* far too busy massing his warriors, no longer interested in understanding these strange invaders he intended to crush with overwhelming force.

Ñamku offered to scout the enemy camp, and Michimalongko gladly agreed, for the *machi* could vanish, leaving no trace. Some said he turned into a bird of darkness, others that he became a disembodied *pellu* … a soul sensed only as a breeze. Perhaps he would discover something Michimalongko did not know already, from moons of fighting *lik winka*.

The *toki* said they would attack at *pichilewechi antu*, whether he had returned or not. Ñamku nodded, stepped behind a huge *peweñ* and disappeared, leaving his husk hanging from a branch like the shells of grubs with claws that clamber unseen from the earth to spread their wings and fly into the night.

The moon-path brought Ñamku to the shore, and he found the *lik winka* where they were said to be. There were guards by fires, standing like posts stuck in the ground, or noisily striding about. Amazing! He was no expert in combat, yet as a Mapuche he knew that warfare often required silence and concealment. Could this be the insolence of the invincible? Maybe they *wanted* to be seen and heard, like *pichiche* in fields of *uwa*, frightening parrots with their shouting. If so, this audacity bred of strength might prove a weakness….

Nothing was white about the guards. Still, their heads glittered no less than the path he had just swum. Creeping the camp, Ñamku saw other *lik winka* by small fires. His eye caught shining, as of silver. The smell of burning meat was everywhere. There were other odors—some unpleasant, most unknown. The *lik winka* had made small *ruka* out of blankets, too small to have fires in them.

One with shadow, Ñamku made it past a dozing guard to behind a blanket *ruka*. Four *lik winka* sat around the fire, gabbling like hoarse geese. And it was true that tails grew on their faces. None was white as he.

He silently mouthed the impossible sounds he was hearing. A *lik winka* belched, and Ñamku smiled, not needing to mouth *that*. He noted that the tails on their faces varied, like the tails of *luan*. Had their ancestors coupled with the four-legged creatures of the beginning? And how had they confused their ends, when even animals could tell them apart? Smiling, Ñamku realized he had lost respect for the unknown he came so far to meet. Michimalongko respected them as warriors, but here he was *mari nufku* from them, and not one was aware of his presence. Emboldened by their blindness, Ñamku wormed his way toward a blanket *ruka*. Looking under the dark wool he saw *lik winka* feet, not bare or in sandals, but curiously covered with what looked like leather. He listened to their *lik winka* babble with strained attention. Forgetting in his curiosity that he was as *pudu* in the den of *pangui*, he crawled closer.

Feet in noisy leather came around the blanket *ruka*. Toward him! The *machi* tensed. Had they been playing with him? Should he run or remain in shadow? Fear deciding, he did nothing.

The feet stopped one *nufku* from Ñamku's head, so close that he could smell them. He waited to die in some unknown way ... and the *lik winka* pissed not far from his ear, long and loud, sighing with satisfaction.

This was the insult before the execution, Ñamku told himself. But he was wrong, for the *lik winka* left. And not long after, another relieved himself where Ñamku had been lying, the *machi* watching from the safety of a nearby tree. He was astounded. A *lik winka* had been close enough to reek—to piss on him!—in a night with a bright half moon! Like blind men they would have to step on him to find him. Perhaps their strange eyes could not see at night. Perhaps blue eyes like blue sky were for the day, and dark eyes for the night. Yet his own—red as sunsets—preferred darkness.

The *lik winka* slept save for the guards pacing in the open, where they were as easy to slip around as slow-moving trees. Ñamku had seen much and understood nothing— except the belch and piss. And none of it had anything to do with the bent stick that was too heavy, the leaves covered in leather, the bone *che*. He had nothing useful to report to Michimalongko save that, as *lik winka* seemed blind in moonlight, it might be better to attack at night. The thought struck him—Were they also *deaf* at night? He risked chirping like insects, subtly wrong. When there was no response he did it boldly, more strangely, taking pleasure in this joke, as Llcflai sometimes did. He could imagine her, with that amazing ear for the sounds of the forest, laughing at his inventions. The guards ignored Ñamku's every nonexistent insect, and he grew wild in his improvisations, now boldly whistling like the birds of day, but the guards ignored this impossibility no less than the snoring *lik winka* warriors.

Flooded by strange joy, Ñamku improvised the sounds of creatures that did not exist. He whistled, warbled, chirped, chuck-chucked, even softly quacked, imagining the impossible animals of his invention—sparrowswans, wrenfinches, ducklarks, quailthrushes, eagleflamingoes, gullpeckers. He created birds until night dimmed, then left his perch for the safety of the forest. The *lik winka* traveled only in crowds and were always noisy—he had been told—especially the enormous ones, so that it was impossible to be surprised by them. Yet bone-deep habit kept him silent in the shadows.

Ñamku was about to step into the Mapocho when he saw a *lik winka* less than *mari nufku* away. He merged into the shadow of a tree, thinking that he had been wrong again—a *lik winka* had stalked him, proving that they could be silent. He did not seem a warrior though, silently sitting with his legs stretched out—a young *lik winka* with hair to his shoulders, no tail on his face, dressed in sand-colored wool. He was looking at humming birds, and nothing silver was on him.

The hummingbirds disappeared, and the *lik winka* looked directly at Ñamku with the impossible eyes described by the messenger—at once blue and green, like a river or the evening sky … like *likan* … like nothing Ñamku had ever seen … like nothing made to *see* with. And these eyes betrayed a perfectly ordinary fear.

The *lik winka* with eyes like sacred stones fled floundering, making immense noise, stumbling, trampling plants, leaving a trail a blind man with no hands or stick could follow, a trail that could lead *lik winka* directly back to Ñamku. Stunned, he slipped into the Mapocho and swam. And not long after he reached the farther shore he heard the sounds of battle. Michimalongko had attacked.

Running swiftly—a distance lengthened by curiosity and old age—then climbing a tree, Ñamku saw the Pikunche fight with order, tenacity and courage, killing many *winka* that were not white, and his heart soared. Then the enormous ones he had heard of—*lik winka* with four legs, two heads, two arms and a tail—attacked, so heavy that they shook the earth. Ñamku did not have to be *weichafe* to know that nothing could stop them, any more than *che* could withstand the great waves *pillañ* sometimes sent from the great sea after they shook *mapu*.

Some *winka* that were not white now were fleeing. The *che* tasted victory, roaring defiance and shaking their weapons in the face of the shining might that rolled toward them at impossible speed. But their defiance, their discipline and strength, their weapons, were as nothing when the thundering mountain struck. They were flung back, hacked, trampled and crushed, on fields green with *uwa, dawe, poñu*. Dying in great numbers they regrouped, returned and fell, fought and fell—waves breaking on the shores of death.

Ñamku could not believe his eyes. The *lik winka* by the river who had eyes like *likan* had clearly been afraid. And the *lik winka* by the fires were not four-legged, enormous—although sometimes they shone like silver. Maybe *lik winka* grew more legs and a second head at sunrise. None of this made sense, but sense was now a thing of the past. Ñamku cursed the *lik winka*, cursed the new beginning they had brought.

In their sorrow the *pillañ* had come as witnesses, and tempestuous they echoed with their turmoil the day that would be forever remembered by the name Welen. Then, hearing thunder crash over the battle, Ñamku saw a shaft of light that was not lightning illuminate the fields of death. Ceasing to fight, many *weichafe* looked at the clouds, crying out '*pillañ*.' Then they were running, cut down from behind, falling like grain to the harvester.

Ñamku cursed the sky.

The *weichafe* of the *aillarewe*—those still alive and not seriously wounded—gathered in a clearing burnt for future fields. There they sat exhausted on cinder, on blackened stumps, discussing what should be done, a few taking turns addressing the assembly of survivors. Many were harshly critical of Michimalongko.

Ñamku found Pichikan and Tuiñam unharmed, covered only by the blood of others. Neither had seen the *lik winka pillañ* in the clouds—the apparition being excitedly discussed. They had shot their arrows then fought with club and spear. Both had struck the mighty *lik winka* but—Pichikan said—it was like hitting boulders, for nothing happened. Each claimed the other had saved his life, blocking blows from the long knives of the *lik winka*. An amazing weapon, this *wif winu* ... silver—not obsidian— and so sharp it cut off heads! Pichikan proposed thicker leather shields, heavier clubs. Tuiñam was for longer spears, and they agreed that never had there been an enemy like this. To fight them was an honor. To lose to them and live was a strange victory.

The *toki* sat in a semicircle, Michimalongko at their center, facing the assembly of *weichafe*. The leader of the *aillarewe* was small but powerful, with pronounced cheekbones and close-set, piercing eyes—the implacable countenance of eagles. He had fought with insane courage, leading the first attack, one of the few to survive. His ribs were cut to the bone— a wound he ignored, too furious at the flight of his *weichafe* to notice. He proposed attacking again immediately, pointing out that many *winka* who were not white and several *lik winka* had fallen. And they had been retreating until the *lik winka pillañ* appeared.

Others rose to speak in opposition, numerous *weichafe* grunting assent and striking *mapu* with the butts of their spears.

The war council was bitter and hostile, worried and divided, argumentative. Bitter, because almost everyone had lost a friend or relative ... hostile in the need to place blame ... worried that *lik winka pillañ* were more powerful than their own ... divided by an enemy without precedent. As for argument, this was usual with Mapuche.

Michimalongko led by a consensus built on reputation, and under him today the Pikunche had suffered a rout so total as to be incomprehensible, with no *ruka* that would not mourn. It was murmured that the *toki* did not have the support of the *pillañ*. The *aillarewe* was disintegrating.

Ñamku went to help with the wounded and found Lleflai cradling the head of a *weichafe* who had air bubbling through a wound on his neck. And when he died they worked late into the night by the light of torches, helping *domo* tend to their sons and husbands. Many wounds were like none he had ever seen—straight, deep and clean. *Weichafe* were missing hands and arms. One—a small hole through him—was dying of thunder.

When Ñamku at last attempted sleep he could not rest, so he set out the unfinished blanket of Rayentru, folded it for Katrinir, and waited in muddled stupor for answers to questions he did not know to ask until—like *cherufe*—Katrinir glowed over the blanket....

Shaking his head with sorrow he said, "*Ayun fotem*—Dear child." And—taking the hands of Ñamku in his own long, cold fingers—he added, "Sleep."

Katrinir—who had not aged one *antu* since his death, and was now young enough to be his child—said only this and disappeared. Sick at heart, weary of body and wearier of mystery, Ñamku slept. His rest was brief, however, for more wounded were brought in. Many of them died that night with the silence that was the courage of the dying, by the silence of the living that was tribute to them.

The war council convening the next morning agreed on nothing. Some *che* from distant *ruka* left. The *weichafe* of the valley of the Mapocho—for whom leaving was least possible—argued the most fiercely. When only two belligerent groups remained, warriors captured in battle appeared, bearing *lik winka* gifts and an offer of peace.

Michimalongko was scornful. Such gifts they had already seen—some were useless *wethakelu* and made no sense, others were ornaments only fit for women. This was less an offer of peace than a bartering of servitude for safety. Nonetheless, some who counseled peace went to the *lik winka*, returning with more gifts. They had listened to an unintelligible speech, yet one thing was clear—the *lik winka* wanted help building *ruka*. This was a small thing to trade for peace, they argued.

Like fat tossed on coal, the realization that *lik winka* had come to stay, taking their land and *ruka*, made tempers flare. Those in favor of war said that it was now inescapable. Those opposed said their staying made peace all the more necessary. If *lik winka* could not be overcome they would have to learn to live with them.

In the end each faction did as it proposed. Those favoring peace helped the *lik winka* build *ruka*, while Michimalongko prepared for war with many fewer *weichafe*, Pichikan and Tuiñam among them.

The Pikunche who went to build *ruka* listened to the speeches of a *lik winka machi* dressed in a black *kepam*. His dress was not surprising—being somewhat like that of a *domo*— yet everything else about him was. He made them kneel when he raised two sticks toward the sky and muttered with uplifted eyes. Ñamku asked them if one stick was short, one long, and if they were crossed. He was told they were. He asked if a *che* hung from the short stick and they said no, they thought the *lik winka machi* was just pointing at *wenu mapu*.

What could all this mean? Being near *lik winka* brought no answers. Seeing them was not enough. Hearing them was not enough. Ñamku had to *talk* to them, but how? Like lost ants maddened by the absence of a trail, a swarm of questions teemed, giving him no rest.

With Lleflai he erected a shelter in the scrubby, dry woods of the Pikunche— little more than a roof over a fire. Having no place of his own he had to leave to talk to the dead. He would set out the blanket of Rayentru, folded to reveal the unwoven section. In front of it he set the bone *che*, the leather *lik winka wethakelu*, and the heavy curved one. Then, facing the unknown and unfinished, he waited for Katrinir. Sometimes he touched these *wethakelu*, astounded that nothing happened when he did.

And when Katrinir appeared he brought patience as his counsel. He added— with a shadow of a smile—that a *machi* who was almost pissed on was a *machi* who might make mistakes. Irritable, Ñamku replied that of patience he had plenty … but he was too old to squander waiting.

"Do not sorrow," Katrinir responded, sorrowing.

"Michimalongko, Pichikan, Tuiñam know what to do," Ñamku complained. "*Lik winka* know what to do. I am the only one lost in a fog, not knowing what to do."

"What do you *truly* want?"

Ñamku said, "To be young, with you again, and apprenticed to a *lik winka machi.*"

"Young as the three *pichice*?"

Closing his eyes, Ñamku saw possibilities flicker on his eyelids like incandescent ants. Of course. But which of the three … or perhaps, all? Had not vision told him that taken together they were the strength and spirit of the *che*?

Katrinir smiled indulgently. "Think it over, Mapuche. But you are cold, old man. Build a proper *ruka* with a fire in it, and a nice place for us."

Four *antu* later Ñamku found the spot deep in the ravine of a mountain flank, far from Pikunche *ruka*. Pichikan and Tuiñam were puzzled … yet not much. From the *machi* they expected the unexpected, and he *always* lived apart. They felled and shaped heavy logs for the roof, arduous work that they turned into tests of skill and strength. Evenings, Pichikan taught Tuiñam the use of what he called the war spoon, hurling stones the size of eggs. And having erected the massive beams, they left for war.

The structure Ñamku had designed was in no way customary—a weighty roof pitched between immense, mossy rocks, cross-beams supporting smaller logs covered with earth. In effect this was an artificial cave, with a hidden entrance reached only by wading a stream whose smooth pebbles left no trace of feet.

When it was roofed, the *machi* began his absences. Lleflai dug a fire pit, removed rocks from the floor … brought in earth to make it level. She wove a door of saplings packed with clay and stone, creating an entrance that vanished to the eye between its boulders. And she planted a forest floor on the roof, including the saplings of mighty trees that would some day root in air.

She snared *degu*. One was pregnant, and soon there were newborn to be gentled. She made rope, clay pots, a loom, baskets and nets. She caught *puye* in the limpid stream. When all this—and more—was done, she needed a garden.

When she mentioned this to Ñamku he replied that nothing could betray the *ruka*. Lleflai whispered, "The *pichiche*!" with the intensity of a scream.

Ñamku sighed, torn between the counsel of the dead—who did not eat—and of the living … who did.

They dug the garden not far down the ravine, where the stream slowed around rich alluvial soil before breaking into cascades under over-arching bluffs. The site was small and shady, yet Lleflai and Ñamku found it good. He, because their presence remained invisible as care could make it … she, because the *pichiche* would eat well.

Pichikan and Tuiñam were with Michimalongko, preparing for war. The immense *lik winka* were everywhere, multiplying like rabbits—despite their size. They thundered about like avalanches, down hill and up, appearing here, appearing there, unopposed and bearing gifts, giving speeches. Sometimes they took prisoners, including women. Often—but not always— *lik winka* raped them.

One of these—named Treytraku—escaped, returning to her husband. To him she said that every morning she was made to listen to *lik winka machi*. After that she worked in fields, planting unknown seed. At night she was made to stay in the blanket *ruka* of a *lik winka* who always had her cook his meat. Then he slept with her.

He was big. Part of his right ear was missing. He stank and was covered with hard things he only took off at night to lie on her. Spitting at the memory, Treytraku said he coupled like a panting dog, with no apparent pleasure. The third night— wanting to die—she bit off the end of his nose and spat it in his face. He beat her senseless. When she came to he was snoring. She crawled away.

Mailef—her husband—picked up his spear and found Pichikan. Together they carried Treytraku—who was near death—to the *ruka* of Ñamku on a hide stretched between poles. Ñamku examined the shattered *domo*, and said there was little he could do.

Treytraku beckoned to her husband from by the fire pit, to whisper in his ear. He nodded an emphatic no. Again she whispered.... Bewildered, indignant, Mailef stalked from the strange *ruka* in the rocks, with its *degu* tame as dogs. The husband's place was by his wife at the *machitun*. He had been ready to support her with his love, to help her heal. He had been rejected in the moment of her deepest need ... and his.

When Mailef was gone Treytraku attempted to sit and failed, gasping with pain, coughing blood. Yet she was able to whisper that she needed to die.

"We will all die," Ñamku told her gently. "Why the hurry?"

She had lost teeth. Her nose, an arm, and several ribs were broken. She had internal injuries. He asked her what happened.

"A *lik winka* raped me. I bit off his nose. He hit me and kicked me with the heavy *wethakelu* on his feet."

"He wore them to lie with a *domo*!" exclaimed Ñamku—astonished into forgetting the suffering that looked into his eyes.

Treytraku insisted. "I *have* to die."

"*Kalku* kill, not *machi*," Ñamku chided softly. "Wait a few *antu*. It will not take long, I promise. I can give you something for the pain."

She persisted. "I need to die *before* Mailef looks upon my shame again." And she was harsh. "Do you always haggle like this?"

"No," replied Ñamku. "But, I could go speak to Mailef. We *machi* are trained in endless talking." Beyond words, the *domo* took a shuddering breath, nodding that she understood.

Ñamku removed his mask so that Treytraku could look into his face, then walked to where Mailef squatted by the stream—trembling with hate and sorrow— to explain to him at length why there was nothing he could do. They returned....

Treytraku had climbed the bench beside the fire pit and hung herself with the rope Lleflai used to smoke meat, so that her feet were swinging over coal. Black *ekull* over her head, she slowly spun.

Mailef tossed her smoldering sandals violently aside and cut her down.

There could be no comfort in words, yet Ñamku said them anyway. "Treitraku loved you very much. She was already dead with shame."

Mailef lashed back. "She was alive and beautiful, before *lik winka* came. The shame is theirs."

The *weichafe* returned to his *ruka*, gave the body to the *domo* of his kin, and mourned. Then, seeing his *kure* laid to rest, he shaved his head. Too full of hate to walk, he ran to war.

Pichikan and Tuiñam visited Ñamku, bringing parrots they had snared for Lleflai, and news…. *Pikunche* helping build *lik winka ruka* said that there was only one *lik winka domo*, who always dressed in black. Her hair was red as sunrise.

Lleflai gasped. Only one, with that many men! She burnt her finger on a pot.

The *weichafe* described *lik winka ruka*. Only the roofs were ordinary. The walls were logs! Imagine cutting down huge trees, dragging them, shaping them, *lifting* them … to make a *ruka* in ten *antu* that could be made in one! Pichikan laughed at the Pikunche, slaving for their enemies. The *lik winka* would not make *ruka* that stupid if they had to do the work themselves.

Tuiñam said that, incredibly, *lik winka ruka* had holes in the walls that let in wind and rain, yet they had no holes for smoke. And their fires were not in pits but inside piled stones. They stuck out through the roofs like hollowed trees.

Lleflai snorted, preparing stew. How did *lik winka domo* smoke meat and fish without a fire pit…?

Tuiñam had saved his most astonishing information. The enormous, shiny *lik winka* were not a single thing. It was a *lik winka* sitting on a beast like a *luan* but much bigger, not as wooly, called *kawell*.

"How does it know where to go and what to do," asked Ñamku.

It was said that they looked into the minds of *lik winka*.

As our dead into ours, Ñamku thought.

Later, in his dark corner of the *ruka*, braiding his long hair, he wondered if *lik winka machi* in their black *kepam* were as curious about *che* as he was about them. What marvels could they teach him…?

A voice not his cried out, "If only I could talk to them!"

Ñamku felt prickling in his arms and feet, as pinions and talons grew. The dark about him glowed. His spirit voice shrieked again. Then—as if insistence were the sun—he soared in clarity, suspended in a shaft of light piercing through cloud to *mapu*.

Folding his wings, Ñamku dropped—a taloned stone.

Below, three dark flecks grew in size.

Ñamku shrieked, "No!"

But the spirit hawk did not falter.

Struggling to free himself from himself, abruptly—as at the snap of a slow-bent stick— Ñamku floated, moon in the air of seeing what could not now be undone….

Shrieking, his spirit struck the first bird—a *traro*—bearing it to the ground in his talons, sending feathers spinning in the wind….

Morning sun shone late in the ravine.

Lleflai stirred *uwa* with ashes, lifting smooth stones—left overnight in coals—into the pot, hearing the hiss.

A hawk shrieked!

She returned to work, leaving Ñamku to his visions.

Wakened by the cry, the drowsy *pichiche* came to sit beside her. Then they were eating *uwa* and tossing kernels to *degu* when Ñamku staggered into her sight. He was unmasked, wild-eyed, long braid unkempt.

Lleflai stared, beyond politeness.

He sat as if his legs had given out.

Knowing he was suffering, Lleflai took his hands and looked into his eyes, seeing there another place, another time. As a hen to chicks, she chuckled softly to him. Then, unbraiding his hair, she felt him relax.

How could she know the *machi* most grieved for her?

Michimalongko was erecting a *fucha pele malal* like the ones *lik winka* built, so high and strong even *kawell* would not get through.

Ñamku went there and talked to Pikunche who had been helping build *lik winka ruka*, and asked them about their *machi*.

They called them *mañke* because they dressed in black and had no hair on their heads. Their baldness differed, though ... and the ruff was around their heads. These vultures mumbled while other *lik winka* listened, making the same long speech every morning while facing away from their audience, going mumble, mumble, mumble, so that even if you knew their language you could not understand a word. Sometimes they knelt. Sometimes they pointed their rears at the listeners. Sometimes everyone mumbled back. *Che* were expected to stand when the *lik winka machi* stood, kneel when they knelt ... but not expected to mumble or point back with their rears.

The same speech every day! Drowning in confusion Ñamku returned to his *ruka*. Orators did not repeat themselves. Also, orators were *weichafe*, not *machi*. They never mumbled and never wore *kepam*. And the *domo* who wore them would rather die than kneel and point their rears at anyone....

Lleflai woke to a pale bulk beside the firepit, her heart sinking with premonition. She dressed quickly, careful not to wake the *pichiche*. Ñamku was masked—a bad sign. And he was stirring coals, watching the glow he created darken.

"*Mari, mari*, Lleflai."

Waiting for the blow she brushed her hair as—far too gently—he said he desired her counsel.

She had always hated compliments, as blindness to her scars—a way of not seeing her as she was. In that sense, compliments were worse than stares. Praise was just one way of not being face to face with her. And now—from Ñamku! She suspected salve for a coming wound.

Seeing dread alter the mask that was her face, the machi reversed his prepared speech, stating the conclusion before its reasons. "It is the will of the *pillañ*," he said—clearing his throat—"that I take Lautaro to the *lik winka*."

The deft hands of Lleflai went numb, dropping to her lap, and she only found the strength to say, "Lautaro…?"

How like her, Ñamku thought, to expect worse, and he proceeded to his argument…. But his careful structure was shattered by her sorrow. Then, he rambled through its ruins as one might look for shards, burnt cloth, unable to rebuild what he did not himself believe.

She wanted nothing of bone *che* … of soaring … of the impenetrable fogs of the *pillañ*. As for new beginnings, every *pichiche* was exactly *that*, needing a mother to begin things right.

"Old *machi*," Ñamku responded sadly, "like the dead, can make mistakes. We are gambling with a precious life, ignorant of the outcome. But such is war. And this one will be won or lost on knowledge. If we lose, the Mapuche lose a child … perhaps. If we win, perhaps the Mapu*che* will survive the coming of the *lik winka*."

Awakened by their voices the *pichiche* straggled to the fire, and were sent immediately to the stream.

"Will he visit us?" asked Lleflai.

"He must, to remain Mapuche, and to pass on what he has learned."

"He will become *lik winka*," Lleflai exclaimed, thinking of her many moons of bitter life alone.

"Lautaro is Mapuche to the bone," Ñamku replied. And—mindful of the listening dead—he added, "Becoming something else is up to him."

"What if he refuses to go?"

"Ask. I do not intend to force this on him."

Two *antu* later the *machi* was fording the Mapocho near the hill Welen, to his chest in water—Lautaro and a large bundle on his shoulders—when thunder rolled toward them through woods at the farther shore. Perhaps ten *lik winka* on *kawell* appeared, approaching with unbelievable speed. Two abreast—striking sparks, scattering stones—the *kawell* surged into the river with a splash so great it created rainbows. Instants later the first *lik winka* stopped his great beast before Ñamku.

He was immense, covered with silver. On his face was a thick, black tail, threaded with gray. He loudly said a few incomprehensible words slowly—as to a *wed wed*. On his shoulder was a tiny and hairy, chattering *che*.

The *lik winka* shouted, gesturing Ñamku to the side with a shining arm … but the *machi* did not move. To allow passage to the huge *kawell* he would have to step off shallows. The bundle that Lleflai had lovingly prepared for Lautaro—blankets, clothes, and food—would be soaked. Ñamku was unarmed, yet obstinately he stood his ground, forgetting that he had a young *weichafe* on his shoulders....

Lautaro nocked a blunt arrow, drew, and shot. The immense *lik winka* clutched his throat. A long and brilliant weapon appeared in his hand.

Ñamku was about to hurl Lautaro to safety in the river when a second blunt arrow bounced off the silver of the *lik winka*. Then he began to roar with laughter through his black tail, bending over his *kawell*. Still laughing, he shouted to those behind him and they surged forward by Ñamku single-file, close enough to reek ... though he did not know what part of that was *lik winka*, what part wet *kawell*.

Lautaro shrieked, "I shot one!"

He was right to be proud, thought Ñamku, for if the arrow had been tipped with obsidian, the *lik winka* would not be laughing. Smiling, he told Lautaro absolutely not to shoot another.

They reached the shore. A short walk brought them to a door in a tall log fence, where a *lik winka* with a spear stared, but did not stop them. Inside there were gardens, *ruka* and ... naked *kawell*! Ñamku had never seen them so, no *lik winka* on their backs. Bare as *luan* they were eating grass, so that what many said was wrong—they were not some kind of dog.

Startled by a voice Ñamku spun to see—it had to be—a *lik winka machi*, for he wore a *kepam* and was bald as *mañke*. His face, hands and head were covered with tiny spots. And hanging from his waist was a bone *che* made of wood! The *lik winka machi* began to babble, incomprehensible as any stream.

Ñamku removed the bone *che* from his pouch, and the eyes of the *lik winka machi* widened, fingers dancing about his chest.

"*Mari, mari, lik winka machi,*" Ñamku said.

Greeting ignored, he was taken by the elbow and rudely led by many *ruka* crowded close together. Were *lik winka* only of one *kuga*, with only one *domo*?

They arrived at a *ruka* made of logs and the *lik winka machi* tapped on the door. It opened....

A *domo* appeared, putting *wethakelu* into her hair, which resembled red gold. She stared at Ñamku with open curiosity.

He stared back through the eye slits of his mask. The *lik winka machi* jabbered.

She was dressed in black also, but the top of her *kepam* fit so tightly you could see the slenderness of her arms and waist ... her mounded breasts. Below, cloth blossomed—a flower opening to the ground. She spoke what Ñamku thought Quechua.

He pointed at himself. "Mapuche."

"Ah!" She called into the darkness behind her. A *winka domo* dressed in vivid colors trotted out the door and was gone.

The *domo* with the red-gold hair had eyes the green of *fucha lafken* … greener than those of the boy he frightened by the Mapocho.

Then—as if summoned by memory—the boy himself walked up behind her, holding the burnt, partly eaten leg of a large animal. He jerked back, startled.

Ñamku was also shaken. Why the leg?

The *winka domo* trotted back with a Pikunche *wentru*. The *lik winka domo* spoke. The *winka* translated into Quechua. The Pikunche translated into strange *mapudungun*.

"She Inedwar, young one Wancardeñam, joyful in front of you as two."

Ñamku nodded solemnly, giving his name, asking about them and their families.

"Big, every one. They thankful."

The *machi* was glad, adding that he had come to speak to the *toki* of the *lik winka aillarewe*.

"Not here, *kawell* walking," the Pikunche translated—whispering in an aside that this was the *domo* of the *toki* Faldifa.

Ñamku had intended to apprentice Lautaro to a *lik winka machi*, but the insane one beside him was out of the question. So he said simply that he had come to apprentice Lautaro.

Inedwar studied the child, who was grimly fingering his sling. She squatted, beckoning with a radiant smile.

The Pikunche translated. "Pretty little man arrive, pretty little man with black eyes, something, something, arrive to me."

Understanding far too much, Lautaro slipped a fat rock in his sling. He was no pretty little man … something, something. He was a *weichafe* with a problem, since he had been told not to shoot more arrows. Nothing had been said about slings, however. Still, he could not throw one at a *domo*—even if she insulted him and was ugly. Her hair, her skin, her eyes were all wrong. Her *kepam* was not a *kepam*. Only her teeth were right.

This was not what Ñamku had intended. He wanted Lautaro to learn from a *machi*—maybe from *weichafe*. But from a *domo*? She could teach him *likwinkadungun*, but what else of use to the Mapuche? Unless, of course, she was *machi*.

The Pikunche said that she was not *machi*, just the *domo* of Faldifa. *Lik winka domo* wore black when their husbands died.

Ñamku asked, was not the *toki* Faldifa alive? What did they wear before the death of their *wentru*, if not black?

Inedwar disappeared into the log *ruka*, and Ñamku examined the *lik winka* youth. On his arms and chest were something like the silver scales of fish—each with a hole in it. Beneath he wore black cloth, tight as a second skin. Under it his *penun* bulged.

The *lik winka domo* emerged with food, and to the scowling *pichiche* she held out charred meat, along with a chunk of something resembling bread.

"Take, eat, she says," the Pikunche translated, unhopeful.

Lautaro took what seemed bread and chewed with a total refusal of enjoyment, fixing the ugliest *domo* ever with a wild stare.

Inedwar asked, "New mother ... why?"

"He has none," Ñamku replied, uncomfortable with the lie.

The *lik winka machi* spoke.

"He asks if you are Keristano. He asks about the Keristo in your pouch."

Ñamku said he was not Keristano–whatever that was. The Keristo in his pouch came from the desert. He said to ask the *lik winka machi* who Keristo was.

"Keristo died for badness. He is the dead son of the big *pillañ*."

Ñamku attempted to understand the dead begetting the dead ... and he was searching for a question so simple that he could comprehend the answer when Inedwar pinched Lautaro's plump cheek. Tossing aside his bread, the child bolted for sanity and freedom.

Inedwar ran after, then the *lik winka* youth, Ñamku close behind. Lautaro was far ahead—already past the fenced *kawell*. But in his way stood a *lik winka* in shining blue, with silver beasts beside him. His voice sang out....

Inedwar shouted something back.

Lautaro had almost reached the river, pursued by the silver beasts. He would be overtaken in a heartbeat. Inedwar cried out again, terror in her voice.

The high voice briefly sang again, evil in its beauty.

The silver beasts spun in their tracks.

Lautaro leapt into the Mapocho, to vanish in a swirl of foam. Then, his head reappeared, bobbing toward the farther shore.

Ñamku slowed his mad pace, only to hear the cries of Inedwar increase. Strange *kepam* flying as she ran, she was shouting with incomprehensible fright. She and the youth with the eyes like *likan* reached the river, waving their arms in the air.

The silver beasts had returned to the *kallfu lik winka*—huge dogs in shining *wethakelu*, Ñamku now realized. He slowed to examine one who could loose such creatures on *pichiche*....

Uwa silk in morning sun, the hair of the *kallfu lik winka* hung from a blue *wethakelu* shadowing his milk-white face, and with his impossibly blue eyes he looked at Ñamku as at a cloud of gnats—barely there ... yet still annoying. His clothes were tight, puffed like mushrooms at the shoulders. The cloth was the deep blue of skies and shining as if wet. The silver dogs panting beside him were somewhat smaller than *luan* but far more massive. One of them yawned—as frustrated dogs will—the tip of his pink tongue curled. His teeth were long as chicken toes.

Inedwar approached and spoke—low, intense—to the *kallfu lik winka* ... then tried to say something to Ñamku. Failing, she sent the youth running, continuing in her argument with the *kallfu lik winka*, hands doing a violent dance. The one in blue—impassive as he spoke—emanated menace as the sun does light.

The youth returned with the *lik winka machi* and the translators.

"Lautaro hit dog one with stone," the Pikunche said. "Nuñofeltran told dogs to eat him."

Two of these—Ñamku decided—could as easily eat Lautaro as ordinary dogs a *degu*. Were all *lik winka* this cruel? He considered Inedwar with new suspicion. Ugly as she was, she had seemed kind.

Turning to him she spoke, animated, as if the intensity of her expression, her flying hands, could make him understand.

"Inedwar sorry," the Pikunche droned "First she think Lautaro eat by dogs. Then she think he die in water. Now that big *pillañ* took him to other shore she sorry. She says, he come back he not eaten. She promises not squeeze his face."

Ñamku replied that this decision was for Lautaro to take. He turned to leave....

Nuñofletran spoke.

Inedwar argued.

The Pikunche translated, "Nuñofeltran asks if you are *domo* or *wentru*."

"I am *machi*," Ñamku replied.

The *kallfu lik winka* did not change expression on hearing the translation.

"It is said—he says—many sorcerers guilty of ... dirty evil."

Beginning to understand, Ñamku did not answer. Was not the *lik winka machi* wearing a *kepam*? Was he not set apart, as Ñamku was? He looked into the eyes of Inedwar.

She looked away.

Ñamku began to walk, knowing she could not stop the dogs, listening for the sounds of death behind him, hearing nothing but his own breathing.

Reaching the Mapocho he slipped in deep, and at last surfaced quietly in reeds. Then—breath by breath—he made his way downriver.

Chapter 12: Malga Malga (Nueva Extremadura, 1541)

There was a time in life—Juan had decided—when you were old enough to listen to Those Who Made Decisions, yet not mature enough to voice your own opinions. This made him an Ear for Problems to be Explored, without the Complications of Response. He was the Ear before which One Rambled. He was a patient and silent ear, weary unto death. And now—Inés needing her ear happy— he was an Ear with a Mouth to Feed.... *Choclo* cakes and blood sausage were the wages of his forbearance.

Seeing that her Ear no longer chewed, Inés inquired if it wanted more blood sausage. And since she—fiery amalgam of beauty, intelligence and purpose— could not be resisted, Juan took more of the black, greasy stuff to masticate. After Pedro left, this morning, Inés had done nothing but ply him with food and worry.

Valdivia had just appointed the government of Santiago, and all were loyal with two notable exceptions—Martín de Solier and Antonio de Pastrana. Not that they conspired in public, but in a small, walled town such things were known. They intended to hand the governorship to De Hoz.

Inés groaned with frustration.

If justice were in her shapely hands—Juan knew—there would already be seditious heads displayed on pikes, leering gruesome warning against treason. There was an iron core to the beauty of Inés. Not her body, but her heart was armored—and this, not just against Valdivia's foes. No doubt, she would fight to the death for him as well.

She shook her head with disbelief. Pastrana? Bah!

Inés paced—for the energies of her anger went to her legs. Three strides brought her to her servant, Isabel. Expressionless as the fireplace by which she squatted, the Inca was frying *choclo* cakes.

Anticipating, Juan gestured his denial. Inés took one and attacked the granitic thing herself.

What she most feared, she said—returning to her litany—was a horde of screaming Indians descending upon a house divided. "We will all die if Valdivia does not do *something.*" How could he refuse the governorship offered by the *cabildo?* The vote was unanimous!

Seas of stress and boredom floated Juan to reverie....

Knight-errant on a steed, he swayed through foreboding forest, the leaves around him shot with shafts of light. Not far away—he knew—was a damsel in desperate need of valor, reclining on oriental cushions in a bower, distraught with thoughts of him. This tapestried scene—which Juan had been elaborating for some time—was rich with detail. Yet never did he dismount, for before the damsel ever came to view his interest veered....

The bower was creamy marble, topped by pennants stirred by languid breezes, surrounded by a garden keeping wild woods at bay. Pedestals for statues—yet without shape—were scattered here and there. Fountains murmured in their basins. In upper stories, alabaster windows framed distant scenes. Priceless carpet and perfumed cushion overlaid the floors. The domed ceilings were intricate and colorful with Moorish carvings....

Deciding to add cascades to a far river overshadowed by a castle on a looming bluff, Juan was framing the panorama in weeping willows ... when he heard Lobo's febrile voice. Inés strode to the door, blocking Juan's view....

The black mask by the river—here without a body—floated in the air beyond. Juan reached for his sword ... realized he was not wearing it. And in the dim interior he perceived the roasted leg of llama on the table, which took on the appearance of a club. Gripping it, he strode to the door.

But the mask was on a body wearing white, merging with exterior glare. And the peculiar Indian seemed to come in peace. Beside him, Lobo frenetically hopped from sandal to sandal. By them both, an Indian child glowered, sling in hand. Juan now regretted that he was holding a llama leg two-handed, much like a bloody mace. Inés glanced over, grin rising to her lips.

Juan bit into the leg. And, chewing with a greasy, uneasy smile, he told Inés about the Indian that had appeared as if by sorcery by the river, wearing that same mask.

Isabel trotted up with a Picunche, and through these translators, Inés spoke to the Indian in white. With shock Juan became aware that the voice behind the black mask was a man's—though sibilant and muffled. He examined his white dress, hanging unbelted from the shoulders to above the knees—too short for a skirt, too long for a shirt. On his hands were tight, white gloves. And—extension of the featureless mask—white leather covered his head and neck.

The Inca *pieza* announced, "War white *winka* head want see."

With a wild leap of intuition, Inés said that Valdivia was on patrol. He was riding, she amended— forked fingers bouncing on a trotting wrist—searching for signs of understanding and failing to grasp the flood that poured out, for foreign languages were always fast, it seemed. But the answer came eventually. "Belong Wispañul, this Lautaro."

Inés smiled radiantly.

She had always wanted a child of her own—as Juan well knew, having too often inadequately filled that void. And now there she was, squatting, gurgling, cooing with the excess of maiden aunts, smitten to her core ... though far as Juan could see this was just another chunky Indian infant—round of cheek, black-eyed, scowling.

Inés went inside saying she was getting food for Lautaro, and *absolutely not* to let him get away! She returned with blood sausage and bread ... the Indian child taking only the latter, with a surly scowl. Responding to Indian grunts from the mask he approached Inés, who embraced him, asking why he was being adopted.

"No mother he."

And who was Ñamku?

The mask was silent, but the Picunche answered.

"Great priest he. Picunche no. Mapuche he. Live south."

Afire with impatience, Lobo had not ceased shifting from foot to foot, and he exploded into language, saying that the white-robed Indian had a crucifix in his pouch. He had seen it with his own God-given eyes. It was old, ivory and gold—perhaps once part of a rosary. Accident may have brought it here, but there was a chance as well—too astounding to ignore—that Christianity had arrived here before the Spanish. For all they knew, they might well be looking at an ancient brother in Christ.

Lost Jews, Juan thought. Why not lost Christians?

The priest interrogated the mask.

"Ñamku he, Keristo no," the wooden Inca intoned. "Keristo Inca land come he." And—after extended discussion with the Picunche—the *pieza* added, "Keristo here, Keristo there," first pointing to the white Indian, then to Juan Lobo.

As the priest attempted to reconcile these laconic Indian messages with ancient history and theology, the mask spoke again.

"Keristo what?"

"Jesus Christ, son of Almighty God, suffered and died for our sins," Lobo replied, crossing himself. Denied facial expressions by the mask, he was pendant on the translators' chatter for some time.

But when the response came it was an utter disappointment. No recognition of any sort!

"*Wispañul* what?"

"He must want to know what *we* are?" Inés said, but the Inca vehemently shook her head. The Indian priest wanted to know what '*español*' meant.

Inés laughed. She had never thought to ask *that*, herself. And in fact she did not know. She consulted Lobo—that expert in too many words—who said that *español* meant nothing, far as he knew. And why should it, she thought? She asked the Indian *what Mapuche meant*.

"People of land."

Another discussion began and Inés—who had little interest in lost tribes, or etymology for that matter—returned her attention to the Indian child she now considered hers. She loved his plump little knees, plump, pouting cheeks. She even loved his undimmed scowl, which reminded her of her own youth. She reached down to tweak the scowl away and gasped, for the little man ran from her like a startled rabbit. She ran after.

Flinging the llama leg into interior darkness, Juan followed. Sweet Saint Francis! The Indian child was heading toward Nuño Beltrán de Mendoza and his ambling wall of armored dogs. And responding to some unheard order, they had sat full in his path!

Inés inarticulately screeched and shot forward, Juan pulling ahead of her. She could run like the wind, but was encumbered by her skirts.

While still running the child whirled his sling over his head.

Inés screamed, "No, Mendoza, no!"

Juan hoarsely echoed her.

The child flung his stone … was by the dogs and heading for the river. Mendoza sang out and the war dogs leapt into a run, like frozen statues given life by sorcery. They would overtake the Indian child, and rend his shuddering flesh….

Inés stopped running, the better to scream. "Do this, Mendoza, and as God is my witness I will have your head!" There was a silence whose length—in retrospect—Juan knew was calculated. But at the time he ran his hardest to avert infanticide.

A single high, inhuman howl. The war dogs wheeled … turned back.

The child plunged into the river. Having escaped the slavering jaws of death, he now would drown!

Inés shouted, "Save him, Juan! Save him! Save him!" Juan sprinted to the shore but before he got there a bobbing head appeared, much too far out for rescue. Crucified Jesus! The Indian child was good as dead, and Inés would never forgive him. Juan waded in to his waist.

Inés splashed in behind him, skirts inflated by the current, holding the dark bundle brought by Lautaro above her head and waving it, as if the child forgot his lunch.

But, miraculously, the head—an animate cork—bobbed until it reached the distant riverbank. Glowering over his shoulder the child trotted into scrub.

Inés was agog, Juan unable to believe his eyes. He rubbed them, scanning the river as if expecting to see some naiad—or large enchanted fish—surface to take credit for the rescue.

Too stunned for words they walked, dripping, to where Mendoza and the masked Indian were staring at each other.

Inés attacked without preliminaries, furious, "Your vicious dogs almost killed that child."

"There is no 'almost' when it comes to my dogs and death," Mendoza replied. "If I wanted him dead he would be."

"Very well then, you *set* your dogs upon that child."

Mendoza was scornful, "That savage brat flung a stone at a bitch worth more than a thousand Indians. What if he had injured her?"

Inés could scarcely argue, having heard similar arithmetic from Valdivia. Therefore she fumed in silence, searching her fury for some scathing formula.

But Mendoza was not done. "Have my head, would you? he scoffed. "I only intended to teach the little savage a lesson."

Mendoza was unfortunately right. Inés well knew that if his beasts had killed the child—even eaten him—he would get a reprimand from Valdivia at the most, and only at her outraged insistence. The Lieutenant Governor had little love for the dogger, yet he invariably leapt to his defense, arguing that Caesar would have done the same.

Oh well—thought Inés—at least she had not made a new enemy. There was no 'almost' when it came to hate as well.

Inés apologized to the masked Indian, saying that this was an accident. She would have welcomed Lautaro in her home as if he were her own.

Isabel translated the Spanish to Quechua, the Picunche translated Quechua to Picunche, the Indian in white spoke, the Picunche translated back. Isabel produced, "Child he decide to."

Thinking she might have understood, Inés sighed, for she was miserable and wet. However, the bundle in her hand was dry. Moodily she contemplated the drip of her skirt, hearing Mendoza ask the Indian in white if he was man or woman. Of course! And why had she *not* thought of this! It was said that Indian priests were *patos*—a wrong profession for one with *this* perversion, if ever there was one.

She stole a glance, irrationally expecting something unnatural to emerge through the slits in the mask—a tongue perhaps, forked and flickering—remembering from somewhere that the Devil was said to have a tongue long as his arm. Justice was quick and rough in the Indies. If Mendoza was right in his guess he might have his dogging after all. The crime he suspected was among the worst, so unspeakable she knew no *real* name for it, just slang.

Isabel eventually pronounced, "Man not he. Woman not he. Priest he." She pointed at Lobo as if his skirt-like habit provided supplemental proof.

Mendoza persevered, icy. Inés sneezed and focused on her dripping skirt, risking only a brief glance at the Indian. Slow, silent, erect, ignoring the bundle in her hands, he was walking away. Inés extended the bundle, but did not call out. Ignoring her he reached the river, slipping in, submerging like a fish returned to water, and she scanned the river for longer than she thought a drowning took. But, nothing. The odd Indian was dead. She shook the bundle, as if to get some sense of what she inherited.

Against all reason Juan suspected the masked Indian was alive. He was a sorcerer after all, and he had slipped into water like an eel. Juan imagined him deep in the dark flood, breathing water that was death to men.

On the morning of June the eighth, 1541, Domingo—*negro* slave and crier to the town—made his rounds, ringing the worn brass bell which summoned Santiago to Mass. Today, however, he was announcing a meeting of all *vecinos* at the Plaza Mayor, on June the tenth. A petition requesting that Don Pedro de Valdivia be made Governor of the colony of Santiago de Nueva Extremadura would be signed by those who thought it right and just and in the best interests of his Holy Majesty, Carlos V, and of all the *cristianos* of Santiago.

Inés paced, worrying, alone in the house she shared with Valdivia—largest in the colony. She knew that all would sign save for a rebellious few. And Valdivia *had* to accept. But then, again, he might not. Only last night he moodily declared he should refuse, as he had twice before. As Caesar had *thrice* refused his crown, he muttered. Opposed by an enemy with formidable claims and a significant number of supporters, he could not afford a hint of impropriety. The *cabildo* offering him the governorship was one he had appointed against the policies of His Majesty, after all, since the governing body was supposed to be elected by the *vecinos*.

Inés countered that the petition was an acceptable substitute. What was the difference between being elected Governor by a majority and being elected Governor by a *cabildo* representing the majority? Valdivia replied that the letter of the law *was* the law. And he returned to his brooding, leaving her chewing angrily on a clove. In war, she decided, Valdivia was like the Caesar he so admired. Yet in peace he could be very much a Jesuit, and if there was anything she hated more than Jews and Moors—these enemies from without—it was casuistry, that parasite within, sucking at the honest Spanish soul. Inés sighed, brushed her hair and put it up with combs, then went to see Pedro de Gamboa about the construction of Santiago....

As he said of himself, Gamboa was born in the middle of the week looking both ways for Sunday. But Fortuna—who cocked his eyes in the first place—amended her decision by putting the left one in an arrow's path. Gamboa achieved some measure of revenge by making himself an eye patch out of Indian hide, and when all was said and done he was not entirely dissatisfied with this lurch of chance. Now he at least knew which way he was looking.

Gamboa was not just one-eyed, he was an *alarife*—that is, he had a royal commission to lay out new cities according to the many stipulations His Majesty,

Charles V, had decreed for the well-being of his subjects. And by early June of 1541 much of his plan for the city of Santiago was done. Streets had been laid out in a rectangular grid radiating from the Plaza Mayor, where the church and the houses of the most prominent *vecinos* were erected. By the hill Santa Lucía, on opposite sides, a chapel dedicated to the Virgin and a windmill had been built. A stout palisade surrounded the colony.

Santiago—that name given to a dream—was now a palpable reality. It lacked only a town hall, where the *cabildo* would convene and justice be meted out, as well as the prison and gallows necessary for that purpose. Lacking also, was an official Governor for the colony.

On June tenth the *vecinos* of Santiago—summoned by Pastrana—signed a petition supporting the appointment by the *cabildo* of Don Pedro de Valdivia, as Governor. A very few—De Hoz among them—abstained. The mandate was overwhelming. On the following day Pastrana presented the petition and list of signatures to Valdivia at the end of Mass. Ignoring the protestations of the Lieutenant Governor the *vecinos* hoisted him on their shoulders and bore him to his house on the corner of the Plaza Mayor....

Too furious for words Valdivia stormed in, slamming the door. Spirits dashed, the *vecinos* huddled, speaking in low voices, shocked at the rebuff. Inés pushed through the crowd to reach the door, hearing the angry buzz....

"Maybe he's waiting for us to crown him Caesar."

"If he doesn't want to be Governor ... I know someone who does."

This last comment she reported to Valdivia, white with fear and grim with determination, for time was short and she had been slammed against her limits. She said, "This day either you or De Hoz will be Governor of Santiago. It is just *that* simple. Forget for the moment that if he is elected it will mean your death on some trumped-up charge. Forget that his election may also mean my death and that of Pedro Gómez, Rodrigo de Quiroga, Diego de Cáceres, Villagrán—the *vecinos* closest to you, the most faithful—perhaps even Juan, despite his youth. Forget all that, just ask yourself who will better serve His Majesty and the *vecinos* of Santiago—you, or that hare-brained, hare-lipped, vicious fop?"

Valdivia paced.

Inés—arms akimbo, green eyes kindled—glowered at her indecisive lord and master.

She insisted. "It is your *duty* to your Emperor to accept."

"You are right ... I must," Valdivia responded, heading for the door.

The *vecinos* listened to his lengthy speech, in which he accepted the governorship as the will of the colony, not necessarily his own. There was cheering, leaping,

clapping. Negrito—who loved celebrations only less than music and potatoes—
danced on Pedro's shoulder.

Inés almost fainted with relief. Still, she managed to wonder at the perfection
of Valdivia's oratory. Had he rehearsed this moment? Was she just another pawn
on the board of his ambition? Had he watched her beg, when he had planned
acceptance from the start? Valdivia *was* sometimes taciturn, yet today's silence
seemed to mask duplicity indifferent to her role. How could he have been false
with *her*, knowing she would gladly die for him?

That day—and after—Inés struggled with the sin of doubt. Nonetheless—
although her faith in Valdivia had been shaken—she continued to believe in him
with her whole heart, whole soul. She still stood firm and upright on this quaking
land, yet it seemed that the foundations of her being had shifted.

The day after becoming Governor Valdivia left Santiago at the head of eighty-
two *vecinos*, all but five of the horsemen, and thirty-six *infantes,* as well as a rabble
of *yanaconas.*

Santiago had been clamoring for an expedition. The city was built and fortified,
a lawful government elected. It was time to discover gold.

The Governor had a second reason for this expedition. His stewardship of the
colony had been not quite unanimously—and not quite legally—acquired. This
meant he needed better communication with Peru. If Pizarro was alive he needed
to know that … if he was dead, likewise. And if the latter, it was imperative to know
who had replaced his benefactor. In short, Valdivia needed a ship, as crossing the
Atacama was both slow and dangerous. And he had been hungering for news from
the north that was not extracted by the unreliability of torture or distorted by the
comedies of translation. They would find and defeat Michimalongo. Then they
could build the brigantine that would put them in touch with civilization.

As usual, word of their coming preceding them, the Picunche evaporated into
their forests. From time to time they arrived at clusters of miserable thatched huts,
where the fires were smothered, the food and animals gone as if by enchantment.

There was no Granada or Sevilla, no Tenochtitlán or Cuzco south of the
Atacama—Juan thought—nothing resembling a city to conquer, just hovels lost
in wilderness. There was no Montezuma or Inca, either. These savages had a body
politic with nothing like a head—no place or person to capture to end the war. Juan
could not imagine how one defeated them, for this was chess against an opponent
that had no king or queen, bishops, knight, or rook … only uncounted pawns that
did not know the rules and hid in thickets.

No chessboard either.… Juan studied the forest rising toward the *cordillera* —
thick as wool on unshorn sheep—thinking that he was not, after years, accustomed
to these mountains. True, he could become oblivious to them. Yet the inevitable

moment came when some accident of light or color, some play of cloud, returned him to that first moment when he caught his breath. Living with the Andes was in some way like loving Inés. There was beauty so great it could not become habit. Was distance part of this...?

Valdivia called a halt. They ate roast meat, cold *papas*. Soon it would be *charqui*, parched *choclo*, and water—which *vecinos* called piss without the flavor. Juan listened to Pedro complaining—he missed wine and pork as always, but today he added genuine Spanish garlic to their absence. Not, he insisted, the tiny Indian imitation. Inés had planted a Spanish patch, yet she would not even let Valdivia touch a clove. Next year, maybe.

Horsemen brought in a Picunche they ran down. As he was uncooperative, Valdivia had him put to the question on the spot, and for the first time Juan witnessed the *strappado*—the most usual torture. Arms behind his back, he was hoisted off the ground by a rope tied to his wrists, and this agony produced no result. Stones were hung from his ankles. He was lifted and dropped. He did not even groan, much less answer questions. Valdivia called a stop, and someone slit the Indian's throat.

"You never know," Pedro commented. "Maybe he knew nothing. Maybe he knew something and decided to die anyway. With these animals you can never tell."

Despite edicts of Emperors and the preaching of priests, Pedro did not believe Indians were human. He glanced at his *hijo*, seeing Juan in one of his trances, breathing heavily. Hearty, he tried to jar him out of it. "You never know unless you try."

The next day another Indian was put to the question. This time—Valdivia telling the *infante* to be more creative—he declared he would perform a 'complete circumcision.' "Not much to his dick though," the torturer complained, flopping the member back and forth, eliciting obscene comments from the audience at this impromptu theater of the Indies.

"Get on with it," Valdivia ordered, half expecting to see Inés gallop up with a squad of disapproving priests.

The *infante's* feelings were hurt. Torture required foreplay, as everybody knew. He was just having a little fun, and giving the Indian a chance to ponder his future. Shrugging, he began to flay.

Juan focused on the tongue of the torturer, protruding from the corner of his mouth. A high whine squeezed itself from the Indian. Results!

Pleased, the *infante* spread out the rectangle he had dissected—perhaps wondering into what curio he could make it—and turned to the *cojones*.

But his work was interrupted when the Picunche said he would take them to Michimalongo.

The Indian was chained to a *yanacona*.

That afternoon—and a good part of the next day—he took them up a narrow path following a stream until it became a gorge cut by rapids far below. The expedition was strung out for half a league. An ideal place for an ambush, thought Juan, hearing a clamor from the van. He tightened his helmet strap. Yet the word passed back was not of battle—the Picunche had leapt to his death, taking the *yanacona* chained to him, and the air was rich with Spanish curses.

The expedition turned back, darkness falling long before they reached the lowlands. They camped in abrupt terrain—no pasture for horses or wood for fires, no place on jumbled stone on which to lie. Juan ate meat that—in Pedro's words— tomorrow would be riper than toe-jam. In armor there was no such thing as lying on softness, and tonight there was no place to stretch out, either. Sitting with their backs against boulders, he and Pedro killed time with talk.

Pedro offered that he had never seen an Indian like the last one tortured. When they wanted to die they kept their mouths shut. When they wanted to live, they talked. They were, in other words, brave or cowardly. This one was smart, instead. He just lost a little too much foreskin. Pedro chuckled—one to relish anything that even resembled a joke about Jews.

You think he was *acting*?"

"He led us to a dead end and killed himself. Lucky he did not walk us into ambush." Pedro complained. "Indians ... it's all their fault."

"Being tortured is their *fault*?"

"They would ask for it, if we did not give it to them."

Juan was speechless—of appalling experiences deliberately endured, the Atacama was as far as *he* had gone, or would.

Pedro mused. "Heathens fight for reasons hard to understand. Aztecs had a 'flower war' in spring to catch captives for sacrifice. Ripped their hearts out, ate the rest. What kind of reason for war is *that*?"

As it was too dark to see Juan's face, Pedro wondered if his silence meant sleep or trance. Little matter, for ideas were coming to him.

"*Cristianos*, who have things, fight to get more. Having nothing, savages just fight to fight." Pedro liked his formula, which made him think of sermons.

"I mean," he amended—feeling with the toe of the mind through quicksand, for solid ground—"that these savages have only hovels, vegetables and fish." He shuddered at these truths, never eating willingly what began life green. And he could not stomach what grew slimy in the sea.

Pedro warmed to the Indian deficiencies in what made life worth living. "No meat, no wine, not even the beers of barbarians. No taverns, indument or priests, no gold, and no God." He crossed himself. "They have women I admit, but all alike—surly and skinny, brutish, good only for emergencies."

Nothing like Liliana and Constanza … or Inés—Juan thought—each with her special beauty.

"When you come down to it, Picunche have nothing to do but fight each other for nothing, which leaves only the pleasure of battle. The Incas and Aztecs, at least, had something decent to wear to war."

Pedro wondered if the thread of his argument had become twisted at some point. "Of course, Incas and Aztecs had cities and kings, gold, other civilized things.

"I know, Pedro, I know. Indians have no wine or pork, taverns, white women, oranges, proper garlic, or God. But why should they *want* to be tortured?"

"Look at it this way. Strip everything civilized from man and all you have left is naked courage—the only pagan virtue—which is why these Indians welcome death."

Like the saints, in a way—thought Juan—and like the martyred virgins who surrendered everything to God, and had only their lives left to give.

"And of course, the ultimate test of courage is torture, especially if it kills you."

Pedro was triumphant, having threaded the labyrinth that linked Indian deprivation to the love of the pain they asked for. And he went silent, less from modesty at what might actually be philosophy, than out of fear of disturbing the delicate edifice of his argument.

'Naked courage,' Juan repeated, relishing the phrase. Torture to the tortured was the courage of those stripped of everything, so that Indians were as godless martyrs…. Then he remembered Pedro's initial argument.

"Indians, who have nothing civilized, fight to fight. So what did you, who have civilization, fight for in Italy?"

"God, gold and the Emperor," Pedro instantly replied, an instant later regretting his outburst, for one could not have more of God and the Emperor.

"And what are we fighting for *here*?"

"Why," Pedro cleared his throat, "*hijo*, in the absence of gold, we are fighting for God and the Emperor … and honor of course."

Juan was thinking that they had suffered to get to *nowhere* for God and the Emperor, fighting people who had nothing but war and courage and wanted to be tortured. The pieces made sense separately, but put together they created something out of Pliny—both impossible and real.

That night while on his cot he decided that Pedro had overlooked much residing in his 'nothings.' If Indians were nonentities living nowhere with 'nothing,' how were the Spanish able to *take* anything from them? And *take* they did—their land, their lives, their work and the product of that work. They took their daughters and their wives—turning them into less than whores, because not paid … etcetera. Indians got God and the Emperor in return, yet the Spanish part of the contract was easy as a *pax vobiscum*. The Indian part was weighted by what was deemed nothing. On the scales of justice, something not of this earth weighed more than a loss of nothing deemed worthwhile on this earth. Weightless angels danced on one side, deprivation on the other. But Juan knew better—gold was hiding under the skirts of Seraphim.

Juan's argument began to limp when it occurred to him that they brought more than the afterlife to Indians. Inés was a crucial figure in all that, with her pork and mutton, vines and lemons, avocados and the rest. Indians could *learn*, also. He could teach them the *romances*. Lobo could expound upon **Utopia**, Aristotle, Erasmus.…

That night Juan dreamed that San Juan Bautista—naked, decapitated, and to his waist in a river—was baptizing a file of naked Indians. With the self-confidence of dreams, San Juan ignored his death and the fact he could not see, splashing water unerringly on Indian heads. Baptized, each new child of God walked on as if there were a path at the bottom of the river, disappearing underwater to reappear at the far shore. There, Inés offered each a gift—olive, rose, grape, piglet, fig.…

The expedition advanced through a forested, increasingly broken plain, pressing on warily through thick growth—*yanacona* scouts on the periphery keeping in touch with coded whistles … an invisible flock of human parrots. Juan noted that fire had cleared the forest floor, sparing the trees, so that they rode over both cinder and green shoots. A sight fit for sermons, he thought—groping for the moral—when arrows began to swish through leaves. To the left came what might have been a death cry, cut off. There was ordered confusion, yelling and galloping, a summoning and sending of scouts … sorties. But not a single Picunche was to be found.

A *yanacona* returned with an arrow through his lung, saying, before collapsing, that the Picunche had laid an ambush.

The guards about the camp that night were many and wary, yet spirits were up. Fickle Fortuna had brought them to the lair of Michimalongo.

They marched in the morning. Encroaching hills compressed the column—the terrain a funnel between promontories. Certain of ambush, Valdivia called a halt. And when Indian scouts did not return he deployed his troops, sending massed *yanacona* warriors to draw the enemy from hiding, taking the initial shock. Disciplined Incas led the way, bright in dyed wool and feathers, followed by half-naked savages of nameless tribes. After them came the *caballeros*, supported at the rear by ranks of *infantes*.

The advance was signaled by a trumpet, which—after all these years—had not ceased to thrill Juan's heart with its prologue. He saw banners fly, heard the *infantes* thud in martial meter. Suddenly, wildly, he thought that not God and the Emperor—not even honor—was what he fought for, but for *this*. He heard the clop of hooves, the muffled hammer of feet, an occasional clang, cascabels.... Pedro rode before him, alert, casual. The chirra-chirra of some insistent bird broke the silence of the forest. Juan did not see arrows rain on the *yanaconas* in the van, simply heard the shouts and screams.

It was impossible to spur his horse however, the *caballeros* before him blocking the way, pressing the *piezas* ahead into the battle, and when Juan rounded the last obscuring trees he saw a meadow flanked by bluffs. There, *yanaconas* were milling and dying under a hail of stones and arrows. Beyond them—blocking the valley—was a palisade of logs higher than a man on horseback, surmounted by a thousand screaming Indian heads. Before the fortification stood rows of sharpened, slanted wooden stakes.

Capering and screeching, Picunche on the cliffs shot arrows and spears at the Spanish as they came into view. Juan saw that the *yanaconas* were trapped—in front by the palisade, to the sides by cliffs, by armored cavalry behind. They did not have room to use their bows and slings—though the air was thick with missiles. From beyond the palisade an invisible multitude of Picunche loosed arrows and stones, an occasional spear.

A squadron of desperate Inca stormed the fortification, creating human pyramids to climb the wall. Picunche brained them with war clubs, ran them through, or simply toppled them onto their own. The few that attempted to scale the cliffs suffered a similar fate, with much farther to fall.

Pulling on his beard, Valdivia scanned the slaughter and ordered a retreat. Wheeling his horse, Juan saw the Indians of the palisade spring up, displaying barbaric paint, waving weapons, and shouting strange words of triumph.

The dispirited Spanish ate, drank and rested, discussing their first true military setback in Chile, as Valdivia conferred with his lieutenants. These savages were learning about civilized warfare, and for the moment they had neutralized the advantages of horse and armor. Voicing the universal opinion of the captains, Pedro Gómez said, "Flank them." Scouts were dispatched to find a route around the palisade.

The lieutenants argued. If this were Italy they would have cannons. Cortéz had cannons. Now that the heathens had learned fortification, they needed engines of destruction. Even a catapult—that primitive thing—might work against this barbaric barrier. Francisco de Villagrán offered—in his impeccable Castilian—that if they could not flank this preposterous fortification then they must perforce go through it. He recommended battering rams. God knows, there were trees enough, about.

Valdivia heard him out politely, though the *vecino* grated on his nerves, irking him with his aristocratically arching nose—a larger version of his own—his aristocratic armor, his aristocratic platitudes … and especially his pointed, aristocratic beard. Villagrán was too much *like* him and far better born. He meant well, tried hard—and sometimes was worth listening to—yet he conveyed the impression that he was the Pope sermonizing swine.

His idea had merit, Valdivia said, but it would kill too many *yanaconas*. There were victories and victories—the best were easiest on the troops. Besides, Valdivia already *knew* what he had to do. Battering rams would work, he said, but constructing them would take too much time. Why not just burn the damned thing?

The Indians scouting a flanking route never returned. And at first light, next day, squads of *yanaconas* protected by borrowed layers of armor ran to the palisade and tossed armloads of brush over the sharpened stakes against its base, filling the space between. Only a few died in the storm of missiles.

Indians on the cliffs released enormous boulders, which bounced like erratic dice down the canyon walls, rebounding at the bottom, insanely leaping across the meadow. One blind stone cut a swath through *yanaconas*. But by then, tinder was thick against the palisade, and archers shot flaming arrows. Soon the brush blazed higher than the fortification, the roaring blaze reaching for the canyon rim. A change of wind brought resinous smoke in Juan's direction. He recognized the odor of burning feathers, roasting meat.

Valdivia pulled back his troops, for no living thing could cross that inferno, and that evening it was only *charqui*, Pedro ebullient nonetheless, for victory was theirs. Wringing his dried meat as if it were a chicken neck, he pointed out that if the Picunche had made a door they could have sortied from it, keeping the *yanaconas* from heaping their brush. These savages may have learned how to make walls, but they still knew nothing about fortification.

Juan's mind wandered when Pedro turned to salients and sapping, trench angles, crossfire, and the outmoded idiocy of crenellation. He had heard it all—or would have if he paid attention. He knew already that fortifications designed to withstand cannon fire were squat and featureless—the architectural equivalent of turtles. Dreaming of his enchanted bower, he added crenellations to the soaring turrets of the castle in the distance, and a touch of fog to its moat.

At dawn Spanish files marched over cinder to confront massed thousands of Picunche ranged into squadrons vivid with barbaric paint. Halting his columns, Valdivia studied the enemy.

Spearmen comprised the first rows, weapons butted in the ground—a deadly barrier. Behind them archers massed, backed by multitudes bearing an outlandish variety of weapons. No doubt, there were thousands on the cliffs.

The Indians' tactics were clear to Valdivia. They intended to stop the *yanaconas* with a storm of missles, as they had two days before. And when the Spanish cavalry charged, the ranked spears would decimate it ... then, the counterattack.

The Indians were doing the best they could with what they had—yet this was not Italy. Even a simple frontal assault would succeed. However, Valdivia did not dream of doing the expected. Much as he loved gambling, when the lives of his men were at stake he did not dice with Fortuna.

Valdivia attacked. Every Indian archer under his command showered the center of the Picunche line with arrows. Then the Inca—the most heavily armed *yanaconas*—hit the same spot like a fist. Those that did not fall broke through the spearmen, attacking archers. Others charged the breach and soon were fighting deeper in Picunche lines. When it seemed to Juan that they were about to be surrounded and destroyed a trumpet sounded.

The *yanaconas* retreated, and the Picunche roared with their coming triumph.

But through the gap the Inca had created *caballeros* galloped, two abreast, wreaking the usual havoc then wheeling to the side, attacking the spearmen and archers of the van, and in the crush the Indian weapons became useless. Like immense boulders, the *caballeros* compressed the Indian ranks against the canyon face.

Juan sat Amadís, with the horsemen of the second wave, watching the implacable advance of the first, cold steel on human batten, eddies of Indians swirling ... falling, then the trumpet propelling him to war. He fought until long after his sword arm was burning, Valdivia sounding the retreat, to eat, rest and regroup. Numberless Picunche had died with not one *cristiano* lost.

Out of arrow range, the captains conferred, Francisco de Aguirre complaining: "Killing gets you nowhere. Might as well conquer a forest by chopping some trees. We have to take their *toki*. But how tell one savage from another? " Aguirre removed his helmet to cool his head, as all pondered the conundrum.

Valdivia did not hesitate. "*Yanaconas* who understand Picunche will attack in the first ranks. When they know the one giving orders, Michimalongo will be singled out and captured ... *not* killed."

They hammered the Indian center, locating Michimalongo at this place of greatest danger, wearing a puma hide, white feathers in his topknot. Alerted horsemen cut through Indians and surrounded him. He attacked first one, and then another, with insane courage ... was beaten back unharmed. He fought until he could scarcely hold his club, but it was not exhaustion that finally made him lean upon his weapon. Picunche were dying in great numbers. All hope of victory was gone.

Juan thought the *toki* suprisingly small—even for an Indian—though corded with muscle and with features of extraordinary intensity. Coal eyes glowed over an aquiline nose. The hide of a puma hung around his neck, long claws dangling. He was painted with black dots. And he wore a single enormous earring, the first he had seen on a Picunche male. Gold!

Michimalongo cast his weapon aside, crossing his arms. With a gesture encompassing the battle Valdivia yelled, "stop," in Quechua. The *toki* repeated the gesture and shouted the same word—in his language—venomous.

Less disciplined than the Spanish, some warriors fought on. Still the moment came when the field became uncannily silent, for wounded Indians—like wounded animals—largely made no sound.

Through interpreters Valdivia talked terms, the *toki* insisting that this was not surrender, but a truce. He wanted no reprisals. He wanted his *weichafe* unharmed. He wanted the *che* left alone.

A commotion interrupted their deliberations. Indians were shouting and backing away from a squadron of *infantes*, leaving them in a circle empty of all but the dead and the wounded that could not crawl. Interpreters told Valdivia that the Indians were shouting, "No nose!"

What had truces to do with noses? The Governor told the interpreters to try again.

Before they did a Picunche detached himself from the crowd—a savage like every other, largely naked, head shaved but for a hank atop his head, with its bouquet of feathers—and walked to the knot of Spanish singled out. Then, stalking the line of *infantes* he stopped, shouting at one who had recently lost the tip of his nose—not in the battle, for it was healing.

The soldier shouted back. This *hideputa* wanted a fight, he would give it to him. And as he could not physically attack when Valdivia had ordered the end of hostilities, maybe a little insult was in order. He made obscene gestures and began to prance as he thought a wild Indian might, brandishing his weapon.

The Picunche knocked his legs out from under with his spear and plunged an obsidian knife deep into his throat. As the *infante* drowned in blood—quiet as any Indian—the nearest comrade took a quick backhanded swing with his sword at the berserk savage, severing his spine.

The Governor stared at Michimalongko with anger and frank astonishment. The *toki* shrugged, starting the process of translation. "*Winka*-no-nose kill wife he. *Lik winka* kill he. I stop no. No can. No will."

Valdivia decided this was an isolated incident—the result of allowing some

Indian village idiot to bear arms—and continued negotiations. What had Michimalongo been about to offer?

The *toki* handed his earring to Valdivia, saying, "Malga Malga." Then and there—as gold spoke for itself—the truce was ratified.

Malga Malga was where Picunche once panned gold for the Inca, and on learning *this*, the Second Coming would have brought less excitement to the troops. That evening they began to gamble future shares, pebbles as their tokens.

All next day it rained as they followed Michimalongo—and some half-hundred taciturn Picunche—to promised wealth.

A depression profound as yesterday's euphoria came over Juan. Shivering in sopping wool, he attempted to understand the profundity of Indian hate. Michimalongo's seemed incomprehensible, that of the Indian that died to kill the *infante* insane. It was puzzling to be hated, and disturbing too—as if you walked around all day with snot hanging from your nose, nobody saying a word. How could they hate him without *knowing* him? God only knew, he had tried all his life to be good, hearing Mass every day when he could. He did his best not to sin and—when he did—repented. Often, he repented *before* he sinned, at the very thought. He prayed too—for the Indians hating him, for Moors and Jews. Not exactly loving all these people he certainly wished them well ... the Moors more than the Jews maybe—for they crucified Christ, and you had to be God to forgive *that*. Besides, everybody knew they used human blood to make their *matzoh*—whatever that was. Father Sosa had hinted at rites in which Jews sacrificed babies, too awful to detail. Yet—even if they barbarically cut off the foreskins of innocent babies—Juan did not really *hate* the Jews. He did not even hate the Aztecs, who ate people. He had to admit that Indians might hate him as part of the package delivered to them by History, but it was not his fault that so many *conquistadores* began their lives as criminals. Juan was deeply aggrieved, resenting the asymmetry of a situation in which he intended to do the Indians good and they did not reciprocate.

The Malga Malga they were led to proved to be a bend in a stream fed by mountain water. A waterfall cut into black rock, cascades tumbling to where the channel meandered through pebbles.

Juan was incredulous. He had not expected rooms full of gold, but at least veins of the precious stuff, or a glittering cliff ... a mineshaft glowing in torchlight....

Michimalongo gestured at the streambed, munificent.

The pebbles that had been the counters of last night's gambling had become the riches of today. Juan had won a seventy-seventh share of what his horse was at this very moment pissing on, and he fought the insane urge to laugh. There were more streams than anybody could possibly want in the Indies. More rain than you could want, too. His teeth were chattering. He yearned for hot food and a warm bed. All the while, Pedro was excitedly pointing out rickety Indian structures by the waterfall.

Valdivia ordered, "Give it a try."

Give what a try? Juan looked about. Not a glint! Fighting a cackle, he sneezed, dismounting to examine what the Picunche had built. Poles supported shallow wooden troughs that scarcely sloped. And that seemed all until the Indians went to work. A hollowed trunk was slipped into a sling and pushed into the waterfall, turning it into a waterspout that could be directed to the troughs. Then Picunche scooped the stuff of streambeds into them, working the slurry with their fingers, letting water move light material down, tossing larger rocks.

A shout, and Juan briefly held the pebble passed around. Resembling a dried, irregular pea, it held no gleam at all. Was this dull thing gold?

He went insane with the rest, yet his heart was not in this madness. All this distance—all this blood—for a pebble he would have walked on and ignored. He was rich—maybe—but his soul was gray as the day, cold as the stones he stood on. Here, gold was just like every other rock, for there was nothing it could buy that man could want. Desperately, Juan yearned for the hearth of childhood, fragrant with olive oil, garlic, and onions—saffron chicken sometimes on a Sunday—Father Sosa smiling by the bubbling pot....

By dark there was enough to fill a heavy pouch, and Valdivia took the gold of Malga Malga to his bed..

Chapter 13: Tree of Justice (Santiago, 1541)

Juan thought he was in the *Santiago de Compostela,* being shaken awake by Pedro ... but there was no ship, no storm. He opened his eyes to a waking dream instead. Wild instinct made him surge to his feet. The earth was a rat shaken by a dog.

He fell, crawled from the tent, fell again. He stood—arms out for balance—seeing *vecinos* getting to their feet ... others on all fours like astonished animals. Trees were snapped by absent winds. Horses reared. The whole scene was blurred by an insane jerking of the earth. Then the indecisive ground made up its mind and stampeded toward the *cordillera*. Expecting to plummet through a hole to Hades, Juan fell on Pedro. About to get up, he found himself in a gentle iron grip.

"No use, *hijo*. No enemy. No place to go. No reason to stand, and every reason to laugh." Pedro was right—this earthquake was a practical joke God was playing on man.

The quake ceased suddenly as it began and men tentatively began to stand. Prophetically, Pedro gestured for Juan to stay down as the earth produced its last, most violent, effort. Every man erect was flung to the ground or capering for balance. It was one huge joke.

Then it was over—save for gentler aftershocks. Trees swayed. Fallen *vecinos* looked about sheepishly, wondering if they could safely stand. When they did, many pushed themselves up in stages, like children learning to walk, wary of being erect. Then the scene turned normal save for curses and disorder. Some tents, a dead tree or two, some branches, were down. That was all save for the eerie silence of the forest. Pedro and Juan checked their horses, found them safe, and ate.

Needing more Indians to work Malga Malga, Valdivia sent for *yanaconas* from Santiago and asked Michimalongo for more Picunche. The *toqui* said he led his people in war. In peace they did as they wanted. And Valdivia's request—he politely suggested—did not make sense. Who would look for *milli* in cold *kuyen*?

The *toqui* was correct. His reluctant summons brought fewer than a hundred *piezas*. In a week—having produced six bags of gold—they said it was time to go home, having found more *milli* than anyone could want.

Valdivia said they could not leave.

He had been pacing, evenings, working out the arithmetic. Double the Indians and in a week you had a dozen bags of gold—six hundred and seventy two a year.

Quadruple the Indians and you had thirteen hundred and forty four bags. The limit to the riches of Malga Malga was Indian sloth.

The Governor decided on five hundred *piezas*. Michimalongo shook his head, incredulous, when the translator explained the impossible figure—which did not even exist in *mapudungun*. The *pillañ* could not order this many *che* to come! Not in *wetre kuyen*!

Valdivia insisted.

Four responded to this summon of the *toqui*—all old men, while ten times that many able-bodied Indians had vanished into the night.

Valdivia's tally of the year's gold evaporated with the morning mist, and Michimalongo did not bother to answer the Governor's angry questions. His shrug said it all.

Enraged, Valdivia was succinct. Either Michimalongo would supply the very reasonable number of Indians he requested or—*pardiez!*—he would have them rounded up and brought in chains.

Here it should be said that, to this point, the *toqui* was innocent of his bargain with the Spanish—which was, that his people would be required to labor in this life for those who made their eternal life possible. Consequently—when Valdivia's shouts were translated to Michimalongo—the terms sounded very much like an intention to enslave the *che*, a dishonorable breach of the promise made in return for being taken to Malga Malga. In fact, this had every appearance of an act of war. Still, the angry *toqui* agreed to do his best.

Through some miracle of persuasion never explained by History, Michimalongo achieved the impossible. In two days many *piezas* straggled into camp—mostly men in their prime, but also women, even a few older children. Nobody ever tallied Indians—which were hard to count as chicks in a spring coop—yet their number seemed approximately right and Valdivia was satisfied. After minor setbacks, his first campaign as Governor was developing into an unalloyed triumph. Clio, that grudging muse, would write his name—and that of Malga Malga—in gold ink.

With so much to do, so few to do it, Valdivia split his forces into three squads, heading the first himself, taking eight *caballeros*, a dozen *infantes* and a quantity of *yanaconas* to the coast to build the brigantine. The second squad—five *caballeros*, ten *infantes* and half the remaining *yanaconas*—were to remain at Malga Malga under the command of Gonzalo de los Ríos. The rest of the *vecinos* and *piezas* would return to Santiago to protect it against a possible Indian uprising. Valdivia selected Juan and Pedro for that duty, saying to them privately that he would feel better about Inés if he knew they were with her.

The evening before he left, Juan explored. Indians worked under the watchful eye of the foremen—*infantes* who knew little about panning gold yet were masters at coaxing work from shiftless savages, making a great show out of snapping their penal whips with a sharp crack. The sound punctuated the melancholy evening, reverberating viciously off stone.... Perhaps it was the quake, but to Juan Malga Malga seemed three parts nightmare, two parts riddle, and one part practical joke.

The nightmare was the labor of the Indians, required to work twilight to dusk in winter, wet and shivering, half naked, scrutinizing passing pebbles. The riddle was the fact that Picunche warriors were willing to endure this discomfort, servitude and shame. Juan knew they were ill armed and next to helpless against Spanish. But he also knew—and admired—their pride and courage.

The practical joke was the gold. Valdivia spent every night at a candlelit table weighing the day's take, apportioning shares, making little piles and big of the dull stuff, and—since portly Luis de Cartagena was in Santiago—having Juan keep tally. This was the labor of Sisyphus, save that instead of rolling one big stone up one big hill you rolled a lot of little ones around on planks, night after night. And since there were more nuggets every evening, the tally had to be redone and once again recorded.

Juan, therefore, was the secretary to Sisyphus. However, it was a labor better than the Indians, he thought, walking by a *pieza* sifting stones, naked as Adam in his leaf, almost. This one was enormous—though not fat—reminding him of a fighting bull, and you could see the muscle work beneath his skin, like an earthquake in meat. Never having seen a white man naked, Juan was fascinated by the sight of hairless Indian bodies exposed without shame, so impervious to cold. With surprise he realized that a long wooden spoon was casually stuck through the belt-like thong holding up the cloth that hid his shame. Deciding that this Indian was some cook, Juan finished his unhappy walk and went to bed.

When he and Pedro returned to Santiago, Inés rode out with Alonso de Monroy to meet them—perhaps four leagues out. Pedro saw that their horses had been pushed. Was this gladness, or trouble?

Juan saw nothing but Inés—her black, broad-brimmed hat blown back, hair brighter than the gold of Malga Malga. Usually, when she rode she kept it braided, in a bun. Today it was whipped to glorious chaos. Reining in her horse she asked for Valdivia, green eyes wide.

"The Governor has gone to the coast to build the brigantine."

As if 'build' were an obscene verb, and Brigantine a notorious whore, Inés stormed, "So he's off to his precious *brigantine*, is he?" Too upset to continue, she fought fury and tears.

Monroy went to the point, "*Caballeros*, we have been struggling with sedition while you were gone."

He explained as they rode on—the revolt of the partisans of Sancho de Hoz, always at a rolling boil, was about to overflow its nasty pot. He and his men, Chinchilla among them, especially Antonio de Pastrana and Martín de Solier— the very men Valdivia appointed to important posts—had become overbearing, churlish, arrogant, intending to provoke a confrontation. He and the *señora doña* Inés had built a gallows as a warning, yet that changed nothing. If anything, the gallows had goaded them. And since word of the gold of Malga Malga reached Santiago, there had been rumors that the conspirators were planning to kill Valdivia, making off with the riches of the colony in the brigantine, their revolt postponed until the ship was finished.

Pedro spat without comment.

Pale eyes expressionless, Monroy said it was good to have loyal reinforcements.

Shaking her head as if to wake herself, Inés smiled at Juan and said that— praise God!—at least they were back safe. She leaned over in her saddle and offered her cheek for the ritual peck, forgetting that he did not possess her mastery of horsemanship. How could he resist this offer, however, blushing with exercise, delicate as a peach? Leaning over on his jouncing mount Juan attempted to make gentle contact and fell short, but at least he did not fall off his horse. Blushing, knowing Amadís de Gaula would have accomplished the kiss with consummate art—Valdivia without disturbing his mustaches—Juan leaned to the far edge of balance, lips extended to help close the gap ... failing again.

Her multitude of perfections must have included a distant knowledge of what it was to be young, in hopeless love, and wanting only to die, for she acted as if the ceremony had been gracefully accomplished. And stealing a glance at saturnine Monroy, Juan saw not the smothered ember of a smile. Either he had witnessed nothing, or he had long ago risen above the amusements afforded by idiocy. As for Pedro, he was violently yanking hairs from his beard, absorbed in devising the many deaths he would deal De Hoz, each more unspeakable than the last. Juan relaxed enough to wonder how Pedro's beard could remain so thick through these harvests of anger.

They rode through Santiago's gate, *vecinos* emerging to cheer the gold of Malga Malga. Everywhere the effects of earthquake were visible. The palisade canted like wheat in a perpetual wind. Chimneys had tumbled. No house was down, yet most were askew. In the central square the gallows stood at a drunken angle, and there Pero Sancho De Hoz and half a dozen others were gathered by the tilted warning.

Slipping a handkerchief from a pocket, De Hoz produced a low, mocking bow. Riding by, Monroy replied with a sour inclination of the head, while Pedro gestured vaguely, with unconcealed distaste—as one might indicate to an innkeeper that the roast is obscenely overdone.

At Valdivia's they found the house damaged but standing, a blanket tossed over the hole created by the chimney when it collapsed. Outside, an Indian turned a side of llama over an open fire. Sitting to eat short ribs they decided that there was nothing to be done. Not without an overt revolt. Not with Valdivia absent.

As *maestre de campo* Pedro agreed, but as the man he was he had to mutter, "I hate his handkerchief!" Pulverizing a rib, he mused, "De Hoz deliberately provokes us, after all. What if I should spit into his fancy pocket by mistake, and he should happen to draw his sword? What if I should happen to kill him in self defense?"

"Spoken like a good and faithful soldier," Inés replied, "but alas, not like a diplomat. If De Hoz dies, Peru—and ultimately His Majesty—must perceive us as blameless. Why else has Valdivia hesitated to kill the hare-lipped ass? But you're absolutely right!" She waggled the rib in her hand to the slow cadence of her thought. "What about a provocation more delicate than spitting in a pocket? What of an insult so almost nonexistent as to have every appearance of innocence? All we need is an incident to unmask their treachery, then we send for Valdivia. If nothing happens we are no worse off. In short, why not have a party with these traitors and delicately goad them?"

This was genius, thought Juan—all that was needed was a spark put to the touchhole of a firearm primed and loaded. And it came to him that dandies could be sensitive about what their tastes in fashion implied about their sexuality—as Mendoza with Enrique. "*Patos*," he exclaimed to Inés. "Why not just discuss your ducks."

Inés grinned. The child was a genius.

The gold of Malga Malga as pretext, she hosted a celebration in Monroy's house, which had survived the earthquake more or less intact. All the principal conspirators, important *vecinos* and priests were invited. She served meat, though in strange form—two of the diminutive deer of Chile, and birds, the larger ones stuffed with forest nuts. There were a number of creatures that looked like large, rounded rats with short noses and hairy tails. And—surprise of surprises!—to prime the intended explosion, Inés provided an enormous quantity of *mudai*—that foul fermented drink the natives made.

Juan assayed a mouthful of the milky stuff, spitting it out. Pedro, however, downed his like a soldier. "Leper's piss," he commented, pouring a second bowl. And he was not the only one to stomach this Indian poison—Chinchilla's thirst, in particular, overcoming his disgust. By nightfall the celebration was a revel, for—deficient as the fluid was in potency—it was being poured into unaccustomed stomachs. Everyone was loud and muzzy, though nothing had yet been ventured, or revealed, by the entire conspiring room.

To polarize her guests, Inés had cunningly provided two laden tables. And polarized they were—De Hoz and company at the one, Valdivia's faction at the other. The tension was palpable.

The time had come to implement their subtle plan: Inés would discuss a problem with her ducks, and every time she said the word '*pato*,' someone would Glance With Significance at De Hoz

When she asked for volunteers, Monroy's expression soured as if the very idea curdled his honor. Rodrigo de Quiroga blushed … but—stuttering—he manfully agreed to try, though he declared himself the worst of actors. And, gleeful, Pedro volunteered. So it was settled. He and Quiroga would deliver the Significant Glances.

The moment come, Inés loudly commenting to Juan that she had a poor duck hatched by a chicken, who had learned everything from this unnatural mother. He had grown up pecking the ground and bathing in dirt, too filthy to float even if he wanted to, which he did not. He was a dirty, perverted duck.

Pedro entered into the spirit of the farce, portentously grimacing at De Hoz every time Inés said '*pato*,' which was often. This was no laughing matter, yet Juan had to fight a grin, for Pedro was no more an actor than Quiroga, glowering from under Knitted Brow and Lowered Lids.

Sensing the tension in the room Negrito bounced on Pedro's shoulder, baring yellow fangs and jabbering at the enemy table as he slapped his bicep, for he was adept at mimicking obscene gestures.

Yet nothing happened. The *pato* lectures, the Significant Glances, Negrito's gestures, were all ignored in the general climate of provocation. The conspirators, who were blind drunk—and equal failures as actors—were engrossed in Seditious Muttering and Deadly Glances of their own.

The Duck Tactic failed. Yet the evening ended in triumph when the other table—desiring to trigger The Event—devised a ruse that the muddy Indian beverage turned insane.

Chinchilla and Martín de Solier began to argue—an altercation that appeared to concern the color of a horse for they were yelling 'roan' and 'liver' at each other.... Drawing their swords they dueled and—with choreographed clumsiness— overturned the candles that lit the room and managed to step on them.

There was a moon this night. However, Inés had hung blankets on the windows as protection from nocturnal airs, and the house became abruptly dark. Juan drew his knife, heard muffled thuds, clangs, inarticulate cries and grunts, stertorous breathing, and … a swish that might have been a sword sweeping by his ear, before a battering ram sent him reeling, tripping, falling. His arm struck cups of the Indian potion, sending them flying in unseen, splattery trajectories, and he found himself lying on a table, sharing that space with the remnants of the feast as an earthquake happened and the table beneath him became a table on top, pinning him down in the company of greasy meat and bones… Unable to get free, Juan suddenly saw light. The reserves Inés had concealed outside ran in with torches and steel, revealing everything.

Martín de Solier was nowhere to be seen. Monroy was twisting the wrist of De Hoz, to make him drop his stiletto. Chinchilla was swinging a drunken sword in a direction that vaguely included Rodrigo de Quiroga. In one corner Lobo frustrated the wild, blind blows of Antonio de Pastrana with a chair. In another—with the hell-sent grin of a horseman of the Apocalypse—Pedro stood before Inés, immense sword in a double-handed guard, crushing her against the wall with the weight of his protection.

The torch put a stop to it all, the conspirators surrounded and outnumbered. Emerging from behind her bulwark Inés asked what this outrage meant—omitting to address De Hoz as *caballero*. Monroy echoed her with icy fury.

Bowing with a flourish that employed not his handkerchief but his stiletto, De Hoz wheezed that this was a mere mistake—ha, ha!—a confusion of identities in the dark, a quarrel simply out of hand. These things happened, did they not…? With a wink he added that the Indian beverage no doubt had addled heads.

Ignoring the offered blame Inés dismissed the traitors without further word, and all weapons were sheathed.

Juan was disgusted. Those who intended murder were free as birds, and here he was forgotten in his pain, lying on smashed crockery and gnawed bones.

Seeing him, Pedro lifted the massive table as if it were air, not oak. Inés delicately probed. A rib was cracked, she supposed. Prescribing rest she said that with such injuries there was not much else to do. Pedro was to take Juan home. She would prepare medicine. And, carrying the child of his heart, Pedro was heading for the door, when Monroy—who had left after De Hoz—returned. They had evidence, he said … witnesses too. He had sent for Valdivia. If all went well the Governor would soon be in Santiago, and God willing, the traitors would dance a *fandango* at rope's end.

Pedro put Juan to bed. Inés applied a wet, warm cloth steeped in her medicine—smelling deliciously of clove—and left exhausted but triumphant. However, Pedro went to bed upset, his topic being medicine. It was well known that the best remedy for almost everything was a plaster of warm guts … known to everybody but Inés, that was. For the life of him—he muttered, dropping onto his grass-stuffed mattress—he could not understand how a tea too disgusting to drink could be good for a pain that close to the stomach. Something was profoundly wrong with *that*. And he proposed his personal theory—that the better the medicine, the more edible. What it came down to is that you healed with either meat or vegetables, and of the two, meat was far to be preferred—raw steak being the specific for bruises, for example.

Unable to sleep as Pedro rambled, Juan analyzed the evening, thinking that it had gone well *despite* their efforts. The conspiracy had betrayed itself *by* itself— volunteering to fail, as it were. He was amazed at the asininity of these men. Their plotting was an insult to intelligence, and a depressing one at that. God was scripting his life in the Indies as a comedy.

Pedro also lost sleep that night, for it was he who overturned the table in the dark, thinking to create a diversion and injuring the child of his heart instead. Also, he had been unable to confess his blunder, the reason being even worse, namely that—*tan cierto como Cristo es Dios*—he would be Juan's death next time around. At the inn in Spain he almost killed him. Now, this ... and the third time *it* always happened. Pedro crossed himself in paternal agony, praying to God the Father, Son and Holy Ghost—as if the Trinity could abrogate the Law of Threes which was His Very Being.

Next morning Juan lay listless on his sick bed, watching an Inca maid work *choclo* paste with stubby fingers, shaping patties that she grilled over coals. Faint smoke rose through the hole that was the absence of a chimney. Pedro had left and returned with the *pieza* and a bowl of meat from yesterday's feast, to build Juan's strength. Shuffling from boot to boot he said he had to be out and about, what with mutiny brewing. The *pieza* would take care of him.

Inés briefly visited, giving the Inca a poultice and instructions. She left, brushing sisterly lips on Juan's cheek, gone to rejoin History in the making. And he was abandoned with a squat, speechless *yanacona*. There, in her things of many colors, she hunkered, as they did. Juan wondered if she would recognize a chair, as such.

Not that she could learn much about chairs from this room, which contained only two mattresses, a bench and a rough-hewn table. The *maestre de campo's* status granted him a house almost as large as Valdivia's—and on the plaza—yet it was next to bare. Pedro disdained comfort, linking easeful furniture to such decadence as perfumed handkerchiefs, and ultimately to cowardice, by a chain of reasoning too obvious to explain. However, Juan had nothing against ease. Although his Bower of Bliss had no chairs, it was provided with carpets, tapestries, cushions, and an invisible kitchen where Moors made pasties delivered by veiled handmaidens materializing as needed. Silent maidens, yes ... but nothing like this Inca incapable of civilized speech. He observed her sourly as she set meat on steaming *choclo*. In moments she would be offering him unwanted food.

Lobo hurried in, his intensity instantly more difficult to bear than boredom. He rattled on in Latin, disapproving of the gold of Malga Malga. He quoted Erasmus. What would Thomas More think?

In due course—Juan merely grunting—he proposed chess.

In such matches, Juan was no less at Lobo's mercy than Indians against Spanish cavalry—although Lobo always let him start with white. Losing did not bother Juan, however, for, like deserts, his boredom focused attention on faint differences in otherwise blank days. He became lost in the beauty of the board of inlaid wood, the ivory and ebony pieces, smoothed by use. He moved them in a sensuous trance, lost in touch, smallness, and elegance. Maybe the Bower of Bliss should have a parquet floor.

The priest attacked without a dream of mercy. And as his ivory armies were crushed, Juan became intrigued by this ritual combat, so unlike the real battles he had come to know. Bloodless and beautiful, this was war on squares, with rules and rulers—as in *romances*—defeat obliterated by resetting the board. Chess was war without consequence, ruthless but revocable, infinite in combination … always the same. On this board nothing was hidden. Here were no secrets … only powers. He imagined a piece allowed to torture—the bishops joining the Inquisition?—yet this was inconceivable in a war without speech, agony or aftermath. And tininess was but part of the enthrallment. The equality of armies, the measured space, was another. The last element eluded Juan until he realized that Inés was the white queen.

Lobo was winning too casually to be drawn into the game. He had thought the boy misguided by Pedro and *romances,* but ultimately bright. Now he doubted his judgment. "Check," he declared, as pandemonium announced the arrival of Valdivia.

The priest scurried out. Juan tried to stand but the pain was too great. The *yanacona* came to prop him, walked him to the door, and he looked out over her Inca cap. In the plaza a whirlpool of *vecinos* milled about Valdivia—who seemed exhausted—talking to Monroy and Pedro. No conspirator was in evidence.

Pedro clanked in, scowling, sitting with a deliberate crash, and slamming the table with his armored elbows. He grumbled, "Valdivia said a drunken brawl is not revolt. Makes me want to puke." He spat instead. Pedro's patience had come upon some kind of inner cliff, and he was falling.

He did not spit again, however. Finding Juan's uneaten meat, he ate, then made to leave with the *chola.* Juan stared, and Pedro paused. "Er," he said. "She is *my* Indian. Got skinny in the desert, but filled out nicely since, don't you think?" He patted her cap as they walked away.

Valdivia spent the afternoon elsewhere with Inés. Lobo reclaimed his chess set and left. Juan was idly gnawing on bones when a second commotion punctuated the Historic Day—shouts and hooves, then nothing. The moment came when Juan, who desperately had to pee, did so, right off the bed against the wall. He had been in Purgatory for an eternity when Inés walked in with a torch, looking about to collapse.

"Are you all right?" she asked.

"What happened?"

"Disaster."

She sat on a bench, ravishing in the warm flicker of light—a Pieta lacking only a Son, a halo, and a desert backdrop.

"What!"

"The Indians rose. All at Malga Malga and the coast are dead. The brigantine was burned, the gold of Malga Malga hurled into the sea. Only Gonzalo de los Ríos and Juan Valiente escaped to relate these horrors." She shook her lovely head in disbelief. So many *vecinos* dead, and she was sure De los Ríos had not revealed the manner of their dying, simply to spare her. "And, oh," she added, spent torch flickering, "Chinchilla got drunk on what was left from the party, and when De los Ríos returned with the news he was so deep in his cups that he rode about laughing at the disaster, shaking the cascabels of a horse's harness like a crazed jester. If I could have my way, I would hang every one of them in motley."

Juan imagined the row of fools in their drooping checkered caps with cascabels, doing their airy dance of death, jingling keeping time to their agony....

He knew Inés had attained some personal limit when she hoarsely added, "As for the Picunche—unholy killers and torturers of *cristianos*—it would not displease me to see them all hung as well. There certainly are trees enough in this hell called Chile."

"Inés?"

Juan had thought he knew her.

"Valdivia," she cried out—revealing what was darkest in her extremity—"has gone with forty, maybe to his slaughter, and why not take *me*? He knows I would fight by his side. He knows I would die for him."

Finally, she cried. And, only when the torch died, did she ask in darkness, "*Y quién soy yo*? Who am I then, to him?"

You are the Queen, Juan grieved in silence. The white. The only.

He woke to soft rain falling on thatch, Pedro in his cot. The Inca maid walked in carrying a rooster by the legs, wings extended and relaxed, accepting fate the quiet way fowl do, yet his head swiveled snakelike, upright—needing to see death in the eye.

"Enough of women's medicines," said Pedro, rubbing his hands together. "You need a plaster of warm guts."

The *pieza* killed and gutted the bird, Pedro applying this acme of healing to Juan's violated ribs. And benignly chuckling, he looked up from entrails steaming in the chill to see his Indian standing idle while fresh chicken went ungrilled.... He scolded her and left, returning with three more roosters—a feathered meat bouquet—when the fat of the first had just begun to sputter. Pedro did not wait, for he liked his chicken pink and juicy. Ripping off a leg, he said that Chinchilla was confined in chains. Valdivia would deal with him when he returned.

"*In vino veritas*," Pedro then pronounced. Distrusting all knowledge that led to words, he yet obscurely felt that Latin was close to God, and this idiom was his favorite.

Juan was amazed that Inés—who had the single-minded attention for sedition that a greyhound has for hares—forgot to tell him. And he was even more surprised that the Governor had acted at last. Biting into his chicken, Juan saw the *chola* standing by, and since her relationship with Pedro had turned her into something like a very, very distant relative, he ripped off a thigh, extending it. She was gesturing her denial when Inés walked in, bearing soup made from leftovers of the feast, smiling. But when her eyes adjusted, she set her kettle down to glare.

"I knew it, Pedro," she exclaimed, arms akimbo, "you *had* to plaster Juan with warm guts! And I suppose you plan to sacrifice those other chickens on the altar of useless medicine."

"They're roosters," Pedro countered, sheepish, reaching for indignation and finding guilt. "Extra ones," he added. He hated remorse even more than pork cut up small in soup.

"Just an excuse to stuff yourself on my animals." And Inés passed judgment. "The dead one is the only one you get."

Pedro glanced longingly at the meat bouquet suspended from a rafter as Inés removed the congealing entrails from Juan's side, cooing pleasant nothings. He wondered which was more embarrassing—being called 'the altar of useless medicine' or having Inés fuss over him before witnesses. She exited with the reprieved roosters and Pedro followed after, muttering 'vegetable poultices' in the tone he might well use to mutter 'water.'

By early afternoon Juan felt much improved. Weary of confinement, he decided on a walk around the town square, where *yanaconas* were repairing the damage done by the quake. He had arrived at the gallows—tilted, still needing a noose—when *vecinos* ran this way and that with drawn swords. A squad of *infantes* trotted by with Pedro at their head, looking both sinister and satisfied.

"What's going on?" shouted Juan.

"They finally did it!" Pedro exulted.

The plaza filled with excited *vecinos* as the squad of *infantes* marched up with De Hoz and his cronies, who were made to stand before Monroy.

"By virtue of the authority invested in me by Don Pedro de Valdivia, Governor of Santiago de Nueva Extremadura, I order you confined in chains until his return, accused of treason."

Pedro left with the prisoners, Inés entering into earnest conversation with Monroy. And when Juan walked over her eyes widened. "What are you *doing* ... *up!*" Then, frowning, "Where's my poultice?" Finally, "You get back to bed, I'll be right over."

She arrived ecstatic, spouting news as she replaced her poultice. Pastrana had sent Chinchilla food. Juan Gómez, the jailer, was watching him eat a chunk of bread when a note baked into it fell out. Both lunged for it but Gómez got it and read—"Do not confess, for nothing is known." Chinchilla, with a mad leap, grasped the message and swallowed it whole.

The Sinister Jesters were at it again, Juan thought, undergoing the vision of a rodent in motley swallowing the evidence of his folly.

"They did it at last," Inés crowed, echoing Pedro.

Juan was wondering, *who* did *what*? The food came from Pastrana, yet Juan Gómez brought it. To include a message in the incriminating loaf—or substituting one—would have been easy. Was it Monroy ... Pedro ... Inés...? In any case this was a brilliantly devious stroke, if such a stroke it was. He studied Inés—fussing with poultices, eyes shadowed by worry—deciding she was incapable of such duplicity. And Monroy was far too honorable. That left just one person, and when Pedro finally arrived—too hungry to turn down soup—Juan put the question to him, "Is it possible that a note got in Chinchilla's bread by some deliberate accident a Benevolent God might wink at?"

Pedro winked, putting a finger to the side of his nose. But never did the *maestre de campo* discuss the mysteries that brought the conspiracy tumbling down. Like the incriminating paper, his knowledge became vanished evidence, digested by the great paunch of History.

At dawn, next morning, black Domingo summoned Santiago to the town square with his bronze bell. Monroy and Pedro stood beside the tilted gallows, to which a noose had been conspicuously attached. The *vecinos* assembled as the accused faced the Lieutenant Governor and the *maestre de campo*, flanked by priests.

"We have evidence of your perfidious treachery to your *vecinos*, your Governor, and the Crown," Monroy declaimed in his uninflected tenor. "Will you now confess before God and man?

De Hoz sneered, but failed to look haughty. Like the other prisoners he was unkempt in hose, boots, a soiled wool shirt, hands bound behind his back.

Monroy nodded to Pedro, who walked the line of accused. They stared defiantly back save for Bartolomé Márquez, who closed his eyes. At a nod from the *maestre de campo* he was dragged to the gallows, whining for mercy. But instead of placing the noose around his neck, *infantes* tied the bound hands of Marquez to the rope and heaved until the weeping man was balanced on his toes. Then Domingo— town crier doubling as executioner—mounted the stairs with his whip, a vicious instrument of seven thongs into which iron nails were braided.

Domingo—History might have noted, but did not—was black as his whip and hard as its nails. Márquez was so horrified he neglected to weep, craning his head the better to see agony approach behind him, reminding Juan of the rooster about to be turned into a plaster of warm guts. Márquez had less self control however, his eyes red and wild, nose running.

Ripping off his filthy shirt, Domingo warmed up with an arc so brutal it hummed like bees. Untouched, Márquez screamed like a dying rabbit, for whippings were far more painful than hangings ... and often just as fatal. The second swing struck full. A second scream ... as tears and snot went flying. The third had blood bright on the whip, dripping nails spattering the audience. Domingo paused, whip hanging....

Something about whipping made one count, thought Juan. And as the number four was building, Márquez screamed. "No! No! I did it! I mean *they* did it! We all did it! I confess! *He* did it! Unable to use a finger, the *infante* puckered his lips, indicating De Hoz with a gesture of his head.

"Do you formally confess?"

Márquez wept before Monroy. "*Sí. Sí.* De Hoz did it!"

"Drop this scum and have his confession taken down."

Luis de Cartagena—returned to his native obesity by the current plenty of Santiago—walked over with importance and sat with the tools of his trade on the gallows steps. There he recorded the entirety of the plot—the names, the plan to kill Valdivia and take the brigantine to Peru. They had conspired since Lima.

The next *infante*—Sebastián Vásquez—confessed after only the second blow. The third—Martín Ortuño—did not even mount the gallows. So it went—Antonio de Pastrana, Martín de Solier, Chinchilla ... De Hoz himself. To the last man the conspirators confessed. All that remained was for Valdivia to return and pronounce sentence.

Late next evening—gaunt, almost, as the Crucified Christ—the Governor rode into Santiago at the head of his men, pointed beard seeming to extend the hollows in his cheeks... There had been too many bodies at Malga Malga to bring back, he said. But they had found three live horses, and they had been laden with tools, saddles and gear, armor. They found no weapons though, and not even an emptied bag of gold.

Valdivia then formally proclaimed, "The *vecinos* of Malga Malga are dead. We buried them except for two we could not find. The brigantine is burnt. The gold is gone. The Indians who did this vanished."

The Governor called a council at his house, and leaning on his scabbard, said, "The savages have not attacked here … yet. But they will. I feared we would return too late. We hurried the burials."

Extending a parchment to Vadivia, Monroy replied that there was more bad news. "Here are the confessions of seven traitors—including their leader, De Hoz—signed, sealed, and sworn to before God and Santiago."

Valdivia ripped off the seal with more sorrow than relief. His eyes were sunk in purplish flesh, and to Juan he seemed far too ancient for Inés. When he first met the invincible captain of Cuzco, his hair was grizzled already. Now—physically— he was much the same. But the fierce flame within now barely seemed to smolder. Perhaps the first defeat of his military career had transformed him, or perhaps the steady drain of living with a Judas.

When the Governor listlessly said that he would "consider this matter" a violent energy swept through the listeners like a wind. Outraged *vecinos* looked about, seeing others equally outraged. There was an oiled rustle in the steel-filled room.

Valdivia continued, "We have lost so many, can we afford seven more? What if…?"

Monroy slammed the confessions on the table and stalked out, too disciplined to speak his mind. Pedro followed, making amorphous sounds of resolve. And when solid, steady Quiroga joined them, he created exodus.

This was the next thing to mutiny, and Juan stood shocked beside Inés in the emptied room, she shaking her head at the Governor with a love no less profound than exasperated. And when she put a hand on Valdivia's shoulder, Juan left without a word.

Next morning, he was discussing the disaster over breakfast with Pedro when Monroy strode up, saying, "I have with me orders from the Governor to execute all the traitors but De Hoz, who will be imprisoned. Martín de Solier will be beheaded, as befits his rank. I would appreciate your help in this matter. We are to waste no time."

Pedro hurried out. There was much to be done, with six men condemned, only one tree of justice, and no executioner's ax.

A gallows big enough for four was erected from logs already cut for rafters—a cross pole supported by tripods not much higher than a tall man's head. As the condemned were to be pulled up—not dropped—they needed to be elevated only until their feet no longer held their weight.

Pedro supervised the making of nooses. Juan helped with the poles, listening to the other workmen.

"Been too long since anybody died of *rope sickness*," said one.

"You better not sneeze, *hideputa*," chuckled another.

The certain, imminent death of others, Juan decided, made witnesses feel more alive, as if last breaths transferred vital force. He inhaled deeply, relishing the light of morning, the cool air. He put his fingers to his throat and pressed, imagining the pain and pressure of the rope. He held his breath.

"Feeling a little rope sick?" asked an *infante*. Juan was not exactly popular with the troops, who considered him useless baggage for the expedition—silly as the potted figs of Doña Inés, and coddled as her pigs. Besides, he read and wrote, like Moors and Jews.

The finished gallows looked to Juan like the ridgepole of a house built for death—therefore needing to provide no shelter. As Spanish drums were not available, the condemned marched to Inca harps and flutes. Standing by the gallows, Domingo wore a pointed hood with eyeholes cut into it, striped and colorful, for it had been made from a poncho. Father Marmolejo, walking backward while holding high a crucifix, led the conspirators—hands bound behind them.

No time was wasted as the condemned had already been shriven. Marmolejo lifted his hand in last a benison. Chinchilla had been chosen to be first—and Fortuna surely chuckled, for this assigned him the only proper gallows. He would hang the highest, but also drop to an easy death. He climbed the steps to the strum and twitter of Inca instruments, remaining firm as the noose was adjusted. Father Marmolejo raised his cross, that it be the last thing Chinchilla saw before his Maker.

Juan missed the moment, bending to scratch his leg as Domingo released the trap, lifting his head when he heard the cheer. Chinchilla was quietly rotating.

The time had come for the remaining four. Márquez was dragged. Vásquez staggered. Pastrana and Ortuño managed walking to the Inca dirge. Father Marmolejo intoned the *credo* as Juan stood on tiptoe, to see Márquez shaking and sniveling. Vásquez was shaking also until his legs collapsed, so that he began his hanging early. Pastrana held firm. Ortuño's eyes were closed.

Juan stared at the back of an *infante*, counting cheers. At the fourth, the rejoicing was interrupted by complaints. On his toes again, Juan saw Ortuño looking back, sticking out his tongue. The accumulating load had made the tripods sag, and as Ortuño was tall he was bearing some of his weight on his toes. Volunteers rushed up to elevate the support. Ortuño's eyes glazed over, and his chin was dripping spittle.

Juan elbowed his way from the crowd, empty of everything but eyes lit by the world's last light.

That evening, while cleaning blood off his armor, Pedro talked about the beheading, which went well. De Solier died nobly, extending his neck without hesitation over the improvised block. Domingo used a two-handed sword, and the head came off clean.

"Amazing, how far a neck can spurt," Pedro mused, "it's like stepping hard on a *bota* of *tinto*." And—wouldn't you know it—the squirt had to come *his* way. "Ah, well." Philosophical, Pedro cleaned on, reporting that Domingo had to pick the head of Solier up by the ears, due to his baldness. He added that the eyes were closed, but the lips were moving.

Juan blanched. Maybe the head was not so much trying to speak as letting the soul emerge. But how, through a head detached? In a church he had once seen a sculpture of a soul—a tiny stone body hovering over the open mouth of its former abode. So, how did the soul of Solier leave the part from the neck down, if the mouth left with the head?

Bluish tubes stuck out the necks of decapitated chickens, Juan knew, and he wondered if Solier's head was like that. Juan knew also that slippery things moved the toes of the severed feet of chicken, making of them marionettes without a body. Were there cords in the neck stump of Solier that you could pull to move his face? Did God so raise *entire* dead at the Last Judgment, yanking on internal things? Maybe he could walk up to Solier's head—now on a pike by the gallows— and, tugging, make it wink ... maybe even talk. Surely not, for if that were possible Cacafuego would long ago have taught dead heads to speak.

Inés walked in, and with a pirouette she sang, "Valdivia is alive, alive." Her lifted hands were pale. Her black skirt bloomed with her spin.

Checking Juan's ribs, she cheerfully declared more medicine unnecessary. Did he feel well enough to help inspect her neglected plants and animals tomorrow?

She came early, offering *choclo* cakes with honey, taking him on a tour of her husbandry. Gesturing with hands holding breakfast, she used her every charm to convert him. There, an orchard. Here vines, for wine and table. Beyond the garden, fallow still. Beside them, pens and coops, easing the transfer of manure. Green eyes glowing, she revealed the harvest of bulging sacks hung in a shed—for seed—explaining that, with luck, they should be baking in the coming year. Most of the garlic had been replanted. What was not, should be wonderfully plump. As for the melons and herbs, they could be enjoyed without delay.

They arrived at the pigsty, where Inés caused a wild commotion by tossing in the last of her corn cake. She had been talking manure, but she turned silent. "Eh?" she urged.

The three sows to survive the Atacama had multiplied into a plethora of pigs, and Juan joined her impromptu jig, ignoring the piercing stab in his side. Pedro would be in Heaven.

The *maestre de campo* returned late in the afternoon with news. Convinced that Picunche were preparing an attack, Valdivia had ordered him to an outpost at the river Cachapoal. There, he was to torture savages for information and destroy whatever fortifications they prepared. He was to take ten *caballeros*, he concluded, unable to look Juan in the eye.

"I know. I know," said Juan.

"Your ribs, *hijo*."

Juan stormed out. And only when he found that his feet had returned him to the pigsty did he remember that he forgot to give Pedro news of pork.

In his bed, that night, he revisited the Bower of Bliss, deciding to elaborate The First Chaste Kiss. However, it grew dark, and the trees pressed. Paths disappeared. Branches clutched and tightened. Juan was more lost than ever he had been before while riding to imagined paradise, in a gloom he would not willingly create. And now his horse was following a glimmering river rushing over rocks far below, where water shattered moonlight.

Dream swallowing Juan's dreams, Amadís galloped unrestrained—for sleep now held the reins. Juan rode through cobwebs in a swamp where creatures flickered, watching him with dim, red eyes. He galloped by skeletons silently gesturing at talking animals, until Amadís stopped his mad rush and hung his head.

Dismounting, Juan walked to the glow of an open door.

Inside, a row of men hung from the ridgepole, faces lost in rising smoke. A cot like his was in the room beneath their boots ... and on it Juan saw himself, reclining.

Cacafuego shambled from darkness into torchlight, his head held high in his left hand. The eyes were closed, mouth moving randomly, as if hoping to rediscover speech by trial and error. And yes, strings hung from the neck. Cacafuego pulled them with his free hand, and his eyes opened. Another pull and he winked. He made his yellow tongue stick out, waggling it obscenely. A leer followed, gruesome and hilarious. Yet at no point did the mouth speak, although moving ever faster. The *infante's* deft fingers flew—as if a milkmaid squeezed expressions from an udder. And it was then that Cacafuego began plainchant with his anus. The head provided a ventriloquistic counterpoint, and he good as sang a *miserere*.

This astonishing performance over, Cacafuego's head took a bow.

And as Juan was wakened by a quake, the hanging dead began to swing like silent bells.

Chapter 14: Pichikan (Malga Malga and Santiago, 1541)

Francisco Carretero was miserable. He had the night watch and it was that awful hour before the dawn. He was famished too, and knew that this morning like every other he would break his fast on rock-like Indian bread that broke your teeth along with your fast. Not many of his teeth were left, all rotted, and they all hurt like hell. And it was raining, cold and fine. And his helmet had a rusted rivet, so water trickled beneath his armor, soaking his shirt, running down the crack in his ass, wetting his hose. Carretero peed, scrutinizing darkness and seeing nothing but dim trees—save for faint shadows that were the fucking horses he guarded but was not rich enough to ride. Not far away glowed the guard fire where his friend Gáspar kept watch in comfort … damn his ass.

At long last, through leaves, Carretero glimpsed the glow of sunrise. His watch was almost over and he could take a crap. He would break his fast, maybe another tooth. He would endure jokes about wet hose. He would sleep. To cheer himself up he remembered the most expensive fuck of his life. She was in a whorehouse run by monks, and he recalled her name, María de la Concepción, as being strange for a *puta*. He remembered even better when her tits dropped down. Her low-cut bodice had offered them up fat and white, like chicken breasts. And when she undid her laces—*Sangre de Cristo!*—they dropped to below her elbows. It was the most beautiful thing he had ever seen…. And it was the last thing he would ever remember, for his helmet clanged, and before he could react there was an instant of intolerable light.

Had he lived, Francisco Carretero might have compared that flash to the backfire of an arquebus. And had he been able to see himself, after, he would know a round black stone had driven his nose deep into his head. The missile remained embedded through his shuddering, giving him what—to one differently educated—would resemble a Cyclopean eye.

Pichikan rejoiced when the *lik winka* fell. Of the two stones he and Tuiñam had hurled one produced a clatter, the other a satisfying thud. But though the guard did not cry out, his *wethakelu* made noise when he fell. They hurried over. The *lik winka* was on his back, mouth open to the drizzle.

Pichikan picked up the spear fallen from his hand and drove it deep into his throat. While he did that Tuiñam took the long knife hanging from his waist. Strangely, there had been no challenge from the other guard. Silent as moths, they hurried to the *kawellu*….

The mighty animals were nervous, stamping the ground. Pichikan and Tuiñam found saplings lashed from tree to tree—the corral for the *kawellu*—and with the heavy, astoundingly sharp weapons they had captured, cut the rawhide thongs that bound them. Slipping from tree to tree they returned to where guard-fire lit the trees, glittering on wet leaves, singling out unsteady drops of water. They hid, not knowing what to do, having expected an alarm followed instantly by battle.

Gáspar Sánchez, *infante*, was half-dozing at his post under a makeshift roof of brush, and the water dripping off it made his fire sizzle in a way that made him sleepy. He tossed more wood on, thinking that night duty could be worse. Francisco—poor bastard—was out in the rain. Thanking Mary for small mercies, Gáspar yawned, scrutinizing the night as his chin began its slow creep down.

He jerked awake … almost toppled into flame. At first he thought he had burned himself—the chain mail on his ass so hot he smelled the wool beneath. That could happen. Once, when his friend, Ignacio Romero, was *ciego de uvas*—grape blind— he passed out on a fire and woke up half-cooked in his armor, steamed in wet wool like a fish cooked in clay. Gaspar chuckled, remembering how Ignacio sizzled when he jumped into a snow bank. Tentatively, he touched the metal over his ass, deciding it was not *too* hot.

Maybe a clang over by Francisco wakened him? Maybe something happened … *was* happening? Maybe Francisco dropped his spear? Leaving one's post was forbidden, but no one would ever know.

Seeing the torch approaching in their direction, Pichikan and Tuiñam melted into shadows, then attacked.

Pichikan leapt onto the back of the *lik winka*—*pangi* on *pudu*. Weaving a sinewy right arm around his neck, he attempted to snap it as they fell … but failed, because of the hard *lik winka wethakelu* on his head. They struggled by the sputtering light of the fallen torch, Pichikan sitting on the back of the *lik winka*, shoving his face into dirt and pine needles to keep him from crying out. Using all his strength he slipped his arms under those of the *lik winka* in a wrestling hold that had often served him well, rolling until the immobilized enemy was turned face up. He would probably yell, but Tuiñam would kill him. They had never expected a complete surprise anyway.

Tuiñam had picked up the torch, intending to put it out, when Pichikan rolled the *lik winka* over.

Eyes wide with terror, gagging, spitting pebbles, pine needles and teeth, the *lik winka* was inhaling, preparing to scream, and Tuiñam crammed the torch deep into his mouth, holding firm against his struggle. The fit was perfect, and *pichilewechi antu* was once more dark and silent, save for the sizzle of blood and spit.

When the *lik winka* stopped moving they dragged him into the forest. Pichikan hooted once, twice … hooted again, signaling with the voice of the *kilkil*—that bird of night and death.

Gonzalo de los Ríos—commander at Malga Malga—rose with the first flush of dawn as was his habit. Strapping on armor, slipping the stench of his boots over the stench of the hose he had slept in, he stepped from his tent into a drizzle that chased the warmth of sleep from his face … and saw that no one was at Gáspar's fire. The *hideputa* was probably off behind some bush, jerking off, or trying to pop the cork of his constipation. Whatever, this *hideputa* was going to wish he was dead. You did *not* leave your post. You could piss while on watch, but you *absolutely* did not shit! Above all, you did not sleep! A shit was a shit, a sleep a sleep, and a watch—damn Gáspar's eyes!—was called a watch for good military reason.

De los Ríos searched, and found, not an *infante* indulging in forbidden acts, but Juan Valiente squatting behind bushes. The commander grunted, smelling what the *negro* was up to. Then the dawn grew too bright, too fast, behind him. Burning arrows arched trails of sparks, thudding into trees and softly quivering in soil. Some hissed in the wool of wet tents. But the sodden cloth would not light, not this morning. De los Ríos drew his sword, taking satisfaction in the fucking incompetence of Indians. And he did not think to wonder why the attack was silent—with not a single savage visible—until he heard the staccato grumble of retreating hooves. Spinning about with panic, he faced the vanishing sound. They were surrounded and without horses—their most powerful weapon, and his necessity, for he was fat and not good on his feet.

He suspected the worst. If Ignacio had not sounded the alarm, he was dead. That would also explain Gáspar's disappearance. De los Ríos hesitated nonetheless— as the distant sound of horses blended into the faint hum of insects—debating whether he should follow or help defend the camp.

It was then the ululation began. Ending his indecision, the heathen whooping filled him not with intended terror but with a calm erected on many hours of slaughter in which weariness had been the greatest price of Spanish victory. Gonzalo de los Ríos was again—so to speak—in his element. But— damn it!—no mount.

He walked, for he could not run in a *caballero's* armor. The camp would take care of itself, and if he returned with even one horse it would swing the weight of battle in the Spanish favor,

He found Carretero dead near his post, face caved in by a smooth black stone, throat yawning crimson, weapons gone. Of course, the horses were also gone. It took no heathen to find their trampled path, even in semi-darkness.

All *caballeros* hated walking—as tiring and ignoble—De los Ríos more than most, for he had been comfortably corpulent until coming to this land of famine, and he retained the habits of his former size. His armor no longer fit, yet he had kept it as a masterpiece both functional and pious—the Stations of the Cross depicted on his torso, front and back. To abandon this work of art would have been sacrilege, even when he fit it like a wrinkled pea its pod. De los Ríos wanted to be fat again. He yearned to fill his splendid armor. Thin, he felt poor. Also, his armor chafed now, especially when he walked. God, did he hate shank's mare!

The sun was well up when De los Ríos stopped walking, seeing that the panicked herd had scattered. A horse plop marked the spot. He was contemplating it—wondering which direction to take—when Juan Valiente ran up babbling, nodding 'yes' to affirm his impossible tale, 'no' to exorcise the horror. Dead, he said, all dead. Truly. *Yanaconas* too. He saw it from bushes ... saw all that awful horror with his very eyes. It was true and terrible.

Stunned, all Gonzalo de los Ríos could bring to mind was that this *negro* had saved his life with a crap.

Whooping, Pichikan ran from blanket *ruka* to blanket *ruka*, cutting the ropes supporting them with his amazing spear, collapsing their wet weight on *lik winka*. Tuiñam and the Pikunche did the same by the light of flaming arrows. Every blanket *ruka* was down.

Lik winka managed to stumble out, confused, and were instantly assaulted. One had a hard *wethakelu* on his head, nothing on his feet. He killed and wounded several, became unable to swing his weapon in the crowd ... went down. Others with nothing on their heads were brained. But most *lik winka*, trapped under wool, were trodden by the dance of victory, worried with spears and clubbed, the wriggling mounds slowly turning crimson until those still alive were dragged out.

Michimalongko shouted, "The *lik winka toki* is not here!"

The *weichafe* paid no attention, brandishing captured weapons, hacking at corpses, removing their hard *wethakelu* and putting them on. One held a severed hand over his head like a cock's comb, crowing—that old joke. Runners had gone for *mudai*, and before long the amazing victory would become a drunken celebration.

Pichikan—who alone had listened to Michimalongko—counted the dead. The *kuru winka* was missing.

The absence of the *toki* was harder to confirm, as almost all the bodies were decapitated. He checked the heads still on the ground, those lifted by the dancers....

De los Ríos ordered the *negro* to pursue the horses, and back propped against a tree, sat to wait. He was weary and chafed, yet this paled by the fact that he had just presided at the greatest disaster of the Indies. And gloom—he thought—was not his natural humour. He was fat, sanguine and choleric by nature, that's what he was. Now he was thin, melancholy and bilious. It came to him that Indians had probably also attacked those building the brigantine. If so they had been trounced by Valdivia. De los Ríos burned with shame at his failure, though it had all been the fault of the damned guards, and he was consigning their souls to the last sulfurous circle of Hell when his helmet bonged like a bell.

Struggling to his feet De los Ríos saw nothing, realizing that *this* was how the sentries died, never even seeing an enemy. "Come out and fight like *cristianos!*" he screamed.

"Fight like men, *hideputas*," he shouted, hearing a whirr by his ear, a thunk into the tree behind him. The stone that fell by his feet was smooth and black.

The next one hit his helmet with a deafening clang, where his face would have been if he had he not looked down. The missiles seemed evil and animate, like malevolent black hornets. Swinging his great sword, roaring—Santiago *y* España!—he charged, defiant of these enemies without face or honor.

Pichikan and Tuiñam found the footprints of the *lik winka toki* following the trampling of *kawellu* and loped after, less intent on tracking than on being ambushed. Yet they found him sitting in plain sight. This was courage, stupidity, or madness. In any case, it was an unexpected opportunity, and from hiding they began to hurl their stones.

The mighty warrior went insane, bellowing, swinging his weapon at nothing. It was like the eruption of a volcano in an unexpected place, such as a fire pit, and Pichikan admired the sight. Then, when the *lik winka* at last stopped fighting nothing and shouted some insult or challenge, he flung a stone that missed. Now the *lik winka* was lumbered toward their hiding place.

They leapt into the open, making obscene gestures. He lumbered faster, stumbling. They ran and hid, throwing stones, popping out to mock him. With *lik winka* you were either dead or laughing.

They returned him to his starting point. He stopped yelling, leaning on his weapon, head erect, and Pichikan became ashamed. This was no turtle, to tease. Inside the shell was a *weichafe* who deserved a warrior's death.

Taking the stinking *wethakelu* from his head, Pichikan walked toward the *lik winka,* bearing his club and the *lik winka* spear he had captured.

They looked each other over, De los Ríos seeing a painted savage, black cloth over his crotch, unremarkable save for his size. He had a Spanish spear however, and the sight made his blood boil, for this trophy surely cost the life of a *cristiano*.

Pichikan thought the *lik winka* looked bloated—like a toad—in his hard *wethakelu*. Did he fill it? Was he willing to be hollow, to seem larger?

"*Dios ayude, y* Santiago!" De los Ríos attacked, yet the Indian merely leapt about, refusing combat.

Having noticed that the *lik winka* took an instant to recover from each huge swing, Pichikan darted in and tripped him with his spear, creating a satisfying crash.

De los Ríos—who had never fought on foot—was stunned. And now the savage was leaning on his Spanish spear, watching him. Not smiling, not laughing, he seemed merely interested, until he heard the sound of galloping horses....

Juan Valiente appeared on one horse, leading another. Approaching, his immense mount reared, striking at the Indians with iron-shod hooves.

Pichikan bolted.

Too astonished to react, Tuiñam fell beneath a blur of hooves. And soon the *lik winka* on their *kawellu* were hurrying toward *fucha lafken*.

Pichikan ran up and saw that blood flowed from the nose and ears of Tuiñam, but he was still breathing. The *lik winka wethakelu* on his head was caved in. Pichikan lifted his friend to his shoulder and ran.

Lleflai, who was bathing in the stream at twilight, heard a cough in the woods. A *wentru* was letting her know of his presence in this way, she supposed, to respect her modesty. She plunged into icy water to her neck, wondering why this man coughed instead of leaving. And who could he be, to know about the hidden *ruka*? How much had he seen?

Another cough.

Lleflai slipped from the water, threw on her *kepam*.

A *weichafe* stepped from the woods.

Pichikan! And ... Tuiñam was slung over his shoulder like *pudu* brought from the hunt! He was covered with dried blood, looked dead, and yet breathed with a soft snore.

"Hurry!" she cried out. "Ñamku is inside."

When the wounds were washed the *machi* said, "His head is broken. Shoulder too. What happened?"

"He was attacked by a *kawellu* that walked like *che*."

"When?"

"Two *antu* ago."

"You *carried* him two days!"

Pichikan shrugged, not mentioning that he had run much of the way.

"He may not wake before he dies."

Lleflai wept for this young man who had been kind to her. Where was the soul of those who lived and would not wake?

"If Tuiñam does not soon awake," said the *machi*, "he will die of sleep."

Hearing a rare uncertainty in his voice, Lleflai said, "I will watch over him this night."

Ñamcu disappeared into his recess and Lleflai went to where the *pichiche* slept. Tucking arms and legs under *degu* pelt she saw two wide-open eyes.

"I will watch with you, *papai*," said Raytrayen.

They shared a blanket, tended the fire, seeing nothing but awful peace on the face of the unwaking, hearing the same soft snore....

When Raytrayen at last went to sleep Lleflai wept, alone with the young man dying of not waking. His face was round and handsome, nose fiercely arched. Wounded, he was vulnerable, childlike. She yearned to touch her cheek to his, cover him with her hair. She felt joy ... and in her joy was horror.

She prayed to the *pillañ*. Let him wake and live to see her. Let his waking save her from herself. Let him live to be her friend—just that—again. Let him open his intolerable eyes!

"Is something wrong, *papai*," Raytrayen fluted, lifting a sleepy head.

"Nothing, Raytra. Nothing." And Lleflai wiped at tears too deep in scars to touch.

The *pichiche* were still asleep when Pichikan left. Painted for war, he said that Michimalongko would soon attack the *lik winka* by the hill Welen, and that was something he could not miss.

Lleflai returned to her vigil.

Tuiñam did not wake that *antu* or the next. From time to time Raytrayen joined her, bringing wood, helping her keep the fire glowing beneath the simmer of a pot.

Ñamku was invisibly occupied all this time, leaving the *ruka* only once. Taciturn, he refused food, nourished by the air as when Lleflai first knew him. Noises of making came from behind his blanket, however. Stone was chipped, wood ground and bored. And at night he spoke with the dead. Lleflai had come to know the other softer voice.

Ñamku smiled at the apparition, not needing to add he loved him, not to the knowing dead.

A shadow of a smile on the bright shadow that he was, Katrinir said, "I brought you what you need."

From darkness he produced the image of a glimmering *wethakelu*—Ñamku's memory of what his teacher once described. Having obsidian, the *machi* set to work, flaking stone that, held to light, glowed green. Too often it shattered, yet by *pichilewechi antu* he had the handful of small points he required.

Searching the forest for wood, he began to assemble the tool the next night, commenting to Katrinir, "You did not call me Mapuche when you appeared."

"You are right ... Mapuche."

Katrinir remembered the Ñamku that had returned from the *lik winka*—confused, depressed, unwilling to talk about what happened by the hill Welen, hiding fear with silence. Scraps of his memory spun into and out of sight, distorted, and Katrinir could not tell how much of the confused dread was real, how much twisted by refusal, how much improved by hope, how much buried by despair. If only for what they had done to Ñamku, *lik winka* were his enemies.

He said, "All *che* must now become something else if they are to remain Mapuche … this I have learned from you. The *lik winka* have made our violence necessary, since they will not let us remain ourselves. They will not let us love what we love, be what we are."

Having fit a shaft to a hole in a wooden disk, Ñamku stopped his work, looking at the apparition with astonishment, prepared to see another Katrinir. Painted for war?

"*Our* violence! You—who would not do violence to earthworms—propose war with the *lik winka!*"

"They will make us strangers to ourselves. This the Mapuche *must* resist. If they make war on our determination, let it be war."

And it was then Ñamku decided that he had been blind to the new beginning. How wrong he had been to think *lik winka* some kind of distant kin! Everything he had imagined about them was wrong. Every encounter was encrusted with questions like barnacles on rock, impossible to pry off.

Katrinir added, "We cannot resist, or fight—much less trust—what we do not know. We need to speak to them."

"Lautaro?"

"Yes, but you took him too soon."

Ñamku voiced the larger question. "Do we have time before they reach the Fio Fio?"

"Perhaps, and perhaps the Pikunche will defeat them at the hill Welen."

"Perhaps this. Perhaps that. Perhaps yes. Perhaps no." Ñamku was annoyed. "It is said that there are many more *lik winka* beyond the great desert."

Katrinir was pensive. "All I have in death, Ñamku, is what I truly loved. And of that you are the greatest part. Maybe you should not ask me about the future."

The *machi* did not respond, feeling too old for this burden he was born to, which seemed both wrong and unfair. Age should bring wisdom. Age gave you eyes.

"Often as you talk with me, you do not yet know death," Katrinir said. "Imagine returning to your *ruka* and finding it gone, Lleflai and the *pichiche* gone, all the Mapuche, all the *ruka* gone, everything you know and love vanished. Imagine returning to find nothing. Imagine being surrounded by strangers and strangeness only."

"I cannot. What one does not know, one cannot imagine."

"You must, for this may happen. The dead are rooted in life. Without these roots, like the *am* of a *kalku* whose ashes have been cursed and scattered, your *am* and mine will wander without a place to rest, for the dead return to memories. And now, imagine *all* that is Mapuche gone, or made strange, for this is what I fear the *lik winka* mean to do to us. The dead will have no living place to return to. Even the *pillañ* will cease to speak, without ears to hear their language.

"You fear for the dead," Ñamku said, astounded.

"*Yamai*."

"I too am afraid," replied the *machi*. Pikunche had been dying of *lik winka kalkutun* against which he was helpless—these deaths brought by spots and heat, madness, vomiting and sleep—sorcery that killed *domo* and *pichiche* along with the *weichafe*. How could *lik winka* wage war on children?

"You must continue in your hiding," said Katrinir.

"And Lautaro...?"

"Remember the vision that named him? Each of the three was born for a reason. For these same reasons they will be protected by the *pillañ*."

"What if he again refuses?"

"Say that it is for the good of the Mapuche. Tell him it is the will of the *pillañ*. If necessary, have Andalikan convince him. If all else fails, tell him that it will be very dangerous."

The *machi* smiled. "Maybe I should forbid it."

Katrinir chuckled, disappearing as he whispered, "Sleep, Mapuche, for the tool is ready and it will soon be light."

Lleflai—who in her vigil had succumbed to sleep—opened her eyes. Ñamku was in black and unmasked, with something in his hand she did not recognize. Fear crawled her body like icy ants.

"*Mari, mari*, Lleflai. It is time. More than two *antu* have passed and Tuiñam has not yet wakened. I need your help."

Lleflai—who had slept in her *kepam*—set aside her blanket.

"Yes, you have time to bathe, brush your hair," said Ñamku. He added, "Take the *pichiche*. Tell them to stay by the stream until we come to get them."

She returned to find Ñamku cross-legged by Tuiñam, whose head he had turned with the wound up. Her soup had been set aside, she noted, and the *machi* was heating beeswax in a pot. Beside him was the *wethakelu* he was holding when she woke, and an obsidian knife, a tiny needle, thread. She stared at the thing on the blanket—a small disk of wood with obsidian points set in a circle, resembling black fish teeth about an absent mouth. A wooden shaft was at its center, and at the end a crosspiece was lashed.... This was no tool she knew.

Patting the blanket as a sign for her to kneel, Ñamku said, "What you are about to help me with I have never done. This may not open the eyes of Tuiñam, but this is our last hope."

Lleflai knelt, eyes enormous.

"You must bind your hair out of the way."

She rolled it behind her head, and he handed her the pot of wax.

"Keep it warm, not burning hot. It should be soft, not liquid."

Lleflai heated the wax, watching the *machi* out of the corner of an eye.

He washed the wound, and *that* was familiar. But after Ñamku washed the head already shaved for war, his every act became unknown, appalling.

Taking the small knife, slowly he cut the scalp of Tuiñam to the bone, made two more cuts, then—delicate as one removing skin from chicken meat—slipped his knife beneath and lifted until he bared a square of skull.

And there it was, bone oozing blood! Lleflai had seen the skinned heads of animals, but this was a *che*! This was her *friend*!

Forgetting her task in her horror, Lleflai saw the *machi* take the *wethakelu* he had made and place it on the wound. Holding the shaft with one hand he pressed, while turning the handle with the other. The circle of obsidian teeth slowly ground into the skull.

"Watch your wax," he said.

She did—heart aflutter—stealing glances.

A circle was being ground about the wound—where the bone had sunken in—and to Lleflai this seemed far worse than having Tuiñam die of sleep.

Ñamku persisted—breath hissing through clenched teeth, in and out—pressing and turning, the rasping making a soft noise that made her want to scream.

"Do not scream," Ñamku said. "How is the wax?"

She felt. "Just right."

The *machi* rasped on and on—with that perfection of attention a raptor has for rabbits—until, carefully he removed a round of blood-smeared bone. Lleflai let out a long, slow breath.

Tuiñam still snored. The whole thing seemed insane, like amputating a bruised thumb.

Ñamku tilted Tuiñam's head to let blood and fluids drain, then applied wax to the cut bone, explaining, "The bone crushed by the *kawellu* was cursed by *lik winka kalkutun*. We will burn it, save the pieces, crush them to powder, and bury them far from Tuiñam."

This explanation did not lessen her horror, and the *machi* nodded sadly, saying, "Think of it as an open door inviting sleep to leave, so that the soul can return."

"His head cannot remain like *that*," insisted Lleflai, peering into the great wound. She could see brains, now that the wax had stopped the bleeding.

"It will not," replied Ñamku, pulling on flaps of scalp, calmly sewing.

When he was done Lleflai thought the head looked like a badly mended blanket. The stitches were small and reasonably neat, but the color in no way matched the skin. Still, she was beginning to hope Tuiñam would live. "He's like a newborn now," she whispered. All *che* began life with a soft spot in their head.

The *machi* struggled to his feet. "Opening this kind of a door for the soul almost always kills," he said.

Lleflai prepared for her vigil, wondering why Ñamku thought that despair was preferable to unfounded hope.

Pichikan arrived at the *ruka* late that night, finding Tuiñam still dead, still snoring. And he examined the strange, stitched wound. When would he wake? he asked. Lleflai shrugged, tears in her eyes.

The *weichafe* decided not to mourn until his friend was buried.

The next morning, proudly, he told Ñamku and Lleflai that the *lik winka* building the *fucha wampu* by the great sea had been defeated, just as at Malga Malga. The *wampu* was burnt. Now Michimalongko was preparing the final battle with the *lik winka* by the hill Welen. *Weichafe* were arriving from great distances. When the *aillarewe* was assembled the *toki* would attack.

Tuiñam lifted a finger.

Lleflai saw, unable to believe her eyes. "Are you back?" she breathed, as if *pellu* were a mouse to be startled back into its hole. "Your friend, Lleflai, is here." Then, realizing that he had not returned to her, but to war, she said to all, "He wakes."

Tuiñam opened his eyes, recognizing the *ruka*. Yet it was a long journey from his last memory to here. He could still see the *kawellu* walking like a *che*, tall as a tree, hard as a boulder. He had been killed and his *am* had flown to the friends about him—that was what this was. He moved a toe. He moved his head. Did the dead feel pain? His head! He reached....

"*Me!*" barked Ñamku.

And after all the explanations, Tuiñam said, "When my little sister was born *papai* told me to be careful of her soft spot. Will mine close like hers?"

"No."

"I would rather die!"

Pichikan was furious. The wandering soul of Tuiñam had returned to his body as a fool ungrateful to the living. Had he himself not carried a snoring corpse for two *antu*? Had Ñamku not done the impossible, creating a door through which his reluctant *pellu* could return? And what about Lleflai, who watched over him without sleep so long she could scarcely sit?

He leapt to his feet with a war cry that would wake the dead, and the inspiration came. Removing the *lik winka wethakelu* from his head, he offered it to Tuiñam. "Wear this and your head will be even harder than mine."

Tuiñam collapsed, eyes rolling up. Then he was dead again, not snoring.

"He needs food!" Ñamku exclaimed.

Lleflai filled a bowl with soup, picked up a spoon.

"Am I allowed to tickle him?" Pichikan yelled, grinning.

"No!" Tuiñam struggled onto an elbow.

Taking bowl and spoon from Lleflai, Pichikan said, "Might as well eat, *peñi.*" He blew on broth.

Three *antu* later Pichikan left, having delayed his departure longer than he wished. If he had missed the battle by the hill Welen, so be it, for his friend was now able to stand.

"You will have to kill ten for yourself, one for me," Tuiñam said, smiling.

Pichikan grinned back. His hair was shaved save for a topknot braided with red thread. And he was painted black from the neck up, which made his grin more brilliant.

While the soul of Tuiñam was deciding to return, Pichikan had labored over the *lik winka wethakelu*, removing the insides, which smelled of swamps and corpses. Using pumice first, then rough cloth, he polished until the whole shone bright as silver, so that you could see yourself distorted on the gleam. Pichikan made faces at himself before lining the inside with tanned *degu* skin and stuffing the remaining space with dried, sweet grass. As the *wethakelu* lacked color, he put green parrot feathers in the holes on the top that seemed made just for that.

Now, about to leave, Pichikan offered the magnificent thing to his friend. Tuiñam grinned, put it on, and rapped it hard with his fist.

Shouldering a *wilal* Pichikan said his *mari mari* and loped off. Stopping by a stream to drink, he looked into the packet Lleflai handed him, finding nuts, smoked fish, dried berries mixed with honey and *degu* fat. He ate and ran, scanning the sky, for part of the plan of battle was to set the *lik winka ruka* roofs on fire.

Michimalongko sat in the circle of *toki*, who were having a heated discussion. The *lik winka* wanted to meet with them, and many thought this a trap. Others maintained that to send no one would make the *lik winka* suspicious. A scarred veteran stood to say, "We have been talking half an *antu*. Let Michimalongko decide if we send representatives or not."

That did not sit well with the majority. Michimalongko rose, quieting the murmur.

"It is the privilege of a *toki*," he cried, "to listen to *weichafe* and so become their voice. And by listening I have formed an opinion that others share. Yet many do not agree with me—these warriors I hold in great respect. How, then, can we act, united? We cannot both send, and not send, *che* to this meeting where—as the *lik winka* claim— we will discuss the exchange of food … a meeting which is probably just more *lik winka* treachery."

Spear butts slammed into the ground until a rhythm built.

"The *lik winka* bewilder our wisdom with their strangeness. They do not look or think like *che*. They do not act like *che*. What wise *che* knows what they know? What wise *che* knows what they will do? What they have brought is worse than war, for their coming has turned our knowledge into ignorance, and the wisest and oldest look upon them as *pichiche* might, with wonder."

His words were drowned by uproar. Many considered his words an insult. More thought that he had spoken well. Michimalongko raised his arms, requesting the courtesy of silence. And his voice became a grating whisper.

"Ignorance must not lead us to words that are *just* words, for we are not parrots quarreling over *uwa* in the fields, fighting with our tongues. Above all, we must not let indecision divide us. The *lik winka* must be fought, for they are cruel and greedy. They *must* be fought, or they will take our freedom from us. They *must*, at all costs, be fought!"

The voice of Michimalongko had risen to the roar of battle. He slammed his fist into his open hand, listening to the thunder of the unleashed anger.

"Will you let *lik winka* take the *mapu* that we walk on, the *mapu* of our fathers, our *pillañ*?"

"*Me!*"

"Will you let *lik winka* take our fields, our food?"

"*Me!*"

"Will you let them burn our *ruka*?"

"*Me!*"

"Will you let *lik winka kalku* kill our old, our *domo*, our *pichiche*, with their *kalkutun*?"

"*Me!*"

"Will you let *lik winka* take *che* working in their fields, walking in their woods, to be tortured?"

"*Me!*"

"Will you let *lik winka* rape our *domo*, and take them to be theirs?"

The outcry drowned him out.

"Are you the *weichafe* I once knew? Will you become their dogs?"

Every warrior, now, was standing, roaring.

Michimalongko roared back, "What good is a fist when the fingers argue about being a part of it? We must strike together or we will fail, for the *lik winka* are more powerful than anything we have ever known."

He ended, "I will not go meet them. But every *toki* who believes this necessary should do so. And I will await their return, hoping that their courage will prove my judgment wrong. But if they return with more *lik winka* lies—or do not return at all—we must fight for our honor, fight for our *domo* and our *pichiche*, fight for *mapu*. We *will* then fight … and to the death!"

Drums pounded as Michimalongko called for those who would meet with the *lik winka* to make themselves known.

Of the many *toki* only seven stood, ignoring cries of disapproval.

"Cowards," hissed the *weichafe* by Pichikan, his own *toki* being one of them.

"They risk their lives in the hope of sparing ours," Pichikan chided. "These are not cowards … but they are fools, for *lik winka* cannot be trusted."

Mapuche had come far *piku* to join the *aillarewe*. Pichikan found them resting from their journey by a stream, making shelters, working on weapons, mixing war paint. With them was a distant cousin, young Naipam—a serious youth with eyebrows forming a single bar over his eyes. Although they saw each only at *ngillatun*, they greeted each other like long lost brothers, kinship being the more precious far from home. Pichikan recounted to him the first battle of the hill Welen, attributing the *lik winka* victory to the silver warrior in the clouds who killed with thunder. *Weichafe* gathered, and Pichikan also told them about the triumph at Malga Malga, as well as of what he heard of the battle of the *fucha wampu*. He answered questions....

Yes, *lik winka* had tails on their faces. They stank like dead fish, too, and wore *wethakelu* that shone like silver. He did not know how many colors face-tails were, or why some of the hard *wethakelu* were brown, not shining. It *was* true that there was only one *lik winka domo*, and she had green eyes, red hair … was spotted. Ñamku said this and he had seen her, so it was true.

Weichafe who would not whimper at the sight of their entrails being unskeined from their bodies, gasped. Pichikan added that she dressed in black like *lik winka machi*.

Ehhh! Was she a *kalku* then, dressed like a *domo*?

"*Me.*"

Pichikan recalled that Ñamku had seen her breasts, which he described as white and spotted. He supposed she had two. And no, he had no idea if they hung between her arms or legs.

If *lik winka wentru* had tails on their faces—someone mused—maybe she was furry.

Pichikan said he did not know.

The *weichafe* decided that she had to be. Only furry creatures were spotted. Someone pointed out that fish and other creatures of the sea were spotted. But the consensus was that he was wrong about a *domo* breathing air. Besides, what creature of the sea had udders … not even seals!

The argument intensified when a *weichafe* argued that no creature of sea or land walked on its hind legs, save for birds. And anyway, no animal—furry or not—had green eyes. There were derisive hoots. *Nothing* had green eyes, so what did *that* have to do with anything?

Nothing living had red hair, either ... feathers, maybe.

Pichikan said that she had hair, not feathers, as his thoughts began to drift.... He knew the invaders as *weichafe* in hard *wethakelu*, mighty but not invincible. Malga Malga proved that, but what of their sorcery? What if this *lik winka domo*— stranger than *lik winka wentru*, and stranger by far than Ñamku—had summoned their *pillañ* from the clouds? He had not seen the apparition, yet Pikunche had been killed by thunder. Uneasy, he recalled that the *lik winka kalku domo* had not been at Malga Malga or the battle of *fucha wampum*. But she was at the hill Welen. Absent at the defeat of *lik winka*, she was present at their victories.

She did walk on her hind legs, he said. Recalling Tuiñam, he added that the *kawellu* on which *lik winka* sat walked on their hind legs to fight, just like *che*. He saw it himself when a *kawellu* killed his friend, making a dent in the hard *lik winka wethakelu* he was wearing. When *kawellu* stood they were five *nufku* high, a *nufku* wide.

No *weichafe* could imagine a beast that size, walking. As a foe this was unthinkable. The *lik winka domo* was forgotten.

No, *kawellu* did not have hands, or talk. They were like huge dogs with feet like stones. And they seemed intelligent. Ñamku said they knew the thoughts of *lik winka*.

Never having seen so many warriors speechless, Pichikan began to enjoy himself. *Kawellu*, he said, wore hard *wethakelu* just like *lik winka weichafe*.

At this point it did not matter to his audience what *kawellu* wore. It was sufficiently impossible that they wore anything at all. A *weichafe* asked the necessary question—How do you fight a beast two *nufku* tall, a *nufku* wide, hard as a boulder, with feet like stones ... a beast that knows your thoughts?

"It gets worse. You have to fight the *lik winka* on its back at the same time. And they carry *this*...."

Pichikan relished their consternation as the spear was passed around. Several unintentionally cut themselves. This was nothing like spears they knew—the long ones with fire-hardened points, the shorter ones tipped with flaked obsidian or flint, for throwing. A warrior mused, "You would probably be dead before you even got to the *kawellu*."

"Many died that way at the hill Welen," Pichikan replied. "*And*, they carry another weapon with no name. It is like a knife, about a *nufku* long, heavy as a club. But its sharpness makes it nothing like a club. I have seen heads, hands, arms, fly through the air."

Weichafe shook their heads in denial, imagining the storm of gore.

"This is true," Pichikan insisted, irritated into exaggeration, "At the hill Welen I was slapped by a flying hand, which left its print in blood upon my chest."

Feeling that he had gone too far—for he had—he planted a seed of thought, "We need spears like theirs, and sometimes they get stuck in *che*."

Turning courage into strategic suicide, a warrior proposed, "So if a spear is stuck in you, run far as you can. And if you see a spear in someone else, pull it out and use it."

This was finally the stuff of war against the impossible. Maybe *lik winka* spears could pierce the hard *wethakelu* that made silver lobsters of them.

Pichikan did not think so.

Where could you kill *lik winka* and their *kawellu*, if not through their *wethakelu*?

Pichikan said the legs of *kawellu* were not protected. But the *lik winka* did not let you get near them. Still—he added—they are outnumbered twenty or thirty to one, or more … and so it went, strategies against an invincible enemy that lasted late into a fireless night.

At first light runners brought word that the *toki* who met with *lik winka* had been put in a *ruka* and not allowed to leave. And the *weichafe* cheered, for this was war.

There was other news. Many *lik winka* on *kawellu* had left and Michimalongko had ordered them attacked far away, keeping almost the entirety of the *aillarewe* near the hill Welen. The *lik winka ruka* were defended by very few. The battle would begin at *pichilewechi antu*, *weichafe* taking their places under cover of darkness.

Pichikan began to prepare for battle, undoing his braid.

Naipam shyly asked if he could help.

A smile faint as ripples over unseen fish crossed the face of Pichikan. Of course, he said. Then he would help his cousin with *his* braid and paint.

They got little sleep that night.

Pichikan was more doubtful of the outcome of the coming battle than he wished, and not because he doubted the skill and bravery of the *weichafe*. He feared *lik winka* sorcery, and the *lik winka kalku domo* haunted him. He imagined her as a beast tall as a tree—dressed in black that parted to reveal spotted udders. Her hair, red as blood and light as parrot feathers, floated in a cloud about her spotted face. Her eyes were the green of the leaves of spring, and, dull as the scales of long-dead fish, they looked into his thoughts.

Very well then, let her know his mind. Let her know that it would be good to die in battle, and even better to die killing a *lik winka kalku*.

In the last quiet before dawn—when the creatures of darkness return to their lairs and creatures of the day begin to stir—no sound betrayed the many *weichafe* beside Pichikan and Naipam, awaiting the signal. Then a startled *keltewe* erupted into flight—crying *piwi piwi*—warning all who chose to listen.

Pichikan cursed both the bird and the Pikunche who frightened it—though he was certain the *lik winka* would not understand what they had heard, even if they had, for their *ruka* were three bowshots away, across meadows and fields of *uwa* and *lik winka* plants.

Prone beside Naipam, he watched the thin moon slip through the tangled warp of trees above him, a bright shuttle. The cry of a *kilkil*—hooted in the distance— was repeated and passed along.

Pichikan leapt from his hiding place. The insects of night sang unheard as he took his place beside *weichafe* he more sensed than saw. And one last time, he rehearsed the plan of battle. Archers should already be in place, blowing on coals kept alive in moss, preparing flaming arrows. They would not see their targets, yet it was known that *lik winka* incomprehensibly built their *ruka* close, in rows—as toads lay their eggs. The roofs would kindle. Sparks would ignite others....

Pichikan looked to his left, for he was at the far right of the line of battle. Heart racing, he saw the dim forms of the disciplined *weichafe* silently deploying—blocks of spearmen at the center, archers and slingmen behind. Every warrior in the wings carried something that might cut the tendons on the hind legs of *kawellu*, if only an obsidian knife. Pichikan and the Mapuche were with the *weichafe* who would attempt to encircle the enemy, attacking from behind.

A *kilkil* hooted.

Sputtering arrows arched over the *lik winka* wall. Spitting sparks as they leapt into the air, trailing flame they lit the scene—a volcano erupting inward.

Pichikan scanned the ranks of *weichafe*, the brilliance of war paint and feathers turned to dark shades of gray by dawn. Shields wet with dew shone dimly.

A dark mass of *lik winka* on *kawellu* emerged through their wall. They cast long shadows, lit from behind by burning *ruka*, hard *wethakelu* glittering red. Pichikan felt unwilling admiration, for they were very few. And, with the sound of heavy sticks on slack drum skins, they raced out, casting wavering shadows, running down archers revealed by the light of their own arrows. Every Pikunche *weichafe* had volunteered for the honor of this certain death, and the *toki* had decided that each *rewe* would send five—these *che* who were now dying.

Flames arched over the wall, their sources one by one extinguished. A thin flame erupting from the ground found a *lik winka* who briefly flared and fell from his *kawellu*. A roar of hate and release came from Pikunche lines.

An answering roar, as the *lik winka* charged, fording the Mapocho, attacking exactly where they were supposed to. The trap was sprung.

Pichikan ran, loping easily in the half-darkness. Naipam tripped and fell behind, hopping awkwardly. "My ankle," he explained, ashamed.

"Can you fight?"

Pichikan could not refuse his cousin the right to combat, yet felt that it would be certain death for Naipam to battle the *lik winka* injured.

Torn by the ambivalence he could not help but hear, Naipam asked, "What would *you* do?"

Pichikan said, "I would put your arm over my shoulder. Three legs will get us there almost as fast as four." Then, arms around each other, holding spears with their free hands, they ran.

They fell and stood … ran better. They crested a low hill laughing, and saw that the *lik winka* had charged in two lines of less than twenty each. The first had driven the Pikunche center almost back to the forest. There the *lik winka* had been halted by assembled hate.

Racing down a slope, Pichikan and Naipam saw *weichafe* enfold the *lik winka*, attacking from behind. The enemy spun about and fought, a *kawellu* floundering to the ground.

They cheered as they ran, seeing the *lik winka* form a circle slowly moving toward the turmoil surrounding the fallen one. Swinging bright weapons, they circled and protected him.

At the bottom of the hill, Pikunche dead and injured were everywhere—trying to crawl or crawling, gasping or silently dying, scattered like *uwa* tossed to birds of death. Blood was spurting, pooled and smeared everywhere. A *weichafe* returned their look with puzzled eyes, holding up a severed arm.

Pichikan looked away. The *lik winka* were now surrounded by hordes of *weichafe* screaming with blood lust. "I am out of the battle,"Pichikan raged, "like the last dog to find a bitch in heat."

Then a sound, behind him! He turned his head, as the battle jerked and spun. Then he was lying with the dead and wounded, seeing *antu* rise above the mountains, scrambling to his feet. He slipped, saw he was standing on a blood-smeared leg, and looked up. The *lik winka* who had been killing archers had finished their task. Racing toward their companions, they were attacking *weichafe* from behind. Naipam!

He found him dead not far away, transfixed by a spear.

Remorse flooded Pichikan, for he had spun at the sound of *kawellu*, putting Naipam in the path of death—perhaps in his own place. Shaking with rage and sorrow, he screamed, then stood on the back of his cousin, working the spear out.

He rolled the body over—brushing dirt from the open eyes—looking for a sign of soul.

He looked up … saw a hawk. He looked down, and a spotted butterfly flew by. The *am*! Unsteady on new wings, his cousin was heading for the Mapocho.

Calmer, Pichikan took the spear that killed his cousin and followed the soul at a dead run, taking the spots as a sign that the *pillañ* intended him to kill the *lik winka domo kalku*. And fording the Mapocho—captured spear raised high—he screamed his hate. Let her hear, who knew already.

Pichikan ran by warriors both dead and wounded. Fires were spreading from dead archers. Ladders leaned against the high *lik winka* fence.

He would know the *lik winka domo kalku* by her black dress, green eyes, red hair, and mottled dugs.

Chapter 15: Apocalypse (Santiago de Nueva Extremadura, 1541)

The trumpet waking Santiago did not wake Inés. Valdivia gone, her sleep was soured by fears for the colony—that incarnation of his genius, as was the body of the soul. How could the place survive, its spirit absent!

She had nightmares, waking from imagined horror to authentic worry, pacing by candlelight. Attempting to fool herself into oblivion, she created waking dreams in which she was Valdivia's wife, the gloom of Chilean forest replaced by vines and orchards, fields of grain extending to the *cordillera*. In such a dream she chose a road, drove her children in an oxcart to a grove filled with golden fruit. They picked oranges and lemons in dappled shade.

A change of scene…. She walked through fields open and immense, in a future in which even the Atacama was irrigated. A breeze created green waves of grain on that bleak sea of sand and niter. The breeze freshened, waves rising, ground heaving, so that Inés scarce kept her feet, waves of grain becoming waves of water torn to spindrift. She knelt to pray, for this storm was worse than the one she had experienced on the Ocean Sea, the captain vowing a pilgrimage to Santa María de Guadalupe if only they were spared. She could just see him….

She *saw* him—kneeling, shouting, vowing to wear a hair shirt if the ship survived.

Over caravel rails, Inés saw the *cordillera* sink into the sea. The captain and his sailors vanished, and she was crawling on rough boards, tasting bitter water, below decks amid the tools, the plants, the seeds, the animals that would create her New World. "My ark is sinking," she thought, despairing. Braced against tufted sheep, she prayed until the oak planks of the caravel became transparent. She touched one, and her hand went through, probing water icy as her skin.

Such was death, she thought. Her ark had foundered. The deep was consuming every seed of her New World. She fought death nonetheless, ensnared in skirts and sinking, seeing the shimmer of the sea surface darken, with its paddling ducks, swimming goats, horses, sheep and pigs. Even the chickens were afloat….

Jerking to her elbows that night, Inés awoke panting with terror, knowing that God had sent her this dream—for as they came to Moses this had come to her, and a fool could decipher *this* one. The ark without a captain was Santiago without Valdivia. The missing sailors were the depleted garrison. The waves were the Indian menace rising all about with the faceless cruelty of the sea.

And until her death of old age, Inés would repeat the miracle of that night for the marvel of others. How, in a dream's parable, she saw the destruction of Santiago before it happened. How—after lighting a candle to the Virgin—she dressed and slipped chain mail over her head, putting on one of Valdivia's helmets, girding herself with one of his swords. How, then, she waited, pacing, praying, wondering if she had only dreamed Apocalypse ... until a trumpet turned it true.

Juan woke to clamor and acrid smoke. The roof exploded, blinding him with flame. He clapped on his helmet, picked up armor, put on a boot ... the heat so intense he hopped from the house carrying the other. He hobbled back through smoke and glowing ash, rescued some of Pedro's things, some of his own, half blind and choking. He made a last trip for his books, thatch above him roaring.

Brushing off embers, he saw that Santiago was an inferno. Blurred shapes of men—lamenting like the damned—appeared and disappeared through smoke. Towers of flame cast immense flickering shadows. Sparks meandered from the sky—a bright snow igniting roofs. A spark storm—Juan absurdly thought—seeing Valdivia's house ablaze. Inés!

Juan ran to the door of Hell, and—arms lifted to protect his face—looked in. His sleeves began to smolder. He held his breath, not to breathe flame. Inés was either dead, or gone.

Returning to his salvage, Juan finished putting on his armor. A *caballero* reined in beside him, unrecognizable, his form swallowed by flame-shot smoke. "Inés is at the gallows!" the apparition screamed.

She was organizing *infantes* and *yanaconas*, mail to well below her hips. On her head was a wobbling helmet. Beside her, Lobo—steel over his habit!—clasped a sword by the scabbard as one might a cross, looking as if about to curse the whole event.

Inés clapped Juan on the shoulder and shouted that the *caballeros* were battling outside Santiago. *Infantes* were stationed on the walls with half the *yanaconas*. Those here were the reserve. Until it was time to fight the Indians, they would fight the fires.

An *infante* guffawed and spat, Cacafuego whooping that it was time to yank out junior and piss the fires out, boys.

An arquebusier yelled forget junior. Why didn't Cacafuego just drop his hose and fart? He would light it with his match. They'd fight fire with fire.

The *yanaconas* did not understand, but they knew bad taste when they heard it, and the few who were not too frightened roared with laughter. Not much white humor existed for them, but they loved Cacafuego.

He was right, Juan thought, in no laughing mood himself. Santiago was surrounded by water, yet the Mapocho might as well be in Spain for all the good it did them. Anyway, there weren't enough buckets in all the Indies to fight *this* firestorm.

Inés shouted, "Climb the roofs not burning—for the love of God!—put out the sparks!" And her good sense sent the *infantes* off. Santiago was burning down around their arses.

Standing beside Inés, Juan saw that her green eyes were fierce in her soot-smudged face—like hot springs in volcanic rock. "*Mierda!*" she yelled.

Never having heard her swear, Juan stared, and thought that, somehow, Valdivia's helmet made the word obscurely right. He turned his attention to Lobo and his sword, unable to believe that this philosophic enemy of war would use the instrument he so despised. "*Dulce bellum inexpertis,*" he taunted, and regretted having spoken. Unlike Marmolejo, Lobo had never fought, yet he knew war. No one ministered to the wounded more gently.

The priest said, "Show me how to use this thing."

"Hold it in both hands," replied Juan, sarcastic. This was *not* the time for the bookish humanist to begin instruction in martial arts. Then—since an armed *cristiano* might make a difference—he was succinct, "A broadsword is more scythe than needle. Cut, don't thrust ... just swing the damn thing hard in their direction." Juan was about to continue when his lesson was put to the test. An ululation rose above the din. Indians inside the city walls!

Then they were visible through smoke, by nightmare light. They must have scrambled over the palisade singly, for it was singly that they were engaging the *infantes* and *yanaconas*. And it was a blessing that they were not organized, since the defenders were at the moment scattered, fighting fires.

A brace of savages sprinted toward them. "I'll take the red striped one," Juan yelled to Lobo, pivoting and slashing into an Indian arm. Experience told him he would be given an instant by astonishment, and he swung at the back of the painted neck.

Lobo was standing on tiptoe over a prone black and white Picunche, attempting to pull his sword from between his ribs. Giving up, he knelt to pray.

"I told you not to stab," Juan grumbled. And he complained, "You missed his heart."

The Picunche was dying, but his eyes were open, hatchet weakly cutting the air. Juan kicked his weapon away and yanked out the sword. "Very soon he will be dead for a very long time," he said to Lobo. "And after you kill more Indians, you can pray for all of them at once." Annoyed that his pupil had ignored his advice, he said this was no time for piety.

"I'm praying for *my* soul," Lobo protested, tears coursing down emaciated cheeks.

"Well, hell, I'm going to fight," Juan rumbled, slipping into Pedro's tone of voice. "You can come with me, or pray, it's up to you."

As Lobo showed no sign of rising, Juan muttered, "Maybe prayer *is* the only thing will save Santiago." And walking away, he yelled, "But if you decide to fight, use your edge, for the love of God!"

Then Juan was using his own, helping an *infante* against an Indian smeared with ochre that fought with incredible speed, courage and fury. Before being dispatched he numbed Juan's left shoulder with his club.

The battle turned into a melee as Picunche spilled over the abandoned palisades. Responding to the logic of survival, the colony formed a line of battle that became a circle shrinking through the streets, pressed by Indians—the savage tide now lapping at the plaza.

Juan took a moment to lean on his sword, fighting desperation as he regained his breath. Only a handful of *infantes* and *yanaconas*—plus a woman and a priest—defended Santiago against an insane horde that would as soon die as take a *siesta*. They would never save the colony unless the *caballeros* returned. In any case, it was too late, so much had already been destroyed.

A figure loomed in Juan's peripheral vision, and he spun about to see Lobo staring at his sword by the ruddy light of the risen sun. As if he were dying himself, the priest said faintly, "I had to kill another. And you were wrong, war is *never* sweet."

"Come with me," was Juan's reply, "Maybe some mounts are alive. The stalls were at a distance from the roaring heart of battle. There the quiet coolness, calm morning light, seemed astonishingly normal as they walked by a floundering, disemboweled horse. Other horses that they passed were dead, or struggling with death in uncanny silence, pierced by arrows trembling with their breathing.

Juan ran through the carnage … vaulted a fence. Rounding a building he surprised a handful of Indians....

They drew their bows. The logs behind him chunked. His helmet whanged and twisted. Blows to his chest made him stagger.

"*Santiago!*" Juan yelled, charging as arrows hammered his mail. Maddened he ran up, cutting through the wrist of one Indian into the ribs of another, then spinning like a lethal top to create space. His edge found flesh, slicing deep into a stomach. Standing in a spray of blood, Juan saw the Indian he had wounded earlier struggling to his feet, and he booted the savage in the crotch. Of the two untouched, one ran. The other held his ground with a spear that was little more than a sharpened stick. But it gave him reach.

Juan dropped his sword and palmed his knife … walked into the fire-hardened point of the spear, so that it pressed into the mail on his chest. He gripped the shaft. Two men at the ends of a stick, they looked at each other.

The Picunche—who would die never realizing that the *lik winka* had gripped the spear with his left hand—let go. He had his hatchet hanging from a thong, the white youth nothing but hard *wethakelu*.

He fumbled for his hatchet, and Juan drove the knife he had concealed in beneath his ribs, turning his back on the death throes. Killing was far simpler than the aftermath—especially with the intimacy of a short blade.

Witness to the encounter, Lobo limped up, looking like a sleepwalker having a nightmare. He whispered, "Just try and vault a fence wearing habit and mail." He shuddered, adding. "It is far too easy to kill a man."

Juan pulled his knife from the corpse—a painted, befeathered, round-faced youth—and said, "Let's go."

Reverting to instinct, the stallions had formed a circle to protect the mares, facing out, so that most Indian arrows had penetrated a chest or neck. There they dangled and bounced, reminding Juan of the *banderillas* of a bullfight. Some of the horses were having trouble keeping their feet, yet all were ready for battle, nostrils flaring crimson in morning light.

Knowing he could not approach these maddened beasts—much less saddle them—

Juan went to the stalls. There he found the horses unharmed, and wasted no time in preparing a mount.

Lobo wrung his hands a moment, then imitated the complex act upon another horse, struggling with heavy leather and ponderous metal. He lifted a breastplate ... could not both swing the weight into place and hold it there to lace it, and moaned. Lifting his eyes to Heaven, Juan said he would help in a moment—thinking that Negrito was more formidable than this bone of a man, and defter.

When at last they mounted and emerged, Santiago's flames were burning pale in the light of day.

As Juan was giving instructions in the sword to Lobo, Inés headed for the house being used as the prison—one of the few not burning. De Hoz was being held there with the seven Indian hostages, and she wanted to be certain that the conspirator attempted nothing in the confusion. Also, she needed the hostages secure, for they might prove to be of use.

De Hoz was at a window, bellowing for freedom, ankles chained. The single guard looked about to spear the foul-mouthed, lisping traitor.

Inés approached De Hoz, who bowed and scraped, saying that all he asked was to fight heathens—*Pardiez!* He needed a weapon. And it would help if someone took his damn shackles off before he burned to death.

Inés swept by him by him to the hostages. Trussed like animals for market, the seven Picunche looked back with black, unfathomable eyes. "Make sure no one escapes," Inés ordered the guard.

She hurried to the gallows to survey the scene from the perspective of the condemned, knowing that she had truly dreamed Apocalypse. The church and prison, the stables—and only two other buildings—were *not* burning and the battle in the streets inexorably pressed the plaza. Every *yanocona* and *infante* was now committed to battle—save for the single prison guard. And the Devil only knew what Monroy and his *caballeros* were doing outside the walls. Killing Indians, she thought—feeling like screaming—as if you could keep from sinking by doing battle with the sea.

Very well then, she *was* dressed to fight, and cinching her belt, she drew her sword. If not for the Indians of the Indies, she was thinking, how good life here would have been ... when she heard the boom of hooves. Monroy and rescue on her mind she turned to see Juan and Lobo, mountainous on their animals. The priest's habit was hiked to his thighs, revealing skinny, hairy legs through mail that he had donned over a priestly absence of hose.

"We fought our way from the corrals."

"Get Monroy! Now!" she shouted. "Tell him Santiago is sinking!"

"Guard Inés," Juan yelled to Lobo. Then it was "*Dios ayude, y Santiago*" at the top of his lungs, sword high, horse at a gallop, charging the street leading to the city gate.

Dwarfing the struggle from his horseman's height—he screamed to be let through. He had a message for Monroy. The *infantes* created space, and Juan urged his horse into the Indians flooding into that breach, hacking at the upturned faces, the hide and wood shields, half submerged in a hostile river of limbs, weapons, and screaming heads, then was through and at the open gate, horse at full stretch over fields, slowing for the Mapocho. At the far shore he picked his way through Indian dead and wounded, pausing to look at the battle he approached, seeing that this was the usual slaughter of savages in Chile, with two notable exceptions— the *caballeros* were surrounded, and outnumbered as never they had been before. He would never fight his way through these hordes, yet Juan spurred his horse. And soon many Indians saw that there was only air between them and one crazy enemy. Then, what seemed to Juan a swelling regiment ran in his direction—ants about to swarm the carcass of a mouse. Unwittingly, he had created a hemorrhage in the Picunche horde.

Monroy attacked the thinning ranks, breaking through toward Santiago.

Juan reined in his horse, arrows pattering about him. Soon he would be in range of spears. He wheeled to lead the Spanish retreat—arrows pinging on armor, one sticking in his saddle. Dismounting at the open city gate, he waited for Monroy and his men to race through ... slid home the twin, great beams.

Then, when he failed to swing onto his saddle he knew he was exhausted, the battle hardly begun, sun scarcely over the *cordillera*. He made it up, however. Settling boots into stirrups and drawing his sword, he charged, crying the name of the saint of battles through a burning throat.

He found Inés and Lobo stupefied, considering an Indian who was bleeding as he crawled on hands and knees. He had run at Inés, holding high a knobby club. Lobo had spurred his horse, swung and missed. Inés—remembering the lesson in combat she overheard—scythed the enemy legs as if they were wheat, reaping wounds so terrible it made her want to drop her sword and bind those bleeding calves…. She dropped her sword.

"*Mierda!*" she screamed for the second time in her life—in the presence of a priest! "We have to kill this man."

Lobo relaxed his rein hand in permission—praying—and the warhorse did the rest.

Retrieving her sword Inés strode away, aimless for the moment, for Monroy and his horsemen were turning the tide of battle, driving the Indians back through corpse-littered streets.

Hooves thudded behind her. She turned, and as she looked up, to see Lobo pursuing her with his inept protection, her helmet tilted down over her eyes. Shoving it back up, Inés shouted, "For the love of God, help others! I can take care of myself."

She slashed off a swatch of skirt with her sword, wrapped it around her head and replaced the helmet—a much better fit—then ran for the prison. The door was open, trussed Indians still in there, but the guard and De Hoz had vanished. Slamming the door shut, she recognized De Hoz by the church, his shackles making him waddle like a duck. He was wielding a spear against a Picunche. Inés ran up with raised sword, not knowing if she was attacking the traitor or the Indian.

De Hoz speared the Picunche, and Inés stopped four paces away. For a disorienting moment she looked at the savage, still miraculously standing, gripping the spear shaft with both hands. Like a backward tongue that had been licking blood, the point protruded from the back of his dark neck.

The tableau ended with his collapse. And putting an unflinching foot on his face, De Hoz worked the weapon out. Inés lowered her own, but continued to hold steel between herself and this intramural Judas, who sought to destroy her lover and her ark, this villain who groped her breast in the night. Consequence, not civilization, held her hate in check. The moment was lengthening toward decision when De Hoz hurled his spear, which was not the death Inés had strapped on steel to meet.

An explosive grunt behind her, and she spun on her heel. Beyond surprise, she saw that a red-spotted Picunche had the spear in his vitals.

"*Gracias, caballero,*" she said—with infinite reluctance—wondering if he had thrown from reflex, or calculation.

"I need these damn shackles off," De Hoz lisped, making for his weapon. "They make me waddle like a duck."

"Monroy has the key."

The Lieutenant was at the gallows shouting orders to *yanaconas* who were levering a catapult onto the platform. Small as the engine was—by standards of European siege—it was yet so ponderous that Inés wondered if the complaining boards would hold. She thought to ask why they were doing this at all.

If it came to a last stand, Monroy shouted, they could fling stones over defenders point blank into Indians. He turned to an *infante* to say that the wedges setting the trajectory would have to be pushed in far as they could, and saw De Hoz.

"Holy Mother of God! What is the *hideputa* doing out of prison?"

Inés shrugged, appalled at seeing the *infantes* from close—their faces turned to masks of dirt and sweat-streaked soot, their gore both caked and fresh. Many were wounded, one with a cut so deep his teeth were visible through his cheek. The boot of another overflowed with blood.

Inés knelt by him. "Water!" she cried. "A clean shirt, for bandages!"

Mulish, Monroy repeated his question.

The *infante* was spouting blood. Inés attempted to stanch the flow by pressing with her hands. De Hoz had saved her life, she said—for the love of the Living God! She needed water and a shirt, not argument!

A soldier said Doña Inés was right. De Hoz *had* fought the Indians.

"Suffering Jesus!—water and bandages," Inés screamed, "or this man will die."

"He'll die anyway," said the *infante* of the blood-filled boot. "Let him die dirty, like he lived. Besides, the only shirts not burnt are on our backs, and you'll find water in Hell sooner than in Santiago."

Inés hacked at her petticoats with her sword, as Monroy freed De Hoz, then bent over her patient, feeling for pulse and finding none. Left without purpose, she wiped her hands on her skirt—fresh blood vivid on black alpaca.

"*Muchas gracias, caballero*," said De Hoz to Monroy—his low bow holding no hint of mockery.

Stiffly bowing back, the Lieutenant grunted, "Find yourself some armor."

And for the rest of that eleventh of September—a confused eternity—Inés de Suárez tended to the wounded and dying by the gallows, which held a catapult and a multitude of stones. All that while, De Hoz fought with ferocity and matchless courage.

Done with the heroism of *romances*, not wasting energy on war cries, Juan simply, wearily, plied his sword. And when at last he rested, noon had doubtless come and gone. God only knew what time it was, with no one asking Him. Like a slowly beating, bleeding, heart, the battle had expanded and contracted beyond counting or remembering, as the Spanish with their horse and armor, skill and steel, drove the Picunche toward Santiago's walls ... only to retreat under the press of wild, fresh numbers that were like ants emerging from hidden burrows—an inexhaustible totality.

Juan killed an Indian, struck into a next. And by his side, Lobo had slain many. But now, of a sudden, he was standing on his stirrups, no longer killing—this, when a break of concentration in battle, as Pedro said, was good as falling asleep forever.

Then Lobo was off, trampling Indians with his horse, yelling "Body of Christ!" at the top of his lungs, heading for the building Santiago used as an impromptu church, which was fiercely burning. Cleaving a feather-covered head, Juan galloped after, and saw Lobo swallowed by the door as by an oven's open maw.

The priest emerged swaying, babbling what was probably Greek, and set down a chalice holding only soot and cinder. Body of Christ, consumed indeed!—Juan thought, smelling burning wool and human hair.

Through chattering teeth, Lobo said, "I was too late." He screamed, "Christ was burning in my hands!"

Juan heard sizzling, decided that sweat was boiling in Lobos' helmet, and— seeing the priest's outstretched palms—knew why he smelled grilled meat. The chalice must have been a glowing coal! "Blessed Mother of God," he breathed.

"Honored be her name," the priest responded, as if Juan had launched a litany. "Blessed be He, Who opened the doors of Hell, and let me touch damnation, for my instruction." Lobo crossed himself, the smoke of incense twining about him.

Incense?

"Christ!" Juan yelled, "your cassock is on fire." He dismounted to smother the glowing hem, Lobo muttering—now in Latin—arms outstretched, burnt face turned to Heaven, as if he now desired nothing less than crucifixion.

Leading both their horses, Juan urged the praying humanist in the direction of the gallows, seeing that the second battle of Santiago was being lost before his eyes, with no miracle in sight. Presently, the Spanish formed a fighting ring not much larger than the plaza. And only the prison was not burning.

So abruptly did Juan stop walking—realization sweeping over him—that the horses bumped steel-clad muzzles into his back. The hostages!

Inés was bending over an *infante* with no feature you could recognize below his eyes, murmuring comfort as she picked at shards that might have been tooth or jaw, dropping them into a helmet as if saving them for future use. Around her, War displayed its spoil—the dead and dying, and hideously wounded, all relaxed by loss of blood, without a thought to the horror they inspired. One—a disemboweled Inca woman—offered the extraordinary whiteness of her teeth to clouds. Juan stared, stunned by the pink of her tongue, the perfection of her cheeks, her round, bare legs. No skirts!

Seeing his stare, Inés said, "I needed bandages. And she wore a lot of wool."

Wool on his mind, Juan saw that Inés had sacrificed as much of hers to bandages as modesty allowed. Her sleeves were hacked at the shoulder. Her skirt—no petticoats!—ended at mid-calf.

Never having seen her upper arms before, much less her upper ankles, Juan cleared his throat, looking everywhere but at the revelation of her smeared perfection. He gestured vaguely at the priest.

Taking stock of the charred, ecstatic Lobo, Inés curtly shook her head. She had far worse to tend to.

The roar of battle had redoubled, hordes of Picunche pouring over the walls and through the opened doors of Santiago.

"This is the end, Juan, isn't it," Inés said, making the sign of the cross, "the end to everything."

He only nodded, thinking how incomparably beautiful, how brave she was. And saluting with his sword, he galloped off to die for her.

Juan survived long enough to find himself far from the plaza, carried there by a flash flood of Indians. He had left his spear in a Picunche, and now was fighting with his sword. He fought thirst as well, fought faintness and a weary arm, fought the dragons of despair. He was unwounded, though. Then the blinding sun whirled into his vision, wreathed in smoke and clouds, and the earth rushed up to hit him.

He opened his eyes to the reek of fire and battle, hellish racket. His helmet was twisted, so that he could see only with one eye. His sword and spear were gone. His damn chinstrap was choking him. Gagging, he was about to stand....

Slammed to the ground, again!

With his single eye, Juan saw he had been thrown clear of his horse. But his boot was twisted in the stirrup, Amadís attempting to flounder to his feet. Juan tried to sit, was flopped onto his back with a bone-jarring thud. And he became aware that a ring of throats was producing the barbaric clamor all about him....

He and Amadís occupied a space cleared like an arena. Unarmed, surrounded by a savage horde, Juan yet felt no horror at the imminence of death. With weariness and ⊠wonder he scanned the chaos of faces, throats swollen with screams that were as silence in the larger noise. Why was he still alive?

An enormous Indian strode into his sight. Like Juan, he was *in* the arena, facing the crowd screaming for blood, shaking a Spanish spear and yammering back at them. Like a metal fragment of Santiago—Saint of War—the bright blade of his spear soared, swooped and winked in the sun, creating the miracle that had spared Juan's life. Yet the savage was not The Saint. Like a warhorse, he was meat and whipcord. His head was painted black. And in Juan's topsy-turvy world, he seemed a monk reversed, for all his hair was shaved—even to his eyebrows—save that a braid hung where a tonsure might have been, a braid twined with coy red thread. Given his nakedness, his male animality, to Juan he was diabolic as the inversions and perversions of the Black Mass. Had he been spared for a fate worse than death in combat? Juan recalled the Aztec 'war of flowers,' waged for captives whose beating hearts were torn out and consumed in an infernal parody of communion.

Ceasing his yammering, Not Tonsure strode toward Juan with every indication of awful purpose.

Damned if he would be gutted like a goat, thought Juan, attempting to yank his foot from the stirrup-tangled boot.

Not two steps away, Not Tonsure stood watching—curious and dispassionate—like a cat studying prey far too slow to escape.

Juan freed his foot. And standing, he saw that Amadís was hamstrung.

The Indian crowd grew quiet, as Not Tonsure addressed Juan with a speech from which he gleaned only the familiar '*winka.*' Prompted by the solemnity of the occasion, he replied, "I am Juan de Cardeña, born in Extremadura. I am almost eighteen years old."

Then, regretting what he had just said as too much like pleading—and even more an epitaph—Juan began the Credo, wondering if he would finish before death.

The '*amen*' left Not Tonsure silent. He gibbered then, before tossing the Spanish spear over. In his astonishment Juan dropped it, to the huge amusement of the Indians, making Juan think that laughter was universal. The Blemmyes, the immaterial Astomi—all the peculiar creatures in Pliny—no doubt they also laughed.

Juan had been offered single combat—more something out of **Amadís de Gaula** than a Black Mass. Now he could die with honor. Impressed by the Indian's chivalry, he removed his helmet and armor until he stood in Spanish shirt and hose—knife still secreted up his sleeve.

Not Tonsure unslung the club Hercules must have wielded, an instrument of death thick as a wrist, longer than legs, ending in a knurled knob. He grunted something as he held it out—no doubt following some pagan rule of duel.

Juan left the spear where it lay, and crossing himself, he took his knife from his sleeve, displaying it as Not Tonsure had … to be confronted by a frowning silence.

He disapproves of my weapon, thought Juan. Not Tonsure will feel dishonored, killing someone with a blade this puny. Amadís de Gaula in mind, he knew the dilemma he had posed to the honor of the savage. Yet he had no way of explaining that he could fight better with nothing else. With a sword, almost. With a spear, absolutely not. His knife was his best hope.

Not Tonsure delivered a short oration.

Juan countered with a *pater noster*.

The Indian briefly gabbled back, the crowd erupting into cheers.

Juan bowed, and—since Pedro was not around—imitated De Hoz flourishing his handkerchief. The crowd cheered again. For all the exotic strangeness of the scene—the plumes, hides and garish paint—it somehow looked familiar. Juan decided that the Indians were taking bets, and wondered at the odds placed on his survival.

Not Tonsure then turned insane—or perhaps simply ecstatic—whooping and leaping, swinging his club with extraordinary speed and bravura, all at a distance that did not threaten. This performance was rounded off with somersaults that made the club an axle to the savage as a meaty wheel.

Astonished, Juan joined the Indian ovation. Half horse, half acrobat, the Indian wielded little less than a mighty oak. He might never get closer to the pages of a *romance* than combat with this Man of the Woods. But—as savages with no written language would witness his death— Juan would be posturing before oblivion. He wondered how they could live in a perpetual present as they did, having no past, no Golden Age, to imitate. What was it like to be a hero, dying forgotten by the printed page?

Juan took no guard, yet he had his reasons. Not Tonsure plied an immense, blunt trunk—nothing like an edge. With the speed of the head he would create an intermittent wall into which it would be death to walk. Juan would only have slivers of time for his sliver of a weapon, darting in when the club changed direction. With luck, he would break the rule he had given Lobo—by killing with a needle.

He breathed, as Pedro counseled. Before a battle— if alive and ready—just breathe, and think you are alive and ready. Then breathe, and think you are alive and breathing. Then just breathe.

The attack came at the nineteenth inhalation, Juan thinking he had counted out more breaths than he had years....

Then he did a desperate somersault. Virgin without Sin Conceived!

Not Tonsure's prancing and cavorting had been intended to deceive. In the actual assault he swung the long weapon by the end as he approached—as Juan had seen—somehow grabbing it near the middle in half twirl, abruptly changing its direction, accelerating its speed, giving it ends blurred like the spokes of a racing wheel.

Cuerpo de Dios! The weapon had, again, just about parted his hair! With an explosive exhalation of astonishment, Juan thanked Pedro for making him practice dodging death, noticing that his knife was in his left hand, now, where it had leapt. Not Tonsure might not expect him to be ambidextrous....

At the next attack Juan hit the ground with a wild, low roll, intending to be as unpredictable as the Indian. This time—had he been Negrito—the club would have parted the hair of his back. Hearing something like distant surf, Juan risked a glance … seeing Indian pandemonium all about him, the roar measuring the miracle of his survival.

Not Tonsure's club began its complicated blur as he raced forward, Juan managing to stay alive again, as a strategy owing much to Cacafuego formed in his mind.

Hands behind his back he strode forward. Puzzled, Not Tonsure shifted his grip to hold his club in thirds. He lost speed and distance by doing this, but was preparing to erect a lethal fence that Juan would have to cross.

Looking right, Juan switched knife hands and lunged left, throwing himself over the club and sweeping with his edge.

Airborne, Juan was pounded on the shoulder by what felt like a horse's hoof. He bounced on the ground—no opponent in sight, just the dirt he was eating. Lurching to hands and knees, he saw Not Tonsure three paces away, striding in. Juan rolled toward death, taking a vicious kick to his ribs, but he had managed to trip the Man of the Woods, who instantly leapt to his feet.

Numb from his shoulder to his right hand, Juan feinted, spun with an outstretched sweep, and was away, the Indian looking down in surprise.

An enemy weapon could guide your blade to the hand that held it, and indeed, a finger was lying on the ground. Bleeding, Not Tonsure was staring at the dusty gobbet.

And it was then that a ball fell from the sky, and bounced.

The rolling ball was not exactly round. Nor was it a ball…. A head rocked to a stop as Juan looked up for the source of this visitation. Disoriented—because the head appeared to have arrived from Heaven—he thought his namesake had come to save him. But why would John the Baptist arrive without his body, or any sign of miracle?

A number of Indian spectators examined the head. Stunned, they repeated the name— Meliwala—and one who might have been a relative or friend knelt beside it. Then, as every Indian faced away in response to shouted cries, Juan saw what he at first refused to recognize—other heads floated above the crowd around the gallows, the grin of death visible even from this distance. Six, he counted. The heads of the hostages were being elevated on spears.

Tearing his eyes from the gruesome spectacle he saw that the head that plummeted into his arena had vanished. Picunche were arguing, some running away. The scene was turning into a disorganized rout. Those remaining approached Juan with weapons lifted, screeching Indian hate.

The time for cunning was past, and Juan crouched with his knife in his only working hand. Unhorsed, unarmored, half-paralyzed, he would only last instants when the circle closed. He counted the breaths left in his life, making them deep, reaching three when Not Tonsure joined him, Juan noticing that he had lost two joints off a little finger, so that his club was drenched in blood. Inexplicably, he was taking Juan's side against his people.

The warriors stopped advancing, looking at each other like children egging their companions on to acts forbidden by adults. At breath six, Not Tonsure said something that made the attackers apprehensive. At breath seven, the stalemate erupted into chaos. The Indians melted away, Juan hearing Spanish war cries, the metallic thud and clang of a Christian advance. He and Not Tonsure became something like a boulder splitting the stream of fleeing Picunche.

When the tide waned Not Tonsure retrieved his finger. Showing it to Juan, and actually grinning, he stuffed it in a pouch that hung around his neck, pointing to Juan then to himself. He was taller than Pedro, with a chest almost as massive. Otherwise, he was lean and hairless. Sweat had made his black paint run, and he was everywhere smeared with blood, making of him a horrific sight—especially grinning, as he was.

Juan was in a quandary. This savage who had done his remarkable best to kill him had also twice saved his life. To thank him would be like expressing gratitude to Mephistopheles for protecting one's soul from lesser devils. Also, the heathen would not be able to tell heartfelt Christian thanks from Cacafuego's 'ask my arse.'

His indecision became moot, for Spanish cavalry was almost upon them, slaughtering Picunche. Irrationally, Juan felt impelled to flee, although Not Tonsure suicidally held his ground, grinning at the doom galloping toward him.

Wildly gesturing, Juan cried out *"No! Por el amor de Dios, no!"*

That halted the *caballeros*, led by Monroy. Beside him rode Inés, holding a bloody sword.

Dear God! thought Juan, she's astride, ankles in full view!

Furious—for Juan had interrupted the hard won rout—Monroy shouted, "No *what...*?"

"I mean, spare this man."

"Are you all right?" Inés cried out.

As for the Lieutenant, he looked like he had just inhaled a fly while at full gallop. An Indian more, an Indian less, hardly mattered, but in his anger he took the time for sarcasm. "Are we allowed to kill *other* Indians?"

The cavalry swept by with a receding thunder, accelerating after the Indians granted precious moments of amnesty by Juan. He asked himself how many would live because of his madness, how many die because of the quickness of his shrug?

Inés dismounted using her horse as shield, perhaps out of modesty, certainly because of the immense Indian still standing there, posing with his club like some uncouth Hercules.

"Are you all right, Juan?" she repeated, reins in one hand, sword in the other.

She was helmeted, armored, smeared with grime and gore like everyone else. However, on *her* it smeared past perfection, and for the first time Juan found his total admiration shaken. Through the worst of the Atacama she had been clean, pale, perfect under her broad-brimmed hat. The enormity of what she had just done gave him a visceral shock, as if on some stained glass window the Virgin wore the armor of Saint George and rode to battle. He saw her framed by a gothic arch, a vision beautiful as abhorrent—*an upraised sword, white horse knee-deep in dying heathens, the splattered gore turned to jeweled glass. Above the carnage gleamed her bare ankles, white as her horse. And, behind her head—a diabolic halo—floated a circle of severed savage heads....*

"Juan?"

The battle had made Lobo go over the edge—which was not surprising, as he had not far to go. But Juan? He was gaping like an idiot after saving the life of an Indian looking much like all the others they were killing.

He did not hear her, for a supposition too awful to entertain was overwhelming him. "The heads...?" he said.

Inés considered her ankles, as if at last aware of how exposed she was. "A shame," she finally pronounced. Then, echoing Pedro, "One does what one must."

One does what one *is*, thought Juan, with an infinite sense of loss. "How could you?"

Inés jerked back as if struck.

"So ... how are *you*?" Her question was a plea.

"Unwounded," Juan replied flatly, turning to Not Tonsure. No less transfixed by Inés than Juan, the Indian leaned on his club, grin gone at last.

"Sheathe your sword," Juan told Inés.

"You're joking!"

Dropping his knife, Juan took a step back.

Not Tonsure was grinning again. He let go his club, pretending to drop it on his foot, began to hop and howl.

First it was like a sneeze when his ribs were cracked—this hiccough that made him realize that they were cracked again—then Juan was beside himself, roaring with torture and release.

Not Tonsure imitated Juan's imitation of the bow of De Hoz, his club a handkerchief—The court of king Perion never saw the like! Then The Man of the Woods loped off, pausing once to hop, howl, and grimace. He scrambled up a ladder set against the city wall, and with lightness astounding for his mass was gone.

Juan at last stopped laughing. Bending over, he took shallow breaths. One side was numb, the other agony. "Don't ask me if I'm all right," he croaked as Inés approached.

"Your horse, your armor...?" She was offended.

Juan looked to where Amadís floundered, saying, "We have to kill him."

"We!"

Inés allowed her beloved creatures to be slaughtered—and ate them with gusto—yet *never* participated in this act. To her mind some animals—like rats and cats—were not innocent. The ones you ate *were*—which was why God put them in the stable at the birth of Jesus.

"It will take two," Juan insisted.

Kneeling, she held Juan's knife as—with a rock—he drove its point into the neck of the obedient animal just behind the head. This killed him quickly, but still the dying shudder seemed to transfer to Inés.

Juan stood stiffly by her suffering, stone clutched in a white-knuckled fist. "Let's go," he said.

Of Santiago's structures only the palisades, a stable or two, and scattered fences survived. In the plaza, the prison and the gallows were also spared. There, the circle of six heads blindly surveyed the scene.

The rest was charred, smoldering, or burning outright. Santiago shimmered like a desert, corpses everywhere. The dying and wounded—mostly Picunche and *yanaconas*, occasional *cristianos*—moaned in a variety of tongues. You stepped over pleas. You trod on blood, careful as you were. In the plaza they at last walked free.

Inés moaned—as if she herself were wounded. "What, *now*?"

Juan shrugged and walked away. Santiago had built its walls around 'nowhere.' And a nowhere is what it had become again. Except that now the walls held memories.

Men stumbled through the nightmare, sorting corpses and artifacts, wondering where to begin and what to begin it with.

By the smoldering coals of his home Juan found his salvage intact. He left it there and walked toward the gallows, seeing a circle of six heads over Santiago, thinking of those towns he had heard of where the landmark was a tower with a clock. Was each head marking every other hour? Six faces had been made into the face of a clock. Where the hands, then? Beheaded clocks, he decided, had no hands with which to tell the time. He felt feverish.

At the gallows Monroy was giving orders.... Dispatch enemy Indians. Pile them with the dead. No one was to be left alive and faking. Spear them all.

The Spanish wounded were being carried to the prison ... where Juan found

Inés. She waved him away with a blood-smeared hand, annoyed. Her eyes were sunk in soot. Juan left.

He found Lobo on the gallows, wounded hands extended to the side, rescued chalice set before him. He was looking at the heavens through the circle of heads above, seeming saint enough to bring a chill to anyone. And he was chanting something.

"*Redios!*" Juan exclaimed. "The Apocalypse!"

You could make up almost anything incredible and it would seem true in The Book of Revelation—especially if it involved the number 7—so that when Juan first read Pliny and Saint John he found them to be strangely similar. Both spoke of ends—in space, in time. Anything went, at the limits of geography and this dispensation.

"The Apocawhat?"

Juan translated from the Latin for the *infante* who had appeared beside him.

"The fifth angel sounded and I saw a star fall from heaven to the earth and the key of the bottomless pit was given to him. And he opened the bottomless pit, and there rose a smoke out of the pit, as the smoke of a great furnace, and the sun and the air were dark with the smoke of the pit."

"Suffering Jesus," the *infante* breathed, "today was in the Bible!"

"And there appeared a great wonder in Heaven, a woman clothed with the sun and heaven under her feet, and upon her head a crown of six stars."

"That makes no sense at all," complained the *infante,* looking up at the circle of six heads. As for stars, there was not a one tonight, what with the clouds....

Soon, rain was drumming on the gallows. Juan cupped his hands to drink as Lobo droned on.

The downpour put out every fire, too late, and made it impossible to light one. Having lost their homes the *vecinos* requisitioned the tents of *yanaconas.* Left with only rain in their lives, many of the Indians vanished north into the night.

The tents were rude, small, few. Inés and other important *vecinos* clustered under the protection of the catapult. Those without tents made do with lean-tos roofed with debris. Men fought for space under the gallows until Monroy restored order. The prison nearly caused a riot, for it was the only dry interior and Inés insisted it was for the wounded—including Indians. *Infantes* were outraged that savages—especially those soon to be dead anyway—were given preferential treatment.

Against the prison wall, Juan constructed a shanty out of charred poles and Indian spears, shingling it with the armor of a dead horse. The rickety structure proved only slightly more comfortable than the downpour.

Inés spent her time with the wounded, working by the light of torches, the center of an infernal scene. When Juan tried to speak to her she said she was too busy, too tired, and he was relieved at not having to apologize. As for Lobo, he collapsed when done with the Apocalypse, and Juan took him to the prison. And when he returned after dark, Inés was gone, but he found the priest packed like salted cod with other wounded who would not—or could not—compete for a larger share of territory. Juan left Lobo there—dry at least—returning to the discomforts of his shelter.

He woke as an ache in the shape of a man—no longer numb, he was able to hurt everywhere. Having worn armor to sleep— more as a protection from the drips than from the Indians—he was soaked nonetheless, hands puckered beneath their grime. The rain had stopped, at least. And the *charqui* he had put under his breastplate was softened by rain and sweat. Chewing the noisome stuff he went to where Amadís lay dead, and somehow the sodden mound—bereft of beauty and vitality—reminded him of the emptiness of his belly. He recruited *infantes*.

Soon there was horsemeat and horse liver being grilled over a straw fire, devoured when barely warm. Replete, he cut meat into strips and cooked it rare, filling his helmet as a peace offering for Inés.

She was sitting in her tent, hugging her knees and looking at nothing. When Juan approached she hardly seemed to notice. "*Buenos días*," he greeted.

Inés responded with a savage laugh. She had somehow acquired a bright Inca skirt that modestly reached the ground. An Inca shawl was over her shoulders— maybe covering armor. Valdivia's helmet was off, however, revealing hair like a mouse's nest. No surer sign of her despair, Juan thought. He wondered if any of her hats survived.

"Food," he said, extending his helmet into the tent.

Her face was bloodless, drawn, her pallor accentuating her freckles. The bluish circles beneath her eyes were brutal. She looked through the helmet full of flesh as if it did not exist.

"It's warm," Juan cajoled.

"I never really had a mother," Inés said from some inner distance.

"Eat," he urged.

She selected a small strip and delicately ate it … chose another with her fingertips—as if a leather Inca helmet were a golden bowl. For all her earthiness, Inés had something in common with the Astomi.

Nibbling on a third strip, she finally thanked Juan, sounding to him like an unwilling child forced into submission.

"*De nada*," he replied, peeved. Though he was guilty of abandoning her in her greatest need, he had cooked her food in penitence. She was supposed to *forgive* him like the Virgin—for the love of God!—and she definitely had *not*. He resented her resentment, which struck him as another *macula* on her perfection.

"May you eat it in good health," he intoned with wooden courtesy, about to leave her with the helmet of horsemeat.

"Might you want to see how the animals fared?" she said—employing the formal 'Quisiera Usted'.

"It would be my greatest pleasure, Señora Doña Inés," he replied in cruel kind.

She ate as they went—perhaps to walk in silence. And when they got to the animal sheds there was little to see and nothing to say, for they were burnt to the ground.

Juan nervously glanced over. The creatures cremated alive here were dear to her—too much so, like the children she never had and now probably never would. However, she betrayed no sign of sorrow.

He brightened. "Look, Inés! Your vines are trampled, but alive. A lot of your trees are standing."

"Let's count hogs," she proposed, sounding pessimistic.

Ash had turned to porridge in the rain, so that—rummaging through the cinders of the sty—Juan turned black as any painted Indian. The pigs had died in a terrified pile, and it was difficult to tell how many. Juan counted trotters, dividing by four. Twenty-seven and three quarter pigs, he pronounced.

Inés exclaimed with waxing hope, "That means as many as three could be alive!"

Juan debated mentioning that pork was fragrant before his very nose at this very moment, hot under dying coal. But he decided to salivate in silence, given her affection for the animals and the present strain on their relationship.

The census of the dead at the goat shed returned the right number—including the kids. This did not trouble Inés, who was buoyed by the hope of a great pig survival. She had never been particularly fond of goats—Juan knew—as the devil's favorite incarnation, having heard her say you could see Hell in the pupils of their eyes—with those funny upright slits. Well, not Hell, exactly, but a door cracked on Darkness.

Juan was about to groan with hunger. The charred pork had been an agony of bliss. Even goats cooked in their wool smelled like ambrosia.

Inés mused, "The Pedros will need to eat when they return."

"Pork!"

"Better than underdone horsemeat," she replied. "But, thank you anyway." Her smile failed.

There was good news the morning after—a boar and a young sow, struck dumb by instinct or terror, were discovered cowering in bushes.

"I knew it!" Inés exclaimed when the survivors were brought before her.

Juan did not know if she was referring to their escape from death, or to the fact that the boar was none other than Don Jamón del Yelmo Negro. In any case Juan was disgusted. She—who now treated him like a pariah—looked about to hug the coward hog.

Invigorated, Inés turned to the immensity of her task. She had the dozen dead pigs, the thirty-two dead sheep and goats, the uncounted dead lambs and kids brought in, as well as piles of charred and soggy chickens. Fourteen horses arrived in pieces, and more were coming. She had a mountain of meat to be sorted according to kind, degree of damage, and doneness.

Identifying hides still good, she organized teams to gut and skin, negotiating shares with the *yanaconas*. *Cristiano* got the hearts, kidneys, livers and intestines—for sausage casings. The Indians would work miracles with the rest, even to the bones and eyeballs.

There was no shortage of half-burnt logs. However, Inés decided against roasting the pigs in pits, since most of the meat was partly cooked already. In fact, pork cut off by the skinners was being passed around in a spontaneous communion—heaven after months of abstinence.

Having no horse, Juan could not patrol, and Inés put him in charge of smoking horsemeat. The men gutting did not know where to put the entrails. He sent them to her. On the gallows platform, she decided, for there they would stay clean, and the juices drain. Hides could be stretched later. What the Indians did not want could be tossed into the Mapocho.

By noon the gallows groaned. Hindquarters and necks were stacked like cordwood, slabs of ribs piled like shingles. Horsemeat—cut into strips for smoking—created a formidable mound. A pyramid of bluish hearts rose like a foothill by a mountain of purple livers. Another—of blood-veined tallow—towered beside it. Like ropes on the deck of a ship, pink-gray lengths of small intestine coiled, here and there.

Done delegating tasks to *yanaconas*, Juan was looking up at the skewered Indian heads—thinking them an appropriate topping for the scene—when Inés strode up and said it was time to start the sausage. He demurred, saying that all he knew of sausage was the eating. She told him to chop innards with fat, stuff the casings with that, tie the ends and smoke them. Simple. No need to bother with seasonings today.

By evening Juan never wanted to eat meat again. All day, those butchering had been consuming flesh and innards, cooked and raw. And the sated workers—all this anatomy at hand—had taken to creating meat jokes. They hung themselves like horses. They made phallic sculptures with eyeballs and sausages, kidneys and sausages, hearts and sausages—the ever-hilarious sausage. They erected huge erections between haunches of horsemeat.

Juan had to go—no home to go to though—and he was wandering aimlessly when he heard the hail and response. Valdivia had returned.

Pedro dismounted by the gallows—center of the ashen desert that was once Santiago—trying to believe his eyes. Masses of raw meat, racks of curing flesh, billowing smoke laden with the odor of—Sweet Jesus!—pork! Santiago was a Hell redolent of Paradise. Horsehides were spread on the ground … and with shock, Pedro recognized the markings of Amadís.

Juan materialized through smoke.

"You all right, *hijo*?" he asked, gruff with profound emotion.

"Fine. You?"

"Unharmed," said Pedro, pointing at the telltale hide.

"Hamstrung. We had to kill him."

Inés ran up from the prison, breathless.

The Governor contemplated her with amazement—dressed like a heathen, outdoors without hat. And her hair had at last won its battle against civilization. In his weeks of absence Inés had aged beyond belief. Only her smile retained perfection.

With a gesture encompassing the ruins, the Governor asked how many dead. "Four *vecinos*," she said, "twenty-four horses, twelve pigs, all the goats and sheep, most of the ducks and chickens."

Valdivia indicated the gallows. "What in Heaven's name is *this!*"

Glancing, Inés saw the row of bluish sausages erect between their haunches. Eyes wide with horror she looked at Juan, who had been put in charge.

However, the Governor was glaring at the impaled Indian heads, not the improvised erections.

She became cool, factual. "Those are the heads of the hostages."

Valdivia was ominously calm. "Can anyone explain why they were decapitated in my absence? Also, why is one head missing?"

Monroy walked up through the crowd. And no other—given his authority, cold composure, and incorruptible honesty—could have done what he then did.

"Señor don Pedro, these Indians were beheaded at my orders. As the battle for Santiago was about to be lost, I decided … hem … to dishearten the savages. This desperate measure was one I would not have taken had you not been gone. Pray accept my sincerest apologies and my offer of resignation as your Lieutenant."

Valdivia—who was nothing like a fool—said talk of resignation was nonsense. Given the extraordinary circumstances, Monroy had made absolutely the correct decision. What he did not mention is that the messenger who summoned him—sent by the very Lieutenant who claimed responsibility for this mass decapitation—claimed that Doña Inés de Suárez, magnificent as El Cid, was the one who did it.

Alea iacta est, Valdivia thought. Leadership sometimes required the tactical suspension of probability. And he asked about the seventh head.

Monroy said he shot it at the Indians with the catapult.

So that was that, Valdivia thought, before announcing that Santiago would have to be rebuilt in unburnable adobe.

Juan went to see how Lobo fared.

Death, good weather—and the arrival of Valdivia—had emptied the prison. There was now room for the Humanist, yet he was tight against the wall, hugging his knees, rocking before the ash-filled chalice set before him. And beside him— appeared from God knows where—were **Utopia** and **In Praise of Folly**.

He was a hero, Juan told him. Everyone said he fought fiercely as his namesake.

Lobo did not even open his eyes. And when Juan returned with hot meat, fresh water, he would not open his mouth to eat, to speak.

Pedro was made lethargic by quantities of pork, verbose by quantities of wine. Therefore, that night he was both lethargic and verbose, and roasting tallow on a stick, he rambled on. In his opinion Inés was wrong in convincing Valdivia to deny Mendoza his request. There was no reason why his dogs should not be fed all that Picunche meat outside the walls before it spoiled. Look at it this way—Indians ate *each other*! And they did worse! Considering sins too foul to mention, Pedro glowered at his crackling, as he lowered it into flames.

There burns an Indian—thought Juan—for transgressions too terrible to be unveiled to innocence.

Sucking on crackling, Pedro resumed. If Indians actually did worse than eat each other—which they did—feeding them to dogs to nourish and train them was justified. After all, Indians were far less valuable than butchered horses, such as Amadís.

Pedro wondered if he had finally gone too far. Like fierce animals, his convictions were restive on the leash of discourse, straining to break free. Now, he thought, they might be off and sprinting into woods. Truculently he crossed himself, intoning an amen ... then repeating his amen—this best word for ending any argument, as raising the level of discussion to the plane of faith made it unquestionable. Amen gave you a fresh start.

The next crackling went to Negrito in a ritual giving Pedro time to think. He needed something brief and final. "Everybody does it," he concluded with a triumphant belch—which was imitated by the *homunculus* in a higher key.

Juan went to the crux. "Lobo says Indians have souls."

Yearning to break that priestly straw in two, Pedro said, "Just a theory." Everybody knew Lobo loved nothing more than contradicting common knowledge. He added, "That priest is crazy."

He probably is, Juan thought, but … *was* he before the eleventh of September? Pedro was too abstracted to notice the child's abstraction, thinking the colony could not now survive. Without food and supplies they could not stay. And without them they could not cross the Atacama. Santiago had run out of miracles.

"So, Pedro, what do *you* say about the seven heads?"

"You know what Monroy claims. And there are those who say Inés cut them off herself."

"That's not *all* they say," Juan corrected in her defense. "Others say she was nowhere near."

"What does *she* say."

"Nothing."

Pedro delivered his military opinion. "She carried Valdivia's spare sword—a light one. Even seasoned soldiers could not lop off heads with *that*."

Juan knew what Pedro meant, having cut into many an Indian neck and never seen a single head fall. So what *was* her part? And what about Monroy? The versions of what Inés had done were many, yet absolutely no one heard him order the executions.

"The Lieutenant…."

Pedro could take no more. "What Monroy did, or had done—as the Governor himself said before the sight of God—was right and just. His decisions are not ours to question."

To the gills in meat and short of breath, Pedro stood, hand on the hilt of the steel God created to defend those defending Him. "Monroy may not have told the truth … exactly. *But*, what he did was his best in an impossible situation, as a lieutenant loyal to Valdivia and a good friend of Inés, for both of whom—as you should know—he would gladly lay down his life."

As you for me, Pedro, Juan thought, wanting to cry at that certainty. And as I for you. The willingness to die for those you loved was the rock on which the God that died for man had built The Church. And risk her life for love was exactly what Inés *had* done, whatever had transpired, with an unflinching courage most men could not command.

"I'm going to see Inés," he said to Pedro, setting off toward her fire.

"*Buenas noches*, Juan," she greeted him.

No helmet. No hat. No weapons. A bright Inca shawl protected her against the evening chill. Her skirt was spread, so that her upturned face resembled the pale center of a flower.

"I'm sorry!"

"You're young. Sit down."

"Pork?" she offered wearily—its abundance a measure of the disaster.

He shook his head.

"Did you manage to save *anything*?" she asked quietly.

"**Amadís de Gaula.** Pedro's clothes. Some of mine. Blankets. Armor. Weapons."

"That sounds like the order of your priorities."

She was right—what you saved from fire said what you were.

"You?"

"Nothing."

"Clove…?" He detected the fragrance.

"I forgot. Just me and my cloves."

Cloven hooves, Juan thought. And—thinking *cloven tongue*—he leapt to his feet, saying he would be right back.

Inés brooded. Juan had more growing to do, yet was already taller than Valdivia, with broad shoulders and deft brown hands that could create the miracle of writing. She wondered if he bedded *yanaconas* … decided not. Juan was otherworldly— that other world being books. He was a mystic of Heavens bound in leather, these places which he could not have in life *or* death. No living human fit the measure of his ideals. And thinking this, Inés damned the queens of his *romances*—women who did not exist and yet ruined the lives of ones who did, when all they did was try their hardest. Long ago, when Juan first talked of love and battles in **Amadís de Gaula**, she decided that those devoted to such things did not want to live before they died. Like martyrs, they wanted nothing more of life than death. Books were coffins for the living soul, she had concluded then, and she had not changed her mind one little bit.

Juan returned and placed a folded blanket in her hands, saying, "It's Pedro's. He wants you to have it."

"*Muchas gracias.* And may I ask a great favor of you."

"Anything!"

"Teach me to read."

"*Por supuesto,*" he said, disbelieving.

"I would have asked Father Marmolejo, but he is busy with his priestly duties and his fighting. He is breeding horses too, and hawks. Also, all he has for me to learn from is a book about the lives of saints, and this other little book listing sins and prayers. There must be more to life than the confessing of it."

"There are few books in Santiago to learn from," Juan told her. "Lobo has his **Utopia** and **In Praise of Folly**, both in Latin. The **Bible** burnt with the church, and it was in Latin too. You don't want to learn Latin, do you?"

Inés laughed so hard she sputtered. "Why learn a language no one understands?" Then an awful thought struck her. "Latin is not what they speak in Heaven … is it?"

Saying he did not think you had to go to school to go to Heaven, Juan summarized, "That leaves Marmolejo's breviary, the *Legenda aurea*, and **Amadís de Gaula**."

"Marmolejo can teach me saints and sins. You can teach me knights and queens," replied Inés. "But all this will have to be when I can see all those little letters by the light of day."

Juan said his good-bye and rose to leave.

"You know," she told him, "it's almost too much to believe."

"Awful. Truly awful."

"I'm not talking about the death and destruction ... think of the survivors. Don Jamón and a young sow. A rooster and a hen."

"Chickens!" Juan exclaimed.

"Saved by a patrol. Two bags of wheat as well. Two volumes of **Amadís de Gaula**. Important things survived in twos."

"What?"

"The ark did not sink! The pairs are signs from God we will survive!"

The colony feasted for two days on pork, another two on horsemeat, and—for a week—on the flyblown rest, recooked to kill the maggots. What remained became too noisome for the dogs.

Then it was sausage and Adam's ale, soon turning into a diet of roots and what could be taken from Indians—*choclo*, roots, dried fish, shriveled *papas* ... nameless foods. And there was little of that, for many Picunche had died or vanished from their huts. Those remaining hid their food.

Torture hardly worked, for in their agony some Indians revealed what they themselves consumed—inedible leaves and mushrooms, roots, wooden tubers, berries that were all seed and stained your teeth. The Picunche seemed to have decided that if they could not eliminate the Spaniards by force of arms they would create a place where they would not want to stay. *Caballeros* rode long distances to plunder Indian huts not yet abandoned, and on these gleanings Santiago managed to survive—not well—the circle of ravage widening. Every Indian female disappeared from a radius of at least ten leagues around Santiago. Yet the warriors remained, creeping through woods, attacking at every opportunity, so that the *vecinos* could only emerge armed. Santiago was under siege.

The eggs of the one Spanish hen to survive were catalogued, and the first one was eaten on the thirteenth day after the disaster. The others were eaten as they were laid, leaving the freshest dozen for the day the hen turned broody. Valdivia shared the first egg with Inés, and felt so guilty that he instituted an egg lottery after Mass.

When eleven chicks hatched the rejoicing was restrained. The *vecinos* would have to wait another avian generation before consuming anything but spare eggs and extra cocks. And yet more generations would transpire before abundance. Fortunately, the climate of the Indies was such they could expect two harvests of grain a year.

With few Picunche helping, and many *yanaconas* dead of fighting and disease—others simply vanished—colonists performed the most menial tasks. Work began on adobe walls constructed of bricks so large it took two men to lift them.

Juan did hard labor. After that, he ate—if you could call it that—and taught Inés to read before dark. He slept, and that was all. The only good news was that the sow was pregnant.

One Sunday early in December of 1541 Valdivia summoned the *cabildo*, saying that it was imperative that Santiago contact the authorities in Peru.

Ten days later, horsemen were ready to ride, for—the brigantine burnt—the Atacama was the only option.

Monroy led the expedition, his companions being Pedro de Miranda, Juan Pacheco, Martín de Castro, Juan Ronquilla, Alonso de Salguero. They would take gold—which Valdivia borrowed from the *vecinos*—as well as letters to Pizarro. God willing, they would return with men, mounts, supplies.

After Mass the delegation mounted six of the best horses in Santiago. No expense had been spared on a display of wealth, to convince colonists to come to Chile, and under the morning light the ambassadors were a dazzling contrast to gaunt Santiago. Their horses were fat and sleek, magnificently armored, caparisoned with cloth tasseled and embroidered, jingling with golden cascabels. Pennants snapped on every spear. On the mirror finish of the armor, blinding reflections of the sun flowed and shattered. And since there was now far more gold than iron in the colony, Valdivia had turned necessity into ostentation, ordering the expedition outfitted with the precious metal. Not just the bells, but the fittings for the swords, the saddles and harness, even the horses' bits, the horseshoes and the very nails that fastened them, were gold. These emissaries beggared the Santiago sending them.

A false El Dorado, Juan thought, as the glittering horsemen galloped off. They belonged in a fabled kingdom paved with gold and emeralds, not in *these* realities. He said his prayers nonetheless, that the deception might succeed.

In the evening—having molded and hauled adobe, weary to the marrow, covered with dust—Juan took food to Lobo. Once in a while, he convinced the priest to take sustenance—not often—and he had shrunken into a mummy drawing reluctant breath. One day Juan contrived to have him swallow stew he prepared from *choclo* and dried *papas* that Pedro brought from a raid on the Picunche.

His teeth moving—mindless as a llama—Lobo stared into inner distances. After Apocalypse he had not uttered a single word, and Juan had gotten into the habit of nattering as before an infant, more to soothe than to communicate. Today he shared the notion of Inés—that Santiago was an ark. God, had revealed this in her dreams, and sent the number two as a sign.

Lobo startled Juan by speaking. "How many arks in the Bible?"

Had the earth yawned to release its bony dead at the last trump, Juan would not have been more astounded. He stared. And indeed, Lobo resembled a resurrected saint lifting his coffin lid, looking about in cadaverous astonishment.

Juan proposed, "Two. Noah's and the Ark of the Covenant."

"Not two, for they are one."

Lobo cackled, enjoying his riddle.

Juan tried to sort it out. There was sense here somewhere, for God had a covenant with Noah. But the one ark held tablets of stone, while the other held Noah and a menagerie.

Lobo chortled, adding, "And the two arks are Santiago." Now he had taken up the bowl and wooden spoon and was eating greedily, as if riddles were a hunger to be solved by spoonfuls.

Fascinated by the immense Adam's apple wobbling between the neck strings of the priest, Juan guessed, "Another ship?"

And, as Lobo licked his bowl, Juan guessed on, "The *Santiago de Compostela.*"

"More!" The priest banged on his empty bowl with his spoon, like a demented child.

"I'm out!" Juan yelled. He was done with patience, out of food, sick of arks.

Lobo stopped banging his bowl. "Out of *what*?"

Juan was on his feet, saying he was out of stew. He was out of answers too.

So light he should have levitated, Lobo still had difficulty rising. "The ship is the answer," he said, shambling for the door.

Juan followed him into a sun that blinded after the shuttered room, hearing the priest say, "We are not out, but in."

"In *what*?—for the love of God!" It seemed to Juan that, by feeding Lobo, he had nourished only his insanity. Bludgeoned by the light of day, the priest—now near collapse—whispered, "*Stultifera navis.*"

"The ship of fools," Juan sighed. "I should have known."

Chapter 16: Dogger (Valley of the Mapocho, 1541)

Bounding over the dead and wounded, swarming up a ladder to vault the high *lik winka* wall, Pichikan scanned the scene, where the bodies of *che* lay like sea wrack left by tides of battle. Some stirred. Some crawled. Those who could run or walk were gone. He had done well not to escape through the door in the wall—*lik winka* on *kawellu* were running down the *che* who did so, a bowshot away. *Kawellu* could quickly turn that distance to none at all.

Pichikan sprinted for the Mapocho, then heard, and saw, a *lik winka* pursuing on a pounding beast. He ran as never before, the river his only chance. When the remorseless hammering was so close the sound seemed to grow between his ears he risked looking back at the shining weapon, and he tripped, death passing him as a rancid gust of wind.

Death was now between him and the river … returning. Pichikan ran behind a tree. And when the *lik winka* thundered up he yelled insults no honor could endure. Pretending to go in one direction— seeing the *lik winka* begin to turn his beast—Pichikan spun, and sprinted toward him.

The *kawellu* reared, too late. Pichikan hit it on the nose with his fist and ran. Then, ululating with joy, he dove into the Mapocho and struck out underwater.

At the other shore, seeing that he was not pursued, he loped through the scrubby land of the Pikunche. When it grew dark he made himself a nest of leaves and grass beneath a ledge of stone. There he slept, warm and dry, although it rained.

Gabriel de la Cruz said that he had chased the enormous savage with the club and the black head—the one whose life was spared by crazy Juan de Cardeña—and that the Indian jumped into the river and drowned. He did not add that the savage made a royal fool of him.

Curious enough to circulate, this news reached the ears of Nuño Beltrán de Mendoza, who did not believe the Indian drowned, knowing that they swam almost from birth, like dogs. Had he not with his own eyes seen one of their whelps navigate the Mapocho? To him this skill was yet another proof of how low they belonged on the ladder of being. However, by their very animality he was attracted. Like purebred horses they had muscular bodies and keen senses, which admirably suited them for his sport. And he had been particularly impressed by the Indian Juan had spared. As a hunter of men he yearned for this kill—not as one of the muddled and forgotten deaths of battle, but as a magnificent animal harvested in the purity of the hunt. Therefore, a brace of mastiffs at the one hand, greyhounds at the other, he went to visit Gabriel de la Cruz, who wakened to the awful sight of war dogs. He screamed, then told his tale.

At the insistence of Inés, Valdivia had commanded that there be no doggings save in battle. Nonetheless, Mendoza was confident the Governor only said this to calm his concubine, as he was too good a soldier to forbid sound military practice. His dogs needed food no less than he needed sport in these humdrum ends of the earth, so he hunted in secret, far from Santiago. But he was bored with the repetitious ease of the chase, even with its climax. The problem was that spoor led you to *whatever* savage. Women and children were not sport but simple meat, ordinary warriors little more. Hopefully today would prove a challenge for his dogs. Last night's rain—by drowning scent—would make the hunt all the more intriguing.

Armed with sword and crossbow, but unarmored—dressed in blue as usual— he set off, lifting his feet from the stirrups when he forded the Mapocho to keep his hose dry.

Mendoza surprised himself by feeling lonely, as solitude was the center of his being and the essence of his *monterías infernales*. There was something absolutely right in being the only witness to the agony of human prey. This focused the pleading and the hate, putting him in charge of life and death. From time to time, he capriciously spared the victim, and that too was good.

The dogger did not understand his present melancholy. He had been wondering, however, what his friendship with Juan would have been if the youth had not turned petty, for he was attracted to him. Not carnally to be sure, but still *materially*—as one admires statues. He was also drawn to the deep, pure spring of violence in him. The youth himself had said he died when young—a statement which shook Mendoza at the time, who thought himself unshakable. Dying young and baptized made of you an angel, airy denizen at the edge of a Heaven which had at its center a God who scolded and punished the sinners of a troubled world, a God who hid under drapery the Organ of Creation—heavy, hairy, pendulous. Angels were not charged with justice or mercy. They just agelessly observed. Mendoza thought that Juan had betrayed these heights he had been granted—the distance and dispassion that allowed you to see men small.

Though he studied the world from something like Heaven's altitudes, Mendoza had never identified with The Father *or* The Son. He was fascinated instead by a painting of the Virgin in the church of the village where he was born. Hovering in cloud, her varnished image glowed through all the years of his youth—the rough execution increasing her allure, in retrospect. On her pallor there was a hectic blush, as from a fever. And Mendoza would never forget the moment the *idea* came to him— that the carmine on her cheeks somehow betrayed God's impregnation.

That day he was burning with fever himself, and mother took him to the church to exorcise his demons. While praying the *salve regina*, Mendoza thought that Mary was hot and thirsty, sick as he, and virgin too. God had *violated* both of them. Mary got sick with Christ, and then got rid of Him, yet the evidence lingered on her cheeks.

For Mendoza, this insight evolved into a personal theology in which The Father was an invisible, impregnating menace. He began to wear broad-brimmed hats and gloves he stitched himself, becoming pale. He acquired an old razor, and shaved twice daily. Boys called him a *pato* and offered to fuck his white ass. It was all funnier than they could stand. Yet they were absolutely wrong. Mendoza hated men as nothing else. Coarse in dress and language, hairy, they were a procession that came to lie on his mother. Sometimes they beat him, calling him a *pato* too, doing unspeakable things that they said he wanted ... as mother watched, sucking on the wine she had been paid with.

Gaspar—Mendoza's given name—vowed never to be like those that covered mother, not dreaming of revenge until one day a large, scrofulous dog happened by, and he tossed him the bone he had been gnawing. By Advent the animal was his shadow. Gaspar called him Hunger.

The day came when he put Hunger to the test, coming upon Rodrigo—biggest boy in the village—bent under firewood on a lonely road. The bully taunted him. Who else had a face white as his butt? Were his nostrils assholes?

Gaspar loosed Hunger.

Rodrigo lost an ear and eyelid. Yet, after, he did exactly as he was told, stating to all who asked that he had been attacked by a pack of feral dogs.

Gaspar trained five more mongrels, which he found by walking leagues. They were everywhere—ignored, unseen as birds—but he wanted the largest. And one day he strode into his mother's hovel....

The men groaning on top of her were usually from the village, but this time it was a gypsy tinsmith who had bartered for a lay. He had spent the night and was banging her again, when—pale as the host, in an outlandish outfit—a boy walked in with a rabble of mutts and ordered him to leave.

Dammed if he would, the tinsmith panted. He had a deal—two fucks per pan. He was coming, not going.

Gaspar whistled softly to his dogs.

The tinsmith had never seen so many teeth before, and his reflex—surging up to where he hung his knife—was a mistake, as he was still coupled to the woman. He rammed her head hard against the wall, which left him encumbered by a helpless, groaning fuck. Backing out, he heard the boy again....

He stood and walked out barefoot—only in his shirt, as he was told. And soon after, the gypsy tinsmith died—although he managed to crawl a distance down the village street, taking the fury with him—screaming, as doors and shutters slammed.

The lack of audience disappointed Gaspar. This was his *true* first communion after all, not that idiotic ceremony dressing him in white, and he wanted witnesses to his power. Also—being no fool—he knew that he needed the villagers afraid. He was confident, however, that no one would talk to the *alguaciles*. No witness would risk being dogged, certainly not for a wandering tinsmith—especially a gypsy. Gaspar had been impressed, himself, by the quantities of blood. He had seen pigs slaughtered of course, but the blood was always collected in a tin for sausage, nothing like what had spurted, pooled and smeared on the street.

He left the village without saying goodbye to the whore that bore him, taking nothing but his dogs, not looking back. But first he visited Rodrigo. Pleasantly, Gaspar told the cowering parents that he was taking their son out for a walk.

For two days they avoided roads, heading south, and Gaspar got all the food he wanted from *campesinos*, generous in the face of his animals. Still—heady as his power had become—he was prudent, taxing only isolated dwellings. He allowed Rodrigo no sustenance, and on the second morning he had him strip, so that his prisoner walked naked all that day, surrounded by dogs, forbidden to whimper, sob, beg or complain. He slept naked that night as well, in the chill of *Semana Santa*. In the morning he could hardly walk, for shaking.

Late the third day Gaspar decided that the place was right, the dogs hungry enough. And, obedient to the last—thinking that only his silence could save him—Rodrigo died without a voluntary sound.

Once in Andalusía, Gaspar became a law unto himself. He trained dogs for fights and races, making enough money to buy purebred stock. He bought fine clothes—always blue—preferring silk and velvet. And eventually, he gave himself a new, far nobler name. He had always despised the wise men....

A greyhound interrupted the reveries of Nuño Beltrán de Mendoza.

With an excitement betrayed only by the rapidity of her motions—swinging her head from side to side—his bitch began to follow an invisible straight line running north. Sure of her discovery she froze, pointing like a weathervane. The other dogs ran up immediately beside her, sinews taut as the twisted rope of catapults. Mendoza dismounted and—taking care not to soil his boots—studied the riverbank. He had known Indians that could track on rock—and of course dogs could—but to him gravel revealed no secrets. Still, scanning the river, he decided that this was the right spot. The shortest distance from Santiago to the water would put the savage on this stony shoal.

Even though it was impossible that he would be followed, Pichikan took precautions, as Ñamku insisted on keeping his place secret from even the Pikunche.

So when he reached the stream that eventually flowed by the *ruka* he crafted faint signs—a smudged heel print in sand, bent twigs, pebbles meticulously nudged from place—that made it seem he followed the bank in the opposite direction. He did this until he came to bare rock. Then he waded the current upstream, stopping only to wash the stump of his finger and tie fresh leaves around it, glad that soon he would be able to amaze Tuiñam and Ñamku, Lleflai and the *pichiche* with the news of the great battle, and his part in it. He would brag a little, and after eating a mountain, sleep forever.

The dogs were puzzled—Mendoza not—when the Indian's trail ended in water. For a half day the rain-eroded spoor had made tracking slow, until it led to where the Indian slept in what looked like an enormous rodent's nest. After that, the greyhounds followed the scent fast as the horse could trot in broken wilderness. When they reached the stream Mendoza did not see the multitude of signs Pichikan had left. However, seeing the mark of a naked heel in wet sand he became indignant, for he was taking the savage seriously and would have appreciated the same in return—along with a great deal of fear. The last thing he had expected was insolence. He was being taken for a dupe. For a Picunche to leave a sign that he could read was a deliberate insult. Outraged, Mendoza vowed to make the death of this upstart slow, and he urged his horse up the watercourse. It was growing late. And here the streambed was flat as flagstones.

Scaling a cliff, Ñamku had discovered a new plant in the subtle strangeness of this Pikunche land, and while savoring the bitter leaf unmasked, heard a distant sound. No question of fleeing down the cliff and upstream to the *ruka*. Swiftly, he climbed to the cliff-edge, vanishing up the tallest tree he found. Then, across a meadow in the woods beyond, he heard the noise of dogs and the drumming feet of a *kawellu*. Was old age murmuring lies in his ears?

A *weichafe* running like a *pudu* exploded from the woods, swerving toward Ñamku. Pichikan! He was headed for the one place where he could make it safely down the precipice to the stream—the faint path he had himself been climbing. Heartbeats later, two glittering animals broke into the clearing, running faster than any creature could, and Ñamku recognized the dogs of the *kallfu lik winka*.

Searching his pouch, clumsy with urgency, the *machi* prepared, seeing that the dogs were closing distance with breathtaking speed. Pichikan would not make it to the stream, but he might make it to his tree if he ran as no *che* ever had before. So intent on the chase was the *machi* that he almost did not see two larger dogs— baying with low, penetrating power—break from the woods.

The shining animals caught up with Pichikan almost directly under Ñamku's tree—no more than a stride from the cliff edge.

Unslinging his club as he spun to face the dogs—the swing a violent extension of his turn—the *weichafe* brained one beast and sent it flying in a spatter of blood. But he missed the other. As it crouched to spring, he slid over the mossy edge of the cliff.

Ñamku watched with horror as Pichikan lost his footing. Slipping, then bouncing on rocks, he dropped onto the top of a small tree clinging to the sheer side of the precipice. It bent and swayed ... did not break.

The *lik winka* dog leapt after Pichikan, stopping short of the edge, uncertain of what to do, then went to lick the crushed head of the dead one. Her mate, Ñamku thought, puffing on his tube.

The dog did not yelp at the bite of the dart on her hindquarters, arching around to snap it off. And only then did the *lik winka* appear in the meadow.

Ñamku looked down at Pichikan. One mistake in grip or footing and he was dead. But, groggy, he was starting to make his way to safety. Ñamku understood his painful slowness, for the tree was rooted in a crevice and—one by one—the roots were pulling out. The branches entangling Pichikan shuddered, dropping with heart-stopping jerks.

The *weichafe* was in the hands of the *pillañ*. If the tree fell, he was dead. But if he made it down the cliff and Ñamku did nothing, he would be torn apart by dogs.

The greyhound was confused, her quarry visible but unreachable. Her mate was dead. The scent of a human she had not been ordered to pursue led to a tree, and up. She made a circuit—cliff, mate, tree—staggering with a weakness she did not recognize as coming death, when she heard a sound and smelled other man-prey. Slowed by stupor she crouched, silently snarling. The man-prey moved into her failing sight, pale against the trees. The greyhound leapt, but—while in the air—was overpowered by a scent that burnt. Her eyes watered and went blind.

Mendoza quickened the pace of his horse as the mastiffs approached the edge of the meadow. The kill was imminent and he wanted to be there to make it slow—though he could not linger too long or he might not make it back to Santiago before dark. As he often did, when the quarry was near he let the dogs run free—the silent greyhounds first, to surprise the prey, mastiffs after, baying to guide his way. Maybe he let them go too soon this time, he thought, seeing a white shadow disappear into forest, glimmering in the uncertain light. Had Mendoza not been riding at a gallop he might have turned in that direction, but—intent on his kill—he galloped after the dogs into twilight intricate with overarching bamboo. Reining in his horse, he saw the mastiffs milling by a cliff edge ... then, to the left, motion. Through a confusion of leaves he saw a greyhound—one!—staggering, floundering, falling, getting up, with nowhere a sign of the quarry. Cursing these thickets that made walking necessary, Mendoza dismounted and drew the sword he had never really learned to use. Snapping branches, getting scratched, he followed the bitch. Was she wounded? Where was her mate?

He stopped abruptly when the noises he pursued turned in his direction. About to whistle, he saw the dog's awful face appear through leaves—eyes blood red and weeping. The muzzle—covered with yellow powder, bright as a flower's heart— swung like a pendulum, vicious with intent. No mercy or recognition there.

Mendoza took a step back, froze. Too late he realized that his own dog had stalked him. And since she could neither see nor smell, he had betrayed himself with his own sound.

She leapt for his throat, the accuracy uncanny, a force mindless as a catapulted stone. Dropping to his knees, Mendoza was struck a glancing blow on the shoulder, and the greyhound's leap carried her over the cliff edge.

Hearing the impact far below Mendoza wiped his eyes, which were stinging, watering. His blue sleeve was smeared yellow. He sneezed, sneezed again. Furious, he hurried to the mastiffs and found them whimpering by the other greyhound. An Indian club explained the death of this dog. What of the one that leapt to her death? What was that yellow powder? What about his stinging eyes and nose, the sneezing?

Cold rage replaced the stately pleasures of the hunt. The mastiffs were better killers than trackers, but spoor had led them to the cliff-edge....

Mendoza saw only an abrupt drop. Big Club had probably been cornered, backed to the cliff and leapt—or been forced over by the dogs—and no one could survive that fall. Either way, the savage was smashed down there under all that greenery. Mendoza took no satisfaction in this unwitnessed death, however, for the hulking savage had cost him two priceless dogs.

Cursing the Indian's heathen soul to Hell, Mendoza set the mastiffs to searching. And they too began to sneeze, snuffling their way to a nearby tree, then in the direction the greyhound had taken. Weeping without sorrow, sneezing without reason, Mendoza let anger cloud his intelligence for the first time in his life, giving the mastiffs the command to track and kill.

Mounting, he heard their deep-throated bass echo through the woods, growing distant. He returned to the meadow to pursue at a gallop, and—mount now running free—wondered if he was being duped *again* as an unfamiliar feeling took his hand to his head. *Virgen santissima!*—no hat. After he had fed this perverted, shadowy Indian to his mastiffs—Mendoza vowed—he would take them upstream to wreak havoc on whatever he and Big Club were trying to hide. He sneezed, and sneezed again.

Ñamku ran through boulders and doubled back, climbing one of them to prepare his darts. Only two left—one for each dog on his trail, so that he could not miss with either one. Yet when they appeared in rapid single file, amazement made him hesitate. These dogs were bigger than *pudu* and far heavier.

Having hesitated too long, he aimed for the second. And the dart took.

Hearing a yelp the first dog spun, presenting Ñamku with only the head and hard *dengu* on the chest as target.

The breeze shifted. Testing the air, the immense dog smelled him, baying.

Ñamku puffed his dart into the open mouth.

Hearing a dog's bay cut off, Mendoza urged his mount to reckless speed— though branches of this green hell whipped him. Even so, it took time to find the mastiffs.

The male seemed to be asleep and having a nightmare, taking stertorous breaths. The bitch was swaying, gagging. Mendoza dismounted ... saw that the male had just died. The bitch was on her knees like a resting llama, shuddering.

Mendoza searched the dogs for wounds, found none. Sorcery? Somewhere in this unholy wilderness without name or feature was a shadowy warlock wanting him dead.

Cranking his crossbow, Mendoza set a bolt. Forgetting to retrieve the armor of his dogs, he mounted and galloped off.

Four days later—famished, weak, erect with fury—he stumbled into Santiago, leading his horse.

Mendoza was a subtle, intelligent man, in the habit of thinking when he rode. The dogs that were his weapons and his shield were his memory as well, making it unnecessary to note or remember his environment. Therefore he became profoundly lost when he struck out for Santiago by himself. He knew the general direction, of course, yet streams and ravines created a haphazard maze, diverting him in unwanted ways through a landscape holding nothing edible. The first night he sat against a tree, sneezing so violently that his muscles ached, sending that involuntary signal to every lurking Indian. He hated his sneezing. It made him feel small and helpless, like a snail without a shell.

The second day he stopped sneezing. But—like a memory burned into his ribs—every breath was agony, throat and nose so raw the very air seemed grit. Finding a river he followed the bank, deciding it was too small to be the Mapocho. Too weary to care when darkness came, he slept like beasts, in leaves.

The third day he found the Mapocho—late—after spending the night in the rodent's nest he had learned to make. And as his horse had gone lame, Mendoza walked. Then it rained. That night he did not even bother to cover himself with wet litter....

To forget his hunger, his shivering, his bleeding and blistered feet, dead dogs—

the very real possibility of his death—Mendoza fantasized revenge, inventing ever deeper circles of the Hell for the Indian in white. Dogs would be far too quick.

And when Mendoza at last walked into Santiago his hose was beyond repair, doublet a shambles, his pallor a peeling itchiness he refused to imagine. Worst was the obscenity his fingers could not leave alone. He was growing a beard.

Chapter 17: Return (Valley of the Mapocho, 1541)

A dog plummeted by Pichikan.

The tree that saved his life had spun away, but not before his fingers found a ledge under which he hid. The dogs, the *kawellu*—maybe even the *lik winka*—could not make it to where he was. And if they did not see or smell him they might think him gone.

He waited in a discomfort so great that little by little it became dangerous. The path down was a seasonal watercourse dripping icy water on him. His face was jammed against wet moss. His holds were slippery, precarious—left hand strangling a small bush, the right wandered crevices in a search for purchase. The exertion of two *antu* and loss of blood had weakened him. The dog sounds stopped, and he heard other sounds above. Only *lik winka* could be that noisy. A silence followed. Then the dog had plunged by.

Something about a fall from such a height made you hold your breath....

Lleflai and Tuiñam sat in the sun, stripping kernels of *uwa* into baskets, engrossed in this familiar task of *pillel cuyen*—moon of planting. They sorted the seed according to kind. Long, blue *uwa* was good for grinding into meal, as were the shorter black ones. The yellow did not keep as well, yet was excellent for roasting. The small, red ones that were almost round—with pointed ends—were for popping.

Tuiñam had been depressed, which made Lleflai talk to him too much and too often, she knew—like a mother babbling at her child to make the hurt go away. Yet she could not stop. Now she was explaining how you had to plant each kind of *uwa* at a distance from other kinds, at different times, or you got strange ones. She held up an example. *Uwa* was like children, she said, when you allowed them to play together some went wild.

Tuiñam thought her hands were truly beautiful, and he was troubled by her kindness, having heard the cruel jokes about the ugliest *domo* ever. But her attention would not have bothered him half so much if his feelings had not gone beyond friendship. Lleflai possessed every virtue and beauty a woman could. She only lacked a face. How important could faces be?

The translucent kernels of the *uwa* that decided to be different—variegated, in their warm bath of light—silenced Lleflai. This was not good seed, yet it was beautiful.... Then she became aware that *she*—not the *uwa*—was being stared at. Fighting the inner beasts of the terror that never left her, she attempted a smile. But when her hand—with a habit born of dread —reached up to cover her smile with her hair, she pulled it over her shoulder instead.

Frozen in mutual tension and embarrassment, they heard a muffled noise not far away. A sneeze! Tuiñam took up his spear, gesturing for Lleflai to take cover. She slid down beside the rock that was her seat. He crouched behind another, scrutinizing the woods that curved around the garden.

A wild call echoed in the ravine. To Lleflai it sounded like an enemy, but Tuiñam sprang up. With a wild answering howl he splashed madly across the stream, to collide in an embrace with Pichikan. They splashed and whooped, pounding each other in an ecstasy of greeting far too great for language. Lleflai began to laugh and shrieked, as they lost their footing, and fell. Like every mother with a baby, she was never unaware of the soft spot on Tuiñam's head—even when he had his *lik winka wethakelu* on, as he did now. Then she splashed up to them feeling silly. They were sitting in the shallows laughing—grown babies indeed.

Pichikan—who had been lightly rapping on the helmet of Tuiñam with his war club—rose to greet Lleflai. But the mighty warrior returned from battle, who could fight *lik winka* and survive, could not conquer his sneezing, his chattering teeth. And his eyes were half closed, the whites scarlet.

"*Mari, mari*, Pichikan. You are cold and hungry. Come into the *ruka*. Eat." She scolded, "You are wounded!"

"Mostly my pride."

Sitting by the fire, eating boiled red *poñu* and ground black *uwa* mixed with honey, drinking hot herb and berry tea—a feast!—Pichikan related his wondrous adventures.

Ñamku joined them when Naipam was being flung a full four *nufku* by the *lik winka* spear. Gesturing for the tale to continue, the *machi* accepted tea as the battle was recounted blow-by-blow. Lautaro cheered when a *lik winka* or *kawellu* was killed or wounded, a lack of politeness not ordinarily permitted. And—when Pichikan described how he had hamstrung the beast of a *lik winka*, bringing him down and challenging him to single combat—even Lleflai was entranced. This was the stuff of legend…. At the end, Tuiñam cried out, "We defeated the *lik winka*!"

"For every dead *lik winka* a hundred Pikunche fell," said Pichikan. He added, "And at least one Mapuche."

"It is an honor to kill—or even wound—a *lik winka*!" Tuiñam exclaimed, forgetting his manners. He would rather have gone with a hole in his head and died, than stay behind the way he did.

Only Lleflai—by stirring the herb and berry tea—interrupted the silence that followed.

Fluid as smoke Ñamku rose, to muse, "Honor and harmony are always themselves, yet no defeat is ever like another."

"Most of the *lik winka* and their *kawellu* are alive," Pichikan somberly commented. "And the Pikunche ended up retreating."

Tuiñam was stubborn. "You killed several and wounded more. Their *ruka* are burnt, along with their food and seed. They will get hungry and go back *piku* where they came from."

This, Ñamku had been hoping also, yet not with the conviction of youth. He prepared a salve for the eyes of Pichikan, knowing that only time would heal his sneezing.

When the *machi* vanished behind his curtain Lleflai put the reluctant *pichiche* to bed, promising more stories for the morning. But Tuiñam had to hear more about the fight with the *lik winka*....

When the *kawellu* fell, Pikunche rushed in to kill the *lik winka*—and it would have been easy.

But he, Pichikan, had not allowed this, since the *lik winka* was his to fight as the one who made the *kawellu* fall. An argument began. Any *weichafe* who wounded another could demand combat to the death. If he won, he could dispose of his body and possessions as he wished. But this was different, Pikunche insisted, since the *lik winka* could separate from his *kawellu*.

They fight as one, Pichikan replied—though this was only partly true, and more important, without precedent. The Pikunche were silenced for the moment, however. And he reminded them of the hunt—The first arrow to wound an animal gave the hunter the right to finish the kill. Was this not so?

As it was undeniable the Pikunche ceased arguing, suppositions writhing like nests of eels in their minds. Pichikan had wounded a *kawellu*, which seemed to make the customs of the hunt apply. But this was war and the *kawellu* fought, which made it resemble a *weichafe*. If so—as the *kawellu* was separate from the *lik winka*—it was something like a *weichafe* with a *weichafe* on its back. This was unthinkable, but only slightly more so than a *weichafe* fighting on an animal. Immutable distinctions were dissolving like familiar footprints in the rain.

A Pikunche yelled over the roar of battle that the Mapuche was welcome to kill the *kawellu* he had wounded, and had a right to the *wethakelu* on it, but not to the *lik winka*.

Pichikan replied that a hunter who wounded a pregnant animal also had a right to the unborn.

All *che* loved good debate—and these matters were intricate. Was a *lik winka* on a *kawellu* something like an unborn child? Were they separate, or was it true—as some said—that a *lik winka* could be taken from his *kawellu* but not permanently, or he would die like an exposed *pichiche*. If they were separate, which one decided what to do? If the *kawellu* was like the mother, then it decided. But every *che* knew that *lik winka* made the decisions for them, and *pichiche* did not tell their parents what to do. Also, there were not a few who said that *lik winka*—like *kalku*—imposed their will on *kawellu* with poisons and spells, as on *ifunche*.

Mother and child, warrior on warrior, warrior on kawellu, *kalku* and *ifunche*.... Or—since none of it made sense—was it *kalku* on *kawellu*, warrior and mother, mother on child? The riot of speculation was cut short when the *lik winka* sat up and looked around.

The Pikunche held back. Pichikan was large, truculent, deadly, and maybe even right. Let him fight and get killed, which would leave them the pleasure of finishing the *lik winka*. If he won—which was unlikely—the *lik winka* would be just as dead. Either way it would be interesting.

"He took off his hard *wethakelu*," Pichikan said, reliving his amazement—the act seeming unlikely as a crab unlacing its shell.

"Some were tied on with string, some with things I saw at Malga Malga and did not understand. Under all this he is not white like snow, just lighter than *che*. His eyes are neither green nor blue—more like pools of water on a sunny day, flecked with little water spiders. His hair is the color of desert sand." He added, "The *lik winka* is not spotted in any way."

Tuiñam wanted to hear about the fight itself.

"I gave him a *lik winka* spear, but he chose a little knife he had hidden in his clothes."

"You said he took his *wethakelu* off."

"Underneath the hard ones they wear cloth."

Pichikan sneezed, Tuiñam rocking on his heels with impatience.

"He is brave—that *lik winka*—to fight with no hard *wethakelu* and that little knife. And he is very fast. He avoided all my attacks—although I came close a time or two."

Pichikan described it all—how he attempted this, tried that. The *lik winka* remained unhurt but did not fight until the last.

"He has great speed, and is unpredictable. You never know where he will be, doing what." Pichikan removed his severed little finger from his pouch and studied it. "Are they unpredictable to each other?" he wondered. "Or just to us." He sneezed.

Sometime during the night Pichikan stopped sneezing, bringing everyone relief, as at the end of a long, unwanted rain. And after bathing next morning, they gathered around the fire.

As his severed little finger was smelly, Pichikan smoked it as he talked. Spinning, darkening, it hung over the flames in dim eddies of heat, creating a focus to his tale....

He admitted to being puzzled at the end. The *kallfu lik winka* and his dogs tracked him. He barely escaped. A dog fell by him when he was hiding from them on a cliff. The *lik winka* and his remaining dogs disappeared along the canyon rim. And when he found the dead dog in the bed of the stream his eyes watered and stung. He began to sneeze.

Suspecting sorcery, Pichikan looked at Ñamku. Disheveled, hair wild to below his waist, he seemed absorbed by the lazy spin of the fingertip.

Lleflai handed him tea, began to brush his milk-white hair.

Ñamku was no real man—and Pichikan had seen his hair brushed before— still, the embarrassing sight caused him to blurt what he had intended to keep silent. "I saw the one *domo* of the *lik winka*. She was on a *kawellu*, holding a long knife, dressed in hard *wethakelu*. I recognized her green eyes, her spots, her red hair."

Pichikan left out the fact that she was the ugliest woman ever—even though this would have been a bitter kind of compliment to Lleflai. He also omitted that no dugs were visible. "She is the only *lik winka* that is truly white," he said. "I know, because her legs were bare to the knee."

Lleflai stopped brushing, shaken by the immodesty of this *domo*, high on a *kawellu*, baring her white legs to strangers. What else was she showing?

"She did not appear to be *kalku*, though her *kepam* was black. She more resembled a *weichafe*. And when she spoke to the one I fought, she acted like his worried mother. Her face is long and thin, not furry. Her spots are small—mostly on her nose—and the hair under her hard *wethakelu* is not red like a *kopiwe*, but more like polished copper."

Lleflai had never seen copper, thinking of it as a rarer, stranger gold. Searching her memory of shades of *uwa* she decided that the hair of the *lik winka* domo was like a color on the most rebellious cobs.

"I don't think she has dugs between her legs."

Modesty kept Pichikan from mentioning that she had bumps under her *wethakelu* where the breasts of a *domo* should be, too small to be udders. He gestured vaguely, half-whispering to himself, "She looked very sad, and not at all evil."

Scrutinizing Pichikan, the *machi* said, smiling, "I think I liked her too. And I know she likes *pichiche*." He smiled at Lautaro's scowl, and—recalling the thrum of pinions—told them of his vision.

He waited—having lost his vision and not yet acquired the eyes of height. And he was cold, as always, when feathers pierced his skin before they grew the down beneath. With painful slowness his legs shrank and hardened, toenails turned to talons.

And the hawk opened his eyes to blindness, Ñamku returning to the cloud that the bone *che* brought his vision. In a whisper of feathers, he was circling, and the cloud buffeted him, turning darker, warmer. He flew out of it into spinning, hot, uprushing air. The tiny glowing eyes of the *pillañ* appeared in the turbulence, also rushing upward, looking at him, sputtering like sparks in an enormous, swirling shaft of acrid smoke that pierced the clouds.

He had flown into vision and been blinded—again!—not by cloud but by the risen sun, and by the fires that roared below. He soared above the battle of the hill Welen, flight sustained by the rising heat of the destruction. And—as Pichikan described it—so it was.

"I flew into vision," the *machi* said to the *weichafe*, "at the moment Naipam was struck by the *lik winka* spear."

Pichikan marveled, remembering a soaring hawk,

Ñamku went on—Lleflai now working on his braid—saying that there was, perhaps, a perspective he could share on the battle. The *lik winka* were outnumbered by the *aillarewe* as a tree trunk by its leaves. Still—although *lik winka* fell—most were left standing when the Pikunche fled. He had seen them by their burnt *ruka*, irate, bitter.

Ñamku concluded, "They do not think themselves defeated. They will seek revenge, and it will be terrible."

Tuiñam was outraged. "They will starve, without food or seed!"

"They do not need to leave, to eat," the *machi* responded, patient. " They will come on their *kawellu* to take our food, killing those who resist."

Ñamku slipped his braid from sight, put on his mask, slipped up his hood. What he had seen was too important to ignore. "I saw the dogs," he hissed. "Like *ifunche*, they know the mind of the *kallfu lik winka*. They led him to us."

"My fault!" Pichikan admitted, hanging his head.

Ñamku ignored him. "In their hunger *lik winka* will go far to find food. The *mapu* of the Pikunche will be devastated by their need, their hate. And their *kalku* will be angry. Pikunche not dead of hunger and war will die of sorcery."

Lleflai could not breathe. She had heard about the strange, awful death that killed with red spots that turned black and burst, reeking, dripping.

The *machi* continued, "Against *lik winka kalkutun* I can do nothing, not in any future I have seen."

Lleflai forgot her place, thinking of the *pichiche*. "We *have* to return!"

Tuiñam glowered at the *domo*. "The women and children can leave. We *weichafe*…"

"For *any* of us to stay would be foolish," Pichikan interrupted his friend, surprising everyone. "We are not Pikunche. We Mapuche will fight when the *lik winka* cross the Fio Fio."

Tuiñam stared at his friend—knowing that nothing resembling cowardice existed in him.

"Well spoken," the *machi* said—having expected more resistance.

Pichikan put the shriveled little finger—dry and black—into his pouch.

Lleflai could have danced, singing like *loika*. They were leaving, returning to life as a family! Lautaro would not be given to the *lik winka domo* who obscenely showed her white legs to strangers! All would be as before! Then like winds of cold *cuyen*, a chill swept over her.... She asked the *machi*, "In your vision did they come? I mean *lik winka,* to our *mapu*?"

Ñamku did not reply, that much of the future being clouded. However, he did not need vision to know their coming was but a matter of time.

Covering her face with her hands, Lleflai whispered, "Did you see *us* return?"

"*Yamai.*"

"When?" She peered at him through rigid fingers.

Remembering the single file of tiny figures far below, disappearing into the blank he flew until he woke, the *machi* said, "We left tomorrow."

BOOK TWO

Chapter 1: Secretary (La Serena, 1545)

The New World had its rats, but not Santiago. This plague of Christendom had sailed to the Indies in the holds of ships, and the enterprising rodents—madly breeding in Mexico—had recently disembarked in Peru. Their journey across the Isthmus of Panama must have been difficult, as it is far easier to be a stowaway in the bowels of a caravel than on a loaded mule. Relying on human transport as they did, no one knows how the first rat Adam and rat Eve achieved the miracle of their journey to rat Paradise ... perhaps half-suffocated in sacks of grain.

In Santiago, of course, there were 'creepers'—as the soldiers called their lice and fleas. Yet, to date, no rats. As if to compensate, the mongrel dogs proliferated more even than in civilization, where they competed with beggars for their sustenance. Dogs roamed the streets as a more dangerous form of vermin, and one day a feral pack contrived to kill a lamb. This soured the benevolence of Inés, who otherwise extended the cape of her protection over all civilized fauna. Lambs were gentle creatures after all—emblematic of the living Christ—while a mongrel most definitely was not. So at her insistence the *cabildo* passed laws to control the beasts. Some were slain, most harried into exile—as suburbanites the feral creatures would eat the animals that ate the crops, and also provide warning against skulking Indians.

So it was that—one morning in the winter of 1544—roaming curs discovered the body of Luis de Cartagena crucified upon a tree. When Juan and Pedro reached the scene, two dogs had already been killed beneath the tragic spectacle, others sent yowling. The crowd awaited the arrival of Father Marmolejo, who would set this savage moment right with God.

Reprisals against Indians were discussed with small enthusiasm. Although the blood-crusted corpse was piteous, Cartagena probably deserved what he got, due to his unbridled appetites. He had, for example, managed to extort and steal food through the famine that followed the second battle of Santiago, so that—insult incarnate—he remained corpulent. Worse was his taste for Indian women, a normal thing save that he forcibly bedded them with disregard to the arrangements they might have with other Spaniards—in a number of cases tantamount to marriage. Given all this, a *vecino* might well have done this terrible thing, masking his revenge with Indian mutilations ... for mutilated Cartagena most definitely was, suspended there for all to see.

Pedro bulked his way up, Juan in his wake. Like other tortured dead, the corpse seemed to him more than naked, the torture exaggerating shame. A tongue darker than a tongue protruded from his mouth, and the milk-white stomach was pendulous over the black wound that once had been his sex. Refusing to think of pregnancy and menstruation, Juan did. He focused on what differentiated this crucifixion from The Sacred One, seeing that—unlike the Son of God—Cartagena had no hands or feet. No nails therefore. He was just strung up with rawhide.

Vecinos speculated that he had been forced to consume his missing parts, so that maybe they were not missing after all. That seemed right, someone proposed, for Luis *had* always been full of himself as an egg, a *huevo*. There was smothered laughter, for *huevos* were always funny, like *cojones*. *Anything* referring to testicles was a riot.

Another said Luis could eat his feet, hands, legs, arms, member, his *huevos* too, and only his fat stomach would be left, a *huevo* without *huevos*.

If only his head could consume itself backwards, inside out, a hoarse voice proposed, he would be left the perfect *huevo*. As the voice had no apparent source, Cacafuego was suspected of ventriloquism.

The general mood was positively jovial when Marmolejo arrived bearing extreme unction. The silenced crowd knelt. Thumbing the sign of the cross, Marmolejo asked if the body was cold.

Whether dogma or just tradition—nobody knew—it was said that last rites could be administered after death if the body was still warm to the touch, although administered it always was, just in case. God's Mercy was a fountain of exceptions to His Laws. That was what miracles were all about.

Juan left as they were taking Cartagena down—an obscene parody of the descent from the cross—thinking that Christ would never seem Himself again. In the Indies there were earthquakes of the mind that shook your every past foundation.

Inés awaited in the new house Juan shared with Pedro. Solemn, she put fingers—pale as lilies—on his mail. "Is it true?" she asked. Juan sketched a gesture intended to communicate 'of course, too bad, so what.'

"This *is* important," Inés responded to his semaphoring, incomparably smiling. And, brushing something nonexistent off his shoulder with proprietary intimacy, she added, "Valdivia will name you secretary. The *cabildo* too, no doubt."

She proved prophetic, telling Juan the next day that Valdivia was ready to 'take the step.' She would pass the news to Pedro, from which point the secret would branch out.

Valdivia counted on this grapevine rooted—so to speak—upon his pillow, using it as a diplomatic tool to test the reaction to decisions still deniable as rumors.

Being secretary had nothing to do with dreams born of **Amadís de Gaula,** yet Juan would get a *repartimiento* and be rich, maybe own an estate the size of

Spanish provinces. He would be able actually to *create* the Bower of Bliss, with Indian maids as servants dressed in some rich imitation of civilization. He decided that they would serve silently, not producing the misbegotten *lingua franca* of Santiago—that Babel born of Spanish, Quechua and Picunche. Not so very long from now, he might find himself being offered dainties by silent, dusky beauties in rustling silk.

But in the Indies, The Bower of Bliss could not exist, Juan knew, so far had he traveled—not so much in leagues as in hope. He last visited the unfinished palace more than two years ago, and though difficult of access, lost in wilderness, Santiago had proved to be the antithesis of The Bower, where desire was never consummated. *Vecinos* casually took Indian women as servants in a relationship that created harems without marriage, walls, or veils. Luis de Cartagena was one such abuser, and Cacafuego had more 'handmaidens' than Queen Isabel.

Here, a bolt of shame struck Juan, since there was no place for dusky maidens in The Bower, even if they exchanged their wool for silk. Despite his every good intention, he could not help but think of Indian women as—in Pedro's words—nothing but nock for man's mettle. It was sad.

Sadly also, nothing of value is what Juan's *encomienda* proved to be—large, but distant, bereft of Indians. He had become the ruler of rocks, shrubs, dust, and the little rain falling on them.

Almost a year later—in September of 1545—Juan contemplated the duck feather he had slit to create a quill, setting this emblem of his profession down beside four others. The letters he had to write were long, and he might need all five. A quill for each of the years destroying his dreams, he thought. Not that he was exactly unhappy as secretary, living day to day with the same day to look forward to, then back at. He told Pedro it was like living a memorized page.

If God wanted to create only pages—Pedro had responded—He would only had made the Bible. Why, then, bother with men?

Juan took up a sheet of parchment, setting it at a slight angle. And dipping his quill, he began the final copy of the Governor's first report to the Emperor—this account of the labor and bloodshed, hunger and deprivation, battle and heartbreak that transpired since Peru....

Above, he put the ritual capitals, "*S. .C. .C. .M.*" (*Sacra, Católica, Cesarea Majestad*—Sacred, Catholic, Caesarean Majesty).

He scrutinized his labor. The script was simple, elegant—as Father Sosa taught him. The periods were squares tilted into diamonds ... and they were not bad. Not good enough for an emperor, of course. Valdivia's harping on perfection had gotten on Juan's nerves.

Now, that hardest line, the first. He had to decide where exactly to begin, centering the text. Taking a fresh quill Juan spun the feather gently on his chosen spot—leaving room for embellishments— creating a dimple visible only to him. Then, inking, he crafted an enormous *C* that swept its black precision to that point—for the first letter was always large, even when not illuminated. As he wrote he would choose other letters to elevate as ornament. Below, of course, the minims were to be kept straight.

Alea iacta est, Juan murmured, somehow seeing the *C* as the arc of a die, and wrote: "*Cinco años Ha que vine de las Provincias del Perú con....*" (It has been five years since I came from the provinces of Peru with....)

Like trees of differing habit, the initial *C*, the **H**, the two **P**'s of the first line towered, ending in flourishes that improvised on their native form. Perhaps it was exhaustion whispering in Juan's ear, but the first line reminded him of Santiago after its destruction by the Indians, the severed heads of the *toqui* at equal heights over the cinders of the city.

He continued: "directives from the Marquis and Governor Don Francisco Pizarro to...."

Juan checked for errors. Consisting mostly of titles and a proper name, this line was easy, having none of the chicken-scratches of the Governor's revisions.

Juan dipped his quill, and wrote: "conquer and populate these lands of New Extremadura, called...."

The letters were parallel to those above, minims straight and square, the serifs not quite aligned. He inked his quill.

"Chile, formerly...."

Clavos de Cristo! Juan did not know whether to end Chile with an *e* or *i*, for it was written and pronounced both ways, and indecision made him spatter the last letter. Cursing, Juan deliberately snapped his quill, inking his hand in the process. And wiping on a sleeve stained with previous error, he knew there was no question of finishing tonight. Was it dawn already? He saw no sign of it through closed shutters.

Valdivia would be furious, and parchment was too precious to waste. Juan thumbed the pages in the press that kept them flat. Thick, rough, too dark, they were horse and llama hide instead of sheepskin—nothing like vellum, which was made from kid. But they served.

After The Apocalypse there was nothing to write on, save for dried forest leaves and the charred margins of surviving documents. In desperation Cartagena attempted records on fresh hides not cured with lime, intending to turn them into parchment retroactively. However, they smelled more of corpse than library, and when they were hung to stretch the mongrels of Santiago made away with several. The resulting commotion—*vecinos* and Indians chasing dogs and their ill-gotten texts— brought Juan running from his bed. One light-footed beast raced to the forest with its prize—for the walls of the city were not yet rebuilt. Three others were surrounded and dispatched. Another almost made it to the Mapocho, but it paused to taste the manuscript, and was skewered by a *yanacona* arrow.

The candle flickered. Juan lit another, sticking it into the same hole in the same loaf of bread. Scanning the one-room hovel in the surge of light he decided that the less you saw of La Serena the better. Valdivia had named it after the city of his nativity, founding it—with thirteen *vecinos!*—over a year ago at the mouth of the river which flowed into the first sheltered bay south of the desert. A fortified port intended as a haven for commerce with Peru, it consisted of seven huts inside a palisade surrounded by the burnt stumps of trees.

Juan appraised the shuttered windows, rough plank door, walls of sooty logs. Rusty armor hung from whittled pegs. The implements of a blacksmith were jumbled in a corner, together with a rusty ax, little else—a hearth of wattle and daub, the table holding the damn document he had worked on for two days, and just ruined. Valdivia had turned his first report to the Emperor into an ordeal of revision. Coughing with the smoke of winter rooms, Juan spat on the rush-strewn floor.

A snort turned his eyes to Pedro—slumped by the hearth, smiling from the far, bright shores of oblivion, his damp cloak emitting plumes of steam—a live volcano too wine-sodden to erupt.

Across the table, Valdivia grumbled in his sleep, head resting on a mailed arm, hand loosely gripping an emptied cup.

He was conquering while passed out, Juan decided, no doubt internally surveying a new boundary to his New Extremadura. But where, in all this, was the woman of his dreams?

This was a question Juan would not have thought to ask a mere two years ago—another measure of the changes since Peru. And he looked over to where Inés stood by the flicker of the hearth—her arms like forgotten sticks. She was lost in thought again, eyes sunk in shadow.

The few Spanish animals and plants that survived the destruction of Santiago had flourished under her tireless supervision in the fertility of the hell that was Nueva Extremadura. By the summer of 1544 there were geese and ducks, chickens and eggs, pigs, as well as lambs and sheep—whose lives were spared for wool. As for horses, there were now more yearlings than *caballeros*. From the last harvest there had been grain, wheat and *choclo* in large quantity, and a wealth of those strange Inca seeds—amaranth and *quinoa*. The orchards, orange and lemon groves, fig trees—as well as the other fruits of Spain—only offered small harvests in the fall of 1545, yet they prospered, a promise for years to come. And—summit to this mountain of plenty—there was now wine of Santiago vintage, when three years ago there had not been enough for Mass.

Inés stopped pacing to stretch, and her spectral hands—severed from her being by black sleeves— floated in darkness. Sensing the intensity of Juan's attention she strode over ... saw the spattered letter. Lifting his chin with a finger to look into his eyes, she smiled.

"Time for bed," she murmured in his ear. "All the others are asleep."

Her nearness had been an ordeal since The Apocalypse. The Virgin simply *could not* hang her halo on the wall, clapping on a steel helmet ... not without consequence to her worship. And neither could Inés wield a sword or behead Indians ... for she had never denied what was accepted—and profoundly admired—by popular opinion.

Juan was breathless. Leaning back slightly, he might touch her. A slight turn would bring into his vision the erotic freckles on her nose. Beautiful in themselves— as being upon her being—they now also had their darker side, inciting him to imagine those he could not see.

She said, "What about a walk?"

He nodded his agreement, knowing Inés meant *exactly* what she said. They would stroll with no purpose other than a walk, stumbling into objects occulted by night. And they would admire the moon, ignored by all but astrologers and navigators.

Juan clapped on his lucky Inca helmet—crimson plumes long gone.

She led silent with preoccupation as he pondered her other eccentricities— cloves, flat black hat, black dress, absurd passion for *fauna* and *flora*—endearing when you knew her. Of these, nocturnal walks were least explicable.

Inés once told Juan about the first time she proposed a stroll at night to Valdivia. He had 'put his foot down *delicately*,' she said, but yelling muscles had bunched around his teeth. And he had replied that he was made too tired by the duties of the day to labor in the pestilential miasmas of the night.

"Miasmas," she had quoted, "When all he did, after, was go gamble and get drunk."

An owl hooted as they approached the shore. Like Spaniards, Indians considered this the worst of omens, and Picunche signaled with the call of that obscene bird of night. What he and Inés were doing was *insane*, in enemy territory. If miasmas did not kill them, Picunche would. Indians were everywhere, shadows yearning to materialize....

The moon was full, low and livid. Trees cast bamboo shadows sharp as knives. Once at the seashore they sat by lapping waves, close enough to touch ...

not touching. Juan listened to the slump and rise of waves, the grumble of worn pebbles, as the moon slid to her rest.

"He's seeing Leticia," Inés stated in a tone so calm, so sweet, one would have thought she commented on astral bodies sinking tired heads into the pillows of the sea. And Juan's heart plumbed his boots, for Inés was right.... Valdivia had always been unfaithful to her—as everybody always knew and never told Inés—however, mostly with Indians, mostly in the field, and far away. Now Leticia had arrived, and that strumpet intended to replace Inés in a female form of civil war.

Juan was torn, despite himself, for Valdivia's wrong might well work to his gain. And he could not comfort Inés without pressing his own suit—at least in his own mind—for to condemn Valdivia was subtly to propose himself. So, he only sighed assent. Relieved that he had a moon to watch, he fixed his eyes upon its set.

In June of 1544—two months ago—the *San Pedro* dropped anchor in Valparaíso. Captained by Juan Bautista de Pastene, the ship brought desperately needed men and supplies. It brought, as well, a bull and two cows—the first cattle of Nueva Extremadura. Five white women also disembarked. One was betrothed to the captain, while the others came unmarried to try their fortunes in these wilds. The mounted messenger preceded their arrival by two days.

There was no road from Valparaíso to Santiago, and since there was only one sidesaddle in Nueva Extremadura, the women were being borne in litters.

Valdivia asked for volunteers to go protect the goods arriving overland. A cheer rang out. *Vecinos* mooed and pawed the ground. Horns and hard-ons were mimicked everywhere. "Beef, beef, beef!" An ad hoc orchestra—including banging on armor and the invention of instruments—accompanied the chant. Juan added to the roar by rasping on his mail with a bone he found down by his foot.

When the escort galloped out the gates—keeping up their chant—he went to stand on the walls beside Inés. Dreary clouds occulted the *cordillera*—a gloom he could almost touch. Soon the overcast began to pour.

Erect, Inés was pale—immobile as the marble she resembled. The San Pedro brought an end to what she once had been, Juan knew, observing that her horizontal hat shed water as a veil. Yet, she would always be The Only One to *him*. A myriad other women could arrive. None could remotely match her. None could take her place. He loved the very rain, as dripping from her hat.

"Beef!" Inés exploded.

"Isn't it great!" Juan blurted, with the alacrity of bad conscience.

"Beef," she accused, peering—as it seemed—into the catacombs of Juan's soul. A tide of blood, unquenchable by rain, rose to his forehead.

"Won't Pedro be pleased," she concluded, scooping up her skirt. And she mooed as she left, giving Juan the proud straight of her back.

That day and the next the *vecinos* of Santiago prepared for *La Llegada*—The Arrival. Haircuts happened. Beards were trimmed. Horses were groomed, cracked leather oiled, armor burnished. Some would-be suitors went so far as to put their houses in order, making their *yanacona* women sweep fouled floors, and strew rush. Others stuffed their mattresses with scented grass. Previously known only at Valdivia's house, tablecloths were improvised from ponchos. And—as the Governor set the style in facial hair—lard was at a sudden premium. A young porker lost his life to the demand.

Inés shut herself in, rain being her excuse.

Ostentatious in his own lack of preparation, Juan watched Pedro fuss over rumpled splendor salvaged from Apocalypse, working at wine stains with spit and salt, stitching loose galloons, fussing over aglets lost to time in who knew what corner of the world, clucking like a mother hen at the ravages of war and wilderness. God only knew, what the current mode might be, he fussed, anything, almost. But, it most certainly was *not* what presently he owned, for change was fashion's essence.

Juan made comforting noises, happy that Pedro was something like himself again. He had been melancholy since the day Juan was appointed secretary to Valdivia, for on that morning the wheel of fortune, which elevated him, had Pedro fall—as if they rode opposing sides. Pedro had been replaced as *maestre de campo* by cold, competent, Francisco de Villagrán.

Valdivia described the demotion as a semi-retirement rewarding valued service. And he gave ·Pedro an *encomienda*. Yet the cutting truth was that Pedro had been put out to pasture because Villagrán was noble and better connected. And Pedro's 'pasture'—his *encomienda*—though huge and not far from Santiago, was composed mostly of high, uninhabited hills. For Pedro this meant there was little labor for his fields, and less gold—*de que comer*, or daily bread, in the language of the *vecinos*.

There was some muttering, as no one was more popular than Pedro with the rank and file. But what many thought—and no one mentioned to his face—was that he was old, impetuous, sometimes foolhardy, and above all, no diplomat. He was an ideal *maestre de campo* for the journey down—that peripatetic war. But now that Santiago was a fact Valdivia needed men to lead an army metamorphosing into a body politic.

Pedro had ignored the sympathy of his comrades—as smacking too much of mutiny—accepting his orders without complaint. Nonetheless, he had been withdrawn, profoundly miserable.

Now, grunting, he was trying on his doublet, and failing at the lacing. His corpulence after the hard years following Apocalypse had become difficult to believe. The largest horses would have groaned, if they knew how, when mounted.

The gates of Santiago seemed to shrink when he rode through. He was Excess let loose upon The Groaning Board.

Pedro rumbled, "Only the hat and boots fit ... barely. And of course, the cloak." After the failure of his doublet, he was not eager to test the elasticity of his last good pair of hose, and he cursed Nueva Extremadura, muttering that everything used to fit when he had all the wine he wanted. Abstinence had upset his humours, creating dropsy due to Adam's ale.

At his meat, next morning, Pedro harrumphed into medicinal cups of red—good for the blood!—mocking the *vecinos* fussing over facial hair. If you wanted to shave that was fine, he said—not wanting to insult his *hijo*, clean-shaven even as a man. Still, hair should never be forced into unnatural shapes, like those bushes in the gardens of Sevilla. He searched for the word....

Juan said, 'topiary.'

Pedro created time to think by freeing gristle with a fingernail, wiping his finding on the bench he sat. "A man is not a garden," he opined. And, as *that* was *that*, Juan emerged into a morning threatening rain.

The messenger arrived as Marmolejo was celebrating Mass. Removing his vestment, the priest announced that—as the host had not yet been consecrated—it was God's will that this sacrament be postponed. Sketching a blessing in the air he scampered out the door after his flock, lifting the skirts of his cassock.

"The second coming," thought Juan, as he waited with Inés on the abandoned city walls. Pedro stood beside them.

Through the doors of Santiago rode triumphant Valdivia, portly, flushed by wine and a hard ride, heading a gesticulating cluster of *caballeros*. After, came laden mules flanked by Indians bent under their burdens—including an anvil in a leather sling, and potted trees not mentioned by the messengers.

Inés crossed herself, saying, "Peaches, as I live and breathe!"

Juan had always been amazed that she could recognize trees without the fruit that gave them name. Yet peach trees they proved to be when she ran up, declaring them desperate for attention.

"Not now Inés!" Juan murmured. As Governess in fact—if not by marriage or decree—her duty was to greet the arrived *vecinos*, who would not appreciate having potted plants welcomed before them.

Inés went to curtsy at the new *vecinos*, then at the women balanced high on litters—invisible beneath their leafy canopies—surrounded by the glittering helmets, soggy plumes and larded hair, of the honor guard.

The *yanaconas* set down a litter before Inés.

A Spanish woman in rich mourning emerged. She was—she stated—Doña Leticia de los Campos Anchos. And in ornate, pious paragraphs, she went on to say that she had looked forward to this moment through the sufferings of her journey as to the cross that marked its end.

Leticia might have spoken better, but the actual sight of Inés de Suárez had shaken her, and her thoughts were racing madly. A curtain had lifted from her ignorance, and the doors of Heaven gaped. Could *this* actually be Valdivia's famous concubine—this stick in ink, this shrouded broom, this far, far less than she?

Where to begin the tally of her imperfections? No style, to begin with. For jewelry only a simple cross—silver no less, common as pewter in the Indies! Then, no makeup or corset! As for the peaks of feminine attraction, they were no doubt ample ... but confined by a black dress of the severest cut. And she had the hips of a nunnery chair—though her waist was damnably small. To boot, her coiffe was perverse—braided high, far more ugly than tonsures. Gauche summit to the whole, the hat was an unfeathered plate. She was, in fact, more *mannish* than many men of fashion....

Leticia almost gasped out loud, knowing that Inés was the only *cristiana* ever to brave the Atacama like a man. There were a few women who unnaturally loved women, of course, yet none flaunted this deeply mortal sin. Was her suspicion *possible*? And even if she was mistaken—which Leticia profoundly did *not* wish to be—how could the Governor of vast territories enter into a relationship with a bone both fleshless and ambiguous?

At that point in her reflections Leticia seriously considered sacrificing her recent respectability on the altar of fame and fortune.

Leticia de los Campos Anchos—History must note—was not her married name, much less some indication of nobility. As a strategy obliterating her origins, it was invented on the putrid cockleshell that brought her to the Indies. Desiring to mask her past in noble anonymity, she reasoned—as there were wide fields everywhere—that her new name would make of her a noble widow without a town to trace her to. And that suited her just fine, for it was to escape her past that she abandoned the comforts of Christendom for travail amid heathens. Not that her past was criminal—oh, no!—but merely "checkered of necessity," as she claimed in the confessional. In the Indies she would reconstruct her distant Spanish history.

In short, Leticia was a prostitute. However—despite her fornications and the fabrications veiling them—in her opinion she was not committing sin. As God well knew, both her profession and her falsehoods originated in her love for her daughter, Concha, who would one day need a husband. And the logic springing from that fact was remorseless. For Concha to marry, she needed to be of good family. And, for *that*, Leticia needed the husband and wealth she never had. And since the truths of the past did not suit the prospects of her daughter, they needed to be refashioned—obviously not in Los Alamos, the small town where she plied her venereal trade, for everyone there knew her, most of the males carnally. As she was a *puta* in a land where only charismatic preachers had a more public occupation, there was nothing to do but leave for worlds unknown—once she had earned the necessary sum—in order to legitimize Concha with white lies. However, inventing a dead husband proved far easier than affording the journey. Her savings from the many years she spread her legs did not suffice for her passage, so that—in brutal fact—she was forced to bed the reeking captain as supplement to the shortfall. And once arrived in Panama she toiled on her back for months in pestilential heat, to earn what she needed to go south.

But as a commodity worth even more than horses, Leticia hugely prospered in Peru. Selling herself for only two years she became obscenely rich, acquiring a drafty palace, jewels, gold, brocades. She was good as noble in everything but nobility, and that was her predicament. To leave her checkered past she had been checkering her present, but—praise God!—each checkered step was an improvement. On the caravel she was a whore with extraordinary tits. In Panama, she transmuted into an abundant widow who sinned excusably, needing to transport both herself and a daughter of tender years. In Peru, she had become the next thing to respectable—considering the character of most white women there. And to her credit, it should be said that through all this Leticia contrived to keep her daughter pure as the day that she was born. For the virginity of her daughter she moaned and bucked in sweaty beds, wanting for Concha better than she ever had herself. The question still remained—Would a wealthy *caballero* wed her daughter?

That question became moot at a banquet that included potentates of Peru, when a man she did not recognize whispered in her ear that he had fucked her blind in Panama ... and how about again, tonight?

Leticia instantly rose to leave the room, and packed to leave, with nowhere left to go but God-abandoned Nueva Extremadura, there to finish tinkering with her history.

How could she have predicted that Inés de Suárez—whose fame reached Spain—would prove emaciated, unattractive, out of fashion? And with an awe that shook her cupidity to the core, Leticia realized that this made of her—a lifelong whore—the rival for a Governor's hand.

She would be cautious—opulent but not forward, of careful cleavage, pious though not somber, not overly merry as a widow. Her slumbering passion would be, not too transparently, unfulfilled, until her pillar of respectability toppled to Valdivia's fatal charm. On the spot, she revised the imaginary date of her husband's death in order to remove her mourning sooner. And, for a prize so rich, marriage would not be strictly *necessary*. Suárez had led the way in *this*, after all.

Pedro commented to Juan about the widow, in undertones, "Color would improve the ensemble. Nonetheless, the cap—crushed velvet!—is superb, the silk of her dress supreme. And—as God is in His Heaven!—I believe the feathers of her cap are pheasant, come from Spain." He hoarsely whispered, "And the corset...!"

He was right to lose his power of speech, thought Juan, for like the Isthmus of Panama, the waist of the widow turned her abundance into nearly separated continents.

"The ruff is Holland—as I breathe and love God!" Pedro said, sighing to his cods as the drizzle became a downpour, struck dumb by what rose and fell beneath the now translucent thing.

Leticia did not mind the damage to her priceless finery—this act of God. If He *chose* to reveal the gifts He created upon her, so be it. And, seeing that Valdivia was stealing glances, she hoped—Hope being a virtue—that he appreciated the contrast between what the Almighty was revealing and what he presently enjoyed with Suárez. Then, with coy cries of modesty, she failed to conceal her abundance with her hands.

At that very moment, Fortuna decided to have the enormous bull that landed with the women charge the gates of Santiago. Those leading him by the ring in his nose scattered, leaving the rancorous bulk free to run. Trampling an Indian, he disappeared in the direction of the gardens.

Inés ran after—toward the fruits of Spain—to save them from the bull. Juan ran after Inés, to save her from the bull. Pedro followed both, to save them.

And as they ran, Valdivia escorted Leticia to the nearest cabin. There, noisome *infantes* were removing wool and armor, building a fire, when the Governor evicted them in various stages of undress. Cacafuego was among them, and—once the door was slammed behind him—he pantomimed in the rain....

Leticia emerging from her litter. Leticia wet. Leticia going 'oooh' and 'aaah,' her ruff collapsing. Leticia giggling, unable to hide the rain-revealed sight—sculpted from the air by Cacafuego's hands.

Then laughter moved him to improvisation leaving fact behind. He swept invisible skirts out of puddles ... tiptoed, so as not to be soiled by mud. He tripped and fell, went 'oooh,' fainted and awakened by fanning himself with a hand. Then—for the eviction had made Cacafuego very angry—he became paunchy, imperial Valdivia, bowing and scraping before a tree become Leticia, twirling his mustaches, ordering that the rain increase or there would be serious consequences. He concluded with a tremolo on his bumhorn.

Having rescued the gardens and secured the bull, Juan, Pedro and Inés returned to find that La Llegada had moved to the unfinished church—largest structure in Santiago—where almost everyone not Indian was now crowded, prematurely sampling last year's vintage by Valdivia's magnanimous decree. The men of power—including the Governor—surrounded the white women, and they, in turn, were encircled by milling *vecinos*.

Inés stopped in her tracks when she saw this. "The wine's too young to drink," she said, and left.

What could Juan do but pretend not to be interested? Given her comment, he was not about to sample the green wine. He listened instead to the animated crowd.

With the ship, the armor, the new blacksmith, arquebuses and gunpowder, tools and provisions, they would be able both to subdue Nueva Extremadura and hold Santiago against any number of hostile Indians—once Monroy arrived with the expected reinforcements, that is. However, the most intense subject of speculation was the white women, and old *vecinos* plied the new arrivals with questions....

Doña Leticia de los Campos Anchos—of the unbelievable second story—was fond of flirting and talking about casting off her widow's weeds. She was also clearly wealthy, for in addition to her enormous trunks she brought with her a small, very heavy, iron-bound coffer kept near her person at all times, the key to which hung from a golden chain between her breasts.

Her daughter, Concha, was a filly of enormous promise—though not yet quite filled out. Shy, perhaps fifteen, she was guarded by her mother as the hole of Hell by Cerberus. Far as anyone knew, Concha never parted her lips to utter word to the opposite sex.

Doña Clara—the intended of Pastene—was pious as any nun, rosary at her waist, black wooden beads worn pale by use. She had not spoken to men other than her future husband until now, engaged as she was in conversation with Marmolejo. He looked glum, having been buttonholed the moment she saw his white hair floating over cuirass, cross and cassock.

The remaining women were cut from lewder cloth, and obviously available through a variety of arrangements. Unimaginably dowdy, they wore the improvisations—part Spanish, part Indian—of all but the richest women in wild Peru. And being unattached, they were the subjects of most interest.

Hermengilda Pacheco—oldest and broadest—wore crimson wool, an Inca hat. A pendant with an emerald big as your thumb hung in her cleavage. She smiled without parting her lips, for her teeth were quite decayed—which made her look deceitful. The lines of charcoal that replaced her plucked brows were running from the rain, and she was complaining that there was no honey for the wine, so that all agreed that she would provide the most value for your money.

The younger one—Juana Montes—wore a striped Peruvian poncho, red cap. She lisped and had a faint, blond mustache. Boldly returning stares, licking wine-wet lips, she stretched from time to time, her poncho lifted by the mounds beneath them. In undertones the *vecinos* were calling her Juana de los Montes Blancos—

Juana of the White Mountains. She caused the coarsest quiet jokes, and when she finally removed her poncho—rightly exclaiming that the thing was sopping—there were audible sighs in the silenced room.

Juan was at the edge of the crowd—on tiptoe that he might see—thinking that, save for Doña Clara, in Spain these women would be bedding swineherds for a pork chop. A rule of thumb took shape—The farther from Spain, the more a woman was a whore. As corollary—The farther from Spain, the richer was the whore. And, as Santiago was farther from Spain than maybe even Cipangu, he should be looking at the richest whores in the world.

The immense exception to his rules of thumb murmured behind him, "Exercising your toes, *caballero*?" Slamming his boot heels down, Juan turned....

Pearls! No less pale than that creamy gem, Inés was magnificent, loosened hair sending back the light transformed. Her gown was cut low, not daringly, yet wonderfully so, the string of pearls suspended over vertiginous space—a precious Inca bridge over the black velvet of her breathing. Her dress—he focused on her dress—clearly intended for this surprise. Brought from Spain? Saved from Apocalypse? Had she foreseen this day? He was outraged she felt the need to compete with prostitutes.

"You're dry," he stuttered. "Almost dry," he corrected.

Brushing a raindrop off a pearl—she commanded, "Take me to the udders."

The crowd parted. And when she took his arm, Juan shuddered.

Remembering that day—sitting by the sea in La Serena—Juan thought that extraordinary as Inés was, she had lost her battle for Valdivia.

"Unhappiness is knowing too much," she said—calm and harsh—face chalky in the setting moon's light.

Adapting celestial mechanics to foundering relationships, she gestured with spectral hands at the coming dawn, saying, "I set, he rises. He sets, I rise."

Juan knew exactly what she meant. Valdivia gambled during the inactivities of peace. Done with his duties, he diced or played cards, drinking himself senseless. He spent most nights out, which was not unusual for a *vecino*, but *he* was the one tupping Leticia.

To Juan's knowledge, Inés never once complained about Valdivia's infidelities. Yet he overheard her exclaiming to Valdivia the night of La Llegada—so impassioned as to forget his presence—that as he loved *her*, he would have nothing to do with 'those women.' The Governor had been infuriatingly reasonable. With so few *vecinos* in his care, how ignore a single one? And since that day their relationship had cooled by slow degrees.

Inés said, "Loving the sun, the moon is filled by sorrow, fullest when farthest from him, drowned when he rises. There is immensity between them when she sets, blind without him. And at last, approaching him she disappears—like a thin slice of orange rind you toss to pigs."

She turned to face Juan.

Seeing her tears, he stood to hurl a fist-sized stone into the sea, exclaiming, "He's not worth it."

He did not say that no one was worth *her,* that no one could be. Nor did he say that she was distant and perfect as the full moon, not to Valdivia but to him, Juan de Cardeña. She had her celestial mechanics wrong.

Devoting a short silence to his outburst, she replied, "He's worth more than everything I am—that's my problem. If a man is measured by his dreams, no one is larger. Valdivia *is* the Indies." Her outstretched arms embraced the mountains, the Ocean Sea.

Am I then *nothing,* Juan thought, having lost my dreams? He complained, "Valdivia is just a man."

"Most men are just men," she said. "Valdivia is not one of them."

She attacked his silence. "He's depressed. That's why he's lost in wine. He needs to go south to complete his triumph. For that he needs men, supplies. He's killing time."

He's killing *you,* Juan thought. And infuriated into cruelty, he snarled, "So what are *you* then, to him? His servant?"

Stung by this asp—these words of years ago—Inés scrubbed a sleeve across her tears, saying, "No need to apologize, Juan. Believe it or not, I *will* survive Valdivia."

They returned to La Serena in sad companionship—not holding hands as they had been known to do, before Apocalypse and Juan's accursed maturity.

Valdivia was pacing by the letter to the Emperor, ruined by an arc of ink. When they appeared, he roared that he had ordered it finished *immediately.*

He had pork ribs in one hand, a cup of the hair of the dog in the other. He was unshaven, sagging mustaches trembling at the tips, for—when angry—Valdivia could shake all over. And his bloodshot glare preserved its legendary power, although—at sixty, or so—he had both feet firmly planted on old age.

"I was about to send a rescue party," he bellowed, having wakened to a crisis while still half drunk and half hung over—that stage of intoxication men were meant to sleep through.

Inés sighed, wooden as a wayside cross. "My fault. Juan was too tired to write, and I took him for a walk."

Valdivia stared with disbelief, face ripening to pomegranate. His cup missing his mouth on its way up, he spilled his wine. He yelled, "Too tired to write, and you went for a *walk*! To rest my secretary! At night!"

He was jealous—Juan decided with euphoria and trepidation—and too proud to accuse her of adultery ... he, a hundred times more adulterous.

"This ... is ... *it!*" the Governor hoarsely exclaimed—pouring replacement wine—'it' having the volume of a war cry. The ribs in his hand then rose and fell— ax of governance descending on the hydra heads of folly and insurrection sprung up during sleep ... which God knew he needed, and his duties made so rare.

Inés knew better than to respond when Valdivia shouted fragments. Surveying his veined nose, flushed face, she left.

The Governor swayed, studying the vacated door, before, with pork as punctuation, he ordered, "No walks!" The ribs thumped Juan's ribs.

"No rest!" Thump.

"Not until you finish!" Thump.

Juan inked a pen.

Juan jerked awake, and reading the letter set before him, realized that he had fallen asleep while recording Apocalypse....

Then I received news that all the natives of this land had risen, creating two armies to make war on us; and I with ninety men went to attack the greater one, leaving my lieutenant to guard the city with fifty, thirty of them horsemen. And while I was fighting with the first, the others attacked the city and fought the whole day with the Christian defenders, killing 23 of their horses, and four Christians, and burning all of the city with its food and clothing and land, leaving us with nothing but the rags we wore to war, the weapons we had with us, two sows and a piglet, a chicken and rooster, as well as a small quantity of grain; in short....

Looking up, Juan saw that Valdivia stood beside him, rage over. The four pages were fine, he said, adding that Juan needed a shave. And he should eat something. Hopefully the letter would be finished before tomorrow, so the **San Pedro** could leave with the offshore breeze.

Juan decided to ignore the wineskin Valdivia set on the table before him. He wanted to brush his teeth with the chewed end of a stick—as Inés had taught him— for his mouth was truly foul. Instead he took a long, cold drink of water from the earthenware Inca jug Pedro brought from Peru—an obese, squatting, naked woman with hanging breasts, the spout originating between her knees. There were riskier Inca jugs, but Pedro had not dared, knowing Inés would see them.

Returning to Apocalypse, Juan became interested in the fact that Valdivia had omitted both good and bad. He was accurate about the crops, yet did not mention that many of Inés' plants survived. And what about the geese and guinea pigs, the *chinchillas*, blankets and clothes, the other sundries rescued? Also there were other survivors—like the Inca jug he just drank from—charred but usable. Many tools only had their handles burned away. The anvil was intact—no blacker than before—as was most of the armor not worn to battle—though the straps and laces were cinder. Coin, too, survived. Parchment had not, however. And, although Valdivia mentioned dead horses, he said nothing about the slaughterhouse at the gallows.

It came to Juan that he was writing on the hide of a horse that died during the description of its own passing. The thought was eerie, perhaps profound. Juan took up the wineskin and had himself a red jet, thinking that to document catastrophe on the hide that it produced was a parable for History—a tale written on the skin of death. Flesh scraped away, what remained was the surface of what happened. You had to remove the bones and scrape the flesh from History, to preserve it. Feeling brilliant, Juan had another squirt.

If History was recorded on the skin of events, did it mean that in some way it *consumed* the flesh? Amadís—the horse—was not mentioned in any letter to the Emperor, nor any of the *yanaconas*—these anonymous dead digested by the earth. And with a reflexive shiver, Juan recalled the day when Lobo explained that 'sarcophagus'—in Greek—meant 'flesh eater.' What he had thought then was that Pedro was in his own way a great sarcophagus, and the idea that coffins were the stomachs of the earth had not left him since.

Juan set down his quill, flexing a weary hand. There were no letters on *his* skin, just a variety of scars—this chronicle making sense to no one else. He was an undried hide, a History still full of flesh that would one day be eaten by the stomach of the earth—unlike this horsehide which would cross the ocean to survive in some imperial library, the horse's death recorded but his name forgotten. On the other hand, his own name would live on that same parchment in that same library, for soon he was to write it....

until this last year, of three, that crops did well— for now we finally are healthy and have much food—we survived the first two before in extreme need, so great as hardly to be described, and many Christians were forced to go dig scallions to sustain themselves, and when these were finished they went for more, and all servants working for us, with all their children, survived on the same, and of meat there was none....

The famine subsequent to Apocalypse was interrupted by Marmolejo and De los Ríos, who walked in armored, having been on patrol.

And as he wrote, Juan half-listened to them debate the fate of an Indian they had captured. De los Ríos recommended torture, Marmolejo some gentler persuasion. The two had locked horns over The Indian Problem many times before, and today—as always—the priest counseled patience, mercy, and force only in self-defense, while De los Ríos argued that you could not convert Indians if they killed those doing the converting. He advocated pre-emptive firmness instead—or in his words,'striking before the iron got hot.'

Like most *vecinos* De los Ríos considered Indians to be something like the offspring of a Jew and goat—beast as to body, Semitic in intention—a composite being that created problems not in conquest but in treating them as human. As beasts they were given man by the Bible to be enjoyed—part and parcel of the bounty God created for the usufruct of the faithful. Being man-like also, and balking at salvation, they became subject to the methods of the Holy Inquisition, as guilty of that most mortal sin—the refusal of God once informed of His Being. Therefore, De los Ríos' solution to The Indian Problem was exactly the solution to the Jewish one. You put the question to them to reveal the sin. Then you inflicted judicious punishment. Any fool who ever attended an *auto da fé* knew this. De los Ríos could not understand why a man of the cloth refused to accept an argument built on religion no less than The Church was built on Peter, who was Petrus, which meant rock, and which stood for Infallibility.

At this heated juncture Inés strode into the room and vehemently sided with Marmolejo. But as the wheels of this argument were clearly mired in the ruts of the past, she diplomatically turned the conversation to her rabbits—that gentle meat she bred in the years of scarcity. You could feed them almost anything that grew on roots, she said, which turned wilderness to edible flesh. What better trade?

Juan thought that paradoxically, her rabbits were another example of the lack of flesh in Valdivia's letter. When he said there was no meat for the first two years he meant Christian fare—pork, veal, beef, lamb and mutton, in the order of preference usual to civilization. Yet during their long deprivation the *vecinos* consumed rabbits and guinea pigs as well as other nameless Indians things. Juan once even had fire-roasted snake slipped steaming from its skin, looking like a long white finger emerging from a blackened glove.

Pedro summarized the meatless years one evening when he was presented with boiled fish. Exploding at the sight of the disgusting, tiny things—served not gutted and beheaded, but simmered whole with roots, so that they looked back from the woody tangle of the bowl—he attained an eloquence born of hunger, and half-remembered cadences of sermons with perdition as their theme. Gesturing at the slimy evidence, he exclaimed, "This is an abomination which savages eat in their savagery, the ignorant in their ignorance, the English no doubt as English, the martyrs in loving suffering, and we, the starving Spanish, only of black necessity. This is not *real meat!*"

The audience cheered—save for Inés, who had worked miracles to coax these fishlets from *yanaconas*.

Pedro then thumped his stomach—turning the emptiness of the offended organ into a drum resonating with rejection. "*Real* meat is big and bloody," he boomed. "*Real* meat has fat outside and a bone in the middle so you can grab it. You don't have to eat it with a stupid spoon."

And Juan remembered that Valdivia had said amen in an undertone, murmuring that there was at least a lot of water in the soup, and—leaving—whispered to his companions that it was time to pee the main course.

As if on cue, the Governor of Juan's troubled memories entered his troubled present to check the progress of the letter, scanning with an eagle eye for changes. His idea of dictation was to indicate the genial—though general—idea, while criticizing Juan's expanded incarnations, at last approving the one he liked, by which act it became the text intended all along.

"Well done," he opined. "Just what I thought, but put to words. Nice minims. Think you can finish in time?"

"*Sí, señor.*"

Preparing a quill, Juan turned his attention to Inés.

Done with rabbits, she was discussing reading with Marmolejo. Reluctant to teach her at the first—for women *did not do* such things!—the warrior priest had reluctantly agreed. If she could ride and kill like a man, maybe she could read like one. He would only instruct her in Spanish, however, not in the little he knew of God's Latin. And the **Legenda Aurea**—as that Life of the Saints was popularly known—was the only Spanish book he owned, other than his breviary. Today Inés had questions about Ambrose, third saint in the text.

Juan returned his pen to parchment at the moment when Monroy and his men—touched by Croesus—left.

Inés interrupted Juan, asking permission to use the other side of the table to practice her reading. She would be quiet she said, bringing a delicate finger to the wonder of her lips. And quiet she proved to be—although Valdivia was not, loudly stuck in conversation with De los Ríos, who was not known for the pleasures of his discourse, harboring few ideas under his helmet, all vehement and changeless.

Juan returned to the chronicle.

Monroy reached Peru in 1542, three quarters starved, and the last quarter baked black—in his own words—with two foundering horses and Pedro Miranda, both so near death that they requested last rites. Indians had stolen the gold Valdivia sent, but he had managed to borrow from a Portuguese priest and persuade seventy *caballeros* to follow him to Nueva Extremadura. Also, at Arequipa he inveigled Lucas Martínez Vegaso—an old friend of Valdivia's—into sending a ship south with gold and supplies.

This ship arrived the month of September of the year five hundred and forty three, and captain Alonso de Monroy with all his people the following December....

Here the page ended. And, preparing parchment, Juan recalled the rejoicing of Santiago. The *vecinos* had been isolated for the greater part of two years, so that his arrival was a bolt of lightning from a cloudless sky, a feast after fasting—although not literally, since the *vecinos* were eating almost well already. The celebration of Monroy's return included roast suckling pig—toothsome, if not bountiful. But sadly pork was almost all that remained of civilization in Santiago, as being able to reproduce itself. The clothes of the *vecinos*—long since turned to rags—had been replaced with Indian cloth, skins and furs, so that *cristianos* could be told from savages only by their armor and weapons. And—as the blacksmith had died in convulsions after eating mushrooms recommended by a guileful Indian—there was hardly a man whose steel did not need repair. Some *infantes* actually had taken up native spears tipped with flint. In short, the colony was mired in savagery. Before long they might forget their mother tongue—along with mother clothing, mother food, mother weapons—for everyone now spoke a patois that wed Spanish to Quechua and Picunche in unholy trigamy.

The **Santiaguillo**—for so the ship was called, although it in no way resembled the vessel that brought Juan to the Indies—carried cloth, iron, armor, and a smith. But above all it brought hope, not just of outliving suffering, but of surviving civilized in the inferno that was Nueva Extremadura.

Excited clapping took Juan's attention from his page. Having finished Ambrose, Inés had turned to Lucy's page. Not bad for someone just beginning reading, eh! She ululated like an Indian, forgetting her vow of silence. And grinning with delight she began to decipher her next saint. "Lucy means light. Light has beauty in its appearance, for by its nature all grace is in it, as Ambrose writes. It has also an unblemished radiance, for it pours its beam on unclean places and yet remains clean."

Juan paused his work, wondering what Ines' own name might mean, for in the **Legenda Aurea** your name declared your essence. If so, it seemed to him that she *was* Lucy in her paleness, and in the radiance she cast on unclean places. She veritably *glowed* with a light not corporeal…. Yet she seemed so vulnerable as she read—he thought—childlike, reminding him of how lost he was when he began his study of Latin with Father Sosa. And thinking that, Juan smiled with fond condescension, as at a tot's first step.

For some reason, Inés always put a finger under the word to be decoded, in this way preparing the way for utterance, since syllables *had* to be pronounced. Concerning reading, Inés claimed—and exclaimed!—that the only real reading was out loud. Otherwise one could cheat with silence, encountering words one did not know. Perhaps Mass had given her the fixed idea, because when reading the register of her voice dropped to contralto plainchant. The effect was unutterably charming, holy in its beauty.

Saint Lucy was born in Sy … Syracuse, Inés read, adding that she did not recognize the place.

Marmolejo did not know it either, saying it was most probably heathen … maybe in Africa.

Valdivia said Syracuse was in Sicily.

Inés decided that the time had come for food. They ate cold rabbit and duck, wheaten bread from Santiago—three days old, not yet moldy—and drank from a skin of wine perturbed by lees.

Juan returned to writing, pleased that he had covered more than a year since lunch. It was now June of 1544, that date he would never forget.…

At this juncture arrived captain Juan Bautista de Pastene, servant of the marquis, Pizarro, my lord and your obedient servant, with his ship the San Pedro, sent by the governor Vaca de Castro to find out about me, loaded with necessary things... and as the captain and I knew each other, and as he was a good man of the sea, so honorable and faithful... I made him my lieutenant of the seas....

No mention of the arrival of Leticia and the whores of the **San Pedro**— or of Doña Clara—not even the bull and cows. Instead Valdivia talked about lieutenants—which was to say power and its delegation. Not that Juan disliked Pastene or regretted his promotion. On the contrary, he was attracted to the genial Lieutenant General of the Seas.

Rotund—profoundly Genoese—he had a thick Italian accent and a wild fringe of fair hair that made him seem a Franciscan out of habit. He was nut brown and clean-shaven, and had blue eyes set in a wilderness of wrinkles caused as much by laughter as by squinting under ocean suns. Overnight, the captain became the most popular *vecino* of the colony. In rough analogy, as the Virgin Mary was mediatrix to the Gods—counting the Father and Son as two—the captain was mediator to the *goods*. Pastene had brought cattle and white women from Peru— and these were repeatable miracles!

Fond as he was of Pastene—and assured of his competence—Juan had to smile at the Emperor's new navy, consisting of one recently named Lieutenant General of the Seas, another captain, perhaps a dozen sailors and, of course, two cockleshells. He remembered enough of shipboard instruction from Gil to know that these wet, bobbing things were nothing like *naos* or caravels, but more like outsized rowboats covered by a single deck, with two stubby masts that gave sailors excuses to elevate their ropes—for sailors had the love of rope deep in them.

On the voyage south the **San Pedro** must have been a sight to strike fear in the passenger and pity in the spectator, so laden that the deck was awash at anything like a rising sea. The cows and bull were tied to one mast, potted plants to the other. The five Spanish women shared the cramped deck with other cargo and caged beasts, Pastene, seven sailors, and the remaining passengers. All were as exposed to the weather as to each other for the whole of the voyage, since the only protection from sun and rain was afforded by spare sails turned to awnings by the sailors. Juan could not imagine how the women managed modesty....

Seeing that captain Juan Bautista was willing and able, in the beginning of the month of September I empowered him—giving him a flag bearing the arms of Your Majesty, and below it mine—to go explore two hundred leagues of the coast and take possession of them for Your Majesty ... and so it was and so he took them.

"*así fué y la tomó,*" Juan murmured to himself, thinking that these words had a Ceasarean ring, a "*veni, vici*" if there ever was one. Yet the journey south had taken twenty-four days—as he well knew, having been a member of the expedition—and here they were condensed to seven syllables. Laughable, if you thought about it.

But of course the Emperor could not have his eye upon the many sparrows of the Indies. Carlos V did not need the details that here crowded life as lice your cot. Ignorance in a way *was* power, Juan decided. The more powerful you were, the less you knew about the more you ruled. Conversely, the more minutiae you were aware of, the less important you were, like the farmer who could name the pebbles of his holding, or the secretary who recorded all the trivia of governance—when not writing to the Emperor. Juan was old hose tossed to the tide, swollen with sand, ponderous and sad ... that's what he was.

He took a squirt from the *bota*, lifted a quill, and began the page that brought his name before the eyes of Clio....

As your majesty will see by the witness that to this gives Juan de Cardeña, my secretary

I came, I saw, I wrote, Juan thought. And I'm still writing, though not exactly what I experienced. And if I'm lucky, I'll finish the damned thing on time.

Hours later he was still transcribing the hell of Nueva Extremadura, turned to paradise by Valdivia....

This land is such that there is no better in the world, to live in and prosper—I say this because it is flat, wholesome, very pleasing; It has only four months of winter.... The summer is temperate and so filled with delightful breezes that all the day one can be out in the sun. There are abundant meadows and fields, for all kinds of cattle and crops; much excellent wood for houses; an infinity of firewood to warm them, and the mines, rich with gold, of which this land is full; so it seems that God created this land just so man could have everything he needed right at hand.

Juan was marveling at Valdivia's hyperbole when Inés finished her first paragraph on Saint Lucy. She insisted on reading texts in sequence—all the way to the end—refusing to begin in the middle. Once, feeling lettered, Juan had explained '*in medias res*' to her, and asked her why she did not explore the *Legenda Aurea*—an orderless compendium if there ever was one—out of order. In her place he would have begun with San Juan, his namesake. She grinned and replied that one day she might find herself.

Perhaps he had annoyed her—smirking in some scholarly way—for she had added that a book was like life, having a beginning and an end. Who wanted to begin life in the middle! *And*, Juan might ask himself why she had chosen Marmolejo as her first instructor in reading instead of some know-it-all of her acquaintance. Chin tilted, looking Juan full in his desire to avoid her eye, she said she was certain that when she reached Santa Inés—should she be in the *Legenda Aurea*—she would be the saint who read her books beginning at the beginning and ending at the end.

Now—months later, and nowhere near the middle—Inés touched Juan lightly on the cheek, smiled, and left, pursued by the clank of Marmolejo.

Juan was contemplating adze patterns on the door, when a timid scratch interrupted his stupor. And at the mouse like sound, he sighed. The Apocalypse had made a saint of Lobo, and no *cristiano* in Santiago was now comfortable in his presence. Excessively holy before, he had been respected but unliked as something like a talking book—the rumor being that, cut, he bled ink. In the minds of *conquistadores* there were only two kinds of saint, Santiago being alone in the only truly good category. Then, there were all the others in the books moldering in monkish libraries where no one read them, such saints as never came down to help you when the battle went wrong. This second kind of saint belonged in Heaven, where they helped you from a welcomed distance—for example, by giving you money, a safe journey, or male issue. Such saints had died long ago and been preserved on earth—if at all—in reliquaries. Saints—*Redios!*—were not supposed to be alive, peering over the shoulders of sinners committing the lapses Christ was born to redeem! Not that Lobo spied on transgression, shunning the commons as he did, engaged in prayer and introspection. Yet whenever he emerged he was avoided as one who had not an evil but a 'holy' eye. Living with a saint is hard, mild though he might be.

The first sermon Lobo preached after emerging from the idiot stupor induced in him by Apocalypse, he cried from the pulpit that he had been the worst of sinners in taking up the sword—when in fact he had been a hero—and that you should not only love your enemy, but also not kill him—which of course you should. After, he had turned to Scripture and the Fathers of the Church so brilliantly, with such erudition and copious recall, that his subversive proposition seemed proved before the horror of his audience. Lobo made the unthinkable irrefutable. No one was happy with that sermon.

Marmolejo had turned scarlet as the cross over his breastplate—that symbol sanctified by the blood of the knights of Calatrava—who girded their swords to rescue Christendom from cruel scimitars.

Valdivia kept gubernatorial silence during the extraordinary performance, all the while destroying the cantilevered symmetry of his mustaches. What to do with this inflammatory saint? He spoke to Marmolejo.

The bluff soldier of God did not know how to make his case, being unequal to Lobo's erudition. Surely, war against the enemies of Christ was holy in the eyes of God, but he could not risk *that* argument, should he be routed. Fortunately—in this battle of right against scripture run amok—he had authority on his side. And he knew an errant sheep when he saw one.... He took Lobo aside that night, saying that, as he had been ill since the battle of Santiago, it would be for the best if he did not preach until he regained his ... hem ... peace of mind. He would be happy to shoulder that duty, also his confessions, other sacraments, and etcetera. Lobo could still say Mass for himself alone, of course.

Now, Lobo—unwanted conscience of Santiago—was at Juan's door, thin hair wild about his tonsure. He was pale. His eyes were fearful. He was a doubtful rabbit.

"Busy?"

"Uh hunh. Take a seat." Juan gestured at the opposing bench, ashamed of his mean-spirited reception.

"Thanks for the company. I'll just say my rosary."

Slumping to a bench—placing a package beside him—Lobo told his beads.

Juan scrutinized his serifs—these flourishes upon the structure Valdivia was erecting for History—and had forgotten Lobo when pages later he came to the priest in the text, at that point where Valdivia praises himself for how well he provides for the spiritual well-being of Indians.

In accordance with the orders of your Majesty, to follow your royal conscience, as well as mine; accordingly there are four priests, three of whom came with me, called Rodrigo González and Juan Lobo, well versed in the conversion of Indians....

The letter was near completion. Done with History, Valdivia was extolling the pieties that justified his actions in something like a political amen.

Massaging his writing hand Juan saw that Lobo's cheeks were hectic—the only man Juan knew who said his rosary feverishly. Scrutinizing the abstracted face—cheekbones like elbows shoved against thin sleeves—Juan wondered how worn beads could create such temperatures.

As the *de facto* doctor of the expedition Inés once said to Juan that Lobo might be consumptive. He was thin enough, and febrile. A persistent cough made the diagnosis plausible. But Juan disagreed. Many *cristianos* were thin and coughed in Nueva Extremadura. Only one of them, however, was a Humanist who had lost his faith in humanity, a scholar who had lost his faith in books. And as a dreamer who had lost his dreams, Juan thought he understood the strange sanity of Lobo. In the alchemy of life, also, the furnace that was his heart was lit under an emptied alembic. Nothing in his life would turn to gold.

The endless manuscript at least was done, last sheet passing scrutiny. Juan interrupted Lobo, touching a finger that seemed a drumstick gnawed to bone. "*Amigo*," he said, "I am done with the letter to the Emperor. Would you like to see your name in it?"

Faced by a stare of horror, Juan asked if he would share his supper, lurching to the hearth. Even such fires as burnt in the hearts of saints needed fuel. He slapped half a boiled chicken on a platter, the succulence separating into its steaming parts. "Eat," he coaxed.

Lobo stared at the offering.

When the monk ate—rarely—it was as if food were atmosphere, necessary for life, but transparent to enjoyment. With a labored grimace intended as a smile, Lobo said, "I am done with both meat and letters."

If so, Juan thought, here burns another library of Alexandria—a Wonder of the World destroyed. He offered that there *had* been lettered saints.

Lobo was cryptic. "Consider the triune duck, a 'trinity' of locomotion—so to say—at home in air, water and land. In two elements the duck attains amazing beauty—angel in the atmosphere, grace upon the aqueous element. Yet *terra firma* turns him into a fool."

Stripped of ecclesiastical duties, Lobo had begun to care for animals, sharing the labor assigned to *yanaconas*. And like a saint deprived of lepers on whom to exercise Dangerous Love without Disgust, he had embraced the most repulsive aspects of animal husbandry, in the process becoming acquainted with what was, to him, a new world.

"Like the duck, I am in my third element, comic and reviled."

Ignoring Juan's half-hearted protestations, Lobo continued. "It is right that the *vecinos* mock me. Still, Dame Folly should be pleased that I failed as Christ did— not mocking mockers, reviling revilers, executing executioners."

The figure of speech was perhaps *polyptoton*, thought Juan, perhaps *isocolon*. Perhaps in it there was some of both. Rhetorical categories could blur.

"If one *must* choose Folly why not that of Christ, that part of the triune God cast out of His Element? I do not think I sin in thinking this—that 'comic,' and 'failure,' are words oddly adequate to what the Son of God experienced while in the body of a man."

Staring at his emaciated hands as he rocked back and forth, Lobo said, "I have decided to return to Spain, to live out my life in a monastery."

Juan shook his head sadly—as when words fail at wakes.

Lobo added, "I have something for you."

He handed Juan an oilcloth package tied in red, frayed string.

Juan unwrapped *In Praise of Folly*, and then ... *Utopia*! Realizing that this bequest dedicated Lobo to a God beyond words, a life without man—speechless with how precious the gifts had once been to the giver—Juan eased the covers open, and both were inscribed by their authors!

"Yes," Lobo said—having failed to read Juan's thoughts. "Providence decreed that these were meant for you." Awkwardly, he took Juan's hand.

"Profoundly, I regret not finding Utopia in the Indies. And even more, I regret not helping create it. In my enthusiasm I did not understand a supremely important thing, which is that rare individuals may possess the qualities necessary to form a perfect society, but that man—in the aggregate—never will. The Indians—whom I imagined as *tabulae rasae*—are no more innocent than the sinners conquering them, nothing like children ready for instruction. They are as depraved as we are—perhaps more—unconstrained by any commandment that I know.

Thomas More believed in the perfectibility of man, but not in his time and place, in a society gnawed to bone by accumulated centuries of sin. *That* is why he created perfection on an island that was elsewhere. And this was *not* just in distrusting the corruptions of civilization. As an islander he knew the virtues of isolation. He knew Utopia needed to be insular lest it be contaminated—or destroyed—by the covetous violence of others."

Here, Lobo mercifully released Juan's hand to gesture north.

"You know well as I that the Inca Empire—model for More's perfection—was far from perfect. In any case, we Spanish have destroyed it. Abandoning my expectations for that society I wandered nameless jungles, deserts, swamps, finding only deepest savagery. Nueva Extremadura was my one last hope."

Juan stifled a yawn.

Lobo turned concise. "What it took to create Eden was God, Adam, a garden, and a wall. What it will take to create Utopia will be a second Adam, a second garden, a second wall."

Juan asked about the Eve of this Eden *redivivus*.

"Eden needed Eve to populate the garden. Utopia needs a second Eve to do the same."

The priest was pacing now, troubled by the sexual matters which destroyed the Garden in the first place. Then, pointing at Juan with intensity easily confused with accusation, he said, "You are the only one I know of in the Indies who could be this second Adam."

Juan's jaw dropped. He willed it shut again.

"All you lack is an Eve, a garden and a wall. Or," Lobo shrugged, "some sort of island." He scrubbed his hands together, radiating gloomy satisfaction.

"Why me?"

Lobo enumerated on fingertips. "You are single, chaste, intelligent and literate. You have the necessary books, minus the Bible ... but we can get you one. You have many of the arts of peace, yet you also have the arts of war, vital to defend Utopia."

To that last issue Pedro responded in Juan's mind—"*Clavos de Cristo, hijo*, this feckless monk is asking you to loan him both your dick and your sword."

Juan protested, "Just me and books, an Eve, a garden, a wall ... and the sword which Eden never had!"

"Aha!" The priest was triumphant. "The fiery angel had one. And what was it for—to keep man in, or keep men out?"

He chuckled, as Juan mulled singulars and plurals.

"Now that God does not walk with us we must rely upon His Word. Eden had God. The Utopia you create will have the Bible, Erasmus, and More."

Juan had been given a triune library. And like the fiery angel, he would be protecting Utopia with his sword. That left the garden and the wall. But it was the second Eve that had him skeptical.

"Who will be the woman taken from my rib...?"

"Why," Lobo murmured, "I suppose you have to find one ... not," he hurried to add, "in Santiago, perhaps in Peru. Providence provides for the provident." Considering his white lie—in the light of the last white women to arrive—Lobo opted for euphemism, "The second Eve could be darker."

Juan had not yet met an Indian he considered attractive. The very thought was outrageous when he had the sublimity of literature, Inés de Suárez, Constanza di Lorenzo for his models. He was speechless.

Lobo sighed, confessing, "I comprehend women even less than swords."

What you comprehend is texts and printing presses, Juan thought. Yet what he brutally said—violating the memory of Liliana—was, "A whore in Sevilla, and the friendship of Inés, is all I know of women." He also did not mention the lingering fever that was Constanza.

"What would you do in my place?" he asked this architect of a second Eden.

"Find an Eve, and leave."

Juan set aside the woman problem. "Where to...?

"Who knows what's out there? Islands, valleys, boundless plains, forests without end.... You could lose all Spain in the crannies of the Indies. As for walls, they can remain metaphors until the despoilers come."

Lobo was delegating hope, without sounding hopeful.

"Someone will *always* want what you have." Juan knew enough of life already to know *that*.

"Then own too little for others to desire. You have the necessary books. All you need is the garden, the woman, and the wall."

Juan did not appreciate this bleak paradigm, even though it sounded a little like a more primal Bower of Bliss. In any case, this was Eden without Eve.

He said, "Your Paradise is a monastery for a man, a nunnery for a woman." Thinking of Pedro, Juan added, "Both eating vegetables."

Lobo was mournful. "We live in the islands of our bodies until death, when we join The Communion of Saints. Until then we are on earth alone, as in a tiny room, while sinners hammer at the door."

With *that* Juan could—at least in part—agree. He knew of no one more capable of being alone, while in the company of men, to the degree that Lobo was ... save for Nuño Beltrán de Mendoza.

Inés—with whom Juan would have loved to share Paradise as with no other—respected respectability too much, and loved him too little, to enter his 'tiny room.' With him, she only slightly stretched the rules she regularly violated with Valdivia. Even Pedro, whom Juan loved as a father, was of a past too different, and of a personality too 'shallow'—the word that unfortunately came to mind. "Being lonely," Juan said to Lobo, "does not make me an Adam before Eve. It's too late for that."

To this, the priest did not reply.

Valdivia burst into the room, enveloped in a scent mingling wine, leather and horse sweat. Inés was close behind. Wasting no time on greetings, the Governor asked if Juan was done with the letter.

"*Sí*, Don Pedro."

Inés smiled, luminous. Clapping her hands over her head she clicked imaginary castanets, her gypsy dance celebrating The Successful Secretary.

Murmuring the rituals of farewell, Lobo left in a subdued flap of sandals.

Valdivia pronounced the calligraphy of the letter excellent, and ordered Juan to take to his cot, sleep for a week if he wanted ... Juan remembering that he had forgotten to thank Lobo.

He slept perhaps ten hours of nightmares half-forgotten, recalling a fetid room shot through with shafts of light that crept the floor like liquid worms.

He woke with Pedro leaning over him.

"*Buenos días?*" Pedro questioned.

"*Muy buenos*."

"You know, *hijo*...." Pedro took his time ... spat on the floor. "You spoke in your sleep and it was strange. Clear as church bells you said that Adam never asked for Eden."

Pedro had spoken better than he meant. To Juan, the realization was like Zeus revealed to Semele, too bright for mortal eye to see—that he was right. Some logic born of dreams took Lobo's idea that every man is a shuttered closure, creating the link between Juan's first memory and Eden.

"And what is this," Pedro added, hesitant, attempting to sound conciliatory as he gestured at the volume on the table. "Not the Bible." This book was far too meager to be holy.

"*De Optimo Republicae Statu, deque Nova Insula Utopia.*"

"Ahhh?" Pedro exhaled, mollified by garble very much like that which priests produced.

"I'm tired," Juan grumbled, rolling over to pretended sleep.

Later, Pedro tiptoed over to pull a blanket over him. And Juan wondered what one could one do about such love as theirs, that, profoundly shared yet left great hollows of the heart. Youth—he decided—was a well of hope not deep enough to last a life.

Chapter 2: Eimi (*Mapu*, 1546)

Millanti ran with speed increased by hate, by pride.

Hate, because his father, brother and three uncles, had been killed by *lik winka weichafe*. His mother and sister, one aunt and seven cousins, had died also, of *wekufu* cast by *lik winka kalku*. Pride, because it was his birthright, for his father had been *werken*—a messenger—and now so was he, loping unknown paths ... so far *willi* that the plants were becoming unfamiliar.

The *werken* also ran with worry. His father, Melillanka, chose his first wife as a *domo* with long legs, hoping with this union based on shanks to increase the speed of his offspring, creating *werken* greater than himself. But he overlooked the fact that she was so absent-minded gossipers whispered that every morning she had to relearn how to boil water. And Millanti grew up long of leg indeed, bringing honor to his *pu kiñeche*, outrunning his father to become the swiftest *werken*. But he was forgetful as his mother.

Being *werken* required great swiftness, greater endurance, unmatched memory. Running like *pudu*—that creature of brief, outrageous speed—messengers also needed the staying power of *peyu*, the turtle—said to doze as he walked. In these conflicting traits lay Millanti's predicament, for while running like *pudu* he seemed to sleep like *peyu* ... wakening at his destination with the message slipping from his mind. Unkind tongues murmured that his feet had to be faster than his forgetting—that is, he *had* to run like the wind, to arrive with something left to remember. Nonetheless, Michimalongko had chosen him to carry the bloodied arrow *willi*....

The words accompanying the arrow were few. However, the *kuga* of Kuriñamku—whose well-being Michimalongko inquired about by immemorial custom—were numerous. Therefore Millanti muttered as he ran to the rhythm of his stride.... Pu, ño, laf. Son, of, Nag, pi, chun. Thud, thud, thud. Pe, ma, ri. Son, of, Lu, pi, trung. Thud, thud, thud....

As *antu* was sinking to the great sea Millanti came upon *ruka* by the trail, and he was famished.

Werken ran with little food, often without weapons, as custom declared they were not to be harmed. And they were instantly recognizable, as the foot of a *pudu* hung from their necks. Given the distances they ran they were often strangers to those they encountered yet were always welcomed. To feed *werken* was an honor.

Millanti sat perspiring—all youth, knees and elbows—on a log bench by the fire pit as *domo* brought him *poñu*, steamed fish, a small bowl of honey. He thanked them, asking how to get to the *ruka* of Kuriñamku, son of Pailakura.

He was given directions that ran a maze of forest paths to the Fio Fio and beyond—right at the first fallen *peweñ*, straight at the fork....

Some messages were private, the bloody arrow was not, and Millanti shared the words of Michimalongko—*lik winka* will soon be coming *willi* and he asks all *toki* to send bloody arrows of their own, rising in arms against this enemy.

An ancient, who had known too many wars, mumbled a toothless curse.

Rabbits were dozing, birds fluttering through the smoke holes to light on branches Lleflai had fixed to the walls, eating from baskets of seed suspended there, singing. She was finishing a broom, tying rush onto a handle with wet *foki*, listening to Wispu, whose ample body shook with laughter, for she was telling a funny story.

Not more than others did Lleflai keep track of *kuyen*, the return of seasons, her own age, or that of the *pichiche*—Did one count heartbeats?—so the memories following her return from *piku* were a pleasant blur in which only the growth of the *pichiche* was distinct.

Lautaro now lived mostly with *weichafe*, seldom eating in her *ruka*. Having chosen the bow as his weapon, he practiced endlessly under the critical eye of Andalikan. From time to time he also took mysterious walks, leaving with Ñamku in the night—wanderings which might last days. These excursions created what she thought of as the night side of Lautaro—his dark thoughtfulness and moody reserve. Of the three who were her being and her breath he was the only one who could embrace her as if not present. Like a far traveler about to leave, his thoughts were already fixed upon that journey.

Laku was devoted to Ñamku, and retained the seriousness of his nickname. Often haunting the night with the *machi*, he was pale, and—Lleflai thought—too thin. Yet there was a twinkle in his eye for her. And somewhere he had learned dry humor. He could appear from nowhere, holding a blossom selected for her.

Soon the *wentru pichiche* would leave Lleflai, and only Raytrayen—light of her eyes, heat of her heart—would remain hers. She had always been beautiful as a child, and she was ripening into the perfection of that promise. Pale as all three were—though definitely *not* like Ñamku—she had a wonderfully rounded face, high cheeks, laughing black eyes, and a gaiety that somehow made Lleflai want to cry.

She had never bound the heads of the *pichiche* with boards to smooth bumps in their skulls, for the three were perfection already, although she did pull on their noses to stretch them into an arch. In so doing, she helped create a beauty in Raytrayen that made her catch her breath with sorrow, a vision that cut deeper than any knife ever could. Of the *pichiche*, she was the one she could not survive losing.

All three would in time abandon her *ruka* and her love—first the *wentru* for war and wisdom, then the laughing, lovely girl, for a man. This was *kume mognen*. And when Ñamku permanently joined the dead Lleflai would not even have a nasty crone for company, for of course Andalikan could not take her into his *ruka*. *Che* would talk if he did. Scarred or not, she was an unwed *domo* not of his *kuga*, and Lleflai could not bring this shame to him and Wispu. Suicide was not uncommon among *domo,* and there were days when she could see no other escape from her future....

Wispu finished her hilarious story. She had not expected laughter, but neither did she expect her audience simply to place a hand upon her own. A familiar doubt came over her—was she administering cheerfulness to scars, as one might useless medicine to the dying? How difficult it was to speak to a face without expression! Wispu leaned over to kiss her forehead. "*Lamnguen*,"—sister—she asked softly, "is something wrong?"

Her denial did not satisfy, and Wispu worked in troubled silence until a polite cough outside the *ruka* announced Tuiñam. Entering, he was welcomed, and he and Lleflai began to discuss brooms—of all things!—she extending her handiwork as if expecting rejection, he praising the well-made thing. A good source of *foki* was not far away, he said. He would be happy to get some for her.

When they went silent, having exhausted the subject of brooms, Wispu knew they were in love, and—fond as she was of both—she grieved.

Tuiñam was resplendent in the *lik winka wethakelu* over the wound that made of him a child in the eyes of *che*. Ñamku had created a soft spot which custom did not allow exposure to the air—in children, the vulnerability was covered with moss until sealed by bone. However, none grew for Tuiñam—though he pounded bones to a powder that he ate, thinking that a body making flesh from flesh could make bone from bone. He was handsome and strong, but his wound tied his tongue. How could one who was as a *pichiche* request a *domo* in marriage?

As for Lleflai, she was what she was.

Pulling *foki* tight with her teeth Wispu thought—not for the first time—that save for her face Lleflai was *kume ad*. She wore her long hair unbraided, free over a supple waist. And the expression that had died in her face seemed to have transferred to her wonderful hands—delicate, bird-like, they were Wispu's unvoiced envy. And now they were white with tension, fisted about the handle of a broom. Deciding that she was a part of the awkwardness, Wispu left.

Not long after, the silent *ruka* was pierced by a sudden shaft of light, extinguished as the door slammed, sending every songbird out the smoke holes. The indignant parrot squawked.

"Tuiñam," Raytrayen cried with the unstinted gladness of the young, leaping, as she still could—not yet a *domo*—into the arms of the *weichafe*. "Tuiñam, see what I found!" She offered a *likan*—translucent, green, smoothed by the sea—also a large fanged beetle, dead and hollow, iridescent.

Both were on a flat black rock by the great sea, she said. Returning, she passed Wispu, who said Tuiñam was at the *ruka*, and she ran the rest of the way. Raytrayen chattered on, rummaging for food, finding fish and *poñu* stew, asking too late for permission to eat, spooning it in cold. She felt something was wrong. Maybe she had offended *papai* by showing the *likan* and beetle to Tuiñam first? But *papai* was never offended. The least of things made her happy.

Ñamku materialized from the back of the *ruka*, silent as fog, unkempt, red eyes uncanny coals in firelight, skeins of white hair wild about his face. He could hardly stand. Soon, he thought, vision, like threshing winds, would blow away the husk that held his soul. "*Mari, mari,*" he greeted, willing himself into the world of the living.

He had built the *ruka* with a hole beneath it, barely big enough to hold him and a few sacred, secret things. There he largely spent his days in sleep and vision. The space was walled, floored with stone, roofed with a wooden lid. Ñamku told Lleflai he was too old a *machi* to live in anything but a cave, yet she was not misled. He desired to be alone with mysteries, his *machi wethakelu* and the speaking dead, but she did not mind. Let him go underground, for she would just as soon not be wakened by hollow voices. If *machi* chose to inhabit graves before their time, that was *their* problem.

Ñamku had just finished a testy conversation with Katrinir.

"So I complain, eh?" he had whined. "So what? I am far too old to be alive. And the old are testy, as you know."

Katrinir had been refusing to give him advice about the *lik winka*—a loving and patient obstruction. He was holding the hand of Ñamku in his long, dim fingers.

Testiness was a wandering anger—thought the *machi*—an anger that forgot where it was going and decided to come home.

"I love you," said Katrinir. "And as I am dead already, the only way you can really hurt me is to hurt yourself."

As I am, Ñamku thought.

Angry at being angry, irritated by his own whining, the *machi* still could not quite forgive Katrinir for abandoning him to decrepitude and worry, refusing help, as if the dead had anything better to do! Above all he was angry at being unable to be truly angry. Such was testiness.

"Simmer down, old pot," Katrinir ordered. He insisted, "Eat!"

But Ñamku was not about to abandon indignation—not just because, should it recede, he would be left depressed, apologetic. Too much, here, was at stake. The fog of his visions had been rent after all these *kuyen*, and through the blank he had seen tantalizing figures—*lik winka* far below heading *willi*, looking like glittering ants. They were coming! And the *pillañ* refused to help....

Returned from the land of the Pikunche, Ñamku began to count *kuyen* for the first time, tying a knot for each in a string—a triple knot for every *mari*—copy of a *winka wethakelu* his teacher had once showed him. Now that he had a string with five triple knots, rumors from *piku* confirmed that the *lik winka* and their *kawellu* were gathering strength. And Katrinir was no help at all.

"I am tight as bowstrings too," Katrinir conciliated. "But the living expect too much of the dead."

"You are *pillañ*!"

"I am that to which the living give that name. However, I, at least, do not have the powers *che* attribute to *pillañ*. All I have is what I have not forgotten of my life, and what I have learned from you after my death. I can assure you that I do not live in clouds, waging airy wars." And with rare melancholy Katrinir added, "Once different, always different. Soaring in your clouds of vision you are more *pillañ*, alive, than I will ever be, dead. Why seek *my* advice?"

Ñamku struck back. "It is not fair that you stay young while I get old. It makes me grouse. I am shuffling sideways like a crab, one eye looking forward at my death, the other back at yours. I am no longer certain I was ever young."

"I died and you did not, old pot. But our love endures, unless *you* stop loving me, for love does not die in the dead."

His fingers traced webs of emotion in the air. "To the dead, memory is *mapu*. Together we formed islands in the past—far more than in the *mapu* of *williche*— each a moment that we lived together. These are islands we can visit...."

Katrinir's hands grew still, despairing of communication, and the silence of time flowed through them both. "There are the islands of my dying, of course— these moments when you say you left me to walk sideways toward your own death. But we visit there—as here—and are we not in love when we meet? So shall we be tomorrow, in love on another island. Because of *you*, our *mapu* together grows ever larger."

One lover incorporeal, the other ancient ... this archipelago of moments begged one important question, or so felt Ñamku.

Katrinir caught the harsh twist of thought.

"I have not been dead that long ... or known many dead well," he offered. "I do not know if the dead make love except in memory."

His fingers began to dissipate, like the chill touch of mist. "Do not fret, old pot. Eat instead, for whether the dead make love or not, I can assure you that they do not eat. Therefore eat, before you forget the taste of pink potatoes."

Ñamku remembered them, these pink potatoes—early, tender, thin of skin like the fingers of *pichiche*, yet gnarled as by old age—the favorites of his love.

A *che* cannot both see and hear in two worlds at once. And so it was that Ñamku did not know about the conversation that took place over his head until after the departure of Katrinir. So now, shaken, he contemplated the silence of Lleflai, Tuiñam, Raytrayen.

"These are signs," he said, indicating the stone and insect in the hand of Raytrayen, thinking that the *ifunche* must have seen her in the grotto—that intimacy opening to immensities.

Ñamku had taken the *pichiche* there when he judged their swimming good enough for *fucha lafken*. But only Raytrayen remained interested, Lautaro preferring the company of *weichafe*. As for Laku, he avoided the power of the place, dreading the change growing in him. He knew from Ñamku that you were attacked by your calling—the power of the *machi* being equal to the strength of his defense. Those easily overcome were ineffectual, given to overcharging, asking a *luan* for a night of singing and fakery. Those who *wanted* power became *kalku*. Laku had been preparing, therefore, for what he could not desire.

So it was that Raytrayen swam the cove alone.

And Ñamku was certain that the *ifunche* had seen her, leaving the *likan* and beetle. Was he plotting something? Was he evil? If not, could he be rescued? The *machi* had to act. These offerings could be a trap, but if the *ifunche* remained uncorrupted Ñamku had to right the injustice he had himself created....

Beetle and *likan*, the arrival of the *lik winka*.... In this there was a pattern, Ñamku thought, like glimpses of a landscape seen through breaking cloud—islands of vision.

"The *lik winka* are coming *willi*," he told his astonished audience.

Millanti sprinted from a forest path into the clearing of the *ruka* of Kuriñam, bloody arrow in his hand. No *werken* he knew of ever ran this far, this fast, and he began the ritual greeting of the *longko* with great pride. Then, disaster, for he began to stutter. "Son of Millale le le...."

No one laughed, for *werken* were to be honored. Kuriñam was consumed by curiosity however, for in his lifetime the bloody arrow had never been carried such a distance. He cut the stuttering short, arms sweeping the air as if to block the swoop of unexpected birds. "Stop, o *werken*! My kin and I are well. Now please, the message."

Miraculously, it flowed from Millanti like the freshets of wet moons, leaving true astonishment, and every *weichafe* roared: "Death to the *lik winka!*"

Kuriñam summoned *werken* to bear the bloody arrow, calling an assembly of all *longko*.

A messenger was sent to Ñamku as well, but the message had magically arrived before the messenger. "Ñamku told us already," Tuiñam said to the *werken*, leaving with the uneasy thought that—through awful arts—his mind could be explored from distances. And why run, then?

The *machi* himself was silent. Unmasked, sad and weary—old beyond belief— he was eating potatoes. Could his words turn life in some different direction?

Ñamku simply said, "Tell the *toki* that I have seen *lik winka* coming like shining ants in dark forests of the future. Tell him to prepare well, for this will be a war such as *che* have never known."

The *machi* was a master of becoming *mapu*, and next morning he was on his back, immobile, covered with small stones, peering through a mask of pebbles and seaweed stuck to wicker. In this way he had made himself one with the grotto by the great sea. Having come before dawn he was shivering, cold as stones, almost blind, full of fright. The *ifunche* might not appear, and if he did Ñamku might not see him through his mask, not against the glare. Yet more than that he feared success. The *ifunche* was no longer the *pichiche* he had given the *kalku*—who was twisted, yes, but had the eyes of every child. Having betrayed innocence, Ñamku dreaded meeting what he had created.

Far from the shore a head surfaced ... sounded. Seals joined it in a roil of feeding. Attracted birds flocked to feast. The *ifunche* disappeared in foam and sparkle.

Raytrayen arrived with the last flush of dawn, whistling to birds, removing her *kepam*, spreading her arms to welcome *antu*. Ñamku closed his eyes, not to violate her solitude. Still, the vision burned upon his eyelids, a pale gold glow on the purple of interior darkness. Slender and erect she stood, body arched, arms white with light.

She was almost a *domo* now—Ñamku thought—lanky as a fawn, both beautiful and awkward. Her mother, Rayentru, had been chosen by the *pillañ* for sorrow, and this had dimmed her radiance, but her daughter glowed like a seashell held to the sun of peaceful days.

The *machi* opened his eyes, and still no sign of the *ifunche*.

Raytrayen returned from her swim shivering. Laughing softly to herself, she stretched out on round black pebbles heated by the risen sun. Then she was dressed and gone, mocking the caw of gulls.

Not much later Ñamku saw the head in the sea again, closer than expected, no longer looking like a seal. Yet like a seal, the *ifunche* was clumsy on shore. Out of his element, he crept....

Intending to rise silently, Ñamku found that his body—too cold and old—failed him. Shrugging off stones, erupting in a racket of pebbles, he was unable to stand.

The *ifunche* did not attempt escape, staring as the *machi* struggled to his feet. And when at last he lurched into the water Ñamku had him by the wrist. Then both were trembling, as much from wonder as from cold....

The legs of the *ifunche* were short and bowed, his feet twisted, torso contorted and burdened by a hump. His head—twisted to the side—was extraordinary, not as monstrous but as perfect. His astonished eyes were large, fringed with heavy lashes. His nose arched from a high forehead with a fierce purity of line. And his lips were cut with a delicacy any *domo* would have envied. The *ifunche* very much resembled Raytrayen, the *machi* realized, astounded, and not just because his hair cascaded to his waist.

"He hates your beauty," the *machi* whispered. "That is why he broke your legs and set them wrong." He pleaded, "Forgive me."

Plainly as the *machi* spoke the *ifunche* did not betray intelligence or recognition, standing without struggling, blank, twisted, desperate.

What *che* does not know forgiveness? What had the childhood of the *ifunche* been? Had he known anything but pain, solitude and a rag around his hips? Could he speak?

Ñamku released him, sat, and removing his mask of pebbles, said, "You are free to go, and also free to stay."

Features wavering in brilliance, the *ifunche* stumbled forward. Eyes on Ñamku's face, he extended a finger....

"These are tears," Ñamku said—certain, now, that the *ifunche* had not been taught to speak. "Tears," he simplified.

"*Kelleñu*," the *ifunche* echoed.

"I am crying."

"I am crying."

Was this a parrot or a *che*? Ñamku wondered.

The *ifunche* said, "I swim in tears." He indicated the great sea.

"You speak!" Ñamku exclaimed.

"Of course I speak." The *ifunche* was indignant. "But do you *hear*? I *have* been speaking."

Ñamku said his name.

The *ifunche* replied that his was Eimi, adding that Chau told him this was name enough when you were the only other.

Ñamku nodded at the hideous purity of the thought. "Now that You are out of *renu* there *are* others," he said. "She for whom Eimi left gifts is one ... and here I am. There are many other *che* as well, each with a name."

You asked, "How do *che* get names?"

"Usually, *chau* gives one to them."

"So I *am* You. Is there another? I mean a 'you' *named* You."

"No other *che* has Eimi as a name."

The *machi* had evaded his question. Family and friends called every *che* 'eimi.' Being Eimi was being everyone, or no one.

"I am the only one to have the name of every *che*!" the *ifunche* cried with happiness.

Ñamku had discovered more than he wanted or expected. This was no mere familiar to the *kalku*. Yes, he was misshapen, yet he had resisted evil with innocence. Denied both goodness and his people, You had found them both.

The *ifunche* cavorted, waggling muscular arms in a dance of his invention.

Breathing more easily, Ñamku looked to where Eimi had been kneeling when he surprised him. On a flat black stone was placed a gleaming wooden bowl. Realization echoed in the *machi*, as thunder wakes sleepers in the night—Eimi was a maker.

Ñamku ran a finger over the shining curves. "Did you make *this*?"

"A bowl. I already gave her my best insect."

The suspicions of the *machi* were confirmed. The bowls, the baskets, boxes and spoons the *kalku* traded for food—pretending they were his livelihood, to conceal his art—had been made by the *ifunche*.

"Her name is Raytrayen," Ñamku said.

"Why did she not leave me anything on the stone?"

"She does not know that You exist. Only I and Chau know." He did not add that Eimi had been seen, and was loathed. Every mother who wanted her *pichiche* to behave invoked *ifunche*. "Eat your *poñu* or the *ifunche* will come get you!"

"Your name was the only other I knew in *renu*," Eimi offered. "Chau keeps a small *che* he made, dressed in white, wearing a black mask. He says you are the only one with white hair and red eyes. He says I have to hate and fear you."

"Why speak to me then, when Eimi are free to go?"

"I hate and fear Chau more than anything. But you never hurt me, even though I hit you with my stick."

Ñamku smiled at the memory.

Eimi drew a deep breath and dove into a sea of fear. "I want to live with *che*, but Chau says they hate me."

"You are too different to live with *che*. But so am I."

"Raytrayen?"

"She lives with me, two brothers, a mother."

"Is *she* different, the only *domo* who is *kume ad*?"

"*Me.*" And Ñamku simplified. "She is very beautiful, but much like others."

The *ifunche* was annoyed. "I have seen *domo*. She *is* different!""

"Yes, but not much."

"Is the mother different?"

"Yes, though not born so."

"*How* is she different?"

"Come see for yourself."

The *ifunche* turned his back ... kicked at pebbles.

Ñamku was gentle. "I will take Raytrayen the bowl. Why not meet her when she comes tomorrow?" Then he put on his proper mask and left.

Raytrayen rose early next morning and left for the grotto. Instead of swimming, she placed a flower on the flat stone where she had found her gifts. She waited, seeing nothing but swimming seals, the swoop of birds.

Lleflai had long allowed the *machi* his peculiarities, but now her *pichiche* was involved. Something was profoundly wrong and she was terrified. Next morning she handed Raytrayen food wrapped in fresh leaves, and she left without explanation.

For three *antu* Raytrayen left early, returning late, avoiding questions, and Lleflai *knew* she was being deliberately excluded. What was happening that could not be spoken? Sick with fear, she could not sleep. Finally she spoke to Ñamku—feeling like screaming—saying that Raytrayen was gone all day, every day, in her good *kepam*. She was no longer around at all, and ... she no longer helped her.

The *machi* replied to her indirections with his.... He could not reveal the existence of the *ifunche* until he left *renu* for good—a possibility more remote every day that Raytrayen returned alone. There could be no half measures.

And, one *antu*, the fears of Lleflai came true. She was grinding *uwa*—birds sitting on her shoulders, singing—when Raytrayen walked up holding the hand of a humped dwarf. His eyes were sewn shut, and—even though his head was turned sideways, not backward—this could only be an *ifunche*, child of sorcery and messenger of death. Having cast a *wekufu* on her daughter, he had come to cast one on her as well.

Lleflai screamed and leapt to her feet, sending birds and *uwa* flying. Holding her pestle high, she prepared to defend Raytrayen, but her trembling legs refused to work.

Eimi—who had been walking with his eyes tight shut—heard the first human scream of his life, and opened his eyes to a sight worse than he could have imagined. Crying out, he ran. Raytrayen bolted after him.

That morning Eimi had put a spoon with a bird-shaped handle on the flat rock.

Raytrayen had never seen anything like it, for *che* did not represent animals— not in weaving, and definitely not on spoons. But—after the first excitement— nothing. She ran her fingers along the carving, stunned by the risen sun, waiting as shadows crept over stone and sand, and birds dove into the great sea. A head appeared....

Eimi came ashore and turned his back to her, still to his shoulders in water.

"*Mari, mari*," she said, standing. "I have been waiting for you, brother."

Preferring more familiar fears, he swam away.

"Return, brother, please!" This was harder than befriending birds.

Eimi paused to tread water ... still facing away.

"I am your sister," she coaxed, extending a hand. "Ñamku will explain if You come with me."

The *ifunche* filled his lungs, closed his eyes, and swam back underwater.

They held hands in silence ... sat.

"Why are you not breathing, Eimi?"

"What?" He squeaked, inhaling.

Humped he was, and warped, yet Raytrayen had never seen eyes as sad or beautiful.

Eimi said, "Chau will wake. If he finds me gone he will be furious."

Raytrayen knew the word, not fury itself. She asked Eimi what it was like.

"Angry is yelling and nothing to eat. Really angry is a beating with a stick. Furious is when Chau breaks your legs."

Raytrayen leapt to her feet. "Brother! You *must not* return!" He said it would probably be all right. *Renu* was big. He could tell Chau he had been exploring.

"Come to our *ruka*," Raytrayen cooed. "You will have a mother ... brothers, too."

As she was beautiful and kind, Eimi allowed himself to be led away. But he could do nothing about the panic that closed his eyes. And he stopped breathing.

Hearing screaming, Ñamku abruptly stood, hitting his head on the wood lid of his hole. With a grunt of pain he lifted it....

Lleflai was holding a pestle high. Raytrayen was running out the door.

But Ñamku knew a shortcut to the great sea.

Eimi—Raytrayen in hot pursuit—almost ran into him.

"*Mari, mari*," Ñamku said, setting a gentle hand on his shoulder. "Welcome to our *ruka*."

Raytrayen took the shaking hands of the *ifunche* in hers. "I am sorry, brother. That was *papai*." She looked at Ñamku.

"The kindest *domo* I know," the *machi* told Eimi, meaning it. "She will welcome you, but it may take a little time. Please return to the *ruka* with Raytrayen. But take your time, I will go on ahead to explain."

Lleflai moaned, whipping her long hair wildly, refusing to believe or accept. She felt horrific shock, as if having fallen from a high cliff she opened her eyes to find herself alive. Then she heard a loud cough from the forest.

The *machi* whispered, "He looks a lot like Raytrayen."

As in cold moons, when *miski* is slow to drip onto the tongue, Lleflai savored the sweet implication late—that in the end, this might be the only child not to leave her. She ran into the *ruka*.

Raytrayen walked up with Eimi, who was silently panting with his eyes wide open, like *degu* scenting fox.

Face veiled by a fall of hair, Lleflai came out the door, a bowl of steaming blue *poñu* in one hand. In the other she held a delicacy Ñamku knew she had been working on for days—dried berries, *miski*, salt, toasted *uwa, dawe*, all fragrant with herbs, unctuous with *degu* fat.

Gesturing to a bench by the stream, beneath the spreading branches of an oak, setting the food down, Lleflai said, "You must be hungry. Please eat." She left.

Eimi devoured *poñu*—in fistfuls—almost the entire dish Lleflai had lovingly prepared for the *pichiche*. No manners here. No comments either—though Raytrayen sighed. Hopefully, love and time would polish this rough stump.

Ñamku went into the *ruka*, where Lleflai was slaughtering her *degu* one by one, stroking them first, then breaking their necks.

She knew! Her favorite pair—supremely fat—was already in a bamboo cage. "We can always use pelts," she said, beginning to skin. "Is there time to smoke the meat?"

"Of course."

She straightened from her labor to wonder, "Does You eat *degu*?"

Chapter 3: Lautaro (Santiago, and *Mapu*, 1546)

There had been temblors in Santiago ... gentle to be sure, yet creating corresponding temblors in Inés—these messages from Fortuna. Frequent, though mild, the quakings did not foretell great disaster. Instead they spoke of a personal misfortune visible with the meat of her own green eyes. Valdivia had been cold and distant—in her presence, that is—being almost always gone in person, having set into motion the machinery of conquest. Presently he was leading an expedition south of the Bío Bío—river boundary of Arauco, and Santiago was a hive abuzz with joy. There would be huge *repartimientos*.

Inés lost herself in labor, organizing matters having to do with food and its bearers—the base of the pyramid that was a moving army, which had the *caballeros* as, in every important sense, the point. This immense task had been assigned to her, keeper of animals and crops as well as unofficial patroness of *yanaconas*—which were the most numerous beasts of burden since, unlike quadrupeds, when they set down their loads they could be called upon to fight. She selected the pigs and chickens to be taken, oversaw the butchering, drying and smoking of meat, the baking of bread, manufacture of cages, making and filling of wineskins ... the thousand other vital etceteras encountering problems predicted by the tremors of these godforsaken lands.

At the moment, she was supervising the rebuilding of an adobe oven that had collapsed upon its bread—a setback foretold by the very temblor that caused it, in obnoxious simultaneity. Masonry did not stand up well to the mobility of Nueva Extremadura, and Indians were secretly amused by these *lik winka* who not only built, but rebuilt, structures that collapsed with every *nuyun*. Chimneys were especially a riot, as useless in the first place.

Juan was helping adze the adobe blocks that created the precise curves of the oven's catenary arch—an elegant structure held in place, not by mortar, but by its own weight—and he was smiling at the fact that the bread survived this falling mass intact. However, his was an inner amusement, as Inés would not appreciate humor about her oven. Juan imagined a dialogue with her....

He—*Drop bricks upon this bread,*
It breaks the bricks instead.

This was the dark, rhymed, alliterative sort of jest that *vecinos* loved in their *dichos* and *refranes*. Juan had created an instant classic, worthy of retelling at a thousand campfires.

She—"You know well as I, Juan, that bread for a campaign needs to be able to survive *anything*."

He—"You could shoot it from cannons."

And She of his imagination became impatient, arms akimbo. Valdivia's aloofness—so visible to friends—had created a reverberation of coldness in her.

He stole a look at the last lodestone for the compass of his heart. Despite work and worry, her black alpaca dress was spotless, hat horizontal. He noted—not for the first time—that she was dewy without actually perspiring. Magic water somehow beaded on her, and bejeweled by the sun she gestured, issuing instructions in the polyglot that had become the *lingua franca* of Santiago.

In the dust and scurry, the hurly-burly, only Valdivia—who was perpetual motion—and the two blacksmiths sweating at their bellows and furnaces, hammering showers of sparks from the metal which clothed war, were busy as she. Yet Inés labored without her customary relish. She had been pensive, snappish.

That evening they shared a meal by candlelight in a silence Juan feared to break, the unspoken topic being Leticia de los Campos. It was therefore as if Inés had read his thoughts when hoarsely she cried out, "Leticia, ha! Belle of the Indies! Ha, and ha! When pigs fly in petticoats!"

Leticia, she continued, was a fat white grub who with vulgar alacrity cast off her widow's weeds no sooner did she spy Valdivia—Inés turning their competition into the wearing of mourning, where she was unmatched. Ha! Leticia was a grub crawled from some slimy, swampy log. She was cylindrical—*Pardiez!*—given a waist by a corset, not by the Almighty!

The competition now had turned to what former times might have been called the lists of waists, yet despite her obvious victory in this arena, Juan was shocked by the pettiness of Inés. Angel that she was, she should *know* herself beyond compare. At the same time he appreciated the cruel accuracy of her analogy. Having seen grubs squashed Juan knew they had no blood or interior organs ... just thick juice that oozed out like porridge. And so it was that the image came to him unbidden, loathsome, vivid....

Segmented, cylindrical, and without waist, Leticia peered at him with beady maggot eyes, pale in the chamber of her plotting. Naked—save for her corset—she created the artifact which was her hourglass form by pulling on her stays ... and worm juice began to squirt from her nipples....

Juan would no doubt have imagined worse, but a temblor recalled him to the troubles of Inés. From the moment that an act of God revealed her bosom to Santiago, the intentions of Leticia had been transparent as her ruff. And yes, Valdivia's eye had wandered at that moment. Yet so had the eye of every other *vecino* in Santiago, Juan's included. However in his opinion, this was what could be considered a natural interest in unnatural phenomena. And feeling inspired by that thought, he said to Inés that, like a two-headed calf, Leticia was impossible to ignore.

Instantly, inwardly he damned his observation, for its echoes of 'beef.' More devastating were the two heads of the calf. And Inés indeed was laughing as he had hoped, yet bitterly.

Men will be men, she was thinking, defending each other to defend themselves, altogether a repugnantly cozy gender. Still, Juan stood out from the rest, so in love with *her* that he was difficult to resist. Always handsome—recently, almost excessively—he would however always be be too young. She had, and would, resist him for their mutual good. Their closeness—a precious thing in this land of blood and sorrow—would be profoundly altered, if not destroyed, by greater intimacy. Besides, Valdivia had not yet spurned her publicly and she loved him still, although no longer utterly. Trouble had aged him. White-haired—where not bald—nose veined by wine, the Governor was now so pot-bellied that his armor had been refashioned in far less Roman form. Yet his eye retained its fire. Mounted, in armor, Valdivia commanded admiration, but unfortunately it was her lot to see him prepare for bed. Perhaps in long relationships we love the person of the past—thought Inés—asking herself if she could become the mistress of the Valdivia she now knew.

She absolutely would—she decided—for, however much his body had decayed, his vital force shone through its carnal envelope undimmed. The fire within was pure Valdivia still ... yet change had thrust itself between them. Could it be—Or was this love's fable?—that he was preparing a necessary separation? Valdivia was certainly subtle enough to pretend a lapse from affection, weaning her with cruel kindness from a relationship that compromised both his authority and her virtue. That distant cloud in the fair skies of the past could no longer be ignored—he *was* a married man. A female companion to the wedded head of a small band of adventurers in a far corner of the world was one thing, an inamorata kept by a Governor of a thriving colony was quite another. God forgave, yet the Holy Roman Emperor did not—who, for all his incalculable wealth and power, lived in the monkish quarters of El Escorial. Whether Valdivia was weaning her of love with kindness or coldness, it came to the same—she had to learn to love him in the past. And to her astonishment, in the past was where she now preferred him. The decision she had been dreading as forced upon her had somehow come about within, of its own amazed accord. She would learn to love his memory.

"Are you cold?" she heard Juan ask, making her realize that she was shaking— out of all control. She nodded a denial, willing her body into submission, looking into the depth of love in Juan's concern. And mad impulse made her kiss him on the lips.

Absolutely chaste as the act was in intention, in commission it was not. Also, for their mutual good, *this* she absolutely could not allow herself. On the spot Inés promised the Virgin that this was Juan's last kiss of *any* sort, save for the airy pecks of greeting. And History proved her firm in the decision, for from the moment of this single lapse she made it clear by every subtle means known to Woman that she and Juan were nothing but best friends, which—contemplated by the eye of a melancholy maturity—was the human relationship most to be desired. Yet before slamming this door shut—in her own *alea iacta est*—she said, "Thank you, Juan, for everything."

Crushed by this formula of deathbeds and last farewells, Juan could only shrug.

Abruptly then, Inés told him she would now devote her life to God—in that way less altering the unspoken subject of their conversation than abolishing its existence. Her transition to the future would be cruel for both, she knew. Yet the time had come for her to love a God who did not age or grow distant—for her own good or not—a God who would not bed a grub. She would pray in the chapel she had endowed, now being built. And thanks to Valdivia she had her own enormous *encomienda*, which would allow her to explore her interests, create a comfortable old age, and—now that the door to respectability had been brutally kicked open—marry.

Dull with sorrow, she asked Juan for his opinion of Rodrigo de Quiroga.

The evening before the expedition left, a *fiesta* was held in the unfinished church. Only *caballeros* were invited, save for Inés—that perpetual exception, and in Santiago something like an honorary man. Carousing at these events was a tradition unquestioned as the Mass before departure, and by tradition also the *vecinos* attended in the armor they would wear, to 'baptize' their steel with wine.

Two roaring chimneys and a half-hundred candles illuminated the assembly. The armor—burnished during idle months of peace—ran with rivers of light. In the smoky din *vecinos* shouted in obligatory drunkenness about lost horseshoes and broken stirrups, arquebus fuses and wet gunpowder. Mountains of food were heaped upon three tables, an immense custard the centerpiece of each. The furor of preparation over, Inés thought that she had finally, truly, handed over the baton, her labor for Valdivia done. Now all she needed do was ply willing sots with wine—the actual pouring accomplished by *yanaconas*, who knew that the drunker the *vecinos*, the more food and drink they could steal when they passed out.

A tremor struck. Cups slopped. Waves formed on custards. Pyramids of fruit went rolling. Drunks dropped … not at all surprised. Those capable of rational movement fled the chimneys—that reflex in an earthquake. The tottering masonry stood, however, settling into a familiar—albeit twisted—form. Toasting the chimneys, someone yelled, "Hell, why not just build them tilted?"

As a woman, Inés was not *required* to get drunk, yet she had achieved a rare, high edge. Mopping her forehead with velvet—not in the mood to spare this sleeve that traveled a thousand leagues—she surveyed the scene revolving like a human wheel about the cockfight. An *inhuman* wheel, she thought, for she detested the bloody sport.

Moody Jerónimo de Alderete—thin as the rapier dangling from his hip— was examining the spurs of his cock and laying a last bet against the rival owner, Gonzalo de los Ríos.

Returned to happy corpulence, that *caballero* sat the floor, strapping spurs to his contender, too drunk to both stand and perform a complex act on an unwilling beast.

Studying the jabbering *vecinos*, Inés decided that none of them—save for Juan, the absent Lobo, and she—were capable of enjoying peace without engaging in some facsimile of war.

Saturnine Francisco de Aguirre counted coin.

Rodrigo González Marmolejo—grown wealthy by breeding horses and raising birds of prey for falconry—was extravagantly betting.

Alonso de Monroy of the long blue jaw—whose eyes, according to Pedro, were the color of spit—managed to remain melancholy while winning.

Juan Bautista de Pastene was murmuring encouragement to Alderete's entry, which he had bet on.

Francisco de Villagrán was arguing about what constituted the perfect fighting cock.

And faithful, wonderful Pedro Gómez—a living wine cask who rejoiced in being filled—winked with exaggeration in her direction. Now, *there* was one who did not care if he won or lost. For Pedro, betting on cockfights was a good in itself.

Her eyes lingered on Valdivia, drunk as she had ever seen him, when she once thought him the eagle on the banner of empire.

Then, there was handsome, besotted Quiroga, stealing secret glances. Tall, slender, dark, intense, he was respected by all *vecinos* for his bravery and incorruptible integrity. In fact he might once have competed successfully with Valdivia for her affection, had he not lacked that spark which ignites volcanoes in a man. Still, she nursed a secret lust for his eyebrows.... Inés smiled at the thought.

Quiroga happening to look over, she let the contact linger, every other eye being on the fight.... All but Juan's ... so that he bit his lip ... drew blood ... heard shouts. A spur badly tied on the rooster of De los Ríos had come loose, yet the valiant animal fought on. His comb was sliced off. Half blind, half spurred, he was in rags, his bright plumage and bright blood spattering the armored circle. He fell … could not stand! The church roared.

Inés turned her back to it all. On the table were the usual wooden cups and Indian ceramic. In a mood to gamble, she had also set out Venetian crystal. So, after pouring *tinto* into a priceless glass she strode out the door, leaving those remaining—and their cocks—to their fates. Once out in the night she asked herself—To what end were roosters brave? Not all animals clung to such insanity, she felt. Juan once told her some philosopher said that man was a featherless biped. Did this mean that men resembled roosters more than, say, fish? Did fish fight to the death? She doubted it. What was *happening* in that church?

Juan followed Inés out, carrying his *bota*, and found her on a bench not far away. Glass in hand, studying the stars, she gestured, and he sat beside her. Silently they toasted, lifting crystal and *bota*. In silence they drank.

The church door cast a sudden shaft of light. A backlit figure walked toward them.

Following the memory of a smile out into obscurity, Rodrigo de Quiroga made out two bulks on a bench beneath a tree. *Cuerpo de Dios!* She was with another! Or, was she there at all? Uttering her name, he might be greeted by baritone laughter.…

Pedro Gómez emerged after Quiroga, singing a *zarzuela*, weaving his way toward the tree under which the drama unfolded. Not quite arrived, he loosed his cod and pissed, groaning with pleasure, as the unseen observers held their breaths.…

Resuming his song, Pedro left.

Inés smothered giggles. Then, when the church door closed, she laughed, and laughed.

Quiroga, all the while, mutely towered.

Men were *mechanical*—Inés was thinking—always going in and out, round and round. This caused her to remember the only complex mechanism she ever knew—a clock on a tower in Sevilla. What a mystery! Seeing it, she had asked herself what the number twelve had to do with time. Why not ten, like God's good digits, given to those made in His Image?

And now—softly burping—Inés contemplated the men rigid beside her.

Juan was recalling Pedro's philosophy of pissing, once shared as he created an X on the unwritten sands of the Atacama. The aim of pissing was to aim, he had said. And he had deluged an ant at the center of his signature with his trajectory—So like artillery!—of which women were incapable. Pissing, a man did not drown something he could not see, taking care not to wet his feet. *Redios!* Would one fire a cannon facing from the enemy?

As for Quiroga, he kept his silence, Pedro having given him an alibi he would rather die than validate. He walked away, dissolving into all-protecting darkness.

Mass was sung next day—at dawn as always—consecrating a departure that would disseminate the word of God. And the *caballeros* thundered off bleary-eyed, ignoring the multitude of *yanaconas* taking up their burdens to trudge after. Observing, Juan stood beside Inés and Pedro, glum. Last night—overly jovial—Valdivia said he needed him to supervise the written business of the colony. Pedro was not going either. Both would look after Inés.

Desiring solitude in the ensuing boredom, Juan spent hours by the pool where he first saw The Indian in White. And with passing time he achieved a quiet clarity of the eye that wed the clarity of the air, itself wed to the silent pool—a trinity of clarities in which fish wheeled and glittered. *Amadís de Gaula*, dreams of the Indies, *Utopia* itself, dissolved like bitter salt in the lucidity that was this void in his attention. Yet—suspended in clarity no less than fishes—Juan could not forget Inés.... Until one day, skittering in the crystal of his sight, a school of fish exploded, creating a void in which a human fish was swimming.

The being erupted up, shattering the continuum of eye, air and water, and then an Indian child dripped impassively before him, naked as any brown egg.

"Child of the Sea!" Magic had come to save Juan's dreams.

"*Mari, mari, lik winka.*"

Then the child mimed covering his eyes, while turning his back to the Mapocho. Juan did so also, and—child himself again—almost began to count to ten.

Then, "*Mari, mari, lik winka.*" A feminine voice....

Uncovering his eyes, Juan saw the Child of the Sea now clothed in Indian drab, bow in hand, quiver at his back. Beside him was a slighter figure. By both a rude raft was beached.

Juan had been asked, he realized, to turn from the nakedness of the Indian girl as she clothed herself. She had a heart-shaped face, a nose both bold and delicate, enormous eyes.

The guard let them through the gates of Santiago, Juan vouching for the armed youth, following him to Valdivia's house, where he set down his bundle and crossed his arms, staring into air.

The bundle pricked Juan's memory. This was the chubby child with the masked Indian—the one who effortlessly swam the Mapocho—no Child of the Sea, merely some savage prodigy. The girl, however, had dropped from the blue. Perhaps The Indian in White sent both. Thinking that these young savages would not know to scratch—or knock—Juan knocked in their stead.

Inés opened the door, looking weary ... snapped erect. And, as there were no reservations in the simple matters of her heart, she exclaimed, "Lautaro! You're back! And how you've grown!"

Transported to happier times, she examined the glowering youth. His refusal to be here while yet present was the same, his crossed arms the same. His bow was larger, sling similar. The bundle at his feet....

"Your bundle!" she exclaimed with joy. Telling Juan to keep the children here—and for God's sake get a translator!—she vanished through the door in clouds of skirts.

She was gone to get the primitive package she had saved—For what, four or five years?—Juan knowing that grieving women treasured keepsakes of their vanished. But since he could not both watch the children and get a translator, he waited until she returned, when with a smile that could melt Toledo steel, she lifted the bundle as a priest the monstrance. Yet the sight—which would make normal men genuflect with awe—left the sullen youth unmoved.

"*Wentru*," Lautaro muttered in disgust, pointing at himself. He would *not* learn from a woman, or he would leave *again*, for good!

Smile turning hesitant, Inés asked Juan where—By the ten thousand virgins!—was that interpreter she asked him for?

Juan returned with a Picunche.

The youth still stood—sullen stone upon his spot—two bundles at his feet.

Inés, now hovering by the girl, beckoned.

The Picunche translated.

"She Winetshwar. She Raytrayen. Mapuche she. The translator pointed south.

Inés considered the youth, the girl. "Tell Raytrayen she is beautiful," she said. "Ask her if she will be my maid. Tell her I promise not to pinch her cheek."

Only God and the translator—certainly not Juan—knew how the Picunche relayed 'maid' and 'pinch,' but Raytrayen took up her bundle. And, beaming, Inés ushered her into the house, saying to Juan that he would have to find something for the surly child to do. She was done with his rudeness. Let him go into a garden and eat worms.

"Don't translate that," Juan snapped at the translator.

"Not know how," the Indian said.

Horses—Juan thought—ignoring him. Unfit for the company of humans, the boy could care for animals. Valdivia's stables were short a lad.

Tremendo—one of Valdivia's stallions—reared at their approach, acquainted with the scent of Indians. Fascinated and unafraid, Lautaro asked, "*Kawellu*?"

"*Ca Ba Llo*," Juan insisted.

"*Ka We Llu*."

Resigned, Juan showed him how to feed the horse, pouring grain into the manger. The youth learned quickly, and then stood in the stall itself, stroking the restive stallion. Juan demonstrated how to rub him down and Lautaro did it well, although he had to use a stool. No language problem here. No scowl either.

Juan introduced himself.

"*Trwandekardeñam.*" Lautaro repeated, solemn.

When he repeated this total failure, Juan corrected only his given name—echoed with nothing like a J, as *Trwan*. He demonstrated this elementary sound—fundamental to his identity—low in the throat, exaggerating. Aware that he must seem about to spit, he changed tack.

"*Car De Ña.*"

"*Cardeña,*" the youth fluidly said, astounding Juan. The *eñe* was peculiar, but there nonetheless.

"*Lau Ta Ro,*" the youth intoned.

Juan imitated—as he thought—perfectly. Sounds were simple for the civilized. They were just there, or not. After all, he had learned Latin while young, pronunciation no problem compared to conjugations and declensions. And he repeated Lautaro's name again correctly, delighting the child—for at some point he had forgotten his native sullenness. With a mocking bow, Juan showed Lautaro the corner where the stable lads slept on straw, then left him to unwrap his bundles....

Inés was home with the Indian girl, saying '*pan*' as she gave her a piece of bread.

'*Pan*' the girl replied correctly, thoughtfully chewing.

"Juan," Inés cried. "Look, she's eating our food! She knows *pan, vino* and *carne*, too! 'Meat' she can hardly pronounce, but she refuses to eat it anyway. 'Wine' she can't pronounce at all. She just spat it out—not on the floor, in the hearth. Such good manners already!" She sprang to her feet, arms outstretched to the marvel. "Isn't she beautiful! I named her Blanca."

What Indian could be beautiful, by you? Juan's inner voice retorted. Yet—dutiful—he scanned the latest maid, who was skinny in a black wool bag, Indian from toe to tooth. She *did*, however, have that astonishingly white smile of savages—when not stained by *coca* as in Peru.

That gave him pause, and in his mind's eye Juan saw the Dance of Death, realizing that not all smiles were equal in that last caper. Indians would dance with better teeth than emperors. What could this mean...?

In any case, Blanca was nothing if not aboriginal, which meant too dark for her name—though lighter than most of her kind. And he was taken by the look in her eyes, at once fearless and appraising. She seemed amused ... about what?

Juan could not know it was his priceless velvet cap that made her want to laugh. It was a gift from Pedro—the only example of recent Italian fashion in Santiago. Somewhat recent that is, for surely its time had passed in Venice. Such was the travail of mode when distant from its source. In Pedro's sad words—It was impossible to both conquer worlds and remain in style.

He had ordered the cap from an Italian merchant in Peru, as the current summit of headgear for young blades of fashion. And he was commissioning the distant future, in effect, for it would take the Genovese many months to return to the fountainhead of indumenta. The act of ordering style that did not even yet *exist* made Pedro somewhat lightheaded, dreaming the impossible dream of every man to whom sartorial perfection mattered—that the merchant could instantaneously return from the Venice of the future!

But, arrived, the headgear—which survived the Mediterranean, the Ocean Sea, the Isthmus of Panama, Peru and the Atacama miraculously intact—was long ago outmoded in Venice, where it counted. Commissioning the future, Pedro had received the past. Gloomily he stroked the pearled and velvet marvel gleaming in the ebony of its lacquered box, as one might a child in its coffin. He was thinking that fashion was by its very nature poignant, as ephemeral. Staying in style was like falling in love with consumptives.

A greater problem…. The cap-of-caps was so formless—save for the leather ring binding the head—as to suggest no ultimate shape. Pouffed? Flattened? Raked? If so, to the side? Tilted to the back? Which way should the feathers point…? Pedro raked the cap left, feathers at the right and pointing back, a subtle, rounded rise in front.

And when he told Juan this was the unique way to sport it, he was not so much lying as demonstrating consummate taste by reinventing what surely must have been.

No less ignorant than Pedro that the cap was destined to be worn tilted to the front, top flat, feathers drooping rearward, Raytrayen was far more ignorant yet, having absolutely no idea of what she saw. Expecting *lik winka* to be unlike anything she knew—alien and fearsome—she found them to be much like *che* instead. None was white as Ñamku or deformed as Lleflai. Most were not as big as Pichikan. They were strangest—as it turned out—not in what they *were* but what they *wore*. The young *lik winka* had a *wethakelu* on his head that looked like striped red feathers on a purple fungus. White, shiny things were stuck there. Big fish eggs?

Raytrayen sniffed, careful not to point her nose in *that* direction.

Marmolejo strode in benignly, booming—with a baritone deepened by war cries and the singing of Mass in open spaces—that it was time for lessons. Having finished more than half the **Legenda Aurea**, Inés could now read almost as well as the good father, by his own admission, yet they had kept their schedule of instruction so that he might help with 'finer points.' Believing—like most *cristianos*—that a lot of learning was a dangerous thing, Marmolejo had piously reined in his own scholarship when he attained the minimum needed to shepherd his flock to Heaven. And he was bothered that a woman—even one that rode like centaurs and decapitated Indians—should want her nose in books. Although not explicitly forbidden, her enterprise gave off that odor of sins not found in missals. Only because Marmolejo expected her to fail had he agreed to be her tutor, and when she actually succeeded—where a woman should not—he felt he had obscurely sinned by helping her. Therefore Marmolejo prayed both for her soul and for his own before he came to language lessons. And it was with horror that Marmolejo had ignored her hints that she might be ready for lessons with Juan—Merciful God!—in reading *Amadís de Gaula*, for, far as Marmolejo knew, this was the only other Spanish text in Santiago, making of it the logical next step. Yet this was not reading as a motion toward redemption. *Romances* made The Great Ladder of Reading a Descent into Hell. Therefore, Marmolejo insisted that there be no *Amadís de Gaula* until after her last saint.

Inés acquiesced, for this suited her nature. Feeling that—as beginnings were beginnings, ends were ends—she always clung like limpets to *whatever* frail bark until it foundered or reached port. For example, she still wore mourning.

She intoned the start of her next saint, Eduardo—Englishman and king— mildly surprised that a country so loutish and peripheral could have produced holiness. Though not exactly formulating this in words, Inés thought sanctity no less Mediterranean than the Church. She was not particularly learned, yet everybody knew that *mapamundi* had Jerusalem at their center, England perched precariously at the farthest outer edge. And *there*—until recently—both the page and the world ended. Little matter that the New World had created expansions to the west, for the cartography of her youth remained that of civilization. Like a sun, the Mediterranean lit further beings less with its enlightenment, *ingleses* receiving only slightly more illumination than *indianos*.

Irked at the raw *englishness* of this saint, Inés was also forced to stumble as she read. Most of the text was in God's good Spanish, but reading, like a pudding grown familiar, was now invaded by ants, the page crawling with strangeness. Eduardo— that name rare in Spain—was not difficult to pronounce. But Ethelredo? Goduino? Alphageo? Canterburi? Grenuich, for the love of God!

Marmolejo sadly shook his head, as at hearing the confession of perversities rooted in deepest Hell. How could men *perpetrate* such words?

Even Juan—who knew more than the doctors of the Church—could not help Inés with these opaque barbarities.

Inés gritted her teeth, muttering through that ivory barrier that—*Redios!*—she could not understand why God did not take the trouble to civilize countries before putting saints in them, knowing full well in His Omniscience that they would end up in books.

Gratefully forgotten, Raytrayen squatted in a corner munching on the food called *pan*, which was bland and not unpleasant. She looked around. Nothing was familiar, nothing right. She wanted to cry … and pee. She tried to memorize her surroundings, as Ñamku said she should. Yet how report what she could not understand or find words for? Even the fire was strange—not in a hole in the center of the *ruka*, it burnt in a small cave made of stones. Above it a huge black slab of meat was supported by a long stick that was impossibly not bending. And fire and meat were the most familiar things. What else to report? *Lik winka wentru* wore *wethakelu* that shone like fish. They ate with *wethakelu* that also shone like fish. The *kepam* of Inethuar was impossibly tight down to her waist, where it opened like a black flower—not to the sun but to the earth. *Lik winka* sat on *wethakelu* that were not logs, though made of wood. They spoke incomprehensibly. And Inethshuar chanted softly to a *wethakelu* in front of her, which was set upon the *wethakelu* that they all sat beside, upon their *wethakelu*. *Wethakelu, wethakelu, wethakelu.* To Ñamku she could only speak of *wethakelu*, for she saw almost nothing with a name. Ignorance of all these things was all she could report.

Like a dry wash in the first moons of rain, suddenly, she was flooded by horror, hearing Inethuar solemnly intone something before her *wethakelu*. Maybe she was the *kalku* many *che* said she was. Maybe she was casting a *wekufu*. Maybe the strangeness of *lik winka* lay not in what they were or wore, but in what they *did*. What was Inethshuar *doing*?

Her ignorance a quicksand in which mind struggled for footing, Raytrayen realized that the suns she planned to devote to understanding *lik winka* might stretch into long moons she could not tolerate. And clasping her knees, she jammed her chin against familiar bones to keep her mouth from trembling. Lautaro would scorn her cowardice if he knew. Even Ñamku—who once praised her silence when he set a broken finger—would wonder. And she badly had to pee—*right now!*—knew no place to do it, had no way to communicate her need. Desperate, Raytrayen remembered her *ruka*, fragrant with familiar food, filled with the song of the creatures of the air.

A half *kuyen* ago—two *antu* after Eimi joined them—Ñamku emerged at first light, wobbly after a night with the dead. Lleflai—who also had not slept—was packing, assigning duties to all save Eimi. Ecstatic at leaving *renu* and Chau far behind, he had shouldered an immense burden, heaped in the basket *papai* gave him. And unasked, he had placed the bamboo cage which held the *degu* on his head. Encumbered beyond the possible, smiling with an excess of perfect teeth, he was ready for any future that had more such moments in it.

Lleflai took Ñamku aside, whispering, "He does not know how to pack. He over-loaded himself. I wanted to carry the *degu* myself!"

The *machi* knew that her rare severity—like a roof upon a *ruka*—hid, and was supported by, resentment. For all his smiling eagerness to please, Eimi did not know *kume mognen*. Free of the cruelty of Chau, he thought all was permitted to those loving one another. He casually spit upon the immaculately swept floor of Lleflai. He ignored the fact that one washed, mornings. And—having learned hugs— Eimi was violently inappropriate, crushing ribs with his affection. It took immense good will not to confuse his happy ignorance with perversity. The list of what he should not have done had no end. He was like a puppy, learning what not do by doing it.

Lleflai was tolerant enough to welcome *degu*—cousins of the toothy mouse— into her *ruka,* yet she had reached her limit. The night after Eimi arrived, everyone else asleep, he had gone to a corner, dug a hole with Lleflai's best spoon, and relieved himself. She—who was serenity and forebearance—went to Ñamku that morning, confronting him with an outraged hiss.

He said, "He has good reason to be fearful of going outside—Kurufil taught him that nothing but hate for him is out there. And he was right—If Eimi is seen by *che* he will be killed.

Ñamku paused for a response, but Lleflai had veiled her face with her hair.

He continued. "Eimi went as far as he could while still inside, disturbing no one. And he buried what he did."

"Dogs do too," Lleflai replied rudely. "Also, he did not wash my spoon."

Ñamku changed the subject. "Have you ever seen such happiness?"

She could not, she admitted—save for perhaps her own, when she became a mother to the *pichiche.*

"Then why not let him bear the burden he has chosen."

Lleflai weighed wisdom against rebellion, then called her parrot to her shoulder and lifted her *wilal.*

Pichikan and Tuiñam were present to say farewell, for Ñamku had insisted on their staying. When the *lik winka* invaded the Mapuche would need every *weichafe.*

Lleflai glanced at Tuiñam, and a tingle—like a frightened mouse— scampered up her back. She would miss the handsome *weichafe* with the ridiculous *lik winka wethakelu* on his head. Blood burned her face.

The *machi* was lost in thought, melancholy at leaving, perhaps never to return. He worried at going *piku* without *weichafe.* Yet Ñamku feared the waning of his powers far more. Since the moment when he first held the bone *che,* many *kuyen* had passed, and he felt decrepit in mind and body, unable to cope with the challenge that threatened the existence of the Mapuche. He was older than he had a right to be, far older than he wanted. And he feared he was too old to do what he must, whatever *that* might be.

Nights, Katrinir argued with him gently, yet Ñamku knew that he was growing weak. His failing eyes were a greater worry—something slow and certain was squeezing vision from him like a strangling vine, and one day he would need no mask at all. Blindness would not much bother Ñamku, for his inner eye was clear. Yet the task he had been called to—the effort that would make the whiteness that was his difference right—required vision in the day. Kurufil would not fail to follow with his vengeance. And in the twilight of his powers, could he stop the *kalku*?

They left, Lautaro leading, Lleflai, Raytrayen, Eimi and Laku walking after. Ñamku went last, to guard against the sorcerer. He had not foreseen that the birds of the *ruka* would choose to travel with them. Lleflai had removed their perches and their food, and a few went out the smoke holes. Others chirped with distress in nearby trees. And when the march began they hovered, twittering above Lleflai, annoying her parrot. Ñamku grew chill with fear, for Kurufil would see, and know.

The *kalku* saw.

He had reached his destination at dawn, climbing a *koiwe* killed by lightning on a hill. He waited, seeing in the distance an agitated flock of tiny birds. There, Lleflai would be with Ñamku and the three *pichiche*. There also—Kurufil believed—was Eimi. He had to pack, prepare poisons and illusions....

Late next day he found Ñamku's *ruka*, abandoned as expected. Beside the stream were footprints—of Ñamku in their leather, Lleflai, and the *pichiche*. One set dragged a foot. Eimi would slow them down.

In the *ruka* Kurufil cast a net over songbirds he found in a corner, pressing a bare foot down on them—not so hard as to soil himself with gore. They were tasty, easy to carry, and cooked quickly over the smallest fire. Then he spat on the carefully swept floor and strode *piku*, thinking the direction provocative. He was fascinated by *lik winka*—who loved gold and silver just as he did. The long-postponed revenge might be instructive.

Ñamku shadowed the track of his companions, vigilant, dozing for short periods from time to time—both day and night—in trees. One evening he snapped awake.

Lautaro whispered up to him that *lik winka* on *kawellu* were behind him on this very path. *Pichi mapu!*" Close!

The *machi* dropped to the ground, and they slipped through bamboo into the forest, hiding in the branches of a *ruili*. Lautaro said that he was scouting when heard a false bird cry and hid. Soon after he saw a *winka*, stealthy, wearing clothes with more colors than a sunset. When he heard *kawellu* he ran to tell Ñamku.

The *winka* scouts passed by them, dark as Mapuche, carrying short, black bows. Silent on sandaled feet, they signaled with birdcalls. Ñamku had seen others like them by the hill Welen.

Lautaro stiffened, for coming down the path he recognized a vision burned into his memory—the *kalfu lik winka,* and his dogs in silver *wethakelu!* He darted a look at Ñamku.

Nuño Beltrán de Mendoza half-dozed in his saddle, mind wandering. With his dogs, their armor and training, he was satisfied—they protected his serenity and gave him status in the colony. Otherwise, he was displeased. His huge *encomienda* was worthless, almost deserted, peopled by sullen savages so plagued by fluxes, agues and poxes he would not feed them to his dogs. Leaving *that* behind, he had ridden to this forlorn corner of the world, wearing tights that were homespun, not silk. And his boots—*Redios!*—were llama hide with the disgusting hair still inside. Yet what most rankled at this moment was that the whore of Babylon, Inés de Suárez—who fornicated with a married man up, on her pedestal, for all to see— dared to sneer down at him....

Relámpago—the lead greyhound—roused Mendoza from his revery, breaking into the stiff-legged, ground-eating lope of his kind, followed by his mate.

Indian scent, thought the dogger. He was a second layer of detection behind Inca scouts, who were far more to be trusted than Picunche, in the brambly savagery of their land. Mendoza urged his horse to a trot, not wanting his dogs to outdistance the Indians ahead, leading him into ambush. About to recall Relámpago, he saw him skid to a stop, then cast about. Mendoza brought his mount to a jarring halt, scrutinizing the forest. Nothing came to his attention in the green proliferation.

Setting his dogs down the path, he returned to reverie, thinking that—had he his way—he would raze everything green in Nueva Extremadura and replant this God-abandoned land with the culinary flora of Spain and other countries lit by the Mediterranean sun—as well as Mexico, Peru, and the Indies—these many lands and wondrous isles that he knew through their spices. The cuisine that would result from this marriage—or harem—of sources, would be unimaginable. And as sometimes he fancied doing, Mendoza decided to create an impossible recipe.

The base—to which he frequently returned—would be the garlic and onions of his youth, tenderly fried. While that simmered he would gut and cut up one of those little Aztec dogs—a *chihuahua,* just the size for a single appetite—and fry him separately. On second thought, he would increase the succulence of that dry, dark meat, marinating it overnight in wine, olive oil, spices. The question then became—What wine, what spices? The Indies provided myriad possibilities dangerous to a hasty cook, as combined intensities could confuse that delicate miracle, the tongue. *Cazuela de chihuahua en adobo* it would be—a Mexican dog stew—but in what *adobo?* He set this matter aside for future moments, though in preparation it came first. Peruvian tomatoes for the foundation, he decided—red, yellow, orange, from the astonishing markets of Cuzco—chopped fine, added to the now golden garlic and onions. Then a number of those tiny, round, red potatoes of the high Andes, could be thrown in, left whole. However, better not add them now, just simmer them in their tender skins until done. The sauce could be poured over.... As this revision made the sauce thin, he reworked the start, adding a quantity of peppers—both hot and sweet—which returned him to the postponed marinade. The Spice Islands now entered into play. He tossed in a stick of cinnamon, four or five cloves, *comino*—for which God be praised!—coriander seed and ten black peppercorns, all toasted, then pulverized in a mortar. Imagination reeling with heady aromas, Mendoza was ready for the marinade. For oil, nothing less than the first pressing from an *olivar* he knew near Córdoba. The question of the wine was subtler. Marsala would add a complex touch—nuances of cork, a certain bite, slight bitterness, and yes, sweetness. The sauce now half-simmered, it was time to add the marinated dog, cover the heavy iron pot and elevate it from the fire, stirring, adjusting coals, creating the slowest of simmers. Perfection would be attained when the vegetables were soft—their every flavor wed—the meat good as falling from the bones. Mendoza sighed with the frustration of palates confined to memory and desire. Retroactively, he grated into the imaginary pot a bit of nutmeg. Perfection...? He sprinkled the dish with chopped *cilantro*, deciding to serve his *Cazuela de chihuahua en adobo* with perhaps a rough Sicilian white—a soldierly wine that would battle the subtle, yet powerful assault upon the palate. After he would sip aged port, and savor a handful of white raisins, assorted nuts. Then he would conclude—as always in his dreams—with a bowl of black and bitter, foaming *chocolatl*, sprinkled with powdered cinnamon.

It was the fate of the culinary genius of Mendoza, thought Mendoza, to create cuisines consumed by the mind. The ingredients—save for the spices—were too scattered in space and time, too perishable, to be assembled in the iron reality of a pot. No matter where you cooked the dish, vital ingredients were elsewhere. No tiny, tender *chihuahuas* in Nueva Extremadura—chicken and *degu* being no real substitutes. Here also, not the peppers, tomatoes and potatoes he required. And regrettably he had long ago depleted his store of *comino*, cinnamon, and *chocolatl*. As for the wines, they now needed to be drunk in memory.

Gloomy, Mendoza imagined himself God the Cook, materializing on summits all over the world, astounding diverse nations with Tablets of Ingredients, blessing these multitudes—as in Indian legends about how some savage divinity gave maize, or this or that, to man. Take ye and eat, for it is strange and wonderful! He envisioned the Aztecs, who had no fats, astounded by butter, lard and olive oil—as of course, they had been. The savage Indians of Nueva Extremadura—

having almost nothing of their own—would have the most to gain. Even proud
Europe—not excluding that pearl of gastronomy, the Mediterranean—could stand
to learn much. What would the French do with potatoes? As for Italians—who
from Roman times considered every other cuisine beneath their notice—what
might they concoct from peppers and tomatoes? Mendoza was embarking on a
recipe that would transmogrify the Italian table when Relámpago returned him to
his time and place by halting in his tracks, a dead Inca in his path....

The dogger could hear the birdcalls of other scouts ahead—all was normal save
for the dead savage and his rigid greyhounds. He dismounted. The *yanacona* had
no visible wound, and his face was not relaxed by that mockery of peace of the
deceased. Fixed in a gargoyle grimace, the open eyes still focused on some last
agony....

Having killed the *winka* with *wekufu*, Kurufil was flitting like a black moth
back down the forest path that brought him, not knowing that the dogger—like
a gambler hoping for a change in luck—had decided to take a risk. Mendoza was
bored and sick of regrets. Unfulfilled by cuisines of the mind, he was gnawed by
that other hunger which had made of him a dogger and brought him to this land.

The *kalku* ran, hoping to reach a stream he not so long ago had crossed.
And now, for the first time he heard the deep and not so distant bay—a growing
sound—of mastiffs loosed behind him. He would have been more terrified had he
known that silent greyhounds outran that cry with their merciless scissored stride.

The stream!

Chest heaving, Kurufil stepped onto the trunk of a tree fallen across it—the
torrent otherwise impassable. Downstream ... the near thunder of a waterfall.
Upstream ... boulders. Hampered by his *wima*, Kurufil jumped to one of them,
was about to leap again. A yowl made him turn to see dogs such as he had never
known before.

Armored greyhounds on the bank—all fangs and howling—were telling their
approaching master the quarry was at bay.

The *kalku* leapt ... slipped ... was swept downstream. A sudden, brutal blow
... his left arm wrenched ... *wima* and *ekull* swept away ... and he was spinning in
an eddy, fighting to keep his head above water ... slammed by a rock and pinned,
arched like a bow at full draw by the astounding force of the current.

He looked, and the yammering monsters were above him.

One leapt, landed with his armored weight, and sank teeth into the arm the
kalku lifted to protect him, snapping it back and forth as he would a rabbit's neck.
But he lost his footing, and—greyhounds not being made to swim raging streams
in armor—disappeared in foam toward the waterfall....

There were deep punctures on the arm of the *kalku*. His wrist was mangled, the palm of his hand ripped off. Better the waterfall than the other dog.... Bones grinding in his arm, he made it to his knees and stood. Downstream ... another boulder. He balanced ... and heard more demon dogs. They sounded bigger, but dead was dead—they could not kill him more. Balanced over the roar of the current, he waited.

The *lik winka* appeared with the quiet of dreams on his immense *kawellu*. Kurufil jumped to the rock ... to the bank ... slipped and landed on his back.

Ordering his dogs to freeze, Mendoza was himself frozen by what he saw—a recumbent Indian woman, wild black eyes fixed on his. Her earrings and the clasp binding her long, wet hair were silver.

Neither sex much attracted Mendoza—sexually, that is—and when it came to dogging, meat was meat. Therefore he surprised himself by ordering his dogs to sit.

The apparition stained with blood stood ... before turning to dissolve into bamboo.

Ill at ease, Mendoza strangely felt that he had looked into a mirror that turned light dark—a mirror nonetheless—then noticed Relámpago was missing.

Mendoza cursed and asked himself—Was that an emerald on her forehead...?

The *kalku* ran *willi*, stopping only to poultice his wounds, too shocked, too injured, to continue *piku*.

Not knowing a *kawellu* could not cross over a stream on a log—expecting at every moment to hear death pound up behind him—Kurufil returned to *renu* half-starved, filled with wonder. Once his wounds healed, he would return north to kill Ñamku and enslave the *ifunche*. And he dreamed of again meeting the *lik winka* with eyes like *likan*. Blue as the mountain lakes of cloudless days, they were absolutely calm.

The *kalku* felt a kinship here, which held an envy known once before, of Ñamku. Kurufil desired the power of the *lik winka*, desired his dogs, desired to kill with thunder. Above all, he desired his eyes. What had they seen when they looked at *him*?

Chapter 4: *Kawellu* (Santiago, 1546)

Having traveled half a *kuyen*, the weary band arrived at the *ruka* nested deep in its ravine, where their efforts at concealment had been perfected by time and *mapu*—the sod roof now a tiny meadow overgrown with mosses, ferns and *chillko*. Lleflai cried out with joy.

Entering, Lautaro whooped, cry amplified by the rock enclosure, and the air was filled with the soft flit of bats erupting by with shrill, high squeals.

The *mapu* of Pikunche was drier than their own, yet that night it rained heavily—and the whole of the next day—so that the usually placid stream roared by. Assigned the familiar task of sweeping up bat guano, even ebullient Eimi was a bit morose. Lleflai made a perch for the parrot, a bed for *degu*. She organized the cooking utensils, stored the provisions.

Lautaro cleaned out the fire pit, lining it with stone. Using the small bow of his childhood—now reserved for making fires—he spun a stick in a handful of the dry moss he carried with him on every journey, to which he added leaves that had drifted into the *ruka* and dried out, and after strenuous labor let out a cry of triumph when tiny flames were dancing. All the while, Ñamku and Raytrayen had been scouring the surrounding forest for what they recognized as edible in this unfamiliar land. That evening they had a wonderfully hot stew—roots, greens and dried *degu*, thickened with ground *uwa*.

The rain stopped overnight and at dawn Lautaro left to hunt under the patter of drops. Lleflai fished the stream with a *chuñidwe*, catching the tiny silver *puyen* herded toward her by Raytrayen.

Ñamku disappeared.

As for Laku, he mysteriously moved rocks in the stream, and then dug between the boulders that formed one wall of the *ruka*. Lleflai thought he was just doing *machi* things. But later he took her inside to show her his creation—a bamboo tube set in packed clay projected from the wall. From it clear water gushed into a shallow pool dug into the floor, lined with flat stone, then down a channel—also lined with stone—pouring back into the pebbled creek, giving the cleft which was the entrance the appearance of a spring. Bamboo pipes often filled the hollowed logs that were used as watering troughs, yet Lleflai had never seen anything like this. Fire was necessary in a *ruka*. But water—inside!—when there was a stream outside the door?

It was Laku's idea, Ñamku explained, returning. The dam that raised the level of the stream was so carefully made one would think *mapu* had done it. And the bamboo pipe was well hidden. Now—he told Lleflai—they could have water and remain concealed.

Maybe she should set aside dried food—she said—smoked fish and rabbit, honey, foods they might need if they had to hide in the *ruka* … and then realized the full consequence of what Ñamku imagined. "No garden!" she gasped.

"Safety is more important. There must be nothing outside this *ruka* to reveal us." He did not correct her assumption that they were hiding from *lik winka*, although Kuruvil was more of a danger and Ñamku had little doubt that the *kalku* would find them. He wondered if his waning powers would be equal to the encounter, for one of them would have to die.

He entered his alcove and sat cross-legged before the flat stone on which he had placed the unfinished blanket of Rayentru. Katrinir no longer needed to be summoned—perhaps because old age had brought Ñamku that much nearer death. His love had taken to materializing dim and glowing, like mist seen through a *ruka* door opened to a night illuminated by the fire within.

"*Mari, mari, Mapuche.*"

"*Mari, mari, Kangen.*" Ñamku knew he sounded tired, bitter.

"You are about to grouse," accused Katrinir.

"My soul feels like a stone swung at the end of a rotten thong," Ñamku complained, "a thong which is about to snap, and send it flying."

"Is the weakness in the thong … or in your will to live?"

Katrinir extended an ungraspable hand. "If the thong breaks, that cannot be helped. But if your failing will releases your *am*, then you are in the wrong. The Mapuche need you. Remember the bone *che* and what you felt when you first held it!"

Ñamku indeed remembered, yet not what he then felt. The terrible thing about forgetfulness was that one did not forget one was forgetting. Living long enough— he supposed—the last awareness would be of forgetting everything. Better to die before. It did not seem fair that *pichiche*—born recalling nothing—did not mind their blank one little bit. He sighed, "I know. To die now would be lazy or cowardly … probably both."

"You are whining." Katrinir observed—not harshly.

"Grouse, grouse, grouse!" Ñamku mocked the mocker, and the tears of Katrinir fell, slow as snowflakes, bright as sparks.

"No one hates like Kurufil, who can track an ant on stone," Katrinir warned, adding that they still needed to decide if Raytrayen should travel with Lautaro to the *lik winka*.

She was not accustomed to pain and hardship, Ñamku said, as *weichafe* were.

What if a *lik winka kalku* cast a spell on her and she died suffering, as so many Pikunche had? And what if she was raped by *lik winka*? They only needed to know how to defeat them. What could Raytrayen learn that was worth this enormous risk?

Katrinir waited out the protest, and then said babbling was not thinking.

"She is my niece. I love her."

Ñamku had invoked an uncle's sacred duty—and indeed, he had promised the dying Rayentru he would care for her *pichiche*.

Katrinir did not mention that Lautaro was also her *pichiche*, observing instead that there was more to life than mere survival.

Ñamku had to smile. "Raytrayen *is* curious," he admitted.

Katrinir prodded. "Do you remember naming the *pichiche*?"

Ñamku did, and Raytrayen had indeed proven to be great in love. Without her Eimi would still be suffering in *renu*. He exhaled deeply, knowing what was coming....

"You know as well as I that *lik winka* will win the coming war," Katrinir said. "And even if they do not, they will stay in the *mapu* of the Pikunche, who are already half-enslaved and half-destroyed. We will have to learn to live with them in peace, or be condemned to endless war."

Katrinir—Ñamku knew—was saying that there was more to being Mapuche than waging war, more to being Mapuche than surviving ... as hopefully more to being *lik winka* than killing, raping and stealing. Perhaps Raytrayen *was* some kind of answer....

"We have an idea of what their *weichafe* can do," Ñamku mused. "We know nothing about their *domo* and their *machi*. Just think what we might learn!"

"Imagine, Mapuche, what *lik winka* could learn from you."

Ñamku remembered the hate of *weye* he observed in the *kallfu lik winka*. Lautaro and Raytrayen might learn to talk to *lik winka* ... but he, never.

The *machi* slipped into the oblivion of the exhausted, and so it was that his decision was reached in sleep. Raytrayen would go to the *lik winka*, learning such things about them as had to do with peace, and, if possible, with healing and sorcery.

In the *lik winka ruka* Raytrayen had managed to contain her tears, yet could not keep her knees from shaking. Maybe *lik winka* did not pee. How did you say 'pee' in *likwinkadungun*?

Done at long last with that barbaric Briton, San Eduardo, Inés smiled across the room at Blanca ... and realized what was happening. She strode over.

Raytrayen whispered, "*Willeñ, willeñ.*" Would Ineshuar understand?

Inés led the trembling child to her private outhouse ... was shocked when Blanca refused to enter.

As to an infant spitting food, Inés patiently explained—for if babies learned by listening, why not Indians? The *infantes*, she said—and most *caballeros*—relieved themselves wherever, even in Santiago, where they liked to use the walls. Never in her presence though, she added, bleakly. Valdivia built this outhouse just for her. Blanca was welcome to use it.

Desperate—unable to understand a word—Raytrayen knew she could not relieve herself in the stench of this tiny *ruka* ... even if she knew how. Why concentrate unburied filth, and then go to great trouble to confine the smell? Why not go out into one of numberless beautiful places in sweet-smelling woods? Having no choice, however, she took the rag Ineshuar handed her, shut the door, and squatted over the stinking hole, holding her nose. Better the forest. But better *this*, than bursting like a crab rotting in the sun.

Ineshuar cooed, "*Willeñ, willeñ.*"

Raytrayen smiled. "*Pan. Car ne. Wi no.*"

"*Vi no.*"

"*Wi no.*"

"*VI no!*"

"*FI no!*"

"Not effffe, beh," Inés insisted. "B de *burro*, beh, beh, beh."

"Feh, feh, feh."

Giggling, Inés embracing the adorable child, saying, "*Vino fino.*"

"*Fino fino.*"

"We had a conversation!" Inés whooped. "And now we're dancing like trained bears!" For indeed they were ... and from the day Inés took Blanca to the outhouse—which she never came to understand—more than mistress and maid, they were friends.

Juan—in sharp contrast—was having problems with Lautaro. Returned to the stables to make sure the lad was settled, he found him brawling.

Outnumbered, Lautaro had held his own. One stable lad was choking, clasping his throat. The other had collapsed, rag to a bleeding nose. Quieting the rearing horses, Juan told the lads they were *absolutely* forbidden to fight. The penalties were severe. These were some of the most valuable horses in Santiago. What if their squabble somehow caused them damage? For an Indian to harm a mount was a crime punishable by death. Why, if an Indian even threw a stone at a horse, the hand that threw it was cut off!

These were not Juan's actual words—History must note—as he was speaking the *lingua franca* of Santiago, a pidgin Spanish stripped of conjugated verbs, with a sprinkling of Quechua, Picunche ... and a liberal use of gesture. For example, his last sentence was: "Indian throw stone horse, Indian hand cut."

Juan drew his sword in non-linguistic communication these lads could recognize—though they could not know that the right hand of blindfolded Justice held this very weapon, as Her left took measure. No more than Juan's own did Her blade need speech to instruct the savage. Spaniards might plead subtleties while being weighed upon her scales, not Indians. For them law was cause followed by violent effect, yet Juan hesitated to elevate his weapon. Peeking from beneath Her blindfold, Justice did not exactly like what She saw.... His duty was to report this fight to authorities that would administer a lashing with a far more serious instrument than a tongue. The severing of a little finger would not be unlikely, also—a punishment much in favor since it scarcely limited the usefulness of servants. So, while the sword of Justice was figuratively lifted, Juan's own dangled from his hand.

He contemplated the intransigence of Lautaro and said that he would overlook his fighting—just this time—drawing a finger across his throat to make the message clear. He left, so unsettled he forgot to warn Lautaro that *negros* and Indians were not allowed to congregate or roam the streets after the curfew bell.

At Ines' place he found Pedro spitting on andirons—admiring the fizz as he gnawed on spareribs incendiary with *ají*. And when his *hijo*—God love him!— entered, he handed over a sizzling slab and his depleted *bota*. He belched ... and was imitated by Negrito—who had seemed to be asleep in his basket. Pedro laughed, then sighed, fussing over him. His little pygmy was getting old. The cold of these parts bothered his little jungle bones.

Then, Pedro waxed philosophical—as often while in his cups—about his cups. Or more precisely, today his topic was the trinity of his ingestion—wine, meat and bread—the last of which might be considered the Holy Ghost, as the least substantial element of his diet.

Bread...? Why did Jesus elevate this offspring of a vegetable at the Last Supper? How could the Son of God call *that* His Body, when He was nothing like a vegetable himself? *Pardiez!* He spat, as punctuation, on an andiron.

With no idea of an intelligent response, Juan produced the rote—Faith was given man so that he could believe in miracles.

Feeling condescended to, Pedro was scornful. "Miracles are *designed* to be incomprehensible, every moron knows that. But they are meant to make incomprehensible sense."

And it was then that a formula drifted, light as autumn leaves, into his ken. "The Virgin Mary was assumed into Heaven. That makes sense since she *should* be in Heaven, the only miracle being *how* she got there. Or take Lazarus, raised from the dead, not turned to vegetables."

Pedro paused, a vision forming in his mind. And he lumbered to his feet, *bota* lifted. "When Faith helps man climb The Mountain of Disbelief he finds Meaning at the summit."

And, squinting sideways at his *hijo*, Pedro squirted wine into an enormous grin.

Juan almost intoned an Amen, for the logic of the parable seemed impeccable.

Pedro concluded. "Therefore—for the love of God!—why did Jesus not elevate pork as his body, wine as his blood? That would take plenty of faith and make a lot more sense!" Then—clubbed by doubt—he sat.

" *Did* Christ eat meat, at all, at the Last Supper...?"

Juan retrieved not a single memory of Christ eating actual meat in the Bible—although the multiplication of loaves and fishes came to mind.

Pedro was wide-eyed. Bread, and no wine, in this second miracle involving food—the only other! Fish, that bloodless flesh of last resort! An unleavened vegetable was the only recurring theme. His path through philosophy—which he had thought to turn in the direction of common sense—had veered into a wilderness where inedibles hooted in the night.

If possible, Juan had been hurled into profounder horror, asking himself what Jesus had in mind when he required that Christians should eat His Body and drink His Blood. The whole thing of a sudden seemed obscene.

Inés interrupted the metaphysical consternation in her house, entering with Blanca. She took in the tableau—Negrito asleep in his basket, Juan and Pedro looking as if they had just seen ghosts.

"You have not closed the shutters to the night!" she scolded. Skirts awhirl, she performed this evening duty, then turned to Blanca—so beautiful, so innocent ... and hers to mold. She had been teaching her Spanish, she informed the men, while setting bread and chops on trenchers. She had taken her to church, where the child learned to cross herself and genuflect.

Raytrayen had been led to an immense *ruka*—tall as trees—where she was made to touch her right knee to *mapu* and move fingers around her body. After, she had been shown many animals she did not know. Still, taken to know the unknowable she had met nothing to equal what faced her now—a *lik winka* who dwarfed Pichikan, so hairy that his nose was less visible than a *pudu* in the woods ... a *lik winka* now picking up a tiny *pichiche* dressed in clothes more colorful than a parrot and placing this strange child on his shoulder. She concluded that they were father and son, checking the feet of the larger to see if he had long, hairy toes … but they were invisible in skins. Raytrayen glanced up to see the tiny, hairy *pichiche* open his lips, revealing yellow fangs.

The apparition walked toward her. Raytrayen poised to run, and was protectively embraced by Ineshuar.

Inés scolded, "Shame on you … you … hulking thing! And shame on your monkey! You frightened the child!"

Pedro was stopped in his innocent tracks. *Cuerpo de Dios!* He was just going to refill his *bota!* What kind of mortal sin was *that!* And poor, insulted Negrito, innocent as Adam before his leaf!

"I apologize for approaching the center of the room," Pedro huffed. And, dramatically keeping to the wall, he headed for the door with a sway that was part wine, part outrage, saying, "I think I will go where I am welcome." Negrito slapped his bicep.

Inés cried out, "Sorry, Pedro!" But he was gone.

Taking a deep breath, Inés returned to language lessons. "*Beh. Beh,*" she uttered, patient. "*Beh de vaca. Beh de burro.*" Lips together she exaggerated, puckering, creating a soft explosion. "*Beh de Blanca. Beh de Valdivia.*" Yet labor as she might the child was mute … and also not eating her pork chops.

Ignored, Juan spiraled down hot circles of a hell of jealousy. Every *beh* Inés pronounced was a heart-stopping pucker for a kiss *he* would never receive. *Beh. Beh. Beh.* She was unutterably beautiful, puckering—even though she sounded a little like a sheep. Dropping his *bota* on the table he left without a word. If Inés preferred a cute savage, so be it.

Sunday dawned, and with every *vecino* not gone south or standing guard Juan attended High Mass. The church was an ambitious edifice which after four years of construction interrupted by constant warfare boasted little more than walls and a high, magnificently timbered roof, its framing supported by hammer beams still being carved with cockleshells—emblem of the city's patron saint.

Today Mass included not only the resounding boom of Marmolejo but—for the first time—a choir of boys trained by Segismundo Buenavida, *infante,* who had been a choirmaster in Burgos until he was surprised *in flagrante delicto* with a castrato.

Buenavida fled Burgos for the Indies. And having always mimicked masculinity of necessity, he aped *conquistadores* perfectly. No one was more warlike, more hairy. No one washed less, drank more, spat farther, or knew more filthy jokes—especially about *patos.* But no other male in the colony was aware that his reputation as the cocksman of them all depended on the fact that he was being whipsawed by the *putas* of Santiago. Once they discovered the reluctance of his virile member, their deal was that he would patronize and pay for nothing … or they would betray all.

So it was that this beard-splitter of repute spent much of his free time—and all his free money—in the company of whores, haggling over the price for their silence in whispers interrupted by false cries of climax.

The great secret of Buenavida had been entombed by the greed of the *putas* of Santiago. But another aspect of the *infante's* past was unearthed one day when Inés came across him as he was—for some reason—teaching an Indian child to sing the *miserere*. On the spot, she resolved to form a choir. And that seed of inspiration today was bearing more melodious fruit than Inés could have thought possible. The unwholesome *infante* was a genius as a choirmaster, spending untold hours in practice with the children, instilling subtle music into tiny savages. In addition he had trained a castrato—a *negro* who, according to law, had his *miembro genital* cut off for forcing an Indian—making of him a countertenor that rivaled seraphim....

Lauthathe thominush omnesh meum, the children sweetly sang.

Sitting on a bench emptied by the expedition south, Juan listened to these voices floating to the ear of God, entranced—while suffering pokes from the elbow of Inés, who was taking credit for the performance.

Lauthathe thominush omnesh tshrekuli.

Every child *is* an angel Juan thought, absorbing the astral harmony, crystalline as music of the spheres. The castrato was extraordinary as descant....

The Mass ended. Uplifted, Juan accepted the arm of Inés. Radiant, she smiled through her black *mantilla*.

Francisco de Quiroga approached bowing deeply, awkward, yet managing not to stutter his inanities. And after the ritual greetings that followed Mass—like sheep herded by dogs of habit—the *vecinos* drifted as a body toward Sunday punishment.

To the left of the gallows stood the *rollo*—an unhewn stone tall as a man, where miscreants were lashed. By it stood the rude block where fingers and toes, hands and feet, were lopped off. Castrations also happened on it—done with the same curved knife used to geld horses and pigs—the criminal arched over the stinking thing, which was caked black with old gore. By it the charcoal stove of the smith shimmered, holding the irons used for cautery.

Pedro Gómez de San Benito presided in his best, sitting in one of the few chairs of the colony that had come from Spain. On his chest was the Inca medallion he considered his informal badge of office.

Juan turned his ear to Inés, who was warding off the fetor of punishment by chewing on a clove and pressing a cloth to her face. With muffled voice she discussed the death of Don Jamón del Yelmo Negro—of ripe old age—whose loins had blessed Santiago with its present wealth of pork, and the surrounding forests with a proliferation of feral pigs deliberately released, as the lean, vicious things were a pleasure to hunt and the best of eating.

A scream cut her short … she took another clove. Remarkable, how they bred—these pigs—she offered. And Inés was justifiably smug, having saved the lives of the ancestors of every porker in Santiago during the hunger after Apocalypse.

Now that Don Jamón had gone to his reward—Juan rejoined—his trotters should be put into a reliquary for Pedro's worship. Inés laughed heartily into her rag, then launched into the promise of the last vintage, which should age well with its tannin. Complex already, there were overtones of strawberry in the *tinto*, of quince in the *blanco*. Turning to Juan, she did her best to ignore the castration of a *negro*, who—according to Pedro's reading of the sentence—had fled his master and not returned within eight days.

Juan spotted Lautaro in the first row of savages, witnessing the application of the cautery.

Pedro proclaimed that the next *yanacona* was sentenced to fifty lashes for being out after curfew. He added that the *cabildo* had, in its mercy, lessened the usual seventy of the punishment, in view of the youth of the offender.

"*Mierda*," Juan exclaimed—though softly—remembering that he forgot to warn Lautaro about this.

Inés studied Juan. Was this a nasty assessment of her vintage? Was he having one of his waking dreams?

"Lautaro," Juan whispered. "I forgot to tell him about curfew." He added by way of self-exculpation, "But he refuses to communicate."

Ignoring the hollow thumping on the rib cage of the *yanacona*, Inés conceived the strange idea that would forever change Juan's life. "You are good at languages, Juanito, so why not learn Picunche from Lautaro?"

"He is Mapuche," Juan corrected absent-mindedly, considering the strange idea. No *vecino* he knew of ever tried to master a savage language—though you could not help but learn just being around them. The exception was Lobo, who was an exception to practically everything, anyway.

Grinning, Juan bet Inés he could learn Mapuche faster than Blanca could learn Spanish.

Inés grinned back. She had never in her life bet money, yet during its course she had played for far greater stakes—including her immortal soul—and she did not hesitate to take him on.

Lautaro's first morning with *lik winka* had been like no other … ever. He was wakened before dawn by *winka* working by the light of torches. "*Kawellu, kawellu*," he repeated to himself, feeding the immense creatures. Clearly they were not dogs, for they ate the food of *luan*. "*Kawellu*," he said, dreaming of sitting on these mighty beings. They were surprisingly obedient, responsive to his touch … and curious, their eyes enormous and intelligent.

Later he was hurried away by a Pikunche and told to watch. "Watch what?" he asked, without receiving a reply. No wonder, because what he was taken to see could not be put to words. He stood in an enormous crowd which was not all *lik winka*—many more than at a *ngillatun*, the *che* fantastically dressed, speaking unknown languages—until a sound which he had never heard made them all go quiet. Two *lik winka* climbed on a *wethakelu*, both dressed in black *kepam*, but they were not *domo* and had shaved a circle from their heads as *weichafe* might for war—though neither carried a weapon. Facing this way and that, one of them spoke to the sky … to himself … to the crowd. He made fire in a shiny thing full of holes, which produced stinking smoke. Then he ate a white thing that did not look like food, and drank something from a shining cup.

When the peculiar incident ended, everyone went to face a large, upright stone. A great number of *lik winka* came out of an immense *ruka* and also faced the stone. No one spoke. Everyone was grim. An immense *lik winka* jabbered. A *kuru winka*—shiny as a beetle with the sweat of fear—was led forward, stripped of clothes. He screamed like a woman when they cut off his *ketrau*. Then they took a *wethakelu* from a fire and pressed it between his legs. It was so hot his blood steamed....

Juan found Lautaro eating in hostile silence with the other stable lads, who stood to greet him in atrocious pidgin. He explained to the Incas that he wanted them to make the laws of the colony clear to Lautaro—especially about curfew, running away, and the bearing of arms within city walls. He also asked them to tell him he wanted to learn Mapuche.

The Incas said to Lautaro that the *lik winka* wanted to learn his language, adding that he also recommended that he carry his weapons if he ever went out after dark. The dogs here were vicious and ran in packs.

Juan sat on straw by Lautaro. The lads were eating chicken. Very well then, let their meal be the language lesson. Pointing, he flapped his arms and crowed.

Lautaro responded, '*Achau.*' And flapping his own elbows, he perfectly pronounced Juan's '*pollo.*'

A word apiece in no time at all, thought Juan. These lessons would be cream on silk. Still, he had to clarify a thing or two. In Spanish, cooked chicken—of whatever sex—was *pollo*. The word for a live female was *gallina*, a live male, *gallo*. So what did *achau* mean? A cooked bird was being eaten, but—by crowing—he might have created misunderstanding. Setting life and death aside for the moment, Juan flapped his arms and crowed again, this time not pointing at the meat.

Lautaro nodded. "*Mai, achau.*"

So the word for 'yes' in Mapuche was the same as in Picunche—which all *vecinos* knew. On the other hand, the lexical issue remained confused, for *achau* could signify *pollo*—rooster, but roasted. The word could also signify *gallo*—as referring to the living beast. *Achau* could also conceivably mean *gallina*, if—as Juan was beginning to suspect—there was only one Mapuche word for this whole avian category.

He resorted to pidgin, hoping that an Inca lad could throw light on the question. But the distinctions he was trying to establish were too fine for the coarse linguistic net he cast. And—as dignity would not allow him to imitate a chicken laying an egg—Juan drew one on the floor with a stick. No comb.

By sunset he was reasonably certain that Mapuche did not distinguish between *pollo*, *gallina* and *gallo*. Perhaps their precision did not even extend to *pollitos*—chicks. As it was almost time for curfew, Juan left. Learning Mapuche had been less cream on silk than rocks on washboard.

At Valdivia's, Pedro and Negrito were gone, Inés saying that Pedro was still sulking. Brightening, she demonstrated the new skills of her Blanca, the child chanting, "Yo me llamo Plan ca." She seemed proud of her performance, unaware that she had just called herself a plank. Juan had to admit, however, that she was closer to approximating the *beh*.

Pirouetting with delight so great she revealed the delicacy of her ankles, Inés performed an impromptu gypsy dance. Clacking imaginary castanets, she sang, "No *fff*! No *fff*! A Spanish sentence too!" She bragged. "Blanca knows *sí* and *no*, some sentences, *and* my name!"

Sly, she inquired, "So, how did it go today with Lautaro?"

Juan embraced the thorns of honesty. "I think Mapuche has just one word—*achau*—for *pollo*, *gallina* and *gallo*. But I'm not sure."

"You learned one word … maybe!"

Sharply, Juan countered that this one Indian word was probably worth three of Spanish. He added that he had confirmed that the Mapuche word for 'yes' was *mai*, as in Picunche. Inés smiled with transparent triumph, needing to say nothing.

And from the moment of that initial exchange, they held their cards to their chests with regard to their competition, commenting only vaguely on progress. Since there was not much else to do they put in long hours—Inés at home, Juan at the stable.

Expecting to learn *winka* secrets having to do with weapons and *kawellu*, Lautaro engaged in the language lessons impatiently, yet discovered much of interest along the way. For example, he learned the names for many of the *wethakelu* that the *kawellu* wore to battle. More important, he was allowed to examine—even hold—a long knife, appreciating its weight, heft, and deadliness.

On the evening of the sixth *antu* after his arrival—night of a new moon—Lautaro decided to inform Ñamku of his progress. He slipped from the *kawellu ruka*, scaled the huge *lik winka* fence, swam the black Mapocho and hid until first light, when he set off, doubling on his trail from time to time to make sure he was not being pursued.

Juan was consternated to find Lautaro gone. The other lads claimed they knew nothing. Cheerfully, they offered that he took his weapons.

It was unlikely that Lautaro was within Santiago's walls, less likely that he left undetected. Yet a hue and cry was out of the question as making the crime public would put a seal upon his sentence ... should he return, that is. Not that Lautaro would, knowing the penalty. Escaped Indians were branded like cattle, and for exactly the same reason—some *vecinos* arguing that they should be branded in the first place, to eliminate later disputes over ownership. Of course, if he did not return within eight days the penalty was castration.

Fretting two days away, one morning Juan found Lautaro at the stable, calmly grooming a horse. "*Mari, mari*," he greeted, cool as Cuzco mornings.

Juan could not *believe* this. Had his warnings not been conveyed? The Inca lads, grooming their horses, seemed nervous.... Deciding to let the whole thing slide, Juan resumed language lessons.

He had a journal in which he jotted down vocabulary and grammar. Nonetheless, after a week he was capable of little in Mapuche, for the fiendish language held sounds impossible to utter or to spell. The **e**, for example, wandered like a drunk from sound to sound—the prodigal vowel seldom returning to anything like a Spanish home. And this errant noise was simple, compared to others. A common one—impossible to pronounce—consisted of an **n** and **g** glued to each other. Harder yet was a **t** followed by **sh** and **r**, all said together—the **r** more pronounced sometimes than at others....

Alphabets founded every language that Juan knew, yet as *mapudungun*—which is what Lautaro called his—had none, he needed to create one. Indians might be given to improvidence, Juan was not. Therefore he toiled in a swamp of rudiments for a week without attaining the equivalent of *amo, amas, amat* ... much less the tenses and structures that would allow him to communicate.

He worked at the Mapuche alphabet from both directions, making Lautaro pronounce Spanish words to learn what he could not say, having him speak *mapudungun* to find non-Spanish sounds. And on the morning of the seventh day—wearier than God—Juan rested to tabulate. *Mapudungun* had an **a,** no **b,** and—beta absent—no proper alphabet. There was no **c** as well—the proper, or soft, **c** that is, for its hard counterpart existed, enabling Lautaro to pronounce the first letter of Juan's last name. As there was a **ch**, Juan made it the second letter of what he called the Mapuche 'alphachet.'

And so it went. The **d** was present only as its distant relative, the **th** sound of

d—as in, say, *nada*. Stretching things, Juan included it as the third letter. Though there was no **g**, Juan surprisingly found an **h** that—as in Spanish—existed only in combination with other letters. There was a normal **i**, but no inkling of a **j**. There went his given name! No Spanish **s** either, although—complicating things— it existed in **sh** and **tshr**. Predictably there was no **x**, which would have been pronounced like the nonexistent **s**. For the same reason **z** was nowhere.

The Mapuche 'alphachet' was a monster of elimination. Such poverty of sound! Yet—turning from sins of omission to those of commission—there was much to twist the Spanish tongue. Of these, the noises Juan decided to spell as **ng** and **tshr** were the only ones as difficult for him as, say, the **j** of his own name for Lautaro. There was also another noise that seemed the bastard offspring of **u** and **i**—that is, you put your mouth in the **u** position and said something approximating **i**. To this he assigned a place next to **u**—because of the lips. So, at last—with no blare of trumpets—Juan had his 'alphachet:'

a, ch, d, e, f, i, k, l, ll, m, n, ñ, ng, o, p, r, sh, t, tschr, u, ui, w, y.

Feeling—in some small way—like God descending to Mount Sinai, Juan shared his findings with Lautaro.

The youth was opaque as he oiled a bridle, uninterested, brusque … and Juan was annoyed. You got the God you deserved. To the civilized, God gave language carved on stone. To savages he gave potatoes.

Juan decided to share his discoveries with Inés, though she was his rival in the wager. These language lessons had driven a wedge between them that he was coming to regret.

She went quiet when he entered, but Juan had heard through the door. Blanca was speaking Spanish—awkward and butchered—like pidgin without Indian in it. However, it was recognizably the language of God and the Emperor.

That evening over wine, sarcastic, he commented to Pedro that Inés was teaching Blanca as one might a child. Being somewhat drunk he laughed unpleasantly, saying she was using the same method an ignoramus uses to instruct a two year old—which is to say none at all. Inés was teaching no alphabet—that first grammatic thing!—nothing phonetic or systematic. She was merely babbling Spanish. And—squawking like a parrot—he imitated Blanca imitating Inés.

Pedro said nothing, well remembering the phrase Juan once taught him—'*in vino veritas*'—perhaps the only Latin not in the Mass that he trusted. However— devout as he was about the virtues of intoxication—Pedro did not believe in being thoughtless with one's friends. Far as he knew his own mother—God rest her soul!—used exactly the same method to teach *him* language. What other was there? Also, he hated words ending in '*ic*,' not a one of which was taught him by his mother. As for the alphabet, he was confident that he would hate it too … should he learn what it might be.

Pedro thought little of women and respected them less—in large part because they let themselves get laid. Yet—had he known Latin—he might have said Inés was *sui generis*, as the only one of her sex who was a true friend to him. And in truth, Pedro was annoyed at Juan's mockery of her, which made him regret his own recent aloofness. However, in sad fact he had far more to lament these days, for he had been excluded from the first major expedition south. Maybe he *was* too old. Also, his armor no longer fit. He had upped his intake of brandy—spirits burning flesh away—yet his previously useful body had taken on a mind of its own. Embarrassingly, these days he had to mount his horse, Chiquito, from steps like an old man. To crown this all, Negrito now preferred resting by the fire to riding on his shoulder. He felt naked without his little friend up there.

Next morning, Pedro found Negrito dead in his basket.

Juan went to tell Inés. He was worried about Pedro, who was simply sitting—chin resting in the hams of his hands—staring at the *homunculus*.

Inés returned with Blanca—as women will—to take charge of death. Placing a gentle hand on Pedro's shoulder, she asked him what to do with the 'poor thing.'

Disconsolate, he said, "It's my fault. All his little life he has been cold because of me. I should have left him in his nice hot jungle."

Sighing, Inés dressed the tiny corpse in wool tights, miniscule poncho, Inca hat … as if that would keep him warm.

Pedro insisted that Negrito be buried, claiming he was no more an animal than all those *yanaconas* they put in graves. Juan glanced at Blanca, who was backed against the wall, hand over her mouth. Her Spanish was not adequate to the insult, he decided.

Now Inés was sobbing at the memories—since she had fashioned many of Negrito's garments, as for a hairy baby. What coffin could they bury him *in*, she blubbered, having bought Pedro's idea.

As his throat was very tight, Juan had to clear it to propose the box for his Venetian cap. The interior was black, after all. And he knew of nothing else that formal, of the right size.

They folded the miniscule corpse into the shining cylinder. Eyes closed, arms around his knees like an Inca mummy, Negrito was uncanny, brilliant clothes reflected by his coffin, colors swimming on the perfect lacquer.

"He looks so peaceful," Inés offered—childless herself—now crying out of all control.

Pedro tied the silk laces of the coffin, and—with no other witness to this impiety—in quiet, strange procession they rode out of Santiago to bury Negrito.

Night after next, Fortuna chuckled and gave her wheel a whirl. Lautaro was returning, having visited Ñamku a second time. He had scaled the walls of Tiako, was almost back to the *kawellu ruka* and flitting from shadow to shadow, avoiding the lanterns of sentries, when he turned a corner and came upon a pack of dogs. He shot one in the throat as it leapt, was knocked down by the others and attacked....

Worried by the lad's absence, Juan had spent this night and the last dozing by the stable in his poncho. Hearing a strangled yelp, he raced out. Drawing, he decapitated a dog, and cut into another. The rest fled.

Combat slows time, so Juan would never know how long it took for him to recognize Lautaro, or know that the lantern of the night watch was moments away. Combat could erase intention also, leaving a skilled body aimless. Therefore, Juan felt as if he was waking from a dream, when the watch entered the stable, revealing with their torches the headless dog on the floor by his feet. Beside him were Lautaro and another dead dog, both covered with blood.

Juan said to the *infante*, "Dogs attacked this *yanacona*. I went to his aid."

"Inside the stable...?"

Vicious as the dogs of Santiago were, they could not open doors. Rudely, one *infante* wondered, "Where's the dog's head?"

Juan wondered, too.

Pedro's investigation created the official version—A pack of dogs attacked a sleeping stable lad, and as it happened, Juan de Cardeña had fallen asleep in that same stable. Wakening after curfew he decided to stay rather than risk a fine by being out after dark. And together they had fought off the vicious animals. As for the dog's head, a blow of the sword made it roll outside.

Skeptics murmured that the blow was mighty, for the head was improbably far away. Yet the rumors by the evening fires faded, as rumors will. Nothing had happened in any case—just some dead mongrels and an injured *yanacona*.

However, Nuño Beltrán de Mendoza became intrigued at this snake's nest of coincidence, and decided to keep an eye on this particular stable lad, suspecting he might lead him to White Shadow.

Not wanting some benighted male to cover Lautaro in a plaster of warm guts, Inés went with Blanca to the stable. Someone had cleansed his wounds—which were numerous but not serious, although a fang had slashed deep by his left eye.

Inés bandaged him.

"*Rathia*," Blanca said, looking directly and passionately at Juan.

Inés peered at the child. What *was* this savage moment all about?

A little nastily, Juan explained, "Blanca cannot pronounce the **g**, **c** or **s** of *gracias*. She's trying to say thank you with the only alphabet she has."

He turned to the intense child and said, "*De nada, señorita. El placer es mío.*" He bowed—a caricature of the court—and deeply regretted *that*, when solemnly she bowed back.

This analphabetic Indian child—female at that—had trusted in him and in his honor, and in return he mocked and patronized. For all his alphabets—*because* of them—Juan had made a farce of her belief in him....

So engrossed was Juan in his internal *mea culpa* that he did not notice Lautaro was bowing also, the youth having to repeat his *rathia* before Juan replied and bowed, sincere at being reprieved. He extended his hand.

Visibly hesitating, Lautaro took the grip.

Ignored, Inés peevishly returned to the last statement actually addressed to *her*. "For the love of God, Juan, Indians *have* no alphabet!"

"They do now," Juan said, thinking that honor could be too much like looking into the sun.

Forty-five days later Valdivia and his exhausted men returned—many of them wounded—a somber cavalcade. After them trudged such *yanaconas* as had not died or deserted, bearing on makeshift litters those who could not walk. And that night was white for Inés, who cared for the Spanish and *yanacona* wounded, assisted by Juan Valiente and Blanca, whose composure and skill were extraordinary. This child flinched at nothing—not at amputations or cautery ... not at death.

The following morning Juan de Cardeña, secretary, recorded this—though not precisely in these words:

On February ll, 1546, Valdivia and sixty caballeros went south with one hundred and fifty armed indios de servicio, reaching the river Maule without incident. Further south there were encounters. The first was with perhaps three hundred Indians, whom it took a surprisingly long time to subdue. That night the camp was guarded by Rodrigo de Quiroga and four infantes, who discovered thousands of warriors about to mount a surprise attack. The savages were fierce, organized—fighting in squadrons, like Germans—so that it was difficult to use horses effectively against them. The battle lasted over two hours, yet victory at last was theirs. Countless Indians were killed, including one of their caciques. However, the Spanish had two mounts dead, many caballeros injured. They also lost more than a third of their yanaconas, with many others wounded. The next day they advanced four leagues, meeting no resistance ... came to the largest river so far seen in Chile, where there was a splendid site for a future city, in a land thickly populated with Indians available for repartimientos. There, also, fell more rain than in Santiago. The soil was fertile, forests so thick that a horse could scarce walk through them. This was a territory well worth conquering—a promised land....

Valdivia's version of events—transcribed by Juan—was radically modified that night by Pedro, who had talked to the returning *vecinos*. "*Hijo*, there is resistance down there you won't believe, once you get to the damn River Bío Bío. The savages there—called Mapuche—are fierce, organized and fight to the death. Absolutely no thought of quarter. Every *vecino* I talked to said that they never saw the like."

Juan said, "Lautaro and Blanca are Mapuche."

Ignoring that—imbibing brandy that both gave pleasure and lessened corpulence—Pedro continued, "Valdivia would not write this to the Emperor, but in that battle by the Bío Bío we were almost defeated. The *yanaconas* were in rout, the *caballeros* forced back by the discipline of the Indians, when the *arquebuceros* managed to load and—*finally!*—discharge."

Pedro had little love for the arquebus, claiming that its rate of fire was such that the enemy comfortably could nap and still have time to wake and kill you. Still and all, he appreciated the effect they had on the savages *this* time—startling them long enough for Valdivia to reform his ranks.

That was bad enough, but there was worse. The next evening, when the expedition camped by the Bío Bío, Valdivia decided that rather than undergo another such attack they would slip away. And so they did, leaving cooking fires ablaze under bubbling pots, propping *yanacona* dead and wounded in the shadows, tying dogs here and there to bark during the night to fool the Indians into thinking they were still there. "Never before has Valdivia stooped to a ploy this low, slinking off like a gypsy with his tail between his legs."

Juan returned to his language journal. *Mapu* meant earth, and *che* meant people, so that the Mapuche were the people of the earth. He also knew that *picu* meant north, making the Picunche the people of the north. He had recorded dozens of other words. A man was *wentru*, a woman, *domo*. Working down the body, head was *lonco*, arm *lipang*, leg *chang*, and so on. *Pichi*—meaning small— was particularly strange as identical to one of the words for piss in Spanish, save that the stress fell on the first syllable. Juan pondered this, deciding to leave it a coincidence.

He now had an 'alphachet' and many nouns. Yet when yesterday he tried to progress to articles, he found that *mapudungun* had no gender marker. And, there was no grammatical number either—like the **s** or **es** added to the end of words that turned one thing into more. How could the Mapuche make sense of the world without *that*? Juan knew that they could count. He leafed to the page where he had recorded their numbers up to one hundred—for they had no more. "I learn ninety nine noun," he muttered, trying to see the world through the eyes of *mapudungun*.

Rolling his eyes to Heaven, Pedro went to bed.

In the morning Juan found Lautaro done grooming Bucephalus—Valdivia's favorite horse, now at stud and done with war—stroking the muzzle of the great, bay beast. Juan straddled the seat of learning—which is what he had taken to calling the unused saddle he sat on in the stable—opened his journal and inked his pen, preparing for the vexing question of the missing plural. And it was then— Fortuna only knowing why—that Juan decided to teach Lautaro how to ride. Why not? If the lad's yearning were a light, the stable would be shining like the sun.

There were a thousand reasons not to. In Santiago there was no actual *law* against allowing Indians to ride, any more than there was a law saying you could not shove a sharp stick in your eye. Yet an instant of glad perversity made Juan's mind. He had put this young Indian at risk in the past, and—even though he eventually saved his life—he still felt he owed him something. How much harm could it do to put just one Mapuche, on just one horse, just once?

He left Santiago astride Bucephalus the following morning, telling the bored guard that the old horse needed exercise. Lautaro trotted beside as many servants did, carrying the bundle that would be correctly interpreted as lunch.

Fording the Mapocho they arrived at a not so distant clearing which Juan recalled—a level valley abandoned by Picunche, fields overrun by waist-high greenery. And there they sat by remnants of a burnt *ruka* in the shade of a tree that the Spanish called an oak after its resemblance to the real thing. Lautaro said it was *koyam*. They shared a lunch as language lesson—*poñu* was potato, *kiñe poñu* was one potato, *epu poñu*, two potato—no inkling of gender, article, or grammatical number for Juan to find. The same was true of *koyam*. One oak, two oak, and no *the* oak. Struck by an idea, Lautaro counted on his fingers, saying *kiñe kawellu*, and of other digits, *feichi pu kawellu*.

Eureka! *Pu*—the plural marker—came before the word! Soon, Juan discovered that only living things could be said as plural in *mapudungun*, the *pu* that made them so unpredictably aided by *feichi*. He pointed at himself, at Lautaro. Holding up two fingers he asked, *"pu che?"*

"Mai."

The lad had earned his ride, and Juan said, *"kawellu."* With no suitable verb available, he gestured. Then, taking Lautaro to Bucephalus, he hoisted a bare foot into the massive stirrup made to take a boot, Lautaro easily swinging to that great height.

Juan was astonished to see the dour youth grin for the first time. And a manic grin it was.

Mania—not instruction—would get him through this experience, Juan decided. Bucephalus was old, intelligent, consummately trained.

He handed up the reins, noticing that Lautaro's feet did not rest on the stirrups, but it was instantly too late to change a thing, as the youth coaxed Bucephalus to a walk with a light tap of heels, then to a canter that left Juan behind, running through plants that came to his shoulders, spitting leaves....

Bucephalus broke into a ponderous gallop, and soon was about to crash into woods. Lautaro had to turn him!

But the warhorse veered from catastrophe at the last moment, and having been shrunk by distance, now he grew—pounding legs invisible in vegetation—a whooping lad riding a living ship on a green sea, the wind of transit creating waves of leaves.

Lautaro was riding without stirrups, at full gallop! Rooted to his spot by stupefaction, Juan remembered his first, failed, riding lesson on Father Sosa's ancient burro, when he had been unable to *move* the obstinate creature.

Bucephalus thundered by without pause or deviation, toward the forest on the other side of the clearing. Juan screamed in useless Spanish—"Rein him in!" Beginning a *pater noster*, he closed his eyes as the cadence of hooves rolled toward disaster.

Then, a silence, interrupted by the rapidly approaching sound of dogs.

Lautaro had vanished into greenery, and—at the far edge of the clearing—Juan saw four of Mendoza's mastiffs erupt from forest like flung stones. This was impossible ... Mendoza dogging *him*! Valdivia would nail his ears to a post! Juan sprinted to where horse and lad had disappeared.

Reaching the trees before the dogs, Juan immediately—and miraculously—found Bucephalus nosing Lautaro, who was unconscious at his feet. Juan vaulted onto the saddle.

Moments later the mastiffs were faced with what they knew and deeply respected. Bucephalus reared, a battlement of meat and hoof between them and their Indian. Not trained to foolishness, the dogs sat panting as Mendoza rode up, reined in, and politely bowed.

Not bothering to return the civility, Juan shouted, "You do not dog *vecinos!*"

Removing his hat to fan his face, Mendoza replied, "Pray sheathe your sword, *caballero*. I was just working out my dogs. I told them to find an Indian, and they did." He gestured with his *sombrero* at Lautaro, still unconscious. "How was I to know that ... ah ... he would be *your* Indian?"

Juan's face grew hot. Was there gossip in Santiago about the time he had been spending with this lad?

"I was just exercising Bucephalus."

Mendoza thought it best simply to replace his hat. Tipping it—and whistling to his dogs—he trotted off, thoughtful.

Unlike her far more educated cousin—History—Fortuna delivers no long-winded, *ex post facto* speeches on the world's stage. Instead She acts with silent purpose, always in the present, behind scenes. And—this might be whispered in passing—She abhors the workings of her pig-like cousin, Chance, with whose rooting Her machinations too often are confused. Mankind says Fortuna's wheel goes high, goes low, yet She knows this to be laughingly naïve, as if, in the complications of their world, humans were limited to simple ups and downs, when every woman and man is—far more than that—a text, which at any given moment is being woven into a greater textile. Mankind lived in fewer dimensions than it knew, and Fortuna considered Herself a weaver in charge of correcting that lack, working on her spinning wheel with threads of lives—distant, or not—creating instantaneous tapestries. And so it came to be, that on this summer day of 1546, Ñamku was a hidden witness to what just transpired, as he had been gathering mushrooms.

Nuño Beltrán de Mendoza believed in nothing decreed by bearded Gods. As for feminine agents said to have powers over earth, he did not believe in Chance or Fortune either, which is why he *never* gambled, preferring to create as much of fate as dogs and his own talents made possible. However he did not, in any way, trust coincidence. Therefore he had been intrigued.

Convinced that Lautaro would lead him to White Shadow, he had bribed the sentries to inform him if he left Santiago. This had led him to discover the apparent complicity of Cardeña. But complicity in what? The time had come to bribe the stable lads.

Juan was unable to revive Lautaro, who had an ugly purple bump on his head. He managed to hoist him to the saddle however, and mounting behind him he returned to Santiago, wondering if Mendoza had seen the riding lesson.

Of the four whose fortunes interlaced that afternoon, Lautaro was alone in being of one mind about what happened—once he had returned to consciousness, that is. Waking, he thought that riding the *kawellu* had been a dream, and it took a moment to sort memory from hope. He knew that he now owed too much to Kardeñam, yet in his joy Lautaro did not care. He had ridden a *kawellu*!

He only told Raytrayen, that day. But in time, what the shuttle of Fortuna had there brought together, History would proclaim.

Chapter 5: Pero Sancho de Hoz (Santiago, and *mapu*, 1546-1547)

Whispering wakened Lautaro in the darkness of the *kawellu ruka*....

The *lik winka* had been defeated at the Fio Fio! The two *winka* pounded on each other, smothering cries of delight. Defeated for the first time! The *lik winka* ran *piku* like frightened rabbits!

Ñamku needed to know about this, and Lautaro slipped into the night.

Scratching at his door wakened Mendoza the very morning after he bribed the stable lads. "Lautaro go, *pathron. Shi, shi*, one Lautaro go."

Mendoza hated pidgin, and his response was carefully grammatical. "*When* did Lautaro go?"

"Now night. *Shi. Shi.* Now night."

Mendoza handed them some of the baubles which *vecinos* called 'Indian coin'—in this case, glass beads. Then he armored six war dogs—two greyhounds in quilted padding, chain mail, and collars ringed with razor-sharp knives, as well as four mastiffs in the same, save that plate replaced the mail. He belted on the sword he rarely wore ... buckled on armor. And taking up crossbow, sword and hat, he breathed deep the morning air, planning to take pleasure in this hunt.

The Indian had a substantial lead ... so much the better. He would silence his dogs and keep them in sight. If he encountered White Shadow, this time *he* would be the master of life and death. One war dog was enough for an Indian and more. Six he could take into battle against hundreds. Today he was as good as Fate itself to savages, and he planned a sad conclusion to their Indian day.

Lautaro swam the Mapocho under a moon. And at *pichilewechi antu* he broke into a relaxed trot, mindful not to leave sign, until in a marsh by a placid stream he came across *pange*—that plant of refreshing pith. Ñamku had told him to take every precaution, yet Lautaro was famished, thirsty, so that he harvested and ate. Feeling guilty, he doubled on his trail and hid near the crest of a hill overlooking a clearing he had crossed not long ago. There, he was dozing when the *kallfu lik winka* erupted from the forest with his dogs.

Lautaro tested the breeze. Finding that he was upwind he relaxed, noticing that—strangely—the *kallfu lik winka* was in no hurry. Stranger yet, the *trewa* were running silent. Maybe the *lik winka* had sent other dogs ahead. They could be almost on him!

Keeping to woods, he ran to where he first saw the dogger emerge into the open, so that—tracking him back—the dogs would have to choose one of two directions. Should he return to Tiako, then, or risk doubling back on the *kallfu lik winka*—shadowing the shadower—abandoning the trail somewhere along the way? Would he reach the *ruka* with hot death howling at his heels?

This day, scrutinizing the forest, Mendoza did not daydream as he rode. And when the greyhounds began to dart about at a marsh he was instantly suspicious. Removing his hat he fanned himself, admiring their perfect training as—finding spoor—the dogs set off toward the *cordillera*.

Something was profoundly wrong. For half of God's good morning his Indian had headed north, so this abrupt change of direction reeked of barbarian stratagem. Uncounted doggings had taught Mendoza the many ruses of the Indian in his woods, and—confident that this one was backtracking—the icy fury of failure began to seep into him. He should separate his forces, sending silent greyhounds racing to devour the insolent native. But what if he was playing an Indian sort of chess that intended for him to release his hounds as he had before, to a mysterious death?

Mendoza's tic began a lonely dance beneath his eye…. Prudence won out, and he let his greyhounds lead him south, ultimately not surprised to be taken to a hill overlooking the very clearing he had recently traversed. The dogger did not relish being led by the nose—especially in circles. However, his fury did not rule out calculation. Toward Santiago lay ultimate failure—whether he killed the lad or not. The only direction that salved his self-respect was north….

Silent as *kilkil*, Lautaro followed the tracks of the *kawellu* to the marsh, where a *luma* overarched the stream. He leapt and caught a low limb, and made his way over water. Holding his bow and arrows high, he jumped, thinking that he had made the choices of the *kallfu lik winka* too many to figure out. Had he gone back to Tiako, or retraced his tracks to here? Somewhere behind, had he left the path undetected? Or—having gotten to the stream—which direction had he taken? His head wounds made it hard for him to smile, yet Lautaro did, going *willi*. Fast as the treacherous footing allowed he reached the confluence with the watercourse that led to the *ruka*. And he waded upstream, satisfied than no one could find his path through these branchings of decision.

But Lautaro had committed to a more arduous journey than he planned. Exertion and loss of blood turned his legs pliant as seaweed in the current that he struggled against—weapons held above his head. Fighting exhaustion, he fell. He stood—skull pounding like a blood-filled drum. Climbing the cascade leading to the *ruka* drained the last of his strength. He fell … was swept downstream.

Lleflai leapt up with a cry, startling the parrot into squawking.

Lautaro put a finger to his lips, poured the contents of the soup pot on the fire, and threw his soggy *makuñ* over the hissing logs. Then he grabbed the parrot by the neck and wrapped it in a blanket until all that could be heard was an indignant, muffled 'aaaack.'

Caught up in the mad spirit of silence Lleflai poured water on the last of the fire, knowing her deepest fears were coming true—*Lik winka* were here! She sat on the blanket that enfolded the parrot, creating total quiet as Lautaro crouched by the door with his obsidian knife. And over the perpetual murmur of the brook, she heard the startle call of her beloved forest birds....

Returned to the marsh, Mendoza asked himself—Why would his Indian circle back, when he knew he would eventually be run down? That left the always-suspect stream.

Having dodged the trees of primitive lands all day—his hat knocked off twice—the dogger realized that an Indian who could swim like an otter could probably climb like monkeys, reaching the stream by way of the large, branchy thing he was now bending to avoid. Mendoza viciously spurred his horse. And his tic turned steady as a clock when he reached a fork of the stream. Having made too many guesses already, he had little to lose by casting yet another die.

Unlike the placid rivulet he had just left, this one ran down mountain slopes, and Mendoza penetrated a steepening ravine. Sheer walls—pressing against the watercourse—shut out the sun, so that he rode in gloom. His dogs were weary, struggling on the banks. The roar of water swelled, and he reined in at the foot of a boulder-strewn cascade. His dogs now sniffed the air, not the ground. Did he smell smoke?

Here—where the stream undercut the cliff—avalanches had created a jumble of rock, an immense sieve for the wild rush of water. The weary dogs would have to struggle through that slippery labyrinth in armor, and he might lose one. There was also a chance that his horse might break a leg in this stream spawned by hell. Intelligence fighting fury, he yearned to dog Indians in more civilized landscapes. Only the thought of walking to Santiago a second time made Mendoza begin the long Calvary that was the journey home. There was no cross he would less rather bear than being played for a fool.

After lifetimes, Lleflai heard birds sing again. Another lifetime later she remembered that she was sitting on the parrot, and she stood, trembling. Like a stalking snake Lautaro slid out the door and returned. Retrieving his smoldering *makuñ* he embraced her.

In *puliwen* Ñamku arrived with Laku to a *ruka* dark and silent, and they talked by a new-lit fire, Lautaro describing what had happened. To have tracked him, the *kallfu lik winka* had to be *kalku*, he insisted, as they ate toasted *dawe* seed.

Ñamku replied that now that they knew *how* Lautaro got here, could he tell them *why* he came? In the excitement, he had forgotten, and he told them of the victory, only then mentioning that he had to risk death every time he came.

"The *lik winka* will kill you if you leave your *ruka* after dark!" cried Laku. "What about *willeñ?*" he challenged.

"You do it inside the *kawellu ruka*."

Ñamku asked about the sound that said you had to stay inside, and Lautaro could not explain it. Loud as a *trutruka*, it was more piercing, discordant, and short. He told them how he got his wounds, and how he had a blood debt to Kardeñam, who saved his life. And—climax to his tale, he proudly said that he sat a running *kawellu*.

Lleflai stopped breathing at the thought.

Ñamku nodded thoughtfully, remembering, and asked how did *kawellu* know what you wanted them to do.

Palpating the tender swelling on his head, Lautaro said he did not know.

How did one guide them, then? What made them go slow, go fast?

Lautaro attempted to explain the reins, the bit and spurs—words which he did not know how to pronounce, *wethakelu* he did not know how to use—only increasing the ignorance of his audience.

Lleflai insisted that *kawellu* ate *che*, refusing to be convinced otherwise.

They talked late into the night, deciding that what they needed was a *werken*, someone to go back and forth so that Lautaro would not have to risk his life every time he came. Millanti would be the obvious choice. Then—as Lleflai stirred the pot in which she was dyeing yarn—they discussed strategy. Days, the gates of Tiako opened. All could come and go. It would not be difficult for Lautaro or Raytrayen to meet Millanti outside the walls. They just had to agree on a time and place. Also, now that the *kallfu lik winka* had almost found them, they had to choose another route.

Juan found Lautaro gone from the stable a third time! Where *did* he go? And why was he insanely risking his life? Pondering the bizarre working of savage minds, Juan went to see Inés … interrupting an intense conversation. She was with Valdivia—he drinking from a *bota*, she darning hose. They greeted him abstractedly, Inés offering her cheek for the ritual peck. The Governor said that in a minute he would need Juan, for they were discussing *encomiendas*.

The growing distance between the Governor and the guardian angel of the colony had not affected her role as counselor, so that bitter souls still whispered that a beast with two backs made the decisions important to Santiago. In this there was some truth—as Juan knew—for when Valdivia conferred with his *cabildo*, his *maestre de campo*, his lieutenants, the matters he brought up had often already been decided. However, it was true as well that—though he often turned a first ear to Inés—he could prove unwilling to agree with her. Valdivia did what Valdivia would, Juan suspecting that he used Inés as a mirror that allowed him to admire his genius in the reflection of that concerned intelligence. The colony would be correct to point out, in any case, that this morning there was no Alderete, no Quiroga, no lieutenant at all, in the room where the most vital and troubled matter in Santiago was being sorted out.

As for Juan, to Valdivia he was not a mirror but a pen ... for the moment set aside. He noticed Blanca in a corner, darning cross-legged on a blanket, and approached her. She echoed his *mari, mari*, smiling that white smile of Indians, and bent to her work. Juan wondered if in fact savages had more teeth than civilized men, as some said. Had anyone counted? How many did *he* have?

At the table the discussion was heated for excellent reason, as *encomienda*s were the inflamed topic of the day. In early Santiago Valdivia had apportioned— and reapportioned—territory and Indians with a fairness based on ignorance. So- and-so was given a valley in which lived an estimated number of *indios de servicio* ... for, of course, you could not accurately count them. These estimates proved to be far too optimistic—especially since the savages died in droves and had been fleeing south—so that *vecinos* who were masters of thousands on parchment, in reality only had a pitiful few to cultivate their fields and pan their gold. This was complicated by the fact that before Valdivia went south he had ordered the *cabildo* to distribute the *repartimientos* of those who went with him, since the pacification of new territories should more than replace those of the expeditionaries. Now that they were back—having conquered nothing—those who had both risked their lives and lost their *encomiendas* were furious. And those who had remained were mulish, claiming that their holdings were no less insufficient than before. In brief, *vecinos* who no longer had *encomiendas* were near revolt, while those who retained them were outraged.

Santiago was in crisis. Such *encomiendas* as existed had to be reapportioned— the thankless task that the Governor and Inés were arguing about. The only solution was to reduce the number of *encomenderos*. Better to satisfy a few than have everyone furious. But whom to divest...? Valdivia and Inés had discussed every *vecino*, he stressing their influence and capacity in war, she insisting on utter faithfulness. That foul seducer of honest men, De Hoz, she pointed out—as well as many of his henchmen—only lived to plot. *That* was where to prune the tree.

Juan turned his attention to Blanca, awkwardly plying a tin thimble and bone needle. The sight of a woman mending a codpiece always troubled him, somehow, and today he thought he caught Blanca stealing glances at his. Was he unlaced? Was she smothering a *laugh*?

He was rescued by Valdivia. Taking up the tools of his trade—ears on fire—

Juan transcribed the Governor's indecisions, remembering the day he decided Valdivia was destined less to govern than to conquer. Although subjugation was out of favor with both Crown and Church—the catechism being that one 'pacified' territories in order to convert their inhabitants—one day in a drunken moment the Governor told Juan exactly what *he* felt....

Indians were by nature sullen, warlike, rebellious, and far too stupid to be improved. Reading them their rights was like preaching to a dog that needed whipping. The only way to pacify savages was to conquer them without unnecessary preliminary words—*Redios*! They needed a mailed foot upon their necks! "Peace by feats of arms," he had concluded, attempting the pith of Caesar. Yet his mot— which in Latin might have been eternal—seemed to have problems with its plurals.

"Peace by foot of arm," Valdivia muttered to his *bota*. "Peace by feet of arms."

Being one to act first and speak later, like Caesar, he forged on. Personally, he did not think it mattered what the Emperor called the process as long as it brought about the desired results. Let it be 'conversion' and 'pacification' that was going on here, not 'conquest,' what did he care? Emperors did what they wanted, including naming whatever anything, anything whatever. And Valdivia went silent, admiring the subtle symmetry of the rhetoric that wine had crafted with his tongue.

Juan had stared, at the time. Accustomed to the wayward mouth of Pedro, he had never expected its like in Caesarean form. Feet of arms?

"What these 'converters' want," the Governor continued, "is a miracle something like the Immaculate Conception—namely, a baby without a 'nasty' act."

About to say that he, for one, was no Saint Joseph, wine-befuddled Valdivia became aware that Inés—who desired nothing more than to bear his child— was listening. And before her he could scarcely voice the fact—to which every *conquistador* would lift his cup—that better to fornicate and not beget, than the reverse. Saying nothing, therefore, Valdivia concluded to himself that 'maculate non-conception' was far, far preferable to such births as were conceived by theologians. Liking the Latinate ring of his formulation, thinking that peace was killing him, he rested his head on his *bota*—creating a lateral fountain of wine— and fell asleep. Inés lifted his head, mopped up, and substituted a folded blanket for the *bota*.

On that now distant day Juan had pondered the soul of the *conquistador*, as exemplified by the Valdivia who left fame and immense fortune in Peru for the receding horizon that was the essence of Nueva Extremadura. And it struck him that this long and narrow land, cramped between mountain and sea—so like a road—could not be better suited to the conqueror's version of the straight and narrow, for Nueva Extremadura was an endless path, endlessly contested. Never so happy as when riding armed into the unknown, the *conquistador* was—in Pedro's words—on the road to 'nowhere.' Arrived 'somewhere' he became restless and out of sorts, out of place. For Valdivia this meant the glory of saddle and sword, or the worry of bench and *bota* in the quarrelsome domesticity he had named Santiago.

The act of naming places—so dear to Valdivia—was the paradoxical key to his soul. Creating a 'somewhere' in which to dwell, he lived an existence that his soul denied. Nothing demonstrated this better than the name he gave his capital— Santiago del Nuevo Extremo—taking the patron saint of conquerors to a new limit. New, because there had been a former limit. New also, because the very word implied another end. Ends without end *were* conquest. And at the new limit you had just created all it took was waking in the morning, getting armed, and mounting your horse to head south, once more on the road to 'nowhere.'

The Valdivia of the present paced restlessly as he scrutinized his changes, trouble on his soldier's face.

Juan set his pen—weightless instrument of bondage—down.

"Copy this fair by tomorrow." And clapping Juan on the shoulder, Valdivia strode out.

The Picunche had been restless, painted warriors sighted. This was a bad sign for—as with fleas—if you saw one there were a thousand others. It was time for a demonstration of Spanish might. He would take two score *caballeros* to run rebels down as an example, brand them if he had time to heat the irons, torture them in any case. Pain and mutilation seldom yielded information—they were just part of the example.

Juan turned his attention to Inés, whose lips were moving as she scanned the list. She sighed—ironically—at being granted one of the largest *encomiendas,* so huge Juan was surprised that she did not protest. Prizing her popularity as she did, he could not understand why she risked odium for more parched land and a few Indians. Her fear that she was losing Valdivia surely had something to do with this.

Baptizing his *tinto,* Juan rummaged through the lean cupboards of winter, finding yesterday's grilled kidneys, boiled red potatoes and stale bread—which he sopped in his cup—embarrassment of an hour ago forgotten.

Blanca—who had not put that moment out of mind—avoided looking at this youth with eyes like skies reflected in a sunlit stream, wondering why he made her want to laugh. Done with mending, she went to show her work to Inesh, who checked it by filling it with her fist.

Juan left, yet not before he and Blanca stole glances at each other, eyes becoming locked by guilt. And what to them was spontaneous embarrassment, to Inés was an awakening of possibilities, since for years she had thought to wean Juan of his infatuation for her. This passion founded on *romances* was impossible in every way, beginning with the inescapable Valdivia, and ending with their disparity in age. Also—as a worried Pedro delicately confided some time ago—Juan … hem … was neglecting the 'father of all saints.'

Inés had to agree with Pedro—although obviously she did not say so. Total abstinence went against both reason and reasonable pleasure. There were scores of young and toothsome *yanaconas* all about, who would happily spread their legs for a mere hawk's bell. What Juan was denying himself was unnatural—as Holy Mother the Church, Herself recognized. Inés was also silently in accord with Pedro that—although the *squandering* of spirit led to languidity—to cork the male was to bottle melancholy. And clearly, Juan had been depressed.

So, Inés was moved to action. She selected the girl considered the most attractive in the racial patchwork of Santiago—called Rosita la Bonita by her admirers. She was the offspring of a half-breed *infante* sired in Mexico—as he claimed—by Cortéz and one of Moctezuma's wives. And, although Rosita's mother was a prostitute, she was white as the host—this, the *infante* was prepared to swear upon the piece of the True Cross hanging from his neck. He boasted of his astonishingly beautiful daughter that she may have been half whore, but she was three quarters white, and the Indian part was royalty.

Whatever the facts, Rosita had nothing of the prostitute about her. By some miracle of the soul she had chosen chastity among soldiers—a virginity incongruously assisted by her father, who was angling for a rich *vecino* who liked somewhat darkish virgin meat.

Inés bribed the father, stripped Rosita of amorphous layers of wool, and made her a dark blue alpaca frock, not cut too low. She trimmed and washed her abundant hair, taught her how to brush her perfect teeth, gave her a clove to chew. Having totally remade the child—somewhat in her image, to be sure—she took her into service as her maid after labors that would have awed Pygmalion.

Tall as Inés, Rosita was lissome in the snug corset of her dress. Uplifted—though scarce revealed—her bosom had a honeyed tone. Dark as Indians,' her hair was made of subtler stuff, and intricately curled by God—a halo for the oval of a face in which the nose of fierce Cortéz found gentler form. Her hands were slender, though not trained to grace. Yet, thought Inés, in this rough diamond it was the eyes—the blue of midnight waters—that truly shone.

However, diligently as she attempted to be the serpent in the garden, Inés miserably failed, despite the astonishing apple she had prepared. For, by creating Rosita somewhat in her image, she forced comparisons in Juan, who refused to rise to suspect bait. More miserably, she failed because Rosita plummeted—being lifted much too high—deep into unrequited love. The fiasco, in short, was total. Where once there had once been a single hopeless passion, Inés had created a second, with its sighs and glances, the infatuated rest. Worse, she had imported into the oiled economy of her household something like a lode of iron that turned every male *vecino* of Santiago into a quivering magnet, while she remained the perpetual north of Juan's own needle.

Inés had crafted the ruination of her peace. *Caballeros* contrived excuses to visit, leering and twirling mustaches. Her evening board groaned under the necessary hospitality. Privacy became a thing of the yearned-for past. And Hermengildo— the swine who begat the pearl—good as joined the family. At wit's end, Inés loaned Rosita to Marmolejo as a maid, an arrangement that had extended into the present, Rosita languishing from a powerfully chaperoned distance.

So that, today, the possibility of creating a more successful Galatea deeply intrigued Inés, and when Juan exited, she dissected Blanca with a woman's eye. The child was slender, yet food and age would fill her out. Darker than Rosita—as would be expected—she was in no way over baked, like *negros* by their tropics. Her rounded face and large, black, heavy-lidded eyes were perfect, while her smile was modest and divine. In biblic dress, she could well have represented the Virgin Mary on the donkey plodding toward Bethlehem.

Inés decided to educate her, not just in language, but also in a Spanish woman's ways and dress, until civilization positively shone through dusky flesh. She rummaged for the mirrors she recently had been avoiding and took the better one—of steel—to teach Blanca the beauty of her face.

Having fallen asleep the second night of his vigil in the stable, Juan was wakened by the very youth he risked a heavy fine to save, and in their whispered exchange Juan understood only two words, *winka* and *kallfu* … but they were more than enough.

He left the stable at the curfew bell to sleep, then was pressed into service by Valdivia. And—until the *código* was finished three days later—little did Juan do but copy and recopy that document which, when promulgated, produced the expected outrage. Like a colony of ants invaded by rude shovels Santiago seethed over its nest eggs, and the months that followed were the darkest in Valdivia's memory. The Indians had returned to rebellious way. And intramural mutiny threatened, De Hoz exploiting the wrath against the *código* to foment revolution, as Inés was tireless in pointing out.

"But what to *do*?" Valdivia exclaimed, gesturing with a gnawed hambone in frustration, the very night after the reading of the *repartimientos*—so quickly had matters come to a head. "My hands are tied unless I have proof. You know as well as I that any move against De Hoz could backfire in our faces."

And yet again, Inés brooded over the unfortunate legitimacy of De Hoz. Though he was laughable as a man, his pretensions were not. His outrageous demands could be interpreted as lawful by whoever happened to be in power in the mutable politics of Peru, and if they took action against the upstart, the colony as they knew it could easily be destroyed.

She and Valdivia went at it for hours, attempting to save the frail vessel that was Santiago, tossing on an Indian tempest, rats of mutiny chattering in the hold. They needed more men to conquer the imagined riches of the south, still leaving enough to defend Santiago. There were two-hundred *vecinos* now—more or less— an immense number compared to the pitiful handful that crossed the Atacama, yet still fewer than required. Their predicament was a vicious circle—they could not attract or keep *vecinos* without gold, land and Indians, and could not conquer gold, land and Indians without them.

No one was more aware of this than Valdivia. Ten months ago—in September of 1545—he had sent Pastene to Peru in the **San Pedro**. With him also sailed Monroi. To them Valdivia entrusted all the gold he had personally amassed, as well as other sums he had borrowed—proceeds of a 'tax' levied from *vecinos*. The gold would purchase supplies that Pastene would bring back by sea, and men and horses that would return overland with Monroi. With Pastene went a number of Indians familiar with the Atacama, who were to bring back news. Yet ten months, three days, had passed, and nothing! Nueva Extremadura might as well have been an island, the **San Pedro** a bottle cast with its message into the sea.

How high their hopes had been ten months ago—thought Inés—recalling last summer. They had sown enough grain to feed two Santiagos in preparation for the reinforcements that never came—and probably never would, because in the **San Pedro** also sailed Ulloa, to whom Valdivia entrusted letters for the Emperor. Ulloa—that Judas! The memory still made her livid. Strange, that after all these years she did not understand Valdivia, who for all his genius could be blind to acts of self-destruction. He would listen to her reasoning and then—as if she were a whining insect—casually brush her off. As when he pardoned De Hoz and his fellow traitors instead of severing their sedition at the root by cutting off their heads. Or—in his latest insanity—entrusting an enemy, fool and bumbler with the future of Santiago.

When Inés found out she actually shrieked at Valdivia that—*Sangre de Cristo!*— putting Ulloa, a lickspittle, poltroon and traitor on the ship which held their hopes was no better than falling on one's sword! The devil only knew what Ulloa would do in Peru, but she would wager her immortal soul it meant Disaster!

Valdivia calmly replied that when the problem was having too few *caballeros* you did not lightly kill any of them off. And she was right about Ulloa—he *was* a despicable lickspittle. However, he had hoped to win him over by conferring a signal honor. Also, he had sent Monroi—whose loyalty was unshakable—to keep an eye on the 'poltroon,' should he wander from his duty.

Inés remained powerfully unconvinced. Every suicide had its reason, yet by destroying himself Valdivia was destroying a colony, destroying a dream, destroying *her*, for the love of Jesus! And—now that her predictions were coming true—she could not bring herself to an 'I told you so.'

Valdivia said that time was against them.

She could not *believe* he was blaming *time* for their problems!

And so it went, they repeated themselves until exhaustion dropped them into bed facing away from each other.

Blanca learned her face in the tense but uneventful months that followed the *nuevo código de repartimientos*. She was more interested in the mirror itself, however, astonished by this *wethakelu* which was full of air as smoke holes are—a solid sort of opening.

"*Espejo*," Inés crooned.

"*Eshpetho*."

Fascinated by the hand-held hole, Raytrayen learned that—like a twisting tunnel in a cave—it could lead elsewhere. For example, she could see the face of Ineshuar, while looking in a different direction. She could also see the back of her own braided head.

"*Nge!*" she exclaimed, pointing at the finger pointing back. "This is not a tunnel, but an eye without a head! Eh!"

Inés—who knew few Mapuche words—smiled a proprietary smile. Her own "Eh!" was the first Spanish that Blanca had taught herself.

But why did Blanca not look at her own face? She explored instead, observing the floor as ceiling, the underside of a bench, the chimney tunneling into the floor. And she studied the inside of her mouth and nose. Why, after these many years of mirrors, Inés wondered, had she never looked at the inside of a chimney or a nose?

Blanca led her outside ... put the mirror on the ground. Heads pressed together they saw—as in a liquid pool—the calm passing of the clouds. And seeing this, Inés inexplicably felt weepy, yearning for an equally selfless eye. A mirror never wept, she thought. Was she making a mistake, teaching vanity to Eve?

The months that followed turned her question moot. Blanca totally lost interest in the mirror, being more fascinated by the animals entrusted to Inés, especially the pigs, goats, cows and sheep. She also loved the orange, lemon, fig, olive and avocado trees—those that bore unfamiliar fruit. Her favorite was the quince, for the aroma of its fruit.

Inés drilled her Spanish until persistence produced a recognizable **j**, an acceptable **b** and **v**, so that Blanca was not now so much making mistakes and retching noises, as speaking Spanish like some gypsy fresh from the exotic distances they came from.

Juan's more systematic instruction in *Mapudungun* ignored subtleties of pronunciation to attack a narrow grammatic front. Personal pronouns soon were vanquished. Adjectives were not that difficult an opponent either. Walls of ignorance were falling. Yet, storming that castle keep—the verb—he found it to be impregnable. By moil and toil he elucidated conjugated endings. *Amo, amas, amat,* for example, were *ayun, ayuimi, ayui*. But the *Mapudungun* verb diverged from both Latin and Spanish with an eccentric dual form—*Ayuiyu, ayuimu, ayuingn* translated as 'we two, thou two, they two, love.' Then came the equivalent of the Latin and Spanish plural—*ayuin, ayuimn, ayuingn* translating as 'more than two, thou more than two, they more than two, love.' But after this beginning—as if the dual form were not bizarre enough—the *Mapudungun* verb swallowed everything in sight, adding interior particles until, like the boa of Panama, it was both long and hideously full. The elements of grammar that had appeared to be missing had been eaten by its verb.

In September of 1547, Pero Sancho de Hoz woke Santiago from sad, suspended animation with his second attempt to assassinate Valdivia—so resembling the first in both form and failure as to be laughable. Pretending to be on his deathbed, he requested the presence of Valdivia to discuss his last testament in private....

In *private*! Inés laughed hysterically until Valdivia said that he would go. At that point Juan, Pedro, Marmolejo—everyone!—shouted that this was madness. They compromised, Valdivia taking an armed escort.

Nothing happened. However, Clio retroactively records that an accomplice of De Hoz—Pedro Romero—was concealed behind drapery, waiting to stab the Governor in the back.

At the time, Valdivia pointed out to Inés that the only sign of treachery was that De Hoz did not appear to be near death. And he refused to take action. The next day—as if to prove how nonchalantly one could look sedition in the face—he left for Quillota. And in his absence the fuse of treachery at last touched powder, De Hoz attempting to recruit Villagra, promising him great rewards if he would only aid his plot. Instead, he went to Inés, who advised him to insinuate himself into the scheme. And she sent a messenger to Valdivia.

On his return, the Governor ordered De Hoz clapped in irons. And as he paced in cloak and spurs, deciding what to do, Fortuna intervened. The messenger from Peru—awaited for two years—galloped up in the form of Juan Bohón, bearing tidings of disaster. Pastene had arrived in the *Santiago,* the ship in such bad shape that it had been beached for repairs. Monroi was dead. And Ulloa had betrayed Valdivia.

Inés turned pale. Valdivia spat. Pedro yanked hairs from his nose. Like a fatidic condor, disaster spiraled overhead. No mention of how all that gold was spent! No mention of supplies, or the desperately needed men and horses!

Valdivia was harshly interrogating Bohón, who knew little about these vital matters, when Pastene himself arrived on horseback. He was exhausted, but able to flesh out the catastrophe.

"To the devil with the details," Pedro grumbled later, eating pig's feet with his *hijo*. As one picks burrs from hose, he was going over the dark fabric of Pastene's narrative with disgust. Sucking gelatin from a trotter, Pedro thought of saying—All right, *hijo*, Monroi was put to bed with a shovel, and this is greatly to be regretted. He was a fine soldier, a good comrade, and an honorable man. Still, the Indies were no convent and Monroi was no nun.... He decided instead to administer sympathetic medicine through song, beginning that ballad of *bodegas* which has as its refrain—"Her black joke and belly so white."

Juan joined in, after a time, in the chorus. They drank to black jokes.

Pedro recalled another ballad, which they sang. They drank. They sang, Juan keeping beat with a drunken boot. And after every song they toasted what Pedro called 'the article'—by a different name each time—smirking like naughty choirboys.

Article?' Juan wondered in his stupor. Why should 'it' be called just about everything, when there were so few words for the ear and belly button? Body parts had their aliases—such as 'bone box' for the mouth. But none rivaled the rich lexicon referring to 'the article,' not even the *membrum virile*.

"Pedro," he asked, "why are there so many words for 'the article,' so few for the nose?"

"No one knows." They roared like dunces.

"I bet I know a word for 'the article' you don't," Juan challenged.

Pedro took the wager, knowing Latin was in his future.

"*Pudendum muliebre.*"

"I lose," Pedro equably conceded. " *That* one I don't know. But I bet I know *more* than you do."

"I go first," Juan demanded—needing every advantage. And with a sly grin he said 'black joke.'

'Quim,' Pedro countered.

'Muff.'
'Miss Brown.'

'Tail.'
'Cock alley.'

'Twat.'

'Mother of all Saints.'

'Bite.'
'Cleft.'

'Shame.'
'Miss Laycock.'

'Pussy.'
'Brown Madam.'

'Nooky.'
'Churn.'

'Notch.'
'Mossy face.'

"You made that *up*!" Juan accused, indignant.
Pedro insisted that—upon his honor!—'mossy face' existed.
'Commodity,' offered Juan, after a pause.
'Crinkum crankum.'
Juan did not challenge him, hearing the insane ring of truth.
'Mother of all Souls,' he muttered, beginning to invent.
Pedro narrowed his eyes. 'Gigg,' he said.
"Gap...! The Gap!" Juan shouted, winds of alliteration blowing possibilities into his mind.
'Upside down jar.'
'Gash,' Juan proposed. Why ever not? And Pedro did not dispute him.
'Mantrap.'
'Mousetrap.'
Bull's eye again! But could he continue to reinvent true entries? And sure enough, 'Low beard,' earned a disapproving lift of eyebrows....
'Dumb glutton.'
'Miss Mossy.'
"Cauliflower," Pedro responded in a cautionary tone—that improbable vegetable the last reference to the locus of man's longing, not invented.
'Miss Orifice?' Juan was stuck in a rut.
Rolling his eyes, Pedro offered 'Cream keeper.'

'Garden of Earthly Delights.'
'Ploughman's pleasure.'

'Adam's Problem.'
'Cock's luck.'

'Delta of Venus.'

'Delta of Penis.'

They rang the changes, Pedro conceding defeat at Juan's 'Other door to Paradise,' for, however versed in venereal language, Pedro was no match for his *hijo* in invention. And he had intended to lose this wager from the first.

They went to bed, and were soon lost in mazes of that other black joke—sleep.

Morning hurt Juan's eyes, and the memory of yesterday was hardly to be borne. He rose nauseous, splashed cold water on his face, broke his fast on goat's milk cheese, strawberries and bread. Since Pedro had already left, he drank water without tint—a practice that his friend decried, as thinning the blood. Glancing at his notes on *mapudungun*, Juan went outside, yawned and stretched, admiring for a moment the false dawn of Santiago—the risen sun still occulted by the *cordillera*, snowy peaks glowing purple and pink. Pissing, as he admired the scene, Juan thought it strange to live in a place with nothing like a horizon for its sunrise.

He found Inés pacing by the door to the bedroom she shared with Valdivia. "He's in there," she whispered, "in bed. He refuses to eat or get up. Maybe you can get him to talk, at least."

Juan tiptoed into shuttered gloom, the Governor acknowledging him with a bloodshot eye. He was in his shirt, famed mustaches a total ruin, white beard very like a goat's.

"Leave me alone," he ordered, "to think."

And 'think' Valdivia did all that extraordinary day, emerging only to relieve himself and fill his *bota*. And when the second morning dawned—the Governor giving no sign of abandoning his bedroom—Inés decided that Santiago needed a distraction. After Mass, she announced that she was donating a cask of *tinto*, another of *blanco*, a roast boar, four fat geese and a dozen young roosters for a festival to be held in the town square. Despite universal gloom, her offer was greeted with a cheer. Inés had not mentioned what the animals were for, but did not have to. Everyone knew that these gifts were a respite from her disapproval of mortal sports. Today there would be feasting, general drunkenness, and the bloody pastimes of the *conquistador* at his leisure—goose riding, cock sticking, pig running.

Juan went to the stable to wrestle with the *mapudungun* verb, in which patterns were emerging. The particle *la* added before the ending, he had found, improbably created the negative. *Ayun*, which was 'I love,' became *ayulan*, 'I do not love.' Today he intended to begin work on the past tense.

Lautaro was done with morning chores, hunkering as he did something to his bow, and they worked in the smell of roasting pork now pervading Santiago. The past tense turned out to be *fu*, another particle consumed by the verb. 'I loved' was *ayufun*. 'I did not love' was *ayulafun*. The *mapudungun* verb as boa of Panama was beginning to lose its strangeness … and so was Lautaro. Juan had never known anyone this young to be as warlike, yet there were times—these days—when he could have sworn he was cracking jokes in his language, which of course Juan did not get.

The church bell summoned Santiago to its festival, and a rowdy crowd gathered around the casks being tapped on the gallows.

Juan took Lautaro to join the fun. Holding handfuls of hot, succulent roast, they cheered the pig running together. Two young boars had been greased, and on the judge's signal their tails were cut off. Squealing with pain and fury, they sprayed blood as they ran. The contestant who managed to lift one above his head while gripping it by a leg and the remainder of the tail could keep it. This difficult act was complicated by the fact that every participant cheated shamelessly, tackling and otherwise attacking anyone lucky enough to embrace a greasy porker.

As a *caballero* Juan merely watched. This was a sport on foot, and therefore for *infantes*—who did not mind indignity. What a riot! Even Inés was helpless with laughter. Lautaro too was grinning, about exactly what, Juan did not know.

Exhaustion eliminated many competitors, who rolled on the ground, laughing and catching their breath. Thirst eliminated others, gone for wine. Eventually only two were left, triumphantly elevating their porkers.

Next came the turn of the *caballeros*, who would compete in the cock-sticking and goose-riding contests. In the first, a dozen roosters were buried to their necks, looking like a row of frantic vegetables. The challenge was for riders to remove their heads with their spears while at full gallop. This was not easy. Also, it was potentially dangerous, should the point seat itself in the ground, unhorsing the competitor. Everyone waited for that mishap, betting on it. But today the audience was disappointed by the skill of the contestants. Cock heads flew.

Goose riding—first cousin to cock sticking—was the last competition. A goose was hung by its feet from a tree, the idea being to ride under it at a gallop while standing on your stirrups and pull its head off with your hand. The risk was that you might be yanked backwards off your mount if the head did not come off. Betting was heavy as to who would get the head, and who would be 'goosed'— that is, unhorsed. And indeed, one rider fell, breaking an arm to cheers and boos. Others missed. At last, one rode in triumph, goose head in hand.

Inés slipped away, and Juan found her at home. Valdivia had emerged from his extraordinary confinement, refusing to share the fruits of his introspection.

The next day—December first—Pastene's ship arrived in Valparaíso. After Mass, Valdivia announced that he was going to Peru. Villagrán would be Lieutanant Governor in his absence.

"*Virgen Santíssima,*" Inés moaned, knowing that Santiago would erupt without

Valdivia. And she led the exodus from the church by going—not home, as was her custom—but to a private garden where she grew the flora of Spain. Sitting under an orange tree, she removed her hat, her combs, shaking her hair loose as Juan sat timidly beside her. She looked through him into the past, the future.

"He wants me to go to Peru, too," Juan told her, wringing his cap.

Inés rescued the priceless object, smoothing feathers as she surveyed the pacific scene.

"Just to Peru...?" There were rumors that Valdivia might continue on to Spain to plead his cause before the Emperor.

Juan shrugged, unable to bear the anguish in her eyes. For Valdivia to have his authority confirmed by the Emperor, he would have to return with his wife.

Removing her glove, Inés lightly placed the coolness of her hand on his. "This is the first time he has kept me completely in the dark," she offered mildly enough....

"When young," she mused, "I liked nothing better than to mount, mornings, and ride until hunger brought me home. The distances I went!" She smiled, replacing the cap on Juan's head, creating a rakish tilt. Surveying the effect with canted head, she said she had been cured of distances.

Juan contemplated the garden, where the resident goose was eating slugs.

"I now prefer walls," Inés said. "Everything in this garden has a Spanish name, you know." Gesturing, she added, "And the sky has what might just as well be Spanish clouds and Spanish birds. *Golondrinas!* God love them!"

Juan agreed, "Very Spanish swallows."

"I hate forests," Inés concluded as she stood, piling her unruly, brilliant hair, creating order with her combs. She unlatched the gate, coaxing the goose aside with her foot, to leave her Paradise—and leave these moments in the sun-drenched garden, forever luminously fixed in Juan's memory. As for him, he was expelled without ever having dwelt there.

In the following days Inés was not so much absent, as absent-minded, until Valdivia taxed both Juan's allegiance and her forbearance. For some days the Governor had been requesting voluntary contributions for his journey, passing the alms plate after Mass and receiving little—the last expedition to Peru, and all its squandered gold, still fresh in the minds of the *vecinos*. Each day his pleadings grew more desperate, compromising his dignity, so that Juan became unable to look Inés in the face. He watched her hands clenching and unclenching on her rosary—like a heart beating to some erratic inner pulse—her fingers turning pink, then pale.

Nights, the tension at the table was palpable. Something was about to break— the only question being what, and when—in a drawing and quartering of the soul. So it came as no real surprise that—in the opinion of many—on December sixth

Valdivia's reason snapped. The day began with the usual entreaties at Mass, save that this time the Governor announced that he was voiding his order prohibiting *vecinos* from leaving Nueva Extremadura. All who wished to go to Peru could do so.

In pandemonium, the congregation genuflected as one, indecorously exiting the church. And two days later, the many who had chosen to leave were at Valparaíso with their hastily assembled possessions, Valdivia addressed the emigrants while standing on a barrel of salted fish, saying that those taking gold were required to release it into the keeping of the ship's captain. They would be given a receipt. On the beach, Juan penned the names and sums, his parchment on a plank supported by a wine cask and a bamboo cage containing chickens. By mid afternoon all the nuggets and coin were accounted for and loaded on the waiting ship. Done, Juan found Pedro and Inés grimly surveying the carnival scene—for Pedro had elected to stay, entrusting to Valdivia what gold he had not gambled. Inés, composed and pale, said this simply could not be, and Juan knew exactly what she meant. Valdivia needed men and gold to acquire men and gold, and he was emptying Santiago of both.

"That many idiots do not fit into one ship," Inés commented, oblique.

Juan nodded, thinking that the gold would fit, the crowd would not.

Valdivia walked up, taking Juan and Alderete aside for a whispered conversation.

Here it comes, Inés thought, hearing nothing of what was said. However, she could see the astonishment on Juan's face—which she read far better than his books. No conspirator, he radiated reluctance.

Inés' love and commitment had been cast aside, yet still she felt her loss as a great burden taken from her, wanting no part of what was being prepared.

Juan and Alderete ambled to the rowboat, where sailors had their oars at the ready. Then Valdivia sprinted seaward as the boat pushed off, hurling himself across the gunwale.

How more comic could this be? Inés wondered, as the betrayed *vecinos* stormed the sea. The only one who could swim floundered far as the boat, to be hit on the head by an oar.

Safely offshore, Valdivia stood to speak, Inés noting that—shrunken by distance—he was no longer laughable. In the burnished wonder of his armor, cloak billowing like the sails of ships propelling men to unknown lands, he looked like a miniature in a military book of hours. This was the Valdivia she once knew— yet a stranger spoke the words he said.

There had been a change in plan. More *vecinos* had elected to leave the colony than the ship could hold. All who contributed to the expedition would have their receipts honored—from his purse if need be—whether they went or stayed behind.

To this before God he swore. And, as seal and covenant, he knelt on a thwart to kiss the image of the Virgin that he had brought to Santiago attached to his saddle.

Juan remained with the Governor in Valparaíso, preparing the departure. Inés returned to Santiago, where—for the first time—she was a bystander to conspiracy against Valdivia.

By order of the Governor, De Hoz had been unchained. Exiled to a distant valley, he had been prohibited from entering Santiago, yet he had managed to conspire by employing messengers. And one day he arrived to lead a triumphant entry into the city, arranged by fellow traitors.

Their clumsy machinations came to the attention of Villagrán when Monroy handed him a letter from De Hoz, detailing his plan, asking him to participate. Therefore—as his first official act—Villagrán summoned the *alguacil mayor*, Juan Gómez, ordering him to arrest De Hoz, who was taken into custody outside the city walls, dismounted. In one hand was the handkerchief with which he was fond of gesturing, in the other, the ceremonial scepter of a Governor—the *vara de dos palmas*. Accompanied by whispering supporters, he awaited the signal to enter and be invested as Governor in the name of Carlos V.

This, Inés learned from Pedro as they hastened to the house of Francisco de Aguirre, where De Hoz had been confined. And there they witnessed the final scene of the tragicomedy that had Pero Sancho de Hoz as its principal actor, this time improvising on a script he had not authored.

Questioned by Villagrán, an *actor* was exactly what De Hoz appeared to be, dressed in magnificent cloth—albeit tattered by the Indies. In purple cap, black cloak, plum doublet topped by ruff, striped silk hose and black suede boots, the pose De Hoz struck was that of a thespian delivering his soliloquy—foot pointed on extended leg, weight shifted back.

Then, stripped of scepter, his every gesture encumbered by shackles, to Inés he seemed shabby, piteous.

He would not reveal the names of the 'other conspirators' he said—for no one had conspired. He merely claimed the scepter to which he was entitled. If anyone had conspired it was Valdivia, who stole what was *his* by right, and the gold of the colony as well.

So it went—recriminations countered by evasions—until Villagrán held high the letter in his hand, asking if he, Pero Sancho de Hoz, had penned this infamous document to Hernán Rodríguez Monroy, which elaborated his treasonous plans. The question was rhetorical, as De Hoz could scarcely deny the flourish of his signature.

The accused lisped that yeth, he wath the author … transfixing Inés. This traitorous clown *had* to know the consequences of what he just admitted. She was disconcerted by his quiet acceptance, for in every way it mimed nobility.

Then De Hoz folded his handkerchief—putting it in that strange thing Pedro called a pocket—preparing for a moment that allowed no gesture.

Villagrán condemned him to death. Yet before he did—as it seemed to Inés—he allowed silence to linger cruelly, making her think that there are moments when time stops, like a clock invaded by eternity. She had time—at any rate—to realize it was more than likely that Valdivia contrived all this by his absence, knowing that as De Hoz breathed, he plotted, that plotting he would fail, and that failing he would be condemned to death. While Valdivia could scarcely execute a rival with legitimate claims to an authority dubiously acquired—his lieutenant could do so without qualm.

Having pronounced sentence, Villagrán was terse. No one outside this room was to be informed. The execution would take place immediately. All would leave together when they had the head in hand.

De Hoz licked his lips, and then crossed himself—Adam's apple bobbing in his scrawny neck.

Marmolejo was summoned for the obligatory shriving, as Juan Gómez went to find Bautista, the *negro* executioner, for no white *vecino* would stoop to this office. All waited in the shuttered room, aware of what was implied by the orders of Villagrán—news of the execution would inflame the partisans of De Hoz, perhaps lead to civil war.

Furniture was shoved against the walls. The condemned—unchained—sat on a stool in the center of the room. Marmolejo arrived buttoning his cassock. Kneeling, he confessed De Hoz in murmurs, but their exchange was interrupted by the *negro*, who erupted panting through the door as the *ego te absolvo* was pronounced. He had been working in the fields and did not have the ax, just a hoe. No hood either. Ax and hood were at home. He had been told to come fast as he could.

Villagrán nodded at the *alguacil*. "Get it over with."

Juan Gómez unsheathed his sword, handing it to Bautista. Heavy as was the weapon, it was no substitute for the ponderous crescent of the executioner. And a human head could be difficult to lop off. De Hoz—who knew this well—did not waver or plead, lips moving in prayer.

In the absence of a block the *alguacil* substituted the stool on which the condemned had been sitting. Kneeling before it, as his last words, De Hoz said that—as the God he went to meet was his witness—he had sought only that which was his by Imperial Decree. "I die for my Emperor and for Spain."

He removed his cloak and folded it ... unlaced his linen ruff—starch crackling in the hush. Placing it upon the cloak, De Hoz crossed himself and rested his head sideways on the stool. And as the circle of soldiers removed their helmets, Inés felt sudden, astounding pity. Perhaps the posture…? On all fours, De Hoz called her beloved animals to mind.

On his knees, Marmolejo kept the crucifix before the eyes of the condemned. Clearing his throat, Bautista asked permission for a practice swing.

Marmolejo prayed—the usual signal for consummation. The *credo* droned. Bautista, perspiring, took three slow swings, each ending poised above the neck. Each time he shuffled to adjust his stance, nervously changing gripImmobile, De Hoz held his breath, eyes fixed on the cross. And at the third slow arc he licked his lips, glancing up at the sword, breathing with a gasp.

Bautista swung in a hissing arc, and did not sever the spinal cord.

De Hoz jerked, head tilted at an impossible angle.

Then he flopped like a half-cut worm as Bautista hacked, turning the stately ritual of decapitation into bedlam. Spectators drew swords and shouted instructions. Damn that incompetent *negro*!

Head off at last, De Hoz most certainly was dead, body shuddering with aftershocks, leaving Inés experiencing unexpected bitterness at this moment desperately longed for, the milk of expectation curdled by success. De Hoz was too absurd, too pitiable—and yes, too noble in his last moments—to be the man she desired dead. And his blood flowed forever.

The circle of *vecinos* stood in suspended animation. Bautista leaned on his sword, drops of blood and sweat beaded on his shaven skull—like separate kinds of dew on the ebony fingerboard of a *vihuela*.

The head of De Hoz ceased its gentle rocking … came to rest on an ear. Much of the chin—along with both lips—had been severed by a wild stroke. The bluish tongue protruded through a fleshless yawn.

Marmolejo resumed his prayers, and by addressing Eternity, returned the room to time. Ever the martinet, Villagrán barked orders.

All replaced their helmets. Pedro and Quiroga left to round up partisans of Valdivia, to escort the head to the gallows. The cloak of De Hoz was unfolded, his body placed on it. The feverish preparations halted as Villagrán dubiously looked from the scraps of flesh that had been the chin and lips to the head they came from. Perhaps he feared that the supporters of De Hoz would be angered by a mutilation, perhaps that the infuriated ghost would appear to him—as John the Baptist to Salome. He shrugged and had Bautista put the gobbets on the cloak. The ruff then was placed on the corpse's chest, and all was wrapped into a bundle. Aguirre scattered straw over the blood while they waited for reinforcements. Then they strode toward the plaza as a compact body bristling with swords and spears—a steel hedgehog. At the center of the mass of men went Inés and the *negro*, who dangled the head by its hair, keeping it low and invisible. The few with De Hoz when he was captured had been immediately—and secretly—confined. However, the many *vecinos* hastily converging on Aguirre's house had not gone unnoticed, so that all armed Santiago was aroused. Hands on hilts, screaming angry questions, supporters of De Hoz stalked the silent phalanx led by Villagrán. Had they been organized, there would have been bloodshed.

At the gallows Bautista impaled the head upon a stake and elevated it. Passionless, Inés ascended the platform to make public her support of Villagrán, who was attempting to be heard in bedlam.

Breathing the clear air of morning, deep, Inés looked over human greed, human fear, human hate, at the looming purity of the mountains, thinking she could learn to love this *cordillera* she once loathed. Cold and barren, immensely cruel, the flayed spine of the land she had chosen as her own was beautiful nonetheless. Years had taught her the many moods crafted on its immensity by sun and storm, passing cloud, snow and moonlight. Yet the mountains had not changed … she had. For good or ill she was here to stay, and she headed down the gallows' steps to breakfast.

Chapter 6: Inés de Suárez (Santiago, 1549)

Recumbent on sun-warmed stone, Inés laced fingers beneath a lazy head. Hat brim tilted against the glare of a January sun, she closed her eyes. Half asleep, she heard hummingbirds, seeing them in her mind's eye. Tiny green and crimson dawns, they hovered over the incandescent blossoms that were their suns— 'Chillko,' Blanca called the heavy-headed flowers.

Inés had surprised herself to find that—not just this astonishing efflorescence— the entirety of the scene surrounding her was lovely. The tiny cove was sheltered on three sides by trees, which made of it a wild room with a window on the quiet river. Brief years ago she would have thought the nameless profusion repulsive— even frightening—absent the improving hand of man. Yet here she was, sinfully *otiose*—relishing this word learned in the **Legenda Aurea**—pagan as some saint not yet struck by the bolt of her vocation, about to fall asleep before breakfast. Valdivia had been gone over a year, and in his absence she was deliciously corrupted, as if her ambitions went with him to Peru, leaving her indolent body behind to ripen. She was a peach warmed by the sun.

"Ineth, Ineth." Blanca's inability to pronounce the Spanish *s* created a charming—almost Castilian—lisp.

Knowing what was coming, Inés lifted her hat brim with a finger, too lazy to sigh.

From their earliest acquaintance Blanca had conveyed—through mime—her desire to emerge at dawn, not just to the outhouse. Inés refused exposing her to the dissipating airs of darkness. Yet Blanca persisted, and the day came that Inés caved in. After that the child left without fail at sunrise to return with her hair sleek, cheeks glowing. Then Inés accompanied her one day when Valdivia had for weeks been gone. Breakfast would have to wait, but who cared, with no master of the house to look hurt and hungry.

Inés knew that Blanca had been bathing somewhere. But in the *river*! *Naked*! A private place, yet still! Wide-eyed she saw her young maid strip as if it were the most venial thing. Undressed, the child loosed hair lustrous as ravens' wings. To her thighs in water, she took leaves from a pouch and pounded them, scrubbing until she was rubrous as the sunrise. Smiling, she slipped into the river.

The very *idea* of swimming gave Inés palpitations. Like every civilized human being, she had an ingrained fear of water that did not fit in tin. However, unlike many of either sex, who would rather die than bathe— and were sometimes buried before they did—Inés was no stranger to soap and water. She made the former from rendered lard, lye and ashes, to which she added ground clove for her personal supply, and every other day she thoroughly cleaned her hair and person. *However,* she did this at home, behind a screen. *And,* she used civilized water— hot, clean, confined by metal—not wild, cold and dangerous, wanting to drown you like this river in which grew nameless slimy things with teeth. Thank you, but no! She would lie in the sun with her clothes on, eyes closed, ignoring this Indian madness. Blanca could plead all she wanted, warhorses would not drag her into the river, bare as an egg!

Blanca beckoned like a siren from her element, cajoling in a Spanish become quite good. *"Ven. Ven, Ineth. Agua eth buena."*

Marveling at her *v,* her *b*—slurred, yet largely their Hispanic selves—Inés also marveled at the beauty of this child that was one no longer. She had never experienced the female nudity of others personally, yet Inés was certain that most women—even, perhaps, herself—would fail the test of emerging from a river naked.

Dismissing Blanca's insistence with a wagged hand, Inés wondered how old the child was. Thirteen? No denying that she was filling out with the disquieting rapidity of that Indian fruit, the *calabaza*. Not that she was *fleshy* to excess, like Leticia—that grub! Oh, no! Nor was she headed for an hourglass figure like her own. Deliciously slender, Blanca was rounded above, and below, the delicate washboard of her ribs. Time had also taken softness from her face, now almost as fierce as her brother's, in some moods—with those high cheekbones and that arched nose. The time had come to display her in proper dress.

Somehow, the decision made Inés feel young and wild. Sitting, she removed her hat, and considered the river. Swept away by a freshet of indiscipline, she removed her shoes and stockings. Then she waded in, lifting skirts, whooping at the chill. Blanca laughed and laughed, bouncing in the water. *"Buena? Buena? Freshca!"* she cried out.

"Not bad," Inés lied. Then, going berserk, she returned to shore, indicating that she desired to be unlaced, and for the first time in her life felt a gentle sun caress her back. She sneezed three times, spreading her arms, taking the temperate heat on her entirety. Why—for so long—shun the sun? She loosed her hair. And wobbling on gently rounded stones—eyeing a school of quicksilver fish with deep suspicion—Inés lowered herself into cold clarity.

After—spread like clean laundry on the beach—they talked.

The leaves they had washed with were *killai.*

Blanca wondered why Spanish women—who did not go to war—painted themselves, while the men— who went to war—did not.

Naked as Eve before creating sin, Inés chuckled. Why did Spanish men *not* paint themselves for war? Leticia as her model in bad taste, she imagined kohl and rouge, lacquered lips and nails, plucked eyebrows, hennaed hair, on various armored men. She laughed so hard she hurt.

In return, she asked why Mapuche warriors painted themselves for war?

"All men are for fight," the child proposed—premise of her Indian syllogism. Living to fight, they had to become men. War paint meant you were a man. Therefore, men painted themselves to become men, to fight.

Amused, Inés thought women like Leticia painted themselves no less for war in a battle of the sexes. Not that the devious strumpet had conquered the Valdivia on whom she set her sights.

After a long and unsuccessful siege on the hand of the Governor she had been tupping, Leticia at last conceded defeat. Pointing what one might call twin cannons elsewhere, she quickly vanquished a *fulano* from Navarra. Rumors—cruel, yet perhaps well-founded—murmured that the copious widow married to become widowed quickly again, her new husband so consumed by some parasite acquired in Venezuela that it was a wonder he survived conjugal duties with a beached whale.

Inés said, "Some Spanish women paint themselves to fight each other, for a man."

Blanca was speechless. *Domo* did not fight *domo*. Well, maybe they did sometimes, but certainly not *painted*. This sounded like *kalkutun*.

Inés, in turn, was attempting to imagine a society with no priests or scriveners, lackeys or lawyers, coachmen or beggars, sailors or merchants, apothecaries or barber-surgeons, and the rest, in short, a people whose men were only warriors. What did Mapuche men *do*, besides fight, she asked.

They hunted, fished, made *ruka*. They burned and cleared fields. They made *wampu*—dugouts. And everything they did was celebrated by getting drunk on *mudai*. That was it. The women did everything else. "Men like roosters," Blanca summarized. "Fight. Do every work the hens."

Inés laughed … and saw that hummingbirds were hovering by *chillko*, shimmering. Looking down at her relaxation offered to the sun—the white body she so prized, save for the freckles—she perceived herself as soft and doughy, like bread let rise too long. What would it be like to dart and float—jeweled—in the air?

The *picaflores*, what were they in *mapudungun*?

"*Pinshe*," was the soft reply, Blanca adding that it had been her mother's name.

Inés knew the child an orphan, yet never pressed her for the tale. Today she heard it all…. How her mother died giving birth to three that should have been smothered with mud. How they had been allowed to live, adopted by a man called Ñamku and a woman called Lleflai.

Smothered with mud! Wondering at the endless strangeness of Indians, Inés fell asleep.

Raytrayen examined Inesh. She was softly snoring, the white of the arm over her eyes resembling milk. In contrast, her hair was startling—especially the bush between her legs, which shone like dark gold. And her spots! Inesh was a white sky covered with dark stars. A sky starting to turn rosy as dawn, she noticed. Touching her lightly, finding her hot, Raytrayen sprinkled water on her face.

Waking naked in the wilderness, for a disorienting moment Inés thought herself in a nightmare. Leaping up, she struggled into her dress. And only after Blanca had laced her, did she discover the shirt she should have put on first. Wadding it, pinning the moist weight of her hair, slapping on her hat, Inés marched for civilization, worrying as she went.

The savages of La Serena had been more belligerent than usual, and if they rose in arms others would join them. Valdivia might well return to find Santiago sacked—if he ever did return, that is, from Peru or Spain, from wherever he might be. No wonder, sighed Inés, that she now plucked the gray of ashes from the fire of her hair.

Then church bells pealed away her troubles. *Sangre de Cristo* ... Mass! And here she was in her worst dress and sun-bleached hat, hair cobbled on her head, shirt a wad beneath her arm! Better death than church like *this*! She flew by the astonished guard at the gate, taking a side street home, Blanca hurrying behind. The *vecinos* would already be congregated in the *plaza*. To remain unseen she would have to go by a back way, crawl through a window—for the Governor's house was next to church, in a proximity that conveyed the close relationship between God and his earthly representatives.

The measured bell tolled implacably, three times three, three times—the twenty-seven peals of the triple trinity—time enough for every *vecino* in the plaza to find seats ... but not Inés. She would be late for Mass. Santiago would be shocked, and wonder.

Hastening around a house Inés almost collided with Nemesis in the person of the former Leticia de los Campos Anchos, whose pudgy hand flew to her scarlet mouth, the gesture conveying that—whatever the disheveled vision before her might mean—it boded wonderful ill. Why haste along a path that led neither to church or home? And ... was an actual *shirt* bunched beneath the arm of Suárez, who was followed by a female Indian child, also half-dressed? Some suspicions bore slow fruit—but O!—they were the sweeter for the wait!

Any other day, Inés might have returned the greeting, vengeful heart delighting in the fact that Leticia was a parody of the caricature she once had been. Prosperity had turned her into walking custard, her bodice a slopping cup. Yet Inés sped away without a word, knowing that she had pressed the seal of suspicion deep into the unctuous wax of rumor.

Miraculously, she made it through a back window of her house unnoticed. As for Mass, she was so late her entry caused a quiet sensation.

Summers in Santiago were fair, Mediterranean. However—cloudless and warm as the next morning proved—Inés was not about to return to the Mapocho. No. Never again, being sunburned for the first time in her life! She glowed from head to toe. Her clothes were agony. And she was spotted as any cow, having been broiled unequally, a crossed leg protecting part of the other—as well as the fount of human fault between—so that she had a half white, half fiery, thigh, while her face wore a pale mask created by her forearm. Mercifully, her back and buttocks had been spared. Every morning Inés thanked the Almighty for His blessings, but today all she could summon was—*Redios!*—she was grateful to be able to sit at breakfast! She was grouchy as a pregnant sow.

Marmolejo strode in—insufferably hale—hooded hawk on a gloved wrist. Too tactful to comment on her appearance, the priest said he had dropped by on his way to hawk ... hem ... with Quiroga. Would she consider also joining him ... hem ... them.

Secretly repelled by the falconry she had a few times practiced, Inés said that unfortunately this morning she was unavailable. And she offered Marmolejo stale bread fried in lard—which seemed to her, on second thought, a representation of her present condition.

The priest rambled, endlessly, about horses and hawks, being an expert in breeding the first, and training the second. Ultimately he arrived at the subject of Valdivia's stable, left in his charge by the Governor. Young Lautaro, he said, was so hard working and talented, that he had not hesitated to promote him to head lad, despite his tender years. Also, the young savage had an uncanny ability to quiet hawks—that least tractable of creatures—so that he swore he fed them—*Tan cierto como Cristo es Dios!*—meat from his naked hand.

Hearing 'naked,' Inés shuddered.

The boy was priceless. If the Governor had not already claimed him for his stable he would have taken him for his own, and for his mews as well. And—here was a good one—Lautaro insisted that his father was a hawk! Har, har. The notions of these Indians!

When Marmolejo left, Inés finished what remained of her baptized *tinto*, idly wondering why savages named themselves after beasts, birds, stones. She tried on Hummingbird de Suárez for size, finding it intriguing. Inés de Hawk?

Lautaro waited outside the *ruka* of Ineshuar, squatting with other *yanacona*, pitying the magnificent bird Kiroka held. What would Ñamku think of a people that enslaved a hawk, deliberately blinding it with leather? No doubt that seeing was the very being of a hawk, and that Kiroka held his namesake dead in soul.

"*Peñi,*" Lautaro whispered to the spirit of the hawk, "when you are released do not return. Fly free."

Marmoleko emerged from the *ruka* of Ineshuar looking troubled and trotted off on his *kawellu*—talking to Kiroka as Lautaro ran behind them. They reached a field so recently deserted that last season's dry *uwa* stood between green stalks sprouted from unharvested ears. There, parrots were noisily feeding. Marmoleko and Kiroka slipped the hoods from their birds … loosed them. With a powerful beat of wings, the two hawks rapidly gained altitude over the frantic *choroy*, fluttering clumsily toward the shelter of their forest. And with heart-stopping speed the hawks stooped, striking in an explosion of brilliant color, bearing parrots in their talons, fluttering, to the ground.

Retrieving them, the *lik winka* urged their horses on, hunting along overgrown trails leading from one *ruka* to another. Some were burnt, others abandoned. Lautaro did not know why the hill Welen had been called that by Pikunche, yet it had earned its name with the coming of the *lik winka*, for around it *mapu* was haunted by the many *am* of *che* who had lost both lives and homes. No wonder *lik winka* feared the night, for here roamed the uncounted dead whose blood was on their hands—lost souls enraged, with no one left to visit but their enemies.

He beat the bush for birds and the hawks did well, downing many, two of which they were allowed to eat. Marmoleko eventually called a halt by an abandoned *ruka*—roof poles visible through decomposing thatch, like the ribs of a huge, dead beast. Yet, unaffected, the spring by it bubbled through a bamboo pipe into a stone-lined hole, overflowing down a mossy hillside thick with fern. The *che* who lived here must have loved this shaded place, Lautaro thought. Springs were reason enough to build a *ruka* near, and this one was on small hill so beautiful it saddened him. He felt the presence of the mourning souls. What did the dead that once lived here think of *him*, who did the will of the *lik winka*? He was no less captive than the hawks on the wrists of Marmoleko and Kiroka. Loosed to fly free, he returned to bondage.

Lautaro looked at the *winka* squatting by him—these ancient enemies become brothers in the family of cowards called *yanacona*. He looked at Marmoleko, laughing as he counted kill, more than half drunk on the *lik winka mudai* they carried in their leather *wethakelu*. He wore a white cloth with red patterns on it, and Lautaro knew it represented the two sticks on which they killed the dead man *lik winka* ate and worshipped—the *kalku* Keshukrishtu.

Suddenly he was overcome with revulsion, not at *lik winka* but at himself. He could kill Marmoleko or Kiroka—probably not both—because they trusted in his cowardly submission. All he had to do was walk up, slash a throat. Lautaro grasped the obsidian knife he carried in his pouch.

But to kill Marmoleko would mean the torture and death of Raytrayen, and Lautaro knew this well, since every seven *antu* he witnessed the punishment of *che* after *lik winka kalku* celebrated the eating of Keshukristu. And he knew also that when *lik winka* did not have the one they wanted, others suffered. If a Pikunche was foolish enough to escape without his wife and children, the right hands of everyone in his family were cut off. Then they were burned on the forehead with the marks common among *yanacona*. How much worse would be the fate of Raytrayen if her brother killed a *lik winka*! Lautaro had heard of the terrible retribution for this greatest of crimes. Hundreds of Pikunche—men, women and children—had been tortured, burnt alive, impaled … *che* whose only crime was being the first to come across the path of the avengers. Lautaro knew—and respected—vengeance. But to kill and torture those who were innocent and unrelated, especially *domo* and *pichiche*, was unthinkable.

Fingering the wood handle of his knife, Lautaro walked over to Marmoleko, who was sitting on a log drinking *mudai* by his *kawellu*, its saddle hung with prey. Repugnant, hairy, unsuspecting, the *lik winka* looked up, offering his throat.

Lautaro did not hesitate, for knowing that he could have killed Marmoleko was a victory in itself. Pointing at the horse, he grunted, taking from his pouch a scrap of cloth he carried to clean armor and harness. Then he wiped bird blood from the saddle of the enemy, spitting on the polished leather—maybe too vigorously—to soften the drying gore.

And that very day—knowing that fires of impotent hate would consume him if he remained with the *lik winka*—he had Millanti run to Ñamku saying that his task was done. He was returning with Raytrayen.

Inés was fitting Blanca for her first dress—a version of her own black, daily wear. Its neckline was modestly scooped, long sleeves puffed, the tight waist accentuated by a blossoming skirt.

Why was Blanca melancholy? Was her swarthy Galatea sulking? Attempting cheer, Inés put her hat on the girl's head—where it settled to the eyebrows—receiving only a forced smile in return.

What a change from this morning! Blanca had clapped her hands with glee when she explained to her—indicating the two bolts of cloth—that she would make her a dress and gown. The first would be black wool. The second would be cut from a bolt of white silk, said to have come from Chipangu, given her by Valdivia these many years ago in an attempt to have her abandon mourning. The gown they would sew later, as it would be a shame to outgrow such priceless stuff.

Inés had gushed, explaining—not just with the pleasures of generosity, believing that Blanca should hear as much Spanish as possible. This teaching method had worked wonders with the child. Also, talking was relaxing when your audience hardly knew a word. Saint Francis of Assisi must have felt similar freedom preaching to the birds—Inés imagined—watching Blanca run enchanted fingers over silk....

Raytrayen was in no way opposed to wearing a *lik winka kepam*, fascinated by this cloth that could not possibly exist—smooth as the skin of a newborn child, lustrous as seashells. What troubled her was the hushed conversation she had this morning with Lautaro, its sorrow piercing her present gladness like a needle. Why *not* want to leave *lik winka*? Standing on the table, she looked down at the astonishing hair of Ineth, who had bone pins in her mouth. She was tightening the *kepam* at the waist, where it was too tight already.

Raytrayen *was* sad … and torn. She liked Ineth very much. Still, no matter how well she treated her, and regardless of the *kepam* she made her—or whether she learned *likwinkadungun*—she would always be a *yanacona* to *lik winka*. Some were treated better, some worse, but not one was respected. Here she would be *ankeñ peñeñ* no less than with Mapuche.

Pedro entered, booming greetings—increasing the odor of the room even as he shrank its volume—growing abruptly silent when he beheld what he thought he was beholding in obscurity. If his aging eyes did not mistake, on the table stood Inés de Suárez in her hat—that singular figure. He rubbed his eyes in disbelief … and a second Inés emerged hatless from behind the skirt of the first, like the villain from the curtains of a drama.

"*Buenas tardes,* Pedro. Sorry not to greet you. I had pins in my mouth." Coaxing the figure on the table into a pivot, she cajoled, "What do you think of my creation?"

Removing her hat to curtsy, Blanca politely offered, "*Buenath tardeth caballero*."

Inés beamed, thinking the charm of the Castilian lisp at least tripled by the dress.

Pedro harrumphed, plucking hair from his beard out of moral indignation. A *cristiano* was a *cristiano*, an Indian an Indian. To put the cloth of the one upon the other was perverted. "I came," he grumbled, "to sup. However, the table is unavailable."

Inés gestured for Blanca to descend and poured not oil, but wine, on troubled waters. Unmollified, Pedro sat to wet his pipes, observing that his great guts were about to eat his little ones, so hungry was he. Blanca brought a trencher, and Pedro almost groaned with disappointment. Guinea pig! Inés persisted in serving this abominable Indian flesh as economical, Valdivia absent. Yet meat was meat.

Stoically he ate, as Inés nibbled on a tiny ham of the so-called pig, which was in fact a fat Indian rat. To top it all, she said she thought it good.

Too much in his present world seemed out of kilter, and Pedro decided to set things right, couching his opposition as philosophy—so as not to be too *personal.*

"Clothes," he asked rhetorically, through masticated bread, "what are they, if not the seal of God on man that distinguishes us from animals, who bare their scandal without shame. Clothes are the outward sign of inner salvation."

He ruminated his formulation. "Only Christians should wear Christian cloth," he concluded, belching.

Aggrieved at this oblique criticism of her handiwork, Inés wagged a tiny leg bone in the air, pointing out that though Blanca was not yet baptized, she could recite the *Pater.* Besides, many *cristianos* wore Inca *ponchos,* Inca hats. Were *these* the outward signs of an inner savage?

Wits fortified by wine, Pedro proposed that beings higher on the ladder of being could wear the clothes of the lower, not the reverse. "A river cannot flow up. Though men wear the feathers and furs of animals, animals do not dress themselves." Savoring the succinct elegance of his solution, Pedro proceeded to higher law—"Christ assumed the cloth of man, but man did not assume God's indument."

With ominous quiet, Inés said that Pedro put clothes on Negrito, God bless his little heart.

Wounded, that Inés had descended from the bloodless voids of philosophy—where he built the battleground—to an item of painful fact, Pedro objected, "He had to wear *something.* He was cold, only in fur." And—as Inés had brought the battle low—he would he fight it low. Voice thick with *tinto* and anger, Pedro said, "Indians are just higher animals in being able to dress themselves. Negrito was maybe just a little lower on the ladder." Setting philosophy aside, Pedro had turned to plant the feet of his belief on the ground of common folk, salt of the earth such as himself.

Inés shouted, "You say Indians are *animals!*"

"Animal enough," Pedro replied with vicious satisfaction. "They have no shame in nakedness. And even when dressed, they wear nothing under."

Remembering the river incident, Inés was speechless.

Then into her silence Pedro delivered a tipsy essay, speaking not just for himself but for all decent *cristianos*—save for a few pale-livered priests. Indians were people the way Negrito was people. Everybody knew that. They had two legs and the right number of fingers and toes, but they lacked a soul. Blanca—he wagered—would strip off her new clothes without a second thought, before their very eyes.

Blanca! Inés scanned the room, found her gone, and cursed the Santiago habit of speaking Spanish before Indians as if they were furniture. Leaving Pedro in mid discourse she searched the bedroom, finding only the unfinished dress, neatly folded, hat on top. No Indian bundle, either. Her little Galatea was gone, out the very window she herself had entered not so long ago. Inés collapsed onto her bed, numb with catastrophe. Then, sick at heart, she returned to the table where Pedro was mumbling into wine, fixing him with an accusatory glare so vicious that he left. And when that evening an angry Marmolejo reported that Lautaro was nowhere to be found, Inés said that she had given him—and his sister—permission to visit their families.

Next morning, she returned to the tiny cove where she had been naked in the sun. Not expecting to find Blanca, she sat and waited an hour anyway, yearning for magic to happen in her life. But no one rose from the waters, like the nymphs of old....

When Raytrayen ran in, insisting that they had to leave at once, Lautaro bundled his possessions and together they walked out the gates of Tiako. As it was daylight, no one noticed or objected. Traveling quickly, they were approaching their *ruka* in the hushed moments before dawn when—silent as a lifting fog— Ñamku materialized before them.

Raytrayen almost screamed. At night the mask was not so much black wood as the absence of a face, all the more startling in its snowy cowl, recalling the evil creatures of legend which, when they opened their mouths, had no teeth or tongues.

"I have been waiting for you." Ñamku whispered, leading them inside.

Lleflai awoke with a glad cry, hurrying to remove the wax on a clay pot of honey saved just for this occasion. How they had grown! How thin they were!

By way of welcome Eimi walked on his hands, making upside-down faces. They all laughed, and the parrot escaped through the smoke hole, complaining with the voice of an old woman.

That night Lautaro and Raytrayen slept under the comfort of the *degu* pelts of their youth, while Ñamku in his alcove whispered with the dead.

Raytrayen opened her eyes to the delight of being home. A shaft of sun illuminated the brilliant parrot eating *uwa* strewn upon the floor. In a corner, fat *degu* nibbled leaves. Whistling, Lleflai summoned songbirds to their seed, which she poured into small baskets fastened to the wall.

Lautaro and Raytrayen went to bathe in the pool that ended the cascade, leaping in from a boulder, kicking in the air, ululating like *pichiche*. Shivering, refreshed, they found Ñamku masked, awaiting their return. When all were sitting about the fire he said. "Last night I saw that Lleflai, Eimi, Laku, and I walked *willi* tomorrow."

Lleflai gasped. What of the other two *pichiche*? The *machi* replied that the future was as lifting fog. He had not seen Lautaro and Raytrayen.

Lautaro did not care if Ñamku had not seen his future—preferring it unseen, for him to make himself. "I will go with you. You may need a *weichafe*."

Raytrayen was as determined as her brother. "Me too."

Lleflai floated to her feet on a tide of happiness ... was stopped by the words of Ñamku. "I did not see your future, but neither did I see you, Lautaro, or you, Raytrayen, leave with us." Lleflai sank to a huddled crouch.

Embers in the fire pit hissed and popped ... and the *pillan* sent a tiny coal flying to glow by Raytrayen's feet. She gasped, not having chosen to be chosen. All she wanted was to leave. This sign was clear, however, and everyone looked at her expectantly. She fought the inevitable. "Ñamku," she said, "the *lik winka* think I am an animal. I heard them say so. How can I *stay* with them?"

The *machi* said that he had learned much from being *kulliñ*. There was no animal that had not been given some great gift by the *pillan*. Even the *kufull*—shelled creatures of the water that no one named a *kuga* after—even they, with no hands or feet, no eyes or ears, being little more than a stomach inside a rock, had a patience that *che* would do well to imitate.

Raytrayen knew her answer to this. "*Lik winka* despise *kulliñ* in the same way they despise us. No *lik winka* is named after an animal. They are not named after anything else in *mapu*, either. They despise *mapu*." She was angry, resentful.

"Are you certain?"

Ñamku trusted Raytrayen, yet was unable to believe her. *Lik winka* were *che* after all, therefore part of *mapu*.

Raytrayen sighed, feeling young and ignorant. Why should Ñamku place this weight on her shoulders when all she desired was to go home? Let *him*, the mighty *machi,* figure these things out. Then—recalling Ñamku had taught her that anger gave bad advice— she said, "I am not sure, but I think so. *Lik winka* never walk barefoot. Never. Also, they crowd themselves together like fenced *luan*."

Ñamku interrupted, "Stepping in their own *ngechin!*"

"Yes! Some *lik winka* do this, but not all ... not Ineshuar. She uses a hole in the floor."

"A hole in the floor!" Lleflai was horrified.

"Not her *ruka* floor! It is in another very little *ruka,* just for *ngechin*. And the hole is not in the floor, but on a *wethakelu* to sit on. I use it too. It stinks."

Raytrayen exclaimed, "*Lik winka* are like *luan* that build fences for themselves." And her insult ran deep, for though *luan* were prized for their wool and meat, they were considered mean and stupid.

Feeling devious, Ñamku commented that just because he did not see Raytrayen and Lautaro leave tomorrow, it did not necessarily mean that they could not.

When neither replied, he said that their leaving might have been hidden by his ignorance. They were free to let their wisdom choose....

"I know, Katrinir," Ñamku admitted wearily that night, "when I said 'wisdom' they were *not* free to choose. I knew it, hating myself. And I hated myself worse when they both said they would return to the *lik winka*."

When Katrinir was annoyed—or sad—he was less visible. Today he was the barest glimmer of his usual self. Still, a glowing hand—chill as the air—touched Ñamku. "Your head trembles on your neck, Mapuche."

As if he needed to be told! Ñamku *knew* he was tired! Tired of body. Tired of living. Above all, tired of *himself.*

"The *pichiche* do not think that they are wise," said Katrinir, voicing what Ñamku thought. "They did what they thought you wanted, because they think *you* wise."

The *machi* moaned, "What kind of love is mine?

"The only kind there is."

"You mean, difficult."

"*Yamai.*"

Ñamku complained, "You are supposed to *help* me, not just echo all I say, like the hills. I have to fight Kurufil before I die. It may already be too late for me to win, as you well know."

"I admit nothing," Katrinir said.

"Laku needs to have his dream, to take my place."

"I am just a fly upon the floor."

"From the time I had the dream that named them," Ñamku mumbled, more than half asleep, "when I first held the bone *che*, I knew I had been chosen, and that they were chosen also."

Katrinir buzzed, a fly.

Ñamku shrugged. "So I repeat myself. Is that worse than your repeating *me*, as I repeat myself?"

His love smiled, lifting a finger to his lips.

"Is love easier for the dead?"

"Not when they love the living."

"I knew it," Ñamku whined. "Now, I do not even want to die."

Katrinir laughed and the *machi* laughed with him silently, trying not to wake the *ruka*.

"I surprised you," he wheezed at last, wondering if laughter could kill the very old … thinking maybe it should.

"I knew you would."

Then Ñamku laughed so hard, so quietly, that it could hardly have hurt more.

The next morning was busily spent packing the few belongings they would carry. Then they ate as much as they could, of what food they would not take.

Ñamku was thoughtful, chewing squash and *poñu* roasted over coal, ignoring the grilled *degu*. And when all were sighing with repletion he stood to speak. "None who are leaving will return. This I have seen."

Lleflai exhaled ... a shuddering relief.

"Now I know what I came here to learn. The *mapu* of the Pikunche has been laid waste by the war and *kalkutun* of *lik winka*, and the *am* of the dead outnumber the *pellu* of the living. I have seen their eyes like crowded stars. They do not speak, and yet they see us. The silent dead are here."

Not even a gnat interrupted. But in the light entering through the smoke hole, motes of dust were trembling. Lleflai closed her eyes with fear.

"You only speak to the dead you love."

Everyone was puzzled, but they *expected* to be puzzled by the *machi*. Still, he shocked them when he added, "I am no less blind than white."

Disbelieving, Laku shook his head.

Ñamku ignored him. "You speak to those you love. You see those that you know.... Therefore, I cannot speak to *lik winka*, alive or dead. They cannot speak to me. I cannot see *lik winka*, alive or dead. And they do not see me. I have become many creatures, yet never one strange as a *lik winka*. They seem like *che*, and are not. They think they see me, and do not. They think they hear me, and do not. Perhaps they see, where I am blind. I do not think so."

Ñamku held a hand palm up, as if to assess its emptiness, and there the bone *che* appeared. Lleflai blinded herself with her hair.

"Keshukrishtu," Lautaro gasped, making a gesture against the evil eye. Raytrayen breathed, "The dead *kalku* that they eat!"

Ñamku went on. "When first I held the bone *che* I thought I was chosen for the new beginning. Now I know I was misled by ignorance and pride. *Lik winka* want to destroy the Mapuche, the Peweñche, the Williche, as they are destroying the Pikunche, and I am powerless to stop them. The thought has come to me that I was chosen, instead, to save your lives, that you might save the *che* ... for there *will* be war with the *lik winka*. You, Lautaro, will fight for your people. But first you must see them as they are."

Lautaro nodded, agreeing. The only problem was the waiting.

"Your task is more difficult, Raytrayen. You must talk to *lik winka,* and not from a distance. Now it is as if the *lik winka* are at the other bank of a great river deep in mist, which they intend to cross. Lautaro will defend our shore. You must swim through blindness toward theirs." The *machi* paused, knowing the cruelty of his counsel.

Wide-eyed, Raytrayen said nothing, tempted to blurt that *lik winka* did not swim at all.

"At the middle of the river—where no *che* can live—you must talk to the *lik winka*. Then, you both *must* return to your own shores, each able to speak about the other."

Ñamku did not voice his fear that Raytrayen might be tempted to stay there—having experienced the seduction of these strangers. They called, like the *shompalwe* of the night, luring the daughters of *che* to that death which was a change of soul. He was handing to Raytrayen not just the task, but also the attraction, he had once thought his.

To Laku he said, "As Lautaro must defend the shore and Raytrayen leave it to return, you must *be* the shore itself, a part of *mapu*. You may wonder how important it is to become what you already are, but I tell you that in the future nothing will be more important than for Mapuche to remain what the beginning made us. I fear this new beginning will create a path for us we did not choose ourselves, for if we do not destroy the *lik winka*, we must share *mapu* with them. Then their power—their difference—will attract other *che* as it attracted me. We must learn what *lik winka* are, not become them. And above all things we must not desire to *be* as they are!

I have spoken."

Saying farewell to Lautaro and Raytrayen, Ñamku did not add that to defeat *lik winka* the Mapuche might need knowledge that would destroy their souls.

The *machi* turned his face *willi*. And—as he himself foresaw—he never returned.

Inés brooded by the fire, contemplating her shrunken power, and change of state. With Valdivia gone, in the eyes of the *vecinos* she was turning into just another woman, which in the Indies often meant a whore—an aging one at that, fortieth year almost upon her. Loathing inactivity, she chopped Spanish garlic, and, as it fried in lard, chopped Spanish onions ... threw them in. Passing up *papas*, she cracked Spanish eggs from chickens whose ancestors had survived the Atacama, determined to make herself a *truly* Spanish omelet—save for the olive oil—with her Spanish hands. And she was almost done when Blanca entered after tapping politely, to stand there in her native rags, the very image of uncertainty.

For Inés the sudden sight almost proved too much—proof of how excessively fond she had become. But she did not break like some egg. Taking a deep breath, she welcomed her, and—in Spanish—asked if she was hungry.

They ate the omelet with fresh bread, Blanca saying that it was good.

Inés smiled. It was the *albahaca* that made the difference, she said, making the child pronounce the wonderful word for basil.

She did not ask where she had been. Neither did Blanca offer explanations. However, a rift had been created between them, never again to be crossed. Inés loved—God knew!—more than enough hostages to Fortuna. Why then dote upon an Indian liable to leave for good, and all too likely to die of flux, or pox? So, that day, Inés rebuilt the moat of propriety separating a servant from the castle that is the mistress. Not that she was unfriendly or unfond, certainly not *cruel* in any way. And she continued to do her best to civilize the charming savage. Indeed—not a week later— she finished her black dress.

Inés was contemplating her handiwork with satisfaction when there was scratching at the door and an Inca unfamiliar to her walked in with Diego de Cáceres. The usually jovial *vecino* was troubled today, saying that the Indian carried a letter to be handed to her only … from Señor don Juan de Cardeña.

Virgen santissima! Expected as the moment was, she reeled … and sat, as the backs of her legs contacted the bench by the table. She searched the face of the Inca extending the sealed letter as if *there* she might read some indication of its message, and all she saw was the **L** branded on his forehead. For an insane moment she attempted to read meaning in that livid capital, then rose to meet her fate.

Dismissing the messenger, thanking De Cáceres, she scrutinized the seal. The red wax on the ribbon that bound the letter was very like the pass of time, she thought, pressing permanent unwanted form on the warm flow of dreams. She did not need to break it to know her life would never be the same again, so that when at last she read, she did not scream….

Juan wrote from Arequipa. The Governor had been dangerously ill, his life feared for. But he was—*Gracias a Dios!*—recovering. They were waiting for him to regain strength before continuing to Santiago. There had been a revolution in Peru and Valdivia was the hero. As head of the royalist forces—answering only to De Gasca—the Governor had brilliantly defended the crown against the rebels, defeating Gonzalo Pizarro and his troops in the battle of Jaquijaguana, earning eternal glory for his name. However, enemies arriving from Chile brought false charges against him—accusations too many and frivolous to repeat. Fortunately, La Gasca had dismissed them as jealous fabrications, and more important, he had confirmed the Governor in his post. However, he had decreed that Valdivia could not continue in his irregular relationship with Inés de Suárez, and was required to terminate it no later than six months after his return to Santiago, at which point the Governor would either marry her to someone else, or see to it that she left the colony.

There was more … Inés not bothering to read. How cruel the sentence, yet how it illuminated forgotten caverns of her Spanish heart! For a mad instant she yearned for the days of glad discomfort in the Atacama, traveling to God-knows-where, bearing the seeds of Spain, riding that blank as if it were a page not just unwritten but unwritable. Now—Spain rooted here—how could she contest what civilization itself decreed?

She summoned Domingo ... had him cry the wonderful news that Valdivia lived, was confirmed as Governor, had fought brilliantly for the Emperor. Soon he would return.

The *negro* left ringing his bell, and Inés realized that, in part, she was weeping because she felt nothing like despair. It would be good at last to be the one determining her fate. No sense in waiting for Valdivia—or waiting out six months—as one who lingers on a deathbed.

Inés turned to the astonished Blanca, mute beside her. "*Lo siento, Blanquita,* but I am going to need the silk I gave you." She had decided to be wed in white.

Still—as a promise was a promise—she took Blanca to the ironbound chest that held her precious things. There, were pearls, gold and silver combs, jewelry she almost never wore, lace *mantillas* she put on for Mass, bags of gold nuggets sifted from rivers by her *indios de servicio*, and ... her few priceless bolts of silk from Cipangu. Inés tried colors against the child's cheek, deciding that red became her best. Taking charge of her life was making Inés giddy with generosity.

Blanca touched the silk—fascinated, but seeming frightened—reminding Inés of moth and candle. However, she herself was done with vacillation. Handing the bolt over, she said, "This is yours. Put it away somewhere, *por favor*. Then please go tell Señor Don Rodrigo de Quiroga that I would be honored if he would join me for dinner, the day after tomorrow.

She needed time to prepare the evening that Quiroga would never forget.

Chapter 7: Kurufil (*Mapu, 1549*)

Rain fell—so fine it seemed suspended in the air. And Lleflai labored behind the *machi*, uncomplaining beneath the cage in which the parrot and a pregnant *degu* kept melancholy company. Laku walked third. Last was Eimi, struggling not to fall behind.

He reminded Ñamku of an ant. And indeed they crawled like insects, the mismatched legs of Eimi granting the *machi* leisure that he devoted to gloomy contemplation. Out of his element in the day, he had also been denied the company of Katrinir at night, and in his loneliness decided that death—for the very old, at least—was less a moment than a process in which you lived increasingly in the past, losing interest in what lay ahead. Long before the end you walked backward, looking back.

If dying was to have the future turn to nothing, so be it. Yet the landscapes in which he knew his love were also shrinking in his memory—a loss he could not tolerate. And so it was that Ñamku walked wanting to die before he became older, walked wanting to die with *living* memories, walked wanting to die before taking another step ... which was peculiar for one upon a journey. Why leave life walking? Why put a foot before another, not wanting to arrive?

A wet bough slapped his mask. Angrily, he swept the air with his hands—as if clearing cobwebs—surprised to be ambushed by a plant ... and he heard the voice of the love living in him—vulnerable as the tiny crabs that inhabit sea urchins, which have no shell of their own.

Ñamku complained, "I am not alone when alone."

"Quiet!" hissed Katrinir. "You are *not* alone. You are leading the living, and they will think you are talking to yourself."

"They know better. Besides, speaking to you *is* like talking to myself! I am always putting words into your mouth."

Katrinir conciliated. "I *know*. But do you have to speak *out loud*?"

Ñamku was done with whispering. "I am done with the future," he asserted with trembling lips. "I do not want to *get* there!"

"What about Kurufil?"

That was—of course—the question, and the source of gloom.

"My burden should rest on younger shoulders," the *machi* insisted, querulous, ignoring his promises to Rayentru, the danger to Laku.

Unsurprised by the silence he had caused, Ñamku muttered, "All right, I will live walking backwards, getting older, losing memory and mind. Hope it makes you happy." He was getting perverse pleasure out of testing the love of Katrinir, slapping him in the face with his old age. Was he *losing his mind...*?

A test. Ñamku called up plants he knew, their names, properties and uses—this exercise of apprenticeship. Having reviewed only *liuto, kulen, pichoa, nilwe*—as medicinal—he objected to no one in particular, "I do remember many plants, but how do I know if one has gone missing from my mind?"

To this no one replied, and Ñamku put a foot before another, thinking that the only way to be alone was truly to annoy his love.

The forest passing by, he returned to the contemplation of a future losing its past, a past losing its future. His memories were not being actually destroyed, he decided, just smoothed like stones worn by water. Easier to handle they might be, yet they were not the wonderful rough things of youth.

This rain was a sign of home, he thought joylessly. Even at an insect's pace, perhaps tomorrow they would cross the Fio Fio, and soon after reach the *ruka*. Yet—walking the beauty of his *mapu*—Ñamku no longer had the heart for arrival, and as one obsessed he returned to memories of his love, who was now suffering that last death which is forgetting.

As a tree, cut, dies—Ñamku thought—and is burnt, releasing its soul as flame, such was his love, alive in being consumed, turning to ashes you could not again ignite. And, thinking this, he began to walk backward, seeing the eyes of the dead in their unblinking multitude. Then—imagining the stars as blind—he removed his mask.

Laku also walked a troubled path. As no *che* truly wanted to be *machi*, he desired the undesirable. It was like yearning to be struck by lightning, and hoping like an idiot for a thunderstorm. Ñamku could well counsel patience, he was thinking, when he heard the *machi* speak in two voices—his argumentative own ... and a softer one, conciliating. The eerie conversation grew heated.

Lleflai stopped in her tracks, blocking the path. "The dead," she croaked to Laku. "Ñamku is arguing with the dead."

Walking backwards now, the *machi* went around a bend, still speaking.

Immediately after, Laku heard a thump. Slipping his tumpline, he ran ... saw a flash of white tumbling down a ravine. He tripped and fell ... slid face-first down the muddy hillside.

Ñamku was twisted on his side in a rivulet swollen by rain, his mouth and nose submerged—one strange red eye open to the sky—unbraided hair undulating like white waterweed. Laku lifted his head and blood poured down the face, pooling in the eye sockets. He pressed a corner of his *makuñ* over the wound.

Eimi ran up, exclaiming, " He is not breathing! Pull him to the bank! Turn him on his stomach!"

Eimi pressed on his chest. Water gushed. Ñamku shuddered, coughed ... breathed in heaves.

Eimi scrambled up the hillside using his powerful arms as much as his legs—a four-legged crab—and reappeared sliding down the hill. From a pouch he took a finely threaded needle, and began to sew the ragged gash on the forehead. "Where did you learn *that*?" Laku asked, awestruck. Ñamku had taught him too, of course, but on dead *degu*, scaled fish.

"It is good that the wound was cleaned by the stream," Eimi commented. And rinsing bloodied hands, he lifted his *makuñ*, reveraling numerous scars on his muscular torso. "In *renu* I fell many times in the dark. Chau taught me how to sew myself."

"Sew yourself!"

Lleflai appeared, sliding down the hill. She rent her hair. She keened.

"He is alive. He is all right!" Eimi scolded. To mourn too early was bad luck.

The *machi*, breathing regularly—if rapidly—was a fearsome sight. Alive indeed, yet *definitely* not all right. His uncanny eyes were open, pupils tiny, seeing nothing.

"If only he had worn his mask," Laku lamented.

"The rain has stopped," Eimi offered—that child born to ignorance and hope.

And what remained of the day was spent sewing a blanket onto saplings felled with a flint ax, creating a litter they could drag.

The next morning the sun shone over a sparkling earth, and as Ñamku remained unconscious they took turns pulling him—which was not easy on the almost nonexistent paths winding through bamboo. Often they were forced to carry him over obstacles, around trees, at times for distances.

Two weary *antu* later they found themselves by the Fio Fio, Ñamku not yet conscious. They built a raft for him, and swam. Then, once they were well out into the current, the *machi* sat up, looked around ... collapsed.

"I am *alive*," he said, annoyed. After that he spoke from time to time, only occasionally making sense—as if communication were a hawk soaring in and out of cloud. For example, he cried out, "The *Fio Fio*," which was a fact. But he added, "The stars can see again." And so it went. Ashore he groaned, "My hip is broken, but ... who needs to walk?"

When Lleflai attempted to feed him honey mixed with *degu* fat and berries he refused, then complained about refusing, "As one half dead, I should have at least half an appetite!"

"Ñamku, you have to eat! It has been three *antu*," said Lleflai. He had always been thin. Now his flesh was tight as drum skins over bone, his soul burning like coals in the sunken sockets of his eyes.

"How can I eat while absent," he objected weakly, going to sleep. Lleflai wandered away through bamboo, weeping.

Finding her, Laku said, "He needs to die."

"He needs to live!" she exclaimed, furious that the *machi* preferred death to his family. "We need *him*!"

Then in Laku something grew—more like nausea than a thought. He shivered, and like a gust of wind it passed. "We all die," he said, pulling her to her feet, and they embraced. Laku rocked her as she wept—as if *he* were the mother. Yet what he murmured was not what he was thinking—Did she not need *him*? And he wondered if Ñamku did not so much need to die—as he had told her—as that *he* needed him to die, to take his place at last.

That night—under the sliver of a moon—Laku found Ñamku whispering to the stars.

"Take my hands in yours," the *machi* said—as never he had before—knuckles cold as pebbles strung on thongs. He struggled to sit, saying, "My death is mine, not yours. We need to talk, so you can take my place."

"Replace *you*!"

Ñamku whispered, "Before Lonkimai speaks there are portents. Souls emerge from the sacred volcano to wander, weeping. *Kuyen* rises the red of blood over *dewiñ*. The *pillañ* send visions so powerful that even those who have never known them before feel them rising as an interior warmth with its own will. So it was when I first saw the *bone che,* and *mapu* foretold the coming of the *lik winka*. So it was and is, and will be, for you.

Forgive me, for I must lie down," the *machi* sighed. Eyes open to the stars, he was silent for long moments before again he spoke, and Laku bent to hear.

"All *che* see, which may seem simple, but is not, for seeing is *mapu* in us, and *mapu* is not simple." The *machi* paused, requesting water. Taking a sip he rasped, "*What* do you see?"

Laku looked about, perplexed. He knew what *should* be out there, but saw almost nothing in the dark. He would fail the test. "I see *mapu* at night, when it is hardly visible. I see many stars and a new moon."

"Excellent!" Ñamku exclaimed, through a racking cough. "*Mapu*! Excellent! Now, let me ask you, "What would *lik winka* see here?"

Attempting to see with the eyes of *lik winka*, Laku failed, and said nothing.

"You have answered my question," the *machi* declared. "What *lik winka* see we do not know. However, of this we can be certain—they do not see *mapu*."

Of course, Laku thought. The *lik winka* did not hear birds at night. How then could they *see* in darkness?

"That *lik winka* do not see *mapu* is the lesson their coming taught me. And that has made me believe that their whiteness is less important than their blindness."

Ñamku slumped. "You are what you see," he mumbled, falling asleep.

Laku kept a vigil dark with guilt. Holding the icy hand of Ñamku, listening to his labored breathing, he willed him not to die. And at dawn, he took the pulse of a neck little larger than a wrist....

Ñamku was distant when he woke, requesting food. Lleflai fed him *dawe* porridge.

"Who need arms?" Ñamku commented.

He ate again that evening.

Next morning he was able to feed himself, saying, "Who needs legs, when you have arms and a big mouth?"

Five *antu* later they reached the *ruka*.

Unable to return Ñamku to his dwelling dug into the floor, they put him by the fire, where he took medicine he prepared himself —the only sign he was in pain. Laku and Eimi repaired thatch. Lleflai released the parrot and pregnant *degu*— who wisely chose homecoming to give birth. Chirping, Lleflai attacked the chores of arrival, happy. She was in her *ruka*, and Ñamku—though he might never walk again—was eating, at least. Better yet, his wound seemed almost healed.

Lleflai began to unpack ... was stopped by the *machi* with words that for all their gentleness cut deep. He desired that she visit Wispu. Laku and Eimi would stay behind with him.

She noticed he did not mention Kurufil. Did he think it better that she feel unwanted than feel fear? Still, nodding that she understood, Lleflai undid the braid of the journey home, veiling her face to walk among the *che*. Then, bent less by what she packed than by her sorrow, she left.

Kurufil's small, black blowgun flickered in his mouth, and he risked the brilliance of a smile against his charcoaled face. They were back!

Drawn by the smell of smoke, he had seen the boy hurry by, distracted. Kurufil shadowed him to the *ruka*, where he was now standing by the fire. Behind the backlit figure he glimpsed Ñamku—prone, unmasked. Kurufil had never seen his face before, and it was uncanny. The glowing eyes seemed to light the place—even though he seemed feeble.

They talked quietly, Kurufil hissing at being unable to make out words, hissing again when the misshapen form of the *ifunche* became visible through the door. Silently, he removed a dart from his pouch, attempting to calm the trembling of his fingers ... failing ... thinking that if he killed the *ankeñ peñeñ* he would die too quickly. Or—more likely—he would not die at all, as Ñamku knew poisons and antidotes.

The *ruka* door closed.

Just as well, thought Kurufil, for time—not rage—was on his side. But, maybe he had waited too long. It would be a shame if the *machi* died in comfort, not suffering and alone, as he looked into his eyes. The *kalku* had promised himself that moment. But first he would kill the others, one by one. He smiled, bamboo tongue flickering through teeth whiter than the moon.

When Laku entered the *ruka* it was warm, dry, filled with the aroma of food.

Eimi was an enthusiastic self-taught cook, having learned in solitude. Kurufil would return to *renu*, hand him things. He would taste them and make something. Out of the cave, his creativeness had gone wild, and the results—owing little to tradition—ranged from triumph to disaster. This night he baked *uwa* cakes with herbs and *trapi*, wrapped in leaves, baked on hot stones, also a pot of black beans and *dawe*. Having waited for Laku, Eimi stirred in fresh herbs. Grinning wide— with a flourish—he sprinkled red flower petals on his black concoction, creating the effect of bubbling lava not yet cooled.

The food was excellent, though unfamiliar, and when Eimi slept Ñamku and Laku conversed late into the night. The *machi* began by repeating, as if no time had passed, what he said four nights ago—"You are what you see."

He went on, "And you see what you are. That is *kume mognen*—the harmony of things."

Ñamku often talked of *kume mognen*, and Laku had observed that—like the *machi*— it took many forms. Tonight it was an immense spider web whose invisible filaments touched everything, so that when a fly moved, *mapu* trembled. All things and living beings were one in harmony, which is why when the *pillañ* sent a message to the *che* they shook not just one thing or two but all of *mapu*, with a *nuyun*. In this way they reminded *che* of *kume mognen*. In this way also they made clear the connection between all things, for when something is wrong for one part it is wrong for the whole, and when something is wrong in one place it is wrong everywhere.

Ñamku took the bone *che* from his pouch, extending it in a cupped and trembling hand for Laku to examine. "That is why, when this *wethakelu* first arrived, there was a *nuyun*. The *pillañ* did not understand what they were seeing. Therefore they knew the bone *che* was not part of *mapu* and *kume mognen*. They knew that the bone *che*, the *lik winka*, their *kawellu*—everything they are, everything they bring—are not part of *kume mognen*."

The *machi* sighed and closed his eyes. Words fell like drops of rain around him, and it did not seem he could catch one.

"In *kume mognen* you are what you see. In *kume mognen* you see what you are. But the *lik winka* do not see what we see, or see what we are. Therefore they destroy both our mapu and us with strange innocence. For all their knowledge, they do not *know* what they are doing."

The mind of Laku spun. He thought he understood, yet what had all this to do with *him*?

"To be one with *mapu* you do not need to be *machi*. You can do much, Laku, simply by preserving *kume mognen*."

This consolation before its need, seemed a prediction. And Laku despaired.

"If you desired nothing, you would not despair," Ñamku chided. "Accept what you are given."

"How can a *che* not desire?" Laku exclaimed. "I want a *name!*"

"Desire what you are." And Ñamku did not mention Eimi.

Silent, Laku clasped his knees like a child in the womb—the position which the living sometimes give the dead.

Ñamku pressed on. "I will die soon, yet hopefully not before you do one thing for me." Handing Laku a small pouch, he said, "Go far and find a sacred place. Fast until the time is right, then chew these seeds and wait for your spirit helper—your *ngen*."

The future he had been living for was here, yet Laku worried he would go too far, not far enough, or in the wrong direction. Or, he would find the wrong place, choose the wrong time. His *ngen* would not come.

Ñamku became impatient, saying, "You could do worse than not be *machi*." And it was then that he revealed the shame so long concealed. "Kurufil was my first apprentice."

Laku leapt to his feet with a strangled cry.

"I gave power to evil," Ñamku admitted, not explaining, thinking—Was this simple honesty, or the vanity of living without excuses? "Yet in teaching *you* I have given power to good."

He extended both hands as if to weigh the air they held. "There will at least be balance when I die."

Laku went limp as a mouse in the talons of a raptor, mind racing with escape.

"I am in no way the equal of Kurufil!"

Then—hot with shame—"Thank you, Ñamku. I will do my best to deserve your trust."

"I never expected less—and for that you have yourself to thank. Now it is time for you to go."

Laku glanced at the pouch he held—all he needed for his journey. Surely there was more to be said and done.

"Kurufil is out there," Ñamku said. "You become *machi* by facing your fears."

Later, the voice of the night whispered, "Not bad, Mapuche."
Ñamku bragged. "All I had to do is trust him."
"All you had to do is fall. You planned!"
"It was my foot."
"Your foot ... my eye!" And so it went between them.

In *pichilewechi antu*, Laku walked toward the light cascading over *dewiñ*, washing the heights with pale color. Avoiding *che* he strode on without eating all that day, that night ... the next day. Perhaps he had walked far enough, for now *everything* seemed sacred, his hunger for food turned into a hunger of the eye. He walked that night, still walked at sunrise, wondering if exhaustion would choose the place. That evening he found himself in a grove of immense *peweñ*, their trunks like posts in a vast, living *ruka*, whose roof let in the night. And his eyes—dropping from the needle-shattered moon—saw *pangi* crouching, looking back with glowing, golden eyes.

Quietly, Laku sat, and cross-legged, he looked into the eyes of his *ngen*, so close that, breathing, they shared the air between. Calmly, Laku opened the pouch that held the seeds.

Eimi woke late, enjoying the brightness—which was *everywhere* when you left *renu*—sneaking in through thatch, pouring through the smoke hole. Laku had been gone five *antu* and Ñamku was asleep, harshly breathing. Eimi went to bathe, returned and dressed. The soup of yesterday was cold, but there was *poñu* he had covered with clay and left on coals. He cracked the blackened crusts, ate the warm, tender flesh. And picking up an ax, he left.

Kurufil threw his net.
A sun erupted in Eimi's head....
And he woke to darkness, nausea. He was trussed with rawhide, heart beating like a *kultrung*. His hands and feet were numb.
The *kalku* bent over him and said, "Now that Eimi are awake it is time to break a leg."
Bats fluttered through the echoes of his laughter.
Ignoring them, the *kalku* hoarsely whispered. "I believe you stole from me, *ifunche*. And I believe that you will tell me where my things are. Then maybe, if you are very good, I will let you live to serve me. However, since I know how stubborn you can be, let us begin with punishment."
Smiling, taking up a large stone, Kurufil shattered Eimi's good leg below the knee.
The *ifunche* bit off the tip of his tongue, but did not scream.
"Still your stubborn self," the *kalku* hissed, striking again. "Very well, sleep if

you can, knowing that tomorrow I will set your leg just like the other. That will unfortunately hurt, but you should thank me for making them the same." Laughing at his little joke, he excited bats into another flutter.

"After *that* I will make you a true *ifunche*—your eyes, mouth and asshole sewn shut. Also—as you probably know—your head should be turned completely backward, and it is not. So, after I improve your leg I will sew your eyes, then your asshole. Maybe I will not sew your mouth, so you can comment on what it feels like to have your head turned all they way around."

Eimi spat the tip of his tongue in his face.

The *kalku* smiled, wiping at the blood with his hand.

"Eimi do not know how hard it is to be Chau when Eimi are bad. I have decided to wait a day to improve your leg. This will give you time to appreciate your pain while I visit Ñamku. I believe he is alone and may want company."

Chuckling, Kurufil went to get the songbirds he had trapped that day. They would be delicious, but gutting and plucking them dulled his pleasure. He considered himself a *domo* as to beauty, yet never had enjoyed the woman's work that for many *kuyen* Eimi did for him—weaving, cleaning, and cooking. Kurufil weighed the pleasures of the leisure created by Eimi's labor against the gratification he would take in his agony and death. Maybe he would just blind him and sew his eyes shut. But then, would he be able to do his work…?

The *machi* woke to darkness, apprehensive. No smoke in the *ruka*. Where was Eimi? Quietly, he called out. No answer.

He explored, pulling himself along the floor with his elbows, ignoring the stabbing pain … but, nothing.

He complained, "I did not plan *this.*"

"Eimi are alive," Katrinir guessed. "Or Kurufil would let us know about his death, to gloat."

Remembering the eviscerated toads of endless moons ago, Ñamku agreed. "He will want to make him suffer, want to let us know he *did*. Maybe we have time."

Katrinir disagreed. "He could show up at any moment, and look at *you*, weak as a newborn."

"Why are you always right," Ñamku whined.

"I had time to think while you were snoring."

"Maybe I should die before he gets here," Ñamku offered—not joking at all.

"You do not need a hip to fly," Katrinir mused….

Sitting with an involuntary grunt—but smiling still—Ñamku countered. "You do not need a hip to die."

Katrinir was speechless.

And Ñamku had also shocked himself. "If I can surprise the dead, I can surprise Kurufil." The *machi* was ecstatic.

Laku shared breath with his *ngen*. And after, he had no memory of chewing—as if light could munch on seeds—for he had turned to light itself. He *was* the sun, his radiance on the countless fingers of the forest, stretched out to reach him.

Sense of time adrift, Laku feared sleep, thinking he would doze, lose himself in ordinary dreams. Returning to the words of Ñamku—bright grains of *uwa* on the grinding stone of memory—he rehearsed what he would do when Ñamku died....

Eviscerate him and dry his body over a smoking fire, then take him to the sacred cave high on the flank of Lonkimai, where he would place the *machi* beside his teacher in a row that stretched—body after body—to the beginning. There, he would take the dried eyes, dried tongue of Kalfuñamku from the pouch at Ñamku's neck and return them to the pouch of his teacher. To this cave Laku would return only if he were *machi*, carried there by the *machi* he had taught. And only if he became *machi* would he bear the dried eyes and tongue of Ñamku in his own pouch—to see through him, speak to him and for him, until his own death.

Become the eye of *antu*, now, Laku shone upon himself in beauty until, with growing thunder, the trees shook—splintering, toppling—as the earth gave way. Body disintegrating, he fell through spinning shards of sun that darkened, the motes of what remained glowing like roaring sand hurtling into night, then swallowed by the cave of death. But, in it, the sudden silence was not cold, the darkness not complete. The file of *machi* glowed like *rapu apeu*—the path of dreams—here in a starless sky, a radiance stretching to the beginning. Bright shone the eyes by their shriveled, silent, smoke-dark tongues....

Laku recognized the last of them. "Ñamku! Are you dead already?"

The *machi* did not reply, indicating the place empty at his left.

And it was that Laku at last rejoiced, knowing he would have a name. But, how return to the body he left behind?

Silence answered his unspoken question with a whisper that grew into a howl. And, as if swept over a waterfall, Laku dropped down to a shining river that was not a river, the phosphorescence of the *machi* reformed into a glowing backbone over which the eyes of Laku raced until—at the end of the cave of death—he arrived at his own skull....

He was an echoing hollow, eyes erupting through the sockets of his head like magma given sight, that *mapu* might behold itself as whole, from high.

Then far he fell, far into blind sleep, waking to weakness, hunger, dark. And, smiling, the one who had once been Laku said his name.

Kurufil left Eimi in *renu*—not before smashing his leg one last time.

Chau gone—panting with agony—the *ifunche* tried to loosen the rawhide binding his wrists with his teeth. But the *kalku* had knotted them wet and—drying—they shrank deep into his swollen flesh. Failing to reach the knots, he crawled that part of *renu* that was kept swept until—far from light—he was squirming, rolling, falling on guano. He had an impossible plan....

Leaving *renu*—as he thought, forever—Eimi had stolen the most precious possessions of the *kalku*, knowing that nothing could hurt him more. He took gold and silver, fine blankets, poisons and the curious weapons that delivered them, antidotes, medicines, wooden spoons, *rali*. Before that, over time, he had also taken other items that would not be missed, such as dried *uwa* and seaweed, needle and thread, rope, and ... a broken scraper. All this was hidden in a remote tunnel so difficult to reach that Eimi had trouble getting there when he was whole. Now—arms bound, leg shattered—how could he reach that obsidian shard?

The *ifunche* laughed ... and sneezed—having inhaled guano dust—not much minding dying at the moment. The joy of enraging the *kalku*, stealing from him—of stealing *himself* from him—kept Eimi moving. His unimaginable pain—his coming death—were well worth it.

The *kalku* reached the *ruka* at sunset, expecting to find Ñamku asleep, finding instead a corpse with not a flutter of a pulse, this insult to his planning sprawled in that indifference to comfort of the dead. Kurufil kicked the mask, would have kicked again, but he had hurt his bare foot. He cursed his foot for hurting, cursed the *machi* for dying, and cursed himself for delaying his revenge. He had allowed Ñamku to succumb without agony or intervention. A great moment of his life had passed him by.

The thought came that perhaps the *machi* had died suffering. Kurufil tore off the mask, and cursed the serenity revealed. The red eyes were open, plump, and moist. Ñamku had not long been dead.

Kurufil spat on the peace of death, pondering vents for his frustration, and decided that the corpse could wait—as could Laku and the others—now that he had a captive. He would blind Eimi, sparing the eyelids, sewing them shut. The pleasure would be worth the trouble of training a sightless servant. Blind, and lame in both legs, the *ifunche* would never escape again. *Kuyen* of slow torture would reveal where he had hidden what he stole.

On the way to *renu* the *kalku* checked his bird traps. Finding turtledoves, he wrung their necks. Softly whistling—forgetting his anger for a moment—he rebaited his traps with *uwa*.

Arrived at the cave, he worked the heavy lever he used to move the boulder that closed the entrance, propping it open with the log kept there for that purpose. Closing the door was a simple matter of knocking the log out. Opening the door from inside was far more difficult, requiring all his height and weight—which was why Eimi would never open it. And, when the lever was inside the cave, so was he. *Renu* was an utter black, embers slumbering in ash. Kurufil strode to the fire pit, habit stopping him at its edge. Fumbling for a stick, he stirred coals to life.

Perhaps he should feed the *ifunche,* making him strong enough he would not faint from pain. He would give him the good news, too—that Ñamku was dead, and the even better news that he had decided not to kill him, only blind him slowly. But, how leave the lids intact? Maybe—after immobilizing his head, somehow—pin them up with needles, dropping coals down on the eyes. He liked the idea of having Eimi's eyes see their last by the very light of their destruction. Kurufil could almost smell the moment. It was time to inform the *ifunche* of his plans.

Gone…!

Lighting a torch the *kalku* explored. Eimi could not be far, but that modest distance included an intricacy that Kurufil never took the trouble to become familiar with, and he almost ran down the nearest tunnel before reason made him stop. The rawhide would hold. Eimi would either fall down some hole and die, or crawl back out for food and water. If he did, his punishment would no longer be so merciful as a mere blinding.

Kurufil plucked turtledoves, calmer at the thought of food. He impaled the tiny bodies, enjoyed their eventual sputter over flame, wondering what revenge was left to him. Of course, he would mutilate the corpse of Ñamku and scatter the remains. But maybe, first, he would find Laku and Lleflai.

The *che* who had once been Laku woke, too weak to stand, looking up the trunk of a *peweñ*, which pointed like an accusing finger at a raucous pair of *traro* overhead.

"*Mari mari.*"

Peweñche looked down at him.

They had come to gather pine nuts they said, offering him some, toasted. They gave him water and covered him with a blanket. Later they gave him tea, dried meat.

When he was strong enough for conversation, the one who had been Laku thanked them.

Puzzled, the Peweñche stated their names, wondering why this Mapuche had so rudely not spoken his, or told them of his *kisuweñ*? Why was he so far from his *ruka*? And why was he half-dead? This reeked of *kalkutun*. Quickly they gathered their things, leaving a basket of pine nuts at his side, not wanting to anger the *pillañ* by lack of hospitality to a stranger—however bad his manners.

His legs seemed pliable as seaweed, yet *Pangi* staggered to his feet. He drank

from an icy stream, ate pine nuts, felt strong enough to walk, soul singing. He
walked, found several large *diweñ*—that fungus which only grows on oak. He ate.
He walked and walked....

He rushed into the *ruka* to find no one there, or signs of recent cooking. The
mask of Ñamku was face to the dust, white tunic beside it, empty as a snake-shed
skin.

Like angry wasps the questions swarmed, and Pangi was in terror. Taking a
deep breath he asked himself what Ñamku would do in his place. But his *pellu*—as
in a vast wood—roamed aimless through past teaching. Having traded his life for
a name, he had found dread, not power, instead. Exhaustion at last brought sleep.

Pangi dreamt he was paralyzed by a wasp, dragged to a sandy cave and buried.
There he waited for the hatch of maggots that would devour him alive.

Chapter 8: *Wichanalwe* (*Mapu,* 1549)

Wispu ran from her *ruka*, fast as her pleasant bulk allowed. Crying with delight, she embraced Lleflai as one might the survivor of a massacre.

Lleflai told her they were back—Ñamku, Laku, and … herself.

Though it seemed strange that the other two *pichiche* had not returned, Wispu did not comment. She led her friend inside, explaining that Andalikan had built her a *ruka*—that rare thing for a *wentru* with only two *domo*. She did not add in the presence of Laku that this was a bitter triumph, for while the place—small but comfortable—was hers, she had given birth to no living *pichiche*, so that when Andalikan was not with her she was alone. Worse was the reason for which she—the first wife!—had been banished from the *ruka* of her husband. Laftuipani, his second wife—who looked like, and bred like, a rodent—had whelped seven pointy-nosed runts, and Wispu had been crowded out by the fertility that the sorcery of the other wife denied her.

Forget all that … Wispu was being *wonderfully* visited. She turned to Laku, exclaiming at his growth, scrutinizing his seriousness for subtle signs that he was *machi*. Yet nothing seemed different or frightening about him.

Laku left soon as politeness allowed.

"Not one to talk," Wispu observed about a silence which could be said to comment on her own tongue. *Domo* were not to speak in the presence of men unless spoken to first. This, however, was not the case with young men. W*entru* were *weichafe*. Returning from war they could take a wife. But, how tell, when *machi* became themselves?

Andalikan interrupted her thoughts with his entrance, inquiring about Lleflai's health, that of Ñamku and the others, demonstrating particular interest in Lautaro. Time had made him fond of the hideously scarred *domo* who helped save his life, yet he could in no way reveal that fact, for *admapu* was *admapu*. He had already offended the accusing eyes of tradition by welcoming *ankeñ peñeñ* into his *ruka*.

Braiding her hair, Wispu gossiped after Andalikan left…. He wanted a third wife—to dilute the misery of living with Liftuipani, in her personal opinion. He had cut timber for a new *ruka*, but Liftuipani had been so nasty about his decision that he had not yet acted.

More news. Melillanka had married Waltuipan—who was more beautiful than ever!—taking her to his *ruka* without her parents' permission. In fact, he almost started a *malon* between their *kuga*, but—after negotiations—they agreed on a bride price. As for poor, young Marifil, Wenchalafken—who was three times her age—had taken her as his fourth wife. And, as he was *longko,* her father had given his permission.

Wispu—who in her barrenness saw *admapu* from the point of view of the children she loved the more for never having had them—strongly disagreed with this decision. Marifil—as the blind could see!—was in love with Weralaf, reason enough not to hand the poor child to an ancient. If she had a daughter like her, she would try to convince her husband to ask a bride price so outrageous that it would make Wenchalafken—who had the breath of vultures—hesitate. But no, he had gotten Marifil for—believe it or not!—two *luan,* ten chickens, five jugs of *mudai,* some clothes … just because the parents of the luckless girl wanted to be related to a *longko.*

Still talking, Wispu began to stir a bubbling pot of dye and yarn.

Lleflai went to the loom set by the door to continue the work there set aside, fixing the warp to the frame, plucking each strand of yarn, adjusting tension. That done she carded wool as Wispu touched on the subject of *kalkutun,* lowering her voice. Paillao had his *uwa* sicken and die when it was no taller than a little finger. And a *machi* found putrid meat buried in his field—that sure sign of sorcery. Lowering her voice further, Wispu said she was certain that Liftuipani had hired *kalku* to make her sterile.

Dogs barked outside….

Tuiñam was out of breath when he entered—no *lik winka dengu* on his head. He had run all the way from his *ruka*—Wispu and Lleflai concluded—the first wondering at the rashness of this public act, the second fearful for the vulnerable head, come all this distance on racing feet.

When greeting one long absent, *admapu* made it possible to converse at length without actually communicating, and this they did, eventually sharing *uwa* and *poñu* stew, until at last Tuiñam walked out into the night swinging the stick they gave him, keeping the coal end alive.

The night was dark as the mood of the *weichafe,* for—by revealing his unvoiced desires—his actions did everything to defeat them. He had no doubt Lleflai was laughing at him and his shiny *lik winka dengu,* even though he did not have it on. The brand he whirled seemed the embodiment of hope kept artificially alive.

As the forest swallowed the glow of the brand, Wispu thought that, like a beautiful snail shell, the most wonderful frienship could hold silent hollows. And she had not just Tuiñam in mind. Why had Lautaro and Raytrayen not returned?

Lleflai was also too aware of this silence she had promised Ñamku. So it was that the two *domo* went to bed sharing everything but their most profound concerns.

And next morning they did not speak of their nightmares before breakfast, for fear they might come true.

So went the *antu*. They finished dyeing yarn, setting the color by boiling it a second time in black earth and putrid urine. They pounded and smoked *loko* over a slow fire—as Andalikan had bartered for that delicacy from the great sea. They gardened. They washed the yarn and dried it on a frame. They wove. The days passed like ants, the *domo* settling into a domestic round so comfortable it mimicked happiness.

Tuiñam did not again visit, and neither did others—especially Laftuipani, making a point of never coming near. However, she could be heard from distances, lecturing her *pichiche* on the importance of avoiding *ankeñ peñeñ*.

Occasionally, formally, Andalikan thoughtfully brought meat, honey, sea salt … other signs of his affection. He also ate with them a time or two, yet never spent the night.

In Lleflai this pleasant routine caused a starvation of the soul that was the absence of her *pichiche*. She worried about Lautaro and Raytrayen, who were in the vile power of *lik winka*. Also, she was tormented at every waking moment by the supernatural battle she imagined taking place between Ñamku and the *kalku*. And what of Laku?

The eyes of Pangi opened to a dark without embers. Disoriented, he remembered being consumed alive by a giant worm. Then, the shape that was Ñamku appeared as a shooting star that fell to *mapu* slowly, alighting beside Pangi. The *machi* had his legs tight against his chest, his arms about his knees.

Naked, and glowing like a firefly, Ñamku approved of the vision and the name. He added, weakly smiling, "I am not dead, just almost."

"Am I dreaming you?"

"Not quite."

The *machi* continued in a diminished whisper, "Trust your dreams, and … please find my body before it is abandoned by my soul."

"Where is it?" Pangi cried. But the glow, like foxfire, flickered out.

Pangi lit a fire by touch, using the spare small bow, the hollowed board, the fire stick left by Lautaro. And contemplating the inconstant flame he had created, he realized that only the disorientation of vision had kept him from finding Ñamku. Yet perhaps the *machi* had *planned* it this way, choosing to meet him as a *machi* first in dreams. With racing heart Pangi removed the mat that concealed Ñamku's underground retreat, and found him there … cold! A faint pulse, though. He covered him with every blanket in the *ruka* and crawled in beside him.

Long past *wun*, Ñamku stirred, complaining when Pangi had him drink from a bowl, "This is *awful!*"

"You should have taught me better-tasting medicine."

Ñamku heaved soundlessly with laughter. Then urgently, "Smother the fire, but use no water. Make it look as if it went out by itself. Then join me in the pit with food and drink, leaving no sign that we are here. The *kalku* will come soon and it will be impossible for you to drag me from the *ruka* without trace. Also, take this comb and put it somewhere."

They hid, listening, knowing at last that the *kalku* had arrived by the silence of the birds, followed by a faint creak, a sigh, a horrid, quiet scuffle above their heads. They waited endlessly....

At last Pangi lifted the lid of their pit into the light of morning. Reporting that the comb was gone, he exulted. "We fooled him!"

"He thinks me dead," Ñamku responded. "And I am inclined to agree with him."

The dose he had taken to mimic death *had* been, almost, mortal, the ruse shortening what little life remained for him—a time in which much needed to be done. If Kurufil thought Ñamku dead, he would attempt to entrap his *am* with spells while it wandered, vulnerable, near the body, turning him into a *wichanalwe*.

Pangi pulled Ñamku out of the pit, put on his mask and headdress, and began to beat on his *kultrung*—as the *machi* was too weak to do this or to chant, though not too weak to join in with his rattle. If they were wrong and the *kalku* was not in *renu* preparing to join them in a battle of spirits—finding them with their bodies emptied by vision—they would both become that horror they were attempting to prevent. He looked at the emaciated Ñamku, who was smiling—which made him look the more cadaverous.

The *machi* said with shaking jaw, "Do not fear, for fear bleeds purpose from strength. Do not worry, for worry is a poultice on a wound that purpose makes unnecessary. If you do not fear, you will not worry."

"The hawk and the puma have no fear."

"A Mapuche has no fear. Our beginning was a battle. We *che* were made to fight."

Pangi drummed and chanted—the tired rattle sometimes joining in. At some point Ñamku said, "Kurufil will want you to look into his eyes. Do not. He will arrive not in body but in power. See what he does." Later he added, "Beware appearances."

Pangi felt his head—that living clay—begin to alter, his skull shrinking as the jaw pressed forward, fur and whiskers piercing through, rustling like dried grass. And at last he shrugged his muscled shoulders, looking at *mapu* for the first time with the quiet of cold, gold eyes, in the forest where he was feared. He stretched up to claw a tree, powerfully ripping down a shower of bark, leaving sign and scent.

He waited then, alert, hearing the rustle of a beetle in dried leaves, the distant drumming which had sent him here, the drumming slowing to the calm beat of his heart....

The *kalku* was not surprised to find the corpse of Ñamku gone. But—although it would have given him great pleasure to kill the *machi* slowly—it was now important to enslave his *am*. Searching the *ruka* he found a comb holding long, white hair. Taking it up he returned to *renu*, whistling, where he began to make the *am* of Ñamku his. He took the mannekin of the *machi,* glued on it every hair from the comb, chanting secret words, smoking his pipe, preparing.

Deep in *renu*, Eimi reached his goal and fell asleep. As time without light is hardly time at all, he did not know or care how much of it had passed when he awoke. He explored his cache with his lips, found the bundle he needed, chewed through the braided bark that tied it, and had obsidian between his teeth. Time was then measured by the back and forth of his jaw, as Eimi—with careless joy—sliced swollen flesh down to buried rawhide. Sticky with gore, he was free! Using the liberated hand he ululated weakly, slapping bloodied lips ... then bandaged his wrist, splinted his leg. He ate dried fruit, putting more in a pouch with other items stolen from Chau. Then—on bandaged hands and one leg—he began the sightless path to freedom. He may have slept a time or two, but eventually he reached that place in *renu* that led to where the world was dark no more.

Eimi came ashore by starlight under a moonless sky such as he had never seen, alive with rippling color. Using a stick to support himself he hurried, and when almost to the *ruka*, was flung down by a violent *nuyun*. Standing, he heard the snarl of *pangi* ... inside the *ruka*! And he trembled with dread as the earthquake shook him. In the distance—like blood from a heart ripped out in sacrifice—fire pulsed from Lonkimai.

Pangi waited—heart keeping pace with the slow, steady throb of the *kultrung*—until the forest shrank around him. He shrugged the trees aside, snapping huge *peweñ* like twigs. He stood, so immense he knew his height not by the trees he crushed but by the dwindling of *dewiñ*—its snows now at the level of his eyes. He coughed his challenge to Kurufil, coughed again as mountains shrank beneath him.

Nothing, no one, could challenge him now, Pangi thought, even though he had suddenly gone blind. No, not blind ... his head was in the clouds. "Ñamku," Pangi roared, shaking *mapu* with his voice, "where are you?"

"Here," was the faint answer.

"Where?" Pangi thundered.

"White in whiteness."

Red eyes glowed through mist, approaching. 'Beware of appearances,' Pangi remembered.

"Beware of *me*," the cloud whispered, as—like a door slammed on sunshine— the cloud went dark, leaving only the shine of the eyes of the black serpent. "I did not expect to find you here, " Kurufil hissed—taking Pangi in his coils—black tongue flickering as it pierced his throat.

They struggled, crushing mountains. Pangi took the serpent neck in his mighty jaws, but—poisoned—he weakened, relaxing into the black embrace.

Hearing nothing more from the *ruka*, Eimi entered during the aftershocks of the *nuyun*. Soot sifted down from rafters and thatch as he searched the darkness, to find Ñamku twitching, mumbling ... and Laku had collapsed by him over a *kultrung*. Both were icy, faint pulses racing. This—thought Eimi—was the work of Kurufil. Ñamku and Laku were dying before his eyes. The sorcerer was *here*, but untouchable. And in *renu* his body would be defenseless in its trance. Picking up a blanket and stick—Eimi hobbled out....

After the *nuyun*, Wispu and Lleflai were again wakened by the clamor of dogs outside their *ruka*. "A puma...?"

Igniting the charred ends of sticks, they emerged whirling their brands and yelling. The uncertain light revealed dogs circling a shapeless mound of wool.

"My blanket !" Lleflai exclaimed—recognizing her work—words lost in uproar as Andalikan and his sons ran up, whirling brands with one hand, spears in the other.

"*Pangi* is under that blanket?" Andalikan exclaimed—attempting to make sense of the confusion seen by spinning light.

"Mine," Lleflai confessed—feeling responsible for what was happening. "I mean, I wove it." And—as it was made for Eimi—a terrible conviction grew.

The blanket parted to reveal a face known only to Lleflai.

"Eimi," she blurted in her horror ... about to cry out *atrutrui*.

Andalikan, barked, "You, who...?"

"*Who* is the *che* in the blanket?" Andalikan insisted more gently, seeing the terror in her eyes.

Lleflai hung her head.

Andalikan headed for his *ruka*. This was no puma, and no enemy *weichafe* either. Known only to Lleflai, he was *her* problem.

"Who *is* this child?" Wispu echoed her husband, once he was out of earshot.

"You," Eimi told her.

"Me!" Wispu mouthed, as the blanket-wrapped child reeled over to whisper to Lleflai, who—frantic—yanked her into the *ruka*.

Eimi waited under a risen moon. Lonkimai loomed in its distance—dark and silent, now. The murmurs in the *ruka* were pierced by a muffled scream....

When the *domo* emerged Wispu wore a blindfold—having agreed to help only if she would not have to *see* the *ifunche*.

The women carried a rafter of the *ruka* not yet built for the intended third wife of Andalikan, following Eimi to that part of the seashore where the paths—avoided by *che*—grew fainter as they neared *renu*. They reached the rocky promontory by the great sea—a dark mass rising from sand like an immense animal half swallowed by the waters of Kaikaifilu in the beginning. Lleflai fell trembling to her knees, wanting to cry out yet fearing to be heard by the evil that lived within. Jolted to a stop, Wispu opened her eyes beneath her blindfold.

Convincing them to pry open the entrance to the unspeakable was not easy, Eimi promising them that—once done—they could leave. Only he would go in. The *domo* did as he asked and scrambled away in a heavy flutter of *kepam*.

Entering familiar darkness, Eimi saw an unfamiliar green glowing in the fire pit—and a shaft of moonlight illuminating a rising twist of poisoned smoke. Coughing, he found Chau cross-legged in his trance. The unmasked mannekin of Ñamku was suspended in the smoke, bound by thongs that trapped his soul. And when the *ifunche* began to release the *machi* from his spirit bonds, the eyes of the *kalku* opened—slow as a black dawn. Eimi fumbled as they focused on him, the pupils immense and blank.

"You," Kurufil said, with a voice from an abyss.

Eimi untied the mannekin, then had it in his hand. He felt faint. His head was spinning.

The *kalku* rumbled, "Do not do this, or I will have your soul as well."

Eimi shuffled to behind the *kalku* ... pressed the shard of obsidian to his throat. Now! he told himself.

Kurufil closed his eyes. But—though he trembled with hatred—Eimi did nothing.

"I would have killed me, in your place," the *kalku* said, eventually.

That, Eimi could not deny. His hate had not been equal to his plan. But what he did next he had not planned. With a shriek he swung his stick, shattering the knee of the *kalku*, spinning him around.

Eimi fell, for only one leg supported him, and he was looking directly into the awful eyes of Chau. *Mapu* heaved beneath him, like an evil, living thing. "I *will* have your soul for this," the black snake hissed, eyes widening.

The soul of Eimi began to flutter from his body, yet he was able to avert his eyes ... to stand ... to stagger toward the door of *renu*. The *kalku* followed, crawling, groaning, suspecting what his *ifunche* was about to do.

Eimi emerged and took an enormous breath, looking up. The shimmer of color had vanished from the sky, yet not the wonder of the stars. He turned to *renu* and—laughing into darkness, ignoring the curses that replied—he knocked out the log that propped the boulder. With a grind and thud the door slammed shut.

And Lonkimai at last erupted, turning the high, white eye of *kuyen* red as blood. Then slow ash fell ... and—at dawn—black rain.

Kurufil hissed as the coils of his body turned to sand, falling from the inert body of Pangi.

Ñamku had been losing his battle with the serpent when it vanished. Now, his soul skipped like a pebble hurled from shore over the heaving glitter of a sea ... slowing ... sinking into silence.

Long ago, Eimi had carved from bone the mannekin that was Ñamku, complete in tiny detail—even to the nipples, ribs and *ketrau*. He had made the clothes as well, and the diminutive mask—as Chau instructed—not knowing what he was doing. Now, he studied Ñamku. Smoke had blackened him, and—where the thongs trapped his *am*—there were stripes that were white shadows of his bonds.

He looked up. The black rain had stopped. A fine drizzle fell clear. Eimi was soaked and shivering with pain and cold. The *ruka* before him seemed a great sheltering beast—thatch coarse and long as the uncut hair of *luan*. He entered....

Ñamku and Laku slept, warm in their blankets ... the breath of the *machi* almost imperceptible, however. Setting the mannekin down—thinking that its safe return might be of use—Eimi brought the dying fire to life. He boiled *poñu* with dried *uwa* and *trapi*, crying and singing as he worked.

He cried. He sang. He wiped tears ... got *trapi* in his eyes. He cried the more. Eimi were home but Ñamku was dying. And it had been your fault for making the mannekin.

Laku woke and slept. He woke and ate. By morning he was more or less himself, revealing his new name. Then he and Eimi recounted their adventures—of the body, of the soul—sharing their worries about Ñamku. Each blamed himself for the coming death—Pangi for looking into the eyes of the *kalku*, Eimi for not killing him, and for the mannekin. They agreed that the *kalku* would not be able to open the door of *renu* for a long time—if ever—even with a pole. He might be buried for good.

Pangi left to get Lleflai.

She arrived, distraught, weeping, and they took turns keeping vigil. The second *antu,* the *machi* opened his eyes, but did not seem to see or hear. They told him what had happened. That evening—the uncanny eyes opening again—Pangi asked Ñamku if his *am* was present.

"Here and there, *machi*," was the harsh whisper. "In and out."

"I looked into the eyes of Kurufil," Pangi apologized.

"You did your best," Ñamku said. "You were strong and unafraid. Be proud, Mapuche."

The *ifunche* confessed, "I did not kill him." He did not bother to explain, for the *machi* knew everything.

"Good," was the whisper. "Better for him to live, than for you to live as he does."

Now Ñamku's hands and feet, his knees, were shaking. He closed his eyes.

"Lleflai," Ñamku murmured with the faintest of smiles, "I did notice, the *antu* you uncovered your shoulder."

At the last—as he could scarce be heard—they crowded by to listen. Ñamku faintly smiled again, and sighed, "I will be back—maybe more than you might want."

Later he was heard to say, "Do not forget the dead, or we lose interest."

Finally, he breathed, "*Mari mari,* Kangen."

Weeping, Lleflai undressed Ñamku. She washed him, combed and braided his hair. At dawn, when she went to bathe, Pangi removed his eyes, tongue and viscera. He dressed the corpse, putting on the mask and medicine pouch. Then—lashed to a rack, arms bound around the knees—the body was propped against the wall. Pangi beat on his *kultrung*, chanting, to keep the spirit of the *kalku* away. Lleflai covered her face, arms and hands, with mud and ash. She tore her hair, crying *atrutrui*. Outside, Eimi hobbled, yelling and beating on the trunks of trees— making all the noise he could to frighten away Kurufil, about to come for the *am* of Ñamku. So they spent that day, that night, but the *machi* did not reveal himself. Had Kurufil stolen his soul? Was he *wichanalwe*? In their grief they feared this.

The second dawn, using the wood of *foike,* that sacred tree—which gives off aromatic smoke—Pangi built a slow fire outside, and they placed the rack holding Ñamku over it. Lleflai was so overcome by the sight of the sunken eyelids, half-open over nothing, that she almost let go her pole—when to drop a corpse was the worst of things!—but she did not. And they began the slow process of preserving Ñamku. The viscera, Pangi ceremonially buried in a hollowed log, along with food, *mudai.* The eyes—pierced and emptied—as well as the tongue, he suspended above the smoke in a small *wilal.* Slowly the corpse turned a shriveled sooty black.

No sign of the *am.* Nor was Ñamku with Pangi in vision. Had he broken his promise to remain near?

When they lifted Ñamku from the rack he was as stiff and hollow as black bamboo. Where the eyes had been Pangi placed seashells with darker whorls at their centers, giving him a strangely lifelike look.

Lleflai washed and dried him, polished the teeth to the white they had once been, and with immense relief, replaced the mask—black wood over black flesh. She slipped on the white gloves, the leggings. Ñamku seemed himself again.

Pangi took the shrivelled eyes, the root-like tongue, and placed them in his medicine pouch. Tomorrow he would take the *machi* to his resting place.

At dawn—having put Ñamku in a large *wilal*—Pangi was about to leave, when a white butterfly came to rest on the black mask. He smiled, seeing it prepare to fly with that pulse of wings that makes one think they are breathing with anticipation. Then—like a leaf with soul and purpose—it fluttered into the air.

Pangi asked the soul—a far off voice—where it had been.

"I had my youth to visit," the *machi* whispered. "And by the way—I was too weak to tell you at my death—you all did well with Kurufil."

"Eimi made it possible."

"Still, I would have been *wichanalwe* if—by fighting Kurufil—you had not given Eimi time."

Pangi asked where Ñamku was during the battle.

"I fought within the *kalku* also … not well, for I was weak, neither dead nor alive, neither this nor that, a hawk become a hatchling pecking at his shell."

"We won, the four of us!"

"A battle which will not be the last," Ñamku replied, assessing the future. "And you might want to lower your voice. Eimi and Lleflai are sleeping."

Pangi returned to worry, whispering, "What will I do about Kurufil?"

Ñamku laughed. "What will he do about *you*?"

Pangi pondered *that* in silence until the *machi* said that he was tired, for dying took a lot out of you. And now they had huge futures in which to talk.

Pangi hurried to ask, "Can Kurufil make you *wichanalwe* still…?"

But what answer there might have been was drowned out by the insects of the night.

Kurufil had failed to enslave the soul of Ñamku, the body of Eimi. And he was crippled. But he was deeply happy in his own way, for he loved nothing quite so much as hate. Fortunately, there was food in *renu*. Water too, in jars. He ran out of wood, however, living under blankets in the darkness, healing, plotting, and hating the bats for flying out.

When at last he opened the door to *renu* Kurufil found his enemies gone, but Lleflai was a friend to Wispu. And he had planned to kill his way through others toward Eimi anyway. He would just work his way in from further out. A little more trouble. A little more killing. A little more time. But also more than a little pleasure.

Chapter 9: Blanca (Santiago, 1549-1550)

The campaign against the rebels in Peru had taken its toll of Valdivia, and he was fearfully gaunt. Yet in Juan's opinion the tribunal after his victories wrought greater havoc of the soul. Eight of his bitterest enemies—Hernán Rodriguez de Monroy, Antonio de Ulloa, Gabriel de la Cruz, Antonio Taravajano, Lope de Landa, Francisco Rabdona, Diego de Céspedes, and Antonio Zapata—accused him before La Gasca, president of the *audiencia* and representative of the crown. There were no fewer than fifty-eight charges, most of them ridiculously petty—of favoritism! Others were serious enough to put his governorship—conceivably his life—in question. Valdivia was accused of wanton executions, embezzling from the emperor's portion, treasonous language, the capricious taking of Indians and land from *vecinos* in order to give them to his friends, forced loans, and ... a notorious relation with Inés de Suárez—which included kissing in public.

La Gasca was magnanimous, confirming Valdivia as Governor, clearing him of all charges but the last. And after that sentence was pronounced—so light as to power, so cruel as to the heart—Valdivia did not break, yet it seemed to Juan that, like crystal with a hairline crack, his soul rang true no longer.

On the journey to Santiago Valdivia collapsed at Arequipa as he dismounted, falling on desert stones. He requested wine, furiously rejecting help, face burning with what to Juan seemed shame. And that night he was delirious.

Nursing the hero, Juan heard more than he wanted about what underlay the accusations of the trial. However, in the midst of much not lucid, one theme emerged dominant and clear. Valdivia loved Inés—not more than power, but far less ambiguously. Conquest was a rat's nest of scheming, politic lies, plots, assassinations, compromises—ultimate self-doubt—while his love for Inés was unalloyed, and perhaps more to be desired as impossible. A married man, Valdivia could no more wed Inés than he could piss upon the cross, like a Moor. And neither could he govern as a representative of His Catholic Majesty with a concubine by his side. The crux of La Gasca's justice was that Valdivia could have Inés or conquest—not both. And, Juan thought, having chosen dominion over love so gnawed at Valdivia that he languished precisely because to be confirmed in office he had denied his heart. Like Amadís de Gaula, he was sick with impossible desire. But unlike the hero of heroes— impossibly!—he had spurned his love.

Juan also was sick at heart, Valdivia's trial having put his faith in *him* on trial as well. Unhesitating, Juan summarily convicted the Governor of failing a hero's crucial test. He had once thought him the incarnation of that present version of knights errant—the *conquistador*. However, it was the love of Inés that pressed the seal of the *romances* on that honor, that splendor. Now, having publicly denied her, he seemed little more than a dishonest despot—no Amadís at all. Valdivia deserved the crisis of soul he had brought upon himself, in Juan's opinion. And if he nursed him he did this for Inés, into whose loyal heart this man would soon plunge the dagger of his treachery. Would she survive the news...?

The days passed, the Governor flirting with death. When it was clear he would survive, Juan wrote Inés a letter. But he had to get drunk to pen it.

The expedition reached Valparaiso in April. In May the Governor still lingered there, fretting about 'strategy' when Juan knew he was just postponing.

One evening, Valdivia liquoring his boots for this journey he could not seem to end, he slammed his cup against the board, exclaiming "I did it all for *her*." *Tinto* dripped from his mustache, thought Juan, like blood from a stiletto.

Juan treasured that commandment of the *caballero andante*—fatally compromised in this case by the past tense—yet he kept his anger to himself.

"People wonder why I left Peru, where I was wealthy as all Portugal." Valdivia gestured expansively with his cup, skillfully spilling nothing. "But does Caesar stop at riches?"

He poured, murmuring, "I know his immortal words—I must admit—only by rote. How I wish I could read Latin. To study Caesar in the original is my greatest dream. Perhaps one day you will instruct me in the language of empire."

Valdivia had asked this of Juan before, and he suspected that if the Governor devoted half the time to ancient language that he did to cards, dice and liquor, he would by now be an Erasmus. Still, as in the past, Juan said he would be honored.

Rapping on his armor with a knuckle—that hollow sound a reminder of the paunch lost in Peru—Valdivia lapsed into sleep at his table. And not for the first time in the last year or so, Juan removed his *bota,* doing the duty of Inés.

At sunset the next day, riders galloped into Valparaíso—Villagra at their head—with news of an Indian uprising in the north. The gold mine was shut down. La Serena had been destroyed. Even the women and children—God have mercy on their souls!—

were slaughtered. Only two *vecinos* escaped the holocaust. Hiding by day, traveling by night, they had managed to reach Quillota.

The news was indeed horrific, yet it returned the Governor to governance. And he barked his orders gratified, Juan thought, perversely, at this disaster that postponed Santiago.

A huge thump on the shoulder, and Pedro—far larger than memory—was there, laughing madly with joy. "*Hijo*, you are a man!" he exclaimed. "*Clavos de Cristo*! My horse gets slower every day!"

"Pedro!" Juan fought tears, thumping back. "Where's your armor?"

"Outgrew my steel."

Pedro was abashed. His magnitude was beginning to perplex him. "The armorer is working on enlargements. And as there was no mail my size—save for gloves and greaves—I wore quilt."

This armor of the Spanish poor slowed—but did not stop—an arrow, did little against a spear, nothing against clubs. With the Indians up in arms, Pedro had gambled his life to see him. Juan shook his head and smiled, thinking that wherever Pedro was, was home.

That evening Valdivia dictated. And after he went to bed Juan talked with Pedro, who was insatiable about Peru, particularly about the battle of Jaquijaguana, which he had Juan endlessly recount.... How Pizarro's men burned the bridges suspended over a mountain gorge. How Valdivia constructed another in the face of enemy fire. How—having crossed the river—they sat their horses until dawn by the valley which gave the battle its name. How at first light the four cannons miraculously brought over the river fired on Pizarro's army. And how the enemy ranks disintegrated once the royalist forces charged, so that the glory of the victory was hardly glory at all, for there had been no battle worth the name—only marching and hard work.

The whole thing disappointed, Juan told Pedro. This was his first battle against real soldiers and there had been no honor in it.

Pedro was differently disappointed. "One does not rebel against the Holy Emperor," he said, crossing himself at the sorrows of civil war, for good comrades had died fighting each other. "God and Santiago were not with Pizarro's men. And neither were their own hearts, either." Juan drank to that, for in his domain Pedro was wiser than philosophers. Pizarro's army had waged war on the collective Spanish heart.

He forged on, to tell Pedro about his own strange adventure. On their way north Valdivia put him ashore at the port of Hilo, thinking that riding overland he might reach La Gasca with important letters more quickly than the ship. But Pizarro's men captured him, and—although he managed to destroy the incriminating letters—he was condemned to death.

"No!"

"Absolutely, no trial either."

Juan would never forget the summary interrogation, the casually pronounced sentence turning the air pellucid, every detail of the horror preserved like bubbles in Venetian glass. A bored, unshaven, armored man, who called himself a priest, took him aside to hear his confession. He could still smell the garlic on his breath. "I think they were just after my horse and sword. They were going to hang me."

Pedro leapt from his seat. "Not the ax! What insolence!" Juan shrugged, for dying just seemed dying at the time. They were walking him to the tree when Francisco de Espinosa—who knew him from Peru— intervened and saved his life. He found La Gasca just before the battle of Jaquijaguana.

The moment came when their conversation was—if not concluded—less relevant than the muzzy pleasures of friendship marinated in wine. Valdivia had begun to snore, the whinny prompting Pedro to mention that his mount no longer would rear at the enemy with him on the saddle, so that recently he had been getting clubbed. Peeling back quilt he revealed a bruise dark as thunderstorms. One thing leading to another, they discussed medicine—leeches as against a plaster of warm guts. This led to the general matter of health in the Indies, Pedro of the opinion that here it was either a constipation due to lack of meat and wine, or Montezuma's revenge, which was due to Indians. Juan agreed. In these wilds there might be gold, yet there was nothing like a golden mean.

On waking, Valdivia decreed that, after the mines were returned to production, they would pacify the north.

The machinery of retribution was set into motion without Juan, however, for the Governor sent him, Pedro, and two others, with dispatches for Santiago. And they rode like madmen, Juan to see Inés the sooner, Pedro because he loved nothing more than riding like a madman.

In Santiago Juan assembled the *cabildo*, delivered his dispatches, gave his report and answered questions. As secretary he also recorded the proceedings— all this like an Italian automaton, moved by clockwork as it played a tune. Where was Inés?

After the meeting he asked a *vecino*, to find out he did not know the ancient talk of all Santiago. Doña Inés had, out of the blue, married Rodrigo de Quiroga. And these days she scarce showed herself in public, save at Mass. However, she was often at the chapel she was having built.

Pasión de Dios! Why had Pedro not told him?

Less walking than borne by dreams, Juan floated through a Santiago nightmarishly emptied of inhabitants—for many were gone, pacifying Indians—a Santiago of unfinished and uninhabited construction, erected for reinforcements not arrived.

The chapel was a raw skeleton of wood, its sacred nature indicated by a makeshift cross, limned against the evening glow. He entered … walked by tools of workmen who had taken up their swords.

Inés was praying, *mantilla* on her head, slipping beads through pale fingertips.

Kneeling, she faced the altar not yet built. Rafter-cast shadows were brutal as prison bars, on the glowing green she wore. Juan was incapable of speech.

"I knew it would be you he sent," she said, half turning and half smiling.

"The dress!" He had never seen her in anything but black. And now … the color of her eyes!

Dropping the *mantilla* to her shoulders as she rose, Inés took up a parasol. With shock, Juan saw gray in her hair.

"Your hair!"

Not up. No hat!

Taking a step over, Inés lightly touched Juan's face. "*Caballero,* you have said enough."

He obeyed with silence, knowing her precautions useless. Without uttering a word he was revealing *everything.*

Oblique, Ines commented, "I almost never ride, these days." She did not mention hats.

Juan was mute as any bone.

"I am deeply glad to see you," she went on. "But—as you know—a married woman cannot meet a man in private, especially when her husband is out of town."

Juan backed away, for she was absolutely right. In the past he had loved her in a suspension of civilization, as if, shipwrecked, they had assumed the savagery of the wild men of the woods on whose shores they had been cast. His had been a forbidden, heathen dream.

Inés smiled at Juan with sad, profound affection, wondering if taking slow steps back at times like this was something knights errant did in books.

"Wait," she said, extending her hand … stopping him in his tracks.

"Don Rodrigo has more than enough servants, so I took the liberty of reserving Blanca for you as a maid."

"Blanca?"

"My Indian girl, " she coaxed. "Surely you remember. I think you will find her Spanish remarkable. She might be of use in your study of her language."

Juan summoned the memory of a thin, young thing in wool … and a forgotten wager with Inés. But, what did an inconsequential servant have to do with the destruction of his world?

Seeing disaster in Juan's face, Inés relented, opening her parasol as she proposed that one last time he take her home. Silent, she did not put her hand upon his arm.

Under the penumbra of the parasol, her pallor was extraordinary. Juan yearned to bend a knee and beg for simple friendship. He was dying to ask about her hat. He even yearned to talk about her pigs, as gladly in the past. In short, he suffered a thousand vagaries of will during their walk, yet walk was all he absolutely did.

And when she reached her door, Inés merely uttered the formulas of parting, not even making the offer of a cheek.

Maddened by her sanity, Juan wandered off. Spitefully he thought that the ash in the fire of her hair betrayed a soul that once lit all the Indies, gone to coal, blaze quenched by sense and sacrament. He had not dreamed La Gasca's sentence on Valdivia—in its unfolding—would also be pronounced on him.

Juan found himself walking out the gates of Santiago, convinced that man was less kept from Paradise by an angel, than by failures of the heart. He roamed through fields to forest, numb, and the bells of curfew did not recall him. That night he slept on chilly moss—Man of the Woods indeed—as armies of reason pacified his lunacy. And when the sun woke him, exhausted, Juan trudged home....

Smoke floated from the chimney. He smelled roasting meat. Light shone through shutters. Pedro must be home, was his dull thought. Opening the door he entered without knock or scratch, and was transfixed. Not the new Inés—prudish and in green—but she of beloved memory, in black, was backlit by the fire!

"Inés!"

She stood and turned … the Indian girl.

With a curtsy Blanca greeted him, "*Muy buenath tardeth, theñor.*" And, placing covered dishes by the candle on the table, she said, "Welcome. Thon Pethro where wonder you are."

All Juan could do was laugh like the buffoon he was.

She smiled from Indian distances, proposing, "*Comitha? Fino?*" She added, "Thon Pethro eat, sleep, but it is chicken roasted left, potatoes with onions, bread." As she spoke, Blanca uncovered dishes in demonstration, reminding Juan that he forgot when he last ate. He sat, sorrow turned to hunger, as if one emptiness could become another. "Holy Mary, wheaten bread!" he exclaimed—through a mouthful of chicken breast, wine and potato—as the girl took a towel off the loaf.

"*Thí,* Thon Wan" she replied, pleased to comprehend, and happy to see him ripping off a chunk—worried nonetheless. Thon Wan ate with the fierce hunger of *pangi*, and his eyes were no less pale. She would much rather be with Thoña Ineth, not just because of her kindness, but because she knew *lik winka wentru* casually raped *domo*. And she had agreed to come to this *ruka* only after Ineth insisted that Thon Wan was a good man, her best friend. But just in case, she had slipped a knife between her breasts.

"*Ay, Díos mío!*" Juan groaned when the glad pressures in his stomach approximated pain, admitting to himself that Inés had amazingly improved the child. Her Spanish was recognizable. Her black hair was neatly combed and pinned up. In Spanish dress she more resembled those dark savages of Spain— the gypsies—than an Indian. Actually, she was better dressed, and far cleaner …

cleaner than *he* was at the moment, for that matter. He ran fingers through snarled hair, pulling out twigs. A small green caterpillar dropped to the floor.

"*Muchas gracias,*" he said.

"*De natha, theñor.*"

Her pronunciation was surprisingly true. The *s* was off, but the *d* of '*de*' was good—nothing of the Mapuche *th* about it. Speaking slowly—in a Spanish amputated for her ignorance—he asked if she 'make' the bread herself.

"*Thí theñor,*" Blanca solemnly replied. Then firmly, "*Theñor,* Doña Ineth not bad Spanish slow speak at me."

Amused by her Indian insolence, Juan took care not to grin. "Perhaps you can teach me your language," he proposed. "I know only the little Mapuche I learned from your brother."

"Not Mapuche, *mapudungun.*"

Of course … the name for the language of the 'people of the earth,' was 'things of the earth.' He had learned this from Lautaro, and it had slipped his mind.

Imitating the teaching style of Inés, Blanca spouted something incomprehensible in her tongue, arms akimbo. And she gestured, head dramatically thrown back. Juan had to laugh at the performance, so exaggerated and yet so right—save for the language. And she was costumed for the part. Yet—when all was said and done— Blanca did not *look* in the slightest like Inés, though she had wonderfully captured her demeanor. In any case, this was not the tongue-tied girl he had once known.

"Will you translate for me, Blanca" Juan requested. But she did not know 'translate,' for Inés had not diluted her instruction in the language of God and conquest with pidgin—much less Indian—teaching her pupil only the purest Spanish through repetition, pointing and mime, so that it took time for Juan to convey the concept of having a word in one language be the equivalent of another. Still—astonished at this early success—he could glimpse the value of what Inés bequeathed him. At his disposal he had—far as he knew—the only savage south of Peru that could communicate reasonably well in Spanish. He would create the first grammar and lexicon of *mapudungun*! There was modest purpose to his life again.

Exiled heart momentarily forgotten, Juan retrieved his journal from the chest where it had long lain idle. Then taking up a pen, sticking a candle in a loaf of bread, he was soon lost in the raveled *mapudungun* verb. Within the hour he achieved a major triumph, discovering the past and future tenses in a number of persons, after learning the word for yesterday—*wiya*—and tomorrow—*wule*— employing them to indicate the time, and using fingers for the number. 'I said,' for example, was *pin*. 'I will say' was *pian*.

To quicken the pace he set aside the verb—rebellious as its speakers—turning to the relative simplicities of lexicon. He had Blanca translate words, transcribing their Spanish equivalents in various categories—food, animals, plants and clothing.

He learned more *mapudungun* this one evening with Blanca than in the weeks spent with her fractious brother. Also, he partially solved 'the chicken problem.' *Achawall* was the correct word, yet could mean rooster also. When you wanted to be specific you added *alka*, which meant any male bird—and, it seemed, the male of other kinds of animals. There appeared to be no separate word for chicken, as cooked.

It was then—while still figuratively in the coop—that he decided to learn 'egg.'

"*Kuram*," he repeated after her. But Blanca had fallen asleep where she sat, as their lesson had lasted late into the night.

Kuram. Juan liked the word. It sounded Spanish. Take away the *m* and you had 'priest.' This made him think of Juan Lobo and the lost tribes of Israel. How was a priest like an egg?

Fearing one of his dreaded waking dreams, Juan looked over guttering candles to where Blanca had collapsed over her folded arms ... close enough that he could smell the pleasant fragrance of some pagan herb in her hair. Listening to her quiet breathing, feeling curiously paternal, he rounded the table and gently touched her arm.

Blanca jerked up and—in one liquid motion—yanked an obsidian knife from her bodice. Leaping to her feet, she sent the bench she sat on clattering. Juan muttered apologies as he backed away, aware that Blanca was a child no longer. And at this moment she was very beautiful in a fierce way.

He put the table between them. To reaffirm the nature of their relationship, he asked her if she had been baptized....

He was not surprised she did not know about baptism. Juan knew Inés was convinced it was the worst of luck to baptize Indians—maids in particular. Not that she disbelieved in the sacrament. O no! It was just that three of her servants had died after being baptized—in as many years—the magic number convincing her that there had been cause and effect. She had her theory—God waited for the moment that made Heaven possible to let good Indians die. Therefore The Almighty was granting heathens what amounted to a stay of execution in order that they might go to Heaven.

This was pure Inés, and Juan was sure that—were she God—this is exactly what She would do with savages whose time came before the fount ... reschedule. However, the clear-eyed devil which is the spirit of humanistic inquiry had prompted him to ask her why God allowed hordes of unbaptized Indians, good and bad, to die exactly when their time had come, not after.

She turned truculent. "God may work in mysterious ways—and that is obviously up to Him. Personally, I sometimes wish that He did not."

Inés was many things, and deep, but she *was* predictably herself. Were she God, *She* would not work in mysterious ways. This made Juan feel inadequate, for he was certain that, were he deified, He would be Absolutely Incomprehensible, understanding not even—and especially—Himself.

"Tomorrow I will explain baptism to you," he told Blanca. And with a 'buenas noches' he slumped onto his cot, enthusiasm replaced by trepidation and distress, for he had just realized that Inés had won her bet, and would never claim her prize. Was it too much to ask—the ritual peck of friendship?

Juan had not noticed—for Blanca's dress was black—that it was bloody. Drawing her knife, she cut her breast. And after Thon Wan went to sleep she took off her *lik winka kepam*, putting it to soak in water. She washed the wound and dressed it with medicinal plants from the rawhide bag Ñamku had given her. Unable to sleep, Raytrayen pondered the surprises of the day. Just when she thought she was getting used to *lik winka*, her perception of them opened on the impossible—like the doors of sleep. Today it had been not so much Thon Wan and his ridiculous clothing—or the language lesson—as the scratching he had done on thin, flat *wethakelu* with a feather, leaving a shiny mark like snail slime, but black, the track of a snail gone insane, going nowhere. The black water Thon Wan used explained the mark, but nothing in her experience explained the *act*. She concluded that he was magically capturing the sounds of speech with his scratches, since—returning to past ones—he could repeat the *mapudungun* she had spoken. Why want a word anywhere but in the mouth? Unnecessary repetition was a sign of idiocy.

Speaking to yourself was also a sign of idiocy, and Raytrayen remembered the many times Thoña Ineth did exactly that while looking at scratches in the *wethakelu* called a *lifro*. These marks were words waiting for a mouth to speak them. Yet why would anyone want to set aside words like dried fruit, when they could be had fresh from the mouth? When it came to words there was no winter, and no need to store them. Raytrayen decided to ask Thon Wan about the black marks tomorrow, and show him that she trusted him. He did not seem so much evil as sad and mourning something.

Her wound had been her brother's fault, she thought, annoyed. He was the one who insisted she not trust *lik winka*. He was the one who said she should never wear a *lik winka kepam*, that it was what the black *lik winka kalku* wore, that Thoña Ineth herself—with her spots, green eyes, and hair like fire—was *kalku*. Learning *likwinkadungun* was a *necessary evil*, said Lautaro, furious, when she replied it was not his place to give her orders. And he had given her the knife. Because of that she embarrassed herself, got cut, and hurt the feelings of Thon Wan.

He had blushed. She wondered if she had, too.

Tomorrow she would apologize.

Juan woke to a delicious breakfast prepared by Blanca. Fried onion rings—crunchy and tender. Fried lettuce—not so much fried as doused with hot olive oil and garlic. Yesterday's potatoes and onions—fried also—to which Blanca added chunks of leftover chicken, all seasoned with salt and a sprinkling of fresh *albahaca*. And crusty toasted bread. All in all, this was a Spanish meal—with the exception of the potatoes, and—that other native of the Indies—hot pepper.

Pedro liberally sprinkled *ají* on almost everything he had for breakfast, his reasoning being that a man asleep was like a fire needing to be revived. And in his opinion nothing did this better than hot pepper and *aguardiente*. He was liberally spicing his breakfast therefore, this morning, drinking Peruvian brandy, and going "Hoo, hoo." He was lit, all right.

"Not bad peckage," Pedro blared—a little crazy with relief. For this last month and more he had been tormented, imagining disaster when Juan found out about the marriage of Inés. Then his *hijo* returned, learned the news, and disappeared. Pedro had feared the worst—insanity ... suicide...?—for he was well acquainted with the moronic notions of love in the *libros de caballería*. But look at his *hijo* now, cool as the *cordillera*, eating with an appetite becoming to a soldier, composed, and as far from suicide as he was from Spain. Pedro had never commented on the transparency of Juan's worship of Inés, yet he had always thought it unwise as extreme, impossible of satisfaction, and derived from the baneful murmurings of literature. Great weights of worry were lifted from him, and he was pleasantly afloat on *aguardiente*.

"Not bad peckage, from an Indian," Pedro roared again, downing a cup as if he had just proposed a toast. He poured another.

Juan was astonished—not that Pedro was three sheets to the wind, at breakfast—but that he was consuming *lettuce*, which he usually referred to as 'the green snot of the earth.' *And* ... he was using a spoon to eat his chicken and potatoes, this implement which he avoided like bubonic plague, claiming it was only less sissified than the fork—which of course, like sodomy, he only knew in theory. He was also eating meat without bone, and calling it good. And finally—in a culminating summit of exceptions—he was praising an Indian with only the very faintest damn.

Blissfully sliding into swamps of stupor, Pedro belched. "Not bad peckage ... from an Indian!" He was stuck in a rut.

Juan looked over at Blanca, apprehensive, seeing that she was basting a sizzling rack of lamb—Pedro's second first course—and flipping bread on the grill. She winked at him over her shoulder.

Was this a Spanish wink learned from Inés, or was it some Indian wink of unknown meaning? Juan did not wink back, unsure as to what that would convey. Replete, he decided now was as good a time as any to instruct her in the rudiments of The One True Faith, preparing her for baptism. And he began *almost* at the beginning—having decided to leave out Adam and Eve, the serpent, and the fatal fruit.

"Man is born sinful," he began, and scrutinized her over tented fingers. 'Original' would be *way* over her head.

Her eyes widened with attention.

"Woman in particular," he corrected.

"*Pecatho?*"

"Sin is doing wrong." That simple truth Blanca *had* to understand. Everyone did wrong—especially the uncivilized.

"Many thing doing wrong. But *what* doing wrong *pecatho?*"

"Sin *is* just exactly that, the doing of wrong." Juan did not mention The Eyes of God.

Blanca wondered why, if doing wrong was 'wrong,' *lik winka* called it something else. She pointed to herself, "I girl. Maybe I wrong. You man. Maybe you wrong. Baby no wrong."

Juan was becoming frustrated. A servant still wet behind her Indian ears was questioning the verities that would save her soul.

Now she was agitated, standing, striding, saying that you had to do *something* to 'do wrong.' Babies did nothing before born. Babies little did *after* born, eat except. Eating wrong?

How could Juan know that Blanca was thinking of herself, who was *anken peñen?* And of Lleflai.

Juan had troubles with her Spanish—corrupted by excitement—yet no problem knowing she was troubled. Somehow he had twanged a raw barbaric nerve. She was correct, however, in claiming that babies do no wrong themselves. Eve was responsible for it all. And, indeed, it did not now seem equitable that the first of evils be visited on innocent children, when an adult committed the original act. But he almost groaned at the idea of beginning at the *beginning*. How explain a talking serpent?

He looked over at Blanca with a curiosity deeply tinged by admiration. She had absorbed that mannerism of Inés—this striding back and forth while attacking problems.

Pedro had polished off a jug of *aguardiente*, about as drunk as he could be with open eyes, thinking that this morning he might get from sleep to sleep without having had a day, and this was fine with him. He was petulant however, at being ignored by his *hijo*, who was discussing theology with a heathen. He had never much liked baptism anyway, as involving washing. It smacked of Jews.

Farting, he roared, "Babies…!" daring the Indian girl to doubt the Holy Bible.

And he concluded with the infallibility of all Popes back to Peter—"Babies are born bad because Eve ate the fruit."

Blanca recoiled from the outburst.

Slyly, Pedro added, "Eve ate it first, and that makes Sin her fault."

Having put the Indian in her place, Pedro passed out—slug on a log—leaving Juan to cope with consequences. Now he would be forced to recount The Fall of Man. Then, the questions....

Who was God? What kind of fruit? Was it spoiled? How did the serpent talk? What did it say? What was a fig leaf ... an angel ... a fiery sword...?

Marmolejo knocked and walked in, Blanca still inquiring. Juan had only managed to explain the fig leaf to her satisfaction—causing her to laugh, with strong overtones of derision.

Deciding that this situation had gotten out of hand, Marmolejo placed a magisterial hand upon her shoulder and pronounced, "All you need do to be baptized, my child, is learn the *Credo.*"

"*Cretho?*"

"A prayer. Don Juan can teach it to you." And Marmolejo ended the botched catechism by saying to Juan, " After Mass, tomorrow morning, I will baptize this beautiful child."

As Pedro was clearly not capable of talking about buying a horse—the errand which brought him—the good priest left blessing all, not without bestowing a parting shot. "Both idiot and Indian can be saved, as understanding is not required for salvation. All it takes is faith, baptism and good works. One does not need the *trivium* or *quadrivium* to go to Heaven." There had always been an undercurrent of jealousy in Marmolejo's admiration of Juan's learning.

Juan failed utterly to teach Blanca the *Credo*, bogged down in explanations that began with why God spoke Latin, and went on to His Nature. How He was three when He was one. How He begat himself. Why He was He, not They, being three. Why He was not a more impressive number....

Next morning Juan led Blanca and Lautaro to baptism, admitting to Marmolejo that he had miserably failed—Blanca only knew the first line of the *Credo*, without beginning to understand it. Lautaro, on the other hand, refused to learn a word.

Marmolejo benevolently contemplated the sullen youth. "No problem. One line is fine, and none will do as well. Just recite the prayer in their stead ... have them learn it later, if you can. We will consider this a baptism of intention. They showed up at the font, after all."

Baptize them Marmolejo did. And from that day Raytrayen's name was Blanca in the eyes of God. As for Lautaro, he became Alonso—Alonsillo to Spaniards, in the diminutive they accorded Indians.

Blanca never apologized to Juan for her mistrust of his intentions—when she had cut her breast. She made amends instead by memorizing the *Credo*, no further questions asked. Alonsillo on the other hand, persisted in his refusal. He was not undergoing daily humiliation in Tiako to learn *lik winka* spells. He was here to learn how they fought. And as *antu* passed, he believed he had.

Having pacified the north, Valdivia sent word of his return to Santiago on the nineteenth of June. And on that date the *cabildo* ordered the crier to proclaim him Governor. The next day the entire population— including *yanaconas* and *indios de servicio*—convened outside the walls to greet the hero of Peru. Waving branches of myrtle and cinnamon, they ran cheering beside him as he entered the city, tossing branches before his horse in a spontaneous echo of Palm Sunday. An arbor had been erected in the *plaza mayor*, and there the *cabildo* ceremoniously welcomed him. From its shade they reviewed the parade of *infantes* and *caballeros*, saluting the eagle of empire.

As secretary to the *cabildo* Juan sat that place of honor with pride. Eleven *cristianos* had left Peru with Valdivia, and now they marched in hundreds! However, of the original eleven, one was conspicuously absent. Inés de Quiroga did not attend the celebration, which lasted for the rest of that memorable day and continued late into the night.

We have Valdivia's triumphant return to Santiago from History, but only Rumor whispers his last meeting with Inés. It is said that when the Governor learned of her marriage with Quiroga he spent days in sorrow, silence and isolation. Told of the chapel she had built in his absence—this penance for their forbidden love— he visited at last to pray. There, *paters*, *aves*, meditation, brought serenity to his spirit, and he had risen to shoulder destiny, when Inés walked in at last. Perhaps he pleaded, perhaps begged or wept. Her will sustained them both, as it is said. And at that chapel Rumor separates the two forever.

Dramatic Necessity suggests that it was on that day Valdivia determined to leave Santiago never to return, seating his new capital in the South. But, be all this as it may, the Governor must have been irked at the alacrity with which Inés had married, because that very evening he proclaimed a bullfight. Two days later a wattle fence had converted the *plaza mayor* into an arena for a celebration that could be said to be the obverse of the coin of Valdivia's sorrow, as—in losing his love—he was also emancipated from her bizarre zoological affections. It was Inés, after all, who had never permitted this most popular of blood sports to take place.

She did not attend the festivities—this slap to her face. Quiroga did, however, along with every other *vecino* in Santiago—save for Juan, fated to be the exception to Spanish impulse. He abstained, partly, to protest this insult to Inés, but even more because he expected to enjoy the bullfight even less than a beheading, where blood at least was being shed for justice. And—since all Santiago slobbered over this formerly forbidden fruit—he left to share a language lesson with Blanca at the beach by the Mapocho where he first met her. There, the uproar was a distant drone.

Fluent in *mapudungun* he was not—confused especially by the multitude of particles devoured by its gluttonous verb. Yet, capable of rudimentary communication, he tried to explain a bullfight to Blanca, succeeding only in making her laugh. He failed to explain a bullfight in Spanish as well. It made no sense to him, either, he eventually admitted—this walled hunt that made a ceremony of death.

Raytrayen was surprised that he did not share a passion so important to his people, having thought *lik winka* alike in purpose and spirit, if not in body. Hesitantly she offered—in *mapudungun*—that *che* had a dish they enjoyed— *apol*—made by slitting the throat of a young guanaco, then stuffing salt and *trapi* into the cut. Hung head up, the animal inhaled blood and hot pepper into its lungs with its dying breaths. Blood filled, spicy, the lungs were considered a delicacy.

Attempting for the first time to meet a *lik winka* 'at the middle of the river', Raytrayen was astonished to see Wan turn pale, grow rigid, sweat and tremble. Without chanting, drumming, smoke or medicine, he was very much like a *machi* in *kuimi*—his trance.

Juan was undergoing reverie instead—for the endless instants it took to die— becoming a young guanaco suffocating in its own burning blood. And—as when, in dreams of falling, one wakes at the impact—he shuddered when it died.

"*Agnus dei*. Lamb of God, who takes away the sins of the world, have mercy on us," he whispered, struggling with the sacrilegious thought that the Mass—no less than bullfights—made a ceremony of agony.

Raytrayen hurried to explain. "My father no eat *apol*, no. Like *apol* not either, me. He eat nothing he become. Animal no. Animal with bone, no. Too, I no eat *apol*." She lifted shoulders in self-deprecation. "I *degu*, fishes, eat."

"He *becomes* animals!"

"He Ñamku because he *is* hawks," she bragged before his innocence. "He other animals too be." She added, "Ñamku be white."

"White! A hawk! Becomes *other* animals…She nodded pleasantly. "*Shi*, hawks. White than more Thoña Ineth."

"White or not, he is a *man*," Juan's outraged intelligence insisted. "Or he could not be your father."

Ñamku was not exactly her father, and not exactly a man, yet Blanca could not reveal these things, knowing what *lik winka* thought about them. She had seen two such *yanacona* punished after Sunday Mass with astounding brutality, forced to watch because *indios* who closed their eyes at punishment were punished also. So, she shrugged.

Searching the marvels of Pliny, Juan found nothing in his memory to rival what he was asked to believe. Yet the rounded Indian face before him was candid as the moon, though troubled by some cloud of thought. And the more Blanca argued in both Spanish and *mapudungun*, the less she convinced him that her father was a Father—*un padre*. That is, he was *machi*, something like a priest of the Mapuche. He was *not* a sorcerer! And—she was adamant—he talked with the dead. Annoyed that Wan did not believe her, Blanca revealed more than she might otherwise.

They returned to Santiago, Juan hammering at the fact that he had actually *seen* Ñamku—though not exactly, as he was clothed from head to foot, and masked. But nonetheless, he was clearly man, not hawk. How explain *that*?

"I have to see him to believe you," Juan insisted. Blanca stopped in her tracks and—without the specter of a smile—intoned the *Credo* in the deepest voice she could muster. Juan laughed so hard he could not see for weeping.

They walked in silence then, she thinking that if Wan *was* different from other *lik winka*, he might not mind her own difference. Their *pillan* was three in one. She was one of three. Maybe it would be safe to mention this ... or was this something *lik winka* tortured you for?

Juan was thinking that there might be something to this girl having a hawk as father. Gentled by youth, her face was still, in profile, fierce—as were her eyes sometimes. And her nose was nothing if not aquiline.

Turning—catching his intensity—Blanca hurried on, looking back, almost running into Cacafuego, who was emerging from the gates of Santiago with two *yanacona* concubines—young and fat, the way he liked them.

"*Caballero*," Cacafuego cackled—ignoring Blanca, reaching for a nostril with the black-rimmed nail of a little finger, searching for snot. He was more stooped than ever, and the hair straggling from his rusted helmet would have been snow itself if not encrusted by passing decades. Now that his every tooth had been taken by decay, he seemed an armored crone.

Juan made no sudden move. "*Buenos días, señor.*"

Declining physically, Cacafuego had prospered otherwise. Previously tricking enemies into death, he was now scamming *vecinos* into poverty. Yet—as the trickery of the moment required him to seem no less poor than the trickery of the past had him incompetent—his prosperity was only visible as a harem of plump, young Indian women. The gold, he buried.

Cacafuego had achieved his every dream. Still, he resented Juan, though not his power as secretary. It was his flawless teeth, and that *something* he seemed to have with women, so that not only was he rumored to have bedded Inés de Suárez, it was common knowledge that Rosita *La Bonita* would sell her immortal soul to have him hump her. *That* hurt Cacafuego. He had tricked men into death. He had scammed men into poverty. But such women as he could not rape he had to buy.

Having mined his snot—deciding to lift his mood—Cacafuego capered, although his heart was not in antic dance today. Then, bending, he wheezed from both ends like an alternating bellows.

Stunned, Juan held his breath.

"Both mouths sound alike, now that I have no teeth," Cacafuego sighed. He mourned, "My *ars musica* remains wordless. And to think once I aspired to plain chant in two voices." Having said this, he created music with his bum horn in a pure—if reedy—tenor, baritone mouth joining in. A wordless melody, this was unmistakably the *Laudate* Dominus ... a *capella*.

Sighing from both ends as he concluded, deepening his stoop into a bow, Cacafuego left with his giggling concubines.

Blanca—staring wide-eyed at Cacafuego's exit—desperately needed the explanation Juan was not about to give. He said, "Sometimes seeing is *not* believing. And do not *dare* recite the *Credo!*"

Valdivia announced the pacification of the south, intending never to return. Magnanimously burning bridges, he distributed his *repartimientos* among the *vecinos* who were to stay, so compensating for the riches they would not conquer.

The day came when Santiago assembled after Mass. The Governor reviewed his troops, horse pacing before the silent ranks, speaking magnificently. The square erupted with cheers, random battle cries, a wasteful volley from the arquebuses. Hearing sounds of war, the Governor's horse reared, striking with its hooves at an imaginary enemy. Valdivia drew his sword to behead an imaginary Indian. No one would ever forget that magnificent moment. Or the next....

The stallion fell back, landing on Valdivia's leg. Paler than The Eucharist, the Governor bit his lip to keep from screaming. The buckles fastening armor to his leg had snapped, and the calf emerged from its protection fearfully bent, not at the knee. Slivers of bloody bone protruded. And when his boot was removed, Valdivia fainted.

Quiroga—who hoarded his wife as misers their gold—did not hesitate to send for her. She arrived at a run, lifting voluminous skirts in a characteristic compromise between speed and modesty. At the sight of Valdivia she crossed herself. "*Virgen santíssima!*"

The Governor opened his eyes at the familiar voice ... passed out again. Ignoring the ruination of her dress, Inés knelt on blood-soaked soil. She had seen worse, yet never in a man that lived to ride again, or walk without a crutch. This leg needed amputation.

Blood was spurting. Using her lace *mantilla* as a tourniquet she twisted with the sheath of Juan's knife, stopping the flow. Then she sent for the butcher and his saw, the blacksmith and his iron. Hearing that, Valdivia said through gritted teeth that *absolutely no one* was going to remove *any part* of his body. That was an order.

Inés lifted her eyes to Heaven, and slit Valdivia's hose. Delicate as was her touch, he fainted again. Turning to Pedro, she said that as God was in His Heaven there would be mortification of this leg if not removed. Better to have Valdivia alive with one leg, than lying with both in his grave.

To Juan she seemed the Pieta come to life—kneeling, grieving, arguing—her magnificently contentious self again.

Pedro, however, was Pedro. "Señora Doña Inés," he rumbled, "*lo siento mucho*, but an order is an order."

Valdivia was hurried home on a litter. Inés cauterized his wounds, and—for hours—labored to return his leg to a semblance of human form, pulling and pushing, kneading bones into their places when possible, breaking off shards when not, using scissors, a small hammer borrowed from the tinsmith, needle and thread. When agony allowed him consciousness Valdivia was dosed with brandy and given an arquebus ball to bite.

Juan had not known a leg and foot contained so many bones—an excess it seemed, for when Inés was done there were leftovers, buried to keep them from the dogs. By nightfall, Valdivia was delirious, his leg a mottled sausage cooking in the fires of calenture.

Marmolejo administered extreme unction. And at dawn—Valdivia breathing still—a Mass attended by the entirety of Santiago was sung for his survival.

For an endless month Fortuna did not decide upon Valdivia. Then—as History would later record—she determined to preserve him for greater horror.

The Governor languished, scarcely able to speak, much less govern. Conquest was indefinitely postponed, and Santiago's days slid by in a limbo of inaction that sapped the spirit of the colony, as if all had been pushing an enormous boulder uphill to a summit, and—when it began to roll down the other side—were called upon to halt the weight. It took every ounce of human will to keep the enterprise from going nowhere.

Juan wandered the mazes of *mapudungun*—a good a way as any of surviving a world without Inés—devoting so much time to the savage language that Pedro looked at him askance. No one civilized *wanted* to learn Indian barks and grunts— and Juan was, if anything, *too* civilized. Could it be—now that Inés no longer dangled before his nose like a forbidden carrot—that he had turned to more wholesome male pursuits? Pedro preferred women meatier, but Blanca was not unattractive. He might have considered porking her himself, had she not arrived with the strictest prohibitions from Inés—which he interpreted to mean this nubile gift was for Juan alone. And now that facts were verifying his surmise—the good soldier kept his silence. A virtual finger to his nose, he made himself scarce during 'language lessons.'

Pedro was wrong, however, for Juan was not porking Blanca. Not even dreaming of it. His language journal—grown to a volume—was bogged down in both grammar and lexicon. He had finished the easy words and reached those without Spanish equivalents—that is, the many plants and animals of the land, air and sea, that did not exist in Spain, as well as pagan objects, rites and customs. Therefore he and Blanca now passed less time in formal lessons, more in rambling through the worlds represented by their languages. Juan was intrigued by the fact that *mapudungun* had no word for 'hour,' or any other numeric division of the day—though there was 'sunrise,' and so on and so forth. Also, while there was a notion of a year, Blanca had no measured idea of her age, and could not be convinced this was important.

Money proved difficult for Blanca. Being 'rich' she could not fathom. To exchange she was accustomed, but why trade gold—which was essentially worthless in her opinion—for something *useful*? Whatever it might *buy*, gold was good for nothing *in itself*. It was stupid to have too much of anything anyway, as attracting envy and the nasty work of *kalku*. Besides, gold was less attractive than *likan*.

"*Likan...*?"

"Sacred stone. Black, blue, green. Volcano make."

She dubiously shook her head when Juan produced a new-minted *doblón*—emblem of the desire of *conquistadores*. She preferred seashells she said, setting a remarkable example beside the coin.

Juan had never thought to scrutinize shells, thinking of them as something to be crunched under a boot when by the seashore. Closely regarded, nonetheless, this coiled home for an amorphous snail had the perfection he had desired for his Bower of Bliss, in miniature. Lambent as marble—though more regularly patterned in creamy white and lavender—the pale whorl was flawless. This miracle was partly in the size—as if a building had been immensely shrunken, which, restored to towering proportion, would continue to demonstrate the perfection of its workmanship. The shell made Juan want to be a mite, the better to explore it as a palace, or to magnify it, so that like a mosque it would dwarf him with alien architecture. Why was he reminded of Moors by this shell? Their domes?

"It *is* more beautiful than the *doblón*," he confessed, feeling argumentative. Yes, the *doblón* seemed crude beside her shell, yet on it was the image of the Holy Roman Emperor! Behind it stood history, power ... God! Whatever the beauties of shells, the *doblón* had not been formed by legless slugs. "Money is what it is as scarce, not as beautiful," he argued. "What is *scarce* is valuable." Let her chew *that* incontestable cud.

Blanca was unimpressed. "What good about rares there? What rares worthless more if," she softly said, "three babies born together, like?"

Juan insisted, "If you can pick money off beaches, where's the worth? Who would trade anything for a shell when they could get all they wanted in a stroll by the sea?"

She lost her poise and spoke her mind. "If *lik winka* think gold good because getting hard, then why not get it *you!*"

Differing beliefs had—abruptly—metamorphosed into a personal assault by one he never thought to harm. Juan felt unjustly injured.

Blanca was not done, however. "Rare, mean *lik winka* want. Hard get, mean Pikunche make too much work to get you from river." Her language was deteriorating.

How right she was, Juan thought, yet how mistaken. And how explain to her that gold had brought salvation to her people, given that no one in their right mind—save for priests—would undertake the deadly task of pacifying Indians without reward? From a supernatural perspective, Indians were getting the world's best bargain—immortal life, just for a little labor while in mortal husk. But Blanca was implacably sub lunar. Unconvinced of the existence of a Heaven, she insisted in taking it literally as the passing clouds—ancestors hovering there—unable to grasp the afterlife as a transcendent, eternal thing.

"You come for gold, just?" she eventually asked.

"No." And Juan was being candid. In what might be called the triune faith of the *conquistador*, gold was the prime mover, yet by its side stood God and glory. How else justify Valdivia, or his own arrival in the Indies? For that matter, how explain what he was doing in this last outpost of civilization, analyzing the founts of conquest with an Indian girl who—far as he knew—did not have a word for 'power' in her language.

Raytrayen was regretting her harshness—made possible by the very friendship it was threatening.

"So, what you come for? I mean one you."

"I don't know." And Juan did not. "I was young," he ventured. "Pedro brought me."

And did not *that* sound halt, he thought—a palming off, of blame. Adding painful truth to the mixture, he said, "I was different."

"*Diferenthe?*"

"An orphan. And I liked reading."

"*Le-er?*"

"*Sí, libros.*"

She knew this word, and turned to inspect his journal on the table.

"Reading, make ashes scratches with feathers?"

Juan had to laugh, before correcting her. "What you call 'make ashes scratches' is writing. And what you call 'feathers' is a quill. As for reading, why, it is...."

He proved unable to explain reading to one who did not know writing in the first place.

Blanca interjected her own theory—"Read is look books, speak scratches."

"Why, yes." Juan was intrigued by her wild discernment. "But only sometimes...."

He had been taught by Father Sosa to read silently, yet the many of the literate did so out loud, or at least mouthed the words. The child was thinking of Inés, no doubt.

Touching the journal with a fingertip, Blanca advanced her theory. "Scratches, these memories."

"Not really."

Blanca was being perceptive, but perversely, unable to be right without giving some pagan twist to truth. So he repaired her wild insight. "Writing is *words. Just words.*"

Blanca mulled this over. Words were sounds, yet memories were silent. Words became memories after they left the mouth. She was unconvinced. And Ñamku always told her to trust her intelligence. She asked, an edge in her voice, "These my words—my *likwinkadungun*—no?"

"Of course."

"I close mouth." And she did, adamant.

Juan's back was up also, so for some time they shared a mulish silence.

Blanca ended the impasse. "No mouth, no word," she said.

Lautaro had sent Millanti *willi* with the message that the *lik winka* were coming. But now that Falthifa rumored to be near death he had a problem—he needed to get word of this to the Mapuche.

The night after the *kawellu* fell on the *lik winka toki*, Lautaro came to the conclusion that he had to be the messenger—as there was no one else to send except Raytrayen. In addition, all the *kuyen* he had lived in Tiako he had been pondering strategies to be used against this enemy, their weapons and *kawellu*, and he had arrived at some ideas that he thought might work. That was perhaps a more important reason to leave as soon as possible.

There remained a question, an obstacle and a problem. The question—what to do about Raytrayen? She was becoming *winka* as the *lik winka*, which gave a traitorous twist to the task Ñamku had assigned her. Lautaro suspected she might not be even willing to return, and that this would have less to do with her duty than with her attraction to the enemy—especially Wan, to whom Lautaro owed his life, but whom he loathed for alienating his sister.

The obstacle—Lautaro hoped to return to his people on a *kawellu*. He would be the talk—the song!—of all the *che*. Even with the support of Ñamku and Andalikan, what *toki* would listen to one who was young, inexperienced, *and ... ankeñ peñeñ*? On a *kawellu*, Lautaro dared dream that they would listen to his ideas ... but as one who worked with *kawellu* in Tiako, he knew how well guarded they were. To attempt to steal one, and fail, would mean certain, awful death.

The problem joined the question to the obstacle. He had to leave with Raytrayen if he succeeded in stealing a *kawellu*, or she would be tortured to death. He *had* to go, but she might not want to leave. He desperately wanted a *kawellu*, but would probably die trying to take one. If so, his message would not be delivered, and Blanca would be killed by the *lik winka* as his sister.

He met her by a well. While drawing water, he told her it was time to go.

"Now!"

"We have to leave."

This was the truth, yet twisted. "The *weichafe* need time to prepare," he said, thinking that if he had time and a *kawellu* he might have a voice among the *longko* of the *aillarewe*.

"When?"

"Three *antu*." By then he would have a *kawellu* or be dead. She had to leave Santiago earlier. "I will meet you at the *loloruka* in four *antu*. There are stores there we need."

"Why not leave together?"

"It would look suspicious."

To avoid attention they would take their possessions concealed under their clothes—one or two at a time—and hide them across the river.

In two *antu* Lautaro moved the few things that he would take *willi*. He still had no plan for stealing a *kawellu*, however. To take one from a stable would not be difficult, to pass the gates of Tiako with it, impossible. He had to get a *kawellu* outside, but how...?

Raytrayen also had a problem, and the third *antu* found her on her knees, looking into the basket where she kept her black *lik winka kepam* and the cloth Inesh had given her. Wan had left, saying he would be back late. It was time for her to go. Raytrayen lingered and was ashamed of lingering. Lautaro had told her to leave nothing behind—not a hair of her head—and to bring nothing *lik winka* with her, or *lik winka kalku* would steal her *am*. But the cloth, the comb, the dress were hers. And she did not so much fear to have her *am* taken by *lik winka kalku* as feel she was leaving part of her *am* behind in these *wethakelu*. She touched the cloth. There was no word for miracle in *mapudungun*, but in *likwinkadungun* it was something real that was also impossible, as *this* was. Yet everything about *lik winka* was some kind of miracle. Could one remain Mapuche and become a *little* like them?

Wan walked in.

Raytrayen had hesitated too long. She covered the basket quickly, feeling guilty in more ways than she could count.

Juan regretted that his hunch had been confirmed. It was his obligation as a *vecino* to denounce her for attempted escape. The sentence would be relatively light—probably just branding. Still, that turned his stomach. And it would be far worse if she were caught in the act. He could not let her try and fail.

"You miss your family, don't you?" he said.

She nodded, relieved that Wan had misunderstood.

"You're leaving Santiago, aren't you?"

Rising, Blanca said she was.

"I'll help you."

Next morning Juan told Pedro he was taking Blanca to the river for language lessons. Casually, he took **Amadís de Gaula** and **Utopia** from the chest where they were kept, saying he would read to her.

Pedro almost laughed at the transparent fib, but kept a straight face. The *romance* was in Spanish, as he knew. But he was no fool to forget that **Utopia** was in Latin. Pedro approved of Juan's humping this toothsome Indian, but was troubled by the lie. He was also unhappily aware that in addition to what presumably was taking place, language learning was going on, which he *truly* disapproved of. As insanities went, the desire to master an Indian language was unique, although relatively harmless. You could teach your child to bark like a dog, but did you *want* to? However, he could put up with this. His *hijo* was subject to hallucinations acquired from books, and he loved him nonetheless. Still and all, to teach Spanish to a heathen was a perversity worse than dressing one in Christian cloth, blurring categories in the hierarchy separating man from animals, having Indians as a buffer in between. The better Blanca spoke Spanish, the more he was gloomy. And he hated the whole thing more at the thought that she would be read to from **Amadís de Gaula**—as if there were a need to fill that emptiness which was Indian mind with one of the few true idiocies of civilization.

Taking up his helmet Pedro clapped his *hijo* on the shoulder, saying, "See you tonight." Being a father had taught him to think twice before opening his mouth.

The plan Juan had formulated was simple. He would go with Blanca to the river and return without her, claiming she had drowned. Improving on this excellent beginning, she offered to take laundry as an excuse for going in that direction.

Lautaro saddled Bucephalus, quietly watching as Wan mounted and left, Raytrayen trotting behind him, basket on her head. Taking a rope coiled on the wall, with pounding heart Lautaro sauntered out the *kawellu ruka*.

Arrived at the ford, Juan and Raytrayen argued. She insisted he go back as planned. But he was not about to let her swim a dangerous river, vanishing into wilderness unarmed and unprotected, especially when she might be dogged. She would go with him, or not at all.

Nose to nose almost—he leaning from his horse, she on tiptoe—they quarreled beside the river that would separate them forever. Frustrated, Juan asked why exactly she was going north when her people lived south ... eh? He had wondered from the start. What did she have in mind that must be done *without* him? Was he aiding in some plot against his people?

His suspicions missed their mark. Raytrayen intended to swim the river naked, keeping her *kepam* dry. Also, there was the promise she made to Ñamku to have the *loloruka* be a secret. But as no one lived there now, perhaps that no longer mattered. And, if she took Wan there, what would happen when Lautaro came? Would he aid her brother in his escape as he was aiding her, or betray him? The escape of a *weichafe*, as she knew, was far more serious than her own. She exclaimed at last, "Family has *ruka*, *piku*, not far. No one live. Things I need. You come, but I have two...."

"Requests. Suggestions. Conditions." Juan added, "Ears. Noses." He was smiling. Blanca's pride, peculiar in one so young—and, yes, the fierceness of her nose—made her pigheadedness comically imperious.

"Leave you *ruka* morning," she insisted, ignoring Juan's taunts. "Promise?"

"*Bien, lo prometo.*" He shrugged. "What else?"

"Look not when *kepam* off, swim river."

"No need to take anything off. Bucephalus can carry the both of us." She was just a girl—he thought—and besides, this would be an unseen violation of the law.

Seeing her reluctance, he added, "No need to worry. Bucephalus is old and experienced."

She relented, and was stowing her things in a saddlebag when both heard the heart-stopping sound of dogs running scent. Mendoza was on their track. And in the wildness of Blanca's eyes Juan saw she was about to bolt like a doe. Then—heedless as he sealed the letters of others—Juan sealed his own fate. Bending to hook an arm around her waist, he heaved Blanca onto Bucephalus, and the horse bounded into the river with an enormous splash, making for the other shore.

Lautaro burst out of *uwa* into woods, listening to the dogs behind him. Their sound was louder, now, than his pounding feet, his pounding blood, his gasping. He hurdled a fallen tree, twisting his ankle as he landed, slamming his head. His ears rang but he made it to his feet, desperately yearning for a glimpse of the Mapocho through the trees.

When excited *yanacona* scratched at Mendoza's door to tell him that Lautaro had left 'Tiako,' the dogger knew he had revenge sweetly in his grasp. The eclipse of Inés de Suárez had altered Santiago's opinion on the matter of dogging. Single Indians were expendable. However, fleeing in large numbers—as they had been— they bled the colony of manpower. Mendoza knew that a dogging within earshot would be welcomed by every *encomendero* as an object lesson to his indolent charges.

Wasting no time in taking up his sword—not bothering with the bladed collars or armor of the dogs—he took four of his best from their kennel. He had one of Lautaro's sandals—stolen by his spy—and once he rode out Santiago's gates Mendoza tossed it to the dogs. They took the scent, leapt forward in full cry, ignoring the silent Indians they passed, frozen at their work by the most chilling sound in the Indies. Soon after—greyhounds in the lead—the pack disappeared into maize. Mendoza followed, his horse creating a furrow of destruction.

The dark figure of a savage emerged from the field and sprinted into woods, pursued by the skeletal greyhounds. Not long after came the clamor signaling the kill.

Not far from the Mapocho, Mendoza found his dogs feeding, muzzles smeared with gore. A mastiff had pulled up wool to expose the belly, was pulling on entrails to get at the heart and liver, his mate working on a thigh. For the moment, the greyhounds made do with the arms.

Mendoza put a handkerchief to his nose, cursing the stupidity of his spy. The moronic Indian must have thought that—in addition to the glass beads of his betrayal—he could steal the sandal of one who would not return, and go work in the damn fields wearing it.

Mendoza allowed the dogs to eat. This misadventure was the fault of the victim after all, and they needed their reward. And only when they had their fill did he set off toward the river, spoor leading him to the ford to which he had tracked the youth before. Pensively rubbing the milky softness of his jaw, Mendoza looked down at an empty laundry basket, abandoned at the shore. Stranger yet—beside it were the huge prints of a warhorse.

To pursue would be foolhardy, Mendoza knew. He was unarmed and unprepared for a long excursion. And his dogs were exercised, heavy with meat. He was loath to take this risk, yet intuition told him he was on the track of something very interesting. It could scarcely hurt to see what sign his dogs found on the farher shore....

There, more hoof prints, and no sign of Lautaro. Hating sweat, Mendoza removed his hat, fanning himself as the greyhounds cast for scent, thinking that nothing made sense this morning. Also, he was angry that the pleasure of the morning's kill had been soured, enough so that he ordered his dogs to track the horse. The rider had to be the root of his frustration.

Not far into the woods the dogs milled about a hollow tree, confused, excited, expecting orders. Mendoza knew them better than he knew most men, and he could have sworn that they had found Indian scent that was not Lautaro's, or they would need no command to pursue.

Savages did not materialize in forests. Neither did they abandon laundry baskets by the river. Smiling seraphically, seating his hat, Mendoza gave the order to pursue and kill. If evidence did not deceive him, an Indian was about to die.

When Lautaro at last glimpsed the Mapocho he heard behind him a sudden frenzy of barking followed by a strangled scream. The dogs went silent. Would he live after all? He limped on madly, pausing only to study the hoof prints he found at the shore before he threw himself into the river. He had been spared. But why … and how?

He had recognized the hoof prints of Bucephalus. This meant Raytrayen was taking Wan to the *loloruka*. Why? She knew as well as he that to return to Tiako after they had escaped would mean torture—perhaps death—for both of them.

The immense *kawellu* leaped, slamming Raytrayen against Wan. Then she was violently lurching, high over water, and would have fallen if his arm were not firm about her. She pulled her legs up to keep her *kepam* dry, too late.

Juan reined in Bucephalus to listen, the noise of their crossing having drowned out every other. In the silence broken only by the breathing of man, maid, and mount there was no sound of dogging. He urged the jittery warhorse to a trot, wishing one could gallop through this wilderness.

Blanca took them to her cache in the hollow of a tree. There she dismounted to retrieve her bundle, and then led the way on foot. Bucephalus plodded after, Juan thinking that—since he had flaunted the law against Indian flight—Mendoza could dog Blanca with impunity, and chills ran his spine. What did the uncanny quiet mean? He prayed to the Virgin to protect this innocent child of God, but he heard baying before he finished his first Ave.

Blanca stopped in her tracks. Juan crossed himself, knowing that there was only one thing to do. But before he could pluck Blanca up she had cast aside her bundle and was running like a deer. Juan spurred Bucephalus down what was no path for a war horse, crashing through bamboo, breaking branches, risking the legs of his mount, still managing to lose Blanca. Then two cadaverous greyhounds bounded by, grinning with effort, pink tongues swinging. Their heads were soaked in blood….

The world turned soundless with the passing of the hounds of death, and Juan witnessed what transpired after—like a monk upon his hushed *lectorium*—as pure illumination. He spurred his horse, breaking through thickets into the glare of a clearing enfolding the bleached framework of an abandoned *ruka*.

Blanca had made it to the other side of the ruined dwelling a dozen strides ahead of the hounds, and was scrambling up a structure tall as a man—the tilted trunk of a tree embedded in the ground, steps hacked into it, a human face carved at the top.

The dogs ran up frenzied, leaping to where she balanced. The larger greyhound seized her bare ankle and did not let go. Blanca screamed as the dog tried to shake her down, writhing in the air with effort. Her bare arms flailed the air. She was about to topple to her death.

"Santiago!"

Juan did not hear—or ever remember—his battle cry, or hear the thunder of Bucephalus surging forward. The vine-lashed frame of the *ruka* exploded as the armored warhorse—like an enormous, living cannon ball—took the shortest path to battle.

The greyhounds heard, and the startled bitch crouched to run, hesitating, for her mate had not released his prey. Galloping by, Juan halved him below the ribs, and reined the horse around.

Bucephalus wheeled, reared, and—with a hoof—crushed the head of the bitch. Then, turning to face the mastiffs just now arriving, Juan clove deep into the neck of the huge male ... could not bring himself kill the other. Not trained in mercy, Bucephalus trampled her as well.

Then, only silence interrupted by harsh breathing ... the thud of an approach ... until blue glimmered through bamboo.

Mendoza leaned on his saddle, surveying the carnage with icy calm. And turning from the convulsions of his dying mastiff bitch he faced Juan, fanning himself with his hat, running fingers through his hair.

"I somehow knew it would be you," he said. "Still, I had hoped for a different ... ah ... outcome."

Ignoring him, Juan glanced to where Blanca was now safely on the ground.

"You cannot let me return to Santiago," Mendoza commented, logical as always.

He was, of course, correct. One trained war dog was worth several warhorses, tens of *infantes*, hundreds of *yanacona* warriors, perhaps half the Indian women of the Indies, and Juan had slaughtered four of these priceless weapons for a scrawny savage. Secretary to the *cabildo* he might be, good friend to the Governor as well, and—for all his youth—one of the most powerful men of Santiago, yet he had just committed an overt act of civil war. This would not cost Juan his head, yet it required the harshest punishment. He would be stripped of his position and *encomienda* at the least, fined and censored without a doubt, possibly even forced to return to Spain in penniless disgrace … unless Mendoza did not live to tell the tale.

"We have had disagreements which I set aside," the dogger continued, temperate. "But what here transpired I cannot ignore."

Juan looked down at his bloodied sword, resting on the oiled leather of his saddle.

"I will denounce you before the Governor and the *cabildo*," Mendoza said, lucid as a fallen angel. "You would be foolish not to finish me."

No trace of irony—or mockery—there, Juan thought, profoundly tempted, thinking also that Mendoza knew he would not kill an unarmed man in cold blood—especially one who once saved his life. The dogger was playing with him.

Mendoza offered that—even with the weight of evidence—it would be one word against another. And Juan had powerful friends, which he himself did not.

"Go," Juan said.

Mendoza smiled. "Don Juan, you have some growing up to do, too late," he replied. And without farewell he reined his horse about.

Fortunately, Blanca was not seriously bleeding. They returned for her bundle and she stowed it in a saddlebag. While lifting her onto Bucephalus, Juan noted the faint aroma of clove, and his heart leapt with memories … only to plummet into despair—for the magic of *this* perfume could not be transferred. Had he been unfaithful to Inés by saving this girl's life?

Bucephalus paced on, Juan deciding that—on the contrary—he had done what Inés herself might have, in one of her magnificently foolhardy moments. He had seen her after all, astride a warhorse like a man, at The Apocalypse.

Abject then—as if, like the Virgin, Inés saw into the hearts of men—he apologized for past behavior. She had been glorious in her armor, and he a bookish fool who failed to love the fierce and loving spirit there, his eyes fixed on a mirage shimmering over the desert of some text. Heartsick, Juan was triumphant still. At last—in some strange way—he had sacrificed everything for her.

Chapter 10: Pangi (*Mapu,* 1550)

From time to time, Blanca asked Juan to halt Bucephalus, sliding down to gather leaves from bushes, dig roots, break twigs. They halted at a stream where she scrubbed her wounds and—pulping her gleanings—put them on her injured leg. For bandages she used more leaves, deftly tied with braided plants.

Leaves and leaves. Twigs and roots. Plants alien as nameless. Juan scrutinized this habitat of the Indian, useful as a source of wood but otherwise to be cleared as dangerous, growing no crops, slowing horses, and concealing savages. Was this actual medicine before his eyes, moved by the breeze? If so, what *else* could Blanca improvise from the salad all about? Indicating the plant she had just used to make cord, Juan asked its name.

"*Nocha.*" She smiled, mischievous, then said they should travel the stream. He helped her up.

Bucephalus walked the current as Juan mulled the insane idea of returning to Santiago and denying everything. He could claim Mendoza staged the massacre of his dogs as a personal vendetta, Venetian in devious complexity. It would be just one word against another, as the dogger himself had pointed out. Ironically, the insanity of what Juan had done would argue for his innocence. What *vecino* would aid an Indian in her escape, and in so doing good as turn his sword against the Emperor...?

A tide of self-revulsion blacked out Juan's environs, transporting him to a visionary gallery of religious paintings of extraordinary color—not a gallery exactly, but a dim vault in which the canvases, like Stations of the Cross, were spaced on stone. Luminous, they lit the church, depicting Juan and Bucephalus in exaggerated attitudes. In the first he was in a Roman amphitheater slaying saints to save a lion. In the second it was Saint George who lay in armored halves as Bucephalus reared to attack the maiden at her stake. But—in this chimerical progression—Juan did not reach the third station of his Calvary, for Blanca slumped against him, fast sleep....

The stream banks gradually steepened into a declivity roofed by the lancet tracery of bamboo, Bucephalus plodding until they arrived at a cascade tumbling over boulders. Mind hollow as his stomach, Juan's eyes took in a crowd of scarlet blossoms with purple hearts—*chillko,* as he knew—over which a rainbow levitated into the slanting light of afternoon. From wall to mossy wall, it seemed to arch the door to magic kingdoms. Yet, beautiful as was this place, it was obviously not their journey's end. They would have to backtrack, spending the night without shelter or food. It was his fault they were lost, but Blanca had been peacefully asleep, cradled in his arm.

Tired—and annoyed—Bucephalus snorted.

Blanca jerked up. "*Ruka!*"

"Here…?" A premonitory shiver shot Juan's spine. One found the Bower of Bliss at dusk, by becoming lost in trackless wilderness … yet Juan had never thought to wade a stream to reach it. Knights-errant did not travel water, although knights at bridges—in black armor, visor down—often challenged them. This made sense, for if knights wandered streams instead of roads, how would the evil opponent know the place to guard? It would be completely wrong of course, to wait *on* the bridge, challenging knights that waded *under*….

Blanca interrupted. "Turn *kawellu, por favor.*"

She took them to a path around the waterfall, so tortured, so narrow, they dismounted to lead the horse. And once they made it up—with a triumphant gesture indicating the blank face of wilderness—Blanca exclaimed, "*Loloruka!*"

Dismayed, Juan saw no sign of a 'cave dwelling.' They were in the very same ravine—wider here, less deep—low shafts of sunlight illuminating *chillko*, a brilliant red above a tumble of unhewn rock. Nothing before him looked like the thatch that made Indian dwellings resemble shaggy oxen—much less the marbled perfection of the Bower….

Juan tethered Bucephalus. Told to wade, he removed his boots and pushed up his hose, as Blanca headed through icy water to a cleft. Squeezing through behind her, Juan was brushed by wings of bats in what might as well have been the door to Hades. Inside, however, was no incubus or demon, no absolute obscurity, Blanca laboring in half-light. The quiet was not total either, the chuckle of flowing water transporting him to the gardens of Sevilla. A flame told him Blanca had begun a fire, yet nothing like the sensuous south of Spain was revealed. He was in a cave with a rough timbered roof—a place for snakes and bears. Chilled by primordial fear Juan fought the urge to draw his sword against the beasts of darkness.

When the fire gave off palpable heat, Blanca took rocks from a cache, revealing a clay pot which she suspended over the fire, filling it with water, dried maize, and … other things. Quietly, she suggested that it was time to care for the *kawellu*.

Her features here seemed right, thought Juan—as through twilight they led Bucephalus to a garden reverted to meadow. Not just her semblance put her in her element, but her sureness in the dusk, as if people were intended to move in gloom. Returned, they ate soup from wooden bowls, Juan learning that he was consuming—other than the dried *uwa* and *poñu* which he recognized—smoked *degu*, and tubers she could not explain.

Blanca brewed a tea she said brought sleep. After, she took a stone shaped like a little finger from the coals, and—holding it with wet leather—cauterized her deeper wounds.

The fragrance of cooking meat made Juan helplessly salivate, and he crossed himself—never expecting to sin this way precisely—in awe of Blanca's silent courage. With a gasp she turned her leg to reveal punctures she could not reach, offering the stone.

"*Cuerpo de Dios!*"

"*Por favor,*" she murmured.

The leg was smooth ... soft ... firm, under the hissing stone.

After, Juan removed his armor and prepared for sleep on straw under a blanket of *degu* pelt. Ermine would not be as sumptuous, he thought—whatever ermine might be. However, tired as he was, he could not sleep for thinking.

"Awake, you?" The voice was barely audible over the faint sound of running water.

"*Sí,*" he whispered.

"I know say *kallfu lik winka* you."

Juan wondered why he assumed she had not understood.

"Why you do, you do?" inquired the disembodied voice.

Juan had no ready answer—especially for himself.

"*Rathia,*" she persisted.

"*De nada,* Blanca."

Yet that nothing was *everything*. Juan had as good as fallen on his sword for her. Or for Inés? Was he *in loco* Inés, as one could be *in loco parentis*? Or was he just plain *loco*—crazy? Ignorance of the etymology that might connect these words hummed in his head like bees disturbed. What did being in someone's place have to do with being crazy? And if a *locus* was a place, where was a madman? Beside himself...?

Then, a last firm whisper in *mapudungun*, "Here, my name is Raytrayen, not Blanca."

"*Yamai.*"

"Say it," she whispered.

And he did. 'Flower in the brook,' indeed.

Juan woke from the nightmares of the night to nightmares of his waking future. There was a disoriented moment however, in which the scene before him was empty of its past ... Raytrayen turning from her fire to smile. Then, memory swept Juan away. What *had* he done? What would he *do*?

"*Buenoth thias,*" she said, offering a steaming bowl. "Sleep late."

Correcting her verb, Juan ate without pleasure, no course of action suggesting itself. One thing was clear— the longer he took to return the more probable his guilt would seem, and the wilder the excuse required. He should have returned yesterday, or better yet, never left at all. Awkwardly thanking Raytrayen, he dressed. Saying a brief farewell he waded despondently into the stream, helmet in one hand, boots in the other.

"*Peukayal,* Wan," Raytrayen said sadly.

Bucephalus was not in the meadow where he had been hobbled! Fighting panic, Juan surveyed the ravine, here widening at a meander of the brook that embraced the meadow. A horse would not by itself thread the maze of stone at the cascade downstream. Nor could he scale the cliffs on either side. So Juan went upstream to where the clearing ended by the pebbled shore, came across a hoof print, and penetrated the dim coolness of the forest, this more silent than sunny place—as if, like flowers, noises loved the light. His breath seemed loud, and time seemed to stop until he found Bucephalus—placid as any cow—tied to an enormous tree.

The peace of the place screamed entrapment, and instinct born of perilous years in the Indies made Juan drop his boots to draw his sword ... too late ... Bright Heaven falling on him as a shower of sparks.

Raytrayen was making rope from *uweñ*—for a *wilal*—her fingers slowed by fears for Wan. She had accomplished little when from the forest beyond the meadow appeared a *kawellu* led by Lautaro! A body hung across it, legs pale as milk. She raced across the stream. Wan was slack, head bleeding.

"You killed him!" Raytrayen screamed at her brother.

"He lives. All I did is drop down from a tree and hit his head."

"This is my fault!" she wailed. "My fault!"

"What!"

"He saved my life!"

"What!"

"Wan killed *trewa* that tried to eat me. Four of them. Huge." She tore the bandages off her leg as proof.

But her wounds appalled Lautaro far less than their collective debt.

Wan groaned, and they took him into the *loloruka*, where Lautaro bound his hands.

Raytrayen was outraged. "He saved my life *and* yours!"

Lautaro bound his feet.

She protested, "He is our *friend!*"

"No *lik winka* is our friend."

"Why did he save us, then?"

"How many *che* has he killed before this day? How many more will he kill if he returns to Tiako? How many will he make slaves?"

The *lik winka* hoarsely said—in his language—"Interesting questions."

Raytrayen silenced him with a finger to her lips, and for much of that dreamlike day she and Lautaro argued. Juan captured only a word—or phrase—here and there, finding the disagreement little more comprehensible than the brook. He grasped the essence of their disagreement, though. Lautaro insisted that he had canceled his blood debt by *not* killing the *lik winka*—which equaled the saving of his life. Also—by capturing him—he was keeping him from killing Mapuche in the future.

Raytrayen scoffed. "I have a great idea. Do not kill him one more time by hitting him on the head again. Then *my* debt will be canceled. And as long as you are 'not killing him' by hitting him on the head—why not 'not kill him' one more time, putting him in *your* debt?"

Her sarcasm was wasted on Lautaro. He agreed that maybe they owed the *lik winka something*, but could they set an enemy free? She said Wan had proved himself a friend by risking his life to save theirs. And casting prudence aside, she attempted to explain how—killing four *trewa*—Wan had angered his people for her sake. Was this an enemy?

Lautaro sneered. The *lik winka* was not just an enemy, he was a traitor to his own.

Did he think Wan should have let the *trewa* devour her?

And so—heatedly—to and fro it went.

When Lautaro left in a huff she came to change the compress on Juan's head—*mulul*, 'good for head hurt,' she said, whispering that Lautaro had gone to the *kawellu*. She began to untie his wrists.

"No!"

Juan had given thought to this moment. "You cannot do this to your brother, or yourself." He did not know how Mapuche treated those who assisted in the escape of enemies, assuming the reprisal to be barbarous. The whole thing should stop here. His treachery to his own people was bad enough.

Raytrayen stood her ground. "I have debt. Too Lautaro. He not kill."

"Are you certain I will not kill him if set free?"

She glanced at the sword set in the corner, betrayed by hesitation. And not for the first time in the Indies, Juan felt what it was to be seeing—as it were—*in loco* Indian. Perhaps this could be attributed to being under savage roof. Perhaps it was Raytrayen, who with her Spanish language, Spanish dress, had blurred distinctions. In any case—and for whatever reason—he had slipped from the axis of his Spanish being, seeing himself through Indian eyes as from outside.

"Lautaro is right. I am the enemy of the Mapuche."

"What?" Lautaro asked as he walked in.

"Translate, *por favor*," Juan asked her, "I have something to propose."

He would surrender his sword, Juan said, and Lautaro shrugged. So what, he already had it.

Juan said that he would swear not to take it or any other weapon up against Mapuche until Lautaro released him from captivity. In addition, he would give his word not to escape. His only requests were to be unbound, and that his possessions be returned to him. He would abide by these promises until ransomed.

Explaining ransom proved less difficult than Juan expected, as the Mapuche traditionally righted wrongs by an exchange of goods. For example, if a woman was raped, the affair could be settled by gifts of blankets, *luan, mudai*.

Lautaro claimed he had everything he wanted, reluctant to agree, until Juan was inspired to propose a horse as ransom—not an old one like Bucephalus. Surely, Juan thought, Pedro would do no less than this for him, even though it was unambiguously against the law.

Raytrayen was insistent too, once she understood. This was the least they could do for one to whom they owed their lives. Also, Lautaro had not quite convinced himself that his debt to Wan had been wiped out by the fact he had not killed him. And so it was that Juan was freed into voluntary imprisonment, although the two Mapuche could not know that this arrangement with no precedent in their culture derived from the *libros de caballería*. But of course, the irony of the situation was not lost on Juan. At long last he had saved a damsel in distress—from dogs if not from dragons. In addition, he had been captured and was being held for ransom. At long last he was *living* the magic of **Amadís de Gaula**, but with Indians.

Using Bucephalus as packhorse they headed for the coast, to give Santiago a wide berth. Since the boots of a *caballero* are not made for walking, by the second day Juan's feet were bloody, almost, as Pedro's morning pork. They camped to let them heal, Lautaro fretting, Raytrayen fashioning Indian 'shoes' from the hide of a *pudu*, pounding until they were softly molded to his feet.

During this forced inactivity, Juan took up the first volume of **Amadís** to read out loud, Raytrayen listening with interest. She had been pondering that external memory called a *lifro*, and—thinking of Millanti—conceived of an actual use for such a thing. She proposed, "A *lifro* is good for *werken* with poor memory." She added, "A book a *werken* running not, carried."

Juan appreciated her innocent acuity. "*Werken* carry writing in Spain, so that they do not have to remember or speak the message. Also, we have a *libro* called the Bible, which is a Message from God."

Raytrayen's features acquired that pleasant blandness with which she underwent salvation—which, for some reason, made Juan feel like the village idiot. Anticipating, he hurried on. "It did *not* fall from Heaven."

She cocked her head, quizzical. Juan wondered how to explain the many secretaries that transcribed God's monumental message. Then the awful thought—like a loose tome dropped from high towers of stacked theology—struck him. Who, in fact—What human pen, that is?—was *there* to record Creation? He bumbled on. "The *werken* was Christ, only Son of God."

"Is writing message?"

"More like a memory," Juan suggested—not so much accepting her bizarre notions, as afraid that she would twist his explanation into some barbaric knot.

"Memory who...?"

"Nobody knows." He knew better than to say the author was anonymous.

Raytrayen belabored her topic. What kind of memory *was* it?

"Well ... it begins with the Beginning."

"Of what?"

"Why, of everything."

She took that immensity in stride. "Mapuche too?"

"Of course. The beginning of everything includes your people."

Raytrayen was triumphant. "*Lik winka* not need Bible. Ñamku know beginning."

"He knows it!"

"See it. Sing it!"

"Water on things everything," she amplified. "*Che* on mountain. Mountain dry." She pointed east.

By all that was holy! Ñamku—who surely never read the Bible—had knowledge of the Deluge! And—for all Juan knew of Biblical geography, as it related to this particular God-forsaken spot—she might well be pointing at Ararat itself, half a world away, east from here if it was anywhere! But, Raytrayen claimed that her father *saw* the beginning, and this could not be. It was equally impossible that he witnessed the ark on fabled Ararat. Juan's reply was therefore harshly instructive. "The Deluge was *not* the Creation, although both are in the Old Testament. And your father was *not* there to see it."

Hurt, Raytrayen watched Wan returning to his *lifro*, cutting their conversation short. Who was *he* to contradict the *machi*! However—she had to admit—sometimes the *pellu* of Wan was also absent from his body, so that he reminded her of a puzzled Ñamku. She smiled—for the *machi* was inconceivable as either young or puzzled—and she concluded that books made Wan go into trances. It *did* seem something like the chanting of a *machi,* when books were read out loud by Ineth. Did she dare disturb?

"Wan," she whispered.

He looked up.

"Memories these, they bring here you?"

"What!" Juan exploded, having just heard her refer to Plato, *anagnorisis,* and the transmigration of souls. How could she know he often dreamed that he had been—if not some noble of Perion's court—at least a lesser, unrecorded knight, errant in past times. "You know of Plato!" he exclaimed in wonderment.

Here, Raytrayen confused the immortal philosopher, *Platón*, with the Spanish word for plate, which she *did* know. Puzzled, she agreed she did. And when that misunderstanding became too tangled to unskein, Juan answered her actual question.

Yes—in a sense—*Amadís* brought him here.

What of good, was these memories?

Of what indeed, thought Juan, pondering the riches in these volumes. Where to begin? What to select? "Listen," Juan said. "And try not to ask questions."

He told her about Amadís de Gaula, child of the sea.

She listened. Yet, although Raytrayen knew many of his words, she could not grasp the whole. She had no problem with giants, as huge *che* … no problem either with sorcerers, as existing, and with castles, as enormous *ruka* made of rock. She understood more or less what the *lik winka* in the *lifro* did, but their motives were a mystery. Amadís had created in her less an explanation than a flare of ignorance—as if one tried to put out a fire with dry grass.

Confusion was so clearly written on her face that Juan ceased his presentation.

"No gold, *lifro* in," Raytrayen offered humbly, trying to understand.

Juan nodded, for she was right, again. No true knight-errant acted out of love of lucre—not even the evil ones. But what **Amadís** was *not* about, was not the point. The immortal manuscript was in a sense a Bible of what was not in the Bible—a book of the earth and not of things not of the earth—making of it the magnificent completion. He would have thought that as a heathen of a warlike tribe whose locus was precisely *mapu*, Raytrayen might at least have caught some resonance of what love and courtesy, honor and glory, might mean. Disheartened, he decided to seduce her with the power of the actual drama. Enough of paraphrases, he would read the Word itself. And as no part was less sublime than another, Juan reverently opened the first volume at random, intoning from the twelfth chapter....

At this time of which I speak king Lisuarte was riding with a company of good men. He arrived at a field that lay between village and forest, where he found Dardan well armed on a handsome steed, leading his friend by the reins of her horse, as beautifully adorned as he could make her. He said—"My lord, order that what is hers be given to this lady. And if there is a caballero who will gainsay this, I will fight him...."

Lost in glorious language, Juan took Raytrayen from adventure to miraculous adventure, ceasing only when he was getting hoarse.

She commented only, shyly, that the *lifro* left out a lot. There were women in it, but nothing about what women *did*, like cooking and weaving. The *lifro* was about warriors who left their *ruka*, looking for love and war. Why not just love someone in peace, at home?

Despairing of finding understanding in one who was both Indian *and* a woman—for nothing was noble about affairs of the hearth, and **Amadís de Gaula** attained greatness precisely by excluding what was low—Juan was astounded when Raytrayen hesitantly added, "I think you leave *ruka* for war look, for love look. War only find." She blushed.

Her interpretation was penetratingly true, thought Juan—though rooted in rustic fact. He *had* come to the Indies looking for the Inés he had not yet met … then lost her. In this, Raytrayen was painfully correct, yet how innocently false was her notion of the *meaning* of war in the *romances*. She did not grasp its heart, which was not mere conflict on a larger scale, a melee of alarums and confusions—tides of steel which left the dead and maimed strewn like so much flotsam on the shores of aftermath. True, in the Indies he had discovered love and lost it. But 'war' here was not as in the *libros de caballería*—a purity of single combat in which love itself, and love of honor, twined. Casting down the gauntlet was quintessential—for love and honor needed challenge to exist—this act culminating in the ceremony of the lists, before the eyes of the beloved being fought for. And her witness was everything—something as the eyes of God made sin the thing it was. Without it, the noblest knight became a brawler. Juan imagined seeing through a damsel's eyes as her world hung in balance at the lists, the knights on weighty horses—her champion and the other—hurtling toward collision like bouncing dice … her fate resolved by a momentary impact.

The impact….

The *point* of the impact, it seemed to Juan, was less a spear's tip than the moment when the putting on of steel assumed a significance which was paradoxically large by embracing one man, one maid—and one other—only. Such single combat was noble as 'single' precisely, unlike a battlefield, where a myriad points, a complexity of edges, blunt forces, elbows and God knows what, plied themselves in every which direction for weary hours. And—not only was such a contest ignoble—ultimately, it could not be written….

"You love the dead," Raytrayen observed at last in her own language, quietly, into his silence. "They talk to you. You cannot talk to them."

Two weeks later—Santiago far behind—Juan was comfortably walking. From time to time they encountered Indians who marveled at the captured *kawellu*, the captive *lik winka*. Sometimes they reached out to touch Juan's arms, his face. He felt like an exotic animal in Montezuma's zoo.

A passing *werken* told them of of Ñamku's death.

Raytrayen went into mourning, doing away with the pleasant moments in Juan's day, when the two would make a game of language as they walked, or in the evening by the fire. He would attempt to explain Sevilla in *mapudungun*, for example, she a Mapuche dish in Spanish. He, bells and hours … she *kuyen*. He, the Emperor … she such authority as existed in their absence of a state. He, the Pope … she the many kinds of *poñu*. Inevitably they laughed, and on the detritus of their failure, as if this chaos of communication were a soil, the germs of understanding grew.

Now Raytrayen walked silent, smeared with an unsightly paste of ash and water—she, who took such pride in cleanliness—lost in memories Juan could not share. The evening came when they reached a river wider than the Guadalquivir … wider than any Juan could have imagined.

Raytrayen spoke, at last. "*Fio Fio*," she called it. And as if the river had returned her to the present, that night she taught Juan the names of unfamiliar stars.

Crossing that immense current was a simple matter for Mapuche, not for Juan. Unable to swim, he rode a raft which held him, as well as the saddle, armor and gear of Bucephalus. Awash on the makeshift platform he felt, if not fear, profoundly mortal. There was no shortage of powerfully swimming, naked Indians to push it, however, as all the local population seemed to be celebrating the triumphant return of Lautaro and his *kawellu*, his *lik winka*.

The hero himself crossed the river without effort, pulled by the tail of Bucephalus, doing everything but yawn to demonstrate his ease to the ululating swimmers surrounding him. But, at the shore, the event became more formal and far grimmer. A long row of unsmiling *toki* sat there—Andalikan and Kuriñam among them—the stone ax head that symbolized their status pendant from their necks. Behind were crowded their armed kin, so that the river strand would have seemed a battlefield, had all been painted. Leading Bucephalus, Lautaro proudly strode to the assembly.

Juan was miserable in soaked hose and shirt. He was also cold, unarmored and unarmed—save for his knife—more than a little frightened too. And he was totally alone, since—as she intended to swim the river naked—Raytrayen went to cross it out of sight, upstream.

Greetings over, Lautaro began a speech in which Juan recognized his capture— the humbling narrative become an epic.

As adopted uncle of Lautaro, Andalikan rose to respond, praising his courage, his wisdom. After, the other *toki* did the same, all concluding by demanding the torture and death of the *lik winka* and his *kawellu*. The consensus was that Lautaro would taste first of the hearts of both.

Not having anticipated this disaster, Lautaro argued that a *kawellu* was not a part of the *lik winka*, as some thought. *Kawellu* were not enemies in themselves. They resembled animals around the house, like dogs, and could be turned against the enemy if *che* became their masters. Would they destroy this weapon given them to use against the invaders?

Jeers and hoots erupted at this revolt against the general will. The assembly began to shout and threaten.

Lautaro leapt onto Bucephalus. The warhorse ponderously reared over the seated *toki*, shaking *mapu* like a walking tree … proving Lautaro right. Extraordinary power was in the hands of a Mapuche! Possibilities—immense as they were vague—materialized.

Lautaro awaited their response uneasily. He had been rude to the point of insult, and his presumption was reflected in their stony eyes.

A *toki*—entertaining visions of his own *kawellu*—rose to proclaim, "I say Lautaro is right. Let the *kawellu* live." Another, and another said the same, until all had stood.

Every eye then turned to Juan. The *kawellu* would live. But why deprive the *che* of the justice, the joy, of torturing the *lik winka,* and the tasting of his heart? *Weichafe* surrounded Juan and Lautaro, shaking spears, shouting, "*L'an!*" Death! Death to the *lik winka*!

Juan had his knife, and he would rather have died fighting, yet—shackled by his promise to Lautaro—there was nothing he could honorably do. With a dispassion born of helplessness, therefore, he saw the tumult grow, demanding his suffering and death. He looked at Lautaro, who returned his look with naked hate. No mercy there. And silently, Juan began the *Pater Noster* that would be his last, seeing that many ululating warriors were dancing now. Others were building a fire….

He was at the hearth of death—Why was he rhyming?—wondering to what awful use they would put these flames. Then he glimpsed Raytrayen—pale in somber wool—working her way through the violence, emerging to take his hand and silently face her people.

The paste of ash and water had vanished. Her hair was sleek and wet, her hand cold. She had just swum an immense river by herself.

"The *lik winka* saved my life," she said quietly to the crowd.

Extraordinary as her act seemed to Juan, he could not begin to imagine its unprecedented *perversity* to the Mapuche. A *domo* was not to speak to *weichafe*—even her husband—unless first spoken to, much less address an assembly of *toki*. In fact, her effrontery was so beyond the possible, that the crowd was shocked into silence. The *domo* had not actually *asked* for anything, yet there she was, holding the hand of the condemned!

The murmuring began, many saying that the three *añkeñ peñeñ* should have been smothered at their birth as *admapu* required. It was time to undo the mistakes of the past. Let the *añkeñ peñeñ* be killed with the *lik winka*! Let them both die!

The triumph of Lautaro was over, his own life now being put into question. Not that his death was being demanded, but the words—*añkeñ peñeñ!*—applied to him as well. And the deep anger—which all his life had glowed like a fire banked in ashes—now blazed against his own people. Very well, let them kill him and his sister. Let them count as nothing what he and Raytrayen sister had done for the *che*, including the capture of the *lik winka* and the *kawellu*.

He silenced the now screaming crowd, shouting that the *lik winka* had saved his life as well. Three times he had to shout this. And then he did not have to raise his voice to add that he would stand by his sister and the *lik winka*. He slipped off Bucephalus. And in an undertone, he spoke to Raytrayen.

"He say promise no more," she breathlessly translated for Juan. "Take *kawellu*, you. Go!"

"Tell him *muchas gracias*, but…." Juan could not find the words to say that this whole thing was a huge mistake.

The *che* near enough to overhear recoiled in horror, discovering that Raytrayen spoke *likwinkadungun*. She was one of *them*—therefore a sorceress. Now, along with 'death' and *añkeñ peñeñ* was heard the cry of "*kalku!*" Riderless, Bucephalus reared at the imminence of battle.

The *toki* were silent. What oratory could channel this madness into the paths of *admapu* and wisdom? Where was courtesy? Where *kume mognen*? Alone among them Andalikan cried out against the frenzy. Then, unable to stem the tide of blood lust, he walked to stand beside Lautaro. And holding his ax high, he created a measure of silence. "*Pu peñi!* I too demanded the death of the *lik winka*. And much as I desire peace among Mapuche, I have sworn to be as uncle to Lautaro and Raytrayen."

He did not need say more. Lautaro would die defending his sister. The *toki* would die defending them both.

The stakes—immeasurably risen—rose again. Recovering from their astonishment, the numerous kin of Andalikan went to stand beside their *toki*, casting aside clothing, massing in urgent, silent order, archers nocking arrows but not drawing.

Every other *weichafe* withdrew to face them, preparing weapons, shedding encumbrances, and—like a receding tide—Pichikan and Tuiñam left behind. They had no need to declare their allegiance, for everyone knew they were as brothers to the *añkeñ peñeñ*—and it was rumored that Laftuiñam had an unnatural love for that mother of monsters, Umeñdomo.

Then, led by Kuriñam, the *pu kiñeche* of Tuiñam and Pichikan separated from the crowd to form ranks by them.

Now, in total quiet, the unequal factions faced each other by the Fio Fio. And all knew that this battle, if begun, would be perpetuated until the Mapuche would be destroyed as a fighting force—so many would be the deaths demanding revenge in a cycle without end.

Juan could appreciate the ironies. A cascade of allegiances had united the Mapuche against each other. By saving two lives he had precipitated a conflict for which these Indians—who had no polity—had no word … for this was civil war. Very soon he would die, and in the process kill more Mapuche than if he led armies. Who could have thought that his affection for two children would shatter their own people! Would Valdivia ever know that his invasion had been facilitated by his secretary's protection of a housemaid and a stable boy? He wondered if those who befriended Indians—like Inés, Juan Lobo, and himself—were paradoxically working harder at their extermination than Spanish cavalry, by corrupting the purity of their hate.…

Had the battle begun, Juan would have died as he had so largely lived—abstracted. But a line had been drawn that no Mapuche dared to cross. Sensing that sudden motion of the part would unleash a tragedy of the whole, the armed multitude was hushed and frozen, in dread of startling war into existence.

Then, an apparition glided between the parting ranks of warriors. Ñamku, returned from the dead! The white form—height exaggerated by his headdress—slowly spun full circle, so that there was not a *che* who did not feel dead eyes had penetrated to his soul.

The mask shrieked, "*Pu Mapuche*, if you would kill *them*, kill me!"

One could not kill the dead, nor could one destroy their power. And Ñamku was right to protect his own from beyond death, *añkeñ peñeñ* though they might be. The listeners—chilled, as by unseen fog—did nothing.

Death-in-life shrieked again. "It was I that sent Lautaro and Raytrayen to the *lik winka*."

Desiring war, Bucephalus stamped the ground, ponderously dancing. Bows and spear points quivered.

"I am proud of Lautaro and of Raytrayen, who sacrificed much by living with *lik winka*. So kill *me*, then, for making them the eyes of my curiosity."

Kuriñam—then, all the *toki*—removed their ax heads, and set them on the ground. To fight the dead was futile, to struggle against their wisdom madness—wrong as their counsel might casually appear. Ñamku had shifted the conflict from their competence—which was war—to his, where the impossible was ordinary.

"Let the *machi* speak," Kuriñam shouted.

Winds of peace blew over the riverbank. Weapons were set upon the ground.

"We are blind!" Ñamku cried. "And the *pillañ* are blind!"

A tremor shook the crowd. Many tested their vision by glancing about. And in fact, *mapu* no longer seemed normal. Yet, *what* were they not seeing? Was the *machi* saying that their ancestors had abandoned them in their time of greatest need?

"The *pillañ* are blind to the *lik winka*, and in yourselves you can recognize their ignorance."

Ñamku gestured at Juan, asking, "Which of you—the bravest, wisest, most experienced—can explain what you are seeing? He looks like *che*, yet does not. He acts like *che*, yet does not. He speaks like *che*, yet does not. He keeps beasts like *che*, yet not the beasts of *che*."

The *machi* was right—the *lik winka* was both ordinary and extraordinary. Helpless, he reeked of danger.

"With your eyes you do not see him."

Was this a deep insult, or opaque wisdom? the *weichafe* wondered.

The *machi* whispered in Raytrayen's ear ... and she in Juan's. "Ñamku want speak *likwinkadungun* you."

Happy to oblige this Indian Lazarus attempting to save their lives, Juan shouted a fervent *Pater Noster*.

The extraordinary sounds—incomprehensible, yet so like language!—drew a collective gasp from the assembly.

Ñamku had made his point. "Our ignorance will not be lessened by killing the *lik winka*."

The crowd muttered, and the *machi* shouted, "You cannot fight what you do not know." The warriors murmured their appreciation. Nothing was more elementary than knowing your enemy.

Ñamku counseled, "*Pu weichafe*, learn from Lautaro. He knows the *lik winka* and their *wethakelu*. He knows *kawellu*. Learn to see them as he does." The *machi* spread his arms, turning, embracing the audience with his gesture.

Approval was slow to come, yet clear—although not total. Many *weichafe* were outraged that the *machi* was giving advice in matters of war—which was insulting. At the same time his words made peculiar sense, since they were planning to do battle with the uncanny. And having a *lik winka* and his *kawellu* in their possession created interesting possibilities.

The *pillañ* wish to speak with the *lik winka*," Ñamku then announced, not inviting contradiction. "I will take him and Raytrayen with me. Lautaro and the *kawellu* will remain with you."

Humming with uneasy comment, the multitude watched the *machi* disappear into the forest, followed by Raytrayen and the *lik winka*. Conflict had been avoided, yet not a few wondered how *giving the lik winka* over *to añkeñ peñeñ* could restore *kume mognen.*

No one was more troubled than Kuriñam—the first to set down his ax. And those who thought he did so simply to save Tuiñam did not do him justice, for the *toki* no more feared an honorable death for his son than for himself. The agonizing truth was that *he* felt responsible for this conflict forced upon the *che*, and he cursed himself for that distant act of insane mercy—small in its own way—from which, as if the three *pichiche* had been pebbles flung into a quiet pond, ripples spread into the future until the harmony of all *mapu* was troubled, trembling. He had disrupted *kume mognen*, then. Now the monsters he allowed to live had attracted disharmonies—like begetting like. The *añkeñ peñeñ* had summoned the *lik winka* by their existence before he ever met them. And the fact that Ñamku—white himself—had been involved, was no surprise.

So that, as *weichafe* crowded around Lautaro and the *kawellu*, babbling like excited children, the *toki* stood aloof. Desperate times called for desperate deeds, and as he could not conceive of a time more desperate, he would seek the aid of *kalku*. Kuriñam could not himself kill the *añkeñ peñeñ* whose lives he had once spared, yet he could see to it that they and the *lik winka* died of inexplicable causes. Like the worms, the snakes, that *machi* sucked from the sick at *machitun*, these monsters needed to be spat out before they consumed the vitals of the Mapuche.

Juan was following Raytrayen—marveling over his release from death—when Ñamku, leading the way, collapsed like a cloak abandoned by its body. Raytrayen knelt and unmasked him, leaving Juan so shaken by what he saw that he had heard her instructions, shouldered his burden and was already struggling down the path before he asked—*Pardiez!*—whom exactly he was carrying, if not Ñamku?

"Brother."

"Hell's spells and wizard's gizzards!" Pedro's mot was ripped from Juan by indignation. He had been tricked—made to think his life had been spared through the intervention of a dead magician when the whole thing was flummery. Indignantly he bleated, "Not Lautaro!"

Raytrayen confessed, "*Hermano otro.* Brother other we call Laku."

So, Juan was laboring under, not so much the living corpse of a swooned magician, as a grandfather who happened to be a brother Raytrayen had never mentioned, disguised as Ñamku. How many layers remained in this Indian onion of deception?

He trudged on with burning legs. "How far?" he croaked when they reached a ravine—for he could go no further. Not down this declivity. Absolutely not up the other side.

"Not far."

He made it to the streambed without collapsing, staggering to rock fortunately flat as tables, where he was told to set down his load beneath an overhang. Juan did not fail to note how carefully their stop had been selected—they were invisible from above, sheltered, and had water. Being a fugitive made him think like Indians. Next—in Pedro's words—he would be 'skulking,' a term which summed all that was ignoble in the savage who would not—By God!—emerge to fight in God's good light.

Bitter memory overmastered Juan with a depth of anguish he would not have believed possible, and he dully watched as Raytrayen tended to her brother, who was stertorously breathing.

She sprinkled water on his face. He woke. Bewildered, Juan saw Raytrayen uncover his legs, to find and unlace small stilts, ending in what had seemed leather covered feet beneath the robe. The sham was more elaborate than he had imagined.

Laku smiled. "I do not fill these clothes."

"Sleep," Raytrayen coaxed.

"He shoves me out my body, then goes away, leaving only air."

"Sleep!"

"Just the air of breathing."

And as they had only what they were and wore, that night the three slept in leaves piled deep, pressed against each other. The next day—dressed as Ñamku— Laku led the way, flitting through the forest like a pallid bat.

Juan lapsed into the relaxation of mice in the mouth of cats, his ease a measure of lost expectations. Fortuna, he thought, expected to sport with him a while longer.

Stopping only to eat this berry, that fruit and leaf—scattering to relieve themselves—mid afternoon found them clambering the flank of an almost vertical mountain, at long last emerging onto the brilliance of a rocky platform.

"*Lolo,*" Raytrayen crowed, indicating the crag before them, whose shadowed flank was swallowing Laku.

God help me! Juan thought. Not *another* cave! In no hurry to enter, he looked back.

Vertigo … and Juan's soul tottered. Immense space plummeted over trees—a perspective extended by the Southern Sea into an infinity melding air and water. Beneath him a hawk slid on wind like a dark bead on some glass thread, recalling Raytrayen's unshakable insistence that Ñamku *was* that bird of prey. And for suspended moments Juan felt something of what it was to inhabit an aerie over teeming earth … to step directly into space, soaring on silent wings like an observing angel. Angels did not flap, he thought, from air to ground and here to there, chittering like sparrows. The unmoved pinions of a silent present elevated them.... And flooded by deep, sudden peace, Juan exclaimed, "*Beatitud!*"

Raytrayen was in awe. As Wan was entering into his trance, she had noticed *pelu*—a fly. Thinking this might be the welcoming *am* of Ñamku, she studied it for signs ... saw Wan extended his arms to embrace *mapu* in that gesture of the *machi* which—even as a child—she never dared to imitate. Now she saw the fly alight on his outstretched hand—the left. And she was expecting to hear the *machi* speak from beyond death when Wan cried out.... '*Feathithud!*' she echoed, shrill with astonishment, release, and a pang of disappointment. Wondering what Wan would think of Lleflai, she turned to enter *lolo*.

About to drop with weariness, Juan penetrated a subterranean obscurity less lit by fire than dimmed by smoke. He rubbed his eyes ... saw a murky shift of forms. Were they smoking meat, or just themselves? Speculating that precisely such interiors turned natives dark as *serrano* hams, he sneezed. A coalescing bulk—Raytrayen—lifted the curtain that closed the cave. Clean, blessed air—and a westering sun—penetrated, revealing sorcery in the dissipating pall. Or was this yet more flummery?
A slender Indian woman stood before him with her head turned backward as the devil's. Or maybe, her feet and hands were turned instead, making of her back the front. Yet this could not be, for he made out breasts beneath her sack.
"My mother, Lleflai." Raytrayen beamed, giving her a hug. "This is the *lik winka*, Wan."
"*Mari, mari*, Lleflai."
"He speaks!" the diabolic vision shrieked.
Shadow in shadows, Pangi gently reproved, "*Papai*, the *lik winka* is our guest. He saved the lives of both Raytrayen and Lautaro."
Lleflai shuddered, whispering. "*Mari mari, lik winka*."
Juan attempted saying that maybe he should go, return later. The first infinitive—he believed—was *tripan*, but the tense, the endings, the accursed particles betrayed him. Lost in the initial verb he never made it to the second, and Juan was certain that Raytrayen was losing her struggle with a smile. Lleflai cut the awful moment short by parting her hair with her fingers and tossing it back, so that the setting sun illuminated her face a brutal pink. Fortunately, it took time for the vision to sink in, and Juan did not recoil.
Raytrayen leapt to embrace Lleflai ... turned to Juan. Catching the challenge in her eyes he said he was very pleased to meet her mother....
He was lying through his teeth, but must have created a correct *mapudungun* sentence—perhaps for the first time—because Raytrayen catapulted herself over to embrace him, astonishing everyone. Livid as sunset, Juan went rigid under the

pressure of her arms and—*María sin pecado concebida!*—unbound breasts! Then, speaking strained formulas they sat down to rude bowls, eating in silence at the Indian absence of a table.

That night, Juan pondered the day. Attempting not to think of breasts—corseted or no— he recalled the epiphany that he experienced as beatitude. Perhaps, emptied of hope, he had somehow been emptied of self, so that his eyes opened as windows through which the world could blow, filling the vacated rooms of his being, making of his eye a transparent cup into which vision poured. This was ecstasy as living suicide, however, replacing man's necessary head with a cyclopean eye detached from its bony home, floating like the moon in crystal spheres. He recalled—while on the cliff—looking over his feet in Indian leather, out at the peculiar familiarity of his extended hands, across the vacancy he inhabited, seeing his 'shoes,' his 'fingers,' only as elements of a landscape. Was this beatitude, to have the empyrean soul estranged, regarding its perishable cage—with its motions and emotions—from perspectives so high that the distance from flesh to Heaven became a gulf *within* the saint? If so, how strangely Christ must have regarded his temporary frame! Not that Juan presumed to the beatitude of actual *saints,* he simply lacked words for the bliss of being dispossessed of self.

The recollection of that moment returned him to a peace that hollowed him with sleep. And he dreamed that he was carrying a phallic Inca drinking vessel through trackless woods, looking for a good place to hide it.

Needing counsel, Pangi did not sleep, waiting until waiting became breathing. As usual, the first sounds were faint—soft as the pop of bubbles in a pot about to boil.

"When will I *see* you, Ñamku?" Pangi was plaintive.

"When your patience is complete."

His patience was exhausted, not complete, and Pangi rebelled. "You know my thoughts, so why not speak them for me?"

"You think I do your deeds. So why do anything?"

"*Yamai!*"

"You think," the voice persisted, "you are not a *machi* in your own right."

"How can I be what *you* did through me?"

"Grouse, Mapuche," a third voice softly mocked—one which Pangi knew from the trances of Ñamku. "Katrinir?" Pangi whispered. A *pillañ,* dead before his birth, was speaking!

"*Mai,*" the mildness responded.

"He means," Ñamku corrected, snappish, "that he is Katrinir in *me* talking."

Pangi laughed. "Two dead voices in the tongue of one," he said. Did he see the glimmer of a smiling face?

"I *am* smiling," Katrinir said. "The Ñamku I am in, is not."

Now Pangi too was smiling, making Ñamku irritable at being outnumbered. "Every *machi* tongue contains other tongues! You both know that! Too many to count."

Katrinir became irritated enough to say, "The living have real problems, *machi*."

"Sorry, Kangen."

And Ñamku *was* feeling sorry, mostly for himself. "I was burrowed into by the worm of blindness, galled, because I thought my whiteness mattered in the new beginning."

Pangi protested. "Do not blame yourself."

"You are *not* proud … not to excess, at least," Katrinir added.

Ñamku glowed. "You are *unmasked!*" Pangi exclaimed.

Katrinir ignored him, sensible. "What *will* we do with *lik winka*?"

Pangi did not answer, now that the voices had boiled out of the pot that was his head. He saw that Ñamku was more or less himself, aglow in customary white, Katrinir a firefly above his head.

"I had thought," Pangi replied, "that the dead would tell me what to do."

"Tell *you* what to do! I am the one that cannot speak with the *lik winka*. I cannot even *see* him, as you said yourself this morning, before *toki*."

"I cannot speak to him, but Raytrayen can," Pangi mused, remembering. "She *sees* him, Ñamku. She truly does, as no one else."

"You mean, as no other Mapuche."

"*Mai.*"

"So do you fear that she will lose her *am* to him?"

"She is being sucked like an oyster."

"Sorry to disagree," the firefly objected. "She is not so much being emptied of herself as filled with *kangen*."

Finding that interesting, Ñamku asked, "At this moment, Pangi, are you Pangi?"

"Yes, and no. And yes—you are both right."

The realization might have been a rumbling drum, for all the time it lived in echoes…. And Pangi acknowledged as the reverberations lingered, "It was I that spoke to the Mapuche."

No response to that. Still, some inner whisper in Pangi insisted that he had been magnificent. And in that dark which blankets sleep and seeing, he knew what he had been and done … and not forgotten.

Chapter 11: *L'Ayem (Mapu,* 1550)

Degu whiskers brushed Juan's nose.

He leapt from bed wearing nothing but his shirt, seeing the astonished four in front of him, sitting about the suspended pot. Four?

Raytrayen, Lleflai, Pangi ... and a *child?*

Bare to his fork, Juan dove for his blanket. *Degu* scattered. The irritable parrot squawked. Birds fled twittering. Clearing her throat, Raytrayen introduced a humpbacked dwarf with raven hair to his waist. Her brother!

Gobbling *mapudungun* greetings, the twisted vision approached, rocking on corkscrew legs. He had the face of a seraph however, and gentle eyes. Heedless of culture and consequence, he was reaching down to touch Juan when Raytrayen halted him, explaining that her brother, Eimi, did not know ... *lik winka.*

The dwarf beamed with a hundred teeth from far too close—his brown, angelic features disquietingly feminine. Juan was astonished that a human being—however stunted, and contorted as a carrot grown in stones—should have been given the familiar pronoun, singular, for a name. The Indies beggared the imagination, he was thinking, groping for his clothes under the covers, but they had vanished overnight!

Tattered they might have been—hose, doublet, cap and cloak, for only they and the belt with its leather bag, his armor and knife remained—but these undeniably ripe garments were his last mementos of civilization. He glared at Raytrayen ... correctly, as her discomfort proved.

Juan absorbed her fatalistic words and gestures, knowing he would not again wear Spanish cloth until his ransom. And to think a girl once his servant was responsible! What was that aberrant celebration of ancient Rome—the *saturnalia?*—when beggars and prostitutes ruled the empire, waited on by emperors? He was absolutely furious.

Raytrayen apologized. Yet she was not sorry she buried his clothes as he slept, for while Wan had left his people, he had not totally escaped their reek. She handed him a worn *chiripa,* a frayed blanket, and they left the cave, after—squirming under fur, invoking saints—Juan had clad himself in primitivity. Mortified, he could have sworn he walked half a league—barefoot, for the love of God!—to a quiet pool in an otherwise restless stream, where Raytrayen handed him a wad of vegetable matter, leaving without a word.

Slipping into the icy flow, Juan did not particularly mind, ascribing his misery to that distant entity—Juan de Cardeña—whose knees protruded from the water, pimpled like plucked drumsticks. The scrubbing hands were dark nonetheless, so that he appeared to wear Indian skin as gloves. Not that they touched the world as Indians did.

Raytrayen returned, long hair sleek, and quietly she led him to a clearing awash in morning light. There, she spread a blanket on which he lay shivering, tight-wrapped—a sausage curing in the sun. Then he observed with astonishment as—planting bare brown feet—Raytrayen rapidly bent at the waist, up and down, up and down, turning her hair into an ebony whip. The stamina! He did not know the word for shiver in *mapudungun*—should it exist—yet it ocurred to him that Raytrayen did not appear to. Pedro would no doubt harrumph, 'Why do fish not shiver?' Yet Juan was not satisfied that God created Indians *that* unlike.

Hair dried, and brushed, Raytrayen reclined on the far edge of the shared blanket, eyes closed to Juan's scrutiny, this girl who swam immense rivers without second thought, and did not shiver … this girl who had saved his life. She had stood beside him, confronting her people out of principle. Courage could be savage, but there was nothing savage about principle.

He muttered "*gracias*"—not having yet discovered a word that by itself expressed gratitude in *mapudungun*. The time for thanks was past but he had postponed—perhaps because it was to a girl he owed his life. "*Digo....*"

"*Sé*," she interrupted what he was about to say, turning her face from the sun and putting a finger to parted lips, appearing to search his features for a signal. She was leaning on her elbow—close!—and she had puckered as she shushed. Were he Pedro, he would have tupped her on the spot. Instead, he held his breath.

"*Qué es un cardeña*?" she asked casually—nothing having happened to make *her* hold her breath.

The syntax was perfect, not the sense. 'What is a Cardeña?' did not signify at all, although, admittedly, it expressed his questioning of self and purpose. He corrected, "*Who* is Cardeña?"

At that point the conversation became raveled in the customary knots of their misunderstanding, Juan eventually discovering that she thought 'Cardeña' was perhaps an animal or stone. He said the name meant nothing, simply referring to his birthplace. "With all its many things," he amended, sensing that the village of his nativity was about to be accused—quite justly—of abject poverty.

"You were name after place you born for!"

Juan condescended. "Your name, in Spain, sometimes tells where you are from, so you do not get confused with someone with the same name from somewhere else."

She exclaimed, "My name mine! Place not name! *Lugar, lugar*! A place is place, have name!" Then, "People from other place no need know me!" She smiled, relishing her Indian solipsism.

Juan explained that there were many Juanes where he came from, including others in Cardeña, which really was not *that* large.

Shaping her mouth into an unvoiced O, Raytrayen argued—jubilant as if predicting checkmate in four moves—that if all these Juanes with the same name were from the same place, their 'two name' did not tell them apart. Better have different name first. So much choose.

Stunned, Juan mentally attempted to parse what seemed very much a verity....

Raytrayen asked what 'Juan' meant, to be chosen by so many.

"Several *santos* in *la Biblia* have the name." And saying that, Juan sighed. As his parents had died in his infancy, he would never know his true eponym. It festered—this thorn of orphanhood.

He shrugged, and said his name was not a thing or animal. And if it meant anything, he did not know what *that* might be. Last names almost always had to do with places and occupations. First names did not mean anything. "Or almost never," he corrected, remembering Constanza di Lorenzo of the bee-stung lips. The time had come to digress … and he offered that 'Flower in the Stream' was a beautiful name.

Raytrayen did not take the bait. "What Cardeña like?"

How explain the destitution, the narrow-mindedness … the distant perspectives on all that was true and beautiful? He said, "Hot and dusty in summer. Cold and muddy in winter."

Nodding—as if that confirmed her every dark suspicion—Raytrayen asked if the Juanes *santos* were alike or different.

"*Diferentes.*" And Juan attempted a joke. "*Mi padre, el padre*—my father, the priest—in that old chestnut of their language lessons—said I was named after Juan Bautista because I spent so much time wandering in fields." He did not add that—allowed to name himself—he would infinitely have preferred the Juan of the Apocalypse, secretary of God, to a voice crying in the wilderness, which more or less summed up his present state.

"O," Raytrayen said, voicing only that charming zero.

She was profoundly dubious about the *lik winka dengu* they called '*religión*.' She could repeat the Credo like a *choroy* but did not understand it. *La Biblia* made her even more rebellious, as seemingly designed to make her feel stupid. She also hated the presumption of *lik winka*, who had taken her true name and given her one she did not want. Angry, she was ready to ask a question she had not dared voice before—Why did *lik winka*, who stank, make a bath into a holy thing, the first one of their lives, and probably the last?

Lost in unvoiced thought himself, Juan was remembering what Lobo in his madness after the battle of Santiago had cried out, that Metaphysics is the bastard child of Ignorance, raped by Faith, and given over to the foster care of Intelligence.

But what the two might next have said, never was....

Lleflai erupted into the clearing, crying, "Ayelewei is dying. Kuriñam has sent for Pangi. There will be a *machitun*."

"Kurufil!" Raytrayen groaned, speeding after her mother....

Juan found the cave deserted save for the several *degu* and the parrot, which was squawking, "*Machi, machi, machitun*." He was maddening, unstoppable.

And for ponderous revolutions of the firmament Juan was alone as Adam before Eve. The first day he spent expecting a return, morose, waking the next morning to darkness and a smothered fire. He found a coal to breathe on ... built a flame. Encouraged, he bound a blanket about his body with a plaited cord. Feeling guilty—as the firewood was not exactly his to burn—he fed the hearth, his thoughts unformed as the inconstant flames.

That night he dreamt that he was John the Baptist, but in Eden, living the loneliness that God granted man as His first bequest—a voice crying in the Garden. And in his dream he paced the high, engirdling walls, discovering that they were cruciform. Eden was an immense cathedral without vault or window, the Tree of Knowledge growing in the altar's stead. And the massive portals of the west wall were locked, studded with black nail heads the size of babies' fists, like those of the city of Sevilla. He was a prisoner in Paradise....

Waking to the morning of the third day, Juan surveyed what remained to burn ... took up a stone ax, and left to cut wood. He labored until late afternoon, faint with hunger. At this rate he would die warm, but soon, he thought, rummaging through the baskets hanging from the logs that spanned the cave.

The *uwa*, the *poñu*—these dried edibles shriveled beyond human recognition— might as well have been the stuff on seashores for all the nourishment they offered in their present state. Juan suspended a pot ... began making soup. Salivating as he stirred, he let time crawl, surveying the cave. And it occurred to him that civilization did not squat about a fire pit, but sat about a board. Impossible to conceive of the Emperor hunkering, bowl in hand. Nor did the Pope sing Mass without an altar. And—to create the sacrament that conferred life after death—The Son of God sat at a table.

Juan tried his hardest *not* to imagine the Last Supper by a fire pit, but the scene began materializing nonetheless—the holy, barefoot, hunkering twelve, in loincloths, surrounding the bubbling vessel, no less undressed than The Crucified Christ Himself! Fortunately, the image faded—as too improbable, perhaps, for not just the table was a *sine quae non*, but also bread and wine. Yearning for that trinity of a Christian meal, Juan fished the pot and found the *poñu* not yet tender.

He studied the hanging nets and baskets of the cave. The kitchens of Spain similarly put food out of reach of the dogs, the occasional cat, and—in farmhouses—the chickens, goats and ducks, particularly the intelligent pig. An absence struck Juan. Nothing *precious* here was stored. There were no locks, chest or coffer … no real door. Poor as he was, even Father Sosa kept the few coins that came his way under lock and key. What would it be like to have nothing worth stealing, to be content with abject poverty, considering it a fault to own more than another, unable to conceive of wealth, not to *have* words for poverty or riches? Juan was reminded of **Utopia**—although the society of the Humanist had in it far more of Inca than of Mapuche, with its rigid hierarchy and organization. And, according to Raytrayen, her people were no more interested in dominion than in riches. No wealth or power, then. No religion worth mentioning that he knew of, except for dead ancestors that could be invoked like saints. No art or learning. No books. And of course, no tables, wine or bread.

He ate unfinished soup. Stuffed—after a period in which greed blotted out consciousness—he was minding the pot, picking his teeth with a splinter, thinking that when you stripped layers from the Indian onion to reach that last savage pearl, all that remained was the will to fight to the death with those who sought to better you. What could be more ironic! Did Mapuche fight in order *not* to eat of the Tree of Knowledge? Was this an Eden perpetuated by some paradoxical virtue, or had he stumbled into fallacy? Something was wrong here, he was thinking, when abruptly he was greeted in *mapudungun* from behind. Close!

Leaping to his feet—knife springing to his hand—Juan spun about … to confirm yet again that he was created to disgrace himself. An Indian woman draped in black was by his bench. Then, the hood shrouding her face began magically—that is, without the intervention of a hand—to lower itself, turning the revelation into uncanny ceremony.

Juan looked away, looked down, less to sheathe his knife than to avoid the accusation about to be revealed. And when at last he lifted his eyes—heavy as cannon in creaking tackle—he was smitten dumb.

She was bedecked with treasure—silver, gold and gems—that must have weighed like millstones. Chains glowed against her dusky, slender neck. Earrings sparkled, making faint metallic noises as she gently shook her head, keeping Juan's eye in the moist dark of hers. A double circlet of gold links bound her forehead like a crown slipped low, from which hung hammered golden suns. The largest—at the center—was inlaid with an emerald glittering like a reptilian eye. Not that there was menace in her smile. Could this be coquetry?

"*Milla*," the apparition breathed, melodious, husky.

Juan knew the *mapudungun* word for gold, yet could not loose the cables binding his tongue, incapable of understanding what he saw. A Mapuche *domo* was wearing a king's ransom!

"You like?" She shook her head—again—with a precious clink of metal. Her smile was brilliant, features perfect in their wild way, a dark oval in which the whites of eyes and teeth were cream in contrast. And the mass of loosed and gleaming, unbraided hair, hung to below the bench she sat. How had it gotten *there*, from out her hood? Regal as queens of Christian demesne, she revealed a hand—tapered fingers heavy with rings, one of which touched the emerald on her brow.

"*Esmeralda*," Juan offered, fortunately not stuttering.

"*Ethmeraltha*."

Become a parrot, Juan echoed her as she gestured toward his stew.

"*Yamai*," he babbled in her thrall—blushing at his lack of hospitality. Gathering a wooden spoon, a bowl—aware that what he had to offer eclipsed even the *ollas podridas* of Spanish inns, which only nostalgia could enjoy—he set the bowl beside the Indian queen.

Gracefully she ate, looking up from under gold.

And thoughts that had been creeping up on Juan, now pounced. Did Mapuche have hidden treasure? Did they have royalty, contradicting everything he knew? If so, where the king … the court? And why was this queen wearing black homespun—a shocking contrast to her jewelry? The questions boiled….

She offered that she once lived near, and, producing what seemed white linen from her sleeve—if sleeve it was—she dabbed soup from her lips. Was this a handkerchief, rare even in Venice?

The *domo* smiled.

Juan stood, all useless thumbs, a blush suffusing his face. He had been tempted … appraised … and she had found him wanting.

"*Trafkiñ*," she said, the word plucking a forgotten note in Juan, recorded in abandoned notebooks.

She gestured with a glimmering hand, making Juan think she was proposing some exchange. What had *he* to trade in the destitution of captivity?

Then—like a dog sensing an approaching presence not registered by man's senses—the *domo* froze, stood, and glided limping from the room.

That she could both limp and glide did not at the moment concern Juan, for he was convinced that Eimi's mother had just left. The resemblance—however masked by gold—was extraordinary, and the limp had created this improbable connection.

Murmuring greetings, Pangi entered, then Raytrayen and Lleflai, both covered with a paste of ash and water, hair clotted and tangled. They sat on a bench, looking like corpses startled by the last trump.

"*Lo siento mucho*," Juan told them, not thinking his *mapudungun* equal to the moment.

Elbows heavy on her knees, Raytrayen looked up to say, "Ayelewei is dead. Pangi performed a *machitun*."

"Dead!" Eimi echoed, shambling in.

"Killed by Kurufil," Pangi specified, with the despondency of one who battled and was defeated. He had failed spectacularly—for Ayelewei was the wife of a *longko*—and he might never again be called upon to heal. Also, it was being whispered that *lik winka kalkutun* had been involved, the rumor said to have begun with Kuriñam himself.

Would these mourners want soup, Juan asked himself. One ate at wakes. He filled a bowl

Eimi stepped up, took a mouthful, and spat it with a glorious smile. Humming, he added pinches and handfuls of this and that into a mortar, grinding, tossing the product into Juan's pot, tasting ... and then they were eating an excellent soup, done at last.

Pangi addressed Juan, and the constant in the verbal flood—like a log bobbing to the surface in a mountain stream—was *trafkiñ*. Juan remembered it as the word produced by the mysterious savage queen.

"He mean you exchange," Raytrayen translated, delicately belching.

"*Your* food," Juan insisted.

"We hungry. Your wood, your cooking, " she rejoined, scraping with fingernails at the gray cake of mourning on her face.

"*Gracias*," Juan said to Pangi. He asked Raytrayen, "Please thank him for saving my life."

"Also," she replied, again scraping at her face.

Juan almost erupted with ill-mannered laughter. How often had *mapudungun* tricked him into equal comedy? he wondered, as Raytrayen luminously smiled at him through ash. Mourning and disaster aside, he felt that this was the silence of companions, and with a casualness made insane by retrospect he described in Spanish the *domo* who had just visited.

"Kurufil," Raytrayen gasped.

Eimi leapt up, dropping his bowl, seizing the end of a smoldering log. Raytrayen exploded into speech, translating.

"Kurufil," the redundant parrot screeched, madly bobbing on his perch.

"Kurufil?" repeated Juan, startled into stupidity.

Pangi and Eimi vanished. Clasping a *degu* to her bosom, Lleflai rocked on her heels, murmuring, "*Atrutrui! Atrutrui!*"

"Bad war," was all Raytrayen said. First, the death of Ayelewei. Now, the *kalku* had returned to the sacred cave.

"Who *is* this Kurufil?" Juan insisted, entrenched in outraged innocence.

Ignoring him, Raytrayen asked what Kurufil had said. And did he *take* anything?

Surprised by the masculine pronoun Juan replied that she had done nothing but eat soup ... and maybe said a dozen words.

"*Thopa!*" she exclaimed with naked dread.

Juan confessed to his abomination. "*Sí, mi sopa.*" He searched her frantic eyes for a key to this Indian terror.

She exclaimed, "He eat! We eat!"

He repaired pronoun and tense. "*She ate. We ate.*"

Raytrayen leapt from his innocent pedagogy as from an asp, and abandoning communication, she babbled across the fire pit in her own tongue, opaque as a distant sphinx.

Shadow in the night, Kurufil had seen them return to the cave he had just left, and became perturbed, for his plans had been going well. The *antu*—not so long ago—that Kuriñam came to him with gifts, making a request blunt as his club, Kurufil had exulted. He refused to kill the *lik winka*, and the angry *longko* strode away, leaving the *kalku* chuckling. He would kill Ayelewei instead, he thought to himself—a brilliant decision. First, Pangi, Lleflai, Raytrayen, Lautaro and Eimi would have their future agonies demonstrated by her death. Then Pangi would be summoned to the *machitun*. Lleflai and Raytrayen would come to be by the side of Ayelewei. If he made the poisons slow, the *lik winka* would be left alone for *antu*.

Poisoning Ayelewei proved easy. The third wife of Kuriñam came to him for *wekufu* to make Ayelewei ugly. Kurufil had her drop pinches of a certain powder in her food, *and* in the herbs she used for healing, insisting that this was important. Therefore, when Ayelewei became ill, she poisoned herself with the teas she prepared, until the day came that she could not stumble out her *ruka* to vomit, half mad with pain, tearing at her clothes, screaming that she could not bear their touch. Ignoring custom, Kuriñam brewed her medicine himself, angering his other wives.

All that *antu* husband and wife argued. Ayelewei—barely capable of speech— insisted that Pangi had to preside at the *machitun*.

Kuriñam angrily refused. Pangi was *ankeñ peñeñ*! The ceremony would destroy *kume mognen*.

No less stubborn, Ayelewei made her unmoved will known with gesture, now that her body was revolting, first stiffening—so that one could tap on her like wood—then shuddering as in a *nuyun*.

When his wife could scarcely moan, and her eyes and ears, her nipples, bled, Kuriñam sent a *werken* for Pangi.

This, the *kalku* learned from the third wife of Kuriñam, who came to him as the ceremony was taking place. Weeping, she insisted she had wanted Ayelewei ugly, not dead.

Kurufil laughed. Ayelewei *was* ugly now, he told her, delighted that Kuriñam was killing Ayelewei himself, by doing the work of *domo*. He imagined the fearsome *weichafe*—all muscles, knuckles and elbows—preparing poisoned teas....

Terrified at dying at the hands of her own husband if her involvement became known, the third wife pleaded for something to heal Ayelewei. Kurufil was unmoved, ecstatic that his poisons had worked so well. Indeed, so deep in gloating was he, that he almost missed the inspiration fluttering by him like a moth.

"Do not blame yourself. Ayelewei is dying of *lik winka kalkutun*."

Fleeing *renu* with her excuse, the third wife spread the rumor.

The *kalku* found out later that Ayelewei had died, yet was still bleeding. Also, rumors circulated that Pangi was a fool unworthy of his teacher—so that Kurufil might be able to have the *lik winka* by making *renu* the only safe place for him. But every *wedwed* who said Ayelewei had died did not know that her *am* remained trapped in her body by his venoms. She would never move—or see—again, but could still hear, still suffer. Too bad he was not there to whisper to the living corpse, letting her know who killed her.

Kuruvil began to prepare his meal, and this reminder of the humiliating servitude of his apprenticeship to Ñamcu brought the death of Katrinir to his mind, so that he relived old memories as he labored....

How crudely he had killed in the infancy of his strength, while still Kalfil! In those *kuyen* he had been proud but tormented ... undecided. Putting on the clothing that declared him *weye*, he discovered not the love he had imagined, but couplings in the forest with *che* who—like himself—were tolerated but taunted and avoided, although Kalfil knew himself superior to those who mocked him. He suffered in solitude, desiring from a distance those who despised him most—the slender young warriors, bodies gleaming like oiled wood as they wrestled, ran, and shot their arrows, hurled their spears....

One morning he went to *fucha lafken*, willing himself cold and unfeeling as a pebble of its shore. A storm approached, flickering with light, and Kalfil faced the fury laughing, stung by spray and sand, pounded by rain. Tasting salt, he bit his lip, and licked the mingling of blood and sea. That day he decided that in the salt of his blood lived Kaikaifilu, enemy of the *che*, and he became solitary and free, at peace. Yet his soul drifted, looking for direction, until the *antu* he attended a *machitun* and saw Ñamku bring a *domo* back from death, dancing, chanting, beating his *kultrung*, spitting the *wekufu* out as a living snake....

When he was apprenticed, Kalfil dreamed of seducing Ñamku and replacing Katrinir. Rejected, he came to hate them both. Therefore he poisoned Katrinir with clumsy inexperience, yet for the best of reasons—as a skinny, odious old hag who obviously detested him.

Killing small birds had always given Kalfil pleasure. He drowned them, suffocated them, and crushed them slowly with his hands, enjoying their tiny tremors. But he found that he enjoyed killing Katrinir far, far more. And when he saw his eyes dim like cloud-hazed sky, Kalfil discovered his vocation.

Having created hate in the only opponent worthy of him, he had gone to *renu* to apprentice himself to the *kalku*, Kuripan, finding him drooling toothless by his fire, ancient and malevolent. Kindred spirits, they were wary of each other from the first.

Kalfil resumed the servility of apprenticeship—which he despised—reaping in return a harvest of dark knowledge.

The *antu* came when the *kalku* lay dying.

He gasped, "You poisoned me."

"*Yamai.*"

Kalfil hummed to pass the time. Now and again he bent over Kuripan to assess the progress of his death, eventually declaring, "I am going to strangle you, or it will be the poisons—not my hands—that kill you."

No stranger to malice, Kuripan did not plead. He whispered, instead, "Fool! Now I will not tell you my greatest secret."

Those were his last words. Kalfil looked into his eyes, slowly pressing on his throat, slowly releasing, savoring each momentary gasp, each feeble kick. When it was over, he lit a torch and strode into the depths of *renu*.

From the first of his apprenticeship Kalfil knew Kuripan was hiding something. He had followed him when he went into the cave, stalking the torch through winding passages that led eventually to a hole into which he crawled. He could have slain him then and known his secret, but he wanted this death more ceremonious.

When Kuripan was dead Kalfil went to the secret, crawling into a chamber— not large, to judge by its echoes—lifting his flame, illuminating an array of baskets. Had he gone to the trouble of killing the *kalku* only to inherit *poñu, penka, uwa*? Hissing, he lifted the first lid.

Unable to believe what he saw, frantically he opened others. "*Liken, milli!*" Kalfil knew silver and gold, yet had never seen the like—*milli* stored like maize! Trembling with nameless lust he lit another torch, and—insanely capering—he emptied every basket, the gold glittering like stars. There were brilliant feathers too, cloth of unimaginable weave, stones which returned light with a fire of their own, and not one *wethakelu* did he recognize.

On that day Kalfil acquired a passion perhaps greater than his hate. He touched it all, lightly—a butterfly over a field of flowers—selecting a necklace. Intricately fashioned, it bore suspended suns. At the center of the largest was a green stone, limpid as a tidal pool. Delighted, Kalfil discovered that it fit his forehead. He found more rings than he could slide onto his fingers. He discovered bracelets, and they clinked on his wrists as he tore off his *kepam*, dancing until he found a feathered cloak—such softness!—in crimson, green and subtle blues, colors without name, billowing as he moved. He put on sandals bound in *milli*, danced in feathers and *milli*, nothing else, until the jounce of his sex became a part of the pleasure. Never had Kalfil felt so beautiful. If only he could see himself! Slow, sinuous in his dance, now, arms over his head, he undulated like a snake, certain of his destiny. To be *kalku* was to be *winka*. He had been born for this....

One of his torches died, returning him to a place with an elsewhere, and Kalfil panted, swaying, seeing that the second torch was sputtering. He kindled his last and crawled in *winka wethakelu* from the chamber of dreams, leaving his clothes behind. Jingling and glittering beneath his upheld brand, he returned to the corpse of the *kalku*—still warm to the touch. And in the light that pierced the smokehole of the cave Kalfil stretched out the weight on his arms and spun—feathered *wethakelu* floating—startled to see light flickering on the walls of *renu*. Reflections of *milli*! He closed his eyes to imagine how he must appear, ablaze. And despite— or perhaps because of—his joy, he found that he was also in great despair, for that which made him beautiful was unknown. He would have given anything to name what he wore. With sadness, he murmured to the silence of the green stone, "You are more beautiful than the waters of the great sea." He felt rejected by the *winka* who had fashioned these wonders, *winka* he had never known and would never know. He wore a stolen dream.

The Mapuche *weichafe* who fought the invading Inca to a standstill destroyed much of what they looted. The remaining *winka wethakelu* was scattered throughout *mapu*—a hidden, secret shame.

Once he was *kalku*, Kurufil made these concealed *winka wethakelu* the price for his deadly arts. He might trade love potions for food, salt and *mudai*, make fields shrivel in return for blankets, but he would not kill *che* for less than *winka wethakelu*. In this way he slowly added to what he had inherited. And he feared he had acquired all that remained until the *antu* that—like a wind bending every blade of grass—word of *lik winka* reached the *che* and drove him almost mad with hope and fear ... the two at war.

Fear kept him from attempting the desert—although *piku* powerfully called.

Yet not the wasteland kept him from his journey, but the terror that once he was face to face with *winka*, he—who despised Mapuche—would be seen as one of them. Not speaking *likwinkadungun*, how could he tell them that in his soul he resembled them? Did he not, as the *winka* did, love *milli*? He knew himself superior to the *che*, but to *lik winka* he would seem like a *pichiche* in her mother's finery, taken without permission. Through their strange, pale eyes Kurufil saw himself as a fool in love with the moon. *That* was the fear. Yet hope raged at this second coming of *winka*. They shone like the sun! They killed with fire and thunder!

Kurufil could not bring himself to act. *Winka* were white as only Ñamku was. Had he summoned his kind from afar? Kurufil despaired, but dared hope again when he heard that *lik winka* loved *milli*, like the *winka* before them. Still he vacillated, until the birds of Umeñdomo betrayed Ñamku and he discovered that the *machi* had gone *piku*. Death it might be to follow, and perhaps he would experience a humiliation worse than death when at last he met *lik winka*, but Kurufil could not let the *machi* succeed where his own fears betrayed him. He had followed Ñamku, consumed by doubt. Would he, or the *machi*, be chosen? Or, both? Neither?

Kurufil remembered bleeding on the bank of the stream, seeing only the eyes of the *lik winka* above him—and like lightning in the night, they seemed to illuminate every other of his wonders. Blue as cloudless skies, they were impassive in the perfect face, white as milk. And, although the apparition wore no *milli*, his hair, falling to his shoulders—twisting like the finest tendrils of a climbing vine— was gold.

Obsessed, Kurufil relived their meeting in memory and troubled sleep. The *lik winka* had attacked him with his dogs, but spared his life. Was this a hateful pity, or something else? Betraying nothing, the eyes reminded him of the pure attention of the snake. The *kalku* found hope in *that*, convinced that if he could he see his own they would have that unmoved stare.

The mangled hand healed scarred, and distorted, yet the *kalku* cherished it, loading it with bracelets and rings, adorning this talisman created upon his body. Like a tree taller than others, lightning had singled him out. Still, he knew nothing about *lik winka*....

Questions without answer, impossible prospects, abrupt sorrows, raptures and suffocations of the soul, turmoil and palpitations—Kurufil lived them all in a cyclone spinning about brief instants of the past. He had expected unknown strength of *lik winka,* not the beauty of this *werken* clothed in blue, sent by the sky. Kurufil was desperately—and hopelessly—in love.

He came to the cave of the *machi* wearing *milli* to tempt the *lik winka*, prepared for the power of that ancient place where he was hated, concealing several of his most powerful *wekufu*. If he was rejected by the *lik winka*, he would kill him.

On the way, Kurufil was light-headed with hope. This *lik winka* would also have skin like milk. In other ways he might be different, yet in his own way as beautiful. Unable to conceive the differences, he imagined him like the first, with blue eyes and gold hair falling to astonishing blue cloth. In captivity, he would be without beasts or familiars, of course, perhaps bound, weakened by the sorcery of Ñamku. How else could he have been overcome?

Kurufil imagined their encounter…. Beautiful, cold eyes would calmly regard him when he entered. He would watch as Kurufil revealed his head and his left hand—laden with *milli*. Wordlessly approaching, Kurufil would gently release him from his bonds. What followed he could not conceive. But he was certain the *lik winka* would be grateful, and more certain yet that he desired *milli*. If all went well he could propose to trade his freedom for whatever mysteries he had to offer. They would become *trafkiñ*. Maybe the *lik winka* could make him white … maybe teach him *likwinkadungun*, or how to kill with lightning. But would he refuse to become *trafkiñ*? Would he have to kill him?

Slipping into the cave, the *kalku* saw no bound figure to liberate, only a dim Mapuche form on a bench silhouetted against the fire, too large to be the *ifunche*. Straight hair fell to his shoulders. He was stirring soup.

Was he being tricked by the *machi* into not seeing what was before him? Kurufil prepared a *wekufu* and greeted the dark figure.

Blanket on his shoulders whirling away into darkness, the dark form leapt, spinning, to face him, crouching with a deadly glimmer in his hand. The *lik winka*!

His eyes were blue, but not cold, face not rounded, nose straight. A closer look determined that his hair was darker than gold, eyes more green than blue. Like a rag, Kurufil collapsed on a bench—looking through the folds of his *ekull*—devouring the beauty of this strangeness. The *lik winka* was slender, with broad shoulders. His lean, unlined face was troubled—the *kalku* decided—by the indecisions of youth.

Kurufil slowly revealed his features, his *milli*, by tugging on concealed thongs. The *lik winka* looked everywhere but at *him*, as if fearful of what was being revealed. And when the extraordinary eyes at last looked into his, Kurufil moved his head gently, making the *milli* shimmer in firelight. The eyes of the *lik winka* widened. Kurufil smiled, loosing his hair to let it fall.

"*Milli*," the *kalku* said. The *lik winka* nodded his head like a *pichiche* scolded, but spared the stick. No wonder he had been captured. He was speechless, shuffling as one in love rejected, more to be pitied than admired. Was he an amputated limb without his *kawellu*? Without his *wethakelu*—shining like the sun—was he a snail without its shell?

Kurufil decided that this was still a warrior to be reckoned with. The shining *wethakelu* he held looked like a different sort of knife. Did it kill with lightning? Smiling seductively, he asked the *lik winka* if he liked what he saw.

When he did not reply, Kurufil wondered if he knew no *mapudungun*, or was a *likwinka wed wed*—if such existed—and the extraordinary thought came to him that he might be turned into an *ifunche*. Kurufil needed facts. Maybe he knew the name of the stone on his forehead. Revealing his left hand, giving the *lik winka* time to appreciate the sight, Kurufil touched it.

"*Ethmeralda.*"

Strange, that the name of a *wethakelu* so wonderful should be so easy to pronounce. Deciding to test his dominance, Kurufil gestured at the soup pot. He was hungry ... curious too. What did *lik winka* eat?

"*Yamai,*" was the flustered response.

Mapudungun!

Kurufil had before him a potential *ifunche* such as no *kalku* ever had, weak enough to be transformed, with immense abilities to be exploited. And as the *lik winka* scurried to fulfill his wishes, Kurufil concluded that he had been poisoned, to be this submissive. He would have to poison him too—at least at first. It would be a shame to break the legs of a youth so well made.

Given soup, the *kalku* relaxed. He knew he was more beautiful than any *domo* he had ever met, yet he had feared he would not prove attractive to *lik winka*, and that uncertainty had been set to rest. He did not need his beauty. He might not even have needed *milli*.

Kurufil tasted, astonished. This annoying blandness was at once over *and* undercooked, depending on the ingredient. He attempted to detect some *lik winka* subtlety so great as to slip by his ignorance, asking himself if he truly wanted to appreciate such food. Would he have to teach the *lik winka* how to cook?

He proposed an exchange, but the expression of the *lik winka*—bland as his food—revealed no sign he understood.

Then, Kurufil heard a distant, faint, *atrutrui*! Ayelewei had died sooner than he planned, and now was not the time to test the powers of Pangi. He could capture the *lik winka* later.

"Pangi!"

The harsh whisper was urgent, and he struggled out of sleep as out of quicksand.

"Ñamku."

The *machi* took form—glow swimming up from depths. Had he come to confirm the failure of his student?

Katrinir—still invisible—was the one to break the silence, quietly proposing that the death of Ayelewei was his fault. He was the one who insisted that Ñamku not study poisons and antidotes.

Ñamku interrupted, rude with love and guilt. *He* was the one who failed.

Pangi insisted that the blame was obviously his, since he presided at the suffering and death of Ayelewei.

The echoes of the outburst had scarcely died when Ñamku called out, "Who else is here?"

A multitude of dead, disturbed, murmured with the dry, distant voices of insects, wanting to be left alone.

Then—near—a familiar "*mari, mari.*"

"Ayelewei!" Pangi and Ñamku cried together.

Katrinir commented, "So far from your body … so soon," expressing what was in all their minds. Her *am* was in danger until she crossed the waters of death to the island Ngulchenmaiwen.

"Not yet gone to the *tempulkalwe*," Ayelewei admitted. "When I heard your call, I left my husband's side."

And on his forehead, like a breeze, Pangi felt a light caress.

Ayelewei chuckled, adding, "He will not know I'm gone."

"Men! she exclaimed. Loving and exasperated, her tone conveyed it all—*wentru* had far too much in common with *pichiche*, that other helpless, cherished burden of her sex.

She became serious. "I am the one to know my death, and I tell you Kurufil killed me, so that no one here needs to take the blame. My husband thinks *lik winka kalkutun* was responsible. Other *che* think so also. Many blame you, *palu*, saying you are unworthy to be *machi*. A few even blame Ñamku for taking *ankeñ peñeñ* under his roof. The only one not being blamed is the one responsible—Kurufil. And here I find you fighting over blame!"

"You are right to blame us," Katrinir told her.

Chuckling, Ayelewei responded, "My death had consequences, and there will be more. The *lik winka* is innocent, yet in peril if he leaves this cave. You, *palu*, have been unjustly dishonored in life, as Ñamku is being dishonored in death. And our people are in danger. Needing to unite against a great enemy, they are divided, all because the *kalku* killed me. Not that I much mind having died. I was old, and I look back on a life lived in honor, love and laughter. But I refuse to be the tool of Kurufil. My honor has been stolen from me, and I will not rest in *kume mognen* until the truth about my death is known.

Ñamku spoke for all, "We are grateful for your counsel."

The voice of Ayelewei became hushed, hesitant. "My husband can be impulsive, rash, extreme…."

The extraordinary afterthought lingered, and no one was eager to comment.

As the only living *che* present, Pangi felt that the weight of action rested on him, and he exclaimed, "What can we *do* to make the truth known? I am the one who can speak to the living, yet no one will listen—not after my *machitun!*"

"All you *machi,* in your wisdom, can decide what to do. I am only a dead old woman," said Ayelewei. And considering her company, she was bold. But the dead are fearless.

"Now, I will visit my husband before I leave for Ngulchenmaiwen. I fear that he will go insane with grief and frustrated vengeance." The fading voice concluded, "My suffering was hard on him."

Sighing with appreciation, Katrinir said that mothers never die.

Ignoring him, Ñamku proposed, "We do not have to kill Kurufil. The truth will kill him if *che* find out. That would not *exactly* be revenge."

Katrinir commented, "Truth does not carry a club."

Taking the sarcasm as assent, Ñamku speculated, "Into what mouth can we put the truth?"

Pangi had a sudden insight, blurting out, "Not just *one* dose killed Ayelewei!"

Ñamku seized the implications. "Who then, if not Kurufil?"

A vicious worm, the question burrowed into the marrow of their minds, until Pangi voiced what all suspected—"Kuriñam prepared her medicine."

"He would *not* kill her," Ñamku insisted, outraged. "He loves her. He humiliated himself to prove it."

Katrinir observed that Kuriñam did not know poisons. Also, Ayelewei, that expert on her own death—the very one who insisted that the truth be spoken—pointed no finger at her husband....

A boulder might as well have dropped among them, its violence echoing in the cave, and Pangi almost keened *atrutrui.* In their horror, the rest kept the perfect silence of the dead until Ñamku whispered, "She knew."

Katrinir added, "She could not tell Kuriñam what he was doing."

"Not if she found out too late."

"Not even before. She saw his act as what it was, and in her love accepted it."

"So now," mused Ñamku, "the question is, how many will her love kill?"

"The question is," Pangi countered, "how can we keep Kuriñam out of *this*?"

Ñamku took his turn. "Also, how did Kurufil fool Kuriñam?"

"Does that matter unless you seek revenge?" This was—of course—Katrinir.

The *machi* agreed it did not matter, but the truth had become a poisonous snake, indifferently striking.

Pangi was practical, saying that only he—of the three—could accuse Kurufil.

"Yes, and no." Ñamku removed his mask to smile.

Pangi reflected. "I am the only one alive, but Kuriñam will not listen to me. Therefore I will not speak."

"Yes and no." Ñamku went silent, plotting.

Katrinir approved. "Why should speech with the living be denied the dead," he said.

Not unlike bats—dark in darkness, silent in silence—the interested dead were gathering.

"And," Ñamku crowed, "we do not need to prove one thing."

Katrinir interjected, "How do we get Pangi in the *ruka*?"

Ñamku was cheerful, "We will think of something."

"What *ruka*?" Pangi exclaimed, annoyed. "What are you *not* saying?"

To which Ñamku—in a much better mood—replied, "Think about it."

Striding down the mountain, Pangi was stifled by the white leather he wore. He had postponed the discomfort of the mask, however. Enjoying the breeze on his face he looked up to admire *mañke*, gliding on the wind like a smooth stone on ice—one way that Ñamku described soaring. He also called it falling without hitting ground. And the puzzled child who heard this became the Pangi who never flew, never wanted to, and never would, the child taught that nothing was more important than to become himself. Now here he was, Ñamku a second time.

Pangi put on the mask, adjusted the headdress. Suffocating, almost blind, he strode on. How could Ñamku dress like *this* most of his life?

"Relax. Who needs eyes? Who needs breath? Think of yourself as dead."

The *machi* spoke through the mask with the voice of Pangi ... then it *was* Ñamku listening to the chink of the sacred stones in his *kultrung*, remembering Pangi, thinking that nothing was more important than to become oneself, but that to be yourself in *kume mognen* required becoming one with others. And the *machi* whispered to the memory of Pangi, "You must see yourself as *mapu* sees you, to know what you are."

Ñamku strode on, breathing easily as darkness fell, hearing in the distance the clamor of *che* by the *ruka* where the wife of Kuriñam lay dead. He strode past corrals and into the fire lit clearing where *wentru* shouted and clashed *palin* sticks together. Every motion stopped and sound was stilled, all eyes turning to the impossible presence. The dead had come to mourn the dead....

Ñamku wasted no time, saying that he had come to honor Ayelewei. And like leaves on snow, his words fell on silence.

Shuddering with dread, the third wife of Kuriñam crawled from firelight into darkness. No one else stirred or spoke.

With the cry of a small, wounded creature, the fifth wife—accustomed to being given the most unpleasant tasks—scurried in the door and returned, saying Ñamku could enter.

Ayelewei was upright beside the firepit, lashed to a rack, feast spread at her feet.

The sweet stench of her putrefaction was far fainter than one might have expected, masked by the aromatic smoke. The *longko*, crumpled on a bench beside the body, raised his head.

Kuriñam was gaunt, disheveled, querulous. "You again," he groaned from the distance of a grief that does not know politeness. "Are you a fly, attracted by death? What do you want?"

"The dead want nothing for themselves," the *machi* said, "save vengeance."

"What does that have to do with *me*?"

Intelligence lived there still, Ñamku thought, and with the voice of the hawk he shrieked, "Listen!"

Outside, the gathered crowd of mourners heard, the crackle of embers interrupting their hush.

And—although the lips of the corpse in no way moved—Ayelewei spoke.

"Kuriñam, my husband, are you here?"

The voice was muted, but unmistakable.

The third wife shrieked, "She knows!" and fainted.

"I am here, *ñuke*," Kuriñam replied, watching shadows flicker on the face that was the death mask of his living wife. "I am here."

"Do not grieve for me. Grieve for my honor, and for yours."

The *longko* stood to look directly into her closed eyes. "*Our* honor!"

"*Mai.*"

Moaning, the third wife crawled into firelight to collapse beside the corpse. Kuriñam ignored her.

Ayelewei whispered, "Kurufil poisoned me!"

The third wife writhed, grinding her face into the dirt floor, tearing her hair. "She speaks the truth!" she wailed wild-eyed, sending muddy spittle flying. Leaping up, she forced her way through the crowd at the door. And every *che* was still, as when in a *nuyun*, after a shock you wait for worse.

"You cannot run from the dead," Ayelewei breathed, and without farewell became a simple corpse again.

The third wife hung herself that night, from a tree not far away. And when both his wives were buried, Kuriñam organized a war party. They opened the door of *renu*, but did not find the *kalku*. Fearing sorcery, they left everything they found intact.

Juan knew none of this, but overheard the conversation Pangi had with Ñamku, Katrinir and Ayelewei. Not that he understood much of the discussion. Still, he was reasonably certain that only one man had gone into that recess forbidden to all but the *machi*, and he had recognized at least four voice, one of them female.

When he confronted Raytrayen, she was defensive. It was best to leave such things alone. In *lolo* you overheard the dead from time to time. *Así es eso.* So is that.

Juan said that *this* 'that' was not *that* kind of 'that' where he came from, but he was singing to the wind. And he did not add that the whole thing stank of sorcery. Marmolejo had told him that *machi* practiced arts far darker than their skins....

His questions unanswered—or unanswerable—Juan had to content himself with seeing Raytrayen uncharacteristically glum, bending over her loom at the luminous mouth of the cave, weaving cloth intended to replace his rags. Her labor of kindness made him regret his inquisition, and he asked about the somber yarn she used. Surely it did not grow this purple-gray on whatever animal it came from.

Raytrayen had to laugh. Of course not, *tonto*, the wool was dyed with the bark of *ngalka* and *tuke*. She laughed again, imagining an animal *that* color.

They returned to language lessons, now hardly to be told from easy conversation. To be sure there were bilingual digressions into grammar and lexicon, although the greatest difficulty remained matters of translation, so that Juan had come to joke that *Feichi nemel kuthaungei rulgenpan meu*--That word is difficult to translate—should be Raytrayen's last name. And as in fact one could not often translate what did not exist in the world of the one into a word in the world of the other, they often needed to describe the indescribable. For Juan—setting aside *machi* and *kalku*, which she refused to discuss—these problems by and large had to do with *mapu*. The elemental world of the Mapuche, in addition to its rich fauna and flora, contained an impressive assortment of demons, monsters, half-human animals, spirits, familiars, and other creatures of the night ... not to mention the roaming dead.

For Raytrayen the pitfalls tended to be cultural. The animals and plants of Spain posed little problem, as demonstrating the diversity of *mapu*. Also, she had become familiar with many in Santiago. Yet she could not, for example, begin to comprehend monks and prostitutes, lumping them into a single category—which Juan imagined that she titled 'sexual excess.' And it was his fault, because one day, while verbally strolling through his culture, he foolishly referred to that venerable Spanish institution, the whorehouse run by monks—a slip he came deeply to regret.

Con nadie no se acostan!

Yes, monks *always* went to bed by themselves. Juan did not mention that some nuns slept in coffins—which seemed strange to him. This was an avenue he did not dream of having her explore.

Family however?

None. They left their families to live together in a big stone *ruka*.

This Spanish reality proved more difficult for Raytrayen to digest even than transubstantiation—with which Juan had tried to impress her once. She had grasped the difficult theological concept instantly, replying smugly that Ñamku transubstantiated all the time while alive, and probably still did, dead. But as for monks, she could not comprehend why *che* would leave their families. Why was abandonment a good?

They were not so much forsaking loved ones, Juan countered, as the things of this world—which included their families—to devote themselves to God.

Díos not in *mapu*! Do monk think *anything* in *mapu* good? Why monk not forsake each other, if in *mapu*? And, finally—contemplating Juan's hasty responses—the incredulous Raytrayen summed up, "Monk think good not *mapu* enjoy. Not not."

Shrugging off Juan's protestations that forsaking the world could lead to higher good, she exclaimed, "Holy no this, no that. No wife. No family. No *mapu*. *No lugar otro*, holy bad."

Juan translated her Spanish into his, and *that* back into what she was saying. If there was no Heaven, the 'holy' needlessly denied themselves the beauties and pleasures of the earth.

"It's just that you don't believe in God," he replied, knowing she would shrug.

She shrugged, turned wooden as a spoon by his religion.

"Do you believe in evil?"

"*Yamai!*"

Juan attempted to understand a world that had no Heaven and no God, just many little earthly devils. Being a monk was being in the world, not of it. Still—having widely traveled *mapu*—he could not begin to conceive that one could call this vale of violence a joy to man. And because, not just his Spanish being, but also his Spanish dreams, were under pagan attack, he became hostile, defensive, asserting more forcefully than he otherwise might that Chastity was a holy thing. One thing leading to another, he made the profound mistake of invoking the Immaculate Conception....

The logic of Virgin Birth was questioned in a hundred ways, and Raytrayen became annoyed with Juan's entrenchment—The Immaculate Conception was not *supposed* to be understood. A miracle was a miracle *because* it was impossible to understand.

Raytrayen stood up, hipshot. Did this mean virgin monks had children without having wives? More miracles? Eh!

Juan attempted to imagine a monk causing virgin birth by *not* penetrating the chosen vessel, just like God. He retained the presence of mind not to voice this, however, telling Raytrayen that monks were not so much virgin as celibate. Still and all, his conscience was troubled, since the promiscuity of priests and monks was the oldest, truest joke in all Spain.

Raytrayen pressed on. If Mary had a husband, what was wrong with *him*, that he did not father his own son?

Faced with Saint Joseph as the impotent cuckold of God, Juan crossed himself, aghast. Merciless, Raytrayen posed her culminating questions.

God *was* the Father of Mary's Son, which is why he was called the Father, no? Then if so, the Virgin Mary was not virgin, was she?

The questions—no less logically compelling than they were sacrilegious— hammered Juan like a lighting bolt. Miraculous birth or no, the seed of God had to have been *somehow* put into its vessel for the fruit to ripen.... Sweet Jesus, the womb! And why had he never thought of it before? The womb of the Virgin was like a garden with walls of flesh and a forbidden door! But where did the forbidden fruit fit in?

Raytrayen insisted, "*Was* Mary virgin?"

"Of course," he replied, managing not to stutter. "It was a miracle. The seed of God was assumed into Mary."

"Assumed?"

"A theological term." The ship of their discussion was transporting Juan to landfalls of the mind he did not dare contemplate. He blurted, "Assume means to rise to Heaven." He corrected, "No! Assume means appearing somewhere, just like that." Then in full and dishonest retreat, he added that 'somewhere' was also sometimes a theological term.

Smiling—and thinking that understanding Wan would precisely take a miracle—Raytrayen felt enough pity to return to her weaving. It was too tempting to argue with him, so that he turned belly up and feebly struggled, like fish in a poisoned stream. All she had to do is ask obvious questions about religion or sex. Or—better yet—obvious questions about religion *and* sex.

Poised at the brink of cliffs of sacrilege, Juan whetted his knife to calm his mind with a familiar act, wondering what made the two of them antagonists in this drama of the Indies, when they so intended to be friends. And the vision of their predicament came to him. Or rather the vision did not come, for he was *holding* it—an edge, with all the weight of the knife and the person behind it, and behind *that* the will and substance of two peoples. He and Raytrayen were edges. Better yet, they were points, each having behind them the mass of a different world, pressing on the skin of the other until, inescapably, they bled. They were tools wielded by their worlds, and it was language that made the pain possible. Language had turned the blind clash of antagonists along an enormous front into single, verbal combat.

"So," Raytrayen commented, "you say *putas* sell themselves for monks."

A beautifully grammatical Spanish sentence, yet so *not* Spanish in substance and intent! Resigned to humiliation Juan nodded, not explaining that the whores kept the larger share of the take, and that the monks looked after their well being. The *putas* were better off than, for example, beggars, as had nothing but charity to feed them. They worked, at least. Many saved enough to buy the roof over their heads. He did not mention the prostitution tax collected by Carlos V either.

She insisted. "*Monjes* good because they 'celibate.' *Putas* bad because not. So…?"

Juan knew exactly where she was going—monks turned sin to profit. Little did it matter that, technically, according to Holy Mother the Church it was no more a sin for a whore to spread her legs than for a man to piss his marrow in her, if she was not married and got paid. Everybody knew sex was *the* original sin, and therefore everywhere.

That incontestable fact returned him to the question of how evil could lead to good? In an imperfect world, was evil necessary to bring about higher things? War was the ultimate example—conquest in particular. He visualized Carlos V—that virtual monk—directing an empire from his cloister, as in the Indies others reaped for him the enormous revenues that fueled his holy wars. And it was then that Juan reached a terrifying revelation—The sinful acts of some funded the sanctity of others. Therefore *conquistador*es were as whores. The difference was, they sold their swords.

Raytrayen looked up from her weaving to see Wan staring at his knife, done muttering to himself and seeming desolate. She had been a little cruel, she told herself, but she had not attacked *him* in any way. Wan looked to be near tears.

Violently, Juan hurled his knife so that it quivered in the floor, crying out in Spanish, "I am a whore for a higher good."

Raytrayen went to where he slumped, back to the fire. And taking his head, she pulled it gently to her stomach, as if he were a child, and only just that tall.

Astonished witness to this moment, Lleflai knew that she had lost her daughter to a man.

Unable to sleep, Juan revisited The Bower of Bliss—so long neglected—thinking to find peace in adding detail—the gardens and vistas, colorful tiles, of the sensual architecture of the Moors. Instead he found an aggravating place, unfinished, lonely and unreal. The thought came that he never created the woman this palace of pleasure was meant to house, which made it something like a casket without its jewel. Had he ever even given The Bower a roof? He imagined slow, cold rain falling on its miraculous interior, soaking carpets and cushions, beading on the marble floor….

He had designed The Bower to be lost to all but two—plus magic servants. Now it was lost to him. He was in an Indian cave instead—a smoky hole in which there were no *houris*, veiled or no. He attempted to picture Raytrayen dressed as Constanza di Lorenzo, transported to the Bower of Bliss. There, she was beautiful indeed, but naughty. He placed her on cushions of the mind, veiling her smile, and—through Moorish gauze—her Indian eyes still mocked.

"Not I, but Spain in me," Juan whispered to himself, wondering if—freighted as they were—he and Raytrayen could ever be together. Again he attempted to imagine her as the recumbent Constanza, now daringly unveiled behind the separating rail—that frame for her perfection. But he could not *see* Raytrayen as pale, otiose, for there was too much dark energy in her. She would probably—athletically—vault the rail to start an argument. After, she would leave to swim the Guadalquivir.

To both, the 'monk and prostitute dilemma' was but one example of a mutual critique that had profound effects. They shared a growing suspicion that—like fish betrayed by ripples on the surface of a stream—something moved beneath their speech, distorting this mirror of their worlds with unseen purpose. And they were both obscurely, powerfully aware of this—that each, by defending separately rooted habit, was discovering a space which belonged to the two alone. And they did this by calling each other into question. Win or lose their battles in this clash of cultures, each surrendered enough troops—so to speak—as to displace them without defense into a no man's land ... a land which indeed did not exist. Ironically, this struggle forged a closeness in which Juan—unable to stray from the cave out of fear for his life—watched Raytrayen weave the cloth of his new identity. And so it was that, as if the two were stones ground against each other by a troubled stream, the mutual erosion of their beliefs—through some slow process—created fit between them. This, they experienced as a discomfort they could not discuss—a sense of loss which occasionally could manifest itself as a manic joy erupting in the presence of the other, a strange volcano of the soul.

Raytrayen asked herself if Lautaro was correct to condemn her interest in what was *lik winka*. And her excuse—that Ñamku had asked this of her—began to seem precisely *that*. But an excuse for what...? The *machi* never told her she would end up in the middle of the river with just one *lik winka*. He did not predict that Lleflai and Pangi, Lautaro, Eimi—all the *che* she loved—would come to seem diminished to her, as if they beckoned from a distant bank, although she loved them not the less.

There were bodily signs of her deep unease. Sitting at her weaving she would grow desperate, feeling she was drowning in ordinary air. Passionately she fought the urge to compare Ineth to Lleflai ... and failed. Remorseful, she pestered *papai* with so much attention that she looked back sadly, black eyes naked in their scars.

Juan struggled with related guilt, feeling his imprisonment as a diabolic form of liberation ... but from what? He made the mistake one day of wondering if—as Lobo argued—man could return to Eden. And inescapably, that night he dreamed....

For the first time in The Garden of his Slumber the sun had set, darkening the scene, which was peculiar in another sense as well, for there she was, aglow in moonlight. Eden was an Indian garden, in which Raytrayen was motionles and bare as the pumpkins pale at her feet. And—merciful God!—she came to life, emerging from rows of uwa *smiling, extending her bare arms with all the innocence annihilated by The Fall....*

Closing his eyes to dreams, Juan woke, thinking that man left an Eden to which he could not return, yet could not survive without the dreaming of it.

A prisoner in a cave, doing little but talk to Raytrayen, eat and sleep, Juan was at loose ends until the day he conceived the project of making chess pieces out of *uwa* dough, which then he dried. He gave them faces. And—since his world seemed upside down—to the black ones he gave armor and weapons, the visors and features of *conquistadores.* The white pieces bore clubs and spears and had the bold, bent nose of Indians. Their king had an ax head suspended from his neck, and so it went.... The castles were thatched like *ruka.* The knights presented a problem—as did the bishops—since Indians had no horses or religious pomp. Juan substituted llamas—even though it made no sense, for no one rode the fractious beast, which spat foul gobs when crossed. The bishops were Ñamku, complete with mask.

Raytrayen witnessed his efforts with a suspicion that startled Juan by having a strong overlay of fear. She explained that only *kalku* created the images of *che,* to use in sorcery. He assured her that these were but pieces in a game, a bloodless war.

The day came when the set was complete and sitting on its board—that is, the squares scratched on the dirt floor. And the first time they played, Raytrayen loudly celebrated the fact that the most powerful piece was a *domo.* Identifying with the queen she delighted in bold and unexpected raids that left her alone and vulnerable in enemy territory. No matter. Ignoring Juan's advice—never presuming to move her 'bishops'—she persisted until her queen was captured. Then she grew bored, until checkmate, when she whooped at being brought back from the dead.

Juan tried to convince her that she commanded an army. But—in her words— she was a *domo,* all the other pieces *wentru!* They start the wars anyway, she exclaimed. Let *them* finish!

Victory came to irritate Juan, the loser laughing and clapping her hands at the pleasures of checkmate. Storm clouds began to tower over the abstract purity of their war. And paradoxically, the actual rift began the day that Juan deliberately let her win—out of accumulated spite—with flagrant sacrifices. Raytrayen was desolate, stonily moving her pieces until the disaster was over, closing her eyes to keep in the tears. She walked away, saying that chess should have more women in it. And from that moment, the pendulum of their give and take—that easy daily swing—hung dead.

Juan made a point of sweeping away the 'board' on the dirt floor. This brutal act, in turn, prompted Raytrayen to retaliate by ignoring her loom, where her work for him approached completion. So the escalation went, until they communicated only with polite banalities—a language so light it could have been squeezed from the puffballs of winter.

To Lleflai, Raytrayen was more than breath itself, and the *lik winka* anguish from the start. Her daughter had returned to her from *piku* as a *domo*, the promise of her beauty so fulfilled that one could scarcely look at her directly—as if she were *antu* reflected on the great sea. Accustomed to the dread of being seen, Lleflai had never thought to know suffering in seeing.... And the day the *lik winka* and Raytrayen became distant to each other Lleflai's instant reaction was a shamed delight. That night she thought to blame the many *wethakelu* with the faces of *che* that he and Raytrayen had moved on the floor of the cave between the lines scratched there—this sorcery in unfamiliar form. But Lleflai knew that she was groping for excuses.

She waited until the *degu* sleeping at her feet were stirring, before—hard and hollow as an eaten clam—she stood to face the day. Lighting a sliver of firewood from embers, she searched in a dark corner of the cave for the basket in which she kept her best *kepam*.

Juan thought he had wakened to continued loneliness, but after he put on his rag to walk to the icy bath that began the savage day, Lleflai invited him to the fire. Giving him a long, hard stare, Raytrayen sat on the rude bench where Lleflai was asking *him* to sit.

They ate in silence, and Lleflai took their bowls. Then, picking up a basket she said she had things to do. Casually, she added that Pangi and Eimi were gone for the day.

Ever the idiot, Juan exclaimed, "Good food."

"You not know, really," Raytrayen said when Lleflai had gone, taking his hand in the soft warmth of her own, "what she did just?"

He never had a chance to respond, for Lautaro strode in, grunting greetings as he unstrung his bow.

Juan and Raytrayen abruptly slid apart, he getting a splinter in his thigh, crying out, "*Ay!*"

Ignoring the alien outburst—direct and intense as always—Lautaro stared a moment at the bare *lik winka* legs, with all that impossibly pale hair, exclaiming, "Where *is* everybody!"

He would have preferred a larger audience, but what he had to say could not wait—He had spoken to the assembled *longko* in council.

Having uttered this calmly, Lautaro then jumped up and down, pounding his naked chest with glee, so that even Juan could understand the astonishment of Raytrayen. A raw youth—an Indian stable boy—had given counsel to the local equivalent of generals.

Pausing in his dance, Lautaro told Wan that his *kawellu* died.

"Too bad," Juan replied, actually relieved that this exquisitely trained and massive weapon was out of the hands of Indians. "But he was old."

Surprised by the *mapudungun*, Lautaro continued, "Some drunk fed him fermented *poñu*, maybe *mudai*. He got bloated and died."

Relieved that Wan was not more upset, he went on to more important news. Ayelewei had been dead but not smelling. *Che* did not know what to do. Some said she was dead but her *am* had not yet left her body. Then the dead Ayelewei spoke, and pointing her finger at Kuriñam, she accused Kurufil of her death, demanding revenge. He, Lautaro, was right outside the door. He saw and heard everything. Also, Wan was no longer suspected of *kalkutun*! And he concluded by imperiously announcing, "You can safely leave the cave, *lik winka*. I permit you, my prisoner, to do so. You can go down the mountain with me." He slapped his chest by way of invitation.

Raytrayen cried out, "What about *me*, brother?"

"You?" Lautaro was confused. "Why, *ñuke*, you can stay with Lleflai." Generously, he added, "You taught him so well you do not need to come. The *lik winka* already knows more *mapudungun* than he needs."

Having made herself superfluous in the world of *wentru*, Raytrayen turned to look at Juan, too angry to cry. What did *he* think about having her ejected from his life, like dirty water out the *ruka* door?

Juan was glad they were no longer enemies, and he was thinking—for no good reason—that she would be ravishing in Moorish dress.

To Lautaro he said, "I have no clothes."

The warrior thought this outrageously funny. He was only inviting him to play *palin*. He tried to describe the game and failed … asking Raytrayen to explain.

She said, coldly, "You hit small ball stick with."

"That's all?" Juan was consumed by doubt.

"*Es todo*," Raytrayen echoed, searching for words to explain that there was more to *palin*—that it might as well be a war fought not with bows and arrows, clubs and spears, but with sticks, that *weichafe* played it to prepare for battle as a demonstration of their courage and endurance, and that players often broke arms, legs, ribs, sometimes their heads. Deaths were not unheard of....

But before she could assemble her sentences, Lautaro interrupted, explaining to the *lik winka* that *weichafe* were curious about him, now that they did not think him *kalku*. There would be feasting and *mudai*. No real need for clothes.

Lautaro was growing angry. He had promised he would bring the *lik winka*, enjoying his importance in advance, and one did not beg favors of prisoners.

"Might as well," said Juan, standing, stretching, feeling that he had been released from dungeons.

Mapuche *domo* absolutely did *not*—especially before others—contradict decisions of their *wentru*, and Raytrayen was paralyzed until she realized there was one thing she could try.

"*Por favor, Wan. No te vayas.*"

Juan admired her immaculate Spanish, and almost perfect pronunciation, hesitating. Why was she asking him not to go? Ignorant of what she was doing—even more ignorant of what she risked—he did not know what to do. He looked down at her clenched hands and wondered what lay behind her words. Was this the banter of the past, taking more serious form?

"*Por favor,*" she repeated.

Lautaro exploded. "What *is* she saying?"

Juan asked her in Spanish, "What *are* you saying?"

"I told him," she replied in *mapudungun* to her brother, "good luck playing *palin* with *weichafe*. But," she added, "he *is* right about his clothes. He can go down the mountain when I finish his *makuñ.*"

Glancing at Lautaro, Juan said, "That's what she said."

Examining the chest, the legs, before him, Lautaro had to agree that the *lik winka* needed clothes. He was darker now, but still reminded him of that white fungus growing on bat droppings. No wonder they covered everything except their faces and their hands.

Chapter 12: *Kuden* (*Mapu*, 1549-1550)

Juan sat on a threadbare blanket under a hazy morning sky, examining the half-gourd he held. *Murkeko*—ground, parched maize in water—again! He could imagine Pedro's outrage—*This is not breakfast, but a barbaric insult to Christian stomachs!* Salivating at the recollection of roast pork—that aura hovering about the memory of Pedro—Juan consumed his gruel wondering why, if Indians had their breads, they did not satisfy the first hunger of the day with a less liquid form of grain.

Cross-legged in the sun, he attempted to figure out the date. Christmas should be soon, and though he would not hear Mass, he wanted to pray on the correct day, at least. He knew he had been captured on September fourteenth of 1549. And after that his captivity became a blur—punctuated by memories to be sure—yet essentially independent of the calendar. Looking out over the ageless ocean, Juan cursed himself for not keeping track. He was at sea in time.

Raytrayen emerged, struggling with her loom. Juan leapt to help, perhaps making a mistake. Now that he was 'going down' the mountain she had been teaching him Mapuche manners. 'Down there' a *wentru* would do no such thing for a *domo* who was not kin. In fact it would be unthinkable for unrelated *wentru* and *domo* even to converse.

She thanked him gently in his language. Their relationship had entered a new phase, every interchange like the adding to a house of cards that might at any moment flutter down.

Together, they leaned the rectangle of smoothed logs that was the loom against the face of the mountain, in the shade. Juan admired her as she wove, sitting on her heels, humming as she tugged at that nameless stick which lifted every other yarn in the warp, deftly passing the shuttle, swaying to the side as she did, packing her work with a comb-like thing. Her slender arms were bare. Somewhere on the mountain, Lleflai was singing with the birds.

"Mapuche have no years," Juan said, attempting not to sound accusing.

He had brought up this subject before, and so Raytrayen was prepared. *Mapu* had years, not *che*, she replied. The years repeated, going around like the wheels on *lik winka* carts, always more or less the same. *Where* one was going was what mattered, not the wheels that took one there.

Her metaphor—purloined from his culture!—seemed so wrong and at the same time so right, that it turned Juan obstinate. If years *were* wheels on the cart of life, they completed their revolution at some point. That should be apparent even to Mapuche, who celebrated their new year—*wetripantu*—though they did not otherwise keep track. Perhaps *that* would allow him to take up the thread of time he had let drop. "Could you tell me when *wetripantu* comes?"

Raytrayen pleasantly shrugged, leaving Juan to wonder if she had understood and would comply, or if, confused, she was sparing his feelings with vagueness. How could Indians look so like *cristianos* and see the same world so differently? With them everything was backward, upside-down and crossways, peculiar as their stars.

Crossways.... And he remembered the day Lobo delivered an impassioned lecture on the subject of the cross, an exegesis hinging on the etymology of 'symbolic' and 'diabolic.' The root of both, he pointed out, was the Greek verb *bolein*, which meant 'to throw.' *Symbolon* meant to throw—or put—together. D*iabolon* meant to throw through, or across. "To throw across!" Lobo exclaimed. "Do you know *what* that means?"

Juan was tongue-tied as Lobo sped ahead, hound of Heaven on hot scent. "Jesus joined earth to Heaven, creating the way between high and low which is salvation. As the man-God, he *is* Symbol Incarnate." The Jesuit paused, thought quicker than his tongue.

Lobo's arguments could leave Juan skeptical, but this one made sense. And for once he thought he knew what Lobo was about to say—that the Devil was a crossroad on a Christian path. But the thesis evolved otherwise. Summarized and stripped of ancient tongues, it ran like this....

The sacred cross was fashioned of sublunar wood upon a Golgotha of skulls and stones, and one might note that the member which was vertical symbolized symbol—which is to say Jesus as a path to Heaven. On the other hand, the horizontal crosspiece symbolized itself, which was to say the material world we walk with the Devil. Therefore the Crucifixion was the symbol which expressed at a higher plane the relationship of symbolic and diabolic, Heaven and earth, spiritual and material, God and man, and ultimately, good and evil....

Juan became aware that he had been staring at the shuttle of Raytrayen—which approximated the dimensions of a coffin in miniature—gliding through the warp. Sweet Jesus Crucified, the loom! The diabolically horizontal thread of life was being passed through symbolic wool, creating a seamless fabric! What could this mean...?

Raytrayen turned, saying proudly in Spanish, "Your *makuñ* is finished, but I tie. You want fringe?"

"*Fleco?*"

She hesitated. "Fringe or fringe not?" Like cloud cast shadow, emotion crossed her face.

Juan hurried to say, by all means a fringe. And only then—oaf!—he realized that she expected a comment on her completion.

He scrutinized the taut, purplish-gray rectangle, with its two off-white stripes. "*Muchas gracias*," he said. "Very nice. *Muy lindo.*" And he *was* sincere. This was in no way Venetian, yet the weave was tight, the stripes and edges true.

She was radiant then—yet not her usual ebullient self—telling him that this was her first … *makuñ*, that is.

Knowing what she said—not what she *meant*—Juan chose to smile, and fortunately, Raytrayen appeared to read this as the human text she hoped for. Then, taking the knapped flint that served her as knife she stood to her work, severing the warp thread by thread, tying the knots that prevented their unraveling.

A freshet of revelation sent Juan's mind tumbling. Mapuche were the people of the earth, he a person of the path that united earth and heaven. Therefore he symbolized the symbolic, she the diabolic. And the *makuñ* somehow depicted their relationship. What *had* he gotten into? What did it mean that he had been 'thrown together' with people who 'threw across?' Did that make his being thrown together with the Mapuche symbolically some kind of cross? Was he being tempted? The *makuñ* was beginning to seem sinister.

She turned from her loom abruptly, interrupting Juan's revery. "I born on blanket, this loom."

The Spanish made no sense … yet Juan suspected he was being honored.

"Mother died on this."

Juan was astonished at the perfection of her pronominal, irregular, third person preterite verb—*se murió*—yet the teacher in him managed not to blurt congratulations. He said instead that he was sorry, at a loss for the Mapuche formula that would suit her revelation. What funerary custom might be involved? He asked what her mother's name had been.

"Rayentru."

"What was she like?"

"She died giving birth to me and to my brothers," she replied in *mapudungun*. "They say she was beautiful, and they also say that she began to die herself when my father died. They also say she wove too well. Other wives were jealous. It is said that sorcery was brought upon her, so that she gave birth to *ankeñ peñeñ.*"

"*Ankeñ peñeñ?*"

Reverting to Spanish in order to mask her confusion, Raytrayen asked if he would like to see the blanket—adding that Ñamku had given it to her before his death.

She emerged from *lolo* with a basket of woven grass, about two *palmos* wide, like others used for storage, except the lid was divided into fourths by paint. From it she took the blanket, meticulously folded. Juan could only see a fraction of a bold, geometric pattern in black, off-white, and a leaden gray so dark it *seemed* black, confusing the eye delightfully. The effect was at once vibrant and subdued, the finish immaculate. Juan was reminded of Inca cloth, so admired by Inés.

"Could you unfold it?" he asked.

"No!"

Raytrayen pressed the blanket to her chest, hastily returning it to the basket. The house of cards was tumbling.

"*Lo siento mucho*," said Juan, suppliant. "I am very, very sorry. I apologize."

Raytrayen tremulously smiled, saying she was sorry too, explaining, "Bloods on blanket." She enumerated on unfolding fingers— "Blood of mother, dead. My blood. Blood of two brothers." Holding up her hand with the thumb folded, she concluded, '*cuatro sangres*.'

At her refrain, like a *vihuela*, Juan resonated with the thought of human sacrifice—Abraham ... the Aztecs—although he knew exactly what she meant. She had once explained to him that Mapuche believed the *pellu* resided in every part of the human body—hair, nail parings, especially blood. Therefore this blanket was soaked, so to say, with the soul of her family. This would make it a profoundly precious thing. Also—potentially—the blanket was supremely dangerous. With it a *kalku* could work deadly spells upon them all, living and dead.

"Mother make blanket for dead father." And Raytrayen unfolded her thumb, completing her family.

Juan could not understand why Indians squandered perfectly good things by giving them to corpses, such as food, drink and clothing. None more than the Inca, who for their king set aside a palace with all its treasures, and his many wives. Indians gave the dead the best they had. But it all was starting to make sense. If there was no 'symbol' for the Indians—that is, no Christ—no union of earth and Heaven, no Heaven at all, then their dead remained Mapuche after death, creatures of the earth still on the earth, presumably with all their worldly needs and appetites.

Juan was about to speak when Lautaro's head appeared over the cliff edge, scowling with suspicion.

He greeted his sister and the *lik winka* gruffly. Saying that he had just been bathing, he entered the cave to emerge with a bowl of *murkeko*, reluctant to leave Raytrayen alone with his prisoner. The fact that Ñamku had asked her to become familiar with *lik winka* did not make her pleasure in his company easier to stomach. *Domo* did not speak to strangers, especially not *his* sister ... especially not with *this* one, an enemy and captive. He glowered at the *lik winka*, sucking loudly at his bowl.

Juan said that it was time for his bath, taking up the old blanket he was sitting on as well as a small *wilal* that held *killai*, a comb, his knife. Unlike Mapuche, who painfully removed what little hair grew on their faces with sharpened shells, he would shave with the perilous ease of Toledo steel.

Scrubbed clean, smooth of cheek, spread out naked in the day to dry, Juan examined his body with astonishment. When first he joined the Indians, the sun had often burned him, he being no more clothed than Christ upon His Cross. Now he approached the brown of natives save where protected by his breechclout. He wondered why Jesus Crucified died in a garment so extremely Indian.

Rolling over to dry his back, Juan returned to the problem of the date. Counting on fingers, he decided he was somewhere in November. And if Valdivia had recovered, he was heading south. The rainy season being over, the time for campaigns had arrived. He could expect to be ransomed soon, perhaps by Christmas.

Eleven years in the Indies had not yet taught Juan to appreciate a Nativity celebrated in the heat. Even so, formerly he had known *when* the celebration was, however misplaced into a southern season. Now it would come and go during his bondage, unrecognized, uncelebrated. When would Valdiva arrive? How would Juan know he was here? How would he get word to Pedro that he was alive and being held for ransom?

Juan brushed his hair—bleached by the Indies, his chestnut mane had faded to a true blond. If it grew much longer he might have to braid it.

"A *chiripa!*"

Raytrayen and Lautaro were eye to eye.

Lleflai stopped patting circles of dough, kneeling with her face in her hands, unable to intervene in the affairs of a *weichafe*—even if he was her son. *Lik winka* did not need sorcery to destroy *this* family.

"You made him a *makuñ*," Lautaro accused, loudly. "Now you insist on making him a breechclout when he already has one!"

"He is wearing a piece of that old blanket we once used to clean potatoes. Besides, a *chiripa* will not take long."

Tension had been mounting in Lautaro as *antu* passed, his sister weaving. He was furious at the delay, and he was furious at the time she wasted with the *lik winka*, not weaving, but chattering in *likwinkadungun*. "The *lik winka* is is *ngillan che*—a slave," he shouted, "and all he does is sit and watch you slave for *him!*"

"He saved both our lives from dogs," Raytrayen quietly replied, "mine from dogs that would have *eaten* me, and we cannot even make him a *chiripa?*"

"We! We! We! *We* are not making him a *chiripa*! *You* want to make the enemy a *chiripa!*"

Raytrayen took a step back and crossed her arms. *Yamai*, she said, that was what she wanted, and that was what she was going to do. He could take Wan down the mountain, she would make him a *chiripa* anyway. She would start right now. This was a matter of honor to her.

Lautaro screamed, "You saved his life too, as I did! Our honor is satisfied! The *lik winka* is an enemy, not your *weku!*"

Hearing this, Lleflai gasped, for he was horribly right. By weaving for the *lik winka*, Raytrayen was treating him as her mother's brother's child—the *wentru* she was expected to marry. And Lautaro was implying that Raytrayen was courting the only man who would wed her—stranger and *lik winka,* an enemy—worse than the *ankeñ peñeñ* she was. Lautaro had touched on the awful subject—unspoken until now—that, as the first born of *ankeñ peñeñ,* custom would only let Lautaro live, if any were allowed to live at all. Raytrayen should have been killed at birth with Pangi. Because they were not—as one of three—Lautaro was *ankeñ peñeñ* himself.

The *kofke* Lleflai had been preparing began to burn, hissing on hot stone.

Raytrayen took two steps back. Wide-eyed, stunned, she searched the face of her brother for the *wentru* she thought she knew. Lautaro could be heedless, headstrong ... yet she had never known him to be cruel. Kneeling, she embraced Lleflai, who was weeping on the floor, her soft sounds drowned out by the screeching parrot.

Eimi limped over, and turning his back to Lautaro, put his arms around them.

Fortuna selected this moment to have Juan walk in, blanket folded on his shoulder. He smelled burnt *kofke*. Damnation! He was famished. Indian bread was just a gritty thing, but he was getting used to these alternatives to starving. "For the love of God, the bread is burning!" he muttered *sotto voce*, words masked by the parrot's squawk. And as he approached the fire pit—eyes growing accustomed to the gloom—he perceived that Raytrayen and Eimi were embracing Lleflai, who was huddled on the floor. Looming over them was Lautaro, now looking over at *him*, fire reflected in his eyes as hate.

Certain that he was the one responsible for this catastrophe, Juan dully thought that the house of cards at last had truly tumbled.

Ñamku materialized, saying, "Do I smell *kofke* burning?"

Lleflai was too terrified to say, or do, anything. She admired Ñamku as no one else, yet had no wish to see him rise and walk while dead.

Ñamku pushed the smoldering bread into the fire. And removing his gloves, the *machi* began to slap dough.

Those who lived with *machi* expected the unexpected, but his fingers were plump with life, not smoked black bones!

Ñamku ignored their surprise. Scraping burnt *kofke* from the heated stone, he rubbed the surface with fat, commenting, "If you ask me, I think there is nothing wrong with being white."

He had intended to lighten the atmosphere, but Lautaro was seething. The first time, his brother had impersonated Ñamku for good reason, now he was meddling in the affairs of his family. Tempted to tear off the mask, he was halted by the trueness of the voice. Lautaro was no longer certain of who, or what, spoke through the mask, yet he refused to be awed. However gently, he was being scolded—whether by a corpse, or not, he did not care. The mask was taking sides with the *lik winka*.

"I do not mean to reproach you, Lautaro," the *machi* said, "just to point out that there is nothing wrong with being different."

Lautaro was outraged. "The *lik winka* is only different *here*, because he is different from *us*. He is not different from his kind. I have seen many like him, with pale eyes, pale hair, these *winka* who kill us and rape our *domo*."

Raytrayen leapt to her feet, eyes blazing. "I think he *is* different from *lik winka*. I *know* this! And how would *you* know otherwise, Lautaro, who spent your time not with *lik winka* but with their animals." She was profoundly hurt, profoundly angry.

Juan also forgot himself, insisting—in Spanish—"I am *not* different." How could he not declare allegiance to his people, with all their imperfections? As the saying went, better a devil you knew than an angel you did not. At the same time— even as he damned himself as a murderer and rapist—Juan was moved. Raytrayen so reminded him of Inés, superb as she defended Valdivia's indefensible decisions.

"You are too!" Raytrayen responded stoutly. Not knowing the word for rape in Spanish, she insisted in *mapudungun*, "You do not kill Mapuche, or rape *domo*."

Juan had to be silent. He had never raped anyone, repelled by this brutality expected of *conquistadores*. And he had never killed a Mapuche knowingly— although he knew some had taken part in the battle of Santiago. Yet he had slaughtered scores of Indians that he no more troubled to number than Indians did their years. And here Raytrayen was, again defending him before her people, not to save his life, but to preserve his character.

Changing to Spanish, now slow, unsure, Raytrayen continued, "I know *lik winka* kill, torture. But you are secretary. *Tu memoria escribes*—You write memories. You do nothing. *No haces nada,*" she repeated, looking into his eyes with pleading. Juan knew she was stating as a fact a question she had never dared ask, one he was too weak of will to answer, now that he knew how much it meant to her ... and how much her faith in him meant to him.

"You have little knife alone," she continued bravely, "to sharpen feather. I see this many time. And cut to eat, cut hair of face."

Raytrayen was right in what she had actually observed. Juan had not killed an Indian for quite a while, certainly not since she became a servant to Inés. By that time Santiago was pacified and he was occupied with secretarial duties. Was she not told about his part in The Apocalypse? This seemed impossible....

Lautaro erupted. "See what you did, Ñamku," he screamed, "A Mapuche *domo* is interrupting the speech of *wentru*! This is what living with *lik winka* did to her!"

"Do not be a *wed wed*. I am your sister," Raytrayen said, low and cold. "I have spoken to you all my life, brother, and you have listened. Are you saying that I no longer can?"

Lleflai moaned. Raytrayen had called a warrior foolish, when the only worse insult was *kalku*. He would be fully in his rights to beat her senseless—even kill her.

"I am saying. . .!" Lautaro shouted.

"Time to eat," Ñamku interrupted, creating a silence due as much to rudeness as to authority. He asked them to sit. There were benches enough, but the mortified *weichafe* squatted, fuming, convinced he was the only *reche* here. The thought burnt in him—He was *ankeñ peñeñ* because the *other* two had been allowed to live.

The *machi* heaped a wooden bowl with *kofke*, stood, and went to each, urging them to eat. And, as without appetite they did, Ñamku recounted the beginning— familiar as breathing to all but Juan. Yet the *machi* did not tell it as he ever had before.

"The Mapuche were created by a battle, and it took place at the shore," the *machi* whispered. "Kaikaifilu, the black serpent, drowned the land and the creatures of the land. On the shore they died, of every kind, and they changed as they were swept away. All that died were changed—by that death which is the sea—into the creatures of *mapu*. Those that drowned became the fish, the seals and whales. Those that died on the shore turned to frogs, toads, and salamanders. The creatures of the land that reached the summit of Trenten escaped unchanged. There the *domo* who survived married *pillañ*, and the first Mapuche were born. So it has been said of the beginning of *mapu* and the *che*. So it has been said from the beginning.

But there is something that the beginning does not tell us. *Che* touched by the waters of Kaikaifilu who did not die survived as different. This has been said as something passed from *machi* to *machi*, that the blood of such *che* lived on in the Mapuche as the *ankeñ peñeñ* who now and then are born. These Mapuche are, and are not, of *mapu*. These *che* are, and are not, *che*.

Kaikaifilu is death to the Mapuche, but he is not evil," the mask whispered. "This thought took time to come to me. Kaikaifilu is the difference that means we cannot be ourselves without becoming other. And I ask you, how do you think the beginning would be told by the children of Kaikaifilu, born of the sea?"

Lautaro did not hesitate. "The beginning would be told as a war they lost."

Raytrayen was restless. Usually she was interested in what Ñamku said, but today she felt the *machi* was digressing. Stuffing *kofke* in her mouth, she took out her anger on the grit of coarse-ground *uwa*.

Seeing muscles knotting in Raytrayen's jaw, Ñamku continued, saying Katrinir thought that, of the *che* fleeing the waters, those who were most frightened of difference ran the fastest and escaped. But those attracted to the difference that was Kaikaifilu ran looking backward, and were slow. So it was that they ran rapidly enough not to be swallowed by the waters, slowly enough that they collapsed safely on the shore. They were not drowned by Kaikaifilu—only touched by him— becoming *che* who continued to exist in some way on the shore, at the edge of *mapu*, different from other *che* not just in being *ankeñ peñeñ,* but also in their attraction to difference.

"These che can become other—as Katrinir did by becoming a seal, as I do by being *ñamku.*"

Lautaro questioned him, sarcastic, "Is it wrong to desire to be like others? Is it wrong to want to be Mapuche, not *ankeñ peñeñ*?"

"Every *che* is given a body for his soul," the *machi* said. That is as it should be. You are right to be what you are, and to desire to be like your people. Yet you must understand that there are those of us who take the shape of *mapu* and its creatures while still living in our bodies as *che.*"

Lleflai was distraught enough to cry out, "But, Ñamku, I am always myself, always *ankeñ peñeñ*. Always ugly, never anything else."

"Umeñdomo, do you speak to birds?"

"*Mai*. But not the way I speak to *che.*"

"Their words are in you and you speak them, yet you do not know exactly what they say?"

"*Mai.*"

"So am I *ñamku*. We *ankeñ peñeñ* can become other—yet not completely. Think of it as being ill with difference, not *dead* of it.

Katrinir thought that *che* are the only children of *mapu* who can become other and remain themselves. But, he said, he could swim like a seal, not *as* a seal. I can see like a hawk, not *as* a hawk. And you, Lleflai, can sing like a bird, not *as* a bird. To many of us who are *ankeñ peñeñ* these gifts are given."

"Gifts!" Lleflai was incredulous.

"Yes. You know the suffering of difference too well. Estranged and mocked, we are rejected when we are not killed at birth. And if we are accepted, it is only from a distance. Often we are feared. It *should* be no surprise for you to wonder why it is a gift to be *ankeñ peñeñ.*"

Lautaro sourly spat, "I would do anything—*give* anything—to be a Mapuche like every other."

"No need for that. You are *reche* already, Lautaro. And think of this—while still a youth you captured a *lik winka* and a *kawellu*. No one else has done this. You are listened to and respected by *toki*. No other youth is. Do you mind being different in this way?"

By way of answer, Lautaro ululated.

Lleflai said, "I have done nothing. I just have a face like the flesh of an oyster."

"Would you exchange speaking with the birds for an ordinary face?"

"*Yamai!*"

"Would you exchange your children for an ordinary face?"

"*Me!*" Lleflai was horrified, desperate—as if her foolish vanity would cause the *machi* to bring this awful thing about. "No! Please!"

Raytrayen leaned over to hug Lleflai, glaring at the mask. Lautaro glared as well. The *machi* had gone too far.

"Accept what you are given."

And from the white pouch at his neck Ñamku took a pendant he held up.

"Katrinir made this long ago, when we first met."

Ñamku stood with the slow care of age. Going to each—not excluding the *lik winka*—he demonstrated the fit of hawk and seal, separate and different, each completed by the other.

"You have been speaking about love," Lleflai decided.

"*Yamai.*"

"You are right, Ñamku. I *am* happy—and grateful—not to have an ordinary face." What she did not say is that she knew the hands she held belonged to Pangi. Her eyes and ears might be fooled, not her touch. This was her child. And he would know she knew.

Like a *werken* who mistakes his path and realizes he has long been running down the wrong one, Lautaro came to a mental halt. By implying that he was the only *reche* here he had insulted those he loved the most. Why? Because he hated *lik winka*. Why did he hate them? Because they attacked the *che* when they refused to be enslaved. Because they enslaved those they did not kill. Because they would not be satisfied until they had killed and raped and enslaved everyone. *That* was what made them enemies of the Mapuche.

And yet…. It was then the thought came to him that would change, not his undying enmity, but his life—the *lik winka* feared people who were not like themselves, killing them when they could not change them. In this, *he* was like *lik winka*. He hated them because they were not Mapuche. In this way, at least, he was no better.

"Enough of stories, Lautaro," said Ñamku. "If the Mapuche are to survive they must fight not just with strength and skill, but with intelligence. That is your part in this coming war, and I know I will be proud of you. You will live and die well, a Mapuche. You will be true to yourself, your *pu kiñeche*, and the *che*."

Lautaro turned to the *lik winka*. "Do you hate me, Wan?"

"No," Juan truthfully admitted. Lautaro hated *him*, instead. And could he blame him?

"*Are* you like other *lik winka*?"

Juan understood enough to be able to say no, in *mapudungun*. He had never wanted to be like most Spaniards, much less the Cacafuegos of this world. His ideals resided in other places, nobler times … in kingdoms of the mind. Yet he had told Raytrayen he was Spanish not so very long ago, and he could not deny that he truly was—even bronzed and barefoot, in a breechclout. Looking pleadingly at Raytrayen, he admitted, "*No sé quién soy.*" And that was the naked truth—He no longer knew who he was, and she was a large part of the problem.

She smiled, and shrugged.

"We need to see *lik winka* with the eyes of a child," Ñamku whispered. "And once we know them in this way, we need to see ourselves through *their* eyes." Swaying with weariness, the *machi* stood. Pulling on gloves he apologized, saying that, unfortunately, he was too old to be alive. And he shuffled into his alcove.

Everyone turned their eyes on Wan, who closed his own.

Raytrayen was the first to laugh, then You—who never passed the chance to do so, even when he did not get the joke. Lautaro roared, after. Even Lleflai was huffing.

"How *do* you see us?" Raytrayen managed to ask Juan, helpless again with laughter until she saw the annoyance on his face, which was answer enough.

When the popping of the fire was the loudest sound, Lautaro said that he was sorry.

"I know, brother," Raytrayen gently replied—even though he had to all appearances apologized to his knuckles.

"Is anyone else hungry?"

Lleflai stood with supple grace, reaching for a hanging basket.

The peace that endured during the weaving of the breechclout was but a truce with doubtful future, and the night before the departure Pangi was depressed, saying so to Ñamku. Yet it was the hovering firefly that sighed, responding, "You think Ñamku would have done it better."

The *machi* said, "You *were* my voice."

"A *che* should be more than the voice of another!"

"Not if he is the memory of memories," said Katrinir, salving pain. "Be glad to be alive," he added, saying that while Ñamku had been alive and he was dead, he missed his hands. Now that they both were dead, he missed his body. He was but a lipless voice.

"Grouse, grouse, grouse," Pangi and the *machi* whispered in unison, not wanting to wake sleeping *che*.

Katrinir continued with no trace of humor, "You do not need to know who you are to do what you have to, Pangi. You did, and will do, what you think is right, which is not easy. No one can ask more."

"But I am Ñamku, not myself, when I act … when I *speak!*"

"No one is himself, alone. We all speak with the voices of the past."

"I learned from you the words I spoke. I did not create what I received."

"As I learned—and did not create—what I taught. As I learned—and did not create—the telling of the beginning. I sing the beginning as it was sung. What makes us all Mapuche is a voice speaking through us since the beginning."

Pangi was somber, doubtful. "Then I am dead."

"*Mai.* As I have always been. That is, more than most," said Ñamku.

"Does the beginning say when *che* learned to speak?"

"It does not. I think *che* have always spoken."

"And we do not know when—or by whom—this gift was given us?"

"By the *pillañ.* No one knows when or how. I think it happened when they married the *domo* of the beginning. Personally, I believe that the speech of the past is in us from birth, as the flights of the past are in the dragonfly when it climbs from water, shedding its husk to unfold its wings."

Pangi was harsh. "I want to live!"

"Do not be hard on the dead who love you, Pangi. You summon us, after all. All you have to do is wish us gone, and we disappear. Then you can have whatever voice you want."

"It is not that easy," Pangi countered, weary. "You are tempting me with what cannot be. You *made* me what I am. Without you I am not *machi*. Without you I am not myself. Without you in me I cannot speak."

"You are not alone. And why would you want to be? We are all as trees whose leaves are moved by the breathing dead."

"Eimi has no past to speak through *him*," Pangi mused.

"He turned his back upon his youth," the *machi* said. "But do not envy him. You would find it hard to have no name."

"His feet are not on *mapu*. He is dancing in the air."

"As I have been known to do."

"It seems to me that we *ankeñ peñeñ* are neither a part of *mapu* or the *che*, imperfectly a part of both."

"But," said the *machi*, "being part of both makes us like *werken*—able to carry messages back and forth."

"It seems to *me* that Pangi is tired," Katrinir said. "He needs sleep."

Pangi ignored him. "So *that* is what you wanted from Lautaro and Raytrayen, to be *werken* between the Mapuche and the *lik winka*."

"Of Raytrayen, yes, in a way. Of Lautaro, no."

"He never was *ankeñ peñeñ*. You knew!" Pangi triumphantly accused.

"Of course."

"How could you do what you did to Raytrayen, Ñamku? Now she will never be herself."

"Why not ask *her* what she is?"

Like foxfire Ñamku pulsed before disappearing. And, distant, disembodied, his voice said that it was time to rest.

Juan descended the mountain barefoot, in armor. Keeping up with Lautaro was not easy. At his insistence he had spent a solid day burnishing, so that now he wore what might as well be metal mirrors. And—though he was baking in his armor like a fish in clay—the only concession he was able to extract from his lord and master was the permission to carry his helmet for the time being. He fanned himself with the ponderous thing.

"The path gets easier," Lautaro condescended. Without their *kawellu*, *lik winka* were like beached whales.

Never having thought to envy the Indian his comfort in the woods—in which, as Pedro said, they were at home like monkeys—today Juan felt the fool.

The path widened and grew loamy, less steep, less stony—although the forest was no less thick. Juan managed both to stride out and remember....

Raytrayen, Pangi, Lleflai, Eimi, had stayed behind. He had thanked Raytrayen for his clothes with verbal paragraphs prepared overnight, hoping he was feeding correct particles to the insatiable Mapuche verb. She smiled with not a trace of ridicule, saying something he did not comprehend in the anxieties of parting. What *had* he told her, in that hushed exchange? Some garbled idiocy no doubt, yet he did not mind, for in that farewell it was as if language did not exist between them, their words mattering less in that suspended moment than her eyes. Surely, in that sadness he was not mistaken....

Mapuche had nothing like villages, yet they had places where they assembled, and into one such clearing in the woods Juan came, clapping his helmet on his head before a crowd of armed *weichafe*. Surrounded, Juan felt not so much frightened as repelled by the mass pressing in, jabbering questions, exclaiming at the miracle of his occasional reply. Fingers in their dozens rapped his armor, stroked his breastplate, helmet, scabbard. Warriors cried out with wonder, seeing their reflections. They made faces, stuck out tongues, moved their heads from side to side, admiring their distorted selves.

Thinking that there was some parable embedded in this moment, Juan closed his eyes and let the murmuring insanity wash over, feeling rivulets of warm sweat trickle, until he became aware that the weight of Indian flesh had parted and *toki* were before him, formally seated on rude stools, ax heads suspended from their necks.

They made speeches—not so much of welcome as of defiance, far as Juan could gather. Raytrayen had told him that they would. And at last, an expectant silence— also predicted—told him that his turn had come.

Throat dry as the nitrous Atacama, Juan did his best with the speech Raytrayen had him memorize—He, Juan de Cardeña, descendant of Adam, who begat Seth, who begat Enos, who in turn begat…. So it went through Mahalaleel, Jared, Enoch, Methuselah and etcetera.

Juan had shamelessly plagiarized Genesis, for—other than his parents—he had no kin he or Father Sosa knew of, and Raytrayen had insisted on long lineage….

He, Juan de Cardeña, was happy to find the honored Mapuche present here in good health. He hoped that their many kin were also in good health. He was honored to be their guest.

The audience seemed politely to approve, sternly listening, some nodding with surprise—not that the *lik winka* spoke well, but that he spoke *mapudungun*.

Encouraged, Juan improvised on Raytrayen's plan, unbuckling his sword and setting it on the ground, saying that he offered this poor gift in exchange for the hospitality of the Mapuche.

And, with this innocent act of diplomatic generosity, Juan created Babel and pandemonium. Only later did he learn that he had proposed the unthinkable. Every *toki* was profoundly covetous of the *lik winka wethakelu*—the mere touch of which was said to kill. Yet not one dared accept it, for the act would seem to reveal to other *toki*—indeed, to every Mapuche present—a pride which would attract the deadly sorceries of jealousy. And in addition, the acceptance of such a gift so great required an exchange, when no *weichcafe* could become *trafkiñ* with enemy.

At the time, Juan did not know exactly how he had disturbed this hive, witness to inexplicable agitation…. When he unbuckled his sword, stepping forward, gift extended in the flat of his hands, every *toki* rose, recoiling into a fighting stance. There were inarticulate cries. Spears were lifted, arrows nocked, long bows drawn taut. Then, when Juan's intentions were revealed as peaceful, the speeches began, insincerely declining the *wethakelu*. The *toki* had become uncertain about this prisoner glittering in the sun, returning a deformed image of the scene.

Pichikan strode up to address the crowd. Elevating the smoked finger suspended from his neck, he announced that the *lik winka* had cut the very finger off, and he had preserved it to remember his courage and his skill. This—and he slammed

Juan on the back no less brutally than Pedro—was an enemy worth having. He would be proud to taste his heart, and he was glad to have him visit.

Everyone breathed more easily. Juan's bravery and skill had been confirmed by a powerful *weichafe*. The warriors decided to ignore the problematic status of the stranger shining like a silver lobster in their midst. In short, they chose to get drunk now, rather than later. Women emerged from the temporary shelters at the periphery of the clearing carrying stacks of flat bread, clay pots filled with *mudai*. The feast began and roared on, unstoppable.

When the muzzy glow of sunset overspread the forest Juan was lying on his back—in a breechclout, out of armor—appreciating the cool evening breeze on his nakedness, swilling the noisome, frothy beverage of these Indians, too blissfully drunk to gag. Thoughtfully, he gnawed upon a chicken leg.

"What is time, after all?" he attempted to say in *mapudungun*—for Mapuche had no word for time as such, only for the day and its parts … the various seasons. He was preparing to make a concession in the philosophical discussion he had been having with Pichikan, his companion of the afternoon, for Lautaro had chosen to spend it with the *toki*.

A fruity belch was the only reply from Pichikan, who was thinking that the *lik winka* might be a warrior, but he was also a *wed wed* when drunk, asking what the 'day' was when even a *pichiche* barely old enough to speak knew that day was day, night was night, and that if it was not the one it was the other, with no real complications in between. Pichikan then wondered if it would be *safe* to taste the heart of this *lik winka*. What idiocies would he absorb along with the courage and the skill? But enough of this nonsense, it was time to find himself a *domo*.

Pichikan was unwittingly right to belch his response, thought Juan, for time is like the air we exhale—in us, all around us. You can count belches and breaths, but time is just *here*, unchanging. Maybe Indians were right not to number it any more than one did air. As Raytrayen once suggested, man might change, yet time itself did not. A heart beat, a clock ticked, yet time did not beat or tick. The question then became—What did mortality have to do with time? Man was mortal … time was not.

Taking two of the drumsticks he had just eaten, Juan moved them over ground like the legs they had once been, which reminded of pendulums. Then, thinking this instant fraught with deep metaphysics, which wed the measuring of time to the dance of death—Juan looked for Pichikan….

The warrior had vanished, and—in the shadows where he had just been—a young *domo,* hesitantly smiling, was pulling on the pins that fastened her *kepam*….

Juan woke, shaken—not by Pedro—a headache pounding in his head like silent drums. And, gratefully, he accepted the earthen jug of water Lautaro handed him. Was the young warrior smirking, or simply squinting with a brutal headache of his own? For that matter, where *were* they?

He looked around…. Sitting in wild flowers in the woods, sometime in the morning—that is where and when Juan was … in any case, not in the shelter. Then he remembered…. Crucified Jesus! The girl had actually exposed her breast!

"I had to track you to find you, *lik winka*. You ran from Choswe like *pudu* from *pangi* last night. She said it was so funny she was not even offended … not until later." Lautaro *was* smirking—headache or no—and in a definitely predatory way. Juan fought a groan.

Lautaro heartlessly continued. Choswe—a widow who decided not to remarry—was considered *very* attractive. And she was telling everyone that she had just come to the *lik winka* out of curiosity, wanting to see what he had between his legs … but there was nothing there.

Juan was thankful to find out nothing happened. As for Choswe's insult, it was totally mistaken. He had a Church with all its teachings—and its Bible—between his legs. *That* was what he had there. He had *the ten thousand virgins* between his legs! He felt like throwing up.

"Also," Lautaro said as they began to walk, "I was not the first to track you." He indicated the ground, Juan seeing there only the innocent forest floor—leaves, both dried and green, a beetle clambering its twig.

"Someone tracked you *before* I did," Lautaro insisted, no longer smiling.

Juan stopped walking, to piss. Why was Lautaro so excited? Maybe Choswe followed him, and found him passed out. So what?

Lautaro thought that something here was wrong. The *lik winka* had rejected a beautiful *domo*, then run off to sleep in woods swarming with the evils of the night. Why…? And he was convinced that Kurufil followed him. Had the two met again? The *lik winka* might be less stupid—and more evil—than he seemed.

Whether memory or dream, a vision seen in moonlight came to Juan—a *domo* whose animate cloth revealed, a perfect oval framed in a tinkling firmament of gold. Again, she said *trafkiñ*….

Perhaps this was a memory of a dream, she so close, the air moved by the slow gold she shook. And Juan remembered feeling chill, when he had never dreamt of cold before.

He floundered from thickets into the light of the clearing and its busy women. Children and dogs ran about. *Weichafe*—strewn like logs where they had dropped—were sleeping. He was reminded of a battlefield.

A child shouted, "*Lik winka!*" Trying to recall in which shelter he had cast off his armor, Juan walked uncertainly into the hush.

Pichikan roared, "*Mari mari.*"

Greeting him, Juan found the armor and the weapons he had shed displayed on a blanket for the admiration of all who passed. The warrior smiled enormously, and Juan's nausea made the teeth of Pichikan seem larger. His hairless torso, corded with thick vein, shone like carved and polished oak. A snakeskin *trarulongko* confined his brutally cropped, shoulder-length hair. Filled with genial menace, Pichikan rumbled with laughter. Picking up Juan's knife, he flicked it over. "I heard that last night you were missing something hanging from you. Was it this?"

Pedro would have fought to the death over the merry insult. But then, he posessed an arquebus that—in his words—never misfired. The image of Pedro clad in a breechclout including a purse-codpiece in its design began to flicker in Juan's inner theater … eclipsed by the approach of an Indian in a Spanish helmet striped black, dotted with crimson, topped with green feathers. Beneath the visor he had plucked his forehead—as did many *wentru*—so that his fierce eyes glittered in an egg-like face. It was Tuiñam, son of Kuriñam.

Juan recalled the imposing figure of the *toki*. He had not forgotten the young warrior in his helmet either, there at the confrontation by the Fío Fío, one of the first prepared to die for him. Honor made for deadly bedfellows in the Indies. Better take an asp to bed, like Cleopatra. Would Tuiñam—like Pichikan—not mind tasting his heart?

Pichikan called for *mudai* as Tuiñam sat by them. And when the *lik winka* politely declined to drink, he was irked. Plenty left he insisted, indicating ranks of what Pedro would call 'live soldiers.' A silent *domo* stooped to lift a vessel and walked up. Then a small child holding a bow appeared from behind her *kepam*.

"My nephew, *pichi* Tropan," Pichikan boasted.

The unsmiling boy—perhaps five or six—had his tiny bow at full draw, squinting down the trembling length of the arrow…. And he shot Juan in the forehead, ululating, as the unmoved woman poured *mudai* into Pichikan's half gourd. However small and blunt, the arrow might as well have been a battering ram, sending echoes of pain reverberating into the dungeons of Juan's headache. Was his status as a prisoner this low? Were *pichiche* allowed to do these things! *Pardiez*, he could have lost an eye!

Pichikan chided his nephew, explaining to him that the head is the worst of targets for an arrow, as too easy to miss and too bony anyway. Might as well try to shoot a foot. Aim just below the ribs, he advised, pouring the child *mudai*, and shooing him out before he shot the *lik winka* again. *Pichi* Tropan was right to assume that enemies should be killed. However, one absolutely did not shoot guests. Knowing that he was reputed to be mindless muscle—so that one of his nicknames was *Penun*—Pichikan felt that today at least, he had been subtle.

Wanting to skin the insolent whelp alive, Juan treated his headache—as Pedro would—with homeopathic medicine. The same silent woman poured *mudai* into his gourd, eyes modestly averted. Had she heard about last night and was smiling internally, Juan wondered, shuddering at his first swallow of foul brew. Llama spit must taste like this, he thought, failing to keep from thinking about the mouths that went into its making.

Tuiñam and Pichikan were discussing the continued absence of Kuriñam. The *toki* was half mad with grief and rage, obsessed, for the death of Ayelewei had not been avenged. When he went to bed he heard her whispering that their honor had been taken. He refused to eat, to sleep, wandering the night with his club, calling for the *kalku* to do battle. Tuiñam shook his head with sorrow. If sorcery did not kill his father, madness would.

Pichikan suggested that a *machitun* might be the answer.

"My father refused that, also," replied Tuiñam—glaring in Juan's direction. "He feels *lik winka* have destroyed *kume mognen*, and that the *che* will not live in peace with each other—or with *mapu*—until the last of them is dead."

The hatred in his eyes made it clear to Juan that Tuiñam passionately believed his father. And no doubt they both were right. Juan was no *kalku*, and had no hatred of these Indians. Nor had he ever fought them. Yet the region around Santiago—home of countless Indians a few years ago—was depopulated now, pacified as much by disease and flight as by war, for which he was no less responsible than every other *conquistador*. What price the bringing of Christ and civilization to Indians? he wondered, as gloomily he drank *mudai*. Maybe Lobo had been right when once he claimed that the crusades—and ultimately the *reconquista*—created a habit in the Spanish soul, which was the need to kill in order to defend and promulgate The One True Faith. This, when Jesus had come into this world to die for peace.

Juan had pointed out to Lobo, on that day, that the crusades were intended to win back the land where Christ Himself was born, from murderous infidels who conquered it in the first place with rapine, fire and sword. 'Reconquista' began with 're' precisely because Spain conquered back what once belonged to her, from infidels.

The emaciated priest had cried out that not just Spaniards, but *all* men, were born wounded by war. A lie had penetrated man's being like a lead ball in his vitals that could not be removed, suppurating there and poisoning his existence at the core.

And brushing wild hair back, Lobo leapt to higher metaphor—War was the mirror in which you saw your enemy as what *you* were, and Christ had come to shatter that awful glass, forever altering the face of humankind, for if—looking into the Countenance of the Living God directly, as a man—you were fortunate enough to see yourself reflected there, however faintly, then you were face to face with Peace, total and absolute … with God, yourself, and with all men.

"Amen," Juan helplessly responded that distant day. Still and all, Lobo had wielded a sword at The Apocalypse, though he lost his mind for doing so. "Can you *imagine* Christ in the armor of centurions?" he had once asked Juan. "Can you see *Him* clad in the metals of war—He, who died that men beat swords to ploughshares?"

Juan glanced at the two *weichafe*—now having a less passionate discussion. No armor there, save for the helmet. No swords or ploughshares either. Difficult as it was to imagine Christ in armor, Juan found it more impossible to imagine Him Mapuche, even in the breechclout of the Crucifixion. As for ploughshares, if these *weichafe* had them and a forge, they would no doubt long ago have beaten them to swords.

Sensing scrutiny, Pichikan turned to Juan, and—shifting register from low Mapuche babble to the loud tones used with misbehaving dogs—said the *toki* had conferred. As no one wanted the *lik winka* in their *ruka,* one had to be built for him. The problem was, no one wanted him near.

Juan downed more homeopathy … and to hell with a place to stay. He would get drunk every day, passing out in wildflowers, alone as the Wild Man of the Woods. He would carve himself a club. The thought came that there was no Wild Woman of the Woods, for him, and a pang of loneliness so deep that it was physical pierced him. He belched. He missed Inés. He missed the smell of clove. He missed oranges and olives. He missed Pedro. He even missed Bucephalus. And—he realized with dismay—he missed Raytrayen more than all of that. Were more recent feelings more intense?

He hiccoughed. He drank. He held his breath, and then he *had* the hicoughs, listening to Pichikan explain that the *toki* had decided there was no reason the *lik winka* could not play *palin*—so like war it seemed appropriate to include an enemy. The game would be the next full moon. Expansive, Pichikan added that he had been selected to lead a team, choosing Juan for his side. He would teach him how to play, he said with a cat-like, mouse-eating grin.

You'll teach me the many ways my head can be broken by your club, thought Juan, squeezing his nose to suffocation. He hiccoughed—time now punctuated by this spasmodic war of the body upon the soul, which somehow figured forth both his imprisonment and humiliation. Five hics later Lautaro walked up in the company of Kanikura, who welcomed the *lik winka* to his shelter—for such it proved to be—offering *mudai.*

Juan tipped his bowl and held his nose, then hiccoughed.

Politely ignoring the strange customs of *lik winka*, the erect old Indian said that he had talked to Andalikan. As uncle to Lautaro he had agreed to let the *lik winka* build a *ruka* near his own. Lautaro had consented to live with him to ensure his good behavior. The *toki* were in agreement. He had spoken.

Kanikura left ... then Tuiñam.

Done hiccoughing at last, Juan was profoundly drunk, and miserably back in armor, listening to Pichikan and Lautaro argue, deep in *mudai* themselves. The *lik winka* needed to practice his *palin*, and Lautaro was insisting that he wear his *wilef wethakelu*.

That was an unfair advantage, said Pichikan. For *palin* you just wore a *chiripa*. Getting hurt was part of it. Was Lautaro going to maintain—next—that the *lik winka* play on a *kawellu?* What was not fair in war was not fair in *palin*.

Lautaro insisted that *wilef wethakelu* were a disadvantage—the *lik winka* could hardly walk in them. Wearing them he could not be hurt, but could not help his team, either.

They compromised—Juan would practice in armor. If that did not work, he would practice without.

And to Juan—barefoot and unhorsed, but armored—*palin* was explained in its bold simplicity. He stood with a knot of young men, naked but for breechclouts, by a small hollow scooped at the center of the playing field—which Juan estimated to be seventy *pasos* long, ten wide. These measurements varied however, as the boundaries were created by the spectators, who did not necessarily keep their places—running after a wandering toddler, finding a stone to throw at a dog, staggering off for *mudai*. Every Mapuche sober enough to stand was there to see the *lik winka* play in his *wilef wethakelu*.

The small wood ball—dark and dented—was placed in the hollow. The object was for a team to get it over the opponent's goal. Juan was told that he could only use his stick. Scoring would be explained later.

In the stick handed to him Juan recognized something like the club Pichikan wielded when he had fought him as Not Tonsure—save for the working end, which was not knobbed but whittled thin, curved gracefully. Perhaps six *palmos* of hardwood, it was light enough to be swung with amazing speed, as Juan well knew from his duel with Pichikan. Useless against armor, on flesh and bone it would be murderous. Juan became glad of his encumbering steel.

Perhaps a dozen bronzed and muscular *weichafe* on each side faced off in ragged lines. Juan and Lautaro standing beside Pichikan. At the center, the sticks of the captains hovered by the ball.

A primitive trumpet blared—a low, discordant moo—startling Juan. He looked for the source ... and missed the beginning of the game. Sticks clanged against his armor.

Indians were receding into the immediate distance. He made to follow, but they reversed course, streaking past, feet and sticks flying.

The howling crowd began to issue derisory cries. The *lik winka* had not used the sorcery of his *wilef wethakelu*—perhaps to move the ball with thunder and flame. He had not even played! The drunken speculation was fierce, divided. Some said the *lik winka* needed his *kawellu*—that immense familiar—for his sorcery. Others laughed. If this was the way *lik winka* played *palin*, why did their *domo* not fight for them?

And who could argue with *that*? *Palin* was a game designed to keep war vibrantly alive, during its absence. *Palin* taught speed and power, cunning, courage and endurance in the face of a challenge stopping little short of death. *Palin* would have been war itself, if murderous energy had not been transferred to the ball— that abstract, shrunken skull. With Mapuche it was usual—when referring to the number of men a leader could count on in a war—to use *palinche* interchangeably with *weichafe*.

Aware of none of this, Juan knew only that he had lost face.

Lautaro—having also lost face—was curt. Practice was over. There was a *ruka* to be built. It was time to go. Next time, the *lik winka* would play in a *chiripa*.

"Next time?" Pichikan objected. "He did not play *today*!" And that drew a laugh from everyone.

Telling Juan to follow, Lautaro strode through the crowd. Stoically following, Juan looked these Indians in the eye, now doing better at recognizing individuals— when once they had been like acorns on their oak. There, was Kanikura. There, the silent woman who had served him *mudai*. There, the naked nephew of Pichikan, drawing his bow....

This time Juan was struck between tackle and *umbilicus*, but—as he wore mail— only his pride was bruised, and he strode through drunken laughter blushing. In the crowd he recognized slender Choswe, with her perfect teeth, and that arched nose of Indians. She was beautiful indeed, he thought, seeing her laugh with the others like an older, crueler Raytrayen. And only when he reached the haven of the woods did it come to him that the truce Mapuche had declared with him extended only to actual war. Playing out of armor, he might well be killed in sport.

Andalikan was polite, formal, cold, for what honor here demanded went against his grain. Tall for an Indian, he stood—arms crossed—before the *ruka* door, barring entrance even as he welcomed Juan.

Materials had been gathered, he announced. The building of the *lik winka ruka* would begin tomorrow. The place was a bit far, yet its spring never failed. For the time being, the *lik winka* could sleep in an old *ruka* where they kept chickens and ducks. The roof leaked, but he did not think it would rain tonight. His wives would bring food. And with that scant comfort, the greeting ended.

To Juan—chafed by armor, famished, bone-weary from a forced march ending at sunset—the offer opened doors to Heaven.

Lautaro was his guard and guide. Trudging through twilight to his coop, Juan ventured to ask him why he was always called 'the *lik winka*.' After all, he had a name.

"Because you are the enemy."

"If I am your enemy, that makes you mine. I call *you* by your name."

"I am one of many *che* who are your enemies. There is just one of your kind here to hate." And Lautaro handed Juan a blanket, saying, "*Lik winka* is the only name you need."

The *ruka* loomed—inky blot in lesser darkness—startled fowl squawking and quacking. Juan wondered how he would find a spot not under some unseen roost....

Two women arrived, one swinging two sputtering firebrands, the other bearing hot food. They left, handing Lautaro one of the strange torches. Whirling, the warrior watched Juan eat, then—shooing indignant ducks away—select a place for his bed. Without a word, he walked away.

Removing his armor in the dark, rolling into his blanket, Juan took comfort in the fact that piled manure was far softer than packed dirt. The place reeked, yet he was full, warm and dry, though sorely aching. Heaven!

Drowned by tides of sleep Juan found time to marvel that the Bower—in its wilderness—had come to *this*.

Chapter 13: *Ruka* (*Mapu*, 1550)

Lautaro could not sleep, remembering....

Playing *palin* in his *wilef wethakelu*, the *lik winka* was a disaster. Might as well have captured a duck, Lautaro thought, visualizing the damp coop where the *lik winka* slept with nasty satisfaction. If only he did not move, not speak *mapudungun!* Better his own babble, masking power like a *machi* in his trance. Invisible in *wilef wethakelu*, thoughts hidden by his speech, there would be mystery in his presence. And having lived with Ñamku, Lautaro knew the power of mystery.

A rooster crowed. He stretched and sat.

Lautaro did not blame Andalikan for humiliating the *lik winka*, by having him sleep in a coop. But his own reputation depended on his captive, so this would have to end. Today they would build a *ruka* for him. And when it was finished, *palin* would become his life. The *lik winka* would run, swing, hit, eat, drink and dream the game, until it was easy as a drunken piss.

Built for one *domo*, the *ruka* of Wispu was small, yet Lautaro spent the night there because it had more room than that of Liftuipani, crowded with *pichiche*. Andalikan had slept by him, unable to leave his wife alone with a grown nephew … also avoiding the whining of his second wife.

Wispu looked up from by the fire, returning the greeting of Lautaro, broad smile on the pleasant roundness of her face. Childless herself, she took the duties of being his *chuchu* with loving seriousness. Smiling back, Lautaro thought that being orphaned could give you more mothers than you started with.

He left to kill his drowsiness with cold water, Andalikan soon joining him. They returned to the *ruka* in the first glow of *antu*, the uncle thinking that here was the one son in whom he took pride, Lautaro that here was his true father. And in these thoughts, in each, there was a residue of guilt....

They drank herb tea, ate *kofke*. And, as the *wentru* were silent, Wispu was also, waiting for them to finish so she could eat—not that she had not sampled as she cooked.

Andalikan brought up the subject of *palin*. Aware of the humiliation the *lik winka* had caused his nephew, he felt the shame as his own. "You need *palinche* to help you teach the *chori* how to play," he said, with a nervous cough. "I would be happy to, and … I have been saving this," he said, extending a stick. It was *koyam*—oak—dried, roughed out, perfectly curved, hardly bending against the knee.

They discussed the coming match—which would be little less than a *malon*—

Andalikan going directly to the point. Not only did players of *both* teams want the *lik winka* dead, there was worse.... *Palin* could substitute for combat when there was a serious disagreement that did not progress to weapons, as in this match. And, as often happened, a *domo* was involved. Marillan—his niece, daughter of Kanikura and cousin to Pichikan—had been abducted by Kuruga, son of Kallfugaru, after his courtship was rejected. Furious, he came with his kin one morning when she was bathing at the stream and took her. Marillan did not just pretend to bite Kuruga, and she squeezed his *ketrau* so hard that to make her let go he had to break her nose. He took her to his *ruka*, but that night she escaped. The next *antu*, when he sent uncles to bargain over the bride price, Kanikura was furious, shouting that no daughter of his was going to marry a brutal idiot. Marillan had been raped and beaten. Therefore revenge was due, not gifts. They would have fought then and there, but the *longko* decided to settle their differences with *palin*.

"There may still be a *malon*," Lautaro spat out, having old scores to settle with Kuruga. Many *pichiche* taunted him in youth, yelling *añkeñ peñeñ*, and he had fought them all, but of these Kuruga had been the worst. Broad and powerful, he compensated for his lack of speed with a nasty slyness.

Andalikan concluded. "Kuruga will captain the other team. If our side wins he and his kin give restitution for Marillan, and she stays in her father's *ruka*. If we lose...."

"She will hang herself!"

Studying his nephew with narrowed eyes, Andalikan said, "Better not kill Kuruga." The *longko* had decided that if there were *any* dead—except for the *lik winka*—a *malon* would be justified.

The dogs announced that *che* had come to build the *ruka*, and Andalikan rose to welcome his guests.

Wispu—her moon of a face tight and drawn—handed *kofke* to Lautaro, saying, "For the *lik winka*, as my husband promised."

The coop was near flowing water, like every Mapuche *ruka* Juan ever encountered. A stream ran by, silver ripples over flat, black stone. In it, step-like fractures—as if hewn for fountains—created tiny waterfalls, reminding Juan of the delight Moors took in the play of water. He washed his filthy blanket. He bathed. Naked, he was scrubbing his teeth with a chewed stick when Lautaro walked up, scowling. Still—blessedly—he had brought *kofke* in a bamboo basket. Juan tied his *chiripa* before the impassive, squatting youth, who assessed him as a butcher might an unfamiliar sort of haunch.

Hunkering was an impossible Indian habit, for Juan—the contortion causing such agony that eventually his muscles seized. So he ate sitting on sun-warmed rock instead, placid as a basking turtle. There was, he thought, an easy satisfaction in having no control over one's destiny. All he needed do at this point in unrecorded time was masticate and swallow, awaiting what the Indian day might bring.

"Come build your *ruka*," said Lautaro.

In the clearing *domo* cooked by fires, reaching into baskets, squirting from bladders, slicing *poñu*, patting dough, wringing the necks of Mapuche chickens—the roosters with their low, cap-like combs, tufts of feathers at the cheek ... the hens, tufted too, laying colored eggs. The men were digging rows of holes—their wooden picks weighted with stones. And with flint axes they were limbing saplings thick as wrists. Naked children were everywhere underfoot.

The bustle ceased when Juan walked up.

Shunned like a leper shambling into town, ringing his forlorn bell, Juan was put to work at the far periphery of activity, on a rise where water seeped. Digging stony soil with bare hands, prying larger rocks with sticks, he created a cavity that filled with water. And, near midday, Juan examined his work with satisfaction. He had created a hole about knee deep, lined with flat stone. He waited for the silt to clear, until the pool became pellucid, a tiny plume of sediment dancing at the bottom. Ignoring his bloodied, puckered hands, Juan knelt to drink, and in the imperfect mirror of the pool saw an Indian.

He examined a blond lock of hair—now more than shoulder length— to reassure himself of his identity. No Indian he, *pardiez*! Then he was wondering why the same sun that lightened hair, darkened skin ... and he was imagining himself transformed into a truly white man by the sun's mysterious acts, pale as a ghost, yet with ebony hair, when he was summoned by a distant hail.

The Mapuche ignored him as he walked into their numbers, eyes roaming elsewhere. He might as well *be* a ghost, Juan thought. Taking a bowl from Wispu to stand blowing, waiting for the soup to cool, he felt his emergent ribs. Vegetables were turning him into a lath.

He started at the sound of an Indian war cry ... reached for an absent sword.

Pichikan ran up ululating, brandishing his club and saying he was sorry he was late. Smiling, Andalikan said that at least he was in time to eat.

The *longko* was fond of his nephew. And he had greater reason for his welcome to be warm. Kurui—his first-born daughter by Liftuipani—who should have married long ago ... had not. Rejected at the *ngillatun* by Pichikan, she had decided she would marry him or not at all, though wooed by *weichafe* Andalikan would have rejoiced to have as kin. Stubborn as overloaded *luan*, she declined. Yet—ignoring custom, and fighting over this with Liftuipani—Andalikan supported her. He loved his daughter. And disappointing his second wife gave him great pleasure.

It puzzled the *longko* that Kurui was born of her mother, for she was nothing like her sisters, with their teeth like rodents. Her marvelous round face made her seem the child Wispu never had. Perhaps, after giving birth to her, Liftuipani had seen the *chonchon*—that winged human head that flew at night, souring the wombs of women unfortunate enough to glimpse it. Maybe she even mated with the monster. In any case, Andalikan was willing to swear that every child Liftuipani bore, after Kurui, was fathered either by sorcery or some malevolent creature of the night. So it was that, as a father, he had been left only with Lautaro—who was like an adopted son—and Kurui, whom he considered to be the only true child of his seed. This made Andalikan indulgent with his daughter. It would cause him sorrow to have her leave his *ruka,* yet he would do his best to help her in her desires. And so—done greeting his nephew—Andalikan told Kurui to bring her cousin food. And let tongues wag.

Well aware that this was a plot against his liberty, Pichikan accepted the offered bowl reluctantly. Looking down at the upturned face of Kurui, he saw that her lips were trembling, as she turned away....

Why marry—Pichikan often asked himself—when there was the meat of *domo* to be had in plenty, with the bones of bondage to be tossed away? The fact that he was *weku* to Kurui made her intentions doubly dangerous, for she embodied the threat of marriage—which, as everybody knew, sapped vitality. Why did *weichafe* abstain from sleeping with *domo* before battle, after all, if this pleasure did not drain them of their strength, like water seeping from an earthen jug? Not that Pichikan abstained at other times—O no!—but *living* with the mild sorcery of her sex milked a warrior of his soul ... and of his will. No wife could refuse the wishes of a warrior, of course, yet they burrowed into the intentions of *wentru* with their soft ways—sighing, getting depressed and losing sleep, making their opposition to what a man wanted known with absolutely everything *but* words. He knew this well from friends who had succumbed to marriage out of pressure from their parents, or out of 'love,' as they said. Pichikan could understand fathering more *weichafe* for the *kuga.* But ... *love?* He saw it as something that ruined marriage, since only if a *weichafe* loved a *domo* would her wiles work on him. Therefore long ago he had decided that when wed—and he could not hold out forever—it would be with a lusty *domo* he could cheerfully ignore. In short, Pichikan did not want to be in love with Kurui.... Yet inescapably he was, having struggled against his feelings since the *antu* he did not dance with her at the *ngillatun.* And, now— predictably—love drained strength from his knees as he saw her walk away, proud head bowed. He stuffed the *kofke* she had given him into his mouth and chewed, staring at the air, trying to think....

Having approved Juan's labors at the spring, Lautaro gave him an ax and took him to where *wentru* worked, some digging holes, others cutting and shaping wood. He handed Juan a log thick as a forearm, had him hack it to a length he specified, pare the limbs flush with the trunk, scrape off the bark. He showed him how a hollow was to be cut in one end—where another log would nest. Finally, he had him notch at intervals.

Juan labored with flint, yearning for Spanish steel. And soon his hands—bleeding from the morning's labor—were also blistered. He was contemplating the damage when Pichikan came and took up his ax. "Time to rest, *lik winka*," he said, swinging with powerful ease, chips flying distances. Fascinated by this violence harnessed to construction, Juan wondered if Mapuche warriors did anything *but* fight … if only with simulacra.

That evening—to avoid his loathsome coop—Juan asked if he could sleep in the unfinished *ruka*. Then, he and Lautaro made beds in rush that tomorrow would be used for thatching. With no Inés to scold him over the dangers of night airs, Juan fell asleep admiring nameless stars.

The *ruka* took shape next morning. Two stout, high poles with forked ends were tamped into the ground, the ridgepole lashed between them. Shorter poles were set as a perimeter—Juan recognizing his contribution—and horizontal logs were laid over their notched ends, creating the outline of the walls. Spaced concavities were hacked into the periphery, for the rafters. Four of these were set and tied by the mid-day meal.

The workers, who had swarmed with the silent intensity of ants, ate and drank in equal quiet—caused by his presence, Juan imagined. But he noticed surreptitious glances, as if the melting of the ice of hate fed springs of curiosity. Heart lighter, Juan ate his *poñu* with appetite. It was fried today, and good.

After the meal, Pichikan called Juan over. He was lashing rafters to the ridgepole, standing on the transverse poles that spanned the walls, placed there to create an elevated platform. Juan asked about the vine they were using.

"*Nupu.*"

Why did the door of the *ruka* face east? Like a cathedral's, he was thinking.

"*Admapu.*"

The back of the *ruka*—where they were now tying rafters—was curved, and as there the poles did not bear horizontal logs, they were setting single rafters. Juan wondered why the end of the *ruka* was shaped like the apse of a church.

"To hold *wethakelu*," Pichikan replied. Descending his ladder he contemplated the knot Juan was tightening.

"What *is* that?"

And Juan became aware that—taking on life from the past—his fingers had tied a sailor's knot learned from Gil … not the one Pichikan had showed him. Then the warrior wanted to learn it. However, his fingers—so dexterous with weapons—were clumsy with vine. Others gathered, also wanting to learn. Juan became the focus of a murmuring crowd.

Perhaps a dozen Indians learned Gil's knot that afternoon, yet none used it on the *ruka* ... *admapu*, of course. But one of them created a knot the size of a fist which he held up for all to admire, exclaiming, "*lik winka peron.*" They all laughed, Juan included. And they all laughed harder when the one who made the '*lik winka* knot' was unable to untie it. From that moment, Juan could not call the Indians exactly friendly—nor did they speak with him—but at least they spoke to each other.

That evening Juan and Lautaro again spread their blankets on rush, this time inside the erected structure, where rafters framed the stars. What a shame to raise tomorrow's roof, Juan thought, for it was a delight to lie in a building that was— in effect—all window. There *was* something sacred about this tiny structure— the orientation, the apse-like end, the peaked roof. His *ruka* was a church in the rough—a kind of personal cathedral. But a cathedral devoted to the worship of what? Enjoying his conceit too much to pursue the questions that would destroy it, Juan simply asked himself why—if the Heavens declared the glory of God— churches had their roofs? And he was wondering why nothing sub lunar declared His Glory—at least in the Bible—when Lautaro surprised him with, "Good *ruka*?"

"Good *ruka*!"

The third morning of construction the weather remained perfect—sunny, with high, plump clouds drifting over the *cordillera*. The clearing was alive with shouts and laughter, for finishing a *ruka* was always good. The men began to thatch the walls and roof from the bottom up.

Juan worked with Lautaro and Pichikan on the roof. They first clambered to the rafters—which were ladder-like, because of the crosspieces lashed to them. From inside Pichikan called out instructions to Juan, until he caught the cadence. They took the bundles of rush he handed them, pressing them together to create a large 'shingle.' A stick was placed across the top and Lautaro passed a large wooden 'needle' through the bundle to Pichikan, who passed it back, as they pulled the *foki* snug. So it went, the 'shingles' snugged against the armature of the roof, the second layer of bundles overlapping the first, concealing the sticks that held them down. The work proceeded rapidly. Not long before dark, the shaggy edifice had acquired its almost completed form, smoke holes at each end of the peak, and—a nicety Juan had not expected—the walls were thinned under the eaves to admit air for the fire. Who would have thought!

Juan contemplated his untidy home—a haystack lashed to the skeleton of a tiny, windowless cathedral—far more moved than he had expected. In the slanting light of evening the rush shone gold against the forest. Behind it, transformed by sunset as by the intimacy of firelight, the *cordillera* for the first time seemed to welcome him. Fool's gold his home might be, and the mountains a fool's welcome, yet Juan was not less glad to have a shelter of his own. Thinking that the *ruka* resembled a broody hen, he placed a hand on the sun-warmed roof. Remembering Inés, he decided on a garden.

Lautaro handed Juan one of the small bows used to make fires, and said that as this was his *ruka*, he should light the first. Working for what seemed the seven days of the Creation, Juan created nothing. *Nihil.* Then ... a tiny glow! The Mapuche roared and clacked sticks together.

Juan emerged to ululate in the cool chiaroscuro of the fire-lit night. Swept away, he shouted in *mapudungun*—no doubt failing to communicate, but who cared?—that all who built this *ruka* had forever earned its welcome. A last cheer, and—whirling flaming brands—the Mapuche disappeared into dark forest paths.

"Rain." Lautaro said, approaching with the large *wilal* containing Juan's possessions. And indeed—Juan saw—battlements of cloud obscured the moon.

The downpour, when it came, created a murmur reminiscent of waterfalls on the new-laid rush, and Juan slid into sleep as into the slow waters of the Styx.

He woke to an insistent, "*Lik winka. Lik winka.*" The sun was already over the *cordillera*, Lautaro a silhouette against the light of the east-facing door, saying, "Andalikan is here with Wispu and Kurui. They have brought food and dogs. Pichikan is here too."

Dogs? Juan knew his guests would wait at a polite distance until he acknowledged them, for nothing like knocking or scratching existed here—which made sense, since most *ruka* had no proper doors. Emerging to welcome them, he was offered two skinny Mapuche mongrels. They had brought cooking pots also, baskets and containers, spoons—the bric-a-brac of Indian households—which the women began silently to unpack, turning the hollow shell of yesterday into today's crude home.

Kurui hung things from rafters, while Wispu heated water in a pot. The *wentru* sat apart, cross-legged on pelts, in Indian silence. Was Juan supposed to speak, as host?

"Good *ruka*," he offered in *mapudungun*, nodding his head like a walking pigeon, with each word. "Very dry." He was under orders from Lautaro to talk little, if at all—except in foreign tongues.

The *weichafe* nodded back, with impassive satisfaction. Lautaro said that Andalikan and Pichikan would help teach him *palin*. But first he had to make his stick. This was *admapu*.

As if on cue in a theater that toured the far edges of the world, Kurui walked up to place exactly that—a stick—at Juan's feet. "A gift from Andalikan," Lautaro commented. "He asks for nothing in return."

Juan knew that no *weichafe* would want to become *trafkiñ* with *him*, and—as sitting he could not bow, and silent he could not be—he said, "Good stick."

The *weichafe* smiled, enigmatic.

Juan had cramps from sitting cross-legged. And he was thinking he needed a civilized chair far more than a crooked stick, when he stood on trembling legs to speak, choosing a passage memorized from **Utopia**. All were agog save for Lautaro, accustomed to *likwinkadungun*. And the warrior was gratified, for—as predicted—his captive was far more impressive when incomprehensible.

Andalikan rose to say that what they brought to the *ruka* was hardly worth mentioning. They would be be using these things themselves in any case, as they would be staying to prepare for *palin*.

No one had explained to Juan that he would share his new home with hostile Indians. He was stunned.

Murmuring farewells, the *domo* left.

And for the remainder of that day, Juan scraped with flint under the dubious eye of warriors who seemed to consider indolence *their* best preparation for the game. By nightfall the general opinion was that—though rough—the stick was usable. Tomorrow they would practice.

The day Juan would never forget began with the usual icy bath—which he had come perversely to enjoy, as a monk, no doubt, his flagellations. After, Juan was led on a run through woods, up and down mountains—distances that would have winded horses. Then, a late breakfast was brought by Wispu and Kurui of—*Redios!*—meat, red and charred, oozing fat and blood! The run had been worth it. Juan gulped his portion like one of Santiago's famished curs, hearing Lautaro explain that the team had to win by four points.

"Just four?"

A point by the other team canceled one of yours.

Seeing realization grow in Juan's eyes, Lautaro added that *palin* had been known to last two *antu*.

"Sweet Jesus!" Juan breathed at that enormity, still mercifully ignorant of what was to come.

They held races barefoot in the field of play, which was sixty or seventy *pasos* long—the perimeter marked with straw—sprint after sprint, with lanky Andalikan invariably finishing first, Lautaro second. Then followed an Indian torture improvised by Pichikan as to who could hold his stick the longest with both arms straight out. This time, Pichikan handily won, Lautaro coming in second. Juan's dismal record remained perfect when he came in last. One seemed to prepare for *palin* by inventing agonies where they did not otherwise exist, he thought. Hopefully, the actual game would prove to be a kindness.

At long last the *weichafe* produced the *pali*—a small wooden ball—and 'played.' In actual fact this meant scrambling at mad speed toward the goals—stones set a *paso* and a half apart at the ends of the field. They took turns, the object being to run as fast as possible without losing the ball—no mean accomplishment on uneven ground. Hitting it hard and sprinting after was fastest, but risky, for the treacherous sphere might careen in wrong directions, allowing a rival player to steal the object of your desire and run the way you had just come from. Sisyphus might have had his hill and boulder, yet he did not *sprint* the slope, thought Juan, realizing that his bare feet were turning to ground meat. The day ended at twilight, they trotting with their sticks—back and forth, from goal to goal—passing the *pali* in complex patterns. Juan managed to shamble with them—and if he bobbled a pass or forgot his battle station, he let the blame fall on *lik winka* ignorance, for he was long past pride.

That evening the warriors conferred around the fire pit as Juan limped out for fresh air and a piss. Swaying with exhaustion, he saw that the full moon had risen over the mountains. Drained, he became a simple naked eye, and the moon the unmoved—yet moving—eye of Night. Never had he been witness to anything so beautiful, pure, and in its own enormous way, so cruel. This somehow *was* the Indies, he thought. The universe awaited man in the sixth day of its Creation, untouched save by the breath of God.

Lautaro emerged to find the *lik winka* staring at the moon and holding his *penun*. He smiled at his student, pleased with the day. Wan had lost every race— yet not by much, against fast runners. *And*, he had not in any way complained about his bleeding feet. Kuruga might be in for a surprise. "Go soak your feet," he said, not unkindly.

When Juan returned to the *ruka*, Kurui was there with a basket containing bread, salt-fried potatoes, and the first strawberries of the season. "*Kelleñ!*" Andalikan exclaimed. "So early!"

Glancing from her father to Pichikan, Kurui modestly replied, "They are small and few," which was true, yet they glowed like coals in a small basket lined with leaves.

"You picked them yourself," Andalikan crowed, crafty … Kurui disapproving with a quick glare.

This made Andalikan rebellious—he being her father, after all—and he proclaimed, "You will walk back with Pichikan."

Kurui had no alternative. Everyone ordered unmarried daughters around—

except for *pichiche* and even younger unmarried daughters. The only escape was the lesser servitude of marriage.

Picking up his club, Pichikan stood, stiff with indignation. Though he was more or less resigned to being in love, he still resented actual *plots* against his freedom.

No flaming brand was needed beneath the moon of this warm night, and they left without, Pichikan striding with rude speed, Kurui trotting after.

Furious as the *weichafe* was, he did not overlook a shadow melting into trees, and he stopped in mid stride—so abruptly that Kurui almost bumped into him. Pichikan saw nothing more ... and heard nothing ... save for the breathing quickening behind him.

She had put her hand on his bare shoulder. Could Pichikan now cruelly stride away, letting the small, warm fingers drop? Was he going stand here like a *wed wed*? He turned, not expecting that her hand would stay just where it was. Then his own was on her shoulder, his back to the moon, her face lifted pale to its light.

"*Ad ngen.* You are beautiful," he whispered.

Then, when she said nothing, he asked her not to cry.

Next morning Lautaro applied vegetable ooze to Juan's feet, which felt far better than Pedro's plaster of warm guts. Smelled better, too. And even better was the change in Lautaro. Nothing was harder than to be alone and hated, Juan had decided, especially when one did not hate back. The profound aversion of Indians made you doubt not only yourself but also the entire Spanish enterprise—whether you called it pacification, or the bringing of the light of God to the benighted. Living with odium was the heaviest cross of his exile.

Putting on the soft footwear Raytrayen had made for him, Juan decided that Lautaro at times resembled his sister. Their noses and their smiles were much alike ... and he was faintly smiling now. He needed his captive to do well in *palin* for the sake of his own reputation, Juan knew. But Juan had his own reasons to master a game that was little less than combat with hostile savages, armed only with a crooked stick. He would have to do his best, just as when he learned the knife from Pedro, who put it simply—A man could do many things badly, and still brag about them after, in a *bodega* ... fighting with Toledo steel was not one of them. Still, survival was not Juan's single motive. Captivity had made him eager to please— childishly so—as if the promises at his capture had sheathed not just his sword but the steel of his Spanish will. Strangely, he *wanted* to gratify Lautaro.

Juan followed him to the *ruka* feeling like his dog, in a state of mind that curiously resembled his eagerness to please the Governor of his days of freedom. What Juan could not understand—now sitting by the fire—was how a young savage could take the place of Valdivia, whose authority derived from the Emperor, himself anointed by God. Did the act of capture create *imperium* on a personal scale, bestowing sovereignty on a savage? Juan doubted this. Was an eagerness to be subjugated an alchemical transmutation of humiliation in the alembic of captivity, creating that higher metal which was loyalty? Indians had captured not just his body, it seemed, but also his resolve….

Pichikan walked into the *ruka*, his greeting all the heartier for being false. Andalikan turned solemn. Lautaro put a hand over his smirk, calling attention to it.

Ignoring these blatant signs that everyone knew why it took him so long to walk a short path in the company of a *domo*, Pichikan noticed that in his absence the strawberries had remained untouched.

"*Kelleñ* anyone," he blustered, picking up the basket, every berry still perfectly in place.

"I am full, *peñi*," Lautaro all but chortled, cruelly patting his stomach.

Andalikan beamed, not even pretending to create excuses.

And when the basket was extended to him, Juan did not forget himself so far as to accept.

Defeated, Pichikan consumed the delicious berries as the dust they were, for this night he had betrayed his teammates by lying with a *domo*.

Andalikan rose, saying that he would go visit his wife. One last night would make no difference.

And once at his *ruka* he woke Wispu, doing a naked dance for her surprise.

Routine declared itself in the wonderful dry days of summer. Endless runs followed a bath at the spring. Then breakfast—which often included meat—was either brought cooked by Kurui and Wispu, or freshly killed by the players, who set snares and hunted during the morning run—usually birds, sometimes *pudu*. After digestion came sprints, followed by tortures designed by Pichikan, who was something like a horse in human hide. After, they raced forever in the game of steal the *pali*. Finally, after eating, they practiced into the declining evening, exploring combinations as to who played what position, who stole the ball and passed to whom—so on, *ad infinitum*—even under moonlight. Juan lived and breathed, and had his being in *palin*.

At some late point the *domo* brought more food, Wispu swinging a brand, Kurui bearing the heaping basket that always contained some delicacy for Pichikan. He did not again walk her back to her *ruka*, yet there was no denying that an unspoken change took place the night he did, Kurui now smiling at him with the calm radiance of the moon.

One day Tuiñam arrived to join the *palinche*, turning the tiny *ruka* into a place crowded with thatch-to-thatch obsession, a kind of calenture of play. Like anchorites perfecting their chastity in the Nubian Desert—high upon a pole—they forsook the world for perfection.

Something like an unwatched pot, Lautaro had returned from the *lik winka* to his people boiling over with ideas inconceivable to them, and one evening he proposed that they play *palin* the way war was practiced in Tiako. Some orders were shouted, he said, while others were blared by a thing like the *trutruka* that had a higher and more piercing voice, so small it could be lifted with one hand. To it, *lik winka* responded like obedient beetles, attacking, retreating, and forming lines.

"A *wentru* with a *pichi trutruka* tells them what to do while fighting!" Andalikan was awed.

"Yes. Falthifa—their *toki*—tells others what orders to shout and what to blow on the *pichi trutruka*."

"How can he do all this and still fight?"

Lautaro smiled mysteriously, saying that *lik winka* battled like what you could call a tree of which Falthifa was the trunk.

"*Mai*," Juan blurted in agreement. Why had he not ever thought of this? The Emperor was the trunk of conquest, Valdivia and the other captains the limbs, while the *caballeros*, the *infantes*, and the *yanaconas* were the leaves.

His brief outburst was ignored, Lautaro going on to say, "Think of it this way, uncle, Falthifa is the trunk that tells the limbs what to do, and each limb tells its leaves what to do."

Pondering the parable, Andalikan replied, "There must be a lot of talking and very little fighting going on. How can they be so *good* at it?"

"The leaves fight while the trunk and limbs are speaking."

Here Juan silently disagreed, for Valdivia and his captains fought hard as anyone. But military exercises in the town square were one thing, actual battle another. No metaphor marched on all four legs anyway, as Lobo once said.

Lautaro appealed to trust, "Believe me, uncle, this *will* work."

"One *longko* with twelve sticks, twenty-four arms, and twenty-four feet?" Andalikan's disbelief had turned derisive.

Juan knew exactly what he was saying. How would this monster march—much less fight or play *palin*—a single head telling all these feet and arms what to do? He visualized a dozen necks— extended in a version of the Hydra—converging to the one head, creating a kind of upside down structure with the head as trunk, marching on its greenery. Then Juan actually *saw* the immense, rootless tree which had the Emperor as its *longko* borne by a myriad leafy feet, not necessarily in one direction, for some were going this way, others that, the necks growing longer as the extremities walked off—to Italy, the Indies— meaty branches stretching vast distances, creating a majestic oak that spanned the Ocean Sea, all topped by the royal head. Yet if necks were limbs, and they the captains of the Emperor, like *atlantes*—those Greek columns in human shape—they sustained the head. And so it went, Juan's visionary structure crumbling when the Emperor's crown sprouted roots stretching toward Heaven....

Lautaro put his *lik winka* idea to the test the next day, blaring improvised signals from the sidelines with a *trutruka* ... failing utterly. The 'language' of the instrument was too simple, new and unfamiliar, to do more than confuse *palinche* in the heat of play, who reverted to ancient habit when they heard low, distracting toots. Ultimately, however, the stubbornness that was the marrow of Mapuche bone killed the exercise. Why should just one *wentru* give the orders? Wanting their servitude to fail, the *weichafe* made certain with ineptitude that it did.

That evening Lautaro was bitter. Had Ñamku been wrong to send him to Tiako to learn from *lik winka*? Had the experience taught him only to feel superior to his people? He was ashamed, for much was at stake.

"Maybe we should replace the *lik winka* with a real player," he said at the evening meal.

Pichikan spoke up, after a silence, "Let him stay on the team, I say."

Tuiñam agreed ... then Andalikan. Still, the decision gladdened no one. And bleakly they stared into the dying fire.

Juan felt betrayed. No one had asked *him* if he wanted to be on the team. So what if he lost this game of theirs for them? Did he care...?

To his dismay, he deeply did. Indians have captured not just your body, but your soul, he decided, when it seems an honor that they desire to taste your heart.

Kurufil was frustrated. That muscled old fool, Kuriñam, had become a nuisance he could not eliminate, wandering outside *renu* shouting challenges day and night. If he killed the *longko*, his kin would not need a *machi* to examine the gall bladder of the corpse to divine the killer. They would come to *renu* despite their fear of his sorcery, as they had before. And *this* time, they might find him....

He remembered the armed *weichafe* who had walked beneath his hiding place, the smoke of their torches making him want to cough. One or two he could have killed, yet not all. His death would have been terrible and slow. He had survived, however, and they had not found his precious cache. Good also was the fact that Kuriñam seemed to be sipping the poisoned teas he had prepared for his wife, as grief and fasting would not by themselves explain his terrible decline. Let the old idiot die, as he soon would. But in the meantime Kurufil had been unable to come and go as he pleased. And he had been frustrated in his attempt to come upon the *lik winka* when he was by himself.

Kurufil had lingered—shadow in shadows—at safe distances, wondering how to kill the *weichafe* and leave *him* unharmed. He could not poison the spring. Neither could he kill the warriors singly—they were seldom alone, and too wary to allow him near.

The night Pichikan glimpsed Kurufil, frustration had brought him dangerously close. And he watched from darkness—too astonished to feel relief—as the *weichafe* and *domo* embraced, kissed, moaned, and like dogs began to couple, standing. He could have killed them, but what he wanted was the *lik winka*. Day after day, he had watched from hiding as he played *palin*, admiring the uncanny eyes, uncanny hair flying with the violence of the game.

Kurufil was again in love, but inexplicably, as with the precious objects of his cache. He was baffled by this love, and as days wore on the futility of his attraction began to seem an imperfection of his hate. Was he drawn to the only two *lik winka* he had met, as kindred souls, or just attracted to what he could not understand *because* they were unlike him? If so, his love did not so much make him different from *che*, as represent ignorance he shared with them, and felt more deeply. Kurufil was frustrated, therefore torn, irritated, his soul a storm-lashed sea. One thing was certain … he could not continue in this futile rage. He would have to act, or hate and yearning would destroy him.

The *palinche* had paused for their midday meal when a *werken* arrived with a breathtaking message—*Lik winka* were coming *willi* in great numbers!

Meat and *poñu* forgotten, everyone began to talk at once, until Andalikan pointed out that the enemy would not arrive for at least half a *kuyen*.

Three decisions were quickly reached. They would continue to practice, as the match was too important to set aside. But since time was short, they would immediately assemble all the players. Finally, they would negotiate with Kuruga to play sooner.

Andalikan left to make arrangements.

Juan's first reaction was euphoria, quickly damped. He had become a tolerated companion of the *weichafe*. Now, because of Valdivia, he was the enemy again.

That night was blustery, a rare north wind sighing through thatch, setting the fire to dancing. And yet Juan quickly went to sleep. Why worry when there was nothing to be done?

He was roused by voices. "*Ngeru! Ngeru! Mena wesha dengu!*"

A fox? Why should a fox be a bad thing? Why should it cause dismay? He fell asleep again.

War cries woke him. The *palinche* were outside naked, beating sticks, creating an immense racket as they ran around the *ruka*, eyes and teeth white in the night, hair flying, sex jouncing, their discord multiplied by the frantic yowling of the dogs, but … not a sign of danger could Juan see. He observed them with astonishment until, at last, they returned to their beds in the false dawn of *mapu*.

When over breakfast Juan asked what all this meant, Pichikan laconically replied, "*Mena wesha dengu. Ngeru. Chiwud.*"

The fox puzzled Juan, not the owl—bird of worst augur. However, the omens did not affect *him*, for how could his luck get worse? He slept again, dreaming that Pedro was beside him, snoring.

Next morning, Pichikan was outside chopping wood, Lautaro rebuilding the fire, and Tuiñam—eternal helmet off for once—filling a pot with Indian gruel. Accustomed to Pedro, who was slovenly about everything but armor and weapons, Juan had not ceased to be amazed by the neatness of these *wentru* without *domo*. Feeling guilty, he tied on his *chiripa*. Postponing his morning bath, he began to sweep the floor. And, accustomed to *mapudungun* as a kind of buzzing in his ears—easy to ignore as sunset crickets—Juan did not realize for some time that he comprehended what he heard….

A fox had barked. Then an owl hooted as it flew over the *ruka*. Separately, these were sinister portents. Together they were disaster, but a disaster of what kind? Usually these creatures foretold sickness to the healthy, death to the sick. The combination could mean worse. Still, omens were by their nature unpredictable, and therefore argued over. Was someone going to get sick, or die? Was *everyone* going to get sick, or—as Tuiñam proposed—did this portend disaster in *palin*?

Rattled, argumentative, dejected, the *palinche* decided on the usual run next morning, before they realized that both dogs were missing. Searching the woods for signs of the supernatural, they came on a decapitated head, set on a flat black stone.

"*Wekufu,*" they cried, contemplating the serpent scratched onto the slate bearing the grisly dog's head. Running for their weapons, they fanned out.

Pichikan found the second head—also set on slate—so that to Juan it seemed buried while wearing a flat stone ruff. What was happening, here?

"*Kalku,*" the *weichafe* murmured, on seeing the second serpent scratched on stone. And they looked toward the Southern Sea, Juan realizing that the muzzle of the second dog was turned in the same direction as the first.

"Kurufil *wants* us to know!"

Pichikan roared that these dogs were a slap on the face.

"His sorcery will make us lose the game," Tuiñam exclaimed.

Then it was, "Kill! Kill! Kill!"

Pichikan and Tuiñam began a war dance, whooping, not hearing when Lautaro quietly remarked, "If he did *this*, then he is not in *renu*."

He was proven right, when they arrived at the cave. The boulder at the mouth was rolled aside. Flanking it, two headless dogs were impaled upright, like sentinels. Between them—blocking the entrance—so small that in the first shock of horror it was not noticed, was a decapitated toad, also impaled.

Juan murmured, "Jesús, María, y José," unable to tear his eyes from this hellish echo of The Crucifixion. Less than Inés—yet much as any normal man—Juan believed in sorcery, and he sensed its nefast presence here. Never had he felt this close to naked evil.

The *weichafe*—every one of whom would spit, laughing, in the face of death—uneasily eyed the iridescent flies swarming on the corpses. Any one of them could be the *kalku*....

How long that buzzing moment lasted, Juan would never know. As wind-borne seeds drift weightless leagues, suspending laws, he lived a dream that did not touch the earth until Lautaro entered *renu*.

No sorcerer was in the enormous bat-filled cave—which without torches they could not explore. No one said a word. And the moment came when as one man they strode toward the light, pride keeping them from running.

The game, it seemed, was doomed before it started. And, back at the *ruka*, they were discussing this when Andalikan returned, successful. The four *palinche* with him were appalled, however, on hearing what had happened. One said that last night he had a nightmare but told no one—for, as all knew, bad dreams shared before breakfast came true....

He was on the palin *field at night, alone, when an enormous snake slipped from the woods, undulating toward him, the night so silent he could hear the hiss of scales on grass. Lifting its head to the height of his, black tongue flickering, it looked at him with the eyes of* che....

"Kurufil!"

No one could blame the *palinche* when he said he could not play. And when he left they quarreled, the other newcomers saying the game was lost already. Andalikan argued that they *had* to try. If they did not Marillan would be given to Kuruga against her will and that of her father. This was a matter of honor. Her rape and beating were an insult to the entire *kuga*.

The newcomers pointed out that they were going to lose anyway, so why bother?

Pichikan, Lautaro and Tuiñam supported Andalikan, who went for *mudai*, thinking this might incline the opposition to his side. But no, when drunk, the *weichafe* began to taunt each other. The situation was turning ugly.

"We need a *machi* to undo this *kalkutun*," said Andalikan.

Lautaro understood too well what his uncle was trying to do. The disagreement was less about omens and sorcery than the unspoken certainty that the *lik winka* was responsible for the coming disaster—if not by *kalkutun*, then by troubling *kume mognen*. And since Lautaro had put him on the team, the problem originated with *him*, so that now even those who supported him were resentful. Teams needed a *machi* to invoke the aid of the *pillañ*, and this team needed one even more, because of the *lik winka*. Ñamku being dead, their obvious choice would have been Pangi, but he had failed his first trial as *machi*. No one was about to propose *him*, yet they could hardly choose another.

Juan was matching the *palinche,* cup for cup, of this liquor cloudy as a blind man's eye, attempting to get drunk enough to enjoy the vile fluid before passing out. He belched, and blurted, "Pangi what? This *machi* no, he?"

Silence and consternation! The *lik winka* who had loomed over the discussion as an immaterial, sorcerous presence, had been forgotten in the actual flesh.

Lautaro seized the opportunity. "*Pu peñi*. Ñamku is not truly dead. I have heard Pangi speak to him."

He said no more, letting implications root. If the 'not dead' *machi* helped, they had a chance to survive the *kalkutun, and* win the game. Spirits lifted, the *palinche* agreed that Lautaro would talk to Pangi. And next morning, when he left to do so, they practiced with remarkable enthusiasm, considering their hangovers. More players arrived that afternoon, bringing their number to fourteen.

That evening—the subject of conversation being sorcery—one of the newcomers recounted what happened to his cousin, Wenchun.

He was courting Pichol, a domo *who lived far away, and one day when he went to see her, hearing the cry of an owl, he got violently ill. He consulted a* machi, *who said that the next time this happened he should plunge his knife into the ground. He did as told and a winged head fell fluttering down, shouting curses, grinding its teeth. The head of Pichol!*

"The *chonchon!*"

Wenchun hurried to her ruka *and found the headless body breathing. He turned it over, ran away, and the next day heard that Pichol had died with her head on backwards.*

The warriors were quite calm about this prodigy. Not Juan, who was thinking that the Indies contained marvels rivaling those of Africa. He yearned to ask about the wings upon the flying head. Were they birdlike—since the creature was named after an owl—or, were they human ears grown out, membranous as those of bats? Wondering about the ears, Juan almost missed the beginning of the next account, about one of Andalikan's ancestors.

Many years ago, as a pichiche, Ongolmo went to the Fio Fio on a foggy morning with his older sister, Lemunao. They were filling water skins, when something moved by the far shore. Mist, lifting from the river, revealed a huge head suspended in the air. Quiet as pudu *hearing a dry stick crack, they saw that the head had glowing eyes and grinned with pointed teeth. It panted like a dog, was sleek as seals, had the ears and muzzle of a fox. The long neck rising from the water was covered with black scales big as scallop shells. Then near them, something emerged from the water like a huge finger growing longer, rising, until they could see it was the tail of the creature tall as trees, a tail that coiled about Lemunao. She did not resist as it pulled her under, for she had fallen in love with* ngurufilu, *the serpent fox. And never did she return, living with him ever after beneath the river....*

Drowsily listening, Juan then heard of *ketronpellun*—a single-footed dwarf resembling a penguin. He also learned about *piuchen*—a flying serpent that sucked the blood of animals and men.

Dreams visited Juan that night....

He walked under a blood red moon ... and under vines, that—as if they shared a single evil—conspired to strangle him. Struggling, he parted them like curtains, opening windows to dim spaces inhabited by monsters that looked back with calm malevolence. Piuchen dripped blood from fangs onto its velvet pelt. The chonchon levitated on trembling, membranous wings, whispering, "I am ostomi."

Night had wed monsters of the Indies to those of **Historia Naturalis***, so that* Ketronpellun *was a penguin on its head, shielding himself from moonlight with one webbed foot—like the monocli of the Umbrella Foot Tribe. Black and white—sinister as an inverted Carmelite—he beckoned, cackling. Then it was witches that Juan stumbled on, exposing flaccid breasts, licking lips on which red paint had cracked....*

Juan woke, yearning for light and roads, Spanish distances.

Kurufil had an insight when he heard the *lik winka* were coming. As when, of shifting cloud, one becomes aware that a familiar shape has lingered there, he knew he was—and was not—in love with the *lik winka* called Wan. He also was—and was not—in love with the *kallfu lik winka*, who was even more beautiful. And all this, he decided, was less contradiction than uncertainty. If he was like *lik winka*, then he was no longer alone, so that, as a child regarded adults with wonder, he could see them as part of his future. Yet, if his attraction was to what he could not be, then his love was the fruit of weakness, making him no better than an *ifunche* yearning not to be *anken peñen.*

He knew then what he had to do. His soul was *winka*, or it was not, and the answer to that lay *piku.* He would go north, therefore, and find the *kallfu lik winka.* The decision was so evident—so *necessary!*—that the *kalku* laughed with delight. Fear had prevented his return—not of the demons that maimed him, but of discovering he was not worthy. And the same fear made him consider Wan desirable. Feebleness and doubt had attracted him to the only *lik winka* he thought he could control. So—as if they had been one from the start—his love for Wan became great loathing. Killing him, he would free himself of fear and become worthy of going *piku.* He would leave *renu* to be *winka,* or to die.

No reason not to kill, now. But whom … how many? Four, he decided—the winning number in *palin.* But first the dogs, letting the *palinche* know a game greater than theirs had begun.

Lautaro returned, saying that Ñamku had agreed to help, and the Heavens seemed to open in response. No Biblical deluge this—a rain of mere days. However—considering the season—to the *palinche* it was a portent. Farmers all to some degree, they rejoiced in the excess, and they practiced in the wet the livelong day, not cold, for this was kind, warm rain. Like children they would break into spontaneous play, have splashing wars, returning to their evening meal mud-covered—people of the earth indeed.

Blessed with dreamless sleep, these days in which the body did its strenuous things Juan discovered a degree of peace he never knew existed—a quiescence rooted in the present, blooming there—so that in the morning when the dawn at last broke free of cloud he welcomed it as pure surprise.

Naked, the *palinche* had emerged to admire the day—Adams wakened from their dreams—when an apparition from another dream materialized at the distant forest edge. Ñamku of the mask was motionless beneath the risen sun, white against the cleansed green world….

He had returned—he shrieked—to protect them from *wekufu.* He would be with them at the game. And he vanished like a breath exhaled.

Seized by an energy that took them all, the *weichafe* ululated, dancing. Sure as sunrise, with the help of Ñamku they would win! They put Lautaro on a blanket … tossed him in the air. And no one was aware—then or after—that the *lik winka* had joined the naked press.

Late that evening, without explanation, Lautaro led Juan into inky woods, where for blind distances they walked until they reached a stream. With curious calm, Juan sat to bathe the soreness of his feet. "Good water," he offered as he smiled into the night—Lautaro more sensed than seen.

"*Lik winka,*" was the whisper slow in coming, "I have a favor to ask of you."

"*Mai.*" Juan was puzzled.

"Hsshrr! *Mapu* has ears," Lautaro hissed.

"I do indeed," the tree trunk that Lautaro leaned on, whispered, and—as if scorched—the warrior leapt away.

Bemused, Juan searched for complications in the gloom.

An intense point of light floated into being in the air, exploding with coruscating brightness. He protected his eyes with his forearm, thought he heard running, peered out at last....

Five *pasos* over, a green flame sizzled on rain soaked leaves, expiring, and by its eerie waver an Indian he presumed to be Lautaro crouched, lifting something. The light died with a spark and hiss.

"Lautaro…?" Juan whispered, blinded, tremulous.

"Promise you will not tell the *peñi*."

Juan wondered how he could disclose what he had neither seen nor understood, as he was led through the forest's clammy touch, until—under palest moonlight—they stood in the clearing scented by the *ruka* fire. There, Lautaro held up an object for Juan's inspection. A shield, round and black, was divided into ocher quadrants by a black cross—eerie Indian echo of Crusades. Lautaro pointed to what might have been long thorns embedded in it, cryptic, "Ñamku saved our lives tonight."

"What!" What *had* he missed?

"Hsshrr," Lautaro cautioned. "You promised silence."

Once in the smoky closeness of the *ruka* Juan thought he would find out what happened, later … but Fortuna knew better.

Four human paths led to that instant of blinding light, and the one that took Pangi there was thorny.

"Go away," he had said, harsh, full of pain. "Stay dead."

The silence of death made Pangi angrier. "I just want to live," he said. "Is that too much to ask?

I want to be *myself*," he insisted, raging at himself, raging at the peace of the dead, which was like diving under water to escape the storm of life—as Katrinir once described it. Now Pangi *was* a tempest. Anger was his life, and *that* was what he wanted. He wanted his life, not their peace.

"You are *piuchen*, Ñamku," he raged. "You suck blood from the living. Being dead is not enough for you!" And, like a mourning *domo,* Pangi tore his unbound hair. "You are jealous of us!" he cried out.

Then he wept until at last he sighed, "Forgive me."

"Can I come out, now?" Katrinir asked.

Beyond smiling, Pangi became calm again. "The question is, can I do this?"

"*How* is what matters," Ñamku insisted.

They planned, lost in timeless concentration, for with Kurufil involved, a mistake would mean disaster.

Pangi woke his brother, telling him that Ñamku had agreed to help. He said to take the *lik winka* into the woods, and specified the time of day, the place.

Ñamku could not help but worry. If Kurufil was watching the *lik winka*, he would know that his challenge had been taken up, and that now their own old game approached its end.

Kurufil respected the woodcraft of the *weichafe* that he stalked too much to risk watching them from close, and so it happened that he witnessed the impossible from a distance—Ñamku emerging into the sunlit clearing! And the high, harsh, distorted shriek of the *machi* was not quite lost in the rustle of the leaves about him. "Is it you," he whispered hoarsely, "or are you Pangi?"

Tricked! Whether this was Ñamku live, or Ñamku dead, he was being taken for a fool. Hurrying with a recklessness he knew insane, Kurufil found footprints familiar as his own. This answer to his challenge was an insult! Wild-eyed, he searched the forest, knowing it was looking back. Burning with humiliation he hastened, promising himself that he would kill soon, in a way that would draw Ñamku out. Then he would kill him too, for good.

He prepared with care, blackening his face and hands with soot—to be, as Ñamku taught him, nothing but the night. After, he waited in starlit dark as from the *ruka* came the sound of laughter and the smell of cooking. He crept closer … was very near when Lautaro emerged with the *lik winka* and led him into the forest. Silent as a bat, Kurufil flitted after. Was this a trap…?

It was.

In furious memory Kurufil knew that Ñamku—not he—planned what happened, including his own hesitation when he heard the *machi* whisper that the forest heard.

Startled by the dazzle of the *cherufe*, Kurufil lifted his hand to kill … saw his victims shield their eyes from light … saw Ñamku also—not where his voice had been—a tree that had the whites of eyes, and held a shield….

Kurufil first ran with the fright of animals, then with the humiliation of a *che*. Almost to *renu* he came on Kuriñam, and, filled with savage joy he asked, "Have you been looking for me?"

The *lonko* was stumbling, weeping, mumbling. Puzzled by the shadow laughing at him, he wiped his running nose.

The *kalku* killed him painfully as he could in the little time he had. Then he hid the body and loutish club, keeping the head. Three to go, he told himself. And smiling, he headed for *lolo*, the head of Kuriñam a satisfying weight.

Andalikan squatted by the spring, plaiting his wet hair, smoking a stinking clay pipe. "*Mari, mari, lik winka*," he greeted.

Juan replied with equal neutrality to one who was no enemy and yet no friend.

Gesturing with his pipe, Andalikan said that today they would go to the *paliwe*, a half *antu* distant. He would not need his *wilef wethakelu*. And the warrior walked away.

Bathing, Juan asked himself if wanting to win in *palin* made him a traitor to his kind. Then, walking to the gruel of Mapuche mornings, he bound his wet hair with a thong.

The clearing with the *paliwe* at its center was a hive buzzing with quiet activity when the team of Pichikan arrived. To Juan, it seemed the field might well have served as the lists for more chivalric times, and he felt a stirring of the wonders of his youth … because this was his first public contest? Despite the somber crowd in black, brown, gray—no pennants, bright pavilions, or damsels in vivid silk— the setting was magnificent. A slope of forest irregularly rose, leading the eye to the impassive loom of the *cordillera*, its battlements immaculate with snow. No wonder the mountains were sacred to these Indians. Like God, they always looked over your shoulder.

The *palinche* descended to the clearing, where the mood was sober as the dress, women busy about fires, men building shelters. Divided into grim encampments, the teams might as well have been opposing armies. Tension was palpable as the *palinche* joined their whispering families. Sorcery was in the air, and listening to those who said Kuriñam was missing…. Still, this was not the first time the old man fell asleep in the woods, only to turn up later. There was talk also about the dead dogs, the disappearance of the *kalku*. And it was said that Kuruga had conspired with Kurufil. Ñamku's promise to intervene comforted some—but not completely—the skeptics not at all. Kurufil was formidable, and unlike Ñamku he still lived.

Juan was ignored. Relieved, he helped Pichikan and Tuiñam make shelters for the *palinche*, separate from those of *domo*. Earthquakes and eruptions would not keep Kurui from Pichikan, however, and she found reason to stroll by, saucy.

That evening, as an extraordinary precaution, both camps posted armed guards by fires burning through the night. The *palinche* perfected their sticks, sighting down the polished lengths. There was the plucking of hair with bone tweezers, the shaving of faces and heads with clamshells—some shaving their foreheads also. As usual, Pichikan opted for baldness about a plait. Others braided and tied their hair in varied ways, including the feathers that would make them light on their feet. Pichikan had to do repairs on Juan's braid, clucking like a mother hen. Then, there were the paints made of charcoal, other earths, and substances Juan did not recognize. The pigments were mixed and pounded—sometimes with tallow— creating unctuous pastes that were mostly black and ocher, but also dull white, somber yellow, lead blue. The *palinche* pounded, looking everywhere but at Juan.

That night he woke in panic, thinking that a vampire bat had brushed him with the clawed velvet of its wings. A dream? Fearing sleep, Juan revisited the blind alley in Cuzco that forever changed him....

Haloed by incandescent copper, the ivory face floated in pellucid altitudes, halfway to Heaven. The green eyes glowed with gorgeous outrage over the perfectly freckled and tilted nose, all framed by the blazing hair....

The hair!

The halo of Inés—to which obsessive memory returned—summed Juan's failure, for he was attempting to recollect what the supreme moment had not collected. Where, the individual wisps, consuming light? Was the instant wondrous as a whole, in which detail swam unseen? Or—as in the parted clouds of altars, betraying Heaven only by escaping rays—did the halo of Inés gloriously announce that her beauty could not be observed *directly*? Lobo—Juan recalled—once said that, as Semele did not survive the sight of Jupiter, a living mortal could not endure the presence of The Living God. Yet, given that God crafted man in His image, could Heaven be reflected on a lower plane? And if so, did man of necessity have to glance aside, to survive? There were paradoxes here....

With a disorienting jounce of memory that took him to the Atacama, Juan saw Inés upon her horse, Blanca Rosa del Desierto. She wore her hat, of course— that dear, flat, customary thing—rebellious wisps emerging, of which no hair was singularly visible. And now, having lost her forever, he had to ask himself if he had ever truly *seen* her? Telling himself that hairs were an innumerable thing, Juan remembered that when—though rarely—in desert heat, Inés pushed up her sleeves, the down upon her arms was limned with light, backlit by blinding suns....

Perhaps God—giving man too much to grasp in the greatest moments he accorded—created that deviation of vision called a halo, to save him from a desire he could not otherwise survive.

Startled, Juan looked up to see Medusa, black braids wreathing her white face....

Lautaro asked, "War paint?"

Chapter 14: *Palin* (*Mapu*, 1550)

Pichikan tilted his head to admire his work, deciding that the *lik winka* looked far fiercer with his face red. Pleased, he took the little finger hanging from the thong around his neck and waggled it.

Numb with consequence, Juan considered the Mapuche dangling—like an obscene lure—that *thing* he considered a bond between them. Everything civilized in him had revolted against being painted, yet when Lautaro led him to Pichikan and his polychrome pots he did not have the heart to refuse. Now—as measure of his hunger for affection in the wilderness—he was red as the little devil cavorting on his left shoulder. All he lacked were horns and a tail.

Juan sighed, remembering the enormous, gentle fingers, solemnly anointing him … and moving him obscurely, for he had a sense of sacraments awry about this Indian laying on of hands. Thank God he had no mirror! In the absence of a glass, however, he had *palinche* all about, daubing *their* faces, shocking versions of his own. Wenchuman was also red, though striped white to his waist. Pichikan—the most appalling—was shaved smooth as eggs up to his braided hank. Below, he was ebony to the neck … and, downward, yellow to his clout. Juan fervently thanked God that his own ochre ended at the chin.

A *trutruka* blared, discordant, and the *palinche* joined their supporters at their goals, where the women chanted—"*Kupapa pali weupe in pu wentru*"—magic words that would attract the ball to where they stood. The men who were not playing hefted *palin* sticks as well, Juan noticed, and though the day was fair the human atmosphere was charged with storms. Kuriñam was still missing—*kalkutun* suspected—as if more were needed to guarantee a ruthless game.

Moral focus of her kin, Marillan was silent amid singing women. Composed, long hair elaborately braided, she brought to Juan's mind Inca children destined for sacrifice on mountaintops. Time passed as, plangent, the women of both sides sang and sang. The *machi* of the opposing team was in his place, but where was Ñamku?

The suspense in this place without clock or bell might have lasted less than half a measured hour, yet when the white form at last slid from trees—silencing the women abruptly as a sacrificial knife—eternities began to lengthen, the figure of the *machi* before them now, snowy as high peaks. Mutely, he faced his counterpart across the field, grasping in one hand a sacred branch, while in the other a white rattle began to chink, chink, chink, like an untroubled heart.

Juan's own heart beat like war drums as Ñamku, swaying, danced to the center of the field. The opposing *machi* in turn danced toward him, accompanied by an assistant tapping a *kultrung*. The clearing scarcely breathed as the dead *machi* eerily sang—hawk headdress swaying over his rival's far more ordinary head.

The ceremony over, Juan saw Ñamku walking up, to him! Juan glanced at the mask, then at the hawk of folded pinions, forever frozen in what seemed a silent scream. Finding no comfort in the unmoved eyes of stone, he looked down to see the *machi* was extending something in an immaculate white glove.... A crucifix?

Juan experienced a profound sense of dislocation, as if waking from a dream in some strange place. He would not have been shocked if the masked figure before him elevated a hand in benison, intoning the "*Introibo ad altare dei*" that began the Mass....

The *machi* said, instead, "I had thought this *wethakelu* meant for me, *lik winka*, but it was never mine."

With Spanish greed Juan grasped the crucifix, contemplating the tiny ivory Redeemer, slumped on a gold cross. His eyes were closed, the emaciated figure lustrous with the touch of long devotion. Nothing could be more profoundly familiar, yet in its context more alien, than this sacred voyager from civilization. A chill swept through Juan like a sudden wind ... the breath of the Paraclete? A realization greater than any he had known hovered at the edge of awareness, refusing to reveal itself. That the crucifix had appeared at this *crux* was a tremendous sign of what? No answer came to him. And glancing up, he found the *machi* gone....

With visceral shock, Juan found himself in a circle of painted savages holding crooked sticks. What he had just received might be a sign, yet it was also a measure of the immensity he had traveled—two oceans, a jungle, mountains, and a desert— this distance separating his Spanish soul from the murmuring Indians all about.

Lautaro stepped from the crowd, asking Wan to elevate what he held, not knowing what Ñamku intended by giving him this *wethakelu*. What mattered was that the entire kin of Kuriñam was now convinced that mysterious power had been given them.

Juan elevated the body of Christ, bemused, as *che* filed by with a blank incomprehension that mimicked worship. Marillan was last—pausing briefly— in wonder that her salvation could assume such unknown form. She seemed so reverent, in fact, that Juan was tempted to make the sign of the cross over the dark child. But he suspected that she would regard any Spanish object—say a mirror, dirk, or purse—with equal awe, not knowing that her veneration was laughably misplaced. Pedro's purse-as-codpiece came to mind, and Juan imagined elevating *it* instead, while gazing into these black eyes in which hope struggled with fear, both mired in Indian innocence.

Wordlessly, she turned away.

He was the focus of her fears and hopes, as the worst *palinche* ever to walk *mapu*, but perhaps invested with alien power at this last instant. Not that Juan felt powerful ... yet he could not shake the responsibility weighing on his shoulders. And, in his mind's eye, Marillan was transformed from the Inca child awaiting sacrifice that she had seemed—a tragic image betraying his expectation of failure from the start—to a peculiar version of the damsel of the joust. Though he would not wear her scarf upon his armor, he *was* her champion, for on him her fate ironically most depended. A chill suffused him to the bone, and—this time—he was certain that the Paraclete *had* revealed His Message. If only Juan had faith, they would win this mortal contest. Marillan would live!

Juan became aware of uproar. The *palinche* were trotting to their places at the center of the field, Pichikan beckoning to him. Insults and bets were being shouted back and forth between the kin of Kuruga and Kuriñam. He heard wagers high as seven blankets.

Yet he could not play clutching the crucifix, nor abandon this precious talisman. He raced to his shelter, slipped a thong through its tiny golden ring, hung it on his neck, and raced back through shouting *che* into the field. Was he being cheered? A tide of fierceness such as he never knew in battle coursed through him ... and joy, that the breath of the Paraclete had touched him. He kissed the crucifix as he ran, and—holding his stick high—sprinted ululating toward his teammates.

Reaching his appointed place, Juan was imbued with an unearthly peace—calm in the hands of God, freed by a Fate that would move him from above. Mildly, he surveyed the crowd defining the boundaries of the field, where the two teams of twelve faced off—in pairs, like pawns in chess—across a distance of a pace or two. At the center, Pichikan and Kuruga opposed each other from much closer, powerfully hunched over the *pali*. Like a mostly naked jester, Kuruga was divided into painted halves, one black, one white. He snarled, immobile....

Juan's personal opponent snarled as well, muttering Mapuche anathemas *sotto voce* ... not one of them comprehensible. He smelled musky, and wore a necklace of large claws. Black puma paw prints were painted on his chest upon a creamy field, reminding Juan of coats of arms. Solid as an anvil, sinewy, filled with menace, he gripped his stick like a two-handed sword. Juan had clearly been assigned one of Kuruga's most powerful and brutal players. He decided to call him Claw.

Time must have passed—and the *trutruka* blared—yet all Juan remembered of the start was leaping back ... the enemy stick whistling by his ear.... And only later would he feel insulted. Naked of feint or ruse, this attack assumed that Juan would take the fate served him as a child his porridge.

"*Mierda!*" was Juan's startled battle cry. He retaliated with a furious swipe, and the world shrank to a duel in which neither dominated, Juan being taller, more nimble, Claw more experienced with his stick. Soon the melee included Lautaro and Tuiñam, who drove Claw back with a flurry of blows. Outnumbered, he was down … Juan's satisfaction cut short by bedlam. Looking up he saw that play had perilously neared their goal. He sprinted horrified in that direction…. Too late!

"*Tripalwe. Koni, Koni.*" A goal! Kuruga's team had scored, and they cavorted like demented goats.

Baleful, Pichikan approached Juan with the other *palinche* of the team. Although the game allowed no formal pause until the end, there was an intermission after every goal—and whenever the ball was driven out of bounds—to allow play to resume at the center of the field. This gave the Pichikans momentary leisure in which to contemplate their failure. No words were uttered, yet the glances of the nine, who had desperately played undermanned, at the three who had not played at all, were eloquent enough. Their painted scowls, thought Juan, belonged in some primitive harrowing of hell.

Pichikan reproachfully shook his ebony head at Lautaro and Tuiñam, though Juan knew he was the foundation on which this tower of fault was built. By escalating a single swipe to personal combat, he had forced his teammates to come to his aid. This might have demonstrated comradeship, except that Juan suspected Lautaro defended him as something like a valuable slave. Worse, the two had assumed that he could not defend himself. But refusing to wallow in self-pity, kissing his crucifix, Juan recovered the peace of purpose the talisman bestowed. He would not fail his team again.

Pichikan spat and said, "Kuruga planned it all." He did not state that the ruse relied on their weakest link—the lobster—for its success.

They have given up on me already, Juan thought, yet something in him managed quietly to say, "*Pu peñi*, trust me."

Startled at the familiarity of his address, the team stared without a word, before Pichikan spun on a bare heel and strode to where the Kurugas waited.

The game began again and Claw—with huge show—swung his stick as before. Juan sidestepped and crouched, one eye on his opponent, another on the furious action, where the ball was lost to view in a crowd of players barely able to swing their sticks. Shouting, shoving, they struck for the ball as teammates hovered, waiting for it to emerge into free play.

Juan had been assigned the position farthest from the center—sometimes reserved for the fleetest, but in his case, simple exile. He could still hope the ball would accidentally come his way.

Of a sudden, the *pali* was not so much passed as wildly ejected, creating a mad dash. The first to reach the skittering thing was white-striped Wenchuman. And as his goal lay beyond the Kurugas, he dashed in Juan's direction, attempting a flanking run.

Faking to the sideline with his eyes, his hips, Juan sprinted left instead, outrunning Claw and breaking free! He bounded like a deer, no one between him and the goal. He yelled, waving his stick. Was Wenchuman blind? No pass came, and—with disbelief—Juan saw *palinche* converge on the solitary runner, creating yet another knot of effort about the ball.

So the game went. Kuruga had assigned Claw to Juan as big and mean, not fast—since the *lik winka* was said to run like lobsters—so that Juan easily outpaced him. Yet as time stretched out without a goal and the ball repeatedly changed hands, no pass came—athough Juan was in the clear five times by any reasonable count. His teammates seemed to think that his magic crucifix affected play by merely being present on the field, oozing auras that had nothing to do with Juan's participation.

Still, the Pichikans were playing brilliantly without him. Coordinated as a flock of birds, they swooped to silent winds of strategy. Several times they almost scored, foiled by the violent Kurugas, who slammed into, tripped, grabbed, and in every other way attacked, not only the *palinche* with the ball, but anyone who might receive a pass. Using similar tactics, the Pichikans relied on them less, playing in looser formation and passing often—except to Juan—counting on speed and skill to keep the ball from the opposing players. Had his team a totem, Juan thought, it would be some bird, for they veritably flew. The Kurugas, then, were fighting bulls. He watched with pride as his team dodged them to steal the *palin*.

He and Claw echoed the tactics of their teams in small, the meaty brute attacking—no other word for it—while Juan fleeted this way and that, avoiding the swings, the kicks at his knees, positioning himself for the pass that never came … the ball a tiny planet on another sphere. Still—as peripheral—he could observe, so that when it came, the score of the Pichikans unfolded before his eyes with a precise necessity. Andalikan—yet again!—stole the ball, passing it through thickets of legs to Chuleu of the black back, but toward his own goal, the wrong direction! This unexpected strategy put the *palinche* in the clear, angling toward the Kurugas goal as they converged.

Never will he make it, thought Juan—sprinting with everybody else—when he saw Pichikan fell the two closest Kurugas, hurling through the air like a log, a self-catapulted missile. Then, granted time and space, Chuleu mightily propelled the *palin* to where Tuiñam waited, so improbably distant that he had been ignored by the Kuruga herd. A heartbeat later Tuiñam scored. He danced, waving his helmet in the air.

And who was now a demented goat? Juan screeched "*Koni, koni!*" wild as the wildest, running to congratulate Tuiñam, when the field took a flip and hit him in the face. He glanced up to see Claw lift his stick, about to finish his dirty work. Kicking his legs out from under, Juan rolled to his feet.

Getting up himself, Claw grinned, and made some unknown obscene gesture, shrugging. Juan shrugged back, too happy to take offense. His nose was broken, but what joy! The slate was clean as if he had never sinned. In some violent Indian version of confession, he had been absolved. The score now again began at zero— though the Mapuche had no notion of that Moorish number.

The day wore on and the game 'began,' again, four times. Both teams played magnificently, a balance of grace and speed against slower power, yet all points scored were nullified. Meantime, the summer sun in no way was reset. Noon came and left with not a break for food—though the players stole mouthfuls in the intervals that restarted play.

They were playing beginnings without ends, Juan weary as a laden mule in the immensities of the Atacama, the ending of his labor a mirage on cruel horizons. He was grateful, though, that Claw had become too weary to attack. Like every other *palinche*, he was haggard under sweaty paint, smeared by collisions. And all were in some way marked by violence—lumps and cuts, bruises, livid welts.

The Kurugas changed their strategy. Rather than running with the ball—leaving them vulnerable to the agility of their opponents—they put it out of bounds. And in the melee that restarted the game they attempted to overwhelm and injure the smaller Pichikans. This was obvious—even to Juan—and to the male kin of Kuriñam it was foul play. *Palin* required mayhem, but *this* was just too much, considering what was at stake! Waving sticks in protest, they howled, yearning to join the violence, and they would have been angrier if their team were not now ahead by a point. Tension was building to crisis.

Pichikan—avoiding a kick to the knee once too often—lost his temper. Turning from the ball to his tormentors, he wielded his stick as if it were his legendary club, the spinning, blurry length creating startled space about him. Andalikan leapt into the momentary void, acquired the ball ... passed to Tralaf. He in turn spun and passed to Marifil, who—pursued by all—ran full tilt toward three Kurugas strung out deep, last protectors of their goal. Quickly the enemy converged, Pichikan and Tuiñam diving into the mass that swallowed Marifil, and—through a miracle unseen by Juan—the ball ejected itself from chaos, propelled with startling accuracy to Lautaro, who outran pursuit to score.

Two to zero! The kin of Kuriñam swarmed the field ululating, pummeling their *peñi*—all but Juan that is, unpummeled eye of the human hurricane. At peace nonetheless, he kissed the crucifix responsible, noting that the *domo* in the sidelines were producing shrill cries of their own, Marillan the only silent one. Erect the maiden stood, with a brave dignity that—Juan thought—would bring honor to heroic times.

Then *palin* recommenced its eternal life, spinning a savage cycle within the larger ambit of Fortune's wheel. There was a change, however, for now the revolutions returned the score to one, in favor of the Pichikans.

The sun declined. The second point came and went no less than five times, cruelly eradicated by Kurugas! Could it be, Juan asked himself, that more than twenty goals had summed to this? Was he too exhausted for arithmetic?

The setting sun now cast deep shadows—of trees, of spectators brandishing lifted sticks. Was Hell like this? Juan wondered, thinking *palin* another Atacama— that inferno without circle or bound. Trapped in a nowhere, you struggled on the broken wheel of time to reach another. Returning to where you once had been, each moment became a memory like the last, until you could not distinguish the weary present from the weary past....

Claw's shadow shifted and Juan looked over. Chuleu was speeding with the ball in his direction, about to be inundated by Kurugas. He tapped the ball to Andalikan, Claw now running to cut him off, leaving Juan to his devices. All Andalikan needed do was pass to *him*, but—as the world's end seemed more likely—Juan sprinted after Claw, and, tripping him with his stick, he dropped him like a sack of stones.

Andalikan now fleeted by, Juan running to intercept pursuing Kurugas, their painted menace amplified by the long shadows of sunset. Then, catapulted into from behind, he was brought down in a confusion of bone and muscle.

"I played!" Juan groaned, embedded in a sweaty mound of *che*. Someone was attempting to cram a stick into his eye. He shoved it away.

Had they scored?

They had not. The ball was out of bounds.

As the teams assembled at the center of the field, Juan managed to admire the scene, the forest glade having a magnificent perspective on the distant sea, where the sun declined in barbaric color, blaring its last. To the east the full moon, invisible behind the *cordillera*, outlined it with unearthly glow. The mountains— lords of all—wore purple velvet trimmed with ermine.

The ball came into play ... and awareness born of danger in the Indies threw Juan back. Still, he caught the stick on the meat of his right shoulder—the price of wandering attention. Claw had returned him to a nightmare in which the Kurugas took every opportunity that the lowering dark provided to do damage. Often as not, now, the *pali* was now being fought for by feel, so that at times *palinche* groped on hands and knees, communicating hoarsely. "I have it! They have it! I lost it! Who has it...?"

As sight failed, the game contracted toward the ball, so that even Juan joined the confusion. The single inviolable rule of *palin*—that the ball not be picked up or carried—was being deliberately broken. However, such dishonesty was useless as no one was allowed to leave the crowd, for fear that he concealed the precious thing. *Palinche* clutched both friend and foe, calling out shibboleths. Juan was pummeled, blind, out of breath.

Fortunately, this eclipse of sanity did not last, a full moon casting light on pandemonium, bright disk soaring. This did not lead the Kurugas to lessen their assault, but the spectators—living boundaries of the game—abandoned their daytime role. Bristling with sticks, they contracted toward players of the opposing team with menace, sometimes tripping them, or conversely, expanded to give their own *palinche* playing room. More than once Juan thought he saw the ball tapped back into bounds, the sidelines claiming this was just a bounce. Under cloak of darkness the spectators were becoming players. The contained chaos that was *palin* was losing its container.

The heavens wheeled, serene, as the moon ascended to its zenith. Insects droned like tiny viols with a single string. A summer breeze brought welcome coolness from the sea…. And the Kurugas scored.

The Pichikans huddled, haggard under midnight light. Juan—who had not really played—was weary as he had ever been, shoulder numb, nose broken. Yet he did not approach the exhaustion of the others, who were bracing hands on knees as if otherwise they might topple.

"We played well," panted Pichikan—his past tense making it a prediction of defeat. To Lautaro he added, "But, *something* has to change."

"Let the *lik winka* play."

Unthinkable before, the idea dropped into the ocean of the team's fatigue without a ripple, *palinche* studying Juan with deadened eyes.

Pichikan shrugged, "Why not?"

Lautaro speculated, "The surprise will not last. We have to be another point ahead."

And so it was that Pichikan's question became a decision never formally expressed, setting Juan upon his final path in a life of many turnings.

Kissing his crucifix, he trotted to his station, thinking that—preposterous as the thought might seem—Lautaro reminded him of that other warrior child, Joan of Arc, who heard the voice of Heaven and obeyed.

Play resumed. One point away from *tabula rasa*, the Kurugas fought with desperate ferocity to regain it—the score that would add Juan to action endlessly deferred. And in fact, the birds of morning were singing when at last the critical moment came….

Kuruga stumbled while in possession of the ball. Tralaf darted in, passing to Marifil. And—like that cruel martial invention, cannon balls connected by a chain—Pichikan bodily flung himself, felling several. Freed to run, Marifil leapt over bodies … sped toward the goal. Drawing near—about to be overwhelmed— he flipped the ball with brilliant daring to Andalikan, who scored!

Quickly the Pichikans took their places, to surprise the enemy while they were still in shock … getting a surprise of their own. Andalikan could not stand—although he tried and fell, leg horribly slack. He was led away, painfully hopping.

Given time to look catastrophe in the face, Juan did so with composure so astounding it merited examination. Was exhaustion a nostrum granting resignation—like the last serenity of the dying—or was his crucifix whispering that God granted victory to the virtuous, no matter what the odds? He looked over at Marillan—erect as a statue in a cathedral niche. What could she now be feeling, her stoutest champion led from the lists? Horror? Despair? What was life without Faith?

The crowd roared.

Tralaf sped in Juan's direction, plying his stick, flanked by Lautaro, their path to the goal blocked by Kurugas on a parallel course. Rocking from foot to foot, Claw looked in their direction....

Juan ambled away, and—in heart-stopping instants—was six long *pasos* into God's clear air, hearing the tap of the approaching stick behind him. In an instant Claw would be swept into play. Juan ran with every fiber of his being.

Lautaro veered from Tralaf. Knocking down a Kuruga, sidestepping another, spinning from the clutch of a third, he bounded toward the goal, pursued. Tralaf passed....

The ball—careening from dream into reality—shot by Juan's elbow … good as gone. Sweet Jesus, crucified! With the leaden feet of nightmare Juan pursued, attaining the wild object as it took a corkscrew leap. In frantic strides he had it captive, and the silent universe—shrunken to the compass of the *pali*—exploded with a roar to fill the field.

Kurugas blocking the goal ran toward him, their feet creating silver clouds of dust in moonlight. Behind, Juan heard pursuit. Cut off!

He swerved, caught the flash of Tuiñam's helmet. "*Santiago!*" He passed … was brutally slammed down.

"*Koni! Koni!*"

At last, just one more point....

Lautaro proposed beginning play just as before—Wan would break away, drawing Kurugas with him, running left. He, Chuleu and Marifil would run right, the pass going to one of them instead.

As Lautaro planned, so happened the play—Juan sped toward the goal pursued by Claw and a Kuruga spotted red. Chuleu took the long pass without breaking stride, instants later closing on the defended goal. About to pass back to Lautaro, he fell! Tripped by a flung stick!

The orphaned ball took on independent life, creating a stampede in which even the Kuruga goalkeepers participated. Like a racehorse spurred, Juan's spent body responded.

Pedro's voice whispered in his ear, "*Not the opponent's knife ... the body!*"

"*What knife? What body?*"—Juan's mind howled, but he saw that only one Kuruga now guarded the goal. He slowed ... changed course, allowing players to speed by until he found himself alone, looking back at the convergence on the ball.

Lautaro dove, in stick first, and—Juan would forever swear—swung while floating in the air, before being blotted by Kurugas, performing a miracle which expelled the ball from the struggling mass in a vicious, flat trajectory that would take it over Juan's head and out of bounds.

Might as well halve a speeding bumblebee with a broadsword, yet Juan swung in the purity of an instant that knew no doubt—less with the practice of battle than with the ecstasy of saints—and with a ringing crack, made contact. Deflected, the airborne ball bounced as it wildly hit the ground, so that only two could quickly reach it now—he and the slate blue Kuruga defending his goal. But, moving at a slant from Juan, the mercurial object continued to improve the enemy advantage. He would never reach it in time....

"*Hijo,*" Pedro whispered, "*corre.*"

Juan stretched out with no notion of exertion or of speed, but of being directed by effortless acts of will—as God is immanent in the whirl of His universe. A heavenly body, he was impelled toward conjunction, free to contemplate the implacably closing distances. One thing was clear—only The Almighty knew who first would reach the ball. He and the Koruga were destined to collide, for to change direction—or to slow—would give advantage to the other. And—while he had to get the *pali* past the Kuruga to the goal—all the enemy needed do was stop him.

"*Ya!*" Pedro roared.

Juan leapt ... swung ... spun. And airborne, he exhaled his soul, falling through showers of stars into black, silent Heaven....

Dim pain woke him, declaring itself instantly as hot and bright. *Redios*, did breathing hurt! Taking shallow breaths, Juan smelled fire. A breeze was moving over him. Something cool and damp covered his eyes, his throbbing nose. "What happened, Pedro?" he croaked, removing the damp rag.

Not Pedro ... but a huge Mapuche, loomed over him. Juan felt a dizzy dijunction of soul and flesh, as if sight and pain were here, while his body remained unharmed in a Santiago he never left. To return, all he had to do was close his eyes. He did, but the well of memory inexorably filled to that last leap.... He sat, fighting a moan.

"We won," said Pichikan, smiling.

"You made the last point," Lautaro added, smiling too.

Stray rays of sun lanced through the shelter's roof. Juan remembered that the game was ending just as false dawn turned true, yet the angle of the sun now told him it was afternoon. His throat was parched, and—in Pedro's words—he was so ravenous, that like a rabbit he could eat a root.

Dark forms materialized, Juan recognizing Andalikan, Chuleu, Tuiñam … the other members of the team, still painted. More warriors crowded into the shelter, armed and solemn, silent. They should be feasting and carousing. Where was the *kawiñ*? *What* was going on?

A thought vivid as his pain shot through him. Was he still painted? At this solemn moment, was he ocher? He rubbed his face, and sighed….

Kanikura entered and spoke, thanking Juan for himself, his daughter and his kin. He was interminable.

Giddy with hunger and thirst, pain and exhaustion, humiliation and gratefulness—the whole cemented into a bizarre amalgam by elation—Juan felt himself about to faint. A second *toki* stepped forward. The air in the shelter grew blurred—as if eyes were windows that let in smoke—and in this murk he droned. The shaded forms began to spin.

Juan closed his eyes … opening them to a circle of black eyes beneath a roof of leaves…. The slowly spinning fabric, shot by brightness, was a firmament seen though green—a Heaven, witnessed through earthly imperfection, revealing The Living God. Then—through Juan as through his namesake, the Saint of Revelation—steeds of vision coursed, hooves madly drumming on his eyelids, as something in him whispered, "Not in our strength, but through the darkness of our frailty, as stars we see Him." And that inner voice returned to Juan what love and memory had denied—His first vision of Inés, her beauty burning like mountain light.

Juan then slept—or fainted—opening his eyes to evening, Lautaro squatting near. By him, a solemn Marillan extended the half of a dried gourd. Juan drank bitter tea, she returning to her fire. And when she knelt by him again, the bowl linked them briefly, he looking into the sloe of Indian eyes. Salvation should have her less solemn, Juan thought, crossing his own. She smiled—faintly—not opening her mouth. Then he saw that a scar twisted her lip … remembered broken teeth.

Sobered, Juan gulped soup, devoured flat bread and roasted *uwa*.

Lautaro materialized, saying it was time to go. Juan painfully followed him out, not failing to notice that the *weichafe* had a full quiver on his back, and carried a long bow, strung. Leading the way, Lautaro was an animate shadow.

Engulfed by forest, Juan blundered through gloom. Ghostly forms flitted by … a flanking guard? Were Kurugas after them? Lautaro hissed him into silence.

At dawn they emerged to where—silvered by moonlight—his *ruka* waited like a shaggy dog. Juan slowly spun, arms extended to embrace the sight, seeing the phantoms of the night appear—Tuiñam, Pichikan, the other *peñi* of *palin,* save for Andalikan. They had been his guards, although he knew not why.

No explanation was offered as the *weichafe* built a fire. Taking dried *uwa* and baskets of *poñu* from rafters, they cooked, communicating with Indian grunts. And after eating, they left, bidding him the briefest of farewells.

Juan was furious. Companionship in exile had been taken from him after what had been—if nothing else—the hardest labor of his life. He had tried his best! He had *helped* them win their game! He had even been injured in the struggle! Two *toki* had thanked him. Marillan cooked for him. Why were his *peñi* so distant when they should have been most friendly?

Lautaro said that it was time to sleep, and gave him the blank of his back.

Juan attempted his first memory of Inés again, and failed. His recollection, gone adrift, brought up scraps of past—flotsam on the restless shores of sleep, swallowed by that bitter sea. And sometime in that night he was visited by his own first memory—*He was burning, tongue thick and dry....*

"I have lost everyone I ever had, and some I never did," Juan mumbled.

"You have me, *hijo,*" Pedro boomed, astride his fine blue mule, Negrito chattering welcome from his shoulder. "You're just peckish," Pedro roared, animating Juan with the volume of his confidence. "You will have pork, I promise, at the next *posada.*"

"We're on our way to Sevilla!"

Pedro did not reply.

"How is Inés ... these days?"

"You have not met her yet," said Pedro, turning cruel absence into light wit—for, God's truth, the pleading in his *hijo's* eyes cut to the marrow.

"One cannot be in two times at once," Juan pronounced, hating the wormwood in that verity. He added, "But I seem to want to be."

"It's the books," Pedro agreed, scowling. Negrito slapped his bicep, and Juan laughed.

Pedro turned meditative. "The notion came to me that you met Inés before the Indies ... hem ... met her that is ... in books." He cleared his throat again. Did his approach smack of reproach?

Juan sighed. "You're right, Pedro. Sometimes I wonder if maybe I loved the memory of a *libro de caballería* in her, more than the woman of flesh and blood."

Pedro produced low sounds of inarticulate assent. Negrito bared his teeth.

"You know," Juan confessed, loud with old anger, "I never forgave Inés for what she did at the battle of Santiago."

"What she did to *herself,*" he added, when there was no response. Even if she had *not* beheaded all those *caciques*, her blood-smeared sword still damned her memory.

This time only Negrito agreed, for Pedro profoundly admired the Inés of that necessary moment, which—far as he was concerned—gloriously had happened.

"Blood … and flesh," Juan mused to himself, calmer. Maybe *that* was his problem, for Inés was absolutely flesh and blood. No book she, *pardiez*! Memories then materialized—Inés paler than parchment pages, her face a milky sheet on which the wonders of her heart were written. Her freckles! He loved that mute alphabet upon her pallor. Lobo might say she was born maculate. And charmingly, she was. He had loved her at first sight, precisely in her fallen state, as Adam loved lapsed Eve. Juan had then to wonder—Did Eve have freckles as a consequence— or prefigurement—of The Fall? Did Christ in this way *sign* his incarnation? Did Oriana, beloved of Amadís de Gaula, have freckles? Were Briolana, Onolaria, Helena, Archisidea—these queens and maidens of heroic pages—freckled? Not a freckle was mentioned in any *romance* Juan ever read … or in the Bible, either. The faces of these books were a blank. What color their eyes, their hair? What shape their noses? The pale ghosts of the ideal hovered as a fog before his eyes.

"They are only Indians, *hijo*."

Pedro—who for years made it his pedagogic duty to interrupt the unwholesome abstractions of his son—had done it again. He harrumphed, to punctuate. "And they are annoyed."

"What!" said Juan, returned to the statement that summoned Pedro and Negrito in the first place.

"You do not lose anyone when you lose an Indian, especially when they are annoyed at you because we are coming, and you are one of us. I mean I'm coming with Valdivia and the others. Not you, of course, as you are here. Take heart."

"As I live and breathe," Juan breathed. "We're invading, south."

"As we speak."

"That's why the Indians are hostile."

"Indians are always hostile. And these are some of the worst."

"We're fighting them…?"

"At the Bío Bío. Stubborn *hideputas*, these Mapuche."

"I should know."

Pedro looked piercingly at his *hijo* … then shook his head.

"I know," sighed Juan, "I look like one of them. And I must seem a clown in a breechclout, on this donkey. You should have seen me with my face red, though." He attempted a laugh, groaning with pain instead.

Pedro's grizzled hair was turning white, his variegated pupils pale. And his armor dimmed, for he was disappearing into mist. "Do not…." the vanishing *conquistador* exhorted.

Juan screamed, "Pedro, don't go! You have to rescue me!"

"*Lik winka.*"

"*No me dejes morir aquí, solito!*"

"*Lik winka!*"

And Juan wailed, again, "Don't let me die here, alone!"

Lautaro had to shake the *lik winka* to wake him, even though he was already sitting up, bleached eyes half open, staring. He had seen trances in *machi*, but never one like this.

They ate, Lautaro brooding over his bowl. Just after *palin* the news had arrived that *lik winka* were at the Fio Fio … and yes, they should have told Wan. But he was unconscious and the team was trying to keep Kuruga and his kin from killing him—as an enemy they insisted, not as the one who got the final point. The *toki* eventually agreed it would be cowardly to kill an unconscious enemy.

Kuruga and his kin departed. Most of the kin of Kuriñam and Kanikura left as well, some remaining to thank the *lik winka* when he revived. However, the *toki* had decided that the *lik winka* could no longer live with *che*, being an enemy. Lautaro had pointed out that he kept his promise not to harm anyone while captive. The *toki* insisted that the *lik winka* divided the *che* at a time when they needed to be united. The *lik winka* would go to *lolo*.

Lautaro felt sorry for Wan, and that was not good. "We are fighting *lik winka* at the Fio Fio," he said as they packed. "They have not crossed the river yet, but they will."

"I know."

He *did* have visions then, like *machi*! And who would have guessed he could play *palin*?

Lautaro said, "You played well, *lik winka* … at the last, anyway."

"Too, that sendball was amazing yours," Wan replied.

Lautaro studied the lean body of his enemy, which reminded him of *winin*— the otter. Wan had become *too* comprehensible. And he was almost as dark as Mapuche. This bothered him, too. He began to pull the heavy load that they had lashed to poles, as the *lik winka* was too injured to help him. And it seemed right to be laden, for his captive had become a burden in ways never expected. Looking back as he walked, he saw him keeping pace with difficulty, not complaining. Lautaro was not puzzled by this tolerance of pain—unremarkable in a warrior— but by his patience with captivity. He recalled his own frustration in Tiako, his refusal to have anything to do with his oppressors, his anger at Raytrayen, who was content to learn *likwinkadungun*, taking on the customs of *lik winka*, dressing as they did. The *lik winka* was like her, in a way. What made him *want* to wear his hair like *che*, dress like *che*, speak like *che*?

The path had become steep and Lautaro set down his load. He drank from his water skin and offered it to the *lik winka*, who was looking back at the great sea glittering through trees. In his *chiripa* he seemed much like a *che*, although too thin and tall. All that bodily remained of his strangeness, really, were his eyes and his hair. The *lik winka* was *too* Mapuche. And for this he was more responsible than Raytrayen, having captured him. Even if sparing his life could be excused by blood debt, he had had no real reason to bring him here, other than a pride that took him to the extreme of insisting that the *lik winka* play *palin*. Why had he done all this...? He had been a boulder on a mountain with the desire to roll, yet unable to control his path ... creating an avalanche he could not comprehend. Something in him had not wanted *kume mognen* for himself and for his people.

They came to a clearing thick with bushes growing to the waist, heavy with berries that the *lik winka* picked and ate. In the distance the great sea was calm beneath the sinking sun, shimmering like fish taken from water. They had traveled so slowly, Lautaro wondered if they would reach *lolo* before dark. He shaded his eyes, and, seeing no smoke over the mountaintop, dropped his poles and ran.

Juan had been thinking about ransom—Was he *insane*, adopting this idea from a *libro de caballería*? Could nobility succeed with savages? Would Lautaro cooperate? If he did, what would Pedro think when he found out? And what if Pedro did *not* find out? What if Valdivia discovered the arrangement? Would friendship cause him to wink at his own edict?

Sometime during that melancholy afternoon they stopped to rest. Looking into Lautaro's belligerent eyes Juan decided that now was not the time to bring up ransom. Exhausted, he leaned against a tree to contemplate the Southern Sea, which mountain height had brought to view. Brilliant—dimpled like steel hammered by a supernal smith—the restless immensity was stilled by distance....

Lautaro began to trot again and Juan struggled after. His feet ached. His nose throbbed. A lancet of pain stabbed his ribs with every step. Scarcely able to walk, he stumbled on, troubled thoughts drowned in pain and weariness as Lautaro mercilessly picked up the pace. Later—the sun low, every step torture—they halted at a clearing crowded with berry-laden bushes. Juan gathered and gobbled as Lautaro climbed a boulder to study the mountain, sniffing the faint breeze like a lost dog. Then, abruptly, he set off at a run, almost immediately lost to view.

Astonished, Juan considered his belongings, abandoned on the path. Not wanting to entrust his few possessions to the weather, wild animals and wandering savages, he vacillated, taking up only the bundle that contained his books. Gasping, he hobbled on. Eventually—in the pink and purple flush of twilight—he found himself on the boulder-strewn slope that he knew was not far below *lolo*. He struggled on. Setting down his bundle to pull himself up the last few *pasos,* he balanced on the cliff edge. "*Mari, mari*," he called out, tentative.... The mouth of the cave was an impenetrable darkness, not even the excitable parrot responding.

Juan had been abandoned, countless leagues from civilization, wounded. About to faint, he sat and closed his eyes. He may have slept, for when he opened them the half moon floated higher over the forests that undulated to the Southern Sea.

He turned to the distant *cordillera,* so immense it dwarfed the mountain on which he stood, and for vertiginous moments Juan *became* the moon, seeing the vast panorama—as he later thought—in eyelight. I am unencumbered as that star, he told himself ... void as a sucked egg. Never had he felt so powerless and insignificant, so far from anything one might call home, so alone and bereft. What remained to him? Not even sandals.

The memory came of Amadís de Gaula, unjustly rejected by Oriana. Having lost the love that was his life, the hero renounced his armor and his horse—these emblems of his being. And taking the name Beltenebros, he assumed a rough tabard of brown wool to live in tears, poverty and solitude....

"*Tabardo de gruesa lana parda,*" Juan murmured—that summation of a hero's dying to the world....

The clout about his loins was also rough, and brown. What better habit for the moment?

Then he remembered and cried out, "My books!" Ignoring weariness and agony, he scrambled down the mountainside.

Chapter 15: Lleflai *(Mapu, 1550)*

Squatting by the stream, Lleflai pounded on the blanket she was washing, taking pleasure in this small, familiar violence. Ignoring the excitement of her birds, she paused to confirm—through a dazzle of leaves—that the day was ending. Time to be cooking, but … no one to cook for. Warmed by sun and exercise she rubbed her neck with hands cooled by the stream. Then she pinned her unbraided hair up in sad admission of her loneliness, taking up her stone to pound again. Lleflai—who was never angry—was angry….

When Pangi ran up the mountain to say the *lik winka* were at the Fio Fio she knew her happiness had ended, and surprised everyone by refusing to leave *lolo*. She would *not* visit her friend Wispu. She did not *care* that she would be left alone. As for Kurufil, maybe he was just *invented* to frighten children. She was staying. Nothing would change her mind. Her intensity shocked even the parrot into silence. Pangi, Raytrayen and Eimi had left, disturbed.

Lleflai had wept. Now she almost wept again, wanting nothing more than to be with her children. And yes, she was in terror of Kurufil, yet long ago had decided not to burden the *pichiche* with her existence … if it came to that. Had they been her children and Ñamku her husband, according to *admapu* the *wentru* would remain near the *ruka* of their birth. Once they were *weichafe*, they would bring wives to join their kin. But these were not her children, and Ñamku not their father. Therefore Lautaro left the cave that should have been his home. And— Lleflai pounded harder, echoing the chatter of the angry birds above—Raytrayen never returned from the *lik winka*. Her body came back, but her *pellu* had been stolen by pale-eyed *kalku*. Raytrayen was lost to her, and this pain she could not bear she also felt as anger. *Admapu* demanded that her daughter marry, then go live in the *ruka* of her husband. But Lleflai—who lived in a cave where it seemed that every custom was at some time ignored—had dreamed that in this case *admapu* would go unnoticed. If she lost Lautaro, it was only fair that Raytrayen should be hers. After all, she was *ankeñ peñeñ* and never courted, despite her astonishing beauty. For this hope Lleflai had been living, but now that *lik winka* were coming she knew—well as her fingers knew her face—that Raytrayen was no longer hers. Therefore Lleflai had denied herself what she most loved. *Domo* killed themselves for less.

She set down her stone to look at the hands Tuiñam said were beautiful. Perhaps they were—as it was said her hair was beautiful. Yet Tuiñam deserved much better, and she was right to deny him too, in *kume mognen*. Yet where *was* harmony, if not with her *pichiche*? Ñamku had never managed to convince her that *mapu* needed creatures of the 'shore.' That was easy for him to say, living at the edge of death. What the *pillañ* had given her was a *mapu* in which she did not fit. Where was the harmony in *that*? And why, of the three *pichiche*, did she grieve most for Raytrayen? Why was it more terrible to lose one daughter than two sons? Because she had grown into the *domo* she herself could never be? Lleflai thought not. Then why had she so desperately desired to keep her, when this would condemn her daughter to live alone in *lolo* with an ugly old woman? For this there were no reasons or excuses.

Too tortured for tears, Lleflai whispered, "You love what you are not."

And nothing seemed more true or terrible than that, for Raytrayen's face was perfect. Lleflai recalled how she had pulled on her nose when she was a *pichiche*, to make it proud and arched. How long, how lovingly, she had worked to make Raytrayen become what she herself could never be, and still…. "I am *not* jealous of her beauty," she told herself, knowing this was true.

Of the three *pichiche* Raytrayen was the one who stayed with her while her brothers were gone—Lautaro learning war, Pangi with Ñamku, talking to the dead. This somehow had seemed right. Then Raytrayen had left too, only to return one awful day from the *lik winka*, emptied of her soul as a broken water pot.

But this last thought was cruel selfishness and nothing else. It was just that Lleflai no longer knew where the soul of her daughter now lived. Changed in ways she could not understand, Raytrayen was going where Lleflai could never follow. And there was no need to feel this as betrayal on her part, for in his wisdom Ñamku had set her on this path. Still it did not seem right—or just—that Raytrayen, who was not truly *ankeñ peñeñ*, was chosen. Her awful birth had been enough.

"Why did you do this to my beautiful *pichiche*, Ñamku … why?"

Weeping at last, Lleflai rocked forward and back, kneeling on stone. "Why? You had good reasons, I just want to know them." And to the silence of the dead she said, "I know you are here, Ñamku. You speak to others, please speak to me. I am sorry to be angry. Forgive me, but I do not understand."

Feeling an unspeaking presence in the forest hush, Lleflai closed her eyes to listen, hearing only her birds, complaining, and the stream. And she felt drained, as if her soul had flowed from her as tears. Bending to see the reflection she usually avoided, in the water saw reflected a second face….

Umeñdomo did not scream—or rise to run—although she knew the *kalku* by his gold. She had not thought the face of death would be this beautiful….

Kurufil came on Lleflai by accident as she was washing clothes at a stream, startling her birds into chatter. Startled himself, he slipped behind a fallen tree. Why was she here, this late, alone? What luck! Unless this was another trap....

Setting down the head of Kuriñam, he watched, annoyed, for here there was no challenge. What was wrong with Umeñdomo, not listening to what her birds were clearly saying?

She pounded on a blanket, seeming angry, saying something he could not hear.

Kurufil quietly approached, she too lost in thought to notice.... Not her birds. The *kalku* cursed them.

Setting down her stone, she pinned her hair up, Kurufil almost exclaiming. He had known about her scars, yet never imagined *this*, like beeswax puddling in the sun.

She chattered as she worked—an angry bird herself. She cried, rocking forward and back, scars twisted by sorrow. Then she was lisping softly. Never had the *kalku* seen anything so repulsive.

And when she spoke the name of Ñamku, Kurufil waded into the stream. Startled, she straightened....

From close, he saw her appalling, upturned face—yawning holes in the twisted nose … moist, lidless eyes.

"Run," he suggested—irritated that she was taking all the pleasure from this killing.

She did nothing but look back.

"Are you afraid?" the *kalku* asked, for she was trembling.

Her arms were long and slender.

Her neck was slender too … and Kurufil slit it.

Looking into her eyes, he stepped away from the blood. She rose with a retching sound and staggered, hands pushing at the air as if that childish gesture would make death go away. Kurufil smiled as she collapsed, head hanging. He bent to wash his knife, waiting for Lleflai to finish with her dying.

The *kalku* was suspicious, for this had been too easy. Where were the others? Kurufil did not appreciate loose ends, and he had imagined a less hasty—much more painful—killing. Now, here he had the corpse of the least important one, with no way to take her to the cave and create a good display. He looked over....

Lleflai lay with her head at an impossible angle, deformed mouth gaping as if the better to release her soul. Her teeth were perfect, though.

He would only take the head, he decided, amused. Two heads were better than one, and he was doing Lleflai a favor by removing that repulsive thing, for the rest of her was very nice.

After, holding the head by the hair, he washed it in the stream until it bled no longer. Humming softly—for he was ahead by two in the game—the *kalku* went to see just who might be in the cave....

When he saw no smoke rising from *lolo,* Lautaro ran down the trail so frantically he leapt over the body by the stream before he realized....

Papai! Beheaded!

And with the idiocy of disbelief he looked about, as if her head had somehow been misplaced.

The bright blood soaking her *kepam* was darkening. She seemed peaceful, with no face to betray her agony. She also seemed very young without her head. He squatted, lifting *papai* from the rock on which she sprawled, arranging her on dry, flat stone. He was washing her blood from his hands when—as if his soul had straddled a rotten limb—something in him snapped. He screamed, and screamed....

Hoarse, he returned to being a *weichafe*. Nocking an arrow he found sign, including drops of blood. Was this bait for a trap? Unwilling to leave *papai* to *mañke* he slung her over his shoulder, knowing he had to find her head before Kurufil stole her soul. Then, with no attempt at silence or concealment, he hastened along the path that was the most direct, and therefore the most dangerous.

He stopped to listen ... heard only forest rustle, the caw of *yeku*. Setting the body down he climbed a *koyam*. And fluttering in the twilight, near *lolo,* he made out a gathering of songbirds, their enraged cries barely audible. Only then he realized that, by the stream, an absence had spoken to him, and that—deafened by grief—he had not listened. *Papai* had never been able to play hide and seek, for her birds were always near.

A *kalku* too could die, he told himself, swinging down the tree, limb to limb. But he had to do what he should have from the first—leave *papai* behind. There was a direct path to *lolo*—short and dangerous—where the *pillañ* had carved the mountain as with the blow of an enormous ax. All other trails doubled on themselves. This one went straight up...

He was at the base of the cliff now, the birds far above him hovering, complaining. Rubbing his hands in dust, Lautaro dug fingertips and toes into cracks, and climbed like a fly until he was above the cave and twenty *nufku* to the side, where the steep shoulder of the mountain rounded. Dismissing the trembling of his body, he crept the slope, concealing himself behind a bush. Had he been seen?

He overlooked the ledge in front of *lolo*—an easy bowshot. There, the ancient *rewe* of the *machi* stood. A loom was propped against the mountain flank. Blankets hung to air. A basket had been casually laid down. Nothing looked suspicious, but what horrors were inside?

Ignoring Lautaro, the fluttering birds of Umeñdomo dove at something concealed by the cliff edge, as at *yeku*. Squinting against the glare of *amuniantu*, taking a deep breath Lautaro drew his bow. And trembling with effort he held his draw, so that Kurufil would see no motion.

Sharp and black against the sky, the slender form appeared....

The pestering songbirds had convinced Kurufil to ascend before dark. He also heard a distant cry not long ago ... so time was growing short. Setting down the two heads he crawled up. Peering over the lip of the cliff he saw a basket, and a loom.

The *kalku* slowly straightened, seeing that the only motion was his shadow on the mountainside, cast by the setting sun. A pebble clattered....

Lautaro cursed as Kurufil looked up, bringing to his mouth what looked like the thighbone of a stork....

His arrow struck true! The *kalku* stumbled back, arms swimming in the air as he dropped over the cliff edge.

Lautaro ululated, descending. He had killed the *kalku* ... avenged *papai*! Her *am* was safe! But in his excitement Lautaro slid too fast down the mountainside, creating a small avalanche. He reached for bushes, wrenched his shoulder, slid faster, landing on his back with a bruising thud. His ankle was badly twisted, but who cared? He hobbled to the verge, seeing no one, alive or dead. *Kalkutun!* Kurufil had vanished! Or, had he transformed into a snake, a twisted stick, or bat?

Descending through treacherous evening shadow, Lautaro discovered his arrow with the flint point shattered. And no blood on it! Chilled by foreboding, he searched, finding not even a snake-like root, until—much like a stone amid rounded stones—he came across the head of Lleflai. He collapsed to his knees. About to touch her face, he noticed a blood-crusted basket with the head of Kuriñam inside. Were there more heads about?

Fighting nausea, Lautaro found no others. Deciding to search at dawn in better light—he took both heads to *lolo*, staggering with sorrow, setting them by the hearth. What now? Their souls were surely near, and he did not even hear a fly. Did *am* remain by their heads, or by their bodies, when they had been separated? Did the soul become confused, and simply wander?

Lautaro was shivering, disoriented. Pale in the gloom, the two faces on the floor seemed to pulse like jellyfish in dark water, and the sight focused his hate— He would find Kurufil and kill him, or die trying. Nothing could be simpler.

But getting to his feet did not prove simple, for a mountain seemed to weigh upon his shoulders. Lautaro staggered from the cave, near collapse. Touching his inflamed shoulder with an icy hand he felt a small wound ... and remembered the sting he had ignored when he shot the *kalku*. Nausea brought bile to his throat. *Wekufu!*

Lautaro retched air … retched again, aware that he had little time. Using his bow as cane he tottered down the mountain through darkness so thick he labored to make progress—ant walking through black honey, boulders rising about him like the heads of disapproving giants buried to their necks. He persevered, blindly crawling, groping, drowsy fingers obeying him only for a time. Faster! Lautaro ordered them, until at last his fingers slept, icy as the stone they grasped. He closed his eyes, and his head became a chilly hollowed space—a kind of cave in which his labored breathing echoed, and there he kept vigil by the dying fire of his thoughts, thinking his comfort surprising. He told himself to feel rage … could not. Wanting to feel grief for *papai* … he could not. Why was he not himself? Questions fluttered through the light of his awareness like bats whose empty home he had invaded. Where was Kurufil? Why had he done this? Why kill Kuriñam? Where, Pangi? Where, the others? What broke the arrowhead? These questions were important but—despite being all that now remained of life—they ceased to matter. Dying was a loss of interest, he supposed.…

As he exhaled his *wekufu*, Kurufil felt a blow over his heart that knocked him back. He tumbled, *mapu* whirling until—with a skull-jarring thump—he came to rest. He sat, felt his throbbing head … touched the *milla wethakelu* over his heart— the pendant which stopped the arrow. And as the moon had risen, Kurufil hooded the glitter about his face, hurrying into mountain shadow. He was abandoning his heads, but they had served their purpose. Lautaro—surely the one who shot him—knew who killed Umeñdomo, and therefore that war had been declared, his side routed in the initial battle. Let him savor *that*. And let all his kin live with the fear of his return. Had only killed Lautaro, that would have been the perfect end to the perfect day.

The *kalku* was almost insane with joy. Death had jabbed him with a brutal finger and he was saved by his *wethakelu*. *Winka* sorcery had protected him. He was—he told himself—not so much running from Lautaro as hastening to join his kind. One *antu* he would return, perhaps on a *kawellu*, and no *che* then would doubt his power. Let them plead, and perhaps experience his mercy … but not Ñamku, certainly not Eimi, Lautaro, Pangi, or Raytrayen. He would crush them like birds in a gloved fist. His own kind had as good as spoken to him.

Kurufil flitted through dim paths dreaming dreams that had been given form the first time he saw *winka wethakelu*, and realized that beauty could be power. Like *filu* he would shed Mapuche skin, revealing his true invulnerable self. How beautiful was *filu*, sinuous and firm! How like a supple bone! How perfect the inhuman distance of his eyes! And how right it was that *filu* was not clothed in soft, disgusting flesh, but in gleaming *wethakelu* of his own!

Hastening *piku*—delirious with hope—Kurufil imagined himself a snake covered with gold scales.

Chapter 16: *Tempulkalwe (Mapu, 1550)*

Always uncanny, *lolo* was barely tolerable when inhabited. And tonight the Stygian entrance promised horrors. In agonies of indecision Juan clutched his books—these tokens of happier times. What had happened to Raytrayen and the others...?

Crossing himself, he shuffled in. Groping, he found a bench and sat, setting down his bundle.

"Lautaro?" he whispered.

"Pangi! Eimi!" he shouted, as fear galloped up from inner distances.

"Raytrayen!" he screamed.

The echoes died, and there was a puzzling odor....

Blindly he crept, making out a dim face by the fire pit. He reached, and when the head he touched rolled into darkness, Juan scuttled crablike out the cave.

There was no mistaking the scars he briefly felt, so to his horror was added shame that he was glad the head was not Raytrayen's. Doing a dance of indecision, he rubbed his fingers over his *chiripa*—as if memories of touch could be scrubbed off. He knelt to pray, but to whom ... John the Baptist, decapitated? For what, too late? He looked up, and saw the moon hovering over him like a severed head. He had to go back in, yet feared what he might discover.

A prolongued moan floated up the mountainside....

Juan scrambled down, scattering rubble, nearly tripping over Lautaro ... who was clearly dead—eyes open sightless to the moon, the pupils enormous, empty of soul as wooden bowls.

He dragged Lautaro by the legs, wincing when the skull bounced on stones. Then with nightmare slowness, he had the corpse inside the cave. Lighting a fire with ash-buried coal, he saw two heads by the fire pit, the second a white-haired male. Neck dark with blood, it grimaced back.

Beyond shock, Juan registered these facts—thinking the second head familiar. Then, lighting a brand, whirling it, he did what he had dreaded, but his search found no other head, or corpse. Calmed, he rummaged through baskets and pots, as it was either eat or collapse. He came across seaweed, which he rejected. Another pot held *uwa* boiled with beans. Devouring this, he made tea. Warm at last, he was keeping house in a horrid dream, coping by not thinking about what might have happened. He asked himself instead what Mapuche did with their dead—burial or a pyre? And what would they do with a simple head? Surely some ceremony was in order.

Feeling stronger he dragged Lautaro into light, thinking to himself that, curiously, the corpse was not stiff. He laid it out, folding the hands, smoothing the tangled hair, closing the eyes, then set the heads beside Lautaro, so that the six eyes made a row. Appraising his work, he put a blanket on the corpse, and considered covering the gruesome heads as well ... decided against. Faces were displayed at wakes along with hands, and it occurred to him that the absence of a body was not all that inappropriate.

Then there was nothing to do but drink tea and eat, avoiding thought. Tonight he would be the only mourner at a grisly vigil. In the morning he would dig graves. If no one else turned up he would improvise some sort of burial rite.

With only seaweed left to eat, Juan sat by the fire, wrapped in a blanket. He chewed the viscid stuff, thinking of coffins to keep dread at bay. How to make one without metal tools? Burying the heads would be far easier. Would baskets or storage jars constitute disrespect? Pondering the containers hanging from the walls and rafters—recalling for a hallucinatory moment the magnificent hatbox in which Negrito had been buried—Juan fell asleep with his mouth full of seaweed....

He walks through gloomy forest in his Spanish finest—feathered cap, velvet doublet, cape, silk hose and embroidered codpiece, cordovan boots. This silent wildernes is not floored with greenery but with Moorish carpet—a fabric into which sinuous plants are woven—and from that tapestry trunks soar like the columns of a mosque, creating geometric vaults. Yet here he is not lost—as in forests he almost always seems to be—in spirit and geography.

Hearing only the soft jangle of his spurs, he arrives at a forest courtyard dimly lit by stars—a sudden firmament—and at its center an unmoving form ... a domo *dressed in some black thing. Smiling, she slips off her hood and shakes her head. The gold and silver, the gems, that frame her face, glitter like the spangled night itself, a miniature sub lunar heaven.*

He slides toward her as on oiled marble, ever faster, and—as the woman towers over him, knows that only distance made her small. Wind roars in his ears ... and now he has to look high to see her, a head luminously severed—like the moon—for the black she wears has become the velvet mantle of the night. She shakes her stars and smiles, mouth opening not to empyrean fires beyond the spheres, but to darkness absolute. Then her mouth yawns wider, eclipsing stars, until all Heaven yawns....

Juan closes his eyes ... screams high as any girl. He screams again. He screams and screams. He spits seaweed, screaming....

And he opens his eyes to find he has not screamed. Instead, Raytrayen stands before him, screaming....

He sits up, and sees that Lautaro is also sitting up, across the fire pit. Lazarus, Juan thinks, too sleep-befuddled for surprise. "You're dead," he accuses. Then something hammers into his back, and under a storm of blows he is protecting his head with his arms, abandoning his broken ribs to their fate.

About the events leading to this moment no one in *Iolo* that night ever did find out—nor could they have. And given the circumstances, even what portion of the tale each separately knew remained unshared for some time. But the immediate misunderstanding was soon resolved....

Returning, Pangi, Eimi and Raytrayen found Lautaro sleeping between two severed heads. Not far away, Wan slept. Jumping to conclusions, Eimi attacked him. Raytrayen leapt to his rescue, and then Pangi. Restraining berserk Eimi had been no easy feat.

When calm was restored, Lautaro insisted that the *lik winka* was innocent. Kurufil had killed *papai*. And, feebly, he told his wondrous story—

How, by the stream, he leapt over her beheaded body. How her birds led him to the killer. How he scaled the cliff to shoot the kalku. *How—with his sorcery—the* kalku *survived an arrow in his heart and vanished. How he found the heads and brought them to the cave. And how he had been bitten by a* wekufu *that burrowed into him, sucking at his soul until he died....*

No one was more astonished than Juan, wakened from one nightmare to another in which dead men rose to tell their tales. In Spain, sorcerers and witches abounded—mostly Jews and Moors who pretended to convert—yet they feared being burnt at the stake too much to go about beheading others. And he could reconcile nothing in this account with the Mapuche sorcerer he briefly met—beautiful, bejeweled, of uncertain sex—somehow escaped from nightmare to wreak havoc in reality. Witches were old and ugly women—at least *Spanish* witches were—and sorcerers generally old men, he was thinking, when Lautaro asserted that the *lik winka* brought him back from death with his spells. He had suspected it all along, he concluded with somber satisfaction. Wan was a *lik winka machi*.

Outraged at being accused of witchcraft, Juan sputtered that what he did was bring Lautaro in by the fire—not that gently, either—and cover him with a blanket, all this by pure mistake because he thought him dead when he was not. A fortunate mistake, he hastened to add. And if some 'thing' had happened—Juan did not know the word for 'miracle' in *mapudungun—he* was not responsible.

However—blither as he might in alien tongues—Juan was not believed. No one was really listening anyway, too absorbed by the catastrophe.

Raytrayen was kneeling at her mother's head, tearing at her hair, crying *atrutrui*. More composed, the men discussed the retrieval of the body. They asked Juan if he had stayed up that night, making noise to frighten evil spirits away ... which he of course had not. Shocked at his neglect of that elemental thing, they set Juan to it.

Obediently, he went outside to bang sticks, inarticulately shouting now and then, remembering that the ancient Athenians—so Lobo said—pounded on kettles at funerals, to keep the Furies at bay.

Pangi and Eimi left, returning with the body of Lleflai and Juan's belongings.

Then Raytrayen had her own, heart-rending, role. She washed the remains—which had been nibbled by small creatures, but fortunately not discovered by *mañke*. She dressed her. And as the severed head would not allow her to be lashed to a rack upright, Lleflai was laid out prone. Also—Raytrayen insisted—her hair was braided so that it did not hide her scars.

The *wentru* discussed the best course of action as Juan clashed sticks outside, occasionally chanting, having progressed from the random noise of idiots to shouted Latin prayer. Why not invoke the powers of God against Indian devils, when his only mandate had been racket, after all?

Lautaro was still too debilitated by having died, to stand, so next morning Pangi left to return the head of Kuriñam to his family. And Eimi went to track the *kalku* while sign was fresh. The *machi* would depart after the burial, to seek revenge.

Evening crawled, then endless night, Juan banging sticks, hoarsely shouting Paters, Aves—rosaries!—while inside Raytrayen kept solitary vigil, weeping, cooking. Mercifully, she brought him bread and a blanket at sunset, hot tea as the night wore on.

Having nothing if not time for thought, Juan pondered Kurufil, wondering if in the books of **Amadís** he had not read—or the burnt pages of those he had—anyone resembled the bejeweled sorcerer. Giving up on that, he speculated about the resurrection of Lautaro, and his own part in the astonishing event. Perhaps his crucifix had an aura—or holy miasma—creating a space in which the Divine voided pagan sorceries. After all, the crucifix was the principal weapon of the exorcist. But why would God take interest in this particular Indian, to this degree? And what did God *intend* by the miracle, had it happened?

However, mostly Juan's mind turned to Raytrayen, unformed thoughts materializing about her coldness—condensing from his melancholy like dew—for she *had* been cold. Not that he expected an embrace when they reunited. And, of course, tragedy had befallen her. Still, she had not so much as given him a greeting, averting her gaze when she brought food, speaking not a word. Wearing Indian sack, ash-smeared face a pale, streaked mask, Raytrayen brought to mind the Furies of the ancients—vengeful, inhuman. And her meditated distance hurt—hurt terribly—so that Juan, banging his sticks, did not know what his shouted prayers were for. Did she, now—like every other Mapuche—consider him an enemy? Did she think him summed by his race? Had she *always* hated him, which made this the unveiling of long duplicity?

Recent, tender fantasies, now were ashes. He was no less alone than the Wild Man of the Woods. Juan cursed Fortuna as a rare, fitful, summer rain began.

Preparing *papai* for burial, Raytrayen felt dead herself, as if the *wekufu* that killed Lautaro sucked out her soul as well. Ñamku once told her that *kalku* poison killed with cold, and cold is what she was, not in body but in soul.

She tore her hair, ripped her face, leaving bloody scratches in the ash. She wept. She cooked. She labored as if inhabiting an ant. The ant knows well the simple things it does, she told herself.

She had to make bread for the funeral—a pitiful amount, for the mourners would be few. And she could not grieve at *that*. Ñamku would know if ants felt grief. Raytrayen decided that they did not, from the way they disposed of their dead.

Unlike Ñamku, who knew how to leave his body, Raytrayen thought she had not so much left it, as been invaded by the work of death. She *was* her work and nothing else, certainly not alive in any important way. Her hands were animals with uncomplicated lives, patting dough, placing it on flat, hot stone.

Looking lost and frightened, a fat *degu* ambled over. She tossed it grain that it ignored....

All the animals knew. The songbirds were mostly gone, though the *choroy* still sat his perch, looking shrunken, saying nothing.

Watching her hands—pale with flour—pat dough, Raytrayen dully thought that there had been no indication of the *am*. No fly. Nothing unusual in fire or smoke. Still the soul *had* to be here, and Raytrayen shivered, tingling with its presence.

"Papai...?" she whispered. "I love you." And she listened....

"Forgive me," she continued without hope, the silence telling her *papai* was deeply hurt.

She had betrayed her, feeling what she felt for Wan.

"*Ave Maria, gratia plena.*"

Outside, he was chanting what she had herself been taught to repeat in Tiako— senseless words, probably something about Keshukrishtu, the *pillañ* they killed and ate as bread. How incomprehensible *lik winka* were! Yet how familiar Wan now was—this pale-eyed *wentru* with hair the gold of *uwa*, startling against the dark of his shoulders. And tall! Tall as his people he had always been, yet he seemed more so after *palin*—having become so thin. This made her want to cook for him, and she felt guilty that she did. She remembered walking into *lolo* only yesterday, seeing him curled beneath a blanket, sleeping like a *pichiche*. The joy!

The joy had betrayed her. Her joy *was* her betrayal. Lautaro was right—enemies were enemies. The pain *papai* felt about her was right too. Her feelings for Wan had made her false to herself, for what was she without family, without Mapuche? She had also been false to Ñamku, not listening to his wisdom, desiring to live where no *che* could. She was Wala, stolen by the *shompalwe*, dragged underwater to his home, where she survived without breathing, never to fill her lungs with sweet air again....

Raytrayen was suffocating. The bread was burning, smoking. She looked at it through tears, not knowing for whom she wept. For *papai*? For *weichafe* fighting the *lik winka* to save their *mapu* and their lives? For *domo* widowed? For orphaned *pichiche*? Or—traitor that she was—was she weeping for herself?

"*Benedicta tu in mulieribus.*"

She shook her head as if to remove a spider landed there. Returned from Tiako, she had talked to *papai* across a distance death only made permanent. If only she could tell her she was sorry ... but she was no *machi*, to speak with the dead. There was only one thing she could do.

Outside, Wan was briefly silent. She imagined him shivering in the rain, bright hair dimmed by night, and she smiled, wiping with the back of her arm at the paste of tears and ash that stung her eyes, for he was probably frightening the *am* of Lleflai more than any evil spirit that might be out there. And, putting warm bread in a *rali*, she stood. Wan was an enemy, but he had saved her life, and in his own strange way was doing his best to honor and protect *papai*. How simple a thing it was for a *weichafe* to wage war, breathing hate clear as the air....

After sunrise, Pangi returned bringing Wispu—not Andalikan—saying that all *weichafe* were assembling at the Fio Fio. Lautaro welcomed them weakly, too sickened by his death to rise. Unwanted, Juan went outside to sit, his back against the welcomed indifference of mountains.

Inside, they ate and drank *mudai*, setting food and drink beside the corpse. *Wentru* were expected to get drunk at funerals, and by *rangiantu* they definitely were. *Domo* were not, yet Raytrayen consumed more than she thought she could.

She was flushed—but calm—as Pangi and Eimi left. Wan went with them—disregarded, unopposed.

They dug the grave by a clearing in the woods—a place Lleflai had loved. Once a garden, it had been abandoned when a spring appeared after a *nuyun*, the earth turning too boggy. *Chillko* flourished there, flaming in the light. Lleflai would work at small tasks in the sun.

Admapu postponed burial until all mourners had arrived, but—as there were no other kin—they did not postpone. Pangi and Eimi carried her on a litter, staggering more from drink than from the weight, but fortunately they did not drop the body—that worst of things. They lowered Umeñdomo into her grave wrapped in a blanket of *degu* pelt.

The *wentru* delivered long drunken speeches as the *domo* wept. After, they set beside her food and drink, some of her things—a comb, necklaces and bracelets, bone needles, woolen thread, her mortar, a *kepam*—those things of life which she would need in death. And, by her right hand, Raytrayen placed a *llanka* for the Tempulkalwe. They covered all with a blanket before the grave was filled, placing logs over the raw earth to protect the grave from animals and evil spirits.

Pangi left at sunrise to follow Eimi. And Wispu returned home.

Juan and Raytrayen were virtually alone upon the mountaintop, as Lautaro spent most of his resurrection sleeping.

They had unsleeping company, however, for the *am* of Lleflai was with them—Raytrayen knew—invisibly. Good as in the flesh, she stood between her and Wan. And across the rift of death she made her unbearably aware of her own distance from the Mapuche, as if *she* had been the first to die, to her mother ... and to her people.

That day and the next, Raytrayen gave herself to grief and labor, for she was—at least while working—a Mapuche *domo*. And she did one other thing the evening of the burial. Taking care Wan did not see, she gathered the things Ineth had given her—mirror, needles, thread, red cloth. And—sealing them with beeswax in a jar—she buried them in a corner of the cave, despising herself for lacking the courage to destroy these proofs of treachery.

Next morning Lautaro stood to say he would leave to fight *lik winka* ... and collapsed. He left two *antu* later all the same, bow unstrung, as he was too weak to string it, and too proud to have another do this for him.

Raytrayen greatly worried about her brother, but she had greater worry on her mind, and after he left she scarcely slept, guilt turning her grief into a corruption of the soul. *Papai* remained in the cave, she felt, because of *her*. Souls lingered by the places and the *che* they loved. Yet nothing was more important than for the *am* to leave after the burial.

"*Papai*, are you here...?" Raytrayen whispered, hearing only quiet snoring from the recess where Wan had moved his bed.

"*Papai*, you know you cannot stay." Raytrayen pleaded. "Please go."

Once breathed out of the body, the *am* was defenseless against *kalku* and evil spirits, in peril until it found the *tempulkalwe*—the spirit guide that, taking the form of a whale, would bear it to the island of the dead, Ngulchenmaiwen. There the soul would be safe.

"*Papai*, please! The *kalku* will steal your soul!"

Frantic, Raytrayen searched the gloom, not seeing what she knew was there.

The *am*—as itself, and not embodied by some other being, or thing—should be visible as a glow, like *cherufe*, and she had hoped that the soul denying itself to her by day would be betrayed by night.

"*Papai*, if you love me as I love you, do not stay! I will wait for your return!"

On Ngulchenmaiwen, Lleflai would be transformed into an *alwe*—a soul no longer vulnerable, but powerful—a spirit that would return to watch over those it loved in life.

"*Papai*, not because of me!"

The invisible soul lingered because of Wan, to protect her daughter from herself. And Raytrayen could not allow—or endure—this.

"I *do* love him. "

And having breathed this truth she could not herself believe, she whispered, "I am sorry."

Yet the night was silent, as Raytrayen knew it would be. Apologies could not undo her betrayal of *kume mognen*. Being *ankeñ peñeñ* was bad enough. Embracing invaders was far worse.

Then she whispered what she must, to Lleflai and the other dead, "I forsake the *lik winka*, as an enemy of my people."

But after those terrible words she did not so much feel that she had reached a Mapuche shore, as that she attempted to fly from a great height and failed. So, it was with sudden shock—as if hitting ground at last—that she saw *papai* blink into life ... die ... glow again. The hovering *am* was visiting as *kudellkiñ*—a firefly pulsing with the cold, bright heart of the dead. Floating, the firefly left *lolo*.

Raytrayen threw aside her blanket and leapt to her feet, pursuing ... to stand on a mountaintop alive with magic. *Kudellkiñ*, everywhere! So many souls!

Papai had joined the dead. Which of the sparks out there she was, Raytrayen could not tell. Yet this did not matter. One *antu* she would return.

"*Mari, mari, papai*."

At one at last with *kume mognen*, shivering in her nakedness, Raytrayen admired the beauty of the night. And when at last she went to lie beneath a weight of pelts, she heard Wan snoring, and she smiled.

In a dark place that held no other place, she was weightless over cold, calm water. There was no other place to walk to, yet she walked not to arrive, her walking saying she was unfulfilled. One did not walk to find the dead, she knew. But she could walk to let them know her need....

Over the water a dark figure slid toward her ... a stooped crone—the tempulkalwe—*guiding spirit silent on her raft, peering from beneath a hood with bright, black eyes. "Get on," the ancient said, and the dark raft changed direction,* tempulkalwe *poling.*

The waters of death were calm, wide and dim. In the distance a single star glowed blue— growing in brightness, not in size—until at last it lit the crone and raft with its cold light ... papai *as well, for it was she who held the glowing* llanka Raytrayen *had placed beside her in the grave.*

Stepping onto the raft, Papai handed the llanka *to the* tempulkalwe, *who hid it in her* kepam. *And with the bright stone eclipsed, the only light was now provided by the* am, *shining on the raft gliding through darkness ... although the guiding spirit no longer poled, having melted into the logs. And the logs—no longer lashed by vines— had grown into each other. Becoming one with the raft, the* tempulkalwe *had turned it into a whale.*

"*I lost my head,*" *the* am *said.*

Was Lleflai smiling? It was always hard to tell.

"*Domo peñeñ,*" *the soul went on, taking the hand of Raytrayen,* "*you have to decide for yourself.*"

"*I did!*"

The hand of the soul was neither warm nor cold, as if not there.

"*I lingered selfishly,*" *the* am *said,* "*to punish you the only way I could.*"

"*Punish me!*"

"*Yamai! I was jealous of the* lik winka.*"*

On the horizon, a dim shape loomed like a black sun rising.

"*Love does not ask permission,*" *the soul added, pensive.*

Ngulchenmaiwen was approaching, and Raytrayen saw that it was wooded, glowing over oily blackness.

"*I came to like the* lik winka, *before I died,*" papai *confessed.*

"*And it has sometimes seemed to me, the soul went on—with that tendency of the dead to generalize—*"*that only unimportant things are given us to choose. I was afraid,* domo peñeñ, *of what I did not know and had to be. With* lik winka *in our* mapu, *nothing will ever be the same again. Ñamku knew this, and you were a part of what he prepared. You must trust his vision.*"

"*I do. I did,*" *Raytrayen insisted with far less conviction than she intended.*

Now Ngunchenmaiwen loomed over them, reflected on the water, lit by motes that were the dancing dead.

Lleflai grew smaller, shining brighter as she said, "*Domo peñen, I am proud of your decision. But you must understand that I was wrong, for I rejected the* lik winka *out of greed.*"

Papai was right—Raytrayen thought—she would have had to choose between them. And at that thought, another struck her....

"*No,*" *the soul forestalled.* "*I did not intend my death. And I absolve you of your*

*promise to me. But as your promise was made to all Mapuche also—and to yourself—
what you do about the* lik winka *is up to you.*"

Raytrayen felt abandoned and betrayed. Where, here, was the wisdom of the
dead?

"*Papai!*"

"*Your decision is not mine to make. I am too ignorant, too selfish in my love of
you, to be of use—for the simple act of dying does not make one wise. I do not know
what here is right, what wrong. Blindly, I would choose for you what I thought would
make you happy … and that is something you can choose yourself.*"

Raytrayen cried out, "*Please!*" For the am *was leaving.*

Lleflai *paused to say,* "*Why not renounce the* lik winka *later? Lolo has long been
a refuge for those like us.*"

The am *flickered like torches about to die, as it floated toward Ngulchenmaiwen.
And throbbing like a heart it said,* "*Do what you must.*"

"*Papai!*"

*The pulsing mote had joined the constellations of the dead upon the island. And
when Lleflai spoke again, Raytrayen was startled to hear the words as a whisper in
her head—*"Ñamku *was attracted by* lik winka *too, you know. But I must leave. I will
return to you,* domo peñeñ.*"

"*Papai!*" Raytrayen cried, arms outstretched. And—as from a far insect, humming
amid many—she faintly heard, "*Give my thanks to the* lik winka, *for all that awful
noise he made.*"

*Then it was only silence as Raytrayen felt weight on her extended hands—two
pots of paint, one red, one white.*

*The whale trembled and was gone, Ngulchenmaiwen disappearing with its
shining dead.*

Juan was wakened by a quake that made the mountain groan and crepitate.
Clay pots clanged like bells. The parrot fluttered off with a demented squawk.
Degu leapt in aimless panic. Dust drifted down, but Juan had buried himself in
blankets. The *machi* dead who had once made the cave their home protected it—or
so he had been told, and was beginning to believe. This mountain was enchanted,
which was well and good, yet he was uncomfortably reminded that the *aquelarre—*
the witches' sabbath—was celebrated on mountain peaks precisely. Was such
protection appropriate for *cristianos*?

Warm in blankets within the bowels of a shaking earth, he thought that—Lleflai
dead and Raytrayen having washed her hands of him—he was good as marooned,
these days. When he dared speak, she responded with laconic grunts, more
short of word with him than with the brooding parrot. And she no longer spoke
Spanish—that enthusiasm of her past—not even a simple *sí* or *no.* He tried to help

her with her tasks—for menial labor had become her life—but his incompetence only added brick and mortar to the wall that rose between them. And now—dawn glowing at the entrance—why was she not up, at work and banging things? The temblor?

Juan put on his *chiripa* under covers, since Hispanic modesty did not allow him to arise as he now slept—naked as an April sheep. He tiptoed out to bathe.

Returned from icy waters, loath to enter *lolo,* he sat on the cliff edge, wet, calm and sad. Ignoring aftershocks, he waited for the fullness of the sun, his thought being that—like a facsimile of the crucifixion—Lleflai's death had perturbed the Heavens. There had been a summer rain the night after—no less rare in *mapu* than in Andalucía … days of dense cloud since. This morning, the earthquake … and presently, impenetrable mist.

He pondered the date. It was mid-summer. Mid-century too—1550, by his calculations. But was it February yet? The imprecision in his reckoning—perhaps a week … perhaps as much as two—for some reason made him most uneasy at the cusps of months. And in this time, what had become of Inés? Of Pedro? Was he with Valdivia in the sea of haze below, working at conquest? Had he remained in Santiago, too decrepit to campaign? Or, was he dead of liquor and old age?

The mist parted far below Juan's feet, a distant forest materializing, soon blotted … yet it transported him to his first glimpse of the Copiapó. Transported in his hopes as well, he saw the future as he had then —distant as it was green—shrouded in the mists of dreams. The marvels that awaited him! But that was August of 1540, more than ten years ago. And the present flooded in, returning him to exile.

Sucked of substance by the risen sun, the mist permitted transitory vistas, and they caused a serene elation in Juan—though he was shivering with cold. Was a hint of a thing better than the thing itself? If so, what did this say about the burnt volumes of **Amadís de Gaula,** read as if through black mist breaking? Can one desire what one can see completely?

Pliny's Africa rambled into the mind. How vast, how rich … yet these windows opened to nothing close, for distance was the necessary perspective of The Geographer. Summing the entire knowledge of his time, he could not linger, composing on a mountain as it were, making of the **Historia Naturalis** a cake confected from every fruit and nut known to man—yet without dough—so that its sweetmeats were crammed in absences…. On the scent of a great elucidation—a perspective on his present moment that would give it dignity and meaning—Juan scrutinized *mapu* through dissipating fog. Was there, out *there*, somehow, the enormous answer to his predicament?

A faint noise behind him….

Raytrayen! He rose, alive with trepidation, and—murmuring to himself that women were the Africa of the soul—turned to face her.

She approached on silent Indian feet, clasping a blanket that she extended, and … her face was painted red. What could *that* mean?

He accepted her offer—a benefaction that shook the moorings of his earth.

She smiled back through shocking pigment, as if expecting a response, although she had herself said nothing.

He noticed now—white dots were dabbed beneath her eyes, in rows upon the red, like tears….

He croaked his thanks.

"*De nada*," she responded cheerfully.

Juan broke into an icy sweat, looking down, to where a circlet of cowries shimmered blue and white—like hollowed pearls—upon a slender ankle. And higher, there was no salvation to be found … her hands folded over the delta with a thousand names. Looking down, again, he saw the blanket he now held.

"*Hace freshco*," she offered, studying his expression.

By the eleven thousand virgins … it *was* chilly! But what did the red face and white tears signify?

Then—like a gargoyle fallen from cathedral spires—awareness crushed him. *He had not put on the blanket!* Besotted idiot!

"Breakfast, you want?" she offered … leaving him speechless.

Waiting out his silence, she invited, "You, me, rot potatoes after," her smile the more brilliant, amid Indian rouge.

"*Bueno*," Juan agreed—to what exactly, he did not know—happy that he had not stammered. And by the time he could manage more complex speech, she was already in the cave.

Now, as if his entire body had been one numb limb, Juan tingled everywhere with sensation, overwhelmed by glee and shame. And, unruly children of the event—in warring camps—afterthoughts competed for attention, making him go hot and cold beneath his blanket, with ecstasy and mortification. But as one accustomed to ignominy, he scarcely cared—a dolt he had always been, and a dolt he would always be, but now he was a dolt with companionship smiling in his future, a dolt who could look forward to communication in his mother tongue. He would not tempt Fortuna by expecting more, but … *what* had he been invited to, this rotting of potatoes?

The skies were blue that day, anomalies of earth and sky having dissipated with the mist, the earthquake as punctuation. That day, too. began the new chapter in Juan's life that he would come to call '*El tiempo de la cara roja*,' for, retroactively, the period that Raytrayen's face was painted red revealed itself as a time set apart—a blessed era, however parenthetical.

Juan enjoyed a breakfast in which *kofke* supplemented *murkeko*—which explained Raytrayen's lingering in the cave—blissfully unaware that there are doors that Fortuna will not open for our desires without closing others. He merely thought She smiled on him that day, for Raytrayen—saints be praised!— was friendly. Little did it matter that she was somewhat ill at ease, and banal, as they shared bread, speaking of weather and the parrot. Would the *choroy* return? Juan devoutly hoped not, but he lied. Her banality carrying the burden of her communication, he took delight in being no less banal in return.

They left the cave bent under heavy, potato-filled baskets, which were supported by tumplines cutting into their foreheads. Juan bore an Indian shovel—hewn from wood—she, an Indian kind of adze. Silently they descended the mountain along a rushing stream, indisposed, for the moment, to test their relationship with speech. Juan particularly did not dare inquire about her paint and painted tears—if such they represented—although he wondered about this savage version of the mask of tragedy of the Greeks.

Raytrayen again brought up the weather—cooler … yet what sun! That topic now exhausted, they discussed birds. Wading the stream, here wider, less rocky, more serene, Juan told her that *pillmaikeñ*—the swallow—darted similarly in Spain. There also, flew *yeku*—crow of ill omen—although its cry was different. So the birds went….

And when, eventually, they set down their loads on a sandbar embraced by a placid oxbow, they had regained a measure of their former ease. Together, they dug a hole in the sand, Raytrayen explaining that they would be making *funa poñu*—rotten potato. The *papa*—she said in Spanish—rot, but stream keep clean, make good. They return in one, two moon … Wan see for self.

Unfortunately Juan could 'see for self' too well in his mind's eye, and 'smell for self' even better with his mind's nose. Having experienced more than one rotten potato, he *knew* what they would return to disinter.

She insisted, *limpia*. Clean potato, like cook. Raytrayen smacked her lips. "*Buena.*"

Juan noted that her *b* was good, though she still had troubles with plural endings.

They washed the potatoes in running water, lined the bottom of the streamside cavity with stone, placing leaves over that crude floor. That done, they half-filled the hole with potatoes, covering them with a second layer of leaves. And after weighting this vegetable grave with more stone, they buried it in sand.

Returning to *lolo*, Raytrayen was silent, Juan deciding that they had restored enough of friendship that she feared restoring more. Could enemies commune?

At the cave—sun well descended—Raytrayen poked the ashes of the fire pit, retrieving *uwa* and *poñu* she had left to roast before they left, still delightfully hot. The parrot returned as they were eating corn steaming on the cob. She welcomed it with glad cries—too effusive to be honest, in Juan's personal opinion. And he watched her feed the obnoxious creature from her hand, then turn to the preparation of some meatless stew. He wondered, sadly, if ever they would talk from the heart again.

Then Raytrayen set down her spoon, firmly. And looking into his eyes she thanked him for saving her brother's life—a quandary for Juan, as in accepting her thanks he would be acknowledging that he practiced Spanish sorcery. Yet the last thing in God's good earth he wanted, at this instant, was giving her the lie. Let her believe he was a sorcerer from beyond the sea. God would register his silent reservations.

She smiled brilliantly and offered stew … said with a little grin that Lleflai thanked him for the noise he made at her wake.

"What!"

But she meant it. Lleflai thanked him from the grave.

"When?" he asked, much too abrupt, imagining words bubbling up through spaded dirt.

"Last night," was the quiet, stiff reply.

"O?" Juan responded, seeking sanctuary in vagueness. "You mean she came to you in dreams."

"*Me*," she insisted—ominously reverting to *mapudungun*. "I spoke with her *am*. Lleflai came to me as *kudellkiñ*. We went with the *tempulkalwe* to Ngulchenmaiwen."

This might as well have been a treatise on celestial mechanics not yet translated from Arabic, to Juan. Yet one thing was clear—Raytrayen had spoken with a corpse, as Ñamku was said to do. Was *she* a witch too?

"Please tell Lleflai that I was delighted to make noise for her," he offered humbly. "When again you see her," he added.

Consorting with Indians, Juan was sliding down the slope of a perdition greased by loneliness. Still, this profound infidelity to Spanish belief troubled him far less than it should, and Juan listened with interest as Raytrayen, sitting at her loom, explained Mapuche death….

In *mapu* the dead roamed about invisible, like Lleflai and Ñamku—and Spanish guardian angels, thought Juan. Then, there were the *pillañ* in the volcanoes, to whom one prayed as saints—resembling the Greek and Roman gods in having powers of their own. The dead were also in the sky, where they fought battles manifest as storms. They were the stars of night as well, and inhabited distant islands.

But as all this was communicated in extremely faulty Spanish, Juan did not know how much of his confusion sprang from misunderstanding. It occurred to him that Mapuche theology was in deep need of an Aquinas to sort the whole thing out....

Raytrayen set down her shuttle, turning from her loom ... yet not to Juan. Cross-legged, she faced the vivid dying of the sun over the Southern Sea, to talk about her father, killed before her birth, and her mother, who died when she was born. She knew little more about them, but added proudly that Rayentru was said to be the most beautiful *dama* of her time.

And so touched was Juan, by her willingness to bare this awful scar, he in no way saw it as incongruous that Raytrayen had called her mother a 'lady.'

Raytrayen's face was turned to sunset, mouth resolute, nose arched and bold— these features wonderfully placed upon a gentle oval.

"Is your mother here, now?" he whispered to her.

"*Mai.*"

He told her that the only thing that he remembered about his family was their dying.

"You live only?"

She turned to face him, profile blank against the ash-gray sky. Still, he did not have to see the emotion he was hearing.

"*Sí.*"

She gestured at the fireflies about them.

"*Luciernagas,*" he said—for indeed, the tiny beings had come alive. They blinked and floated, mortal mirrors of eternal stars.

She broke into his thoughts, recounting her journey to Ngulchenmaiwen.

Juan was seduced ... if not quite convinced.

"So, these are souls?" he said.

"*Quién sabe?*" she responded, rising.

Had she misspoken? Was she being flippant, or profound ... or simply just the irritatingly Mapuche self she could be sometimes?

Juan followed Raytrayen inside the cave, where she lit two long splinters of wood, handing him one. In their small globe of illumination beneath the earth— red face tilted up—her painted tears were bright and steady. How she had grown!

"How old are you?" he blurted.

Like fuses, their splinters sputtered....

"What a *lik winka* thing to want to know," she said, ambiguous.

Juan hurried to his cot, splinter dying on the way.

Reviewing the day's events, that night, he was of two minds or more. They *had* communicated. Yet he could not shake the feeling that the intimacy was at *his* expense, she so very Indian that it grated. Putrefied potatoes! And she had dwelt on the habits of her dead....

"Not machismo, but *Ma-pu-chismo*," Juan thought to himself. The war betwen them was not of swords and arrows, but of customs and beliefs. Was she trying to convert him, with her rotten potatoes and pagan theology? Or was she simply holding up before him what *she* had to offer?

Out of fairness, Juan decided to give the reverse a try, beginning with the afterlife—that last subject of her day....

"So where Lleflai go, death after?" the Raytrayen of his imaginary essay asked.

"To Limbo," Juan responded, slamming that unpalatable fact on the table of discussion. "She was good—according to her Indian lights—yet could not go to Heaven unbaptized." He amplified, "Her *am* went *directly* there."

Juan was thinking—but not saying—that her soul did not wander the earth, and absolutely did *not* speak to the living.

The Raytrayen of his essay sighed, unconvinced.

"Her *am* was released through her mouth," Juan conciliated—for this might be the only belief here held in common. "As for Limbo, it is at the edge of Hell, yet definitely *not* Hell. There is hope for those who enter there."

What *kind* of hope Juan did not know, for argument and perplexity summed the History of Limbo.

Raytrayen sighed again.

Juan pressed on, saying, "Hell is down."

There was no doubting that ancient verity, agreed to even by the Greeks and Romans. How far down, however, had never been made clear to him—though much farther than any Mapuche soul appeared to go. "Not down a volcano," he anticipated, seeing the light of understanding dying in Raytrayen's eyes.

In truth, Juan always had trouble understanding Limbo—that muddled threshold to Heaven, existing only for some. There was the *limbus infantum*, composed of innocents who died before being baptized. There was the *limbus patrum*—for Limbo also hosted the good patriarchs of the Bible, deceased before baptism and Christ. And—Juan now realized with profound misgiving—there must surely be a *limbus indium*, although not even Lobo's learning touched on a destination for those like Lleflai, kept by geography from baptism and the Word of God.

Too many questions were in the air about Limbo, chief among them being when—and even if—a soul was elevated from its vague murk to the sight of God. Anyway, who took interest in Limbo except theologians? Juan could not recall it portrayed on churches or in illuminations. Heaven, Hell and Purgatory, yes ...

Limbo no. It was impossible to *see* a realm where infants in swaddling clothes swam through dim, perpetual cloud, in the company of bearded prophets and patriarchs. And now ... Indians? Was it heretical to think Lleflai had reason to linger near the Raytrayen she loved? The fireflies of these mountains haunted him....

Thus, by dint of imagined sighs, the Raytrayen of Juan's venture in fairness was a devil's advocate that night, calling into doubt the certainties to which he tried to sway her. The more he thought, the more confused he grew. And the more confused he was, the more he feared that Pedro would appear to him in dreams. Given his father's robust beliefs, how would *he* judge the Indian depths to which his *hijo* had descended?

Savage habit could steal a Spanish body—Juan had learned—but could it steal a Spanish soul? What if he actually enjoyed putrefied potatoes. For after *that*, what?

Chapter 17: *Kutran* (*Mapu*, 1550)

Eimi followed Chau without pausing to eat or rest, stopping when it became too dark to track. Squatting on a rock, You ate cold beans and *poñu*, thinking that Chau was going *piku* when You did not expect this. If Chau kept traveling through the night, You might lose him.

Shouldering his load You crashed through bamboo in the dark. You would die horribly if Chau heard, and yet You pressed on, at last stopping by a stream in the faint first glow of *chipanantu*. Glad to have survived the night, You ate, waiting for the sun to rise, then searched the stream bank. The *pillañ* smiled, for he found a well-known print in clay, and there were others. Following, You discovered a nest of fern and leaves where Chau had slept, and You resumed his pursuit, alert. Chau should be close....

Then, sudden as a clap of hands, You heard *trewa*—a deep clamor. Terrified, he ran, stopping as the awful sound faded. They had the scent of Chau, not his.

You hurried *piku* fast as his twisted legs allowed.

The sound was powerful, chilling—close!—approaching Kurufil. The *kallfu lik winka*! He fled—terror overwhelming joy—until, mastering himself, he turned to face the fear that he had traveled to embrace. Hooding himself, he waited with hammering heart as revelation rushed toward him....

Two *trewa* erupted into sight. Two more ... and Kurufil was surrounded by their frenzy. *Wethakelu* glittering, they leapt higher than his head, barking and slavering, baring immense teeth. Eight or nine of them surrounded him now—the last to arrive the size of *luan* but more massive—so close he could smell them. Yet they did not attack. Like a beast loosed in his breast, a wild hope leapt.

The *trewa* went abruptly silent, sitting. Kurufil heard hurried thuds. The sound slowed. He lifted his eyes as branches parted....

The *kallfu lik winka* sat high on a black *kawellu*, not wearing cloth, but bright *wethakelu*, so that he shone with the cold fires of the moon. His eyes!

He looked down at Kurufil with a blue, impassive gaze. Lifted by the breeze— they were so fine—wisps of hair the gold of *uwa* tassels escaped the *wethakelu* on his head. His face was perfect, smooth, unlined, the white of summer clouds, or milk.

Kurufil allowed his hood to fall.

The *kallfu lik winka* spoke....

"Well, well, what have we here?" said Nuño Beltrán de Mendoza.

He had been riding the van with his dogs, to run down Indians and take them back to undergo the question. By and large this was a futile exercise—the savages of these parts being headstrong as a drover's mule, sooner perishing under torture than parting with information—yet Mendoza did not mind, for his dogs got Indian meat. He had an unspoken understanding with Valdivia that—given the cruel necessities of war—what happened unwitnessed did not happen at all. Like the trees of theologians, Indians dropping in their forests without sound, did not drop at all.

Futile as they were, these *monterías* were entertaining nonetheless. Mendoza did not fish, preferring more momentous game. Still, he thought of dogging as akin to angling. His dogs were a kind of line, connected to him by training and devotion, their jaws a sort of hook that 'set' itself out of your sight. And the first glimpse of what he had 'hooked' always gave Mendoza its pleasurable shock....

This one was a woman, and her black hood slid down as of itself—revealing silver ... massive Inca gold.... And—*Cuerpo de Cristo!*—an emerald!

"Well, well, what have we here?" the dogger repeated, at a loss.

Mendoza did not believe in repeating himself ... or in being at a loss, for that matter. And he loathed astonishment—that crass emotion of the less worldly. Therefore he was aggravated at the sight of her extended, languid hand, which was mutilated yet slender, heavy with rings, and as if offered for a kiss. Attractive—though in a definitely dark way—she brought to mind pampered Aztec princesses.

Then, with a shaking her head, she created tinkling music.

Whatever the Indian meaning of this tableau, Mendoza was now a much richer man. He said, "*Señora*, we meet again."

Gallantly he bowed, savoring the ironies. This was the Indian his dogs ran down some time ago—the one that got away. Reminded of tales in which a poor fisherman finds a jewel while opening the stomach of his catch, Mendoza admired the emerald on the circlet that bound the Indian's brow, the bracelets on her wrist. She was not offering her hand to be kissed, he decided, but in this wordless way saying, "*Caballero*, we meet again." The gall! However—considering what she ultimately offered—Mendoza found the insolence quite tolerable. Had he his blue silk hat, he would have doffed it. Instead, removing his helmet, he shook his hair loose. This Indian was far too valuable to be dog food. And he was not about to share her with Valdivia.

You crawled through bamboo and thick *kulkul* ... heard *likwinkadungun* and stopped to listen. The *lik winka* spoke again. You crawled over silent moss, and moments later, through *kulkul,* he saw. You gasped.

Morning light poured into a forest clearing. Chau wore his black *kepam*, but on his head, hanging from his ears and on his wrist, he had *winka wethakelu*. Shaking his head, he blazed with light. Around him were glittering dogs, their bared fangs long as the little finger of You—*trewa* so large he could have put his head in their mouths. Over them all—immense—was a *lik winka*. Separating one leg from the *kawellu*, he dropped to the ground with a thud, and—saying something in *likwinkadungun*—held out the shiny bowl he had been wearing on his head. Chau remained expressionless, unblinking as a snake.

You knew he was too proud to let his horror show. And You was glad, seeing Chau strip himself of *wethakelu*, putting them in the shiny bowl of the *lik winka* until it was almost full. You was happy as when first he escaped *renu*, for Chau loved his *winka milli* only less than himself.

The *lik winka* took the leather pouch *chau* had in his hand, looked inside … threw it down. And saying nothing, he poured the *milli* he had taken into a *wethakelu* hanging from his *kawellu*. Returning his bowl to his head, he pulled himself up. Then—whistling so softly You could scarcely hear him—he thudded into the forest, glittering like a lake through leaves until he vanished.

On his chest—through *mapu*—You felt the heavy pacing of the *kawellu*.

The *trewa* in the clearing growled with profound menace. Heads low, long tongues hanging, they surrounded Chau. Were they about to eat him? You hid his eyes. The thumping feet of the *kawellu* echoed his racing heart. You looked….

Four *trewa* … Chau facing them with an ear cocked, as if appreciating the sounds they made. Calmly, he bent to retrieve his pouch. The *trewa* barked … tensed to spring. Chau froze and straightened. Then, herded by the dogs, he walked away.

You fought the urge to follow, knowing he was lucky the *trewa* had not caught his scent. Better track them later. He lay on cool moss to wait in shade, caressed by fronds. He slept. And when Pangi wakened him, *antu* was not yet overhead.

Two greyhounds led the way. Flanked by another pair of dogs—part greyhound, part mastiff, a combination of speed, ferocity and size that he esteemed—Nuño Beltrán ruminated the astonishing turn of his morning. This Indian clearly had valuable information. More loot might well be concealed in these wilds, and who knew? Maybe there existed another Indian empire, rich as the Incas'. Richer. Had he stumbled into fabled El Dorado in this casual way? Too bad he hardly knew a word of Indian language, or he would have questioned her on the spot.

Had he been overly impulsive, taking her treasure, when by law it was to be apportioned by shares to the expedition and the Emperor? But how could Valdivia find out, when Indian women were almost never put to the question? He would simply claim he needed another bearer—for, in truth, one of his had died of pox. And once she was his, he would interrogate her through an interpreter. If he found out about more treasure, he could get it during his *monterías* with no one the wiser. If she revealed an entire Indian empire, he would magnanimously share the information, demanding a finder's share. Nuño Beltrán was not accustomed to flights of fancy but he definitely had them now. Quite possibly, he held the key to the doors of El Dorado, whose streets were paved with gold....

So lost in golden dreams was Mendoza, that the growl of his dogs came as a shock. An armed, half naked *yanacona* soundlessly materialized through trees, three others after, stolid Indian faces empty. Scouts.

Horsemen trotted up, reining in, Mendoza recognizing them as Juan Godinez and Gregorio de Castaneda.

"*Muy buenos días, caballeros,*" he greeted affably ... inwardly dismayed, for his mastiffs and his captive were not far behind.

"*Muy buenos, Don Nuño,*" they replied, cold, polite.

As always, Mendoza appreciated their distaste, knowing it a part of the respect he and his dogs commanded. Yet today he was not happy with this chance encounter ... and far less so when a file of *infantes* trudged up, to slouch over their spears when they saw the *caballeros* were conferring.

"You captured an Indian," Gregorio de Castaneda observed—for, as Mendoza feared, his mastiffs and his captive had caught up.

"Just a woman."

"Hmmm?" Castaneda inquired, wondering why this was 'just' a woman, not a warrior that could be questioned. And why had Mendoza not fed her to his dogs?

Always up for rape, the *infantes* crowded in, stopped in their tracks by the snarling mastiffs.

Quietly in their midst, the Indian stood, her face shadowed by black wool.

"One of my porters died of pox," Mendoza said. "I captured a replacement." Indian women were almost as durable as their men and considerably more docile. No one would question his decision.

"Why four dogs, Don Nuño, for a woman?" The question came from an *infante* with an untidy mane of soiled white hair hanging from his helmet, its steel so fouled one could not see through filth to rust.

Cacafuego nauseated Mendoza, and not just with his fetor. As a caricature of civilization he was worse than Indians, reflecting on what was Spanish from obscene intramural distances. But—damn his eyes!—he was right to ask his question.

"*Sí. Porqué?*" other *infantes* chorused, curious as to what the Indian hood concealed.

Mendoza attempted a smile, and failed. Dismissively, he waved his hand as if to say, 'a simple oversight,' then whistled. Three dogs abandoned their captive, one remaining.

The *infantes* surrounded the woman … then approached her. The dog that was guarding her growled.

"As I said, she is mine," Mendoza snapped.

Cacafuego replied with a polluted smile, "Of course, *caballero*." Then he pranced and cackled, farted, and—as the message was too complex for his bum hole—said, "Surely you will not mind, Don Nuño, if we peek at your new porter's face?"

Mendoza shrugged.

Cacafuego slid down the hood, and—since, like many *infantes,* he chewed *coca*— spat copiously in appreciation of what he had revealed. "Prime Indian mutton," he declared. The *infantes* coughed and blew their noses with their fingers, suppressing smirks and hoots. Mendoza was reputed to wear the hat of sexuality askew, but the most oblique reference to *this,* in his presence, was attempted suicide.

Still, the dogger sat his horse as if noticing not a thing, and the matter would no doubt have ended there, save that—with trouble's talent—Cacafuego spied gold through wool. He clutched and ripped. Pins snapped….

Now, naked to her slender waist, the Indian clutched her dress.

Cacafuego crowed loud and long—the perfect rooster.

"*Cuerpo de Dios!*" Juan Godinez exclaimed, crossing himself, for nested between virginal breasts, was an Inca ornament—or amulet—representing the sun. Ponderous on its chain, looking back with eyes of emerald, this was a treasure to itself.

"You hid it," Mendoza shouted truthfully, also warding off suspicion that he had hoarded. Damnation!

"Get that thing for me," he barked at the *infantes.* "I will personally hand it to the *cabildo*." And lifting the pendant high, he addressed the *caballeros.* "We need to know if there is more. My captive must be questioned." Turning to the *infantes* he ordered, "You will guard the prisoner. See to it that she gets safely back to camp."

Oily as always, Cacafuego inquired, "*Señores*, might I have your kind permission to see if she is hiding more, somewhere…?"

The *infantes* leered, recalling conical breasts.

Gregorio de Castaneda gestured his approval, intrigued—it took a shifty *infante* to fathom shifty Indians.

Cacafuego tore off her dress, flourishing it like a *torero* executing a brilliant pass, and saw….

Black hair hanging to below her waist, she was delicate as a girl filling into maturity. Her waist was small, and her hips only slightly rounded. Arms rigid by her side, with fierce intensity she was looking at Mendoza.

Seeing what was between her legs, the dogger gagged. She had shaved—or plucked—her triangle, and from that smoothness hung male tackle, small but unmistakable. He looked astounded at the breasts, the face, realizing that she still stared at him, lips moving silently.

"Well, well. What have we here?" Cacafuego cackled. And, one by one, the *infantes* diverted their attention from the delicate monster to the dogger. Had Mendoza *known* what he was bringing back to camp—as he declared—for himself?

Mendoza's ears were burning in his helmet. Then something in him broke. And like a cretin—yelling, *"Hasta la vista, caballeros"*—he spurred his horse into the forest, Inca pendant forgotten in his hand. The other *caballeros* galloped after him.

Left unsupervised in wild woods, every *infante* was thinking the exact same thing. Illiterate to a man, when it came to orders they were masters of the letter of the law. They were to bring the monster back—*but*—no mention of how quickly. As for 'safely,' that clearly meant the prisoner should arrive alive enough to talk. She, or he, was going to be tortured anyway.

Still they hesitated, studying the Indian aberration, resentful that their primal urges were confused. How could God allow that face—those breasts!—to coexist with that crotch? Not a few felt that the situation required punishment. Unused to complexities in lust, they yearned to correct this aberration with their spears by giving her, or him, what after all was called a gash, to fuck. In short, they were shaken to a man. Still—when all was said and done—their collective appetite was whetted.

Me first," said Cacafuego.

The other other *infantes* leaned on their spears to wait....

Scrutinizing the contents of the leather bag Kurufil had abandoned, Pangi said, *"wekufu."* Not long after, he and You found a trampled place. They recognized prints of *kawellu, lik winka* ... and the *kalku*. What had happened here?

They searched....

Che had spit here and there. They found the *willeñ* of *che* ... piles of *kawellu* dung. There was trodden blood, and long, black hair flung aside. Sniffing, You said it belonged to Chau. They were about to leave when You glimpsed a scrap of black through leaves—a *kepam*, blood on the muddied wool, but not enough to suggest a mortal wound. This place had a violent tale to tell....

They were looking at each other with wordless speculation when the *kepam* that they were both holding thumped. Pangi jerked—yipping with pain and surprise —an arrow hanging from his ribs.

The arrow fell. Another whistled by as he sprinted into the forest.

You ran in the opposite direction, crashing through brush, hearing pursuit.

Knowing he could not outrun a warrior, he stood, back to a tree, unarmed, for at some point he had dropped his club.

A *che* appeared—not *lik winka*—bow in one hand, knife shining in another. Scarlet feathers dangled over his grinning face, which was striped red and gray. He looked something like a Mapuche at war, but when he spoke he might as well have been a *trewa* barking.

In a fighting crouch the *winka* shuffled, obsidian knife extended. Suddenly, he slapped the back of his neck with his free hand, as if bee-stung. He spun, and— seeing nothing—turned to You again, moving slowly ... then more slowly, until he did not move at all. Eyes unfocused, weaving like a drunk, he fell with blind eyes open, snoring.

Pangi walked up, leather pouch in hand. Kicking the *winka* to see if he reacted, he probed his own ribs. "A scratch," he said.

"You were lucky. His arrow was slowed by the *kepam*."

"What *happened* to Kurufil?"

Eimi shrugged, as if to ask—How much revenge suffices?

Scanning the forest, Pangi said they could not stay. And he smiled at You as at a *pichiche* taking his first steps. "I am glad you are all right, You," he said.

You smiled back. "Me too."

They returned to *lolo* on the evening of the fifth *antu*, foot-sore, famished. Raytrayen—who was grinding flour outside—greeted them with glad cries, surprising Pangi with her painted face. He did not ask why, and she did not explain.

He described their journey of revenge, leaving out the hair of the *kalku*, his bloodied *kepam* and the spilled blood—no need to horrify with what they did not know. He left out the *winka* with the striped face as well. The *kalku* had gone far *piku*, and had been captured by *lik winka*. That was revenge enough.

Raytrayen spoke of how she journeyed with *papai* to Ngulchenmaiwen.

That night Pangi sat cross-legged listening to Ñamku, who sounded sad. Astonished he exclaimed, "You *saw*!"

"What happened was very terrible."

These words being like a branching trail, Pangi pondered his direction before saying, "You are right, Ñamku, I do not want to know."

"Revenge is poisoned fruit."

"Yet *you* saw." Pangi was remorseless, asking, "Can the dead close their eyes?"

Silence crackled like a fire.

"*Should* we close them?"

"*Mari, mari, Katrinir*."

"*Mari, mari, Mapuche*."

"What Katrinir means by calling us Mapuche," said Ñamku, "is that he does not believe in revenge." Clearly, the *machi* was irritated.

"How can a *che*...?"

Ñamku interrupted Katrinir, "let violence to a loved one go unpunished? My thought exactly."

"Remember Kalfil," Katrinir suggested.

Ñamku was no more than a wavering glow as his love quietly continued. "You were right to be attracted to him. And I do not mean his beauty. He could have been a healer worthy of your teaching."

"You are being cruel to Pangi, and to me!"

"A *machi* can have more than one apprentice," Katrinir responded sadly. "I do not mean to insult Pangi. I just thought that it was time to speak this truth."

Ñamku was puzzled, belligerent. "What about us? I loved *you*!"

"I know."

Ñamku reconsidered. "Do not blame yourself, Katrinir, for Kalfil. You did not make him *kalku*. You did not *make* him kill you."

"He wanted you too much to share. That led to wrong, but his evil did not make my jealousy right."

"You never told me," Ñamku objected.

"My jealousy changed *you*."

"I was the one who set Kalfil on his path."

Like insects droning in a *ruka*, words wandered through Pangi, seeking escape. He said, "I have always been jealous of him, Ñamku—not Kurufil, I mean, but Kalfil, before he became *kalku*."

"*Mai*," the *machi* replied, mournful, "Still, I had to tell you, so you would know what shaped me. You need to see through my eyes to take my place."

Pangi sighed. "I am still jealous, wanting to be what Kalfil *might* have been. He knew what he wanted. He knew who he was. *That* is what I want, not *what* he wanted."

"Most *che* want too much and do not know what too much is." This was the rueful kindness of Katrinir, scattering blame to the winds.

"They want *kangen*," Ñamku weakly joked.

"Kurufil definitely yearned for something else," Pangi pointed out, somber. "And it led him *piku*."

The last whisper of Katrinir was soft as the rustle of winter leaves. "No need to fight to take the blame. Kurufil was the one who did the yearning. If that led to our revenge, we can forgive ourselves."

And the silence created by his words blew like a steady breeze.

"*Lamngen!*" Raytrayen was gentle, urgent....

"*Mari, mari*," Pangi said—mouth all salt and sand—attempting to focus on his sister. Kneeling, she extended a bowl of *murkeko*. He felt stiff and light, empty as dried reeds.

Taking the offering, he staggered to his feet, spilling a little. With a cry of concern Raytrayen helped him to the fire. Fists propping her chin, she studied him, face freshly painted. Rows of neat white dots ran down the red.

"My ribs are fine," he said smiling, "but sore."

"You have to dress the wound."

"I will after I wash."

"You did not tell us all that happened, *piku*," she accused.

"*Yamai*." Pangi was very cheerful.

Exasperated, Raytrayen shook her head, then went to pull *poñu* from hot ash, sprinkling salt, chopped herbs and *trapi* on them. "I heard you talking to Ñamku," she murmured.

Pangi embraced the subject. "I am happy being who I am, *lamngen*. And I am glad to be with you." He was thinking that—painted—Raytrayen seemed to glow with gentle heat, gleaming hair tossing back the firelight. His sister was very beautiful. She was also, clearly, annoyed.

"You may ask," he argued, "who is this Pangi who is glad to be with you, and I must say I do not know. Maybe he is clothing on a corpse. Maybe he is a skin over an absence, making noises like a drum."

Raytrayen groaned. Living with *machi* was not easy.

He smiled, said he loved her, and went out. Closing his eyes to the sun, he shivered with pleasure at the touch of a breeze. Returning from death was an assault of feeling…. He was flayed. He was a wound in the world. The insides of his eyelids glowed like coals. A *diuka* sang.

Pangi opened his eyes to see Wan looking *piku*. There, smoke clouded the horizon.

Sitting on the cliff edge, having bathed at the stream, Juan was waiting for his hair to dry before he bound it. The morning was warm and hushed. Birds called through haze. Insects murmured like whisperers in a church. *Up here* time was suspended as in enchanted castles. *Down there* Clio was afoot. Somewhere on that expanse, Valdivia—like a living pen—was scripting his eternal self, while on the mountain only the day-to-day existed.

History surveyed a world lit by greatness, but—Juan reasoned—not exactly. On Her Scene, the pen illuminated nobility and excellence alone. And thinking this, he envisioned the world as Clio saw it. The steady glow of Spain and Italy in the far distance, where nothing of true note went unrecorded. Beyond them, the dim Germanies. To the left, the Low Countries flickered with their sudden flares—

wars, Erasmus. By them, the gloom of England ... Thomas More burning like a torch in a shadowy cathedral. As for here—the benighted Indies in which he sat and dried his hair— this vast expanse was lit only by the dying bonfires of Mexico and Peru, erratic sparks shooting into darkness, the most brilliant being Valdivia.

Juan recalled the moment in which the Governor had him write his name for History—*Juan de Cardeña, escribano mayor del juzgado, y mi secretario*—and ... saw smoke to the north. As he lived and loved God, Valdivia!

"*Mari, mari,* Wan."

Pangi blinked at him like an owl, peaceably smiling—though he was gaunt as a fasting saint, his ribs pierced like Christ's. Still smiling, he disappeared over the cliff edge, no doubt to bathe.

In *lolo*, Raytrayen gave Juan breakfast ... spicy! He told her it was delicious, not mentioning the smudge of hope on his horizon, for it brought war.

Eimi rolled off his cot to join them, eating prodigiously, sharing his food with the *degu*. Hair sleek, Pangi returned, wound dressed, announcing that he was going down the mountain.

Sent for water, Juan saw that the smoke had dissipated, and was relieved. Returning, he found Raytrayen sitting outside *lolo*, looking with disgust at a ragged *chiripa*. He sat cross-legged beside her to share the disapproval, knowing how long it took to weave the most modest Indian garment. This loincloth was truly tattered.

"*Wentru!*" she exclaimed, as if that said it all—Going off to war and ruining their clothes! Taking up a needle, she began repairs.

As she was the one to bring up the topic, Juan risked discussing Mapuche manhood. "Is Pangi he, you know, *wentru*? Is he man, you know, or is he ... you know?" Juan was aware of no word in *mapudungun* for what Ñamku apparently had been. And Juan *was* curious, that one who was an abomination in the eyes of God and civilized man should be so revered here—though at the same time somewhat shunned.

She smiled like a cat replete.

Annoyed at her relish in his discomfort, Juan asked baldly, in *castellano*. "Is Pangi a *pato*, as Ñamku was?"

She stared in wide-eyed disbelief and collapsed, convulsed by laughter ... stopping to moan ... only to laugh again.

"Ñamku is a hawk, not a duck."

Then they were laughing together, Juan *seeing* Ñamku as a duck with a black face. White was *perfect* here—far better than for a hawk—which made it funnier.

Paroxysms dying, Raytrayen said that *machi* did not have to be *weye*, but Ñamku once told her that a *domo* lived in every *wentru machi* ... a *wentru* in every *domo machi*.

There was a time when Juan would have dismissed this Indian paradox out of hand, as a rephrasing of evil, for was not a *pato* exactly *that*, a woman somehow living in a man? But today, Juan accorded Raytrayen's words consideration. Was not 'a woman living in a man' a mingling of categories that were holy *ab origine*, as created separate by God? Was not The Creation itself a cascade of separations— beginning with light from dark? What sense did it then make to say, that—in the universe God intended —*in* darkness there was light …or that the Heavens, which He created separate from earth, were *in* it?

Of a sudden Juan realized that he just might be questioning Christ Himself, who was Heaven Come to Earth … then remembered Lobo's version of the cross on which God died, as that place where Heaven and earth intersected.

Calmed, Juan sighed and crossed himself, turning to that later moment of Creation in which woman was separated from man by the taking of a rib. He sighed again at the conundrums there. And with humble curiosity he asked, "What did Ñamku mean by what he said".

"*Weye*," Juan repeated—absorbing the word—asking why Pangi *pretended* to be Ñamku.

Raytrayen went rigid, their communion in laughter vanishing. "That *was* Ñamku," she insisted, her Medusa stare turning Juan to stone.

"Ñamku is *dead*," he dared protest, appalled that Pangi could be possessed by a corpse—or conversely, possess one, which seemed even more evil. Dead, did the *machi* now enter into living men as he once entered into animals while alive?

"How hard is that to understand," Raytrayen challenged, "for one who believes in Keshukrishtu?"

"What!"

"Is Keshukrishtu dead?"

Juan looked to Heaven, source of fire and brimstone, home to The Living God whose name she had taken tremendously in vain. And mispronounced!

"Yes, and no," he sighed, yielding ground on the battlefield of argument. He hoped she would not ask him to explain, knowing that she would.

"Is Keshukristu *kofke*?"

She meant the communion wafer, of course—transformed into the body of Christ—and Juan profoundly regretted that distant day in which he thought to amaze her with the wonders of transubstantiation. For yes, through Indian eyes it made more sense that one man should become another—even dead—than that the corpse of God should resurrect as bread.

Dismayed, Juan transubstantiated transubstantiation in his mind, into a protean *machi* who became other creatures in life, other men in death. And the analogy was clearly diabolic, for it was the Devil that entered into black cats and goats, and possessed men without becoming them, therefore needing to be exorcised. God did not *do* these things. He entered into bread instead, in which form He was taken into man, but … what about the Holy Ghost—that tongue of flame entering the apostles, not making *them* Divine? Nor was God made into them by this penetration. It seemed that God could become dough, yet not another man or animal, Jesus being the exception. Yet, once transformed to man, he then transformed to bread.

Juan was to his eyeballs in quicksands of theological mutation, Raytrayen's question still hanging. Was it heresy to believe that bread remained itself after consecration turned it into God? Vaguely remembering one of Lobo's discussions of apostasy, he muttered 'consubstantiation.'

Raytrayen rested her case with silence, more than a little smug.

Juan was eventually rescued by Eimi, who emerged to play wild melodies on his *pifalka*, more pagan than Pan—that glad, goat-footed god.

The northern glimpse of smoke remained just that, leaving the horizon of Juan's hope blank. History might well be in the making, down below, but on the mountain, time just rolled its heavy wheel.

Juan and Raytrayen were often left alone by Pangi, who one day brought news up to the mountain—there had been a great battle by the Niweketen. Many *weichafe* died. It was said that a *lik winka* died as well. No word about Lautaro, save that he was *piku*, fighting.

Later there were confused accounts of skirmishes. Valdivia marched here, marched there, along rivers, to the coast. Weeks later Pangi reported that *lik winka* were building an enormous fence by the great sea. Tall as two *che*, it held *ruka*.

Juan interpreted this to mean that Valdivia had built a fort at a harbor. And still no word of Lautaro.

This was a somber time upon the mountain, the war below creating internal conflict in those above. For Pangi and Eimi—both attached to the *lik winka*, despite his being born an enemy—this was a minor skirmish of the soul, manifest as occasional embarrassment. In Juan and Raytrayen, however, this was internecine war, as neither could unambiguously desire victory for their people. Nor was the war below something they could wish to vanish, Valdivia miraculously withdrawing, for along with him would go Juan's hopes. This was a prospect Raytrayen knew he dreaded—though he never said so—and in her love for him she also dreaded it. So, to the degree their love was deep, that deeply were they turned against their own.

On the mountain, no news from below was good. And yet one *antu* Pangi brought worse. Mapuche were dying—not just *weichafe*, but *domo*, *pichiche* and the old. Agitated, Pangi said it was the most horrible *kalkutun* you could imagine. He had seen a child die blistered, looking as if she had been slowly roasted.

The pox! Juan was stunned. It was deadlier than a thousand Valdivias, and he was in terror that it would ascend the mountain. Not here! Not Eimi, Pangi ... Raytrayen! He had come to believe this place was made safe through alien magic, yet remembered Father Sosa telling him of the many who sought refuge from the plague in churches, dying dreadful deaths.

Without looking at Wan, Pangi described the horror in a monotone, and when done, challenged him with a look. *Was* this *lik winka kalkutun*?

Spaniards got the pox, just not like Indians. For some reason, to them it was not as fatal. Could Juan say that the pox simply perched upon his kind, like Negrito on Pedro's shoulder? Could he say that they did not have the slightest idea of the nightmare that had come to visit, that this disease—along with others—had totally depopulated Hispaniola, where Columbus first set foot in the Indies, in less than a generation? All he could tell them was that he was sorry—and he truly was. But he said nothing.

Pangi wearily continued. The *machi* who conducted *machitun* were also dying, so that now many were refusing to heal, saying this was a sorcery they did not know. The families of the ill were so desperate they even asked *him* to do *machitun*.

Now the *machi*—and Raytrayen—looked to Juan with wordless pleading.

Merciful God, they expected him to perform miracles! Juan jumped up, shaking his head, ignoring the disillusionment written on Raytrayen's face. They were obscenely wrong to think him a *lik winka machi*. He was not a sorcerer of *any* sort!

Pangi said he was going, anyway. Someone had to try. And he left without another word.

Juan knew the *machi* risked returning with disease gibbering on his shoulder, endangering the life of everyone on the mountain with his courage and innocence. Still, he said nothing. He and Raytrayen hardly spoke, in fact, save that the next morning she told him what Pangi had said in private—that many *che* thought Wan responsible for this *kalkutun* ... but not she, not Pangi.

Gone nine endless days, Pangi stumbled in one evening and collapsed.

"No touch!" Juan cried when Raytrayen leapt up. Looking wildly at her brother, she took a second step.

"*Me!*" Juan yelled, stopping her with the desperation in his voice.

Hand clapped over her mouth, she stifled a scream. Pangi was going into convulsions.

"I *will* take care of this," Juan insisted. "You and Eimi *have* to leave!"

She took another step.

"Now!" he screamed in mortal horror.

She vacillated, swaying.

Pangi jerked and writhed. Covered with a paste of dust and sweat, he looked like he was prematurely mourning his own death.

"I will take the *wekufu* from him," Juan said, and at this promise of the impossible Raytrayen and Eimi backed into the night.

Juan washed Pangi, as much to cool as cleanse him—for he was burning like an ember. Lucid for a moment, he complained through chattering teeth of headache, nausea. Whining like a dog, he returned to his convulsions.

Watching over Pangi that long night, cooling him with water, Juan said Paters and Aves, Credos, until the sanguine humours waned and his patient shivered. Covered with blankets, Pangi slept at last.

Juan found Raytrayen and Eimi awake outside, sitting against the *rewe* under morning light, wrapped in blankets covered with dew. Their shadowed eyes were enormous as they looked up....

"Pangi sleeps," Juan said.

There were conflicting theories about pox. Most thought that—like the plague—it was visited on sinful man by God. Some believed that it was caused by nefast conjunctions of planets. Others said that the Jews—blamed for almost everything—poisoned the wells. Learned physicians, on the other hand, maintained the pox was caused by an imbalance of humours, the excess emerging through the pores, causing the characteristic exsanguination. Then, not a few attributed the pox—and most disease—to the miasmas of the night. In brief, there were myriad theories as to pox, yet Juan had never heard of an actual cure. Of it, you either died or you did not. Almost all Indians did.

Raytrayen stood—real tears smearing painted ones—eyes dull in her red face. And only then did Juan remember Lobo's passing mention of Averroes, who believed that smallpox produced undesirable humors needing to be excreted, which made red, a warming color, the specific for that disease.

Juan told her to paint Eimi's face red, too. Also, he needed what red paint of hers was left.

He found Pangi in convulsions, foaming pink at the mouth, for in his delirium he had bit his tongue. Juan painted his face red—where, as he knew, the rash would first appear. Working steadily through the day, Raytrayen prepared more paint. That night she and Eimi slept outside again. In the morning Juan told her to go down the mountain to a *ruka* where no *che* was sick of *kalkutun*, for he had remembered what Lobo told him of Italian plagues, and how those who could—the wealthy—fled cities for the country. Like the pox, the plague was a curse of crowded places. How ironic, then, that it should visit Indians who had nothing you could even call a village! There was no place to escape *to* in *mapu*, where everyone had 'a place in the country.' Ironic this might be, yet also cause for hope. Still, disease itself caused Mapuche to congregate at *machitun*, which meant that their rite of healing could turn deadly.

He told Raytrayen that—as she valued her life and that of her brother—she would visit no one with *kalkutun*.

She said she would stay with Wispu.

Eimi said that he would go to *renu*, since Chau was gone. He trotted off.

And Juan was left alone with Pangi on the mountain.

The wheel of time ground to a halt in the night that was the cave lit by perpetual flame. And to a large degree, what then transpired went unremembered. Being much the same, memories melded—a confused reality not to be told from nightmare. Juan would doze, dream he was in the cave, and not exactly know when he wakened. Disease came to resemble the eternity of which it was the threshold.

On Pangi's face the pustules swelled, spreading to his chest, more heavily to his arms and legs, and Juan painted them as they appeared. In time much of his skin was bubbling like thick stew. Some pustules burst, releasing foul, yellow pus. Juan washed and painted. With passing days the eruptions turned to cratered scabs. And Pangi's fever waned at about the time the pustules first appeared. This meant that—as if pox were designed as torture—Pangi became aware of the horror that was his body. He felt scalded. The lightest touch was torment. And when he slept he raged.

Juan did not know exactly when the impossible idea was born—that Pangi might survive—perhaps when his dreams became more lucid, thought healing before the body. At any rate one morning Juan dared emerge into the light. Two weeks had passed, he estimated. Pangi was eating solid food and sleeping peacefully. His scabs—almost continuous on his face and hands—were turning into scar.

Juan shaved and bathed. And, thinking that one paid dearly to survive this death, he set off down the mountain.

She was waiting on the path—wide-eyed, fearful, fragile.

Seeing his smile, she leapt into his arms. Embracing, they hopped and whooped, a four-legged child.

"Pangi lives," Juan confirmed, leaving them clasping hands, for to let go or not, to look away or not, seemed equally impossible. She took charge, leading him by the hand in to *chuchu*, saying she had to know.

Wispu was delighted, plump face wrinkled like a raisin by her smile. Hugging Raytrayen, she shyly asked her if the *lik winka* would like food.

They ate *kofke*, *uwa*, and stew, in silence. But, generously as she had extended her hospitality, Wispu could not have the *lik winka* in her *ruka*, especially since her *wentru* had gone to war … although she did not say this of course.

Raytrayen left with Wan.

He did not have the courage to tell her about Pangi's disfigurement, asking her instead how long it had been since she left the cave. She said less than one *kuyen*.

And more than a day, Juan thought, with melancholy derision. She had not counted either, but what Mapuche did? Taking a deep breath he told her that Pangi was fortunate to be alive, and lucky he could see.

"See?" Raytrayen stopped in her tracks, all gladness fled, not fooled.

"Many are blinded by the pox."

Juan blundered on, dragged by the momentum of his plan. "He has scars," he confessed. And those were the last words they exchanged before *lolo*.

Pangi was sitting by the fire, blanket around his shoulders. Raytrayen took a tentative step ... then looked at Juan.

"*Mai*," he said, and she rushed forward to embrace her brother, showing no sign of being affected by his scabs. Turning to Juan, she asked if he could eat—and in truth, the fires of disease had left Pangi a cratered skeleton.

"*Yamai*."

What should Pangi eat?

"Food."

Juan relished her newfound humility. His stature had changed, now that he was a healer—a situation as undeserved as it was disconcerting—and he felt no less happy than deceitful, sitting down to eat.

Pangi grinned toothily at his sister, reminding Juan of a Peruvian mummy.

Next morning he left to find Eimi, with elaborate directions, but one forest path was the brother of every other, the hills and hollows kissing cousins—and there seemed to be a 'large oak' at every fork—so that when at last he reached the Southern Sea he was truly lost. Untroubled, Juan admired the jumble of black rock, pounded by creamy surf. He unbound his hair, exhilarated by the waves and wind, the spray, the blue immensity. And—as here there was only north and south—undiscouraged he walked *willi*, leaping from rock to rock where the shore became precipitous. Then, taking off his sandals, he walked barefoot on the sandy beaches of the coves, hair whipping like a flag. And despite the violence of wind and sea, he was at peace. Being lost was good today. Simple walking was good today. Therefore he walked, and in the end did not find *renu,* or Eimi.

Eimi found *him,* a head sleek as a seal's appearing in the sea, an arm improbably gesturing. Soon he surged powerfully ashore through surf, soaring on crests, swallowed by hollows, at last emerging to stand before him, fingers blue with cold, smiling with the face of a tawny angel.

Juan was led to *renu,* where the entrance yawned like the mouth of Hades in a tumble of baleful stone. Larger and draftier than the mountain cave, *renu* was also far more sinister. Murkier too, walls lost in gloom, despite a shaft of angled light cast by a high aperture that howled with wind. Juan threw on the poncho he had been carrying, squatting to watch Eimi build a fire, and uncomfortably he searched the shadows, for *renu* was vast. Satan and a thousand witches could revel here, invisibly, with all their goats and crazed familiars. Juan shivered with more than cold.

They ate. Then—without a hint of explanation—Eimi handed Juan a lighted torch. And taking several for himself, lighting another, he limped into the bowels of darkness, beckoning.

"*Me!*" Juan cried, surging forward in his fear of abandonment, Eimi's light receding. He trotted to catch up, terrified. Like a huge instrument of torture, the walls and roof closed in, Eimi ambling into a maze. Would they emerge, ever? What if their torches died! Juan broke into a cold sweat, fascinated as a moth by the flicker of his own flame. He cupped it with a hand, protecting it from absent winds.

They came to a larger chamber, where the ceiling exploded into fragments chittering like damned souls, rushing by with a soft flap.

Bats!

Juan dropped his torch, and the primitive thing snuffed out. Aghast, he groped in stony darkness, fearing what he might touch. Finding nothing, he hurried after Eimi's flame, bumping into cold, sharp stone and stumbling, catching up at last.

Eimi handed him a light he lit with his own, and they walked endlessly before stopping at a wall. Juan felt a swell of hope, for surely this was the awful journey's end, But … Eimi disappeared beneath a ledge. Juan followed, more in dread of being left alone than of whatever might come next. Mercifully, the passage was short—though cramped—and soon he stood by his guide, who was elevating his torch. Holding up his own, Juan exclaimed, "Sweet Jesus, crucified!" He rubbed disbelieving eyes … yet the vision did not cease to glitter in the velvet casket of the dark—pagan riches a stunned intelligence could not grasp.

"*Milli,*" Eimi offered. And he began to say more, when part of the treasure moved … and began to crawl toward them!

Juan screamed, scuttling out the chamber, scraping against jagged walls. His torch went black and he pressed on, borne by tides of panic. Fumbling, he felt space over his head and stood, took a blind step….

And only then did he examine memory, to find the terror he had fled—face framed in gold, pustular meat, tears of blood, teeth of ivory….

Something touched his leg.

Juan screamed and leapt away, slamming into rock. He tottered, head floating in a cascade of stars. A brighter glow....

Eimi!

They walked, and to Juan their shadows seemed less created, than held at bay, by light—incorporeal stalking beings that would take on flesh, attacking if their last torch went out. They stopped to listen.

Juan heard it—a soft scrabble.

"Eimi...?" the darkness asked.

"Chau." Eimi's face turned rigid with an inhuman snarl.

The apparition touched their palpitating globe of light with the glitter of a hand, and what had once been Kurufil—shadow in a world of shadows—said, "*Lik winka.*"

His voice was a rattling whisper and his head trembled, gold unsteady in reflected flame. Otherwise he was invisible—black *kepam* in a black cave, black lips, dark pustules on his face, his hands. Kurufil was lost in darkness, only riches casting back the light. Shaking his head, making the gold dance, he shuffled forward.

They threaded the labyrinth backward, Kurufil at the edge of vision, stumbling as toward a mirage of dawn.

The *kalku* fell. "My torches went out," he rasped, sounding strangely apologetic.

"Good," said Eimi.

"I went *piku* to the *lik winka.*"I know. I saw."

Not a sound, save for sandals and bare feet.

"I killed a *lik winka,*" Kurufil wailed.

Eimi spat.

"They took my *milli!*" Demented echoes turned his howl into a cry of multitudes, for they had reached the chamber of the bats, now flitting through torchlight like lost souls.

"*You saw it all!*"

"*Mai,*" Eimi lied.

The *kalku* fell again, and Juan glimpsed an extended hand, all pustules save for the nails, the gold.

Eimi entered a narrow passage.

Juan heard the pursuing word, "*Ko!*" desperately shouted, echoing. Would the *kalku* be entombed alive?

When at last they made it to the fire pit, Eimi asked, "*Lik winka kutran?*"

"*Mai.*" Torchlight was treacherous, yet Juan was certain that the *kalku* had the pox. He shuddered at the memory—of gold embedded in flesh as if in suppurating dough, long hair brutally cropped short. And who knew what the *kepam* concealed...?

Eimi did not respond, simply pouring all the water he could find into the fire. And they closed the boulder door of the cave behind them as they left.

These few hours beneath the earth made Juan think that there are events like caves themselves, containing chambers never visited. What happened to Kurufil, *piku*? How had he escaped? How returned to *renu*? How had Inca treasure made it there?

Juan was in the dark, and not a word did Eimi say about it all on their journey back … or ever. To Raytrayen and Pangi he gave the barest sketch. Kurufil had *lik winka kutran*, and would soon die.

In Wan's absence, Pangi had decided that together they should descend the mountain to replicate the miracle of his healing, and Raytrayen had prepared more red paint. But the *machi* could hardly stand, so that Juan had no difficulty postponing the departure.

He was becoming adept at women's tasks—cooking and weaving mostly—baskets, not cloth. It was amazing how difficult the most primitive task could be.

"If only Lautaro could see you," she said mischievously one evening as Juan was fumbling with reeds that were doing their best not to become a rounded form. He became annoyed, saying in Spanish, "Would you have me make a spear or chip an arrowhead? " It seemed to him that *weichafe* had precious little else to do—when not fighting—other than prepare to fight, or rehearse the fighting of the past. In this they were like Pedros with no interest in indument.

Raytrayen said that she was worried. "Will you and Pangi be safe?"

Juan wondered how she could both talk and weave so well, at once.

Pangi descended the mountain by himself, shouldering a *wima* that included red paint, having decided to prepare the way for Juan with living testimony to his healing.

Left with Raytrayen, Juan explained to her that pox was a kind of fire—that is, it was a *kalkutun* which smoldered whether the victim died or not, a sorcery that could spread to others, as to kindling. To put fires out, one scattered them. Therefore this *kalkutun* had to be scattered too. He added that the fiery nature of pox explained the healing power of red.

Some things he did not tell her. He had toyed with the idea of dressing like the 'beak doctors' of Italy, who ministered to plague in broad-brimmed, flat-crowned hats, a long cloak and a black bird's mask, but decided against. He would feel an imbecile, walking the forest *that* dramatic, even if he could recreate the costume.

One day Pangi returned, reporting that *che* were willing to let the *lik winka* attempt his kind of healing. Some were more desperate than hostile. Many felt that their own *machi* had failed them.

When they walked down the mountain, Pangi commented to Juan that it was too bad he was not on a *kawellu*.

Indeed, thought Juan. He could appreciate how a horse would contribute, not to their art, but to the acceptance of it by Mapuche—although this would be ironic homeopathy. However, this excess of fantasy would only call attention to his failure. He was tempted nonetheless, seeing himself for the first time as a *caballero andante*, peculiar though this incarnation of that ideal might be. Dismounted, unarmed and unarmored in the Indies he might be, but, he *was* errant for the first time with the mission of helping the helpless he encountered, and all this for a lady, in a sense. Not that the analogy did not stumble. He had a squire of sorts, but his 'sword' was paint.

A frightened child ran up … said his mother was dying. They would give the *lik winka machi* two blankets, a *luan, uwa*, if he would perform a *machitun*.

Juan's heart sank at this enormous misplacement of Indian hope, and—this '*alea iacta est*' upon him—he followed the trotting child.

She was on a cot attended by an ancient *domo*. Wild-eyed, trembling—but lucid—she said her name was Paillalafken. She apologized for sending a *pichiche*. Her husband and grown sons were gone.

The pustules on her face had burst, and Juan concluded that she was at the crux—life or death to be decided soon. He said he would do a *machitun* as *lik winka* did, chanting in *likwinkadungun*, while his assistant played the *kultrung*. He would also paint her, to take the *wekufu* from her. The *machitun* would begin immediately, no one to be invited. And Juan concluded with a lie—He would accept no payment, for this was what *lik winka machi* did. Paillalafken accepted, making Juan think that, as *machi*, he could violate both custom and decency, like jesters in courts of old.

He painted her—although he thought extreme unction far more fitting. He chanted parts of High Mass—Pangi improvising on his *kultrung*. However, he did not dance or speak in tongues. And all that evening, and that night, and the following day, Juan washed pustules, painted and prayed, as Pangi played his drum.

When it was clear that Paillalafken would survive, her relatives were summoned. Juan wiped paint from his patient, ceremonially burning the rag. He chanted a Pater, explaining that fire had been returned to fire. When the fire went out, he said, the sorcery was over. And at the *kawiñ* that followed he became insanely drunk.

The news spread so fast that Juan was still hung-over when he began his next cure, after journeying half the day. Hours later, his patient cured him of omnipotence by dying. Juan convinced the family to burn both corpse and *ruka*—

returning fire to fire. The disbelieving crowd might have been less inclined to accept, if not composed of women and children, the infirm, the old.

Juan's adventure would have ended there, except—while failing to cure infallibly—he contained the scourge. Where he did *machitun*, many *che* survived. Where he did not, they died like flies. The Mapuche came to believe that *lik winka kalkutun* was indeed like fire—and spread like fire—taking measures to contain it. Juan's reputation became that of one who could control the flames of sorcery.

For a month Juan performed *likwinkatun*—as *che* called his outlandish ritual— 'healing' only three of sixteen. Yet this huge failure had its small reward, for the Mapuche were beginning to accept him, and he came to realize that as *machi* he had a role that a *lik winka* could play. Respected, not embraced—definitely feared—he was a necessary evil. No one called him *chori* any more.

The day came when he and Pangi had finished a cure and were on their way to *lolo*. Extenuated, they rounded a forest bend....

Weichafe strode up. Painted for war, wearing feathers, puma skins, tooth necklaces, foxtails ... they were bleak and armed. Andalikan stepped forward, glowering....

Juan's gaze was drawn to the tallest warrior.... Millanti! And, at the center of his face, a yawning wound. "Merciful God!" Juan exclaimed, feeling faint. Millanti's nose had been cut off!

The warrior stepped forward, arms extended ... and where his hands had been, were nothing but the scars of cautery.

Juan recoiled as Andalikan confirming what he could not believe. There had been a battle at Penko. The *lik winka* captured many. And Falthifa had their noses and hands cut off ... *epu pataka weichafe*.

"*Me!*"

Juan was unable to believe. Two hundred warriors! A *conquistador* sometimes needed to be cruel, yet never had Valdivia done anything like *this*.

Lifting his spear, Andalikan surged forward, for no one gave a *weichafe* the lie.

Saved by an immediate apology, Juan returned to *lolo*, his days as a *caballero andante* ended.

Chapter 18: *Machitun (Mapu, 1551-1552)*

Clio records that Valdivia built a fort at Penco as a base for his pacification of the South. There—on March 11, of 1550—a battle took place. The Mapuche had been unremittingly hostile, and at dawn they surrounded the garrison, attacking in great numbers. Fifty *caballeros* sallied under the command of Jerónimo de Alderete, wreaking such havoc that they created rout. Horsemen pursued the fleeing Indians, killing many, taking prisoners. Valdivia had the hands and noses of these captives severed.

What Clio notes, she does not always elucidate, but in this case Valdivia defends his actions in a letter to the Emperor....

This was done because I had sent often to summon them and bid them come in peace, telling them for what purpose Your Majesty had sent me to this land, and they had received the message, and had not done as I bade them, and this seemed best to me for fulfilling Your Majesty's commands, and the satisfaction of your royal conscience; and so I sent them away.

Valdivia did not clarify what was different about that bloody day in March. He had not done anything like this before, and by the standards of the time he was not a ruthless man. Possibly his character had suffered—as some historians suggest—absent the gentling influence of Inés de Suárez. Or, since the Mapuche were proving more intransigent than their northern cousins, he may have thought that their extraordinary stubbornness called for extraordinary measures. Or, perhaps, Valdivia simply had a fit of rage and did not know exactly why he did this grisly thing, so that his decision remained sealed as a coffin, even to himself.

In any case, Juan's understanding could not penetrate the cruelty of Penco. As a soldier he was far too familiar with brutality ... with severed hands for that matter—having cut off more than one in battle. What he could not understand about Penco was its deliberate excess. This decision of Valdivia's was something he could not *imagine*, not only as grotesque, but also as unnecessary. Indeed, the 'message' the Governor sent to the Mapuche on that day suggested to Juan that, to Valdivia, the cruelty of conquest had become its own reward.

Brooding on his mountain, Juan became convinced that there was a message here for him as well—carved into Millanti, as it were—for Valdivia's act was needless in the profoundest sense, as serving an unworthy purpose. Call it *pacificación*, or *conquista*, and excuse it as you might—say, the bringing of eternal life to heathens—but Juan found he could no longer accept the dissemination of salvation by force of arms. Then—since rejoining Valdivia would have him take up his own sword—he had to ask himself how he could do so in good conscience. And so it was, that Juan contemplated Valdivia's opaque brutality as a prisoner the blankness of his walls.

However, in defense of Valdivia, History says that the 'message' sent from Penco to the Indians was unique. He spent the next seven months engaged in the more usual cruelties of war, pacifying the region around the fort with enough success that he founded a city he named Concepción, there appointing a *cabildo*, erecting the obligatory 'tree of justice,' distributing land and Indians. When his rear guard was secure—in mid February of 1555—he at last crossed the Bío Bío with one hundred and seventy. In March of that same year, by the banks of the river Cautín, he erected a fort some thirty leagues to the south—La Imperial. And on the fourth of April the Governor went north to Concepción to winter with twenty, leaving the balance of his troops in the more southern fort under the command of Pedro de Villagrán. Then, that spring, the Governor returned to La Imperial with reinforcements—about a hundred—issuing *repartimientos*. In October of 1551 he constructed a fort at Arauco. And in November he marched his pacification south....

These nineteen months that Juan remained out of the eye of Clio on his mountain, Valdivia arrived below, built a fort, and passed him by. This, Juan knew only from the Mapuche—reports which he assumed to be a stew of errors. Time proved him right when Lautaro at last arrived with first hand information, for as the struggle with the *lik winka* moved south the young *weichafe* was brought home again. He sent word of his safe return with Pangi, yet did not walk the path to *lolo* until fall—sometime in May, by Juan's calculations.

Lautaro had only a vague notion of the chronology of Valdivia's progress, since as a Mapuche he had no calendar. Nor could he name the cities founded. However, he retained vivid memories of the many skirmishes—and the several pitched battles—in which he had participated, including Penco.

Knowing the outcome, Juan listened to his account with palpitating heart, awaiting an aftermath which his horror had embellished. He had imagined severed hands and noses piled on long tables—a horrific parody of the excesses of a banquet—or catapulted from the fort as a heavy, bloody rain....

But the reality proved different, Lautaro in no way accounting for what had been cut off. The *weichafe* had been disarmed and taken inside *fucha pele malal*. It was early afternoon when they began to emerge—a long, slow, silent file—the process lasting until the gate was closed at sunset. *Epu pataka mari pura*—two hundred and eighteen—Lautaro concluded, underscoring the scale and horror of

Penco with a precision uncommon in his people. He added with quiet pride that not a cry was heard outside the walls....

Juan felt the burden of Penco personally. Little comfort that Raytrayen cast no blame—that even Pangi did not—for in past months Juan's status had with time insensibly changed ... not only on the mountain, but below. Perhaps this was because he *had* helped—and was still helping—heal Mapuche. Perhaps this reflected his small part of the victory in *palin*. Perhaps this was due to the fact he was no longer *lik* and scarcely *winka*, as he spoke and dressed—acted!—much like *reche*. For whatever reason, Juan's origins had been curiously dissociated from his present being by most Mapuche. They did not consider him one of their own, of course, yet he was somehow not lumped together with those actually warring on them. To Juan this was a bewildering generosity, and it struck him that to these *che* it was as if—through some strange parthenogenesis of the Indies—he had sprung unarmed from the forehead of Lautaro. Not that the process by which Juan lost his past was talked about, or planned. It happened by quiet general accord, as the benevolence of towns will turn a blind eye to congenital abnormalities. The attitude simply grew, in a community that had been deserted by its warriors. And this growing unanimity was perfected by Juan's acquiring a Mapuche name....

Since early in their relationship he had been 'Wan' to Raytrayen, despite the fact that to Lautaro and every other Mapuche he was 'the *lik winka*.' This token of friendliness on her part—casual enough in Santiago—in *mapu* represented her unique solidarity with him. Then, when Lautaro went to war, Eimi and Pangi took to calling him Wan as well—and through the *machi* this name spread. 'The *lik winka*' became 'Wan' to all ... but not for long, as someone thought to add a sound to the incomprehensible *winka* name—so like a moan—making of it Uwan. The invention spread, as resembling the perfectly good word for maize. And it seemed right, for his hair *was* dark gold.

Curiously, when Lautaro returned to *lolo* he had absorbed these transformations. He arrived projecting no hatred, calling him Uwan from the start. And when he recounted battles with the Spanish he did this as if Juan were inoffensive as a fireside bench.

Juan might have been more surprised if Lautaro had not changed in other ways as well. He was now full-grown—perhaps seventeen or eighteen, though with Indians it was hard to tell. And unremitting war had made of him a man. Taller, more muscled, he moved like a forest cat. Head shaved for battle, he was a chilling sight, even unpainted and in repose. Quieter—more serious if possible—he spoke with a new formality that Juan knew to be an echo of Mapuche oratory.

During his absence Raytrayen had changed too—although she still painted her face red—filling her *kepam* more ... and differently. Like her brother, she was quieter, more assured. But she was also easier to be with, less prickly and tart of tongue. And above all—like a stabilized top—she had found a calm center for her spirit, bringing a steady axis to the insane spin of their relationship. Juan was now the one more troubled, more erratic, so that despite the difference in their ages she had ironically taken the role of older sister, dispensing comfort and advice.

The return of Lautaro clouded this precarious harmony, and, like heat lightning, tension crackled in the air. Relations shifted, Raytrayen now treating Lautaro as Mapuche *domo* did their *wentru*—never initiating conversation, serving him first at meals, and so on … Indian courtesies she did not extend to Pangi or to Juan. This irritated him.

Lautaro was irritated also, *because* of Raytrayen. He left his sister a *pichiche* and returned to find a *domo* scandalously living with a *wentru* not related to her. An *antu* had passed since his return and he remained shocked. She was so at ease with Uwan—more so even than with him. And while her new formality was an honor, Lautaro thought there was a trace of mockery in her seriousness. Also, what could that red face mean? He was convinced that it had something to do with Uwan….

Raytrayen was quietly bent over his *makuñ*, making repairs by firelight as Lautaro brooded, studying his sister as he drank *mudai*. How *kume ad* she had become! He could not blame Uwan for being attracted, especially since the fault was his, leaving them unsupervised for *kuyen*. He also could not blame his sister for becoming a *domo*. And he had never expected to be gone so long—that other matter contributing to his gloom—for he was no longer certain that the Mapuche, with all their courage, fighting skills, and overwhelming numbers, could defeat the *lik winka*. Countless brave *weichafe* had died already. And enemy reinforcements kept arriving….

Had Raytrayen just smiled at Uwan? Or was it fire-cast shadow? Uwan did not seem to notice, carving his *wutru*.

He was *too* intent on that spoon, Lautaro thought, with anger.

The knife Uwan was using glittered bright as mica in the sun. How perfect *lik winka* weapons were! Yet it seemed to Lautaro that the blade looked out of place in the dark hands of Uwan, who was wearing a *makuñ* and making a *wutru*, *trarilongko* binding his long hair. Lautaro could not deny it—Uwan now was in many ways *che*. This he had not expected on his return. He had feared he would corrupt Raytrayen. Instead, she seemed more Mapuche than when he left, and not a word of *likwinkadungun* had he heard from her. Lautaro was confused. Worse, he was beginning to like Uwan. He could even understand how Raytrayen might be attracted—not physically of course, for his face and nose were long and hideous. Still, he appreciated how she could admire him as a *wentru*. Lautaro knew his courage, his fighting skill. He had also been true to his word, remaining in a captivity he hated and could escape. *And,* he had saved the life of Pangi and others from *lik winka kalkutun.*

Lautaro did not like liking the *lik winka.* He did not admire his admiration for him, either. Nor was he grateful for all the gratitude thrust upon him by this enemy. Consequently, it had become difficult for him to like, or admire, himself. Because of Uwan he was at war with *kume mognen,* and this absolutely had to stop.

Downing the last of his *mudai,* Lautaro lurched over to rummage in a corner, returning to light a torch at the fire. "*Pulluuyu,* Uwan," he grunted, striding out.

Surprised, Juan rose unsteadily to his feet. Where could they be going now, at night?

Raytrayen smiled and handed over an unlit torch.

Lautaro strode, whirling his brand, Juan hurrying after. In a cocoon of inconstant light, they walked the path along the mountain stream where they all bathed. Passing that familiar spot—and eventually the bend where Juan first made *funa poñu* with Raytrayen—they arrived at a pool where the water was deep, sliding by like black silk. Removing his *chiripa,* Lautaro waded in, slow as herons, torch held high. His hand darted in … pulled out a fish. Glittering, the bright creature flung quicksilver drops through torchlight. Grinning, Lautaro waded back.

Kauki, Lautaro called his catch, which resembled mackerel. And after dropping several into a sack, he lit Juan's torch.

Yet try as he might, Juan failed at fishing with his hands. Attracted by his flame, the gleaming *kauki* surged like living steel, and he touched—yet could not grasp— the darting things. All the while Lautaro's hand—a heron's beak—shot in, and out with prey, until his torch went dark and the sack heaving on the shore was full.

They put on their clothes—such as they were—Lautaro studying the bright firmament above them.

The sack convulsed … went still, Juan thinking it a good thing fish died in silence. He wondered if they suffered and feared death, deciding that they did. Otherwise, why struggle? And he wondered why, if God gave them the ability to suffer and die, He did not give them voices.

"I never should have captured you," Lautaro said quietly enough—adding that he had wanted a *kawellu* and Juan became a part of that. But the *kawellu* was dead. Two harvest *kuyen* had passed, and the *lik winka* were not defeated. This war would be very long, very hard, and very bloody.

"*Yamai.*" No harm in agreeing to the undeniable.

"Where did *lik winka* come from?"

"España." And Juan explained, "*Kamapu piku.*" Far north, indeed.

Not to confound Spain with Peru, he tried to say they came from farther than far north—the other side of a great, salt sea. Not the great sea of *mapu* either.

Ignoring Juan's paragraph, Lautaro simply stated, "You *lik winka* will never leave."

To that, Juan had nothing to say.

"Maybe we can force you back to Tiako."

Juan shrugged under cloak of darkness, thinking *'buena suerte.'* Not even rebel Spaniards had defeated Valdivia, and they had cannons, horse and armor.

Sensing the depth of his disbelief, Lautaro grew aggressive. "*Lik winka* are not good at *everything.*"

Juan scarcely needed to be told *that*, after his failure in fishing with bare hands. As he suspected, he had been brought here for a lesson in humiliation.

"What *lik winka* do, they do well, yet there is much they do not do themselves. I saw this in Tiako. Slaves cook and clean for them, hunt and garden for them, care for their *kawellu*. Slaves do everything but lie on their women and go to war for them. They are like those ants with enormous jaws that only fight, as their smaller brothers labor."

There was some justice in Lautaro's analogy, Juan supposed—though he did not know these ants he spoke of. However, did any of this increase the chance of Mapuche victory, if fighting was what the Spanish did better than even civilized armies?

"*Lik winka* do not know *mapu*. You build walls, roofs and fences to keep *mapu* out. Your slaves touch *mapu* and its creatures for you. Your *kawellu* walk *mapu* for you. Your *trewa* kill enemies for you. You are powerful in your *wethakelu*, yet in them you cannot touch your enemies. Therefore, in your strength is weakness."

Juan thought that *here* was at least one *lik winka* 'touching' *mapu* in the middle of a forest, in the middle of the night, half naked in miasmas without the benefit of a torch. He at least was deep in Lautaro's precious *mapu* with a casualness that would have been unthinkable scant years ago. It made him sad to be at home in wilderness.

"*Mapu* will defeat the *lik winka*."

Lautaro rose to his feet as for a culminating point. And standing beneath starlight, he said, "I would not want to be *lik winka* even if I could, for without *mapu* I would die. Without *mapu* I would not *want* to live."

Juan rose as well—the lesson seeming over.

But Lautaro was not done. "Falthifa spoke to the *toki* at the Fio Fio. I was there. He said that he came in peace and that he wanted us to be at peace. He also said his *longko* would be our *longko*. He said he came to give us your *pillañ*."

"I know—the *requerimiento*."

Lautro harshly laughed. "We have *longko* of our own, *pillañ* of our own."

Then he accused. "I have been to Tiako and seen what the Pikunche exchanged for peace, *lik winka*. Ñamku sent me there to learn what you are like, and now that I know, I prefer death to peace in slavery."

Juan recoiled, at the hate and venom in Lautaro's voice.

"I told the *toki* of the Mapuche that I was a slave in Tiako until I escaped, taking you and the *kawellu*. I told them that the Pikunche, their *wentru*, their *domo*, their *pichiche*, are slaves—those few that survived *lik winka* sorcery. I told the *toki* that the Mapuche will be also become their slaves if they make peace. I told the *toki* this, and they listened.

You can tell Falthifa this yourself, *lik winka*—The Mapuche would rather die than become his slaves. You can tell Falthifa this as well—We do not want, and will not have your *longko*, your *pillañ*. You can tell him he can kill so many *weichafe* that he cannot count them, and this will make no difference. You can tell him that he can cut off our hands and noses, and this will make no difference. You can tell him that he can rape our *domo*, and this will make no difference. You can tell him that even if he kills our *pichiche*, this will make no difference, for the Mapuche will not be his slaves. You can tell him that if he kills us all, our souls will haunt him in the *mapu* taken from us. You can tell Falthifa that the Mapuche will fight him, and that fighting, we may all die, but that he will never make us slaves."

Then reaching down to lift the sack full of fish, Lautro added, calmly now, "I have decided to trade you for a *kawellu*." And delivered of that cold enormity, he strode away.

Next morning he left, saying that he would be with Andalikan, adding that he desired Raytrayen and Uwan to follow him as soon as they could. Wispu would be happy to take Raytrayen in. Uwan could stay in his own *ruka*.

At some moment Juan had discovered that—although he did not actually *relish* rotten raw potato—the shocking stuff was palatable, as bland. And on the evening of Lautaro's departure he found himself eating the mealy stuff with Raytrayen. They had gone out to admire the wondrous shimmer of the sky that Lobo called the *aurora australis*. Pangi was gone, as someone suspecting sorcery done to his fields. And, since Eimi slept, they were alone.

"*Funa poñu?*"

Juan's attention wandered from the crescent moon above the sea—honed sharp as a Moorish scimitar.

"Ugh!" he said, taking another.

Not rising to that worn lure, she commented, neutral, "Lautaro has changed."

"A *weichafe!*"

"More than that ... a *longko*. "

"So young!"

She shrugged beneath the pale fires of the sky. "*Longko* listen to him."

Juan recalled that Alexander the Great died at the age of thirty-three, having conquered the known world. Lautaro was what … eighteen?

"Uwan?"

Backlit by unearthly ripples of the heavens—seas of light over a lightless sea—her face was a gray oval in which the chalk of painted tears glowed, as if with the light of corposants. Her intensity radiated like unnamed heat.

"*No estás contento aquí.*" Her low voice was firm.

He told her about his ransom.

Barely audible, she replied that this would be good for him, looking out into that distance where obscurity wed night and sea.

She was a disembodied voice—the speaking dark—and for mad moments Juan recalled the oracle at Delphi.

Without entering into explanations he said to her that he did not want to rejoin Valdivia. Not now. Not really.

"*Vete a Santiago, pues.*"

These past days they had been speaking *mapudungun*, and momentarily she had enchanted Juan by reverting to his mother tongue, in the charming lilt of a Mapuche *domo*. So beguiling was Raytrayen, in fact, that he had drawn a long, long breath, before he realized the implications of her suggestion. He could go north to be a secretary of a pacified place, in no way militant. He would be a simple man of contemplation, a monk in his *scriptorium*…. "I will!" he exclaimed, leaping to his feet, prepared to soar north on the wings of the instant.

"First, the horse," Raytrayen commented. "Watch out for the cliff," she warned.

That simply, Juan's future left the wilderness. At peace, he saw the *aurora* vanish, blotted by cloud. And a chill wind slid up the mountain, bringing slow, fine rain.

He followed Raytrayen into the cave, insisting to himself that this weather was *not* an omen, Fortuna being too aware of his total unimportance. The winter rains of *mapu* were simply here to stay. War would go on furlough. It would be too wet for the matchlocks and too wet to march, or the feet of the *infantes* would rot in their boots, the horses mire. Valdivia would hole up in some fort of his creation, drinking and gambling until the time came to fight.

"*Buenas noches*, Uwan."

Some imp in Juan—irked that she had spoken first … again!—asked Raytrayen why she no longer spoke first to Lautaro, when she did to *him*, the perverse sprite whispering that this was disrespect.…

"*Y quién quisieras que yo fuera?*"

Who, indeed, would he have Raytrayen be? And—he marveled—her subjunctive was no less perfect than her pronunciation!

She confronted him arms akimbo, reminding him that there was a slender waist—and not so slender hips—beneath the hang of Indian sack.

"*Nada más que tú.*"

She shook her head with fond forbearance at this insistence that she be herself—as to one not yet mature enough to disabuse of fictions told the young.

Juan returned her *buenas noches* thinking that—*mutatis mutandis*—Raytrayen sometimes *was* Inés. Uncanny....

Maybe all wonderful women were—in some deep place—alike.

A day was spent in preparation. And laden like peddler's donkeys, they set out the following morning through fog, wearing layered wool. *Pukem* was upon them, and all that chill day they walked through intermittent rain. Then, once at the *ruka* of Andalikan, they discovered that he and Lautaro—all the *wentru* for that matter—were gone. Wispu said they left for *fucha lafken*, to the *fucha pele malal*.

She was the only one to greet them—Liftuipani making a point of not emerging from her *ruka*.

Juan and Raytrayen were welcomed into Wispu's tiny dwelling, where she managed to ignore his presence. They sat—the weary visitors—clothes soaked, steaming in the fire's heat little less than the soup in the pot before them. This was no weather for fighting, Wispu commented into the air, ladling into bowls. The *wentru* would soon return, she hoped. She asked Raytrayen if Uwan might like some of this poor soup....

To be invisible as ghosts was disconcerting, yet Juan was grateful at the offered bowl—the first, as was his warrior's due. However—not to abuse hospitality—he ate hastily and left, asking Raytrayen to thank her.

He found that his *ruka* had survived more or less sound, but was fireless, musty. And the roof leaked—not badly—Juan wrapping himself in a blanket beneath the drip. But he had help thatching next day, for Pangi arriving while Juan was wondering what to do. And together they amicably labored to turn the abandoned place into a home. Roof repaired, they stacked wood, liberated the spring of its debris, rid the clearing of emergent forest....

One day Pangi returned from a *machitun* bearing a basket of squawking chickens. Two dogs trotted by his side—these omnipresent guardians, tolerated and unloved. They built a shelter for them, another for the chickens. The *machi* walled off a corner, where he kept what he needed for his secretive profession. There he slept and meditated. He also built his first *rewe*, hewing steps into a log, erecting it at a slant outside the *ruka* door, where it faced the rising sun like the bowsprit of a buried ship. A human face was carved into the apex, and it was adorned with branches of *foike*—that tree sacred to the Mapuche. Precariously balanced—Pangi climbed it to pray at sunrise, without fail.

Not a *kuyen* had passed when, furtive, Eimi hobbled in the door one evening. He had been to *renu* and not found the corpse of Kurufil. Maybe the *kalku* had wandered into a remote passage to die, maybe survived by sorcery, or turned into a bat. But dead or alive, *che* or bat, You feared that Chau would steal his soul, so he had been living in the woods. Juan and Pangi took him in, despite the risk. Eimi could always hide in Pangi's alcove if visitors surprised them.

Raytrayen and Wispu came from time to time—not often or for long—always during the day, always together. As a married woman Wispu's reputation was at stake, despite her age. In Raytrayen's case, *admapu* would not so much forbid, as misinterpret, her familiarity with the *lik winka*, assuming a relationship that was not there. Uwan could be considered one adopted into the 'family' of Ñamku, a kind of cousin in a household that evaded category—and as a *lik winka* he evaded most classification on his own—but whatever else he might be, Uwan was *wentru*. They were no longer on the mountain, and *admapu* was pitiless here below.

Left to his devices, Juan slept or simply dozed in his cot under murmuring rain. Sometimes he read—rarely and with little pleasure, for **Amadís** had become too remote for his fantasy to travel the huge geographies of mind involved. Sometimes—draped in sodden wool—he wandered muddy forest paths, alone in the perpetual twilight of these winter days, until his feet puckered like prunes. He attempted failed conversations with Eimi from time to time, the *ifunche* no less taciturn than cheerful—like an exclamation point without its sentence. And Pangi was almost never there. Success had made him very busy indeed, for many *machi* had died of *lik winka kalkutun*.

This reverse of fortune was a blessing in its way, as Pangi provided for them all. He would return with *makuñ*, baskets, spoons, and bowls. He brought Raytrayen a small loom and wool. He provided smoked fish and *loko*, dried *poñu*, *uwa*, salt and more … all this when *che* were starving.

Winter always emptied Mapuche stomachs. However, privation threatened earlier this year, more brutally. The *weichafe* had been gone two growing seasons, leaving the fields untended. Many *che* had abandoned *ruka* close to *fucha pele malal*, where the *lik winka* killed the men or took them as slaves, and stole their *domo* and their crops. Those displaced moved inland, arriving only with what they could carry, to be taken in by relatives—for Mapuche took pride in their hospitality—and in these *ruka* more *che* were now eating what little food there was. Refugees with no kin built rough shelters in the woods, fending for themselves. The cold *kuyen* had scarcely begun, yet many *che* faced starvation. *Weda antu*—the 'bad days' before the first green sprouts of spring—were here far too early, as the *weichafe* still alive came straggling back from war.…

Lautaro was with them, reporting to Juan that that Falthifa was *kamapu willi*.

The exchange for the *kawellu* could not take place. With an unreadable expression, he added that Mapuche would have to learn to live with war as with a mother-in-law. Grim—but chuckling—he left to hunt.

Ransom postponed, a wet and hungry winter loomed, Juan often finding himself alone with Eimi—that cheerful cipher. Pangi was seldom around, as the damp of *pukem*, the privation, the over-crowded dwellings, had brought disease to the Mapuche. So, sadly, the *machi* had more employment than he could cope with. Raytrayen and Eimi helped, preparing potions, salves and infusions according to his directions, as well as other less medicinal preparations—love potions and abortifacients, for life went on. But he still had no one to assist him at *machitun*, no *dugulmachin*—or helper—and one day he asked Uwan to do this for him.

Juan instantly refused. He knew no chants, and did not begin to understand the complicated ceremony. Above all, he would not be able to recall the words of Pangi when in ecstasy he spoke in tongues. How could he, when he struggled with the simplest *mapudungun*?

Pangi countered that assisting was more a matter of spirit than of language. This was a communication of souls. As a *machi* Uwan would understand the meaning beyond the words. He would *see* what he said, Pangi insisted, full of faith.

But no, Juan would not participate in this farce—a heathen one at that, which might well damn his soul. He would continue as he had, presiding over *lik winka* disease only, leaving native maladies and sorceries to Pangi. He was adamant. Yet all his sound objections and rejections came to nothing when Kurui—beloved daughter of Andalikan and future wife of Pichikan—was stricken by *kalkutun*....

When Andalikan had returned from war, Liftuipani attempted to convince him to kill Uwan as a *lik winka* and sorcerer. Infuriated when he refused, she left for the *ruka* of her father. With her went Kurui, for even though her daughter was full-grown, as unmarried she had no real voice in her affairs. Delighted to have Liftuipani gone, Andalikan did nothing to oppose her, although he missed his cherished daughter.

And ironically, it was at the *ruka* of the father of Liftuipani—far from the *lik winka*—that Kurui began to shake and burn. Learning of this, Andalikan brought his daughter home. He knew this was not *chafo* his daughter had—that cough common in cold moons. Nor was it *aling*—a fever caused by emerging into sunshine in the winter. Clearly, this was a far more deadly sorcery. Andalikan, his brothers, and Pichikan conferred. They needed to summon a *machi*, but which one...?

Juan invited them in, wondering what this solemn invasion meant. Not having seen his teammates in *palin* for over a year, he was prepared for long Mapuche salutations, but Andalikan cut them short, saying that Kurui was dying of sorcery, and they had come to request a *machitun*. Sadly, he was convinced that his wife, Liftuipani, had done this terrible thing to her daughter—of whom she had always been jealous. And she was angry with him at the moment, also. Therefore he requested that Pangi preside at a *machitun* for Kurui to remove the *wekufu* from his daughter and determine who was responsible for the sorcery. He concluded by saying that Pichikan would also speak.

The *weichafe* stepped forward—seeming to fill the interior with his shoulders—saying that in his opinion Kurui was not suffering from Mapuche *kalkutun*, and did not need a Mapuche *machi*. She was the victim of some kind of *lik winka* sorcery instead, and Uwan should be in charge.

Andalikan then said that since he and Pichikan did not agree—and Kurui was dying—they had decided to ask both *machi* to examine her.

Pangi and Juan left as soon as they had gathered up the paraphernalia of their healing arts.

Andalikan's brothers and their wives, as well as *pu kineche* who lived near—more men than women—were already crowded in the *ruka*. Kurui was barely conscious, tossing on a blanket on the floor, delirious, perspiring. Moaning—*Are, are!*—she was ineffectually tearing at her clothes.

Wispu sat beside her—wrinkled old face contorted with anguish—holding the wandering hands of her daughter, crooning what sounded like a lullaby. And Raytrayen knelt by Kurui's head, wiping her face with a wad of moss dipped in cold water. It seemed to Juan that every relative that could fit was crammed into this space without window. The overcrowded *ruka* was silent, stifling, smelling of smoke, ripe urine and wet wool. Juan noticed that the *weichafe* were unarmed, but some bore *palin* sticks—a sign of future mourning, he supposed … therefore not of confidence.

Pangi knelt beside Kurui, asking Andalikan how long she had been sick.

"*Kula antu.*" Sometimes she shivered from cold, he added.

Juan had seen ague before—that disease in which the sanguine and lymphatic humours went to mad extremes, at war. But all he knew about a cure was what Inés had told him—Bleed a fever, feed a chill.

"*Escalofríos,*" he murmured, for Kurui had begun to shiver.

The word created an awed hush, every Indian eye turning to the *lik winka* … speaking in tongues already. And under the weight of their attention Juan shrank into himself, wanting to laugh hysterically. How could he go through with this?

Pangi took over. He and Uwan needed to examine Kurui, he said. Everyone should leave except for Wispu and Andalikan.

All filed out the door—Juan observing Raytrayen's exit with regret. Then he looked down, and saw Wispu undressing Kurui. Her breasts were bare already! He ripped his eyes away.

Andalikan was contemplating him strangely—not because his daughter was being peeled like a peach before a stranger, Juan imagined, but because he, the *machi*, was *not* scrutinizing her nudity. He was *supposed* to be studying the beautiful Kurui closely—So help him God!—when the only woman he ever saw naked was a whore. And, as the Crucified Christ was his witness, that solitary time he never dreamed of scrutiny below the navel, her breasts being as much sin as he could handle.

Eyelids trembling in their effort not to close, Juan looked down again. Kurui was nude now, moaning as Pangi examined her from the head on down, lifting her eyelids, looking in her mouth, her nose! What would he *not* peer into next! Panting with panic, Juan saw the *machi* slowly make his way down the body glistening with perspiration. He paused at the navel, studying the involutions as if they were an enigmatic text, and moved on to what, for Juan, was *terra incognita*....

When the final revelation came, Pangi did not have to spread Kurui's legs, as they parted with the oblivious lewdness of delirium. And so it was that Juan finally witnessed that unknown to which Liliana's hand had led his lower self. Trembling, he made the sign of the cross.

Appreciating this ritual act, Andalikan quietly exhaled.

Pangi stood, for Juan's turn had come.

Kurui softly moaned.

Juan moaned as well.

Kurui moaned again, arching her back.

Then, through some miracle, the power of motion was granted Juan. He knelt, took his crucifix, and held it over the body of temptation. Closing his eyes he prayed that the demon of lust be taken from him, prayed not to remember the vision moaning naked in his memory, prayed to Saint Anthony—tempted anchorite—prayed until his arms were trembling of their own extended weight ... Kurui stretched out nude beneath his cross, her elemental mystery a pink, unopened flower in damp moss....

Shaking with the effort not to see what he was seeing, Juan opened his eyes to find that Kurui—unclothed in memory—was clothed again, and a question was in every troubled Mapuche eye regarding him. What kind of inspection *had* his been, eyes squeezed shut? Forestalling, Juan told them that—in vision—he had summoned his *pillañ*, Saint Anthony, to do the examination for him.

The Mapuche sighed, in their relief.

Pangi whispered that he had found no obvious sign of *kalkutun*.

Juan whispered back that he thought Kurui had the ague. But was it a Spanish or Mapuche ague? Did Mapuche get ague, at all?

Kalofio? Pangi shrugged. He never saw *kalkutun* like this before, yet that meant little, inexperienced as he was. And he had no notion of what *kalofio* meant, so it might well *be* what Kurui suffered from. He asked Uwan—Was this *lik winka kalkutun?*

Juan did not know, suspecting not. Sorcery existed in Spain no less than here—though in civilization it was less common—yet he profoundly doubted that Hispanic black arts had caused this illness. Seeing that they were getting nowhere, with a mutual nod, Pangi and Juan united their ignorance and leapt into the unknown, saying that they would both perform the *machitun.*

Relatives filed in, commenting in hushed voices. Pangi placed a branch of *foike* by Kurui's head, and a branch of a plant not familiar to Juan by her feet. Beside her he placed bowls holding twigs. He asked what Kurui had been given for her fever.

Killai he was told—just the juice of the crushed leaves. Nodding his approval, Pangi readied his medicine. He handed a bowl to Juan, saying Kurui had to drink it all.

Kneeling, Juan tilted her head back, and found it hot as hearthstones. He brushed strands of hair aside, poured between swollen, parted lips. Kurui was rosy, gleaming with perspiration, panting, eyes rolled back. She moaned … moaned again. Her illness mimicked every sign of lust Juan knew! Praying to Saint Anthony, he backed away, as from the queen of Sheba in revealing veils.

Juan planned what to do when his turn came. Red paint was out, as Kurui did not have the pox, and he did not think red a specific for the ague. Otherwise, he had the crucifix—already used—and his knife. He could bleed her fever, if only he knew how….

After considering—and rejecting—a plaster of warm guts, he decided that he could no more heal Kurui than he could banish her nudity from his memory. Profoundly relieved that he was useless, Juan prayed. Pangi would have to save her.

Into a bowl the *machi* poured brown syrup, green matter, and … the liquid contents of a Mapuche chamber pot! Juan gagged as Pangi deeply drank of the obscene decoction, offering him what remained.

"Leper's piss," Juan murmured—Pedro's worst insult for bad wine. Panicking, he stared into the stinking amber tea, which was cloudy with God knew what. Gagging, he lifted the pagan chalice and closed his eyes. He drank, praying he not throw up….

History did not witness the answer to Juan's prayer. Nor did the cosmos—which remarked with gravity upon the death of Christ—comment on his sacrifice in this land of casual earthquake. Mapuche eyes themselves—once Juan had opened his—seemed to approve, yet they could not peer into his awful depths. To them this was an ordinary thing, common as a sacrament in Spain. How could they plumb his abhorrence—both physical and metaphysical?

"What have I *done*?" he said out loud.

"Ya, ya, YAI!" the *ruka* roared, frightening evil spirits with pandemonium.

"Ya, ya, YAI!" the *ruka* roared again.

Deafened, nauseous, disoriented, Juan saw the *machi* beating his *kultrung*, discordantly singing, this barbaric plain chant accompanied by pounding that went on … and on….

The tempo eventually increased. The spectators danced, women swinging burning sticks.

The *machi* leapt over Kurui's prone form—back and forth, back and forth—beating his *kultrung*, chanting until night fell, the fire pit casting infernal shadows on the walls. The air was rancid, smoky, and Juan was smothering, drenched in sweat. Like spinning fireflies, bright spots swam in the smoke-clotted atmosphere—sinuous as desert air. And every shadow undulated, as if the overheated scene were underwater.

Pangi undressed Kurui a second time, ringing her naked form—which glistened like a wave-washed stone—with twigs he took from bowls.

The *ruka* spun. The floor trembled as with earthquake. And now Juan was on his knees, afire, his skull a heated, hollow thing. Like Kurui, he panted. Like the shadows in the *ruka,* he swayed, flower on the dancing floor … floating … soaring now, a wind-borne seed. And freed of his body's husk he hovered, burning over Kurui's head. He was a Pentecostal flame.

"Ya, ya, YAI!"

Juan opened his eyes. The *ruka* was larger, dim and vaulted, crowded. But the *che* had shrunk to dwarfs clashing sticks that—like the staff of Moses multiplied—turned to writhing snakes.

"Ya, ya, YAI!"

By the fire, the *machi* danced, as shadows swarmed the walls. Chanting, he walked on coals, then immersed his arm in fire to the elbows, so that his fingers kindled. He picked up coals, scattering them on the floor … then on Kurui, where like tiny suns they glowed on the night of her *kepam.*

"Ya, ya, YAI!"

Like Pangi, Juan was burning and unburned, the *ruka* looking at him with its many flaming eyes, and he walked on burning water toward the woman moaning on the floor, blind….

He was blind. No matter, for he was a Pentecostal eye, disembodied as the moon.

Then he was a Pentecostal moon, seeing his mortal body from above—eyes closed, hair bright, drenched in sweat.

The moon saw Juan take his knife by the blade—damascene wavering like water, upright as a crucifix.

The *ruka* roared. And the roar faded....

High, faint, remote, Juan heard his name as he floated out the smoke hole, and he drifted into clouds disturbed by thunder from a distance, as when summer storms recede.

"Juan de Cardeña," an irritated voice called out, again.

"Saint Anthony!" Juan exclaimed. "Thank you for answering my prayer," he amended humbly—wondering if genuflection was appropriate in a place without a floor....

He was answered by a dismissive grunt.

"My pig," the saint apologized. "Like a third leg, he goes with me everywhere."

"What!" Surely not to Heaven, Juan thought, startled by the notion of a pig in glory.

"This is not Heaven," Saint Anthony corrected. "I have descended very far indeed. This pig is just my symbol, as you know."

"No ... yes." Juan was bewildered.

The saint explained. "He represents lust of every sort—my specialty as a saint. I call him 'Sin,' because he is exactly *that*, yanked out to where I can put a ring through his nose."

Sin squealed defiance, with disconcerting human overtones.

Ignoring him, Saint Anthony reproved Juan, saying, "You prayed to the wrong saint."

This annoyed Juan. "You *answered* my prayer! Kurui was naked and I did not feel temptation, though I saw *everything*!"

"Sometimes you get what you need without praying."

"You mean, without the help of Heaven, I still felt no lust!"

"Correct. What you are doing without my help—as you so naively state—is growing up, despite yourself."

Juan did not appreciate hearing *that*. It seemed to him that Heaven was belittling his fervent prayer. Pedro would definitely have felt lust in his place, and he would not have prayed not to feel it either!

Sin snorted in derision from on high, departing with St. Anthony.

"Sometimes you can pray for the wrong thing." This was another voice, wise and kind, sounding like a far more tranquil Lobo. Birds harmoniously warbled.

"Saint Francis of Assisi!" Juan welcomed.

"You are wondering why I have come, Juan, as you did not pray to me. But think about what is happening, to you and to Kurui. Think of what you feel." The voice reminded Juan he never had a mother....

He confessed. "It did not matter that Kurui was beautiful and naked. What mattered was her dying."

Saint Francis was silent, though a mourning dove hoo-hooed, much like a mellow Inca flute.

"A child of God is dying." Juan repeated—now thinking like a saint. And, clear eyed, he faced his fears. "I am in terror that she will die," he said to gentle Saint Francis of Assisi, "because of *me*. I am no physician. What I am is a *fraud*. Her life is in my hands, and I don't begin to know what to do."

The saint sympathized. "Knowing little is the human lot."

"Help me, please!"

"I am no sawbones, either."

"But her life is not ultimately in my hands," Juan said, thinking like a saint again ... and a melodious chorus approved.

More comfortable now, Juan confided, "You know, for some reason I felt that illness had turned Kurui into the incarnation of lust. She reminded me of the queen of Sheba tempting Saint Anthony. Now, I think she is more like your birds."

"Innocent, and rendered yet more innocent by delirium, a beautiful child of God," the saint concurred—yet with that rising tone that asks for more.

"I wanted Kurui to *deserve* to die," Juan whispered in awed repugnance of himself. "I wanted her to be sinful, so I could blame *her* both for her death and my lust ... when all the guilt was mine."

Saint Francis was unwavering. "You were beside yourself—of four minds, when Heaven last lost count. The important thing is listening to the inner voice which summoned me."

"You came to save me from myself!"

"You are not listening, Juan. I came to have you *listen* to yourself. Neither God, nor the saints, nor the angels in Heaven, can instill virtue in a man. Right impulse lives in you, or it does not. We are but midwives to your good."

At that, it all came clear for Juan. "What I thought lust was what Lobo calls *caritas*. I did not covet Kurui because I was in love with her as innocent. And loving her innocence as one might that of the tiny creatures of the woods and fields, I feared her death. "

Thrushes sang angelically.

"Yes, my son, but are you not saying that some evil part of you prayed not to be involved ... or to love? Have you thought to ask yourself why you feared love, as innocent, in the first place?"

"Not until now. In her illness Kurui is like one of your songbirds. However, she is also a beautiful woman ... though Indian." And having said that, Juan felt the bewildering satisfaction you get by taking a knife tip and cutting out a tick fat with your blood. "As if lust—not love—was all I could feel for a Mapuche," he concluded. "You know, I would not have thought a *domo* like her beautiful, short years ago."

Reflecting on what he had just said, Juan commented. "I think that you would like Lleflai."

A *loika* sang assent.

Saint Francis said, "One thing at a time. Perhaps you might introduce us in the future. We could share the songs of birds we do not know."

Juan hardly heard, mind having wandered off. "Drinking that awful stuff Pangi gave me was the hardest thing!" He shuddered at the memory, yet pride was stirring in him.

"You drank Indian piss as an act of love," the saint conceded mildly. "But, child, the fears that brought you here are keeping you from returning."

Invoked, dread flooded back. Decision also. "I will return to the *ruka* and pray for Kurui."

"Pray indeed … but also bleed this child of God. The Almighty is not about to hold your knife."

The gentle voice faded—the singing birds as well—floating into altitudes….

"I will," Juan promised Heaven, feeling himself sinking through cloud with a slowness that reminded him of grain in honey. The glow that was the smoke hole grew, below … then clouds and flashing lights rushed by. A fiery furnace swallowed him … exploded … spat him out

Floating above himself, Juan was again a Pentecostal eye, seeing himself kneeling by Kurui, knife poised, hair a white flame in the darkness of the *ruka*, surrounded by glittering eyes.

Then as if will were air, Juan breathed himself into himself, seeing with eyes of flesh his own dark hands, dark legs, black *chiripa*. My hair—which I do not see—is bright, he thought, while the eyes I see my darkness with are light. The eyes making me *lik winka* cannot see themselves. In this there was a paradox—or parable—he could not linger to examine.

And swaying with a weariness that moved him like the sea, he let the knife sink of its own weight….

"What happened? Where am I? How is Kurui?"

Juan was prone on some wonderfully unmoved thing, hearing his questions as he asked them….

His lips were numb. Light lanced through his slitted eyelids, so dazzling that he could not recognize the face above—haloed, indistinct. His head was pulsing like a drum, mouth full of bitter grit. Never had he been so dry. He was the Atacama on a cot.

"Kurui is better, Uwan. You are in your *ruka*, and I am going to give you water now ... if you can open your mouth without asking a question."

Blissful water—cool, unmixed with anything.

Juan groaned with pleasure ... groaned with the pain of having groaned. He lifted his lids again, allowing daggers of light to penetrate his eyes.

Pangi sat by him, smiling crookedly.

"I know how you feel, *peñi*," he murmured.

"What *happened*!" Juan asked, as Pichikan and Andalikan entered.

"You were *kuimin*—in a *machi* trance," Pangi explained, searching for words to describe what he had witnessed. "You knelt with your eyes closed, holding your knife over Kurui."

That was exactly what Juan remembered, but what about his vision—or audition—of the two saints, the pig called 'Sin,' the warbling birds?

"You held the knife over Kurui, and Andalikan grabbed your wrist. Ignoring him, you spoke with your eyes closed. Sometimes you said the name of Kurui. Once you mentioned Lleflai. Mostly you spoke *likwinkadungun*. I am sorry that I did not understand you."

Pangi was ashamed. The assistant was expected to remember *everything* the *machi* said in trance—however nonsensical—so that it could be interpreted. He had failed.

Dismissing the apology with a casual hand, Juan was stung by an insight sharp as wasps, for he had bared the whole of his squalid soul before Saint Francis. To all Mapuche what he said had been oracular babble ... but not to Raytrayen. Merciful God in Heaven!

You had a conversation," Pangi continued, "with the dead. *Epu pillañ*—two spirits—were in you, each with a voice. And there was another *pillañ*." The *machi* paused, hoping Uwan would explain the bestial noises.

Juan muttered, "The *pullu* of a speaking animal."

Pangi took the *lik wink*a oddity in stride. "After you spoke with the *pillañ*, Andalikan let go your wrist. You opened your eyes and cut the hollow of her arm with your knife—slowly, carefully—filling a bowl with her blood. You did not drink it, just set it down. Then you collapsed."

Juan could have cheered, but was too weary. Through some miracle, Kurui had survived his incompetence! Then —Mother of God!—the thought came. Had Pangi consumed hot human gore in his stead, as at that apex of pagan horror, the Aztec pyramid?

"One more thing," the *machi* said, intense. "Before taking blood from Kurui, you said the name of Kurufil."

Juan could not see this in the fogged mirror of his memory. What else had he forgotten?

Pangi was jubilant, and sinister. "I *knew* he did it."

Pichikan added, "Pangi took the *wekufu* of the *kalku* from Kurui! He sucked it out her forehead—a small, black, living snake!"

Andalikan nodded his assent.

Juan crossed himself in awe, sagging back into his cot.

"I threw the *wekufu* in the fire," Pangi concluded. "Also the bowl of blood. Then I took the ashes across a stream and scattered them. The *wekufu* will not return."

"Well done," said Juan, and fainted.

Chapter 19: Pedro *(Mapu, 1552)*

Two *antu* later, Kurui was weak but lucid, healing.

Liftuipani had hung herself.

Juan was a hero. And Pichikan more or less adopted him, killing time in his *ruka*, bringing *peñi* to enjoy these bachelor quarters. Unmarried warriors all, they included Juan's companions from *palin*—Tuiñam, Wenchuman, Marifil, Chuleu, Tralaf, Anileo ... and also Millanti, who bore Juan no grudge for his shocking amputations. From time to time Andalikan joined the younger warriors. Lautaro sometimes came as well, formal in the company of the boisterous *weichafe*, as if attempting to seem older—yet Juan might have been unkind in this assessment.... Lautaro's demeanor—martial, hieratic—recalled Rodrigo González de Marmolejo, in whom war wed religion. Lautaro reminded Juan of a crusader without a cross.

The *peñi* also sometimes emerged to hunt, to fish, sometimes to participate in the bizarre challenges improvised by Pichikan, such as the running-one-legged-long-jump, and log-relay races. They also engaged in the more usual contests—holding a war bow drawn at full extension, wrestling, running and swimming races of all types and in all weathers, as well as the obligatory target practice with sling, arrow and spear. From time to time they organized long and violent sessions of *palin* on a field turned into a swamp by rain, and from these contests the players returned battered and exhausted, covered with winter mud. Juan participated to the best of his ability in everything but swimming ... also passing on Indian weapons. Time however, made him expert in *palin*, which had become a passion for him. Only elongated Millanti could run faster, and only over distances.

For the first time in his life Juan had the friendship of companions of his age, so that in the winter of 1552 he was as content in exile as he could be—either brutally exercising in cold rain, or being smoked like a herring in a cramped interior—actually *enjoying* this austere Mapuche regimen. Still—he thought—no Indian pleasure should surprise one who had come to like rotten raw potato.

He feared for Eimi however, who roamed the unhealthy woods of June alone.

And, Juan sorely missed Raytrayen—though she must despise him after his babbling to Saint Francis at the *machitun*. What was worse, Juan often had to miss Raytrayen in her presence, for they came across each other, now that she was the close friend of Kurui. With Liftuipani buried, Raytrayen was good as family in the *ruka* of Andalikan. This meant that she and Juan were frequently together—always in the presence of *domo*, however. And when they spoke it was in *mapudungun*.

With Raytrayen therefore—*in* Raytrayen—Juan missed his native tongue. On the other hand, he was proud of his growing mastery of hers, able to produce its clotted syntax almost with the ease of breathing. Magically, also, he had acquired the ability to utter sounds impossible for a *cristiano*—the savage *n*, lost in sinuses, yearning to be *g*, the protean *e* metamorphosing into everything but its forthright Spanish self....

Pichikan took his *peñi*, Uwan, wherever his endless energy led, visiting relatives and friends. Not that they went far—and certainly not fast—since the forest paths were quagmires, and the many streams in flood. Swollen by incessant rain, they could only perilously be crossed, sometimes on logs, rarely on dugout canoes, most rarely on primitive suspended bridges recalling those of Peru. As for the rivers, the *weichafe* simply swam them when no *wampu* were available, placing their clothes and weapons on improvised rafts. Juan, however, straddled these unsteady platforms, paddling and kicking as those who had already crossed with ease watched from the farther bank. Though solemn, they were roaring with inner laughter, Juan was sure.

Travel would be easier in *karu waleng*—season of green things—Pichikan assured him. They would go to *kawiñ* together, *peñi!*

Juan was as fond of the bluff warrior as a man could be, but Pichikan was precisely that, a man. Perhaps Inés had predisposed Juan to the company of women, for there were moments when, as if Pichikan were the sun, the energy he generated cast enormous shadows of that which he was not—impenetrable gloom, for there was nothing there to be experienced. In contrast, Inés and Raytrayen had depths to their shadows, as in the pools of placid summer rivers overhung by trees. However clear the water, one could only see so deep, and there at vision's edge sub lunar mysteries swam, no less removed than Heaven, the more wondrous as being both near and unattainable. In contrast, Pichikan—God bless his oaken heart!—was rudimentary as his club. In no way stupid, he was yet in absolutely no way deep, demonstrating no interest in Juan's past or culture—save for martial things. And he was puzzled by questions about his people, unable to conceive of a different perspective. To him what was, was—which was to say Mapuche—and that which was not Mapuche did not merit interest. On the other hand, his *mapu* and people were to him uncomplicated, unquestioned and unquestionable, so that he could become annoyed that what to him was evident as his thumb should come under scrutiny. This made him a terrible interpreter, and Juan definitely needed interpretation of the world in which he was immersed—not just *mapu* teeming with its fauna and flora, uncatalogued by any Mapuche Pliny, but more important, the inexplicable behavior of the Mapuche themselves.

Consider the seven deadly sins—that bedrock upon which the Fathers of the Church constructed the architecture of right behavior. Beginning with Pride—Satan's fatal fault—the Mapuche took greater pride in nothing else. As for Lust—perhaps the most mortal of the seven—these Indians fornicated outside the bounds of marriage freely and with the lightest heart, as if promiscuity were akin to sipping from a common bowl of good, hot soup. Had they anything resembling the Sacrament of Confession—which they most certainly did *not*—lust would be the last thing whispered through the grate. So, sin-by-sin, the mortal gamut went. The blackest Christian faults were as lilies to Mapuche, though there did exist haphazard zones of gray. Not that good and evil were here a diabolical inversion—a parody which turned Christian evil into their good, for—as if throwing random darts—these Indians created their own mortal sins where Juan never knew them to exist, or imagined that they should. To mention one extraordinary example, they thought it the worst of things for a man to speak to his mother-in-law. Who would have thought!

All that winter, therefore, Juan was lost, ensnared in the thickets of an Indian moral forest, desiring the guidance of Raytrayen. And when November came he required counsel even more, for Pichikan kept his promise to take him everywhere, especially to *kawiñ*. Amazingly, they managed to attend a wedding, two funerals, the building of a *ruka* … even a *machitun*.

Pichikan attended *kawiñ* to eat, drink and be merry. But he also went, as he candidly admitted, to 'bump into' Kurui—a naked euphemism, if ever there was one. In brute fact, Pichikan and Kurui went to *kawiñ* to copulate in the woods. They were in virtual rut. And should Juan have retained any doubts about what was going on, they were obliterated by the gleeful indirections of his friend, who dropped hints without a tinge of shame.

What disturbed Juan most was not so much their sin, as venial. No … what grated was the flippancy with which the unblushing lovers regarded their fornication—Kurui not mourning her irreplaceable virginity. And Juan could not comprehend the role of Andalikan, who was in a position to enforce some parental moral code, however primitive. Not the licentiousness itself, the *attitude* toward carnal union—expected, as of goats—agitated Juan, for in this crucial aspect of civilization Indians saw nothing like a sin. To them sex was an easy good—as if the apples of Eden were a fruit consumed without consequence!—when, where these apples were, *there* guilt should also be, for without repentance how could God forgive? Lleflai's *degu* came to mind, copulating by the public hearth … though to their credit they gave birth in secret. Still, Juan could not shake the suspicion that—without the *knowledge* expelling Adam—these Indians had remained within the walls of Paradise at the price of existing like small, furry beasts.

All this would have bothered Juan far, far less if The Degu Of Concupiscence Without Guilt had not wandered into his own affairs....

Juan could not have helped but notice that nubile *domo* at *kawiñ* had been eyeing him with more than simple curiosity. Imagining that these black-eyed maidens, tawny and rounded, were simply piqued by his extreme degree of strangeness— as by the fiery peppers that they loved—he considered their maneuvers less provocative than embarrassing. And there, the matter of flirtation and abstinence would have remained, if the Choswe of Juan's past had not reappeared in a present complicated by alien culture. She was some kind of distant relative of Pichikan, it seemed, and that November she managed to attend every *kawiñ* to which Juan went, so without fail that conspiracy had to be suspected. Fortunately, at no time did Choswe bare more than her intentions, as she had two years ago. Nonetheless, by the many wordless means known to woman, she communicated that she would not mind chancing upon Uwan in the woods. And if Juan had any doubts about *that*, Pichikan dissipated them, for Choswe had her reputation....

She had been in love with Antemil, who promised marriage, but did not take her as his wife, abducting her cousin Paillalaf instead. Choswe was shattered by his broken vow ... pregnant as well. So when her *pichiche* died at birth, the rumor spread that in her outrage she had summoned a *kalku* who performed *koftun*— that is, her newborn was killed, and his testicles roasted over a slow fire.

Juan shut his eyes, and crossed himself.

Pichikan explained that *koftun* was sometimes requested by unmarried *domo* to make false lovers impotent, and—although no one had accused Choswe of anything—the *pichiche* was in fact buried the day he was born. Soon after, Antemil became fearfully ill. And it was whispered—Pichikan whispered—that before Antemil died his testicles turned hollow as gourds abandoned in the sun, so that they rattled through all his agony.

Pichikan paused to examine Juan, who was slack-jawed with disbelief.

"Terrible way for a man to die," agreed the warrior, adding that when Antemil was buried, Choswe announced that she would never again marry.

Shock had addled her wit, Juan presumed, allowing eccentricities. To the Mapuche she must be a sexual version of the village idiot.

Pichikan winked at Juan—man to man—saying that in renouncing husbands Choswe had in no way renounced *wentru*. Unmarried, she had given birth to a *pichiche* who was *kiñe ñuke, mari chau*—a one mother, ten father, child—and ... now she had set her eye on Uwan. Chuckling, Pichikan batted his surprisingly long eyelashes. And with a last bawdy wink, he put a period to his tale.

To Juan, this barbaric round of love and death turned on an axle of horror—even if it was nothing more than rumor, for apparently such abominations *did* take place. Yet when he protested, Pichikan stressed not the killing of an infant—*and* the roasting of his pea-like genitals in a pot!—but the weakness of the father. Epulef should have acted on the duplicity of Antemil, before the whole thing came to sorcery. Also, Antemil merited at least temporary impotence for his betrayal of Choswe. When all was said and done, Pichikan attributed this death to the incompetence of the *kalku* performing the *koftun*.

When Juan was speechless, he exclaimed—What did *he* think Choswe should have done, betrayed and rejected by both lover and cousin, publicly humiliated, abandoned pregnant in her father's *ruka*...?

"What about the innocent *pichiche*?" Juan countered, naked outrage in his voice. What did the blameless infant *do*, to deserve his awful fate?

Pichikan shook his head with fond pity, as at a brother born a *wed wed*—who, through the workings of affection, was not loved the less. Shrugging meaty shoulders, he said that many *pichiche* died before—or after—they were born, maybe most of them, who knew? *Pichiche* died, and who was counting? Besides, those who did not just die were sometimes killed for good reason—when not wanted, for example ... or when more than one was born.

Juan knew argument was useless, for Pichikan was invoking *kume mognen*. Multiple births were to him some kind of discord, yet how did one proceed from *that* to the fact that the tiny testicles of an infant had been roasted? Harmony, hah! A human life a 'sour note,' hah and hah! As if infanticide could restore their precious *kume mognen*! Harmony? Horsefeathers! Bloody King Harod was laughing in his grave.

Refusal turned Juan into a sexual fort unto himself—Christian ramparts rising impregnably in the wilderness—until she who caused his walls overflew them like a swallow, one November day.

This was a lovely, temperate season—*mapu* in verdant bloom. Juan went with Pichikan and Tuiñam to build a *ruka* for a family displaced by war. Andalikan, Wispu and Kurui went too, but not Raytrayen.

The hive of activity was a clearing overlooking a lake, giving a magnificent view of the *cordillera*. Women cooked in the shelters that ringed the work, *pichiche* bound into *kupulwe* near them. Children old enough to be liberated from that captivity toddled up, to stare at Juan. He patted their solemn heads, on his way to find Tuiñam. Then together they cut, barked, and shaped rafters, Juan relishing the smell of fresh-cut wood. There was solid satisfaction in erecting shelter with one's hands, he thought.

Choswe—being present—found reasons to approach, languorously giving Juan the eye. Scarlet blossoms were woven into her long, black braids, and—to cook!—she wore a necklace of shell and bone with matching *trarulongko*. Mother-of-pearl pins secured her *kepam* as well. She was a jewel gorgeously set. Thinking Antemil a total idiot, Juan plied his tool.

When labor ceased at dusk the food was plentiful—though much consisted of the roots of winter and the greens of spring—Juan particularly enjoying the coiled, steamed shoots of ferns. *Mudai* made its inevitable rounds. Pichikan had vanished into the forest, and Juan supposed Kurui was with him. Andalikan and Wispu were off to talk with friends.

Not wanting to be surprised alone by Choswe, Juan sat by Tuiñam, both of them working at getting drunk. He stole glances at his companion's helmet, which today was covered with green and yellow feathers. Smiling to himself, he wondered how *weichafe* would adorn their horses if they had them. He imagined a warrior on a feathered steed, wearing a feathered *yelmo*—the top and bottom of a *caballero andante*, so to speak—with the knight between three-quarters naked, painted bright as a ceramic pot....

The helmet was not the only Spanish artifact Juan knew of, strayed from familiar origins. He had seen a warrior lifting a tattered shirt upon a stick, much like a captured flag. Another *weichafe* that he knew of reverently kept a mailed glove in a pouch, as if it were the bone of an authenticated saint. He had been shown a necklace fashioned from the points of crossbow bolts, looking like so many rusted teeth, and heard of an arquebus subjected to a Mapuche exorcism, then burned and buried. A Spanish boot had been similarly exorcised, the ashes consumed in *mudai* by *weichafe* desiring to take into themselves the power of *lik winka*. They were odd, funny, and sad, these captured things.

Juan felt exactly like them—displaced, ludicrous, misunderstood ... yet at the same time somehow numinous to the *che*. Maybe irony was one perspective of displacement. In him—who knew the place in the tapestry of civilization from which they had been torn—these objects were heart-rending. But the Mapuche saw them as akin to comets from a void—fallen fragments of Heaven. This might explain Choswe's baffling infatuation. Juan was not just a stranger, he was strangeness itself come from the blue, his presence amplified by the absent whole he represented. Yet that coin had its other side. He felt hugely diminished without his Spain. The lack that magnified him in the eyes of Choswe, shrank him in his own.

Tuiñam poured *mudai*. Nodding simultaneously—one, two, three!—they downed their bowls, then belched in unison. And they laughed so loud, so long, Juan knew that he was very drunk.

"I am much like your helmet," he confided, and—whatever he might have said in *mapudungun*—Tuiñam took it as the greatest joke. They howled and pounded on each other.

Inspired, Juan outdid himself. "I am a featherless biped," he said in Latin, and they roared.

Juan's head was spinning. He sank onto his elbows, wiping tears, belched the memory of his meal, and slid into vortices of sleep....

On a forest path he came across Tuiñam *wearing his helmet, arms rigid at his side. Approaching,* Juan *saw that this was a log carved into human form, instead—a buried post, much like a* rewe. *And on the helmet were not feathers but a green and yellow fungus. He touched the face upon the rotten log, and it crumbled. Insects fled as the helmet rolled upon the mossy forest floor....*

Juan woke, Tuiñam saying to him with a sly grin that Choswe came while he was sleeping. Sobered in more ways than one, Juan determined to remain alert this night.

When the *ruka* was finished late that evening, the *kawiñ* began. Pichikan did not wander into the woods, ambling about drinking *mudai* instead, eventually returning to the shelter. Eerie, a *pifilka* played, much like a throaty bird. There was quiet conversation, laughter. Replete—and only slightly tipsy—Juan basked in weariness as in a bath.

Without warning, Wispu stepped from her shelter. The assembly went silent as she sang.

Before Juan realized what had happened, it was over. She had dreamed of a deer, but so what? Yet the Mapuche murmured their approval. Had she sung well ... though to him the melody was no less short than it was discordant?

To Pichikan, he whispered, "What was *that*?"

"The deer is a good animal. This means Wispu is happy with Andalikan."

A second *domo* sang....

Juan could not believe what he just thought he had just heard. This woman dreamed of shit! And even if she had, why *sing* it before all!

Pichikan—stage whisper no quieter than before—said her *fillka* was about to marry.

No more questions for Pichikan, but Juan thought he had a chance at grasping something, here. Another woman was coming to join the household, and *domo* married to brothers lived unhappily together so often that it was commonplace for them to call each other *medomo*, or shitwoman.

Another song.... This *domo* dreamed of a vulture, and Juan was willing to bet anything that this said nothing good about her marriage. Pichikan whispered—mercifully low, this time—that her husband did not satisfy her sexual needs.

This husband—the first *wentru* to sing—responded, surprising Juan by professing his love.

Another *domo* sang about a bird Juan did not know—the *tregul*. Her husband was *overactive* in her bed. Another dreamed about a fox ... and her husband was a ne'er do well. Both of the accused responded, not with anger, as if airing their soiled laundry in public was a trivial thing.

Juan had figured one thing out—*domo* were venting feelings as song, when custom scarcely allowed them to address *wentru*, much less strenuously complain of anything. They were not dreaming of animals, birds and excrement ... they were airing emblems of their discontent—save for Wispu. Juan wondered if custom allowed Mapuche *domo* to express their love directly, an intriguing reason to wonder what Raytrayen's paint might mean for him.

So absorbed in personal speculation was Juan—that he did not notice Choswe had emerged from her shelter until she sang....

No dreams or emblems here. With no possible misunderstanding, this was Choswe's song of love for him.

Juan did not rise to sing that he dreamed of a green and yellow helmet turned to fungus. Nor did he wander into the forest for a chance encounter. He did absolutely nothing, for not a single Spanish instinct was operating at the time.

Somewhat like Pandora's box, Choswe's song sprang open during Juan's walk home, love emerging in unfamiliar form. Was this pity touched by fear ... a twisted *caritas*? Or was it that love offered could not be denied, for its own blessed sake? Was he so deep in need, he was in love with love?

Pichikan remained an implacable two strides ahead— no matter how Juan hurried—until at last he stopped to turn and say, "Choswe has her pride." Black accusation was in his eye.

"I cannot sing in *mapudungun*."

Shaking his head, Pichikan pondered the strange disability. "Choswe sang the song of a *wentru*," he said at last, draping an arm heavy as hawsers over Juan. "She must be desperate."

Desperate is what Juan was too, but about *what* precisely, he did not know.

Raytrayen maintained her cool distance when he returned—though she must have learned of Choswe's song, and this made him feel rebellious. Why was she so taciturn when, as he had found, *domo* could be forward? He felt he had churlishly refused a gift generously offered. Why not stroll into the woods at the next *kawiñ*? Sing in *mapudungun* he could not, yet he could manage *that*. With neither having sinned, he could restore Choswe's pride. No woman had ever professed her love for him—much less this publicly!—and Choswe's wild song echoed in his heart. In some peculiar way he truly *was* in love....

One morning not much later, Pichikan erupted into Juan's turbid moral situation, insisting that he go with him, bringing his *newen*.

His weapon? A surprise attack! Juan leapt for his knife—which was never far, like Pedro's memory turned to steel.

Fucha winu—the big one—Pichikan insisted.

Juan retrieved his sword reluctantly—that icon of his enmity to Mapuche. He buckled it on ... was hurried away without breakfast, scabbard banging on his hipbone. Racing down forest paths, Pichikan told him that *pangi* had attacked the *luan* of Epulef.

Epulef...?

The name seemed familiar, and Juan found out why when he got there. He was Choswe's father ... and there *she* was when they emerged into the clearing, aiming a smile at Juan from where she cooked. He froze at that as at an arquebus, match above the touchhole, primed. And every *che* present paused to appreciate the drama. An Indian ambush, Juan told himself ... and not just for *pangi*. Redemption was being offered him.

Juan woodenly smiled back, and jerky as a puppet with important strings detached, he turned to the *weichafe*. The hands of time again began to crawl.

Wentru were modifying the corral in which the *luan* had been attacked. Having built up the sides they were now working on an addition—a constricted passage ending in a blind wall. *Pangi* would be trapped there, unable to turn around.

All happened as planned, save the end....

The *weichafe* waited, downwind from their trap, Juan squatting by Pichikan as the purple glow of sunset faded, sky deepening to nocturnal blue. Nameless insects whirred like spinning tops. Juan was immobile for a lingering eternity, thighs burning, until—when in his suffering he had decided he could squat no more—Pichikan levitated from by his side, a meaty moth.

Juan ran, legs numb, to where arms and spears were rising, falling, in the darkness. Hearing the mind-searing scream of *pangi* he did not pause, possessed by war. The puma leapt from his imprisonment—so high he blotted stars—and dropped upon a man....

Swinging at the hissing whirlwind, Juan felt the familiar impact of edge on flesh. *Pangi* spun, the gold eyes finding his, and—in an instant like a cobweb snapped—he soared. Juan whirled, struck the whirlwind ... was struck. He almost fell, and then was looking into golden eyes again, so close he could have touched them with his steel, if not his hand. He could *hear pangi* breathe—a living tremor of the chest—for now time crawled with legs of centipedes, granting Juan the leisure to realize that he was wounded … and that *pangi* was wounded too. Mutual shock was granting them a brief communion.

Pangi leapt….

Juan was a rag doll flung across a room, the rending fury on him … and then peace. He curled in a protective ball, gasping as hot weight was lifted from him.

Recognizing a face, he said, "*Mari, mari*, Pichikan."

"*Mari, mari, peñi.*" The smile was enormous with relief.

"*Fucha winu?*"

Where *was* his sword…?

"In *pangi.*"

Juan was bathed in gore—no way to know how much the puma's, how much his. Leaning on Pichikan, Juan hobbled to a nearby spring, where he was told that, with the first swing, he slashed into the shoulder of the cat. The second cut his neck, *pangi* spurting blood. And when he sprang, Juan pierced him through-and-through.

Weichafe gathered, murmuring their witness, Juan knowing their respect misplaced. Not knowing swords, *pangi* had simply impaled himself.

The world spun and Juan sank to his knees, thinking that he must have lost blood.

He was rushed to a *ruka* and set down. Then the *weichafe* hurried out, as if they had ministered to a drunk. Abandoned by his *peñi*, Juan closed his eyes to the familiar sight of sooty *ruka* rafters, and sensed coolness on his burning ribs….

Choswe of the brilliant smile was tending to his wounds, not smiling. And she seemed so devastated—applying salve and bandage—that an emotion greater than compassion flooded Juan.

"*Mari, mari*, Choswe," he said, attempting an honest smile.

Startled, she looked into his eyes, lips wobbling. Juan was too weak to panic as silently she shook, tears dripping like forest rain onto the leaves placed on his wounds. He reached out to touch her cheek, wondering if her sadness meant he was about to die. Then Juan did not pass away, he just passed out….

Reviving bound as any mummy, he saw that Choswe smiled at him by the hearth with brilliant shyness. Then she left, as *weichafe* solemnly filed in— Pichikan, Epulef, Millanti, Tuiñam.

Epulef—bandaged much like Juan—thanked him for saving his life, praising his courage and skill. He concluded by pouring into his hands the claws and fangs of *pangi*, saying he had earned them and should have a necklace made to honor the event. Maybe he could take a *real* Mapuche name. Grinning, Epulef said that he knew of no other warrior named after a vegetable.

The *weichafe* left. Juan slept and woke, then slept again, and modestly Choswe nursed him. Clearly, this gentle *domo* was incapable of the atrocity ascribed her.

Days passed, and the moment came when—bending to examine his dressings—
Choswe murmured, "You are getting well, Uwan."

Thanks be! He grinned lustfully at Choswe, tossing civilization to winds of
change.

She produced a soft leather pouch and removed a necklace.

Bewildered, Juan exclaimed, "*Kume ad!*" And it *was* beautiful in its Indian way.
Between the fangs and claws of *pangi*, symmetrically arranged, Choswe had set
patterns of blue and black stones—the *llanka* and *likan* sacred to the Mapuche.
Juan slipped this savage ivory on, over his crucifix.

Having admired her handiwork in its intended setting Choswe left, returning
with a *wentru pichiche* perhaps four years old. Solemn, he stood obediently beneath
the firm shelter of her hand.

"My son, Antemil," Choswe said. "Will you touch him, Uwan?"

Juan did—a puzzled laying on of hands upon the bony shoulder of this child-
with-ten-fathers. What had happened to the lusty *domo* and the outspoken
courage of her love…?

Choswe left to return alone. And, arms folded, she watched Juan calmly from
by the Indian absence of a door. However courteously, he was being dismissed.

Returned to the embarrassment that was his destiny, Juan stood to fuss with
his baldrick, reluctant to depart—the serpent with the meaty helmet whispering
to him that he was misunderstanding Choswe. After all, Mapuche women made a
play of being forced….

He buckled on his sword, she telling him that he had spoken in his sleep.
And—as he walked out—she added that his *mapudungun* was really very good.

Juan healed scarred—elevated welts on his chest, legs and stomach, others less
serious on his face. His emotions were quite another matter. He attended *kawiñ*,
yet Choswe never passed near, to smile in his direction. And of course, she never
sang for him again.

Clio did not give Juan time to brood over what might have been—or for that
matter, *should* have. Valdivia had constructed a fort to the north, a few days' walk
away, ending the truce imposed by winter. Sporadic fighting resumed. Pichikan
and his *peñi* stopped visiting. Violence was in the air, when one evening Lautaro
visited to talk about the ransom.

Juan had given the matter thought. It would be easiest to write Pedro a note,
but he could not even read his own name, signing it with an X. And for the note to
be read by someone else was out of the question. He had decided to write Lautaro a
message, to be delivered with a shibboleth that Pedro should recognize by sight—
the frontispiece of **Utopia**.

Lautaro left. Days passed. Juan fought depression, knowing nothing, for he was an eddy in streams of Indian communication. But—as if to compensate—Pichikan confided in him, announcing that he intended to abduct Kurui. And he wanted his *peñi*, Uwan, to take part.

Juan more or less knew the Mapuche version of marriage. Nothing like a priest involved. No vows. No participation of pagan gods. What mattered was the bride price, and long negotiations took place over this mercenary question. And when a deal at last was struck, the glad event was stark, the bride leaving her father's family without pomp or ritual to live with her husband, this anticlimax drowned in an immense *kawiñ*.

From Hispanic perspectives, a Mapuche wedding distressingly resembled the purchase of a cow, thought Juan. But, they could be complicated by turning into abductions. Sometimes *domo* were unwilling, or the parents refused to grant consent. Sometimes a family could not—or would not—pay the bride price. And there were times when *weichafe* stole their wives out of sheer high spirits....

This was the case with Pichikan, even though his mother was the sister of Andalikan. Kurui was the child of his mother's brother—by far the preferred relationship for marriage, for whatever Indian reason. And—God knew!—Kurui had no objection to being tupped by Pichikan, in or out of wedlock. Yet he proposed an attack on the *ruka* of his future father-in-law with the intention of violating his daughter.

Troubled to his Spanish core, Juan asked why.

"*Chem meu?*" Pichikan replied gruffly, cut to the heart at having a high moment of his life questioned by his *peñi*.

Why not, indeed? And Juan said he that would be happy to play his part.

Pichikan planned the abduction no less carefully than Valdivia his pacifications. They would leave tomorrow at moonrise. Only Pichikan and Tuiñam would carry out the actual invasion—for there was little room inside the *ruka*—going before the others, upwind of the dogs. Marifil, Chuleu, Tralaf, Wenchuman and Uwan would wait at the forest edge to intercept those who emerged. Millanti would create confusion.

The abduction went exactly as planned.

The high-pitched scream emerging from the *ruka* had the true ring of outrage. Dogs barked and leapt about. Millanti roared—an army to himself. The abductors dragged Kurui out by her legs, naked and violently struggling. Slinging her over his shoulder, Pichikan ran. Kicking the innocent air while pounding on his back, she screeched like a forest cat.

Those who emerged to defend Kurui commenced a battle without weapons, but with violence far greater than the lusty farce required, thought Juan. He wrestled, lashing out blindly at opponents who apparently saw in the dark. He was kneed in the kidneys, butted in the nose, slammed into, by body parts that felt like oak. At some point a dog—ignorant of the ban on serious damage—bit into his ankle, refusing to let go. Juan shook him off to hobble after his *peñi*, unable to recall when last he had such fun.

At the ruka of Kuriñam there was a victory celebration—as if they had returned from a just war, with valuable loot. Pichikan strutted, proudly displaying the purple bite-marks on his shoulders. Kurui sulked ritually in a corner of the *ruka*, guarded by the *domo* of her new home.

The next day Juan limped away on familiar forest paths, taking with him the thought that—while his body had learned to find its way in a strange land—his Spanish soul had strayed. Only ransom could rescue him from *this* direction.

Three *antu* later—eleven after Lautaro left—Raytrayen came to visit by herself, saying that there was a *ngillatun*, and every *che* not gone to war had left to pray. The moon was waning. It was the perfect time to plant, she said, handing him a hoe.

He led the way, dancing to the unheard music of the hoe become a flute, goat-footed Pan himself. After, he rode the innocent hoe-horse of childhood. Then, the magic hoe became a broom sweeping the path before Raytrayen … he strewing imaginary rose petals. At last—swaying to absent swells—the hoe become a mast transforming Juan into the captain of the ship of fools. And when they reached the garden—fool of gladness—he piped a silent song that turned his hoe-flute into a hoe again.

Together they hilled *poñu*, pulling moist soil to the crinkled intensity of dark green leaves—their purplish tint telling Juan that these tubers would be blue. He grinned. She grinned back.

Now, they were weeding onions. Stealing glances at Raytrayen, Juan knew he had never witnessed anything so beautiful as her composure. How difficult, to be faithful to their friendship, yet not a traitor to her people! He foundered in storms of the soul, while—navigating similar seas— she sailed halcyon days. Like the fabled bird, she emanated peace.

Calmed by her calm, Juan hoed onions with an attention he had never paid the pungent things before. How extraordinary the hollow shoots, unique in taste and form! Nipping a tip, he chewed. Why onions were more extraordinary than blue potatoes, he did not know. Not just the onions but also the *poñu*, the entire garden for that matter—bathed by light, ringed by forest walls, yet with a sloped perspective on the distant sea—was transfigured. Raytrayen, he decided, created about her a nimbus of lucidity. Mediatrix of sublunar spaces, she granted a new vision of the world….

"Time to plant *uwa* … Uwan."

They smiled at her little joke, she pouring gold into his palm.

He built a row of hills, a perfect grain in each. Unique, discrete, they were time become material—these moments transporting him to confession....

"Choswe sang for me at a *kawiñ*," he said.

"I heard."

"I did nothing."

"You do not know how—or what—to sing."

Raytrayen put a seed to bed ... leaned on her hoe.

Why did she repair her white tears daily? Was she Penelope to his Ulysses?

The quiet potency of her eyes overcame him, and Juan confessed it all—his lust for Choswe, her chaste healing of his wounds, culminating with her rejection....

Raytrayen remained tranquil, yet Juan felt she held her hoe at a military rest.

"Choswe never had *koftun* done," was all she said.

What is happening between us? Juan's mind screamed. He had bared his soul to earn her mercy, not to correct a rumor!

And it was then that—with the exquisite sense of timing that distinguishes Fortuna from simple chance—She cut their conversation short.... Eimi hobbled up screeching, "*Kuru winka!*"

Juan and Raytrayen dropped their hoes.

"Run!" Eimi shrieked, wobbling toward the forest edge, Raytrayen bounding after him.

A *negro*? Juan scrutinized the forest ... saw nothing. Considering the seeds in his hand, he returned to planting, knowing that stubbornness could not restore the magic of the day.

Not long after, the predicted *negro* ran up, arms flailing, shirt tattered....

"Domingo!"

The town crier of Santiago recoiled. "You are dead and far away," he screeched. Sinking to his knees he crossed himself, muttering what were probably African exorcisms....

Juan found Raytrayen in the *ruka*, cooking. Convincing her that Domingo was harmless was easy—she knew him from Santiago. Convincing *him* that Juan was alive and in a Spanish body—not dead and reincarnated as Indian—proved impossible.

But Juan was hungrier for information than for food.

Domingo told him that Pedro Gómez was in the near-by fort. And no, he had not seen the Indian who used to work in the stables—Indians all looking alike to him, always coming and going, dying, being replaced....

Valdivia had left for Santiago. No idea of when he would return.

Doña Inés de Suárez…?

She lived in seclusion, although she spoke to the *cabildo* when Don Juan disappeared. Many Indians had been tortured when he died.

"I am not dead," Juan insisted, as if the words could absolve him of the suffering he had caused.

Raytrayen rose. The *ngillatun* had just begun. She could return tomorrow.…

Domingo thanked him for the food after she left, saying he *had* to leave, now … he knew of a pass over the *cordillera*.…

"War dogs!"

The *negro* nodded fearfully.

Juan handed him a skin of water. "Go, now! God speed and good luck!" Domingo was certain to need both. An escaped slave, he was certain to be dogged.

Raytrayen arrived early next morning.

Juan had scarcely slept, for the dogs of war could not be far behind the *negro*. He feared the disease of war as well, feared that what food there was after a hard winter would be plundered, feared for every Mapuche that he knew. Above all, he was terrified of what might happen to Raytrayen, Kurui, Choswe—all the *domo*, young and beautiful.…

Valdivia would apportion land and Indians—*repartimientos* that would include every Mapuche *domo, wentru and pichiche* living here. Some uncouth stinking soldier probably owned Raytrayen now—or soon would—someone who could rape her with impunity and leave her bleeding in the woods, or if more civilized, take her as a concubine.

Juan considered going with her to *lolo*—for the place was defensible, even if discovered. But they could hardly leave Eimi behind. And even if all of Juan's Mapuche 'family' took refuge in the cave, *che* would soon be returning from the *ngillatun*. Juan had to confront Nuño Beltrán de Mendoza. For an insane moment Juan contemplated his armor … yet, in the end, he only wore his sword to the garden. They planted *uwa*, stopping to eat at midday. Raytrayen—who had not commented on his weapon—said that she was worried about Eimi.

"Me too," Juan honestly replied. He chewed on scallions wrapped in bread, listening for the dogs.

She heard them first, leaping up with consternation in her eyes.

Drawing his sword, Juan told her to run to the *ruka*. He had planned exactly this—to intercept Mendoza on Domingo's trail. Raytrayen fled, lifting her *kepam*. Slender legs flashing in the light, she disappeared into woods.

Juan knew that his duty was no less simple in conception than impossible to execute. Alone, unarmored, and on foot, he had to stop the dogger. To succeed he would have to kill Mendoza, which he obviously could not, though he might dispose of a dog or two before dying. Surprise was on his side however. Perhaps some stratagem? He was rehearsing improbabilities when Domingo rendered every one of them impossible by sprinting into the clearing. Too out of breath to speak, he vanished after Raytrayen.

As Domingo's scent was fresh, Juan cursed Fortuna, having lost his chance of beguiling Mendoza with some fiction. He had also lost his choice of battlefield, for the *negro* would lead the war dogs to Raytrayen. Sheathing his sword, Juan ran, passing the exhausted Domingo before he reached the *ruka*. There, Raytrayen crouched in Pangi's walled-in corner. And when the *negro* eventually staggered up, insane with dread, Juan also shoved him in.

As there was nothing more to do, he thought to pray, but did not, noticing a tumult of cloud boiling from the sea. Thunder rumbled closer, inexorable as the approaching dogs. Maybe the *pillañ* had come to help Raytrayen, Juan thought, with a rictus of irony ... but, too late to wash Domingo's scent.

When the dogs were close, Juan drew his sword, ignoring the first fat drops of rain. Two greyhounds in spiked collars and quilted armor—the silent van—pounded into the clearing just as it began to pour. Barking furiously as a signal to their master, they darted, out of reach of Juan's sword. He held his guard, wondering if the larger, more heavily armored dogs which followed, had been ordered to kill.

The mastiffs ran up and joined the greyhounds, circling Juan with jaws and steel. Clearly, the dogger intended to be present at his sport.

Backed against the *ruka*, Juan considered an attack ... but the dogs would overcome him. And there *was* a faint chance that he might fool the dogger into mercy. In any case he hesitated too long, the rain now so steady, so heavy, he did not hear the horse.

A *caballero* materialized through sheets of silver water, towering over him, face a shadow without feature under his visor, drawn sword resting on his saddle. This was odd, for Mendoza affected going about unarmed, claiming that his dogs were all the weapon he needed.

"As I live and breathe what have we here ... an Indian with a sword!"

This offense was punishable by death, yet Juan said nothing. The cracked treble was not Mendoza's. Nor could the rusted armor possibly be his....

"Just kidding, Don Juan," the *caballero* cackled, "fancy meeting you here." Hooting, he doubled over his saddle, wheezing with nasty pleasure.

"Cacafuego!"

"Don Caca de Fuego to you, *theñor*, if you pleathe." Lisping like a Castilian noble, striking an arrogant pose, he signaled his dogs, who sat.

Despite the pouring rain, the dogger removed his helmet, perhaps to cool himself, more probably because he wanted Juan to see him gloat. "You may well wonder at my change in statuth, Don Juan, but much hath happened thince you tho unfortunately died."

Cacafuego coughed—so hard, so deep, he seemed to be bringing up his entrails. Hawking, he spat a wad, making Juan think that all four horsemen of the Apocalypse were here before him. War, with his signature sword and armor. Pestilence of the hollowed cheeks and red-rimmed eyes, liverish lips. Famine, for his flesh was but a wrinkled stocking on a skull. And he was Death as well, to be sure, for that is what he brought to Juan and the Mapuche.

He *smelled* dead too, and the devil only knew what dissolution his armor concealed. "Not just disease ... *coca*," Juan told himself, as the *caballero* retched and spat. Evil and insane Cacafuego had always been. Apparently, he was now drugged as well. With Mendoza's icy strangeness he could possibly have reasoned, not with *this*. What had kept him alive this long, he assumed, was the foul horseman's manic urge to brag.

"Too high and mighty to converse, even in your present Indian form?" Cacafuego hissed, anger oozing through some chink in his noble role—however briefly. He removed a handkerchief gray with ancient crust and waved it grandly in the rain.

"Mendotha left Nueva Ethtremadura for thome reathon, returning to Peru."

Juan said nothing, having noticed that the *rewe* with its chopped-out notches stood not far from the shoulder of the enormous warhorse.

"I bought the dogth from him with my thavingth, though he wath reluctant to thell. I wath forthed to part with an enormouth thum."

Planning a miracle, Juan tensed.... And, sensing something, the dogs snarled.

"You mutht thmell like a thavage," Cacafuego commented, malignant. "Nithe cruthifix, though. I like your tooth necklathe, too."

"Coward!" His taunts had touched Juan's quick, and he was ready to end it all.

"*Coño!* You are a fucking renegade."

No trace of lisp—only malice steeped in hate. Cacafuego had just pronounced a sentence of death, as there was no possible clemency for deserting to the enemy. In the eyes of the law he was justified in killing Juan on the spot. And—though feeding a *cristiano* to his dogs could be considered an exaggeration of justice—who would know?

"Speaking of fucking renegades," Cacafuego yelled, "did you see the fucking *negro* my dogs tracked right to this place? Fucking Domingo wouldn't just happen to be inside the Indian shit hole behind you, would he?"

A bird cried near—a warning call—and a stone clanged on Cacafuego's armor. His mount reared.

No less surprised than the dogger, Juan was inspired to shout, "Indian ambush!"

A second stone hit Cacafuego on his bald pate, thud audible above the rain.

Crying out, the dogger spun his horse to confront this threat cloaked by the forest, dropping his helmet so he could wield his sword two-handed. The superbly trained dogs whirled as well … away from Juan.

Eimi tumbled from a near-by tree with a thump, having lost his balance slinging stones, and he was crouching, wild-eyed.

As by a sling—an unthinking stone—Juan was propelled. Two stuttering steps, one enormous bound, and he leapt over a crouching mastiff. Another leap and he was on the *rewe*, finding purchase on the last notch. From there he flew, slamming down astride the haunch of the horse, behind Cacafuego … and he instantly put his knife to the unshaven throat.

"Call off your hounds," he ordered, gagging at the overpowering proximity. The dogger whistled. The dogs sat.

Eimi hobbled into woods, safe for the moment, but this lethal game was not yet played out.

"Your sword," Juan told Cacafuego, "drop it." The dogger did.

"Your knife."

Cacafuego reached behind his head with the thumb and forefinger of his left hand, producing a throwing knife, which he dropped.

"Your other knife," Juan guessed, certain that Cacafuego had at least another weapon. But the dogger shrugged.

Juan had no time to waste, and he cried to Raytrayen and Eimi that they should go with the *kuru winka* to *lolo*, quickly as they could. He would lead the dogs away and join them later.

The warhorse cantered into woods—greyhounds leading, a pair of mastiffs at the flank, the other pair taking the rear. Juan was surrounded … and in a curious predicament. He could hardly return to the fort, bringing a witness to his crimes as his captive, not after having aided a renegade—two, if you counted Raytrayen—especially not when he was a renegade himself. He could kill Cacafuego, of course, but the dogs would tear him limb from limb the instant he attacked their master. Dismounting would mean instant death. And as the horse could not outrun the dogs, this was stalemate. However, he could lead the dogs away from Raytrayen, Eimi and Domingo. The fort lay in a direction away from *lolo*. And—blessedly!—a torrent was erasing all evidence of their escape. He thanked the Saint of Sudden Downpours—should there be one—as the horse cantered on, Juan thinking that living with Indians had made the thud of hooves on loam far louder.

Cacafuego farted—foul and long, but inarticulate. Startled, Juan almost slit him ear to ear.

As he was unable to duck his head—knife tight against his jugular—the dogger had been riding with an arm raised to protect his face from bamboo. Ominously docile, he was surely plotting something.…

They had traveled perhaps a league, when at last he spoke. Unctuous, he begged that, should he not survive this day, he be buried in Christian soil.

Juan went on high alert. When Cacafuego spoke, it was a cloak for daggers.

The *infante* whined, then, that he was sick. He had to cough, and the knife was awful tight. He had cut himself a little just by speaking, and a cough might kill him. He had to spit bad, too.

"Cough and spit, then," Juan replied, easing pressure on the knife.

Cacafuego's lifted hand clutched Juan's wrist, and his other hand dropped to his boot.

An icy coal slid along Juan's ribs.... But he had already killed Cacafuego. The dogger slumped gurgling, head half cut off, spurting bright arterial life. Juan groped for the reins.

The dogs attacked, leaping for Juan's bare legs.

The immense warhorse reared, an instant biped. Spinning and kicking with powerful grace, he was a formidable defense all to himself. As Juan's part consisted in not falling off, he embraced the shuddering corpse of Cacafuego.

A mastiff had his brains dashed out. A greyhound bit into Juan's arm. Taking skin and flesh, he fell, was trampled, dying howl cut short. The fight was going fairly well in fact, until the horse reared and something smashed into Juan's head— so hard it rang with church bells. Reaching for the pain, he began to topple toward to his death, but—through some homeopathy of fate—grasped the very limb that struck him. Then he was unhorsed and hanging, swinging like a pendulum, as a battle of masterless animals raged below. He swung a leg over the limb. Fangs barely missed his foot....

Juan's levitation caused the battle to wind down. Embraced by his war saddle, Cacafuego slouched in gore, genuinely dead—at this very moment, no doubt, attempting to steal the keys to the Pearly Gates. The surviving dogs ceased leaping but did not leave—alert and deadly—as the sun ran its course.

At last the warhorse broke into a weighty trot, heading for his manger. The dogs milled indecisively for a moment, then grouped into the order in which they ran—minus the dead—and loped away.

Juan reached his *ruka* too weary and sore, too troubled by the future, to be glad to be alive. He had time until the Spanish retaliation, he knew. The rain had eased. He had to go. Stuffing his armor and books—and as many of his Mapuche things as he could—into a large *wilal*, he stumbled out into the night under his burden.

Raytrayen wept when he arrived at *lolo*, stopping short of an embrace. And he told her what had happened as she dressed his wounds. Then they sat to eat fresh mushroom soup with wild onion, *trapi*, and dried *poñu*, unable to ignore the disastrous promise of their new lease on life. Domingo had departed to cross the mountains. Eimi had gone to watch the sunset—as he said—and after he would watch the stars. He did everything but wink.

Juan tried to conclude the conversation interrupted by Domingo. "I…"

Raytrayen touched a finger to her lips.

"Choswe…."

She touched her lips again, shoulders lifting in an Indian version of 'who cares?'

Was she making a Mapuche molehill out of the Spanish mountain of his betrayal, when his repentance was sincere? Juan would have preferred having sinned, and being shriven, to having his betrayal taken lightly.

"When I hear speak to you him *lik winka* outside *ruka*, I know with dog kill you he," Raytrayen said in a *castellano* corrupted by agitation and recent lack of practice. "I you alive glad." As if she would not have been next to be devoured!

Juan pondered the oblique response. Was he forgiven as *surviving*?

She was urgent. "Alive, you Uwan, yes. But *lik winka* you kill, two dog, will not return bad be?"

Juan sighed, appreciating Raytrayen's generosity. She thought he had traded her life and Domingo's for his own ransom, when he had simply been the marionette of Fate, his head a block of Spanish oak.

"No one will find out," he told her gently. "The tracks are drowned in rain. Cacafuego is dead. And dogs do not tell tales."

But Juan could not ease his own conscience. Cacafuego was a man of rotten soul, and he was glad—God forgive him!—to have slit his throat. Yet there was no escaping the enormity that he was Spanish.

Hesitant, Raytrayen said that last night Ñamku came to tell her Uwan was alive. And he warned her that no *che* could live in the middle of a river.

Right, thought Juan—he *would* drown if not returned to Spanish shore, in sorrow and confusion.

Eimi rushed up, crying out that Pangi was coming.

Hard on his heels came the *machi*. He had been sick with worry, he said, returning from the *ngillatun* to find everyone gone. Outside the *ruka* there were the hoof prints of *kawellu* and enormous *trewa*. He had hurried to the mountain, hoping the *lik winka* had not killed them all.

Raytrayen looked at Juan, looked down.

"We are all tired," he said, "and I am going to bed." Oblivion seemed the best reason to have survived. He hoped he would not dream….

Stung by wind borne brine, he walked the mineral flats of the Atacama—blank, and void of life—the blinding desert of his waiting. Lips blistered by the desert winds of time, he searched the chalk horizon. A mote appeared…. Veiled by the dust of the future, his coming years rode toward him, glittering. A voice cried out….

Raytrayen was kneeling by the fire pit, gathering shards of earthenware, looking at him strangely.

"Sorry to wake you. I dropped a *challa*."

Juan knotted a *chiripa* under cover, and then went for water. Enough of nightmares, there were a thousand living things to do. The morning was sublime, the Spanish fort a distant cloud upon the prospects of the day. He bathed. They ate. Juan and Eimi went to cut firewood. The planting of the garden could wait another day.

Next morning, striding down the mountain to retrieve the firewood, Juan heard *kawellu*. Cacafuego's vengeance was riding toward him!

He bounded from the path and hid. Peering through leaves he heard a cadence of slow hooves, pebbles rattling down-slope. Three war horses? Impossible!

The hoof beats turned into a temblor of the ground, and Juan saw Lautaro mounted, leading a riderless horse. Then…. "Pedro!" Juan screamed in disbelief, fighting toward him through armies of bamboo.

"*Hijo!*" Reaching down, Pedro laughed, and laughed, crushing Juan's hand.

Lautaro slid off his horse. "Uwan," he said, stern, "tell him the path ahead is too steep for *kawellu*. Tell him I will give them food and water, and get them ready for the night."

Pedro raised a doubtful eyebrow at Juan's translation. Unhorsed in the hostile heart of Indian territory…?

"Trust him," Juan said.

"I already did, *hijo*," Pedro said, dismounting. And taking tottering steps, he abruptly sat on a log, eyes narrowed by suspicion as Lautaro vanished with the horses. This was insanity, but…. Shaking his head, removing his helmet, he turned to Juan. "As God lives, you are a miracle, " he said, rheumy eyes ablink. He crossed himself. "*Hijo*, years ago we thought you dead."

Juan was bewildered by the havoc time had wreaked on Pedro. Not that his decline surprised, given his sixty some odd years, but his father—whose essence was immensity—was approaching frailty. Only his nose had increased, in size and crimson bloom. And not a trace of 'indument' remained.

"Good to see you, too…."

Words were failing both.

"Lost my appetite when you died, *hijo*," Pedro said, correctly interpreting Juan's dismay. He plucked a white hair from his beard and studied it.

"But I am quite alive, as you can see."

Pedro sadly smiled. "You still have the knife I gave you."

Juan looked at the weapon—forgotten in his hand.

Pedro offered him a cylindrical oilcloth packet produced from a mailed sleeve, his hand trembling uncontrollably as his smile—not simply out of emotion, Juan supposed, but from a life marinated in wine.

"This knife is the most precious thing I own," Juan told him, close to tears with the uttering of that simple truth. And he busied himself with the packet. As expected, it was the frontispiece of **Utopia**.

"How did you know this was not stolen?"

Pedro snorted. "Over your dead body."

"What if I *was* dead?"

"I gambled. Odds were against me, but what could I lose?"

"Lose? Juan said, thinking, three horses and his life! "How did you know to bring the extra horse?"

"That savage is persistent."

"His name is Lautaro. The third horse is my ransom."

"That is what ... er, Lautaro, told me ... in so many words," said Pedro with disbelief, living a nightmare from which he could not wake. He heaved a gusty sigh. "I knew that one day books would get you into serious trouble." He stood, looking about to faint.

Juan propped him with an arm. "What's the date?" he asked as they struggled up the mountain.

"December of 1552. How long since we were last together, *hijo*?"

"Three years and three months, more or less."

Pedro did not comment on the cave, once they arrived, having traveled beyond astonishment.

Raytrayen and Eimi were gone to garden, Juan imagined, and he offered Pedro what remained of breakfast—*murkeko*, warm in a thick ceramic pot, and bread.

"Sorry, Pedro. No meat. No wine." And, as if the words were a spell causing an enchantment to be canceled, Juan saw the cave as Pedro must—poor, dank and gloomy, primitive beyond belief.

"Your hair," Pedro commented, "is ... blond."

"The sun," Juan said, thinking that Pedro had not said anything about the length, or the fact that it was braided. Such were the charities of deep affection.

With a grimace, Pedro consumed the Indian abominations he had been given, as good soldiers must while in the field, where living on was everything.

Juan explained his capture and the ransom, not his years with the Mapuche.

Pedro said that Valdivia was in Santiago arranging Alderete's trip to Spain, as he intended the court to reward his old friend and comrade for faithful service. And he would bring back Valdivia's wife, as La Gasca ordered years ago.

He sketched out the last campaign, enumerating the forts created, going south—Concepción, La Imperial, and then of course Arauco, not so far away, where Lautaro found him. Valdivia intended to go further south when he returned, but in his personal opinion the troops were already spread too thin. The Indians here were fiercer than Picunche. Better organized. The war parties were larger and more hostile. No major battles had been fought, and some said the savages of the South had been taught their lesson. Pedro very much doubted that, however. "Things are too quiet here, *hijo*," he concluded, storm clouds on his brow. "This is the eye before the hurricane."

Juan tilted the subject to Inés.

And from that glad place they wandered into their past, relaxed at last, memory another sort of wine. The journey to Peru. The *cordillera*. The Atacama—somehow the more dear as terrible, and shared. Funnier too, as if the impossibility of living on became a joke when you survived. The postures of death!

And they at last arrived at that nameless *posada* where they met—Juan's first drunk, though he had simply gone to get communion wine for Father Sosa. Laughing, they relived the night. How Pedro absolutely destroyed the place in a brawl, defending his honor against insult. How the next day he paid with Indies gold to have the place rebuilt in stone, saying he needed a place that did not fall down about his ears in which to lift his cup.

"Never had that *pueblo* seen the likes of you," Juan crowed.

"I can be eloquent when drunk," Pedro admitted. "And do not forget my indument!"

"Without equal!"

"In the courts of Venice, even," Pedro exaggerated, reverent before splendors past.

"Your codpiece-purse!"

"Negrito!"

"His hats! His codpiece!"

That led them to the superb black box in which the poor dear had been buried....

And, as at a funeral one shares loving memories of the departed, Pedro related how at a banquet in Peru, Negrito—trained to do it in a chamber pot—shat in Gonzalo Pizarro's huge Inca wine cup, after which he made a leg, sweeping off his feathered cap.

Juan suspected this verse from the thick Bible of Pedro's past to be apocryphal. Still, he had to roar, and they were whooping out of all rational control when Raytrayen and Lautaro entered.

She greeted them with a curtsy that was extraordinary, considering her Indian wool, her painted face.

"*Muy buenos días, caballeros.*"

When all were seated and silent, she cooked, and they ate.

Raytrayen curtsied, departing to garden. Lautaro followed to guard the *kawellu*, telling Juan that at dawn they would leave for *fucha pele malal*.

Juan confessed to Pedro that he had killed Cacafuego and two of his dogs, explaining how events unfolded.

Pedro nodded his head. "The horse brought him back. No sword, no helmet, head half off and two dogs missing. The place was uproar when I left." And, plucking a hair from his ear, he added, "In His perplexing wisdom, God fashions some men out of turds, not clay."

"Cacafuego was a comrade," Juan insisted, correcting his teacher in the curriculum of war. Why was he so desperate to have done wrong?

"Cacafuego was shit in boots—which explains his name, and probably his breath."

Sensing that the conversation was heading nowhere even vaguely good, Pedro underscored the obvious—"*Hijo*, self defense is allowed by every law of God and man. Besides, how will anyone find out? You *know* I will never breathe the slightest word."

Juan drove the dagger home. "You have to return and tell them. There is no other way."

"What!" Pedro struggled to his feet. "By all that's holy, *hijo*, I most certainly will *not*! You killed a *caballero*, a capital offense! And then ... the dogs!" He almost moaned, "You will most certainly be beheaded, if not hung!"

"I know, Pedro."

The matter had taken on its logic, and he said, "Look at it this way, I killed Cacafuego and his dogs, but if you do not tell it as it happened, the Mapuche will be punished for my crime."

Gasping like a landed fish, Pedro searched Juan's eyes for the dementia surely living there. Finding only sadness, he slumped onto his bench, vitality drained from his mortal jar.

He complained, "I'm tired, *hijo* ... all the time, of everything. Of pork! Some days I'm too tired to get dressed."

Juan took both gnarled hands in his. "I'm sorry, Pedro. Believe me, I did not plan *this*."

"Don't cry *hijo*. Don't cry."

Then, "You ... ah ... feel something for the girl with the painted face."

"I love her no more than I love you as my father."

Last meetings could be first confessions, Juan told himself, numb with misery.

Pedro was diplomatic. "She speaks very well, considering ... *castellano*, I mean. She curtsies, too."

Juan was irritated that blinders could be worn by best intentions. "Her name is Raytrayen. It means Flower in the Stream."

"I have known not a few Rosas," Pedro responded, peering into the bleakness of Juan's eye....

"All right, *hijo*. Since you insist, I will go to Arauco, telling all that you killed Cacafuego and the dogs. But I will *absolutely not* reveal your whereabouts."

"*Gracias.*"

Pedro ruminated crime and consequence. "Valdivia just might be lenient. You were always a favorite of his. And, speaking of favorites, why not go to Santiago after all the commotion is over? Inés is worshiped there, as you know. She will cast the mantle of her protection over you."

Which was what Juan originally intended. However, intervening disasters had made the plan so fantastic that he constructed a fiction of his own. "Maybe the fort will be gone when you return—made to disappear by the spell of a powerful sorcerer. All my problems will be solved."

Pedro crossed himself at this temptation dangled before Fortuna's nasty eye. "*Romances* do not solve problems in the real world," he said. And sensing unholy presences in the cave, he sat, insisting, "We do not live in books."

Lautaro was awake all night, guarding the *kawellu*, thinking. The *lik winka* were mighty, yet could be defeated on foot. *Kawellu* could not carry them everywhere. They became tangled in forest, mired in the mud of *pukem*. They could be lured to a place like one he knew by the river Tukapel. And now he had a horse!

But he did not. When he returned to *lolo*, Uwan said that he had thought it through—their deal was canceled.

Furious, Lautaro drew his knife.

Drawing his, Juan crouched.

"*Me!*"

Raytrayen leapt between them extending her hands, palm out, to her brother and to Uwan.

"*No!*" She cried to Juan in *castellano*.

And—in both languages—she said that they would have to kill her first.

Lautaro left with Pedro and the *kawellu*.

The weeks lingered. Summer overspread green forests with blue haze. There were rumors of engagements with *lik winka*, so distant as hardly to seem real.

Pestilence returning, Juan offered help that Pangi could not accept. *Weichafe* swarmed near, he said. Among them were Kuruga and his kin, all sworn to kill him.

Pangi performed *lik winka kalkutun* himself, painting his patients red, drawing their blood when they had fever. Against fierce resistance he isolated them, like *domo* giving birth. And he insisted that all they owned be destroyed by fire, whether they died from sorcery or not.

Juan had loaned Pangi his sword, which the *machi* drove into the ground by the head of the afflicted. No harm in having the rood at these events, Juan thought—even in warlike form.

Summer wore on. Marooned on a tranquil mountain, Juan did not descend to the human storm below. Raytrayen and Eimi kept him company. And Pangi—who had been living in Juan's *ruka*—rarely visited.

But one day in March he unexpectedly appeared, saying he had bad news, with a priestly tone reminding Juan of prayers before decapitations....

Raytrayen gasped and took a step back.

Juan began a *pater noster* ... did not make it to the *qui est in coelis*.

"Andalikan is dead."

Raytrayen sank to her knees whispering, "Wispu?"

Pangi shrugged, saying he did not know.

Raytrayen leapt up, ran out....

Slow to react, Juan at long last found her weeping as she embraced the knees of Wispu, who had hung herself from a tree not far from the ashes of her *ruka*.

Unable to bear the sight, Juan walked away to find that his *ruka* was also ash, though there were buried coals he could not touch.

Chapter 20: Raytrayen (*Mapu,* 1553)

She was grinding *uwa*—flat palms pushing on an elongated stone with the wonderful cadence of waves on a calm day. Hearing the crepitating grain, admiring the shift of muscle in the round, brown arms, Juan asked himself how a sight so simple could so move a man. Nothing he and Raytrayen did, or said, seemed to have changed since the December day in which he confessed his love for her to Pedro … the day he had not left her. Yet all was different, for every shared moment with her had become a precious, fragile thing … precious *because* fragile. Perceiving her as one departing, he recorded every instant for the day he would be gone. And their escape from death together confused his love of her with love of life itself. *Mapu* was transformed for Juan, that day, in ways making him think that love resembled air, embracing everything transparently. Like air, love clung to all it wed. Love was a clarity abolishing corporeal separation. Love was the crystal substance on which Heaven's ponderous spheres depended, with their sun and planets, moon and stars. And, yes, love was like these last warm days of April—a harvest joy, profound and melancholy, as all harvests were. Love was an autumn moment seen by winter's eye.

"Uwan?"

Fondly as she glanced over, Juan knew he was remiss, and pouring his prepared measure on her stone, he returned to husking … stripping leaves crackling from the ears, and—with a twisting hand—releasing grains that were like sleeping stones. Intense, translucent, they were garnet, obsidian, amber, and vermilion dark as clotted blood. These were living jewels, soon to be ground to dust.

"Lautaro has returned."

A short earthquake to be sure, yet it opened fissures which plunged Juan to last December….

When Raytrayen intervened, Lautaro sheathed his knife and left with Pedro—so abruptly that there was hardly time for a good bye. What the *longko* had been doing these four *kuyen* Juan absolutely did not know … although Raytrayen might, from talking to Pangi, who visited from time to time.

The day he left, Lautaro joined the unmentioned world below, with all its blood and strife, suffering and disease, tragedies large and small—a world Juan and Raytrayen could not ignore yet did not willingly evoke. And now Lautaro would be ascending to their peace, bringing with him storms of History….

Raytrayen was serene, finishing her work. Rising, she poured flour into a bowl beside the hearth, and left. Juan followed, watching as she prepared to weave on the stone entablature outside the cave, which reminded him of the forecastle of a ship … the *rewe* a bowsprit pointing at the distant sea. Beside it he had created wooden braces that allowed her loom to stand, so she could both weave and face her loved perspectives. She knelt, hands flying over lead-gray yarn … then leapt to her feet….

Returned, Lautaro stood in the commotion like a boulder parting mountain streams, his hair shaved for war into a horse's mane. Yet—armed—he was in no way hostile, delighted to see his sister. Eimi, he patted fondly on the head.

Juan merited a greeting, and he noticed that a stone pendant hung from Lautaro's neck—the *ulme kura*, worn only by *longko*! Also, from his right earlobe dangled a flattened stone on which the quadrants of *mapu* were incised—that other symbol of Mapuche leadership! No one mentioned any of *that*, however. They ate and talked… though not about the war below. Lautaro commented, matter of fact, that the *lik winka* and his *kawellu* had returned safely to *fucha pele malal*.

Raytrayen asked about the ugly scar running from his eyebrow to his jaw. Lautaro shrugged. "A Pikunche knife … and that reminds me." From a leather pouch he produced a black and shriveled thing, looking to Juan like the dried mushrooms Indians ate. "I smoked his ear," Lautaro said—voice low with hate— "as a reminder that we must unite or be defeated." Removing a *pifilka* from the same pouch he extended it to Eimi. "I made this from his thigh bone."

Eimi piped a melancholy tune, Juan wondering why they all seemed sad to him, these Indian melodies.

Inscrutable as the *cordillera*—and no less bleak—Lautaro stated that he was now *longko* of the *aillarewe*. And he gazed toward the sea, as if his dreams still resided in horizons, requiring no excitement where he sat.

Military head of all Mapuche, who resisted authority like no others! This was the stuff of legend! Yet Juan was not surprised. Lautaro's fierce purpose abolished age, as in the Alexander who conquered Greece before he grew a beard. He brought to mind Valdivia also, in matters of the martial soul. In both—through alchemies of honor—the base elements that were ambition and the will to power were sublimated into virtue.

"Why did you *lik winka* come here?"

If ever there was an enormous question that lumped Juan indifferently with characters of different stripe, this was it. And, indeed, why leave civilization for the brutal gamble that was the Indies?

Juan had no answer Lautaro could comprehend. To *him* place was everything, while Juan had not so much gone anywhere as created a rosary of departures, in that sad respect a *caballero andante*. The obvious response was that *conquistadores* came for gold and God—The Immense Syncopation....⊠

Yet Juan said nothing of the sort. Ironically, the vision that took Valdivia south resembled Lautaro's own, the difference consisting only in the sizes of their worlds. Alexander as paradigm, Valdivia conquered in a map made enormous by Marco Polo and expanded by Columbus, intending to perform expansions of his own. As for Lautaro, he desired to dominate the entirety of his *mapu*. In both, ambition expanded to known bounds, as wine fills its skin. Though the distinctions here were obvious, it seemed curious to Juan that the *reconquista* united Spain to expel the Moors, much as the Mapuche now were united against the Spanish. This bizarre parallel led to the irony that Lautaro owed his present power to Spain. Without it he would just be another Indian—a leaf lost in his forest.

Lautaro elevated an eyebrow....

"Can you say that you regret our coming?" Juan at last responded.

The young *longko* studied him. "Maybe you *are* a *machi*, Uwan," he replied, with a truly carnivorous grin. "You speak a lot like Ñamku."

"Let me ask you this. If Tren Tren erupted from his volcanos when we *lik winka* came and drove us all into *fucha lafken*, what would you think of *that*?"

"I *am* Tren Tren ... but I might want to keep your *kawellu*."

"What about our *wilef wethakelu*?"

"*Me!*"

At that, Lobo's voice spoke in Juan....

Forget true religion, forget writing and mathematics, the trivium *and* quadrivium, *the aggregate wisdom of civilization—Aristotle!—forget civility in its myriad forms, architecture of any sort, not to mention government, cities, towns, roads and bridges, ships, the clock, the compass and the astrolabe, forget books and writing, the legacy of man to beyond the Greeks, forget everything but horses, and toss the rest into the Ocean Sea!*

The voice nagged on, yet Juan found himself more interested that a *weichafe*—steeped in warfare as the body is in blood—should reject its most advanced technologies. War was about winning after all.

"*Fucha winu?*"

"*Me!* "With *kawellu* we can live as we always have, and perhaps with the *ofitha*, the *chanchu*, that are also in their way a part of *mapu*. But the *wilaf kalkutun* of the *lik winka* would steal the *pellu* of the Mapuche. What kind of victory would make us the slaves of things?"

Shiny sorceries? Juan scrutinized the damascened miracle that was his knife, wavering like ocean waves beneath its oily sheen. Was this deadly artifact precious only as Pedro's gift?

"We do not want your *kalku* Keshukristu, either."

Lautaro contemptuously indicated the crucifix around Juan's neck. "He can return to the *fucha lafken* from which he came, to join the serpent Kaikaifilu."

Suffering Madonna! Juan crossed himelf at the sacrilege, for, baptized, instructed and unrepentant, Lautaro could burn in Hell for this.

The warrior mirthlessly smiled as with his thumb Uwan traced the form of a knife on his head and chest. An enemy he was, and an enemy he would remain, despite his reluctant admiration for him ... despite Raytrayen.

Uwan could return to the *lik winka*, Lautaro said. He released him from his promise. And he had to leave immediately. As valediction he added, "*Kume pellu*, Uwan, I hope we do not meet again." And he padded silently away.

Juan sensed Raytrayen behind him ... turned to face her. Arms rigid at her side, she searched his face with intensity so difficult to bear that the eternal fool in him awoke.

"You heard Lautaro?"

"*Mai*, but Ñamku told me earlier."

Juan distrustfully examined a beetle droning by in clouds of wings. Was this an honest insect or another incarnation of the pesky *machi*?

"*When* did he tell you?" Juan was aggravated by the lack of privacy among Indians, whose interested dead were everywhere.

Crinkles tightened the corners of her eyes. "Ñamku spoke to me one beetle, two butterflies, and twelve clouds ago," she said.

"I know," he admitted, smiling "I count everything."

"Not really, Uwan. *Lik winka* mostly count time and gold, which makes you only partly guilty." She walked away, gesturing for him to follow. "Let me show you something."

They descended the mountain flank far into a valley, along a rivulet through pathless forest he had never walked before, so lush they floundered in green seas. Forced into a terrestrial form of swimming, they came to ancient groves rising beyond sight—huge mossy branches arching over the dimness of cathedrals—until they halted at a clearing that seemed to Juan a chapel. The delicacy of fern composed the floor, under bamboo. Juan looked up....

"*Kopiwe!*"

"*Mai.*"

Juan knew the flower of that climbing vine, yet never had he seen anything like this astonishing display. Clusters of fluted and inverted, brilliant crimson cups, floated through a lace of light, the half-glimpsed blossoms vanishing above, there displaying their glory to birds and angels only. Glowing—coals in color, stars in number—the *kopiwe* made of their little place a universe. And man's timeless soul must sometimes become his eye, because Juan never knew how long the vision lasted.

Returned to time by fine rain falling—the drops of which not even seraphim could count—they journeyed back to *lolo* through darkening twilight, the brook their guide. And at some point Raytrayen took his hand, leading him through an obscurity with no path or guiding star. Juan was Orpheus in an inverted universe, led from Heaven into darkness by Eurydice.

Glowing with desire the *kopiwe* climbed, seeking light, and yet the blossoms faced *mapu*, she told him. "This, Ñamku said."

Juan was selecting from his possessions for the journey to Santiago—a meager accumulation for half a life. Over-burdened he might be, yet not by material things. He took the bundle of his books, though he had ceased to read them. No matter, for like reliquaries they contained what was dead, but remained precious.

They sat outside … the rain of yesterday—winter's augur—done for now. Low skies, a penetrating chill, had lingered to late morning. Raytrayen kneaded in a wooden bowl that was blackened by both time and touch. Rocking over the pale dough—inhaling with the back, discussing *kopiwe* with the forth—she created unrhymed verse in *mapudungun*, parsed by human breath at work.…

Ñamku said that kopiwe
Are the soul of the Mapuche,
Many, like the che … *yet one.*

Rooted like che, *in* mapu,
the kopiwe *emerges into light,*
but in the dark of mapu
roots reach out like fingers,
sending up more vines.

So no kopiwe *blooms alone,*
every flower joined invisibly to every other.

Rooted in mapu *like* kopiwe,
the che—*many in the light of* antu—
are one in the dark of mapu,
born from the same seed.

She paused to look at Juan, assaying.

Silent, resentful, he folded a *makuñ* and set it on the bundle of his books, asking himself what her little fable said about *him*, a rootless soul. One seed indeed! She bent her head, resuming her kneading and her narrative....

Born to light, but blind,
kopiwe *grope for* antu,
circling up....

Rebellious, Juan felt like shouting that fables concerned animals, not plants, and with good reason, for plants were *not* like people. Plants did not move, communicate, or in any way interact. They just grew where God or a gardener put them. And plants were definitely not made in His Image. Had Aesop ever written, say, *The Ox and Squash*, or *The Carrot and the Crow*? Of course not. In life, as in fables, vegetables were created to be eaten. Why then was Raytrayen pointing out, however obliquely, that—as a *lik winka*—he was excluded from her pagan communion, especially on their last day together?

She abandoned her dough to demonstrate the circling of the *kopiwe* with a vine-like arm dusted with flour, slender index representing the growing tip....

"*Slowly circling. Always up, always circling, with the patience of the blind desiring touch. And the* kopiwe *that finds a tree embraces it, circling always in the same direction, up and up.*"

Either her work or the fable was now complete—or both—or Juan had somehow communicated the extent of his resistance, for Raytrayen took her bowl into the cave.

Obstinately, he remained outside with his basket, packing the sum of a life into its small span. His books were the Spanish foundation—for he included no armor, as he would be on foot. And as Pangi still had his sword, it would also remain behind. Good riddance, and let it heal! For sentimental reasons he included a *rali* and spoon he had carved, and clothes—which carefully he folded—the wool woven by Raytrayen, fashioned into simple, useful garments. She was preparing food for him to take as well, he knew, allowing room for that.

The thought came that his *wilal* was an hourglass—a figuring of time as fate—and of a sudden Juan could not breathe. Iron hoops tightened about his chest as he contemplated that last space which Raytrayen baked to fill. And lurching to his feet he walked away ... as if man can leave the sands of time behind.

He walked endlessly, blind will his only guide. Perhaps he passed the chapel of *kopiwe* in the night—he could not tell, although he walked under the cold sickle of a moon. And at some moment he sat down, back against a tree. Arms around his knees, he slept.

Waking disoriented, he remembered ... and he almost laughed, for he had attempted to leave leaving. Of all people! And now Raytrayen's fable lingered on his mind. What *was* this place, if not more plants than anyone could want? Selecting a nearby fern, Juan pissed on *mapu*. He could abandon this green excess, but could he *live* without Raytrayen? Never had he felt such pain.

He drank from the brook he had followed down—placid here—which told him that at some unnoticed point he left the mountain. And, oblivious to hunger, blind to the forest, to everything but postponing, Juan began to walk upstream. Could he steal more time with Raytrayen? Perhaps. But why delay? There were a thousand reasons not to, including Pedro, civilization, and the danger to his immortal soul.

Take Raytrayen with him? Absolutely not! Uprooting her, to whom place was everything—this *mapu* in which her *genius loci* rooted. How could he conceivably remove her from her land and family ... her dead?

So, Juan's internal battle raged, as the mountain slope grew steeper, the brook more agitated in its descent. He climbed—light-headed on this second day of failed escape from fate—allowing the voices of his past to join the argument....

Pedro said, "*Hijo*, if you love her, take your chances."

Lobo opted for a sacrifice—however great—that returned one to the salvation and civilization.

Inés advocated the fierce following of the heart ... to the farthest bound of common sense.

Father Sosa whispered that he was sorry he ever handed him a book.

Juan arrived at the *kopiwe* clearing, and explored the shallow bowl, green walls spangled by a crimson crowd of flower. At the center was a quiet pool arched over by bamboo, where the stream bent. He drank, contemplative, seeing that a very few *kopiwe* were lily white. Some were white-streaked, reminding him of Raytrayen's painted tears.

He lay on sun-warmed stone beside the pool and closed his eyes, delaying the return that meant departure. He listened to the birds, the brook, imagining that his thoughts ran clear and cold as mountain water. Perhaps he slept, perhaps not, but when—startled by a shadow—Juan looked up, he knew that he was dreaming....

After, he would think of Adam waking to his Eve. But at the time he simply did not know what he was seeing—a backlit figure blotting out the sun—familiar. The skirt! That hourglass figure! He would have blurted out 'Inés,' yet did not see the necessary hat. He blinked and stood.

"Raytrayen!"

And there—in blissful living fact—she was.

"*Muy buenos días, caballero.*"

Her face was rosy ... paint scrubbed off. And—as God was in His Heaven—

she wore Spanish dress. He was reminded of angels in illuminations, displacing earthly robes into the sky.

"You washed your face!"

Her dark eyes blazed.

Juan noticed that her bodice was cut down to a tender wave of flesh, on which not pearls but cowries glowed.

"The dress! The crimson silk! You must have sewn it all yourself."

Juan babbled like the clear brook running by, although his mind was silted by desire.

"Uwan?"

Her hair was unbraided, wonderfully free, bound by a circlet of *kopiwe* echoing the crimson of her dress. Who could have known Valdivia's intoxicated cast of dice would land that bright bolt here? The waist was pinched. The long skirt bloomed— owing everything to Inés. Still, what cut Juan the most was not her heart-wrenching impersonation, but her willingness to be what she was not, in order to be loved.

"Uwan!"

She was chiding him correctly, as one who could postpone entire lives with wrong attention—these existences to be lived later, if at all. Yet she was also wrong, for much like her once painted face, his deferral intended mutual good. It just so happened that babbling was one mask he knew … his silence was another.

"*Llévame contigo,*" she pleaded.

Take her with him! Could he even dream this? Not if his love included a measure of respect. Juan recalled Pedro's looking at Raytrayen, as at a bitch taught to walk on her hind legs, when she addressed him in *castellano.* To Spanish eyes unaccustomed to her Indian beauty, her wild intelligence, she would be an animal in silk.

Raytrayen must have washed off her defenses with her paint, for she begged. "*Por favor.*" And her tears ran paths never before depicted until—blinded by her hands—she turned away, pride drowned in grief. Juan gasped and slid a finger down her hair. She shuddered, turning, reaching....

Joined by fingertips, they created a quiet circle through which enormous energies were surging. Then she rubbed the two-day stubble on his cheek—maybe impish, maybe just releasing pent-up greed—hands having appetites of their own. In any case, when at last she smiled, the dam broke. And at some point their clothes were swept away.

On the bank by the brook—tangled all that afternoon as only the undressed can be—they loved each other on warm rock, sometimes stealing onto cooler soil, softer fern. At times they slipped into the truly chilly pool, smiling with their heads floating above that mirror of the sky.

At times they talked ... not much. For example, Juan exclaimed, "You brought food!" while greedily consuming bread.

She replied, "I waited all day when you left without your *wilal*. This morning I came, hoping to find you here. I knew you would be hungry."

And that made Juan attempt a lascivious leer—his first. Raytrayen laughed, naked as Eden's apple beneath the eye of the still innocent sun. Maybe Juan should have stopped chewing before he leered. Maybe untutored lust should first be practiced with a mirror.

He placed a fern on her gently mounded delta—a scanty frond, nothing like the chaste leaf worn by Eve, for through it knowledge easily could peep. In return she placed a fern on him, then flicked it off.

"Why is he dark?" she asked.

His sex, Juan realized, luxuriated in a last bastion of Spanish pallor. A little Indian was hiding in the bushes of his loins.

Attuned to the harmony of their sphere, Raytrayen crooned, "My little Mapuche," patting his little Indian....

Later—shivering in the twilight, no matter how tightly they twined on cooling stone—they dressed. The wheel of night spun on, causing Juan's numerical demon to become aroused. "How far do you think the stars are, up there?" He added, smiling, "Not a measure you can take with butterflies."

She rose to an elbow to look into his eyes and said—in *mapudungun*—"The stars are here, not *there*, Uwan, just as you are."

"Tiako is farther."

Having attempted a Mapuche concept—awkward sorcerer that he was—Juan had uttered the spell returning them to time.

"Uwan," she said, sitting, "you *have* to return to Tiako. Many *weichafe* want you dead. Kuruga and the warriors of his *kuga* are near. All of them have sworn that when they find you they will torture you to death and eat your heart."

That gave Juan pause. "Lautaro tried to save my life by telling me to leave?"

"You have been making honor difficult for my brother."

"What did he say about your coming with me?"

"Nothing."

They had returned, full circle, to her initial plea. And Juan knew she would not beg again.

"*Llévame contigo*," he begged instead.

"What! Where? *Here* is the only place I know."

Juan said, "Here is better than anywhere that I have ever been."

And as they could find nothing more to say, on fern they slept together.

"*Uwan?*

The susurrus of an insect spoke faintly in his ear.
"*Ñamku…?*"
Juan opened his eyes to nothing. *There had been an angry edge to his response, he knew, at this invasion of his dreams.*
"*You are annoyed to have me visit, Uwan.*"
Yamai! *Juan did not appreciate having his feelings announced to him—an echo before he even spoke. He protested: "You Mapuche dead are everywhere. In dreams!*"
But, far more than aggravation, he had a disquieting perception that reality was a frail raft afloat on dreams, and now a storm was gathering.
"*All* che *are creatures of the shore, Uwan,*" the machi *observed. "Katrinir would swim far out into* fucha lafken, *from where he would return quite blue, you know. He frightened me, and yet he returned.*"
"*I have been called Child of the Sea,*" a hollow voice announced.
"*Amadís de Gaula!*" Juan exclaimed, searching the gloom. He heard clanks, and there *the paragon of knights now was, afoot. His armor gave off pale light—as if reflecting an absent moon. He was a tower of gleaming steel, the plumes of his helmet soaring high, lost like smoke in darkness.*
The faint glow of the caballero andante *illuminated Ñamku.*
Suspended in the air like a black moon, the mask said, "Mari, mari, Amadís."
Offended, Juan exclaimed, "Ñamku, you do not know him! You are Mapuche and cannot read a book, let alone the immortal pages of **Amadís de Gaula**. *And even if you could, you can't pronounce his name!*"
"*A caballero is always courteous, hijo, even to peasants.*" Amadís *lowered his enormous weight onto an unseen, groaning bench.*
"*What is 'a book?' the mask inquired, chuckling.*"
Ignoring the machi, Juan became aware that the visor of Amadís was lowered, with not the glimmer of a living eye through the slits. His hero had at last appeared— invisibly!
"*A long-dead* chori, *hollow as a flute,*" Ñamku *commented.*
Amadís let the insult pass, apologizing, "Books retained my mighty deeds, but lost my features in the process. I suppose I have blue eyes. Gauls do."
"*Forget your eyes,*" Juan said. "*Why* are *you here?*"
"*I was summoned by your need for counsel.*"
Ñamku complained, "Why not just tell the child—out and out—that he has found a love not learned in books?"
The knight of knights replied, "Do you imply, señor, *that the love that lives in the* libros de caballería—*such as my own—is something less than Juan might find by living in a savage land? Do you insult the fair maids of my glorious time?*" *The unseen bench supporting Amadís creaked mightily as, tilting to his feet, he placed enormous hands on an enormous hilt....*

If the mask did not apologize, Juan knew, the hero would cleave it like an olive. But first Amadís would have to cast his gauntlet, and so reveal his hand. Juan waited....
"Listen," the mask hissed," to the birds!"

Juan woke to Raytrayen beside him, propped on an elbow, listening. Then she undulated backward into fern, finger on her lips. He undulated after—doing in this strange Rome as its strange Romans did.

Hidden by the damp, green cool, Raytrayen radiated fear as the silent sun its heat. But the birds, screaming messages at *her*, did not communicate with Juan, at all. He listened to these outbursts in some chirpy tongue, until he heard a human voice, and—through thick frond—saw legs muscular and bare. More legs appeared, to total eight....

The strange *weichafe* bent to drink.

"How much farther, Kalfu?" asked one of them.

"Two *antu* more, perhaps."

These were warriors from afar, thought Juan, *weichafe* who would torture him with delight, make flutes from his long bones, a meal of his heart! His breath slid, silent as needles through silk.

Filling their water skins, the *weichafe* vanished, leaving Juan with strange elation and a palpitating heart—for he had done as Indians did—until he realized Raytrayen's fear had been for him.

On her back now, eyes closed, breathing deeply, she was faintly smiling, making Juan think of Lazarus learning life again. He kissed her eyelids and confessed. "When the *weichafe* came I was dreaming of Ñamku. He told me to listen to the birds. He warned me."

"He likes you," Raytrayen said, opening her eyes, still smiling.

They bathed and—cold and clean—Juan told her he thought he would remain on the mountain for a while. Head tilted like a bird, she nodded with delight.

Hand in hand they followed the stream. Juan gathered a *kopiwe* and threaded it into her hair—a living ember that, in its location, surpassed the passion of the rose. He kissed her bare shoulder.

Bare! Married *domo* wore their *kepam* this way! She had made her silent promise, and what had *he* done, but grope and copulate!

Juan stumbled on a root ... cleared his throat. "How do you say 'I plight eternal troth to thee' in *mapudungun*," he asked her.

"We do not say 'I plight eternal troth to thee' in *mapudungun*."

And so, by laughter they were wed.

Yet though the brief rite was over, the marriage day was not. And if—in Juan's opinion—simple minutes were riches for the avarice of love, a winter on the mountain would exceed the accumulated wealth of man, come spring. Then they could just walk away—as now they walked—in love without a roof above them.

He tried the thought out loud, "*Esposo andante....*"

Something here was wrong. A knight could be errant, but a husband?

"*Esposo andante, con esposa,*" he amended.

Seeing that Raytrayen was pendant on his words, Juan hoped her Indian notions would not make her overly submissive, as a wife. So, lovingly he offered, "You may speak to me before I speak to you."

"I have. I will," she replied.

Her *castellano* was perfect. And Juan thought that—had it been Latin—her asyndeton would have been worthy of a Caesar.

Chapter 21: Clio *(Mapu, November and December, 1553)*

In the millennia of her existence History had been the mistress of countless men, and Valdivia was one of them. She suspected that he never loved the wife he left in Spain. But far more to the point, She knew he loved Inés de Suárez as much as men could love a mortal, so that when he abandoned *her*, History was certain of his worship.

Loving him in return, Clio observed as he marched south in the spring of 1553, enlarging the theater on which her blood-soaked dramas were played out. She recorded every sword he sank in earth, taking possession in her name—Purén, Los Confines, Tucapel. These forts Valdivia founded in a season's conquest were hers to claim as well ... and would be hers long after he was dead.

Still—lauding the victories of the knight who could be said to wear her scarf—Clio was ignorant that Valdivia's very love of Her would prove his flaw. With Caesar and Alexander as his exemplars, desiring to subdue as much world as possible, Valdivia sowed his seeds of conquest thin. Purén and Tucapel, for example, were each garrisoned by a mere dozen Spanish. Valdivia commanded a thousand men in steel south of the River Bío Bío, but they were scattered through enormous territories or sent on far-flung expeditions.

For this, Clio might note, the Governor had ample precedent. If the conquests of Mexico and Peru created a historical arithmetic—a ratio of armed Spanish, to gold and territory acquired—Valdivia could expect to subjugate the whole of the remaining south with merely reasonable effort. And, as he knew himself to be at least the military equal of Cortéz and Pizarro, we should not be surprised that both Valdivia and Clio took the pacification of the Mapuche lightly. Unlike the Aztecs and the Incas, these were disorganized and scattered savages, without proper weapons, proper armies ... without even an Indian civilization.

Therefore History expected to repeat herself that spring of 1553, with the triumphs of Valdivia, and only the ironies of retrospect would reveal that Her counsel led the hero to desire too much, too soon, for as the Governor divided and sub-divided his forces, the Mapuche were discreetly massing theirs, the blood-tipped arrow carried everywhere.

Yet the Governor was no fool, and when—submitted to the *strappado*—Indians told tales of rebellion, he immediately dispatched Gabriel de Villagra to reinforce La Imperial, sending Diego de Maldonado and several armed men as reinforcements for Tucapel, as well. But an enormous force ambushed Maldonado before he got there. Retreating, he left three Spanish dead. At Tucapel, Mapuche entered the fort under guise of bringing fodder for the horses, their weapons concealed within ... and attacked.

Led by Martín de Ariza the garrison fought back, taking many prisoners, although most of the Mapuche dissolved into the forest, emerging to fight back. Ariza then led several charges, killing and wounding scores. Ignoring their losses, the Indian squadrons withdrew to reorganize. By sunset—several of his men wounded, all of them exhausted—Ariza knew they could not last much longer, so he dashed out the brains of his prisoners with an iron bar and rode away under cover of darkness to join Coronas at Purén.

The Mapuche sacked, then burnt, Tucapel—the name that Clio would one day give this crux in the Spanish invasion of the Americas. But Valdivia would not taste the fruit of this retrospect....

Usually, it is in this chapter of her chronicles that Clio introduces Lautaro with a puzzled flourish—this Mapuche, little more than a boy—as an Indian version of a *deus ex machina*. How else explain what happened on that fateful spring? Something, or someone, must have caused the Indians to exceed their primitive capabilities. Retroactively musing, Clio has been known to assert that, as a stable boy, Lautaro acquired knowledge of horses and Spanish weapons that he transmitted to his people, giving them a tactical advantage they would not otherwise have had. Of course, such reasoning might be considered an insult to the Mapuche—as if without this young Prometheus of the Indies they could not have defended their land. But, it must be pointed out, Clio does contradict herself. Some accounts incline the blame for what transpired at Tucapel toward a deep-rooted Mapuche genius for war. We must not forget that this same people brought Inca armies to their knees not so very long ago.

Be all this as it may, when with creaking tackle Clio lowered Lautaro onto her stage in 1553, he was lurking in the wings.... He had both a Mapuche and a Spanish name ... and an age—approximately eighteen. Yet he had no family, no documented history, and—above all—no line to speak in the astounding drama of the time. Like every other Mapuche, Lautaro had no recorded past—making him an enemy of both Spain and History. He would have lived, and died, with anonymous multitudes of his people, had he not battled Clio's hero. There is no question that Lautaro played a heroic role in the events unfolding that Mapuche spring. However, in what way he did so—and to what degree—History will never truly know.

This much Clio states.... When the *cristianos* fleeing Tucapel arrived at Purén with news of insurrection, Alonso Coronas—commander of that fort—requested reinforcements from La Imperial. As chance had it, Juan Gómez de Almagro had just arrived from Santiago with armed men, and he rode to his aid. On the fourteenth of December—third day after his arrival—Mapuche attacked with what has been estimated to be between four and twelve thousand warriors. Almagro sallied to encounter this horde with seventeen *caballeros*, four arquebusiers, and some three or four hundred allied Indians. They charged three times, but the Mapuche had modified their strategy, battling in orderly squadrons bristling with spears, using long clubs to appalling effect on the horses. With two mounts dead, several soldiers wounded, Almagro retreated into the fort. After his men had rested, the captain sallied yet again, and this time the Indians fled. Almagro sent a message to Valdivia, reporting a great victory.

The Governor was troubled by this rebellion, and irritated by its location as well, for these very Indians were his vassals in the enormous *encomienda* he had granted himself south of the Bío Bío. Their uprising also threatened nearby Quilacoya—his property—where gold was being panned. Therefore Valdivia organized an expedition. Assembling forty *cristianos* in Concepción, he left—not in any hurry—passing by Quilacoya, where he spent days seeing to its defense. There, he received notice of Almagro's 'victory.' Sending that captain word to meet him at Tucapel, he departed on December 25th. Encountering no resistance, he arrived at Arauco, where he increased his force to some fifty *caballeros*.

After hearing his customary Mass, Valdivia departed Arauco on the morning of the 23rd, marching inland, south, to Tucapel, whose palisades had been erected on the foothills of the coastal range. Only sixteen leagues distant, his destination was two hard days away, for the forest was dense, the route abrupt. Unopposed, he spent the first night at Labalebu. Worried by the absence of hostilities, the next morning he sent five men to scout the route.

The scouts did not return … and, late that morning, Valdivia came across a strange gage upon his path—an arm, of which the hand was wearing a Spanish glove. What this grisly challenge brought to his mind, no man will ever know. History notes that he had been talking of old age and the settling of his affairs, so that in that gage perhaps Valdivia saw the end of his ambitions. Or perhaps, he perceived it simply as just more flotsam cast upon the shores of conquest.

In any case, Clio knows this—Valdivia rode to Tucapel. And there, the ruins of the fort still smoldered.

Chapter 22: Tucapel (*Mapu:* November and December of 1553)

Smoke was rising to the south—the distant plumes twining in a dissipating braid, arching toward the *cordillera*—not the scattered Mapuche fires Juan was accustomed to. This was a Spanish fort, burning....

Having been gardening with Raytrayen, Juan slid a supportive arm around her waist. The past winter they had existed in a time outside of time, like the polished stones of streambeds, the clear, cold months flowing over them. On their mountaintop they were—if not untroubled—undisturbed. Now, leaving was upon them. The journey to Santiago would be perilous, and there Raytrayen would live in exile, for Juan's sake.

Her rare scoldings were in *castellano*—as if the ventriloquism of an alien tongue shifted responsibility from her uncomplaining Mapuche self—yet she did not reproach Juan now, although he knew she had the right. Since April, what he had put off was not his leaving, but the revelation of his decision to remain with her. And—as he found himself again unable to confess—he said instead that they would 'see what tomorrow brought.' Visibly dubious, Raytrayen had no reply to *that*. And the rest of that November morning—as if man is a cart driven to meet fate by habit, whatever the mental freight—they planted as one did in spring.

Distraught, Juan violently hacked the earth, Raytrayen calmly following, sowing, humming, softly singing, nesting seed into the soil he so brutally prepared. Juan wondered at her tranquility, planting what she knew they would not harvest....

"Our *pichiche* will be a boy," she cheerfully predicted next morning, as they lingered under *degu* pelt.

"How do you know?"

"I have not been morning sick. Not pale. Separate goods, but together certain signs."

Juan knew better than to praise—or correct—her *castellano*, much less question her Mapuche lore.

"Wonderful," he fervently replied—and full of wonder he was indeed, nestling against the Raytrayen who believed this child of hers would be born to exile. What extraordinary faith she had in him and heartless Fortune!

How long, since she told him she was pregnant? Four months—give or take a week—and somehow he had not gotten over the astonishment. He caressed the swelling of her stomach, the satin of her breast. *This* was something he had not become used to either, that so much of love resided in simple touch—without the spectacle, the pomp and trumpets of *romances*. What he felt for Raytrayen had nothing to do with pageantry, yet Juan would not alter a thing they had together. With her he was a happy troglodyte—or would have been, if his people had not visited war on the Mapuche.

Kissing him softly, Raytrayen rose to dress—shadow in familiar shadows. Rebuilding the fire from embers, she suspended the morning pot, then lit a wooden splinter to search a dark recess of the cave, the tiny flame wonderfully singling out her face, serene with attention. Yet Juan knew she was now always absent-minded to some degree, communing with the hidden life within, her interest everted like a glove. He deeply prized her affection for their child, yet still found it odd that she murmured messages—or sang softly—to this tiny messenger not yet arrived. Indeed, her enchanting habit of treating this absent infant as one here already reminded Juan of the way the Mapuche perceived their dead, as if not truly gone. And since the human soul surely inhabits man before remembrance—recalling that his own first memory was of his mother's death—Juan wondered what this woman without name might have whispered to him in that silence before recall, what songs might have been sung to him by unremembered love....

He joined Raytrayen, who was sitting cross-legged on a blanket, waiting for her pot of water to get hot. A bowl of the dried moss she had retrieved from darkness rested on her lap. She teased the crinkly stuff.

"Dried moss for breakfast!" Juan exclaimed—part of him not jesting, for with Mapuche one never really knew.

Grinning, Raytrayen said she was making a warm cap for the *pichiche*. And— God's truth—there had been no end to her doting labor. The many squares of cloth, both new-woven, and cut from old. The *kupulwe* she designed and he helped construct—that tiny, confining shelter with a miniature roof to protect the newborn from the sun, so that he would not grow up freckled ... or cross-eyed, which was worse.

Such preparations his Spanish ignorance could grasp, yet much else about her pregnancy remained mysterious as the Indies beneath Juan's feet, with all their quakings. There was the time Raytrayen cracked an innocent pale-blue egg into their meal, and perceiving a double yolk, recoiled in horror, refusing to touch both the pot itself and the shell she had let drop. Juan had to toss out all that perfectly good food. He half-believed her explanation that double yolks would cause the birth of twins ... still, other things she did were inexplicable. For example, now she always scurried through the entrance to the cave, both out and in. And when he asked her why, she took offense, saying slowly—as to a *wed wed*—that surely he was not about to ask *her* to linger *there* ... in her condition! Would he next require her to eat a *crab*?

Pregnancy had added unexplored territories to their relationship, but after that opaque rebuke Juan had given up on questions—such as why she no longer sat on wood.

Breaking their fast with *murkeko*, they left to bathe—reversing the natural order of Mapuche mornings, for these days Raytrayen did not emerge except in total daylight, avoiding even the false dawn of *mapu*. And Juan respected her reluctance. Nocturnal miasmas—or the lingering monsters of the Mapuche night—might harm the delicate *pichiche*.

Returning from the stream, Raytrayen organized her seeds, then—taking up their tools—they returned to the glorious November morning. Soon, Juan knew, he would be gardening in nothing but sandals and *chiripa*.

All appeared good and right about the day … but all was not. Never had Juan known such joy as in this winter with Raytrayen, yet the thought that what they shared existed in unstable balance was never far from his mind. He was reminded of felling trees, when—hearing deep fibers groan—one sets down the ax to step aside, for soon the poised magnificence will fall of its own weight....

After the fateful morning when they saw smoke by the river Tukapel—for that, Raytrayen said, was its name—nothing happened for two ordinary days spent under a benevolent sun, until Pangi and Eimi walked into the cave with news of terrible *lik winka kalkutun*—so widespread that there were too many ceremonies for the *machi* to perform. Several *che* had requested Uwan, for it seemed that his reputation as a healer had grown while he was on the mountain, absence turning him to legend. Eimi added that he thought it safe down there for Uwan. All *weichafe* had gone *willi*, except for those too wounded to fight, or too sick with *kalkutun*. How could Juan refuse this cruel excuse Fortuna had created for him to linger...?

He left next morning, bearing his sword of healing and his pot of ocher. Two days later he began a *machitun* for an ancient Mapuche—a certain Penkru. And at that ceremony, heartsick and lonely, Juan drank the foul decoction prepared by Pangi, even though he had sworn never again to do so. He would drown his troubles in this Indian version of Delphic madness, and he certainly could use advice from Heaven....

Shuddering, he downed his bowl. And when the *ruka* began to spin, Juan planted his sword in the floor beside Penkru, and then painted him red. The time had come to pray, but as lust was not an issue here, he did not summon St. Anthony and his obnoxious pig. Instead—unable to recall what saint was charged with pox—he prayed simply for Heaven's help.

In time, Juan's body exhaled his spirit, which ascended through the smokehole high into turbulent—then peaceful—cloud.

A melodious contralto greeted him, *"Muy buenas noches, caballero."*

He turned to the sound. "Saint Lucy!"

She was a less nebulous portion of the shifting whiteness, her countenance taking on lugubrious expressions Juan did not think she intended. Yet, ambiguously materialized as she was, Saint Lucy was identifiable by the icons she held—the eyes plucked out at her martyrdom, upon a platter.

"I'm seeing!" Juan exclaimed, astonished that he had gone from the audition, to the *vision,* of Higher Things. Who would have thought, though he was nothing like a saint!

Considering him with empty sockets, Saint Lucy said, "Not as well as I do."

Juan examined the salver she extended, reminded of the servants in the palace of Giambattista di Lorenzo. Oddly, the eyeballs were fresh and whole—like hard-boiled eggs—not bloody and not dried, at all. They were shifty instead, refusing to look at him directly. But then, the entire saint was shifting.

"You're slobbering. Your eyes are bloodshot. Your nose is dripping," Saint Lucy pointed out, maternally.

Wiping his nose with a sweaty forearm, Juan wondered why—from Heaven's crowd—he had been sent *this* obscure saint. Because her feast day neared...? In mid December, was it? What *was* her specialty?

"I am said to specialize in the dark days of the year. But I like to think my powers have more to do with second sight."

Of course! A net of unseen connections materialized in Juan—as cobwebs magically form across familiar paths. For a moment he contemplated the gossamer obstruction.

"Would you like to meet Ñamku, Saint Lucy?" Juan asked. "He, too, is dead, a saint of sorts. And he wears the smoke-dried eyes of his teacher in a pouch around his neck."

"So thoughtful of you ... maybe later," the saint replied politely, with what was perhaps a smile. Juan noted that her lips moved independently of her words.

So vague and plump, so pleasant, was this Saint Lucy in the clouds, that Juan made bold to ask why *she* of all the saints was sent to him.

"You mean to ask," she responded, "what part of you was praying to my specialty."

"Why ... yes."

"Then, Juan, that part of you which says, physician heal thyself."

Remembering his patient, Juan exclaimed, "Selfish again! Dear God, I have to bleed him!" He bid the Saint good-by, and—boulders of mortality refastened to his soul—accelerated downward.

Plummeting through the *ruka* smoke hole, he saw himself kneeling, swaying, about to collapse beside a dark-clad, white-haired form. And although the *ruka* was pulsing like a smoky, hollowed heart, he managed to bleed the shuddering child of God.

Juan was unconscious when Penkru died. And in the coming weeks he assisted at four more *machitun* with little more success—two patients surviving, while five others perished in unimaginable suffering. Surprisingly, the *pu kiñeche* of the departed appeared satisfied, though sad. Pangi explained that in their eyes all *lik winka* were *kalku*, and they gave him credit for trying his solitary best, pitted against that awful multitude.

Nonetheless, Juan considered every death he supervised a personal failure—not of the competence he had not, but of his *caritas*. His love, his prayers for his dying patients, did not suffice, even though the saints unanimously insisted that his dejection was a form of pride. The outcome was up to God.

Juan did not cease to talk to Heaven, imbibing the foul brew of vision until he came to see the saints quite clearly—although in stylized form. Much about these conversations with them he remembered, yet he forgot much more, so that God only knew what he babbled while his eyes were in the sky. And all this seemed to have no bearing on his success or failure as a *machi*. But, whatever he might see or say after he levitated through smoke holes—those Indian doors to Paradise—Juan found he had a new perspective now, returned to the sub lunar world....

Mapu was more vivid, sharper-edged, and shrunken, making him suppose that monkish illuminators saw the world this way, for he had acquired their eye for smallness. Not that he now focused, say, upon a freckle of his arm. Rather, he now perceived the world as *composed* of tiny parts. Before, seeing a *koyam*, Juan saw an 'oak'—the tree's attributes allowing him to dismiss it as recognized. Now, he scrutinized the lobed leaves in their specific vastness, so tempting him with their proliferation that he yearned for the impossible—which was to know the subtle differences of each one singly. The desire to come near as he could—taking in the whole of *mapu* in the embracing compass of his eye—had become the motive of Juan's perception. There was no such thing as near enough, however, since proximity turned every nearness into distance. He approached the *koyam*, then its leaf ... there perceived the tiniest of ants, his eye a huge, observant moon over an insect world. Juan decided that—casting aside matters of the soul—the Great Ladder of Being could be considered a spherical progression. And this led him to conceive an onion peeled, layer-by-layer, to what vision could not reduce—a miniscule globe that for some reason he imagined as looking back. Perhaps, for this, the insects were responsible.

The Great Onion of Being—and its corollary, the Irreducible Eyeball—came to Juan while he recuperated from *machitun*, for the healing ceremony was like a disease unto itself, the days between transfigured by the lingering effects of visiting the clouds … and by spring also, for *mapu* was in wondrous flush. But, in nasty contrast to this prodigious flowering, the world of the Mapuche was being transformed by disease and war.

One day, walking to a *machitun*—a journey lasting from one twilight to another—Juan counted nine smokeless *ruka,* of twelve. Yet these tragedies seemed trivial in the vastness of their wooded stage. Happy *mapu*—blooming, thriving— did not care about her *che.* Arriving, he and Pangi found the two they came to cure already dead, six others dying—an entire family which soon expired. They set fire to the *ruka,* corpses laid out inside. And with the kin of the dead they capered, shouting and beating sticks, dancing until timber turned to coal.

That spring a vague and obstinate revolt was brewing in Juan. He had decided that he was something like a wound into which vision rubbed its salt, and he made the mistake of saying that to Pangi.

Scarred face passionless, the *machi* shrugged—as if to say, 'such was healing, this taking the disease of others into oneself.' Yet it was Juan, never dreaming of sucking *wekufu* from his patients, who found himself unable to spit them out. And he refused to drink the *machi* brew again.

The outbreak of pox was eventually contained—all the sick recovered, recovering, or dead.

Juan returned to the mountain consumed by grief, extenuated.

But what a restorative joy, seeing Raytrayen! She insisted that her belly did not matter and they made love everywhere—the usual cot, the garden, the woods…. They were shameless as little hairy beasts, yet with a bliss Juan doubted God had granted *degu.*

The garden was flourishing … *uwa* to Juan's waist when he returned. The squash blossoms—golden trumpets with furry tongues—hummed with bees. And listening to that happy drone while hoeing some days later, Juan saw in the distance a huge plume of smoke. He crossed himself. The fort at Tucapel was burning! Dropping his hoe, he raced down the mountain….

Pangi said he knew nothing about it. And no one else admitted to a thing—a conspiracy of silence that Juan could hardly blame. Ironically, all the closest friends he had were *weichafe* gone to battle … save for one, as it turned out, for stork-like Millanti visited next morning.

Having carried the bloodied arrow, he enumerated the many places he had been. And after that—he said—he had taken messages for, and to, Lautaro, *longko* of the *wichanmapu.*

The *werken* droned with the uninflected voice of Memory, Juan not interrupting, for one did not. *Werken* were priestlike in an Indian way, so much did the Mapuche prize remembrance. And Millanti had in truth been Heaven sent.

No one—especially the Spanish—could know more about the ongoing war, except Lautaro.

Valdivia relied on the capricious results of torture for military intelligence. Lautaro, on the other hand, had hundreds of his spies in the enemy camps. He knew precisely where the Spanish were, how many and how armed. He often knew their destination when they marched. And he did not have to scheme to have these agents in place, for the Spanish simply captured them—the *encomienda* system amounting to an involuntary infiltration. Millanti knew more or less what Lautaro knew, which is to say far more than Valdivia—or History—about Tucapel....

The fort had been destroyed. Several *lik winka*—and some of their *kawellu*—were killed. Many *weichafe* died. Most of the *lik winka* escaped in the night after killing their prisoners, crushing their heads as if they were chickens, not *che*.

Millanti narrated—taking forest trails of the mind toward the present—Juan thinking that Tucapel was the greatest setback suffered by Valdivia since the burning of Santiago. He wondered if Pedro was dead....

Then he jerked as if slapped, for the *werken* was speaking the moment they were living. *Lik winka* were on their way to the *fucha pele malal* burnt by the river Tucapel. Lautaro had summoned every *weichafe* able to fight. And he had sent him here to tell Uwan.

Millanti smiled faintly—far more horribly than he intended, due to his missing nose. And much as Juan considered him a friend, he wondered if he had come to warn him, or to gloat.

"How many *weichafe* with Lautaro?" he asked.

"Never have so many gathered in one place."

"How many *lik winka* with Falthifa?"

"*Rangin pataka*—not many on *kawell*."

"A half hundred!" Juan's heart sank, yet this did not necessarily mean disaster.

"How many *winka weichafe* with the *lik winka*?"

Millanti snorted. "*Epu ... kula ... meli pataka*." He drew a finger across his throat—that universal gesture—clearly not considering the Indian allies any kind of problem, however many their hundreds.

Juan *had* to warn Valdivia. He slung a water skin around his neck and ran.

The sun was low when the *werken* caught up, *wilal* on his back, forked sticks lashed to his arms. He loped easily beside Juan, light as *pudu* over rocks and fallen trunks.

"Do you know where you are going, Uwan?" he asked, not out of breath at all.

Not out of breath himself, Juan said he did not know, exactly. Did it matter? Given the geography, by going *willi* he could hardly fail to miss both armies.

"Then follow me," the *werken* said, running ahead. And Juan noticed—after some time—that the messenger's tireless legs chose paths not always entirely south. However, they made far, far better progress than he would have by himself.

"Why are you helping me?" Juan asked, as they paused to fill their water skins at a stream, for Millanti had to know he ran to warn Valdivia.

"You are my *peñi,*" the messenger replied.

Peñi or no, Juan thought, Millanti could only help him in good Indian conscience if he thought him good as dead … which probably he was. Armed only with a knife, he could not dream of surviving the bloodthirsty hordes stalking Valdivia. And should he slip through their numbers, what would the Governor do about the murder of Cacafuego?

They ran on. And when the sun had set they ran by a half-moon's light. Juan's breath held, but his legs were beginning to rebel.

They sat, perspiring backs against a mossy log. Millanti produced balls of *ñachi*—coagulated blood mixed with salt, fat and *trapi*—which Juan had come to enjoy more than the blood sausage of his youth. They devoured the fiery stuff as clouds obscured the moon, Millanti saying that it was now too dark to run.

They slept … were wakened by a *diuka*. Light grew over the *cordillera* as they ate and drank, and then they ran through twilight, angling up foothills. Under a burning sun they crossed ravines, splashed along a stream, clambered over one ridge and then another, each steeper, until they came to one so vertical Juan was pulling himself up bush by bush—wondering how Millanti managed without hands. Reaching the top at last, Juan momentarily forgot his quest at the sight of rolling, green infinities.

He smelled smoke, and glancing down—bird in his altitudes—he saw the far away ruins of the fort at Tucapel. Above a cleared plain sloping to the river, they smoldered. And there, armor sparkled like shards of glass. Valdivia!

Juan had to ask himself—why had the messenger brought him to this aerie, not the fort, when *werken* were good as the geographers of the *che*? He turned to Millanti, who was calmly sucking on his waterskin; unreadable as the rock he sat.

Looking out over vertiginous space, Juan forgot his anger. The forest edge that overlooked the fort had become an angry anthill, swarms of *weichafe* emerging.… Sweet Jesus Crucified, the trap was sprung already!

Distance—and History—lent some measure of objectivity to Juan's horror, however, and he concluded that Lautaro had chosen his ambush poorly. Cleared ground sloped to the river, which here was an omega meandering around the mountain spur on which the fort had been constructed. And the River Tucapel had cut both sides steeply, so that the battlefield was bounded by ravines no horse could manage. But, neither could the Mapuche outflank the Spanish. The battle would be fought in the open, on a narrow front. Valdivia could not have chosen better ground for cavalry. This would be butchery, and Juan's heart trembled at the thought of all the *peñi* maimed and dead.

Weapons erect, Mapuche spearmen deployed like deadly fields of maize, to bear the brunt of the Spanish charge. *Weichafe* behind them were armed for closer combat with clubs and axes. Upslope, archers and slingsmen assembled.

By the marshy river shore, *caballeros* had formed three squadrons, a rabble of allied Indians at their flanks, for the river would protect their backs.

Valdivia's tactics were obvious. A squadron of horsemen would charge. Replaced, they would retreat to rest. Near-naked warriors could not long resist the carnage wrought by horse and steel. Yet—as the uncountable thousands of Mapuche formed their ranks—Juan began to have his doubts.

Trutruka bellowed. *Machi* praying at the flanks called for the aid of *pillañ*. Warriors flowed in ordered seas, while the squadrons of *caballeros* were perhaps a dozen each.

What noise reached Juan was an erratic hum and—briefly—the spectacle was magnificent. Pennants flew. Horsemen glittered. Mapuche massed, their barbaric color framed by green. This seemed more the diagram of a battle than the brutal thing itself....

Bugles!

A far roar ... and *caballeros* galloped, armor shattering the sun.

Trutruka!

Weichafe howled and ran, not breaking rank.

The Spanish charge sank into the Mapuche like a boulder, becoming an eddy in an Indian sea. Spears rose and fell, blown by winds of violence.

Juan put his knife to Millanti's throat, and looked into the unwavering eyes of the messenger. Had he been led to where he was, to see—and only see—his comrades die?

Shrugging and sheathing his knife, Juan turned, saw warriors swirling around a fallen *caballero*. Not far from him, Mapuche—perhaps a hundred—were being herded by horsemen to the cliff bordering the plain, leaving corpses strewn like multi-colored Indian maize. Some made it to safety. A few tumbled to their deaths. The *caballeros* spun their mounts to gallop back over the field sown with bodies, dispatching the wounded foolish enough to rise.

Juan could stand no more. He turned his back to the battle and scrambled down the cliff, grabbing bushes, seeking cracks in rock, risking death at every moment to hurry to his death—though there was nothing down there he could do. When the cliff became a brushy slope, he turned and sat, dug in his heels and slid, seeing that the second Spanish squadron was engaged.

The field was bright with Indian bodies, but orderly ranks continued to emerge from the forest to take the place of the dead. The Spanish third squadron was in reserve, and soon the Governor would commit it too, probably himself as well. Despite the horrific slaughter in their lines, the Mapuche remained disciplined, unwavering.

Having fought in armor, Juan knew the stifling heat, the wounds, the weariness of the *caballero*. Usually, this was the only price the Spanish paid for their carnage in the Indies, and yet he saw another horseman downed.

Pebbles showered by, and then … Millanti slid into Juan, hard. They tumbled distances at the mercy of God and the mountain, coming to rest not far from the river.

The *werken* breathed, and would not wake….

Setting his water skin beside him, Juan forded the Tucapel and scrambled up the steep bank on the other side, where he found a corpse striped black with yellow dots. The headdress of the *weichafe* was fashioned from the head of *pangi*—lower mandible removed so that teeth of the upper jaw rested on his forehead.

Juan put it on and climbed. The flap behind would hide his hair, and—as the headdress matched his necklace—he now presented a creditable Indian whole. Except, of course, for his blue eyes….

He came across a *weichafe*, right arm almost cut off. Shivering—although the day was warm—the warrior asked for water.

Having none to give him, Juan hurried on, muttering a *pater noster.*

The continuous roar of battle—punctuated by the occasional flat snort of an arquebus—was now a thing hardly to be believed. He made out Mapuche battle cries—*Lape! Marichewe!*—the clamor blowing over him like hurricanes. And at last—through leaves—he saw the backs of screaming archers at the forest edge, loosing ragged clouds of arrows. Beyond them, the battle was invisible.

Then, as Juan crept the edge of the ravine … painted, armed Mapuche sprang from the forest floor as from the teeth of dragons. Surrounded!

Juan drew his knife.

"*Me*," a harsh voice warned….

Juan came to, face down, wrists bound. His head pounded. The pain was blinding.

Brained but not dead, he thought. And he was tied, so he could be tortured before dying. He had heard *weichafe* brag about eating the flesh of enemies before their living eyes. Had he been brave enough to earn that honor, not having fought?

Rolling onto his back he saw Pichikan, who passed a hand before his eyes to see how he reacted. Concern shone through blood-spattered paint. "Uwan?"

"Why am I alive?" Juan asked—head too addled for a proper greeting.

"Lautaro told me you would come when you found out. And he said to the assembled *weichafe* that you were not a *lik winka* any more, because you were married to his *deya*, and the *che* who killed you would have to fight him too."

"He said *that!*" Juan was awed.

"*Yamai.*" Pichikan thumped his chest with a finger. "I also stood, to say you are my *peñi.*"

Juan changed the subject. "How did you find me?"

The *weichafe* shrugged. "Lautaro planned it, sent Millanti."

Having been led by the nose to bondage, could Juan complain at being tricked into surviving?

"I am *tied up!*" he objected, clamor of battle rolling over him like surf.

"I cannot free you unless you promise not to fight."

"Fight whom?"

Pichikan roared … and roared. And he was still laughing when he cut Juan's bonds, handing him his knife.

"Defend yourself then, Uwan," he said, waggling the little finger hanging from his neck. "There are *weichafe* too stupid to be afraid of you, of Lautaro, and of *me.*" He loped away with his companions.

Juan stalked the forest edge with no sense of how the battle went, longing for perspectives. Finding a likely tree, he climbed, and swaying high in branches saw the third squadron now committed—all the *caballeros* fighting in a shallow crescent slowly driven back. He saw as well that the allied Indian flanks were shockingly thinned. Knowing he could not allow his forces to be circled, Valdivia was retreating to the river.

This is greatest captain of the Indies, Juan insisted to himself, unable to believe what he was seeing. *Cristianos* he knew were dying. Was Pedro one of them? The *caballeros* visibly were fewer—and surely so weary as hardly able to lift a sword. All the while, the disciplined Indian thousands were pressing the Spanish back, and back—lapping waves of an advancing tide—not just with weight of numbers but with astounding courage, for they were being slaughtered.

Bugles in the din … and Valdivia withdrew, abandoning his baggage.

Juan thought this was a desperate gamble, intended to divert the Mapuche into looting. Yet their attack did not falter, while—at the sound of retreat—Valdivia's allied Indians fled like hares. Pursued, they floundered in the reedy marsh cupped by the river bend, where they were slain by arrows. Now, the heartbreakingly few *caballeros* left were being pressed to the marsh as well…. Unscrolling the progression of events, Juan knew he was not the only one to be led here by the nose. Lautaro had planned it all. The surviving Spanish were mired, on exhausted mounts, with no possible escape.

Juan swung madly down the tree, unable to bear the thought of Pedro tortured, mutilated … eaten! He sprinted into the field of battle, where the surviving horsemen now struggled in the marsh, surrounded by warriors clubbing them and their mounts, thrusting with spears, dragging them down.

The battle of Tucapel was all but over, and the looting and killing of the wounded had begun. Juan ran by ululating *weichafe* swinging clubs, hacking with axes at bodies writhing on the ground, rising with dripping heads.

Juan neared the marsh—where the last of the battle was playing itself out—combatants obscured by curtains of splashing water. Mud coated everyone and everything….

Three *caballeros* erupted free to reach the shore. Juan recognized the armor of Valdivia under mire. Then he heard his father's battle cry….

Pedro was not thirty *pasos* distant, on foot. As if standing on earthquakes, he swayed, keeping dozens at bay with slow sweeps of his enormous, bloodied sword. From the distance allowed by their spears the *weichafe* taunted him, battering his armor, darting in and out like hounds baiting a bear. Pedro toppled.

Juan slammed into Mapuche backs, shoved through the throng of warriors, and reached Pedro. His back was against a pyramid of bodies of which his horse was the base, and he was drawing slow circles in the air with his sword.

Kicking the nearest warrior in the stomach to make room, Juan faced the ring of spears, knife ready.

"*Fotru*, Uwan!"

Tuiñam—the *weichafe* he had just kicked—was staring at him in disbelief.

"Uwan!" the shout was echoed, astonished warriors drawing back—a wall of points and edges.

"This is my father," Juan shouted in *mapudungun*, knowing that, here and now, he could not trust the ordinary power of these words.

Pedro was slathered with mud as a summer boar, face contorted by the mask of battle….

He tottered and collapsed.

Juan knelt to take his hand … said his name.

"You have the eyes of my *hijo*," Pedro answered, drooling blood … and smiling when Juan removed his headdress.

"I am very thirsty, *hijo*. Did you bring wine?"

His eyes closed. His hand tightened … trembled … dropped.

"*Sí*," Juan lied too late, and leapt to his feet when a *weichafe* walked up.

Painted—just as for *palin*—Kuruga wore a necklace of Spanish ears today. And he held a huge sword high.

"I am happy you are alive, *lik winka*. Now I can kill you," he roared.

"*Me!*"

Juan looked up.

Lautaro sat a warhorse in the silence he had created. And he asked Juan who this *lik winka* was, that he would die for him.

"My father."

"Your *chau* widowed many Mapuche *domo*."

"He's dead," Juan insanely apologized.

Kuruga insisted, "Uwan must die, too!"

"Uwan is my *ngillan*," Lautaro replied, harsh. "I do not like to repeat myself, but if you kill Uwan you will have to fight me too."

Pichikan shoved through the crowd to stand by Lautaro. Leaning on his long club, relaxed and radiating menace, he did not have to say a word.

Juan said, "Let Kuruga fight me. There will be no revenge if I die. And if I live I can go free."

"Death to all *lik winka*!" the crowd howled in protest. Spears were shaken, clattered.

Lautaro shouted, "If Uwan lives he will have four *antu* before he is pursued. If he dies, there will be no revenge."

Kuruga haggled. "One day's start,"

"Three," Juan countered, causing a clamor that Lautaro had to still.

"Agreed. The weapons?"

Kuruga elevated his captured sword.

Juan raised his knife, to hoots of derision. Judging the climate good for negotiation, he said, "If I win, I can bury my father, and his body will be left in peace."

Kuruga spat.

Lautaro lifted his spear. "So be it."

The crowd of *weichafe* spread out, creating a human fence bristling with weapons.

Juan bound his hair, the Pedro in him whispering that mobility was the first commandment of a warrior.

Lautaro called out, "To the death … begin!"

"Economy," whispered Pedro, for his *hijo* was very weary.

Juan took a deep breath … waited.

Kuruga darted in sword high—*Marichewe!*—weapon accelerating in a bright arc, as he had seen it used to devastating effect by mounted Spanish.

Leaning just far enough to the side—damascened steel hissing by his head— Juan leapt in and sank his knife below the ribs, twisting as he it yanked out.

Bleeding gouts, Kuruga jumped forward, sword high again. Juan spun, and— with weary mercy—struck to the heart.

Kuruga toppled like a tree.

The crowd went silent with disbelief. So simple the death … and no magic in it! Lautaro raised his spear. His warhorse reared.

"Uwan will bury his *chau*, and no *che* will disturb the grave. When he leaves, he will have three days before he is pursued."

There was grumbling from Kuruga's kin—who felt that the burial should form part of the head start—but they were derided, for Uwan won in a fair fight.

The assembly evaporated to kill and loot.

Juan turned to squat by Pedro—dead on his pile of dead.

Lautaro slid from his horse, saying, "I think Ñamku chose you for my *deya*, Uwan. And why he selected an enemy, I do not know. But I know this about his choice—you are a *weichafe* I respect."

Looking up, Juan said nothing.

"You love Raytrayen?"

"I would die for her."

Lautaro vaulted onto his horse, saying, "You probably will. Why did you not leave when I told you to?"

Juan chose not to answer, asking instead, "Falthifa?"

"Captured … wounded."

Then, with a chilling smile, Lautaro kicked his horse into a trot and rode away.

Juan was left with Pedro's corpse, Kuruga sentinels circling a bowshot away. Pichikan, Millanti and Tuiñam stood guard beside him.

Then, as if the depth of burials had something to do with love, Juan dug late into the night with Pedro's sword, using Pedro's helmet as his shovel. Briefly, he slept. Waking, he ate bread that Pichikan found in Valdivia's baggage.

The grave was finished near midday, and he slid Pedro in feet first. He washed his face with water from the river, then held the hard, cold hand and prayed—*aves* and *paters* that asked for nothing—before he climbed out to bury him, thinking that no sound was more hollow, and more terrible, than that of soil falling upon a human chest. Over the mounded grave he placed Pedro's helmet to mark the spot. Beside it he stuck his sword upright—a soldier's crucifix—and went to rejoin his *peñi* by their fire.

Pichikan, Tuiñam, and Millanti were cooking horsemeat on their spears, whispering excitedly. Hearing Valdivia's name, Juan asked what had become of him.

"Dead," Pichikan said.

"How?"

"Clubbed. Too soon, some say."

"Was he … eaten?"

The faces of the warriors went rigid.

All the answer he needed, Juan thought wearily. It was time to go.

He filled his water skin from the river, and when he returned Pichikan said they would stay to make certain the Kurugas kept their bargain. Uwan would have to return by himself. They would catch up later....

"Lautaro called for no revenge."

"Uwan," said Pichikan, "they *will* come after you."

Millanti added, "When you are followed, I will run ahead to tell you."

Tuiñam asked, "Where will you go?"

"I do not know." And—to his astonishment—Juan did not.

Pichikan said, "We will track you from the cave."

Chapter 23: Mountain Pass *(Mapu,* December, 1553*)*

Pedro was magnificent on his fine blue mule. Dead, he had taken to appearing in Juan's dreams dressed as when first they rode to Sevilla.

"*Hijo,* we had happy days."

Balanced on Pedro's shoulder, Negrito groomed his master's beard. Unlike his master, he had not been fixed in time by dreams, sometimes sporting outfits from the future, and at others some he never wore. Tonight he sported a crimson and black Inca poncho, yellow Spanish tights, a padded and embroidered codpiece. No cap.

"Amen," Juan said, heaving an internal sigh. And indeed, had he the wine of dreams, he would have drunk to *that.*

Licking his beard for last night's pork, Pedro inquired, "Do you really want the opinion of a dead old soldier?"

"You were—and are—the only father I ever knew."

Coughing to conceal the depths of his emotion, Pedro said, "Very well, *hijo*. As you cannot stay with Indians, you must return to us. Not to the dead I mean, but to the Spanish. And as there is no East or West in this peculiar land, you must go North or South. That leaves Santiago only." Fatalistic, Pedro shrugged. "Inés will not let them behead you, I am sure."

Better off without a head, Juan thought—which summarized his life. In Santiago he would be a murderer and pariah, however obscene his victim. Therefore he would be poor, for his *encomienda* had surely been redistributed already, and no one in his right mind would have a criminal as secretary. In consequence, since all he knew was how to write and fight, he would become an *infante,* or earn a pittance scripting letters for illiterates.

Pedro said, "You will be indeed be poor. And ... hem ... there is the matter of your Indian."

"Her name is Raytrayen. She is my wife," Juan protested.

Morose, they rode through an Andalusian village—walls blinding as linen hung in sun. They passed a *campesino* limping on a peg leg, no doubt a veteran of foreign wars. In the road ahead, the Emperor's messenger rode toward them on his mirage.

Dreamed beginnings are not the same, thought Juan—weighing present against past. The same Pedro in the same finery ... the same blue mule ... the same monkey ... the same road white with dust. Yet all had changed.

"Thank you for burying me, *hijo*," Pedro offered, tugging hairs from his ear. "Not that I much minded passing, as being old and sad. And I fought well at Tucapel. But I would have hated to have Indians eat my flesh before my eyes."

He added, cheerfully abrupt. "*Voto a Dios*, that was quite the fight with the painted Indian. You were very economical. I could not be prouder."

Juan had to smile—for Pedro would never change—and thinking that, he realized he was no less happy than in 1539. They absolutely *did* have happy days. That, too, would never change.

He asked Pedro, "What does happiness require?"

"One dreaming, and one dead."

"Seriously!"

"Just us two, *hijo*, though I would miss Negrito and my indument."

Pedro understood. Happiness simply required another, a journey, and a dream.

"You dreamed," Raytrayen whispered in Juan's ear.

"What did I say?"

"That we will cross the *cordillera*."

"Do *you* think we should?"

Nibbling on his earlobe, she murmured, "Though it is summer, we might need fur boots and hats to cross the mountains. And as it happens, I made some."

"What are you talking about?"

Eimi was grinning. Setting down his laden *wilal*, he strutted in his version of what Raytrayen called '*botas*.' They had the leather out, pelt in, and were fashioned into a garment, so that they ended at his armpits—he was so short and mountain snow presumably so deep. A fur hat was pulled to below his ears.

At the entrance Pangi squatted, scarred face passionless.

"He said that we will cross *dewiñ*," Raytrayen translated, adding to Juan in *castellano*, "You needed resting. Now we leave."

They set off, Juan thinking that laden as they were, walking at Eimi's pace, they would be overtaken by Kurugas. And to defend against seasoned warriors he had a pregnant woman, a healer and a dwarf ... and of course, the loving dead.

They walked the mountain flank to the plain. Speed being everything, Eimi madly moved his twisted legs—two strides to their one—a prodigious demonstration of courage and endurance that only postponed fate.

The fourth night they made camp beside a stream meandering through a grove of huge *peweñ*—trunks straight as if designed by carpenters, craggy bark softened by the gray-green drip of moss. Through their high and spiky tracery—a ghost—the snowy peak of a volcano loomed.

"The stars are with us," Juan quoted Raytrayen, lost in love and admiration of her.

"*Yamai*," she replied, taking his hand.

He insisted, "We will live."

"We *will*, Uwan," she replied with a smile. "And beyond these mountains we will have our boy. Maybe he will have your eyes, your hair."

"Eyes like fish, hair like ash."

Not particularly wanting his child to be different from the Indians of their future, Juan asked himself if his son—with his mother's Mapuche blood and his own violent seed—would grow to be a warrior, nothing more. And, before he slept, it came to him that he was leaving Arauco not because of danger, or out of love. He was less going anywhere than fleeing war.

Millanti caught up next morning, Spanish daggers lashed to both arm stumps. The *pu kiñeche* of Kuruga were not far behind, he said—ten at least. There would have been more, he added, but when they cheated and left early in the night he, Pichikan and Tuiñam killed one each. The *peñi* should arrive before the enemy.

Juan surveyed their surroundings—the high foothills of the *cordillera*—for they would need to make a stand. They had been following a stream, at an altitude that stunted the forest. This open place was not the spot.

They hurried to where the stream carved a steep ravine, and boulders created rapids. Here they would not be outflanked. Nor could the Kurugas mass their attack, taking advantage of their numbers. Juan told Raytrayen, Pangi and Eimi to press on. If it came to the worst, he said, better that some survive. He lied, of course—knowing that the Kurugas would not be satisfied until all were dead—yet the three hurried upstream, laboring under their *wilal*.

Peering around a boulder as the slow sun spun its round, Juan counted breaths, fighting the dread that said against these odds he could not save his wife and unborn child.

At the forty-second breath Pedro commented, "You have surprise on your side, *hijo*. And—as I always say—one defender is worth three attackers."

Smiling, for Pedro always *did* say that—yet noting to himself that here the ratio was five to one—Juan thought, "*Gracias, Pedro.*"

At breath two thousand eight hundred and thirty two—minus those uncounted during Pedro's interruption—Pichikan appeared, hurrying up the watercourse, Tuiñam close behind. Wasting no time on greetings, they all agreed that this was this was as good a place to fight as any. The pursuit was very close.

They hid, two taking each side of the stream—Juan with Pichikan, Millanti with Tuiñam—the ravine sheer behind their backs.

Eighteen hundred and twenty-two breaths later Juan saw the first Kuruga—

gray-blue, wearing a fox tail. After him came one striped red like the tights of the Negrito of his dreams. Others hurried around the bend. Merciful God … eleven!

Juan slid his head behind his rock.

Twelve breaths later, he looked at Pichikan, relaxed over his club, attempting to judge the precise moment of the attack, when—*marichewe!*—across the stream Millanti leapt, striking with twin knives. The blue Kuruga of the foxtail dropped.

Another—blue and yellow—now was turning, hatchet poised over Millanti.

Juan was on him instantly from behind, arm around the throat, knife into his kidney, producing an involuntary scream. Juan spun to see….

Back against a boulder, louder than waterfalls, black-headed Pichikan held his own against four, huge club no less blurred by speed than wings of dragonflies. A Kuruga was crumpled at his feet.

"Look left, *hijo*," Pedro shouted.

Juan did—the Kuruga almost on him—and dropped to a knee. He cut as the club whistled over his head, dropping a body spraying blood. A clang….

Tuiñam, having taken a blow to his helmet, fought against two.

A third Kuruga, face down in the stream, struggled to his knees. And … beside him an archer at full draw….

"Millanti!" Juan screamed, hurling his knife, burying it below the archer's ribs. Too late! Millanti reeled and fell.

Now a red-spotted Kuruga, hatchet lifted, splashed in Juan's direction, not three long strides away. Seeing Juan unarmed, he took his time, painted face an awful mask of rage. Groping, Juan found—and flung—a stone. The Kuruga took it on his shield, laughing. Then his head jerked…. He slumped and dropped.

Looking up, Juan saw Eimi hurling yet another rock from high.

"*Marichewe!*"

And from the same cliff edge—battle cry high and clear, Raytrayen heaved a weight that she could hardly lift, with a frightful accuracy granted by her *pillan* … or Juan's own Heaven.

Seeing her Kuruga fall—the fleeing of those still able—Juan's legs gave way. And he knelt on stones in flowing water, chuckling like the idiot of the village he so long ago had left.

Pichikan and Tuiñam dispatched the wounded enemy, who accepted their deaths as the stoics all Mapuche seemed to be. The nine corpses were stacked on a sandbar to let the *pu kiñeche* of Kuruga know what here had happened, and to warn against pursuit.

Millanti soon died of the arrow in his liver, and they buried him when he stopped breathing. The parting then was brief, for the remaining Kurugas soon would be on them.

Pichikan offered Juan his smoke-dried little finger. In return Juan gave him his ivory cross. "*Trafkiñ*," was the word they used.

What could be more appropriate, Juan thought sadly, as his *peñi* turned to leave, for they had shared so much already, not just mementos to be suspended from the neck. And—Pichikan and Tuiñam did not have to breathe a word of this—as The Living God existed, the two would set an ambush for their pursuers in which they would be frightfully outnumbered. Juan did not dare contemplate their failure.

"Raytrayen," he said, turning, wanting to compliment the wonderful accuracy of her rock. But she was too absorbed in looking up the mountain to reply.

And she was right to be in awe for, here, east was more a wall than a compass point. Until this moment— obsessed with pursuit—Juan had not much noticed where they were going, attention devoted to their backs. But now he knew exactly what was on Raytrayen's mind. Through some miracle they might survive the Kurugas, but could they survive the immense peaks above them, over which storm clouds were gathering?

Eimi splashed by to lead the way, smile wide as Caribbean beaches.

That night they camped in stunted vegetation, waking to cloud so thick they hardly saw their feet. Following the stream that Pangi said would lead them to a pass, they came to patchy snow … put on their boots and hats. The snow deepened as they climbed, burying all but the running water of the stream. For hours they floundered in this summer miracle, Juan taking turns breaking path with Pangi, until both were exhausted and Raytrayen took her turn. They climbed, changing lead, losing all sense of time until, numb and blind, struggling through squalls and drifts, they became disoriented. Pangi insisted that Ñamku traveled with them, telling him the way.

They fought on for yet another day. And when evening blued with night, they dug a cave in snowdrifts, eating food thawed by their mouths. There, they made a human pile under every blanket they had brought, and all the clothes they were not wearing, so cold that no one slept, entombed in whiteness, waiting endlessly for signs of dawn.

When the wait became intolerable, Juan fought his way out through drifts, to find the storm had passed. Stars shone through ragged cloud, steady as levitated pearls. Around him, absolutely everything was white. No sound at all … but east, a glow through overcast….

An arm slid about his waist.

Juan turned to a Raytrayen tremulous with cold, and asked, "What *is* down there?" If this was death at last, he had to wonder what would be missed. Maybe another Indian civilization. Maybe the fabled kingdom of Prester John. Maybe even Eden ... for who truly knew where it resided?

She said, "*Mapu* is down there, Uwan, and *che* that with stones tied to thongs hunt huge birds that do not fly, but run like men."

"O!" Juan said—not at this marvel that could well belong in Pliny's swarming pages—for, through dissipating cloud, he had just glimpsed his first true sunrise of these many years, a far, hot light.

"O!" Eimi echoed, floundering up ... to his arms in snow.

And Pangi joined them as a sunny morning declared itself.

Ñamku had led them to a snowy saddle between peaks. Lakes glittered far below, half-glimpsed through cloud. And crimson rags of storm revealed immensities stretching to the risen sun. Cheering, the assembled travelers went to pack.

Juan lingered for a moment, though, overcome by the beauty of a future that so easily could end. Kurugas storming into memory, he hurried to the snowy cave.

Raytrayen—back turned—was wrapping oilcloth with blankets....

"**Amadís de Gaula**," Juan cried out—for he had thought to leave at least that much of errant youth behind ... hard as it was, for books drove deep, sly roots into your soul.

Caught in the act, Raytrayen began a second packet.

"**Utopia!**"

She concentrated on her task, jaw clenched in disobedience.

Juan crawled through snow to the resolute back ... and taking a long, black braid, kissing its tip, he said, "That weight is mine."

Raytrayen answered with a passing smile, brilliant as a comet.

Once assembled at the watershed, momentarily the four ignored the dawn, turning to face a past blued by mountain shadow.

Much they had shared, much not, Juan thought—when at last they walked together, down from that divide—but only he had turned his back on History.

Afterword

Having defeated Valdivia at the battle of Tucapel, the Mapuche continued to fight the Spanish. Led by Lautaro, they besieged the city of Concepción. Valdivia's successor, Francisco de Villagra, assembled an army that included cannon, and was defeated at the battle of Mariweñu on February 23rd, 1554. Concepción was abandoned and sacked.

Attempting to attack Santiago, in April of 1557, Lautaro was killed and dismembered, his head displayed in the Plaza de Armas of the capital. The Mapuche fought on ... and on. In 1598 there was a general uprising leading to a six-year struggle that culminated in the elimination of all Spanish settlements south of the River Bío-Bío, with the exception of the island of Chiloe. And in 1643, the Spanish signed a treaty conceding autonomy to the Mapuche in lands south of the river Bío Bío.

To make a long war short—though there were intervals of peace, the Mapuche fought the 'War of Arauco' until the 1860's, when Chilean forces at last occupied the land that the Mapuche had defended for three centuries.

All this is History.

And *Arauco* is 'historical' as I could make it, although the sources frequently contradict themselves.

All the significant Spanish characters are taken from History's pages, with two notable exceptions—Nuño Beltrán de Mendoza, and Cacafuego. The first— whose name alters that of a renowned dogger of 'the conquest'—I include in the assumption that the attested Spanish custom of dogging in the Indies made its way south from Peru, although to my knowledge this is not recorded in the annals of Chile. As for Cacafuego, he is my tribute to the fact that, while in the mid sixteenth century Cervantes was not even a glow on the literary horizon, this was the high noon of Rabelais.

Incidentally, 'Cacafuego' is the anglicized version of the Spanish '*Cagafuego*,' or, 'Shitfire,' a character transferred to the popular imagination of England from Spain, described in Captain Francis Grose's wonderful eighteenth century compendium, *A Classical Dictionary of the Vulgar Tongue*, as "a furious braggadocio, or bully huff."

As for Juan de Cardeña, he presumably wrote his own name for History, since he was Valdivia's secretary. However, I abstract his presence from Her pages earlier than She does, while providing much detail about him that She does not.

Pedro Gómez de San Benito was noted by History also, as a *maestre de campo* to Valdivia. As for Marmolejo and Juan Lobo, they were priests with Valdivia's expedition, the first described as a *clérigo batallador*, although there is no record that he displayed the cross of the knights of Calatrava. Juan Lobo may also have been a "battling cleric," since contemporary accounts state that he fought like his namesake—the wolf—at the second battle of Santiago. No mention is made of his Humanism, however … that is my personal nod to the powerful intellectual currents that helped make the invasion of the Americas what it was.

And finally, the incomparable Inés de Suárez—the original impulse for *Arauco*—died of old age in 1580, briefly surviving her husband, Rodrigo de Quiroga.

No one really knows the Mapuche as they were, when—clothed with alphabet and steel—History invaded *mapu*, for the Mapuche had no writing of their own. With profound irony, the document which brought them to the eyes of Europe as 'noble savages' in 1569—Alonso de Ercilla's *La Araucana*—presented them in heroic verse (*octava real*) owing as much to classics like Vergil, as to the books of idealized chivalry—*Orlando furioso*!—that drove the Quijote to his 'madness.'

Through a further twist of irony, Geronimo and his people were at last defeated at much the same time that the 'War of Arauco' came to its putative conclusion in another hemisphere. One difference leading to the simultaneity of these 'Indian' outcomes is that the Mapuche had no huge continent to separate them from the advance of the invaders, and to retreat into. They fought their war on a narrow front, squeezed between the Andes and the Pacific. But whatever the disparities—which are many and important—they defended their *mapu* for three hundred years, in one of the longest recorded wars of History. When Jamestown was founded in 1607, they had already been fighting the Spanish for over a half-century! Had Chile been closer to Spain, or had there been more for the Spanish to covet in lands south of the River Bío Bío—in the way of gold, silver, and etc—their long delayed 'pacification' might have come sooner. Still and all, there can be no denying the extraordinary achievement of the Mapuche. I ask the English reader, as an exercise of the imagination, to imagine—*mutatis mutandis*—the westward advance of European settlers in North America halted at the Appalachian Mountains until the presidency of James Buchanan, by a 'native insurgency,' settled by a treaty that granted them all lands west.

Of the Mapuche in *Arauco*, only Lautaro and Michimalongko are historical, the other indigenous characters of necessity invented. Glaringly, I omit the *toki* Kaupolikan from my tale—a 'sin of omission' I deemed necessary as the novel was long and complicated enough without him, despite his importance to History. And I am also guilty of many 'sins of commission.' There is absolutely no record that Lautaro was a triplet, as a conspicuous example. Here, as elsewhere, I painted in the blanks created by the fact that the Mapuche had no historians of their own.

As for the lives, customs, and society of the Mapuche in *Arauco*, the Spanish first recorded them, if at all. And as one might imagine—however well intended these interpretations of an alien culture—they had their biases. In addition, the very fact that the Mapuche retained their land and their autonomy for centuries, passing on their past as oral tradition, contributed to the subtle erosion of the record of what once had been. And as a last exacerbation, due to simple contact with European settlers—and to proselytizing by their priests—Mapuche culture was subtly altered over time. All this goes to say that inescapably *Arauco* makes only educated guesses as to what the Mapuche of its pages were in the sixteenth century. But what I depict is faithful as I could make it given the sources that I had, and I apologize for any egregious errors.

Aspects of Mapuche culture continue relatively unaltered to this day. As one illustration, aboriginal *ruka* are still being built—largely as anthropological exercises, much as plains 'Indians' might construct *tipi* to celebrate continuity with their past. In partial contrast, ancient Mapuche instruments ceremonially used today tend to survive in altered form. For example, the *trutruka* is often tipped by a bull's horn, although the Spanish brought that beast to South America. Contemporary Mapuche food is another instance of the complexities of assimilation, as incorporating Spanish introductions—wheat, lemons, rice, the meat of horses, sheep and cows, etc. And as a salient example of a more debatable change, we can be quite certain that the Mapuche of the sixteenth century were polygamous, although in the present they are far less so. So it goes....

Other facets of Mapuche culture—particularly those that infringe on European taboo—are more equivocal in their transmission to the here and now. Present day *machi* are women, by and large. Yet evidence exists that at the Spanish advent *machi* were often men, and not infrequently homosexual. But how interpret what was first recorded— and demonized—by the Spanish, from the perspective of their culture and religion? And—attacking this problem from the opposite direction— how recreate the shamanism of the past by examining the *machi* of today, given the gnawing tooth of time and the constant pressure of Spanish/Chilean values on the Mapuche? In her fascinating anthropological study of contemporary *machi*, **Shamans of the Foye Tree**, Ana Mariella Bacigalupo, argues that theirs is a ritual "co-gendered" sexuality, not limited by their biological sex or their everyday gender identities, but by ritual relationships involving spiritual kinship, spiritual marriage and spiritual mastery. That is—to simplify her argument—Mapuche *machi*, of whatever biological sex, are female as receptive to spirits, and male as spiritually masterful. On the cover of Bacigalupo's work a male *machi* is depicted holding his *kultrung*, dressed as a *domo*.

All these caveats intend to say that, as a novel out to tell its tale, *Arauco* could not linger over elements of the past laden with conjecture, complication, and controversy, as a scholar would. Therefore its representation of Ñamku does not delve anthropological detail, any more than the sounds of *mapudungun* are presented as a contemporary linguist might. The sexuality of Ñamku, *machi* of the Mapuche—and whatever gender might have to do with his spiritual role— is represented as the thing seen 'darkly' that it was through a sixteenth century 'looking glass.'

And while on the subject of Mapuche shamanism, one final detail—I assume the ritual comsumption of *Datura stramonium* by the *machi* depicted in *Arauco*. The nature and progress of the characteristic 'visions' that this psychoactive plant induces are those of the novel.

As forensic pathologists 'flesh' skulls with clay, I have attempted to give human face to events that are far less easily reconstructed than one might think. I refer not just to the Mapuche—their spoken past receding into mists of memory, there to meld with myth—for Spanish History does little better with all its texts. Notably, She recounts little of the origins of two principal Hispanic characters in *Arauco*— Inés de Suárez and Pedro de Valdivia. Their meeting—which profoundly altered both their lives, and History as well—is essentially the stuff of legend, much like their final parting. As for Juan de Cardeña—our 'hero'—he first emerges from the wings of History's stage no less stripped of past than Lautaro.

Valdivia did not just found—and name—his cities. Naming was part of his conquest, as a seal upon the taking of the land of others. But the Mapuche, as 'people of the land,' did not subdivide the soil they walked with names denoting ownership. Having no concept of nations as well, they had no idea of boundaries enclosing a huge, named area, much less for a sovereign ruling that whole. They called the other 'people of the land' they knew by the directions in which they lived—the *pikunche* of the north, the *williche* of the south—or, in the case of the *peweñche*, by the trees on mountain slopes which provided the pine nuts that were the staple of their diet.

In light of the above, I titled my novel '*Arauco*' with trepidation. Although the word is apparently of *mapudungun* origin—*ko* being the word for water—the aboriginal Mapuche did not so name their land, any more than they have ever called themselves *araucanos*. And so it is, as the Mapuche had no name for their own land, that the Spanish named it—and its future history—by default.

Having pointed out the differences between the Spanish and the Mapuche of the time, I should stress that both lived to fight, and superbly did. Pushing those they called *moros* into the sea, the Spanish kept on going—so to speak—by taking to that same sea, west. The *reconquista* of Spain segues into the *conquista* of the

Americas. The same Spanish courage and fighting skills that defeated the Moors were transported there, the same technologies of war adapted ... yet serving what might be called upended purpose, at a time when an inverted cross identified a Mass as black. Having 'liberated' their land, the men of Spain—done wiping the blood of *moros* from their swords—invaded the distant lands of those they called *indianos*. And in the mirror that was the eyes of those they now battled, some— obviously not all ... not always—saw themselves reflected there, as the enemy they knew for centuries.

Alonso de Ercilla fought the Mapuche as a soldier, and in **La araucana** he wrote this about his part—"*what I am doing, I condemn as evil.*"

Cervantes read these words, as did his Don Quijote de la Mancha. And it is worth noting that Ercilla's text is one of the three spared the bonfire of such books as spurred the 'madness' of his hero.

A Mapudungun/English Glossary

Pronunciation of *Mapudungun*, simplified

A, as in the A of America

CH, as in the CH of *choose*

D as in the TH of *the*

E, as in the E of *end*—but actually runs a far greater gamut

F, as in English

I as in the I of *iguana*

K, as in English

L, as in English

LL, as in the Y of *yes*

M, as in English

N, as in English

Ñ, as in NY of *canyon*

NG, resembles the ending of *ending*—disconcertingly to be found at the beginnings and middles of words

O, as in the O of *or*

P, as in English

R, not as in English, more like the Spanish R, as in *cara*

T, as in English

TR, is a complex sound, not to be found in Spanish or English, combines T, S and R as something like 'TSHR'

U, as in the OO of *cool*

UI, is not a diphthong, for the mouth shapes an U and says I

W, as in English

Y, as in English

Note: diphthongs resemble those of Spanish.

Ad: Exterior aspect of things.

Admapu: Custom, tradition.

*Adwe*n: Close relatives. A person who shares your customs.

Ailla: Nine.

Aillarewe: (See *rewe*.) Literally, nine *rewe*, therefore a large gathering of Mapuche.

Am: Soul as separate from the body, living on after death. Also *alwe*. The soul, while in the body, is *pellu*.

Amuyu: Let's go.

Añkeñ peñeñ: Deformed child.

Antu: Sun. Or day.

Are: Heat.

Atrutrui: Cry of sorrow.

Ayulaimn: You do not love.

Ayun: To love.

Chaiwe: Basket, or sieve.

Chamall: Breechclout (also chiripa).

Chau: Father.

Che: Person.

Cherufe: Fox fire.

Chillko: A fuchsia (*Fuchsia magellanica*).

Chiripa: Breechclout (also chamall).

Chiwud: Owl (bird of ill omen).

Chomellko: Edible sea snail

Choñchoñ: In Mapuche mythology, a fatidic nocturnal bird in form of a human head that flies by using enlarged ears.

Chori: Lobster.

Choroi: Green parrot with a dark red tail (*Enicognathus leptorynchus*).

Chuchu: Maternal grandmother.

Dawe: Quinoa.

Degu: Small rodent native to Chile (*Octogon degus*). Easily domesticated, and edible.

Dengu: Thing, of affairs. See
  wethakelu.
Dewiñ: Mountain range. The Andes.
Deya: A man's sister.
Diuka: Finch endemic to Chile
  (*Diuca diuca*).
Diweñ: Edible bracket fungus that
  grows on oak trees.
Domo: Woman, or wife.
Dumiñ: Darkness.
Eimi: You (familiar, singular).
Ekull: Rag, or shawl.
Epu: Two.
Feichi: This.
Filew: The ancestral spirit of all
  machi.
Filu: Snake.
Fiu Fiu: River called the Bío Bío in
  Spanish.
Foike: Tree sacred to the Mapuche
  (*Drymis winteri*). *Canelo*, in
  Spanish.
Foki: A vine.
Fotem: Child of the father.
Fotru: Interjection. Exclamation.
Fucha: Old man, as a noun. Big, as an
  adjective.
Fucha lafken: Great sea. The Pacific.
Fucha pele malal: Big wood fence. A
  stockade.
Ifunche: Mythological being,
  variously described (the name also
  variously spelled). A deformed
  child taken into the service of a
  kalku, or sorcerer. The *ifunche* has
  its head turned backward, and
  walks on one leg since the other has
  been broken and attached to the
  back of its head. The *kalku* sews all
  the orifices of the *ifunche* shut.

Kaikaifilu: Mythological snake living
  in the ocean.
Kallfu: Blue.
Kalku: Evil sorcerer, or witch.
Kalkutun: Witchcraft.
Kangen: Something else.
Kawell(u): A horse. *Mapudungun* for
  the Spanish word, *caballo*.
Kawiñ: The drunken celebration of a
  glad event.
Kechu: Five.
Keltewe: Lapwing (*Vanellus chilensis*).
  Bird common in Chile, black and
  white in flight, with a shrill warning
  cry.
Kelleñu: Tears.
Kelleñ: Strawberries.
Ketrau: Testicles.
Kewen: Tongue.
Kepam: Mapuche woman's 'dress.'
Kilkil: Nocturnal pygmy owl
  (*Glaucidium nanum*).
Killai: Tree with a saponiferous inner
  bark (*Quillaja saponaria*).
Kiñe: One.
Kiñeche: Relative (*Pu kiñeche*:
  Extended kin).
Kisuweñ: People belonging to the
  same family.
Ko: Water.
Kofke: Bread.
Koftun: The killing of a newborn child
  and the roasting of his testicles:
  a revenge of unwed Mapuche
  mothers on unfaithful men.
Kollof: Edible seaweed (*Durvilleae
  antartica*). *Cochayuyo*, in Spanish.
Konchatun: Ceremony in which two
  men sacrifice animals for each
  other, making them special friends
  who call each other "*koncho*."

Koni: From the verb 'konn,' to enter. In!

Kopiwe: Evergreen climbing vine, and its flower, indigenous to the 'Valdivian' forest of Chile (*Lapageria roseae*).

Koyam: Oak.

Kudañ: Testicles.

Kuden: Games.

Kudellkiñ: Firefly.

Kufull: Shellfish.

Kuga: Family.

Kula: A bamboo (*Chusquea quila*). Quila, in Spanish.

Kulkul: Fern.

Kullkull: Aboriginal instrument, tipped by a cow's horn in modern times.

Kultrung: Drum of the *machi*.

Kulliñ: Animal.

Kume: Good.

Kume ad: Beautiful (see *ad*).

Kume mognen: Good living, or the harmony of things.

Kume pellu: Good luck.

Kupulwe: Mapuche cradleboard.

Kurawitrutref: War spoon of Pichikan.

Kure: Wife.

Kuru: Black.

Kutran: Disease.

Kuyen: Moon, or month.

Lafken: Lake, or sea.

Laku: Paternal grandfather.

Lamngen: Sibling.

Lape: War cry, "Death!"

L'an: To die.

L'ayem: The dead.

Likan: Sacred stone.

Lik winka: White foreigner (see *winka*), or a Spaniard.

Liken: Silver.

Likwinkadungun: Spanish language..

Loika: Meadowlark (*Sturnella loyca*).

Loko: Edible ocean mollusk (*Concholepas concholepas*)

Lolo: Hole, or cave.

Longko: The head. A leader.

Luan: Llama or guanaco.

Llanka: Sacred stone.

Machi: Shaman, healer.

Mai: Yes.

Machitun: Healing ceremony of the *machi*.

Maki: Small tree with an edible berry (*Aristotelia chilensis*), sacred to the Mapuche.

Makuñ: Poncho.

Malon: Feud.

Malle fotem: Father's brother's nephew.

Malle ñawe: Father's brother's niece.

Mañke: Condor (*Vultur gryphus*).

Mari: Ten.

Marichewe: A war cry of the Mapuche.

Mari mari: Mapuche greeting. Literally, "ten ten," or a hundred.

Mapu: The earth.

Mapudungun: Language of the Mapuche.

Mapuche: Person of the earth.

Me: No.

Meñkutoki: Crested sparrow indigenous to Chile (*Zonotrichia capensis chilensis*). Chincol, in Spanish.

Meulen: Whirlwind.

Milli: Gold.

Miski: Honey.

Mognen: To live.

Mudai: A fermented beverage.
Mulul: A vine (Ribes cucullatum), *zarzaparrilla*, in Spanish. A compress made from it is said to be good for headaches.
Murke: Toasted flour.
Murkeko: Toasted flour and water.
Newen: Force. A weapon.
Nge: Eye.
Ngen: A wild spirit that comes to the *machi* in vision and offers its powers.
Ngechin: Excrement.
Ngeru: Fox.
Ngillañ: A man's brother in law.
Ngillatun: Sacred ceremony of the Mapuche.
Ngollife: A drunk.
Ngulchenmaiwen: Island of the dead (which some equate with Isla Mocha).
Nalka: Rhubarb with edible stems (*Gunnera tinctoria*). A black dye can be obtained from its roots. *Pangue* in Spanish
Nupu: Tree with an edible fruit (*Lardizabala biternata*).
Nuyun: Earthquake.
Ñachi: Dish prepared from coagulated blood, salt and hot pepper.
Ñamku: Hawk (*Buteo polysoma polysoma*).
Ñawe: Father's daughter.
Ñocha: Plant of the *bromeliaceae*, leaves used to make baskets.
Nufku: Measure equal to the distance between both hands extended out.
Ñuke: Mother. Maternal aunt.
Pali: The ball with which *palin* is played.

Palin: A Mapuche ball game played with curved sticks (the accent is on the second syllable).
Palinche: *Palin* player.
Pangi: Puma.
Papai: How children address their mother.
Parufe: The central, sacred circle of the *ngillatun*.
Pellu: Soul of a living person.
Penun: Penis.
Peñeñ: Child, with respect to the mother.
Peñi: Brother of a man. Also a greeting between men.
Peron: Knot.
Peukayal: Good bye.
Peuko: Hawk (*Parabuteo unicinctus*).
Pewen: A small fish.
Peweñ: A coniferous evergreen tree (*Araucaria araucana*), *araucaria* in Spanish.
Peweñche: *Che* who live on the mountain flanks, and eat the pine nuts of the *peweñ*.
Piam: "It is said," or gossip.
Pichi: Small.
Pichiche: A child.
Pichi mapu: Close.
Pifilka: A whistle, or flute.
Piku: North.
Pikunche: People of the north.
Pillañ: A spirit governing natural events. An ancestor. A volcano.
Pillmaiken: A swallow (*Tachycineta meyeni*).
Pinshe: A hummingbird. See *pingda*.
Piwicheñ: A flying monster, and vampire.
Pingda: A hummingbird (*Sephanoides galeritus*). Also *pinshe*.

Poñu: A potato.

Pu: Pluralizes living things (*pu kiñeche*, e.g.).

Pudu: Tiny deer.

Pu kiñeche: Immediate family.

Puye: A small fish.

Raki: A bird (*Ibis melanopsis*). The *bandurria*, in Spanish.

Rali: Wooden plate.

Raytrayen: Flower in the Waterfall (a name).

Reche: A true Mapuche.

Rengi: A bamboo (*Chuscuea coleou*). *Colihue*, in Spanish.

Rewe: A pole set in the ground. Formerly it stood for a subdivision of the Mapuche. Also, a section of tree trunk with steps carved in it so it can be climbed used by *machi* in their ceremonies into present times. Branches of the sacred trees—*maki*, *triwe*, and *foike*—are tied to its side. The face of the *filew* of the *machi* is carved at the top.

Renu: Sorcerer's cave.

Ruili: A large tree (*Nothofagus alpina*).

Ruka: A Mapuche dwelling, its wood frame thatched with rush.

Shompalwe: A mythological Mapuche creature living in water that steals a woman and turns her into a *wala*.

Tempulkalwe: A mythological Mapuche whale/boatwoman that takes the souls of the dead to Ngulchenmaiwen (the versions are many).

Tiuke: A large, hawk-like bird (*Milvago chimango*).

Toki: Literally, a stone ax. A battle chief wears an ax head pendant from his neck as symbol of his leadership.

Trapi: Hot pepper.

Traro: A falcon (*Caracara plancus*).

Trarulongko: Headband.

Trengko: Mockingbird (*Mimus thenka*)

Trentren: A mythological Mapuche serpent, that sets out to dominate the land and its volcanoes, and is defeated.

Trewa: A dog

Tripalwe: The goal, in *palin*.

Triwe: Tree sacred to the Mapuche (*Laurelia sempervivens*). *Laurel*, in Spanish.

Trutruka: A Mapuche musical instrument, tipped by a cow's horn in modern times.

Umeñ: A bird.

Umeñdomo: Birdwoman.

Uwa: Corn.

Uweñ: A reed used for making rope.

Waillapeñ: A monster.

Wala: A diving bird, a coot (*Podiceps major*), which constructs a floating nest and has a mournful cry.

Wampu: Dugout canoe.

Wed wed: Idiot.

Weda: Bad.

Weichafe: Warrior.

Wekufu: Projected evil, which the *machi* can remove from the sick person as a small object or animal—perhaps a sliver of wood, or snake.

Welen: Sorrow.

Wentru: Man, or husband.

Wenu: Up. The sky. The weather.

Wenu mapu: A spiritual dimension located in the sky, where Mapuche ancestors and deities live.

Werken: Messenger.

Wetripantu: The New Year.

Wethakelu: Thing, of an object. See *dengu*.

Weye: Homosexual man.

Wichanalwe: Soul captured by a *kalku,* and enslaved.

Wichanmapu: From *wichawn*, to ally for a common cause, as for war. The alliance of all Mapuche.

Wif winu: Long knife.

Wilal: Net bag.

Wilef: Brilliant, or shining.

Wilef wethakelu: Shining thing.

Willeñ: Urine.

Willi: South.

Willin: A nutria, or otter (*Lutra provocax*)

Winka: An Inca. Not Mapuche. A foreigner.

Winu: A knife.

Wutru: A spoon.

Yamai: Yes indeed.

Yeku: A crow-like bird (*Phalacrocorax brazilianus*).

Yupe: Sea urchin.

21213451R00371

Made in the USA
Lexington, KY
03 March 2013